A FATAL MERCY

A FATAL MERCY

The Man Who Lost
The Civil War

A Novel By
THOMAS MOORE

GREEN ALTAR BOOKS
Columbia, South Carolina

A FATAL MERCY: THE MAN WHO LOST THE CIVIL WAR
Copyright ©2019 Thomas Moore

Published by Green Altar Books, an imprint of

Shotwell Publishing LLC
Post Office Box 2592
Columbia, South Carolina 29202

This is a work of fiction based on historical events and historical figures.

Cover design by Boo Jackson Designs
FIRST EDITION

ISBN- 13: 978-1-947660-19-9
ISBN- 10: 1-947660-19-5

For Rhonda
With love and gratitude.

Part I
Chapter One

Gettysburg, Pennsylvania, July 2, 1863. The Second Day.

Hell uncorked and overflowing, madness heaped on madness. Drayton has been at war since June 1861, but has never witnessed such ferocious fighting. Confederate regiments marching shoulder to shoulder across the Emmitsburg Pike plunge into a storm of Union musketry and cannon in a wheat field and peach orchard. Federal artillery cuts down gray-clad soldiers in bloody furrows. Ignoring their losses, the Southerners advance under their high-pitched yell. The Federals fall in equal numbers, but stand their ground.

The lines of opposing infantry are now too close to reload after firing their one round. The battle descends into a frenzied man-to-man encounter. Snarling and cheering, Blue and Gray grapple with bayonets and swords, using musket butts as clubs, slashing with knives, teeth, fingernails.

The wheat was breast-high when the assault began. Drayton can follow the tracks of soldiers through stalks crushed to earth, like the wakes of ships at sea. Splashes of blue are visible in the trampled grain. The dead in butternut grey blend into the landscape, with blood-red smears to show where they have fallen.

The din is incessant and mind-jarring. Solid shot screams overhead, setting teeth on edge. Bursting shells spray fragments over attacker and defender alike. Wounded men still on their feet emerge from the veil of dust and smoke and stagger to the rear. Those hurt too bad to walk lie in the stubble uttering inchoate cries.

General Longstreet, commanding the assault, has advanced with Kershaw's Brigade of South Carolina infantry as far as the Emmitsburg Pike. Wreathed in smoke, Kershaw's men charge into battle as the General shouts hoarsely and waves them on with his hat. Longstreet turns in the saddle to Drayton. "Your people are fighting like very devils," he says.

Drayton is proud of the men of his state, but he can only manage a choked reply. "Yes, sir, but the devils are fighting back." *My brother is in that hell. .*

Young, gallant Ransome FitzHenry, with whom he's just exchanged a

1

brief word as his brigade waited for orders to join the assault on Sickles' Third Corps.

A shell explodes nearby in a gout of flame, smoke, and soil. Horses shy sideways. Drayton pats Beltane's shoulder and soothes him with a few words.

"Let's not give them an easy mark, gentlemen," says Longstreet, beckoning to his staff. "This place has become a slaughter pen." He gallops along the rear of the advancing Confederates. They cheer him as they march forward at shoulder arms, heads bent forward into the gunfire as if in a gale.

With the death of Stonewall Jackson three months earlier at Chancellorsville, the Army has come to regard James Longstreet as the most skilled of Lee's subordinates. General Lee calls him 'my old warhorse.' But now a frown etches Longstreet's bearded face as the fire from the wheat field deepen into a deafening roar. He slaps his right hand with leather gauntlets, peering into the chaos of the developing battle as if weighing his next move. He brightens as decimated Federal regiments break for the rear, then scowls as fresh units replace them. The Yankee line is eroding, but somehow still holds under the slashing Confederate attacks. Both sides are fighting with a courage and self-sacrifice seldom known in the annals of warfare. Every man, North and South, seems to recognize this encounter will decide it all. But it has become a grinding battle of attrition. The Confederates can't keep it up for long. They simply don't have enough men.

A galloper arrives, reining in breathlessly. "Sir, General Law's men have taken that huge pile of huge rocks yonder to the south. And the Yankees have been cleared out of the valley beyond it."

Lieutenant Colonel Porter Alexander, commanding Longstreet's Corps artillery, canters up and salutes the General as Drayton edges aside. The 27-year-old 'Ned' Alexander is one of the Army's most talented engineers and gunners. The officers look down at the map while Longstreet stabs it with a gloved finger.

"General Law's men now hold that rocky place," he says, pointing at a tumble of huge boulders quickly dubbed Devil's Den. "It's a natural fortress from which to launch an attack. Here. This high ground is where we must try to turn their flank. It appears undefended. Now we must turn them, turn them!" he barks. "We must end this folly of attacking their strength."

"That height beyond the valley, that hill called—"

"Sugar Loaf, according to the locals," says Major Moxley Sorrel, the chief of staff. "But the map shows it as Little Round Top."

Colonel Alexander studies it through his glasses. "It's good ground tactically. It will be hard to get our guns up that rocky slope, but I think we can do it."

"It dominates the Federals' left flank. It's the key to the whole Union position," says the General. "You *will* get your guns up there, Ned; especially your long-range rifled guns. From there you can enfilade the entire Union line. Then Meade will have to withdraw. Yet we have such a grip on him now he will not be able to withdraw in good order. His only choice will be to attack us on that hill or flee in disorder. Either way spells his destruction."

Alexander nods in assent; scratches some notes in his order book.

"General Lee came north hoping to end the War with one great deathblow to the enemy on his own ground," Longstreet continues. "The opportunity appears within our grasp. Up there, on Little Round Top."

"General," says Alexander, "Yankee signalmen were reported on top of the hill. How do we know it's not defended? The Yankees could be hidden on the reverse slope as they were on Culp's Hill. Let's not repeat General's Ewell's setback yesterday on Culp's Hill."

In addition to his skill as a gunner, Alexander is also a pioneer in military signaling. He's not one to overlook a Union signals detachment.

Longstreet pauses. Drayton has heard his tactical doctrine many times. Secure a strong defensive position and let the enemy break themselves on it, as they did at Fredericksburg in December 1862. Well aware of what rifled muskets and cannon could do against massed troops in the open, Longstreet clearly abhors the thought of ordering his Corps into such an attack.

"Yes," the General says. "We must know before we send the men forward *en masse*." The thunder of the guns from the killing ground beyond the Rose Farm increases. They can hear the shrill keening of McLaws's Division attacking the Federals in the peach orchard. In his mind's eye Drayton can see the bloodletting, feel the sway and tension of battle. The General studies the smoke-wreathed field again and turns to his staff.

"Gentlemen, we must stop this battering head-on and get around their flank, or we will be bled too dry to exploit our success. Mr. FitzHenry, I have a task for you. And that splendid horse of yours."

All eyes turn to 2nd Lieutenant Drayton and his stalwart gelding. Longstreet murmurs to Major Sorrel and Colonel Alexander. They nod in confirmation. Drayton has only recently joined the staff, but feels he's proven himself as a scout. He takes a deep breath, occupies his mind with re-checking the girth while awaiting his orders. The July is pungent with odors of gun smoke, human sweat, wet wool, and horseflesh.

The General motions to him, pointing toward Little Round Top. "I want you to ride to that hill and see if there are Yankees up there. By the grace of God it appears that General Sickles left it uncovered when he moved forward from Cemetery Ridge. But we must be certain. Do you see the eminence I mean? There, about a mile to the southwest. On that horse you can get there in a few minutes. And be inconspicuous. Don't alert 'em that we've taken note of the place."

Drayton studies the height through his own glasses, fine Swiss optics that Cecilia had given him when he set off to war. Little Round Top is studded with boulders ranging in size from a breadbox to a locomotive.

"General, I can be at the base of the hill in a few minutes. But you see how rock-strewn it is. I'll have to go up the slope on foot. Wingéd Pegasus himself couldn't ride up terrain like that."

"Yes, yes," Longstreet says. "In that case you'd best get moving."

***

Beltane is an Irish hunter, a dappled gray of 16 hands with black points, as beautiful to behold as he is to ride. He and his master have become something of a legend in an army full of fine horses and expert riders. Even the Virginians, who act as if they alone invented horsemanship, admire the firm of Beltane and FitzHenry Ltd.

Tossing a salute, Drayton takes off in a canter to the southwest. He follows concealing dips in the landscape. Slower, but his mission is not to get himself valiantly killed. His task is to get there and back with vital information. Drayton rejoices again he's not in the infantry, although the danger he feels heightens with every step. He breathes deeply to still the thudding of his heart. But he resolves to succeed, for he sees what Longstreet has just seen plain and clear — if the Army can occupy the hill, if Ned can get his guns on the heights, the South might win this battle and end the killing.

Reaching the sprawling granite mass of Devil's Den, Drayton pauses to confer with an officer, a bearded giant. He reins in and salutes. "Lieutenant FitzHenry, Sir. I'm from General Longstreet, with orders to scout up the hill yonder. Have you seen any Yankees digging in up there?"

"Colonel Oates, Fifteenth Alabama, General Law's Brigade," the smoke-begrimed officer returns the salute. "No, Lieutenant, we've seen nothing of the enemy up there. That don't mean they aren't there, however."

"Well, that's what I aim to find out, Lord willing."

"We just had a hell of a fight here in these rocks," says Colonel Oates. "It was so confused that we've gotten all mixed in together. We have to re-organize. But Lord willing, we Alabamians will take that hill when the order comes."

Drayton regards the nut-brown infantry, many of whom suffer the lassitude that washes over men after desperate battle. Most lie in the rock-bound shadows, gathering strength for the next push. Some of the prone figures are the dead.

"Yes, Sir," says Drayton, "I believe you will. You've got the toughest looking folks I've ever seen. Until then, please inform your sharpshooters I'm up there."

He puts heel to horse and trots into the valley between Devil's Den and the hill, now 400 yards away to the west. Across his front a stream meanders through marshy ground. Plum Run, he recalls, from the General's map. His horse shies at the smell of blood and viscera; jigs away from a handful of cattle carcasses, their entrails bulging horribly. Drayton urges the horse across the mud-lined ditch. Bel leaps it easily, but tosses his head with impatience at the sticky soil clinging to his fetlocks. Finally they reach dry ground where the hill slopes upward. The stone carpet thickens.

Drayton tethers Bel by the bridle to the bole of a fir tree, then knee-halters him as an added measure. He doesn't want the horse bolting away if startled by a stray shell. Bel hates hobbling, but stands patiently.

"Sorry, old boy." Drayton pats his neck. He retrieves the Spencer carbine from the scabbard and checks the Navy Colt in its holster on his right hip. "I'll be back shortly." He looks deep into the horse's liquid eyes, certain his equine friend understands.

Trailing vines clutch at Drayton's ankles. The smooth leather soles of his cavalry boots slide off stone. But he clambers to the summit.

To his relief and surprise, there are no Yankees on Little Round Top. The handful of signalmen observed earlier are nowhere to be seen. And no Federal infantry or artillery lying in ambush behind the crest. To the south looms Big Round Top, higher than its neighbor but too thickly covered with trees to be useful tactically. No enemy visible there, either.

Flitting from boulder to boulder, tree to tree, his grey shell jacket blending into the shadows, Drayton stalks the northern verge of Little Round Top, its rocky summit open to the panorama below. The view staggers him. From here he can look down the length of the Union lines along Cemetery Ridge. It's an artillerist's dream, to be able to fire in enfilade on the enemy from an impregnable height.

Up here the noise of battle is muted. In the distance ant-like figures scurry forward to reinforce Sickles' collapsing Union salient. Tiny horses, guns, and ammunition limbers jolt toward the churning cauldron where Longstreet's First Corps grapples with and Sickles. He sees with Olympian clarity how the drama could play out, for the hill dominates the most direct routes from the Union lines toward Washington City. If Longstreet's men can seize the heights,

Meade will be turned. He'll have to retreat *and* at the same time have to avoid the Taneytown Road. Yet how can he? Incredibly, this commanding position remains unguarded, for the moment, at least, nor even noticed by the enemy. Lee and Longstreet are right: the War is going to end in victory right on this desolate height. And he will have helped bring it about. Now he must get back and report the prize awaiting them. In warfare time is everything. Mere minutes can make the difference between victory and defeat. He begins the descent.

Partway down the slope he hears voices above. Yankees! Are they infantry, or perhaps only the signal party returning? He climbs onto a granite shelf supporting two towering monoliths and crowned horizontally by another. It's a natural post-and-lintel formation, a *trilithon*, a miniature Stonehenge. The space between the two uprights provides a window from which he can observe without being seen or hit if fired on. He peers upward through his glasses.

On an outcropping at the summit he spies a man in the uniform frock coat of a senior Union officer. He's a slight, hawk-faced man with a bristling mustache and hooded eyes under a black brimmed hat. Oblivious to the danger below, he stands in full view on the platform of rock, scanning the valley below with binoculars while speaking and gesturing — inaudibly to Drayton — to a younger officer at his side. *He sees the importance of this hilltop, too,* Drayton realizes.

Instinctively, Drayton brings the Spencer around on its sling and up to his shoulder. It's a weapon taken from the Yankee horseman he killed at Brandy Station, one of the new repeaters firing fixed-case ammunition from a magazine in the stock. It's fast and accurate. From his stable position he can easily pick off the two Yankees. He's a fine marksman as well as a horseman, and it's barely 40 yards. His sights settle on the senior man. His finger slowly tightens on the trigger.

Almost without thought or will, he releases the tension on the trigger. It's one thing to kill an enemy face-to-face who's trying to kill you. But to shoot down two unsuspecting men from the rocks and shadows — that isn't war, it's murder. Cecilia's image has eddied in his mind between him and his targets, smiling her grave smile. She'd hated the coming of this war as much as he had, fearing he'd return hardened and brutalized, *if* he returned at all. For the sake of their great love he promised not to let it transform him. How can he go back to her with the knowledge he's shot down unsuspecting men from ambush?

Perhaps there's no room in this titanic struggle for one's own private feelings, but he wants to embrace her again with hands unstained – and more, with heart unstained – not blighted with the blood of wanton murder. Yes, he'd killed two Federal cavalrymen just weeks before, fighting hand-to-hand at Brandy Station. Then it had been a matter of sheer survival. This is different.

Cecelia's dark eyes speak to him, encouraging him to be the man she believes him to be. *Very well, then.* He's a Christian gentleman – well, Christian of a sort — not an assassin. But he still has his duty to perform. Silently he slips off the rock shelf and threads his way through the tangle of boulders downhill to Beltane. The horse whinnies in relief and tries to stamp off the hated hobble.

"Be patient, old boy," he soothes, removing the restraint and swinging into the saddle. Now it's a race. He must get back to Longstreet before the Union officer can report his findings. It will take the Yankee a half hour or more to make his way down the north slope and back to Meade far in the rear. Drayton has a head start and a fast horse.

Slogging across Plum Run, he dashes south with the vital news that Little Round Top is theirs for the taking. He takes the most direct route, exposing himself to Union guns, for vital minutes are ticking by. Speed is the handmaiden of victory.

Chapter Two

Drayton FitzHenry, Professor of Classics at the College of Charleston, was usually pleased to see his brother, but not today. Cabell was in town for the *S.S. Caledonia* trial and had dropped 'round to the office after recess of court. Sitting in the leather wing chair across the desk, he tossed a printed card on the blotter. Drayton saw it was an invitation, an invitation to relive what he'd been trying fifty years to forget.

"Cabell, you're as crazy as an outhouse rat if you think I'm going to Gettysburg. Why would I go back to that hellish place?" Swallowing a surge of anger, Drayton gripped the armrests of the office chair till his knuckles hurt.

Cabell recoiled. "Let's not quarrel again. Please." He offered a pewter pocket flask across the desk. "Take a drop with me."

With reluctance Drayton poured an ounce of bourbon into glasses on a silver tray on the credenza. Handing one to his brother, he sat back in his creaky swivel seat and sipped warily. The red-gold liquid glowed in the late afternoon light from the high windows behind them. It was Kentucky bourbon, potent yet mellow. His brother drank only the best.

"Now," said Cabell, "I'm asking you — just listen. It'll do you a parcel of good."

"All right, I'll listen. But you're wasting your breath."

Cabell gestured with his cane to the printed card on the desk. "Read the damn thing. All of it, please."

Drayton picked it up again and read aloud the legend across the top. 'United Confederate Veterans. Committee on Gettysburg Celebration, July 1-4, 1913.'

"Celebration!" He flung the card back on the desk.

"You didn't read it all," Cabell complained. "There's to be a reunion in July, a three-day encampment at Gettysburg to commemorate the fiftieth anniversary of the battle. All us veterans are invited to take part, North and South."

"And you didn't answer my question. Why would I want to go?"

Cabell ignored him. "The state of Pennsylvania is hosting the event. And the Federal government. They'll provide shelter and meals, courtesy of the U.S. Army. The UCV are encouraging us to attend." His voice rose with excitement. "It'll be an event of enormous national significance. Nothing like it in our history. Or anyone else's, for that matter. Don't you think the Old Cause should be represented?"

Drayton drained his bourbon and said, "*Causa finita est; arma locuta est.*"

Cabell shrugged. "You know I've forgotten my Latin. Except for the legal terms."

"It means: war has spoken; the cause is finished."

"Now there you have it wrong," said Cabell, growing heated. He waggled a finger at his brother. "Issues settled by force are never truly settled. They're bound to re-assert themselves, in other times, in other ways."

"Perhaps," said Drayton, leaning back with both hands on the desk. "But they're settled in our time. We resorted to force, and we must live with the verdict of force." He poured himself another finger of Cabell's whiskey.

"Then go with me to lay Ranse's ghost to rest," said Cabell.

Ransome FitzHenry, their late brother, had been the youngest. For reasons Drayton never understood, Ranse had chosen the infantry instead of following his brothers into the cavalry. He had died at Gettysburg on the Second Day.

"Let the dead bury the dead," Drayton said with an indifference he didn't feel. He turned and peered out the window. The loss of Ranse was still an open wound of the soul. Ranse had left no children, no widow, no grave. There was only the cenotaph at Cypress Stand. It was as though Ranse had never been, his existence swallowed up by time and fate.

"Then go and lay your own ghosts to rest."

"I can do that here in Charleston. I sure don't need to travel to Pennsylvania."

The two men fell silent. Drayton stared into the amber heart of the shot glass as if it contained a solution to the impasse. His brother filled the awkwardness with a dyspeptic rumbling in his throat, but said nothing. Though he'd grown stout in his 77th year, Cabell had lost none of his commanding presence. He was bearded and bald, except for white tufts around the temples.

Drayton admired his brother but hated the way Cabell pressed him, as if he were in the defendant's dock. Yet in a way, he was — in the dock of his own conscience. He'd tenaciously guarded a secret for fifty years. For fifty years Cabell had tried with equal tenacity to uncover it. A trip to Gettysburg would be Cabell's best opportunity. And his last.

"You speak of other times in the War," said Cabell, softening his tone. "Rarely, but when asked. Yet never of Gettysburg. Why is that?" He grimaced and rubbed his leg, taken off by a Union round shot during the Petersburg Campaign in 1864. Drayton reached over and replenished Cabell's glass.

"Because Gettysburg is where we lost the War." *Not just a battle lost, but a way of life, everything.* "Why do you want to go back and serve as stage props for the Yankee narrative of the War? What good will it do?"

Cabell took a cigar from his pocket, offered one to Drayton, who declined. Cabell brushed a few grains of tobacco from his blue serge suit.

"I confess I don't understand you," said Cabell. "You ought to be glad of the chance for reconciliation. You were the only one of us FitzHenrys who opposed the War in 1860."

"You believed we would win. I didn't. I only went to war to preserve the family honor. And my own, I suppose."

Cabell nodded. "Yet you fought like a demon at Brandy Station. Killed two Yankees in single combat. And with a damn saber, no less. Lost two fingers." He gestured at Drayton's mutilated left hand. "After fifty years I thought *you'd* be the one most ready to forgive and forget."

"I've forgiven the injuries done to me. But it's not my prerogative to forgive the injuries done to others. In neither case can I ever forget. Fifty years, a hundred years if I were to live that long. Makes no difference."

"Fifty years and you've never moved on. Yes, we lost Ranse and Father. You lost your wife. Believe me, I know how much you loved Celia. But she's *gone*, Drayton, gone. She'd have wanted you to live your life, not remain mired in the past. Think of the Reunion as an opportunity to heal. That's the only reason I'm proposing it."

Not the only reason, Drayton mused. "There are things I can't explain, Cabell, not even to my own brother. Not even to myself."

Cabell was nothing if not persistent. Drayton braced for a final salvo.

"You remain as cross-grained as ever," Cabell grumbled in a voice that was both supplicating and commanding. "But I urge you to consider the idea. I'll bring Tommy up to the River next week for his regular visit and we'll talk again. Promise me you'll keep an open mind and not decide anything until then."

Drayton promised nothing but allowed the possibility to linger in his mind.

Cabell's cigar aroma brought him back to the present.

"You ought to give those up," Drayton said. "They'll be the death of you."

Cabell laughed. "Doc Craven has ordered me to give up drinking, and Nellie won't let me chase women. If I have to give up cigars too, then I might as well *be* dead."

"We both ought to be dead. It's a miracle we survived." Drayton touched his chest where he barely escaped a fatal wound on the Third Day at Gettysburg.

"Then let that be your reason," Cabell said. "Go back and give thanks. In the place where you encountered God's mercy."

A long silence followed.

"It was not a mercy that I lived," Drayton said. "It was a punishment."

***

Departing, Cabell left the invitation on the desk. Drayton understood it was not by accident. He remained seated for a while lost in his recollections. The joys and the sorrows balanced each other in equal measure. Finally, despite himself, he studied the printed card, putting it down, then picking it up again.

The Angelus began to peal at St. John the Baptist, sonorous and stately. Not to be outdone by Catholics in Anglican Charleston, St. Michael's began the antiphonal tolling of the hour at Meeting and Broad. Six P.M. Past time go home. Annalee would be fuming at the back door by the time he arrived. Drayton stood wearily and stretched. Closing his files, he turned off the gaslight and shut the door to his office.

Mrs. Poteet, the Department secretary, plain but pretty, got up behind her desk with a smile. She stood every time he entered the reception area, though he'd told her repeatedly not to. Recognizing it was a gesture of respect, he'd finally let the matter rest. His remonstrances had no effect, anyway. The main thing was her unfailing pleasantness, and he wanted to keep it that way.

"I suppose you heard," he said with a tilt of the head toward the inner office. "Nothing escapes your notice around here."

"Yes," she nodded, still smiling, but offering no opinion.

"Well, aren't you going to tell me I should go back to Gettysburg? That it will do me a parcel of good?"

"I think *you* should decide, not me, not Mr. Cabell, not anyone else. In the meanwhile, I'll tell you only to go home. Mrs. FitzHenry will be wondering." Though Drayton was old enough to be her father, she addressed him in a manner that was motherly and deferential at the same time.

"No doubt," he grumbled. "Why are you still here, Mrs. Poteet? You ought to have left an hour ago."

"I didn't want to leave until you did. In case you needed anything."

Drayton chuckled. "Am I so needy? I thought I was doing pretty well keeping decrepitude at bay."

"Decrepitude? Ha! You'll outlast all of us."

"Not likely," he murmured. "I've been here twenty-three years. I'm surprised they've let me stay on this long, with just the one class to teach."

At the coat tree he began to shrug into his overcoat, the Donegal breadeen he loved so well but seldom needed in temperate Charleston. Mrs. Poteet stepped from behind her desk and held the garment while he thrust his arms into the sleeves.

"Oh, Professor, you know Classics wouldn't be the same without you. You made this Department."

"If so, my day has come and gone. I'm just a relic now."

"No, a symbol."

"Mrs. Poteet, you don't need to do that," he said as she helped button the coat and arrange his scarf.

"Says who"?

"Says I. I'm grateful your kindness, but—"

"You've been enormously kind to me. Would you deprive me of the pleasure of reciprocating?"

"Well, no."

She handed him his tweed hat. "And you show everyone in this Department nothing but kindness, even those who don't deserve it."

"We all need kindness, whether we deserve it or not."

"That's just what I mean. When my Lanny died, you showed up with your carriage, drove me to the church, and stood in the downpour at the cemetery holding me under your umbrella. I'll never be able to thank you."

"I know how terrible it is to lose one's beloved."

Mrs. Poteet came forward to open the outer door. He raised a hand.

Now don't you go waving me away," she said. "My father fought with Hart's Battery. I can still remember the tales he told about you. You're a genuine hero of the War, yet you never speak of it."

"I am *no* hero. What we had to do in the War... It's better not to speak of it."

She held the door open for him. "It's always the heroes who are unassuming. Like you. Not like the braggarts in Charleston."

Let them brag, he thought, exiting the office and descending the stairway. *They're not the ones who lost the War. I'm the one who lost it.*

Chapter Three

Charleston, South Carolina; March 1913.

At last. Annalee heard the back door to the kitchen squeak open and shut. She wished he would use the front door like proper people should. But Drayton liked to sneak in the back and creep down the hallway to his office. All right. She understood. He wanted a few minutes of solitude. But not at her expense — she was his wife of twenty-seven years. She confronted him before he was through the kitchen.

"Why are you late?" she said. "Supper is getting cold."

"Sorry. My brother dropped by the office for a while."

"Your brother." Annalee couldn't help the hostility, an attitude she held toward anyone asserting a claim on her husband's attention.

Drayton nodded wordlessly and stepped into the hallway toward the drawing room.

"Don't tarry. Supper is ready," she commanded with folded arms.

He reported back for supper, dutiful and chastened.

"Well?" said Annalee, as she passed him a platter of fried pork chops. Instead of the formal dining room, they used a small oak table in a corner of the kitchen, where she found it easier to serve meals.

"Well what?" Her husband was looking at some sort of printed notice as he ate. He was always reading at meals, a habit she thought rude. When reproached, he would agree it was rude, apologize, and promise to desist. He would comply for a time, but sooner or later fell back into the old habit, though he would always engage her readily enough when she initiated a conversation.

"What did *he* want?"

While she waited for an answer, her husband rose slowly from his chair to select a bottle of wine. She had served only water, though she knew he liked wine with his meals. But wine was expensive. He seemed to be fixated on the labels on various bottles. She despised his pretensions as a wine connoisseur, and now she was certain his languid movements were intended to annoy. But she kept her silence, unwilling to give him the satisfaction. Finally he chose a bottle and set about it with the corkscrew.

"In fact, Cabell wants me to travel with him to Gettysburg this summer," he said. "Seems they're organizing an old veterans' reunion."

He gestured toward the cards on the table. She reached over, picked them up, then tossed them back at his place with contempt. "Is this a practical joke?"

"Well, no. It's real. It's being billed as an historic moment of national healing and reconciliation between North and South. Perhaps it will be. Who can say?"

"I hope you told your brother you have no intention of going with him."

"Yes, that's what I told him. I have no intention of going." He sat again with the wine bottle and two glasses at his elbow. He offered to pour her some, but she declined.

"Well, then," she said, with triumph.

She didn't like the look he gave her. He said, "Just for the sake of argument, tell me why I shouldn't go. So that I may be better reconciled to my decision."

Ignoring his sarcasm, she replied, "It's the *principle* of the thing."

He straightened, with one arm resting on table top, twirling his wineglass and watching intently as the ruby-red liquid swirled inside, coating the glass. She braced for the scathing words she knew were coming. But his tone was gentle, almost professorial.

"Have you ever noticed?" he said. "We could be talking about the weather or the price of peaches or the cut of a woman's skirt, and you never fail, within minutes, to bring the conversation around to 'the principle of the thing.' Now I regard myself as a principled man. Yet until we married I never realized that the Cosmos contained so many intransigent principles."

"You needn't be condescending. I *am* your wife, and I have a right to my opinion about things that concern us both." She might have some wine after all. She poured a few ounces, measuring carefully lest she take too much.

"Yes, you do have a right," he said. "But I should think you'd want me to go celebrate the Lost Cause. You're a charter member of the UDC. You're always first on the scene at Magnolia Cemetery to decorate the graves on Confederate Memorial Day. In fact, there's no more conspicuous Southern patriot in Charleston than you."

She felt her face turn hot, and her jaw clench. She took a deep sip and replied, "I feel an obligation to honor the sacrifice of my late husband, even if you don't care to take part. Perhaps it's because you gave only two fingers. He gave all — his life."

Drayton sucked in a deep breath. His eyes blazed, and she realized she'd gone too far. She tried a placating tone. "Anyway, you ought to see that traveling to Pennsylvania is a preposterous idea."

"Why is it preposterous?"

"First, you are not a young man anymore—"

"None of us veterans are. It is the fiftieth anniversary of the battle. That is the whole point."

Rushing on, she said, "You promised to finish your next book. We need the money, and you barely earn a pittance teaching at the College. Look at this house, falling down around our ears. It needs repairs. Lord knows I've done my best to give you a good home. It's time you took some responsibility for it, too."

She braced herself for an angry reply. But he said nothing, only seemed to sag and grow smaller. She'd won — again. He looked up at her wearily. "My dear, I realize it's your home. You never let me forget it. I've done all I can to support you and pay for the upkeep and improvements. But there are limits to what a man can do, especially when he passes 70."

She felt aggrieved. Why did he blame her for wanting him to write another book? The War and its worse aftermath, Reconstruction, were long over; but Southerners still struggled economically. There were few paths to affluence, especially for someone like Drayton who was trained as an academic and had few other skills. He'd done well despite the obstacles. Couldn't he understand her desire to keep things ticking over as long as they could? She hated to treat him as little more than a cash cow. Yet a husband was obliged to support his wife. There was no statute of limitations on that responsibility. At 73, he might not be able to work much longer. The money from Isaac had long since run out. Whatever it took, she would never go back to those dark days after the War. Nor was it wrong of her to want the latest inventions to save time and labor — motor cars and telephones and especially the new gas range she lusted for. It cooked with a twist of the wrist and flick of a match. No need to split and haul firewood and kindling and coax it into flame. She was tired of a woman's drudgery. She was no longer young, either.

Before she could organize these sprawling thoughts into an answer, he said, "Well, don't fret yourself. I told you I'm not inclined to go."

She stifled a satisfied smile, and could only hope he took her reaction for gratitude and affection. Stepping forward, she patted him on the shoulder, then turned and went wordlessly to the kitchen sink to clean up the dishes. She could tell he'd been hungry. She also knew she was a fine cook. The meal was tasty, even if eaten in silence, as was now their habit.

Jacksonboro, South Carolina; April 1913.

Drayton came to his feet stiffly as the Charleston-Savannah train slowed to a creaking halt in Jacksonboro, thirty miles southwest of Charleston on the west bank of the Edisto River in Colleton County. Besides the tiny depot, the hamlet boasted a few clapboard houses, a country store, and a post office. But Drayton felt an attachment to the otherwise nondescript place — it was the whistle stop on the way to his weekend retreat, a site he referred to simply as 'the River.'

His family's rice farm on the Edisto, Cypress Stand, had been burned by Federals raiding upriver on steam launches near the end of the War, in January 1865. At the height of Reconstruction, when most Southerners were destitute, and with help from his Princeton classmates, he'd managed to publish a successful book, *Man of the Hour*. It was a study of the Roman statesman Cicero and his defeat of Cataline's conspiracy in 63 B.C. His publisher urged him to write another, a project long in mind that became *Twilight of Liberty*. The second book had become a standard college text on the collapse of the Roman republic and its degeneration into empire. Both found a wide readership among the public beyond the textbook market. The books provided enough income to build a small cottage on the bluff above the River near the ruins of the old home.

For his river cottage Drayton took the name Tusculum, Cicero's country retreat in the Alban Hills north of Rome. Much to his surprise, when many South Carolinians were barely surviving the ravages of the War, he found he could make a decent living in the classics, of all things. The broken planter class still wanted their sons to be gentlemen, which required a passing familiarity with Homer and Plato and Xenophon, with Livy and Tacitus and Cicero. Socially conscious Northerners, even while occupying the prostrate South, mimicked its manners, or tried to. They wanted their sons to be gentlemen; and the South remained the template even in defeat. Drayton thought of himself as one of the Athenian captives of Syracuse in the Peloponnesian War who escaped slow death in the quarries by teaching Homer and Euripides to the sons of their captors. Only those who possessed the great literature of the Greeks in memory returned to tell of the disaster that befell Nicias and the Athenian army.

His joints and his back ached. His chest hurt deep inside and he was often short of breath from the old wound in the sternum at Gettysburg. He didn't know how much longer he'd be able to do this. Nevertheless, Drayton struck out on foot for the final two miles south, following a sandy track along the Colleton

County side of the river, which glinted palely in the January sun. Before the War Shortbread or one of the house servants would have met him at the station with the barouche and fine pair of matched bays for the ride to Cypress Stand. He cast his mind back, seeing them vital and strong against the roseate glow of late afternoon. They were gone, yet their names whispered in the winter wind among the pines. Shortbread and his twin Shadpole. Junius. Maum Biddy. His celebrated Beltane. And his boon companions of the Army, all killed untimely in battle. Preston Hampton, the General's son, lost at Burgess Mill during the siege at Petersburg. The gallant John Pelham, the Army's best horse artillerist, fallen in a minor skirmish at Kelly's Ford when he had no business being there. Another fine gunner, odd little Willie Pegram of the wire-rimmed glasses, dying scant weeks near the end after getting married. And his own brother Ranse, who had, like Biblical Joseph and Benjamin, been the joy of his aging father.

Above all, there was the lingering pain of the departed Cecelia Sullivan, his first wife, whom he'd called Celia. Was it disloyal to his present wife that he should think Celia's name, see her face, with such persistent longing? Was it folly to remember her so poignantly after fifty years? After all, he was married and the father of a son. A dissolute disappointment of a son, but his name and blood nonetheless.

Tiring from the hike, he settled on a fallen pine next to the road. As he rested, for perhaps the hundredth time in as many days he retrieved from his side coat pocket the miniature Celia had given him in 1861 when he departed for the War. The image was an exquisite rendering by Charleston's famous Charles Fraser, finely wrought on enamel and framed with gold. The likeness had been set into a solid brass oval, thanks be to God, for the metal base had saved his life.

Or so it seemed to him at the time. Later, after Gettysburg, as he lay wounded and pondering what had happened, he scoffed at himself. It was his second wound. The first was the loss of two fingers to a Yankee sabre at Brandy Station. This second was far more serious, his sternum fractured and his heart bruised by a grape or shell fragment that ought to have killed him. Yet he lived. It was baseless sentiment to think that Celia had reached across time and space to save him. Still, on the eve of his departure for the War he had made her a pledge touching on the very nature of their love, and he'd honored it. In his fevered mind, this vow had empowered her to come between him and the near-fatal projectile that struck him on the futile Third Day, the climax of Gettysburg's stupendous slaughter.

Gettysburg, Pennsylvania; the Third Day; July 3, 1863.

The greatest artillery barrage ever to convulse the North American continent began at 1:00 and subsided around 3:00 PM. Porter Alexander, in command of Longstreet's artillery for the attack, had pounded the Union positions on Cemetery Ridge with 170 guns until ammunition began to run low. The earth quivered under the relentless roaring, booming, and barking of so many guns. Coiling smoke and plumes of dust obscured the targets, rendering further aimed fire ineffective. Colonel Alexander warned the General that his batteries had done all they could to soften up the enemy position.

With deep reluctance General Longstreet gave the order. 14,000 Confederates of the divisions of Generals Pickett and Pettigrew emerged from their assembly areas in the woods along Seminary Ridge. After forming in double lines for the attack, they stepped forward to beating drums, aiming at the center of the Union line along Cemetery Ridge, a mile across open ground.

Drayton sat his horse quietly with Longstreet and his staff. Awestruck, he could only imagine what the grand assault must look like from the enemy's vantage point; that is, from the front. From behind the lines he saw a steel-tipped wave of butternut grey surging across the landscape toward the smoke-crowned heights across the valley. The regiments marched in near-perfect step, their ranks dressed as if on parade, red flags in the van. Here was war in all its fearful splendor.

As the brigades approached the Emmitsburg Pike and the center of the intervening valley, Federal artillery opened up. Still the Confederates marched on, struggling to cross the stout fences lining the Pike and now within musket range. There the killing was at its worst; the fences slowed the attackers, forcing them to bunch up as they clambered over the rails.

The battered regiments re-formed on the other side of the Pike and continued up the slope. He could still hear in memory the vast moan that rose above the bloody field, the collective death sound of hundreds of men dying under the massed Federal rifle and cannon fire, a sound lodged deep in his soul and never to be forgotten. He had never heard anything like it on another battlefield.

Ignoring the bloody swaths being torn in their ranks, the Confederates filled the gaps, closed on their colors, and pressed forward. They angled toward the center of the Union position marked by a stone wall and copse of trees. General Longstreet watched through his glasses with deepening dismay etched in his face.

Suddenly he exclaimed, "Look there! Kemper's men are going to be flanked. General Pickett can't see from his post for the folds in the ground."

A sizeable party of Yankees, perhaps an entire regiment, had left the main Union position and wheeled right to enfilade the extreme Confederate right flank, composed of Brigadier James Kemper's Virginians.

The General's worried gaze fell on Drayton. "Mr. FitzHenry, get forward quick as you can and warn General Kemper his right is about to be enveloped." He pointed and Drayton followed, taking in the threatening scene at a glance. "He's bearing too far to the center and leaving his right exposed. He must refuse his flank or guide more to his right to engage those Yankees. Go now! Quickly!"

Heart drumming at the thought of entering the maelstrom of death, Drayton spurred Beltane forward, gobbling ground and leaping the fence along the Emmitsburg Pike that had slowed the assault so lethally. He reined in as Beltane pawed the air. Grey boys nearby cheered at the sight.

The scene about him buffeted the senses – surging motion, deafening noise, acrid smoke, and the coppery stench of blood.

"General Kemper!"

The heavy-set Virginian turned, imperturbable. Drayton glimpsed that the art of battle was to maintain your sanity while chaos throbbed in your ears and in your eyes.

"Sir, General Longstreet says look to your right! See that little knoll? The Yankees are about to come up there in force. They will have your right in enfilade as you press forward."

General Kemper stared and nodded and was about to give his orders — too late. Always the story of lost battles: too little, too late.

Years later Drayton learned it was two Vermont regiments, the 13th and 14th Infantry under Brigadier George Stannard that took up the extended position on the Confederate right. As Kemper's men rushed toward Cemetery Ridge, the enterprising Vermonters, out ahead of their main defense line, rose up and poured a devastating fire into the Confederates' open flank. The Virginians fell in heaps. Since the Southerners faced 90 degrees away from the Vermonters, they couldn't return an effective volley. Instead they shied away from the unexpected blast and herded left toward the center, entangling themselves with their fellow Virginians of the brigades of Garnett and Armistead. General Kemper tried to correct the drift, but the mind-shattering noise and the momentum of the charge made it impossible. A moment later he was wounded and had to be carried from the field.

In virtually the same instant a heavy blow hit Drayton in the chest. All about him turned incandescent white, then black. He felt himself falling, but had no recollection of actually hitting the ground. *So this is what it's like to die*, he thought.

He felt a deep but not a sharp pain across the entire top half of his body.

Pain, but no fear, only a profound sadness that he wouldn't see Celia again, nor Ranse, nor Cabell, nor Father, nor sit again on the veranda above the glimmering Edisto sipping iced cordial. He felt consciousness ebbing away, and a resignation settled over him, bringing a degree of peace, suddenly offset by curiosity. How did one actually die? Was there a … a formal procedure in passing over? Would he be met by anyone, a committee, so to speak? He hoped it might include his mother, who had died when he was young, and whom he'd hardly known.

Sometime later he came to, realizing that such thoughts were the thoughts of the living, not the dead. Along with the pain. Iron claws gripped his chest, and each breath was agony. His sight cleared and he saw Beltane staring back at him, his large eyes full of equine concern. The blessed horse had remained by him amid the shelling instead of running away as any sensible animal would do. Men included.

How long he'd been unconscious he couldn't tell, but the din of gunfire had subsided, and amid the roaring and buzzing in his brain he heard muffled cheers from somewhere up the Union-occupied ridge. With an effort he struggled to one elbow, despite the nausea and excruciating bolts that shot through his chest. Banks of smoke were lifting but still obscured the landscape. He couldn't see much of the Union lines, only grey forms in retreat, individually and in small clumps. Some limped on their muskets, some helped others arm-in-arm. The Grand Charge had failed. Lee's Invincibles had been vanquished.

A weaponless young man scurried past, tears streaming down his cheeks. Hardly able to catch his breath, Drayton rasped, "Here, friend! Give me a hand."

The fellow stopped and stared, as if encountering an apparition, then stepped forward and slid strong arms under Drayton's back. "Sir, you're bad hurt. Can you rise?"

"Lord willing," gasped Drayton, swaying to his feet in spite of the pain. He noticed for the first time that his chest was a smear of blood. The young man handed him Bel's reins.

"I can rise, but I can't ride."

"Then I'll help you walk," said the young soldier, evidently glad of the opportunity to aid a comrade, and perhaps also explain why he'd come away with no musket.

Gripping the stirrup leather with his right hand, and with the soldier supporting him on his left, Drayton struggled back to Longstreet. The General managed a brief approving nod in the midst of planning to repel a possible Union counter-attack. His fellow staff officers laid Drayton gently on a blanket in the shade and peeled back his blood-encrusted jacket and linen shirt.

"Well, lookee here," said Sergeant Simms, the staff medical orderly, tracing the shape incised in Drayton's flesh. "A perfect oval." He fished inside Drayton's torn gray uniform and brought out the bent miniature. "Right over the heart, too. Lieutenant, you're lucky to be alive."

Celia had come between him and certain death, although the impact still left him badly hurt. Badly enough to be invalided home, as it turned out. The brass was deeply dented by the strike of the flying ball, the enamel cracked, and the visage all but ruined where enamel chips had fallen away. All but the eyes, those dark searching eyes that had captured him long years ago. The eyes still peered out above the cracks in the broken surface, warm and serene and mischievous.

Such interpositions were common in the war, with tons of lead whizzing over every battlefield. Countless times he'd heard about someone saved from a Minié ball by a pocket Testament or a Bible in a haversack. His old comrade Calhoun Sparks had once escaped injury when a ball struck the eyeglasses he carried in a breast pocket. Only two days ago the Army was abuzz about Confederate General Harry Heth's narrow escape as the battle began. A ball had struck him in the head, but he was spared by the thickness of newspaper he'd placed in the hatband of a new hat to improve its fit. Some cynics wished the ball had hit lower, since many blamed Heth's rash acts on the First Day for the unwanted battle in this unexpected place. But alas, there was ample blame to go around, starting with General Lee himself, although Drayton dared not utter the thought.

Jacksonboro, South Carolina, April 1913.

The memory faded, was placed back in its proper file and the war relic back in his pocket. Drayton continued his walk. Almost home now. There was much to do to prepare. His grandson Tommy was coming to visit with Cabell.

Annalee never accompanied him to Tusculum. One obvious reason — Celia was buried nearby at the ruins of Cypress Stand. He tried to be understanding of his wife's jealousy of one so long dead. For the sake of good form he always asked her to come with him. She always refused, and he was content. Years had passed since he blamed her or himself. Marriage was one of those institutions from which the participants perhaps expected too much; although his marriage to Celia, brief as it was, had exceeded all expectations. When he wed again Drayton had resolved to rise above this lamentable human tendency. He felt he'd done his best despite undeniable errors, but to no avail. He had even kept Annalee's secret, unasked and simply for her sake. She didn't know that he knew the truth about her late husband Isaac Joyner. If he had his secrets… well, Annalee had hers, too.

He stopped for a moment to enjoy a great blue heron taking to the air, following its ungainly glide to the far bank. These birds were actually grey, though with a bluish cast, and he wondered why they were called blue herons. The blue and the grey. It seemed he could never escape the reminders. Still, the sight lifted his spirits. He trudged on, and the rhythm of the hike stirred up his thoughts. Thinking of Annalee began to crack his wall of resolution. For the first time since his brother's visit at the College he began to consider the Gettysburg trip in earnest. Annalee didn't want him to go, and suddenly this seemed an argument in favor of going.

He and Annalee had lived together long enough to scour away the feelings that had first brought them together. It was like overdrawing one's account, since the initial affections didn't regenerate themselves. For his part at least, what remained was a residue of superficial good will, overshadowed by the knowledge of their incompatibility and the steady, unfolding display of her controlling nature. He strove to be kind, to show understanding and compassion, as spouses should. For her world had collapsed in 1865 as it had for all Southerners. But her response had been an unseemly grubbing for power and control over everything within reach. Nothing was more corrosive to a marriage. In a sense, the War went on, its effects reverberating down the decades since 1865.

Drayton sought no power. What he wanted was understanding, love, and intimacy. But Annalee was a shrewd woman. Long ago, he understood she'd sensed a wound deep in his soul. Drayton had never told her of his wartime experiences. He suspected she believed his diffidence flowed from guilty feelings for the dead Cecelia. In fact, there was a kernel of truth in her suspicions. But once again and as always, she misread him. Nevertheless, he was not whole within himself, and the knowledge had become her chief instrument of manipulation. Hearing Cabell's news of the Gettysburg reunion must have dismayed her. If the reunion brought reconciliation with himself, it would jeopardize her power and control. What irony, he thought. Power and control. Met by the natural human impulse to resist power and control, especially when exercised by an alien, hostile people. It was why the South had gone to war in the first place.

Chapter Four

West Bank of the Edisto River, April 1913.

Cabell Heyward FitzHenry bounced along the clay road from his farm at Green Pond in Colleton County to the Edisto River in an old-fashioned, one-horse buggy. At his side was his grand-nephew, Drayton's grandson, Thomas Preston FitzHenry Junior. Tommy was a bright twelve-year-old, tall and thin. His adolescent loose-jointedness reminded Cabell of a young colt not sure where to put his feet. He seldom spoke unless spoken to. When he did speak, he surprised his elders with his discernment. Cabell attributed this precocity to the failure of his family – an alcoholic father, with whom he lived in Beaufort, and a mother who had absconded to parts unknown. Did she flee because of her husband's drinking, or did he drink because she had fled? No one knew, except possibly Tommy, who wasn't saying. The rest of the family, with typical Southern reticence, refused to speculate on the matter openly.

Driving a spirited Cleveland Bay required constant attention, a tiring exercise for a man of 77. He let the boy handle the horse from time to time for the experience, until the animal detected hesitant hands on the leads and became restive.

"Here. Let me take over," said Cabell. They rode in silence for a while.

Tommy said, "Grand-Uncle, why don't you get one of those motorcars? I've been seeing the new Ford Model T's in Beaufort. Wouldn't it be easier to drive one of them than a horse and buggy?"

Cabell could have easily afforded one Model T. "I've thought about it, Son. But driving the damn thing would require me to operate three foot pedals, and ... well." He tapped his wooden leg. "Anyway, horses don't break down or have flat tires."

"No, sir. But motorcars don't colic or founder and drop a shoe," Tommy replied.

Cabell laughed. *He's sharp, this one.* "True, son. And saddles don't come off motorcars in midstride. Did I ever tell you about the time...?" He paused, recalling a moment of fear and excitement almost as vivid in memory as it had been in reality.

"Yes, Grand-Uncle? Tell me what?"

Yes, indeed. Tell me what? says Tommy. For a Southerner there was usually a story at the root of every very impulse. In this case, one of gratitude. Drayton had saved his brother's life in 1862, and Cabell had always been generous in acknowledging the debt. True, his curiosity about Drayton's war experience intruded in the relationship. Even a touch of envy intruded, since Drayton was accounted a hero while Cabell's war service was, if not ignored, deemed unremarkable, and despite the loss of his leg at Burgess Mill. But *au fond* lay a deep sense of obligation and duty, more than one might normally feel toward a brother. He owed Drayton, and he was going to re-pay. He'd drag him by the collar to Gettysburg if that's what it took to heal his brother's wound of the soul.

Like most men, they found it difficult to express the love they felt for each other, all the more so because it was deep and heartfelt. Cabell was determined not merely to express it in words, but in action – to perform a service even if it went against his brother's inclination. He would have to use all his powers of persuasion, something a good lawyer ought to find doable. Thinking back to the War, he knew he owed his best efforts to the brother who'd spared him from captivity and possibly saved his life. It was natural to love one's brother. But what he felt for Drayton – gratitude? admiration? concern? – extended far beyond the normal ties of kinship.

"Tell me what, Grand-Uncle?" Tommy insisted.

"Wait till we get to Ashepoo, Tommy. It's too hard to talk over the road noise. At Ashepoo we'll have a bite of lunch and I'll tell you then, or while we ride the ferry over."

They stopped at a tumbledown shed at the Ashepoo River crossing. Lapstrake siding had come loose and protruded from the outer walls. There were gaps in the cedar shingles. And the plank trestle tables in front were weathered and covered with graffiti carved into the wood. But the old black couple who ran the place served the freshest, tastiest seafood this side of Charleston. Man and boy busied themselves with reducing the mound of fried clams and boiled shrimp, and sipping sweet iced tea.

Tommy laid down his napkin and said, "All right, Grand-Uncle. Time for that story."

"Ah, Mistah Thomas, Are you sure?" Cabell teased. "Another old war story?"

"Yes, sir. I love those stories about you and GramPa and Cal Butler and Wade Hampton and all."

Cabell reproached himself for putting the boy to the test. He stared at him and said, "What's the point, son? Today it's a different world. The Yankees won, we lost, and the country has moved on. The North is enjoying what they call the Gilded Age. Do you know what that means?"

"I think so, Grand-Uncle. Gilded means golden."

"That's right. Our Northern industrialists possess wealth that oriental potentates could only dream of. The South has been looted. The Indian tribes have been reduced to beggary. America defeated Spain the year you were born and took over its global empire. Don't you think that makes the War Between the States irrelevant? Who cares if us old Confederates cling to our lost cause and tales of gallantry?"

"Well, GramPa told me..." The boy's face wrinkled with the effort of recall. "GramPa said 'courage and fortitude are never in vain.' And he said, 'no good cause is ever lost because *all* good causes are lost causes.' I don't exactly understand that last part."

"He did, did he? Well, he's right. It's time for the story then. About your GramPa's courage."

Prince William County, Virginia; December 1862.

The moment that might have been Cabell's last but for his brother came at the end of 1862. He and Drayton served in the 2nd South Carolina Cavalry, posted in Northern Virginia since July 1861. Winter was upon them, a harsh season for these men from the Low Country of South Carolina, where snow and ice were a rarity. Cabell, a second lieutenant, commanded a platoon of the Beaufort District Troop, now part of the 2nd South Carolina Cavalry Regiment.

On a bitter night in December, Lieutenant Colonel Calbraith Butler, the regimental commander, called a council of war at his bivouac. Captain Thomas Screven, commander of the Troop, and his company officers sat on empty ration crates around a cheerful fire of pine knots while Colonel Butler outlined a grand raid on the Orange and Alexandria Railroad, the main supply line for the Federals in Northern Virginia.

Until now, most of the Regiment's service had been dull and routine. They had taken part in Stuart's epic ride around McClellan's Army back in the spring of 1862, but had mostly missed the dreadful battle of Sharpsburg on Antietam Creek in Maryland in September. Now the war seemed to have sneaked off to a quiet place for an unauthorized spot of leave. The hours crawled by in a tedium of picket duty along the Occoquan River. They served as couriers for the higher-ups, which at least got them out of camp. They spent most of their waking hours enduring the never-ending guard mount and horse-care fatigues in camp. It was disappointing as well as boring, since they'd ridden off to war with images of Napoleonic cavalry in their heads. Southern horse soldiers envisioned themselves riding with Murat at Jena, plumes flying and bugles blaring; or at Eylau, one of the great cavalry charges in all history. Compared to those images, their war had been dull and insignificant. But things were about to change, if only slightly.

With a gloved finger on the map, Colonel Butler traced the railroad from Manassas Junction running southwest below Warrenton and through key points in their area of operations.

Butler wore a grin that appeared diabolical in the flickering firelight as he issued his orders to Captain Screven. "Tom, I want you to spread your troop along the railroad between Nokesville and Bristow Station. Your primary mission is to gather intelligence on enemy movements. But when you have the tactical advantage, stir 'em up a bit, with minimum risk to yourselves. We need prisoners. And of course we want fresh horses, tack, weapons, and supplies."

Captain Screven nodded and said, "Colonel, could you be more precise regarding 'tactical advantage?'"

"Well, surprise, mainly. That will offset their greater numbers. And I hardly need add, there are no better horsemen or marksmen than the Beaufort District Troop. That ought to be advantage enough."

As the platoon leaders rose to join their men, Butler added, "Gentlemen, until now our cavalry duties have been routine. But that is about to change into something of a more strategic nature. In assuming an aggressive posture, General Hampton wants to keep the enemy confused and off balance." He spoke of newly-promoted Brigadier General Wade Hampton, in whose Legion they served. "Our attacks must force the Yankees to deploy more troops to guard the railroad, troops that might be used elsewhere against General Lee and our main forces. That's all I need say at present."

Screven looked tellingly at Cabell and his platoon leaders. Something major was clearly building up for the spring. A campaign to take the War into the North was the rumor. Into enemy territory, where the land hadn't been devastated as in Virginia.

Drayton, who had never aspired to military rank, was a private in Cabell's platoon. Hundreds of the sons of the Southern planter class preferred to serve as enlisted men — 'gentlemen rankers,' they were called. Returning from the command briefing, Cabell nodded to his brother, who tossed him a casual salute.

"Are we finally going into action, or continue to sit here and put down roots?" Drayton asked.

Cabell said, "Oh, you'll soon be getting all the action you want."

"It's not what I want," said Drayton. "But Beltane is getting soft and wants to do some real open-field galloping. And some forage. We've depleted all the food sources around these parts."

"Right. We have orders to raid the Lincolnites at Bristow Station. Let's hope for new forage for man and horse, new mounts, saddles, and tack, and whatever else we need. Join your platoon. We'll be moving out in an hour."

Cabell confirmed final details of the order with Captain Screven and Colonel Butler, then led his platoon from the regimental bivouac across the Rappahannock River. Other platoons departed along different routes. Riding around the Federal picket line, the South Carolinians made their way quietly along hidden paths toward Bristow Station. Talking was strictly forbidden. The only sound was the occasional snort of a horse, clop of a hoof, and jingling of tack.

Arriving just before dawn, Cabell posted his horsemen in a dark copse of pines on a slope above the rail-bed. Since they were almost always outnumbered, the Confederates had to rely on guile, creative tactics, and superior horsemanship. Cabell's plan was to lure the enemy into ambush at the verge of the woods by attacking with a small number as bait, then turning and ostensibly fleeing. He intended using the fenced fields to keep the pursuing Yankees out of pistol range. Federal cavalry couldn't – or normally wouldn't – jump fences, a skill the South Carolinians were long used to. Hadn't Colonel Butler boasted that every man of the Beaufort Troop was a natural-born rider? All they needed was to put a few fences between them and the enemy. The Yankees would stop to pull down the rails, giving the Confederates time to escape.

After an hour's wait, a patrol of Union cavalry came into view along the rail cut, numbering about 30 men. Cabell ordered two squads to wait in ambush in the screen of trees. Drawing his Colt, he nodded toward the first squad and whispered hoarsely, "Let's stir 'em up!" He led the squad galloping from the trees and whooping like Apaches, taking advantage of those critical few moments of surprise when the enemy's response is frozen.

Their pistols popped sharply in the crisp air, and two bluecoats toppled from their saddles. The tactical aim was to cause a 'scatterization,' but without being scattered themselves. Maintaining unit integrity was hard for fast-moving cavalry.

Cabell emptied one of the two pistols he carried, as did his troopers, then wheeled and dashed for the pines, jumping a split rail fence. As expected, it delayed the Yankees, who stopped to kick down the rails before pursuing. But they were learning. They kicked them down from the saddle instead of dismounting, which gained them a few valuable minutes in the pursuit.

Another fence, and Cabell's horse Jolly sprang up and over. Cabell felt a lurch and a sinking sensation as he landed hard on the other side – on the ground, not in the saddle. At first he couldn't tell what had happened, then saw the girth had parted. He'd come off when the saddle shifted, landing heavily on his left shoulder. Only the springiness of the deep winter broom straw spared him injury. Struggling to his feet and regaining his breath, he glanced back anxiously at the Federals, then to the fleeing Confederates. He expected his brother to swerve and pick him up, and felt a surge of hot anger as his brother continued to flee. Where *was* the damned rascal?

Turning, he saw Drayton was pursuing Jolly. The horse had been trained to stop when his rider came off. But the flapping saddle had panicked the animal. Jolly ran on, and with a head start. At a hard gallop, his brother quickly caught him up, even though Beltane was bearing rider and equipment and Jolly was bare. Drayton leaned over his neck like a Cossack and grabbed the bridle. He turned smoothly back toward Cabell, who watched transfixed at the display of horsemanship.

Drayton guided Jolly to Cabell, slowed to a trot, and tossed him the reins. Cabell grabbed mane and reins with his left hand. Riding bareback, he followed his grinning brother, pounding across the fields scant yards ahead of the enraged Federals, now deprived of their prisoner. They entered the woods while the Yankees slowed. At precisely the right moment the two hidden squads erupted from hiding, Colts blazing, killing and wounding several Bluecoats and routing the rest.

Later, on a Yankee mare and leading Jolly, they rode home, surfeit with prisoners and captured supplies.

Cabell, said, "Brother, that was a splendid piece of riding. Not to mention you saved me from being shot. Or captured. "

Drayton laughed. "Well, it was Jolly I was trying to save. Officers we have and to spare. But you know how desperately we need good mounts."

Tusculum Cottage, West Bank of the Edisto, April 1913.

Cabell and Tommy reached the cottage on the Edisto by mid-afternoon. Drayton met them at the foot of the porch smiling broadly. He embraced his grandson and shook hands with Cabell. As he unhitched the horse to lead it to its stall and hay, he told his kinfolks, "There's a fire. Go inside and get warm. Tommy, there's hot cocoa on the tea caddy by the hearth." The waning April day had grown chilly, and Cabell was feeling it in his bones. He was glad of the cozy refuge.

Later Drayton spread a country supper from local sources — roast duck with oysters, wild rice, boiled cattail roots in butter, corn muffins with Tusculum honey. Warmed inside and out, the brothers decided to enjoy a *digestif* of the local peach brandy with coffee on the verandah where they could watch the sunset. In comfortable country tweeds, they took their drinks overlooking the River, while Tommy had another mug of steaming cocoa.

Cabell said, "Still living off the land, I see." He sighed deeply.

Drayton asked, "Brother, aren't you well?"

"Just feeling my seventy-seven years" said Cabell. "I feel as though I'm nearing the edge of the eternal abyss." He paused and sipped. "But if my time is drawing to a close, I think I've run a pretty good course. And every day has been a gift of God since Burgess Mill." In this sharp fight in 1864 near Petersburg a cannon ball had taken off his leg at the knee. Thomas Preston Hampton, for whom Tommy was named, had died in the same fight in the arms of his father, General Wade Hampton. Hampton's other son, Wade Junior, had been seriously wounded in the back as he bent over to give aid to his younger brother. For a time, General Hampton thought he had lost both sons.

Cabell and Drayton had made it through four years of bitter combat more or less intact. But, as Drayton never failed to remind him, they *had* lost, as attested by the blackened ruins nearby. The skeletal chimneys mocked him with a lingering regret for the grace of a time that was irretrievably gone.

Sniffing his brandy, Cabell said, "I suppose the approaching end of my days makes me appreciate this place and the time here with my kin all the more. The Yankees may've destroyed the old house, but they couldn't destroy the land or the River. And thanks to you, Brother, they couldn't steal it, either. The land and the River are what you and I love most."

Cabell smiled as Drayton quoted the well-loved lines: "*Thank Him who placed us here / Beneath so kind a sky.* "

"Good old Henry Timrod," said Cabell. "He was a particular friend of yours, wasn't he?"

"No, not a particular friend. He was a decade older than I. But I used to listen to him read his verse at Russell's Bookstore, down on King Street. It was the nearest thing in Charleston to a literary *salon*. Gilmore Simms was usually there. And Basil Gildersleeve, who inspired me to study the classics. And the Charleston fire-eaters. Timrod and Orr and Paul Hayne and Barney Rhett."

"And you had the temerity to argue with these giants. I recall it was your self-appointed mission to prevent the War," said Cabell, a little sharply.

"Yes, but I was the youngest among them, and they paid me little mind."

"No more than you pay me," said Cabell. "But for your sake, I hope you'll listen to me this once. Did you at least read the invitations?"

Drayton nodded. "Actually, I did."

He took out the note card from Mrs. White of the United Daughters of the Confederacy, and read aloud, 'This gathering at Gettysburg is to be a great Peace Celebration where the gallant survivors of both sides will come together to cement the good will and friendship that have gradually been forming for the good of the country. On the battlefield of Gettysburg was shown the highest devotion to country, and it will make our old heroes happy to revisit that spot made glorious by their heroism.'

Again, Cabell heard a note of some old secret rancor when Drayton said, "I may be old, but I'm certainly no 'old hero.'"

"Well, that's beside the point. It will do you good, I think. A catharsis. Gettysburg was an epic, and as a scholar of the classics, surely you love epics. You were there, in the midst of it, like fighting before the walls of Troy."

"In deference to you, Brother, I've begun to consider going. But I still haven't overcome my doubts. I really don't understand this need of war veterans to go back to the scene. I think we'd want to stay far away from such places, not go back to them."

Cabell disagreed. "Something profound happens to men at such places, something that may require a return visit to finally understand the meaning of it all — the violence, the pain, the loss."

"Well, at Gettysburg I'd feel as the captives of ancient Rome must have felt in a Roman triumph. Paraded behind their conqueror in chains along with the spoils before all the people to see. A spectacle of imperial domination by Rome. Humiliation and submission of the conquered." Drayton retrieved the bottle and filled their cordial glasses.

Cabell said, "I think you're wrong there. In fact, the way I read the invitations and other notices, the event is intended to do just the opposite, to assuage the humiliation of the conquered, to remind us that now we're all Americans, North and South."

"Perhaps. But I fear it's just a more polite version of the Roman triumph, delayed fifty years."

Cabell frowned. "You play your part well, the Stoic Greek, the stern Roman. But you don't fool me, Drayton, I know something gnaws at your insides. You're not… not a *settled* man. Not since the War."

"Brother, you're a wise man in many ways," Drayton said. "I've always respected your insight. But we're different, you and I. Your own wisdom deceives you in certain matters. It seems to have escaped your notice that my war experience differed from yours, and that I have good reason for not wanting to be reminded of it. Especially at Gettysburg."

Cabell persisted. "This encampment is supposed to be a time of national reconciliation. Can you not be reconciled?"

Drayton stood, resting his hands on the porch railing and drinking in the late afternoon landscape. Cabell's attention was inexorably drawn to the injured hand, puckered over with scar tissue.

His brother responded after a long pause, "I could perhaps be reconciled with our Northern brothers. They were valiant men. Most were good men. But doesn't this reunion mean we must be reconciled with their version of the past? Don't you think we're being invited to Gettysburg to serve as foils for their …for their propaganda? Remember, Cabell, the propaganda of the winner becomes the history of the loser. And with this I can't be reconciled."

"I see no reason to think propaganda is the purpose."

"Big Brother, don't deceive yourself. The Yankee narrative of events has become the official and only acceptable version. You know it as well as I do: arrogant Southerners rebel against the sublime Union in order to maintain their evil institution of slavery. Father Abraham descends from Heaven on a golden cloud, bearing the Emancipation Proclamation in one hand and a sword in the other. Virtuous Northerners take up arms to put down the traitors, free the slaves, and preserve a government of the people, by the people, and for the people. Then Lincoln is martyred and becomes our secular Christ."

Cabell snorted. "Well, yes. I'm afraid you have it there, in a nutshell."

"This narrative has become so deeply entrenched – it's even taught in our own Southern schools, for God's sake," said Drayton, whirling and chopping the air with his right hand. "So deeply entrenched that nothing can ever shine a ray of light into its darkness."

Cabell frowned. "I don't deny that's the official version. But we Southerners will always know the truth of why we fought. It's lodged deep in our hearts, and they can't take it away from us."

"No, not from us. But they can take it from him and future generations." Drayton gestured toward his grandson, who listened intently to the exchange between grandfather and grand-uncle. "Who controls the present controls the past. And who controls the past controls the future."

Cabell looked at Tommy and smiled. "Then it's up to us to pass on the true history, to make sure our descendants understand. I for one aim to use the reunion for this purpose. Why, they're even going to allow us to fly the Battle Flag alongside the Stars and Stripes. The North needs us now. The old bitterness is healing on both sides. You need healing, too; and this trip is too important an opportunity to pass up. To come to terms not just with the past but with yourself. You served with distinction in the War. Yet sometimes… well, I don't understand, but sometimes you act like you're ashamed of your war record. Instead you ought to be proud."

"It's too late for that," Drayton said. "The years take back the laurels they gave to younger men."

Cabell was at the limit of his patience. "Ah, well, I've said all I will on the matter. Have it your own way, as you always do. You're as stubborn as a three-legged mule." Then he sighed. "Anyway, I'm too old and too busted up to make the trip, much less get around if I did. I'd need a helper."

Tommy's head shot up from his chocolate. "Grand-Uncle, I could go and be your helper." His eyes gleamed with a fierce light. "I want to see where Grand-Uncle Ranse picked up the fallen flag and charged the Yankees."

The brothers glanced at each other, Cabell with amusement, Drayton with alarm. Tommy seemed to have grown an inch as he spoke, and his thin chest puffed out.

Drayton reproved his grandson mildly. "Tommy, you know your Great-Uncle Ranse was killed in that charge." *Killed.* A weak word to describe what really happened. But at least he'd died instantly and hadn't lingered in agony, like so many others.

"Oh, yes, GramPa, I know." The boy's eyes shone fiercer yet.

Cabell smiled consolingly and said, "Tommy, I'm sorry to have to tell you that children are not invited. However, you might go as one of those new Boy Scouts. The Boys Scouts in Pennsylvania have been given the job of squires, so to speak, for the old fellows. They're expecting 40,000 old soldiers. Two troops of Boy Scouts from North and South Carolina are going along to help take care of their grandpas. Would you like to become a Boy Scout?"

Tommy smiled, climbed out of his chair, and approached the two old men. He said, "Oh, yes, Grand-Uncle. Does that mean I can have a uniform?"

"Uniform?" Cabell saw the concern deepen in his brother's face.

"Yes, GramPa. The Boy Scouts wear khaki." It was a new word in the American lexicon. Tommy pronounced it British-style, COCK-ee. "Just like the Army men wear. And you also get a campaign hat, just like the soldiers."

"You've been studying on the subject, I see," said Drayton.

"Oh, yes, sir." Tommy's face glowed in the setting sun. "I want to be a soldier when I grow up."

Drayton looked at Cabell, shaking his head. "It's the curse of our race – the lust for military glory. Perhaps we ought to go to Gettysburg and let him see the *other* side of military glory."

"Then I can go, GramPa?"

"Well, it's not entirely up to me. Your father will have to agree. But if your Grand-Uncle Cabell and I explain that you'll be learning a history lesson, I think he might let you. But I haven't decided whether I'll go myself."

Chapter Five

Early the next day Tommy came onto the porch, his eyes shining at the view of the River and a flight of great egrets, the morning sun tinting their white plumage in gold. He hugged Drayton and took a chair. His grandfather pushed a mug toward him and a tray of corn muffins. He asked, "Do you want your chocolate, or have you grown up enough to try coffee?"

Tommy smiled shyly and said, "Coffee's too bitter. But I'll try it if you think I should."

"I think you should do what *you* want, not what someone else thinks you ought. But most people do find coffee more bracing when they get older. Just the thing in the morning to chase away the night's cobwebs and put you in the frame to hear an old man's tales."

The boy tried it. Drayton poured in plenty of cream and sugar, but Tommy's nose wrinkled. "I *might* could get used to it," he said. Drayton laughed and nudged his cocoa to him.

They sipped their hot beverages in companionable silence until the egrets took silently to the air, standing out brightly against the black of the river.

Tommy asked suddenly, "GramPa, it's so beautiful here. Why doesn't GramMa ever come with you?"

He paused a long time before answering, knowing instinctively it was a significant moment. He could do no less than answer truthfully, yet he didn't want to poison the boy's feelings for his grandmother. No words of malice riding on words of truth.

Finally he said, "Son, I think she feels uncomfortable here. There are too many sad memories at Cypress Stand, too many ghosts of the past."

Tommy gestured toward the ruins. A hundred yards away from the blackened brick-and-tabby foundation lay the family cemetery, obscured in the early morning in the gloom of spreading oaks. A low wall of worn mossy brick dating from before the Revolution enclosed the plot.

"You mean...*her*?"

"Yes, I think so." A wise question from one so young. Obviously he'd heard bits and pieces of the story.

"What happened to her, GramPa? Why does GramMa always shush me when I ask about her?"

Looking into his eager, trusting face, he wanted to say to Tommy, *It was too beautiful to last. Like this farm. Like our lives before the War. But don't tell him that. Give him hope. He will come to know despair soon enough, when he is old.*

It appeared this was where his account of the past would begin, unexpectedly. But it was impossible to explain to a youngster the lingering passion for one long dead, and the absence of passion for one to whom he was married, when it was the boy's own grandmother. Drayton wouldn't lie, but neither would he burden the boy with knowledge too far above his understanding.

While the memories rushed at him and caught at the filaments of his heart, he realized the time had come to share Celia's history with the boy, even if only a bare recitation of fact.

The silence hung heavily. Drayton said finally, "Well, Tommy, she was my first wife. She died of typhus while caring for sick Confederates in the little army hospital at Jacksonborough, where the train stopped. It happened many years before I met your grandmother Annalee. It was during the War, while I was away fighting in Virginia."

"How did you meet her, GramPa?"

"How? Ah, Thomas, that is a story all in itself. A great love story." *That is what will survive of us. Our love.*

Charleston, South Carolina; January 1860.

Drayton was surprised at how glad he was to be back in Charleston. He'd spent the last 18 months touring Europe and had enjoyed the great cities of the continent. He had studied in Berlin under one of the great Greek scholars of his day. He'd studied under the world's leading expert in the burgeoning field of Greek archaeology. It had all been broadening and stimulating. But no city was as fine as the city of his birth. Now that he was home, he supposed the coming spring season would bring scores of female relations of Charleston's families to town, the so-called 'fishing fleet' looking for husbands. He would be in great demand after his sojourn in Europe. But he was weary of designing women and empty socializing, and hoped to avoid his own family's pressures to get married. Let him live a little first, enjoy his new horse, think about what he'd absorbed on his Grand Tour.

And that was mostly what he did – especially reliving the time he'd spent in Ireland. Like most Southerners, he was 'blood proud,' and wanted to learn more about the origin of the family. He explored the places in Leinster associated in family tradition with Meiler FitzHenry, a Cambro-Norman lord and the first of the name to come to Ireland, with Strongbow, in 1170. Meiler's father was Henry FitzHenry, an illegitimate son of England's King Henry I and Nesta, daughter of Welsh prince Rhys ap Twdyr, or Tudor as it came to be spelled in English. Thus the family claimed to have both Plantagenet and Tudor blood, even if both came from the wrong side of the blanket.

He'd spent hours tramping the scenic Wicklow Mountains, deeply moved by Glendalough, the Valley of the Two Lakes, with its spectacular ruins of the old monastery, and the breathtaking view from the Sally Gap. Then he'd traveled to The Curragh, visiting old FitzHenry lands along the way. He called on Archibald Rowan of County Kildare, one of the last United Irishman of 1798 and his grandfather's friend. Now in his 90's, Old Rowan kept Drayton enthralled – and appalled – by tales of the 1798 Rebellion, giving him a glimpse of the 'last splendour of the Gael.'

But what stayed with him most vividly was the first encounter with his great horse. The animal was out of Crough Patrick, the legendary Thoroughbred from County Mayo that won the Stewards' Cup in 1856, the first Irish horse to capture this top honor in racing. He was five, not quite yet a 'made' horse, but with some good training under him. The local lord, the Viscount Breconsfield, had been using the horse as a field hunter. The Viscount had just died, and some of his estate was being sold off to pay gambling debts. Drayton heard about it just in time.

The Viscount's chief trainer was Art O'Leary, a small arthritic man who'd once been the lord's jockey. He greeted Drayton with a warmth that grew even warmer when he learned his visitor was a wealthy American. Might he be in the market for a horse, Art wondered. Drayton fretted over the difficulty of transporting him home.

"What's his name," Drayton asked.

"Bel-tawn-ah," said Art, pronouncing it in the Gaelic. "Or Bel-tane, as the Sassanach say."

"The Sassanach?"

"The English."

"And what is Beltane?"

"Bealtaine is the first of May, a celebration of spring," Art explained. "It's also the Irish for the month of May, the day he was foaled. The same day as we hold in the ancient tales that the Men of Dea came across the sea in a mist to do battle with the Old Ones who lived in Erin. The lord trained him for a hunter and rode him to the hounds 'til he died last month. But Bel is destined for more than chasing fox. The old people say he descends from Enbarr of the Flowing Mane."

"An Irish race horse?"

"Ah, to be sure. Enbarr was the horse of Manannán mac Lir, the sea god of the old Irish. Enbarr could ride across land and sea and never be caught, nor ever harmed by mortal man."

"Then he would be right at home in Charleston by the sea."

"Aye, likely so. This horse was born to be a war horse. But the only war horses in Ireland are those of the English. And you'll pardon me for saying so, but we're not after giving this horse to the English."

Drayton saw the gelding was agitated. The grooms were reluctant to come near him. "Is he up like this all the time? Has he kicked or bitten any of the grooms?"

"Divil a one. He can be fractious, though. He's put the fright on 'em, sure. He was gelded late. But he just needs a friend, now the old lord is gone. Of the right sort, that is."

"Is he fast? Has he raced, or only hunted?"

"Aye, he is fast, though he's not a sprinter like some of our Irish Thoroughbreds. But he has bottom. For the right master he'll go far as well as fast, and never give up till his great heart burst within him."

Beltane's head was elegant and perfectly proportioned to the body. His ears were on the short side, his legs straight, with slightly more bone than the English Thoroughbred. For strength, Drayton realized, and from the blood of his great-grand-dam, Irish draft, to be sure. He had strong, supple hindquarters and a straight back, neither too long nor too short-coupled. What captivated Drayton most was the curious, intelligent eyes, as if he was eager to be part of whatever was going on about him. At sixteen hands and change, he was big. And spirited, but not mean. It appeared to Drayton his fractiousness was simply a matter of picking up the fear and anxiety of the grooms. They fed off one another. If the animal was sensitive enough to read the negative signals of a groom, then he could equally be reassured by Drayton's affection and self-confidence. As Drayton studied the horse, suddenly the task of shipping him home seemed less daunting.

"Mr. O'Leary," Drayton said, walking 'round the horse. "Could you please have the groom walk him, then trot him on the longe?"

Art took the longe line and whip himself, though the whip proved unnecessary. Beltane moved out briskly through his paces. As he circled, Drayton realized he was falling in love. With the trainer in charge and not the skittish grooms, Beltane walked square and level. His trot was lovely, collected, soft and slightly springy instead of long and rangy. And the canter — it was pure poetry. He circled in both directions, moving straight ahead with no dishing or head-tossing or mixing his leads. At the trot and canter, his poll was up and nose down, framed in a very businesslike manner.

Drayton felt Beltane's legs, and found no swelling or heat in the joints. He lifted the feet and saw they'd been well cared for. His hooves were slightly larger than the average Thoroughbred's, bred for the springy turf common to Ireland. Drayton stroked his neck in large circles, spoke to him soothingly. By inspiration he began to croon the songs of Thomas Moore he'd learned in Wicklow. The horse's ears pricked up and he turned curiously, as if no one had ever sung to him. Drayton breathed lightly into his nostrils, removed the longe line, and slipped on the bridle. Beltane stood patiently.

"Here sir, will I saddle him for you?" Art offered.

"No, Mr. O'Leary. If I can ride him bareback, then I can ride him under tack. If I can't ride him bare, then I will never ride him."

It was a splendid ride, and Drayton understood Beltane was satisfied. The horse consented to leave Ireland and come to America, like so many Irishmen before him.

***

After a stormy passage from Queenstown, with the usual winter gales in the Atlantic, Drayton disembarked at Adger's Wharf in a city that seldom changed. He supervised Beltane's unloading, stabling, warm mash, and a rub-down, then walked to the FitzHenry home on East Battery and Atlantic Street, a pre-Revolutionary mansion with a commanding view of Charleston Harbor. Skies were cold but clear, and he caught the last of the Yuletide celebrations with his father, his brother Cabell, and Ranse, who were eager to see Drayton's new friend. A few days later he strolled up to the College of Charleston to call on Alston Cowles, his former Classics professor.

Cowles was a large man whose corpulence strained against the fabric of his grey suit just short of popping the buttons. He stood and gestured Drayton into his office, lined with hundreds of books, but otherwise a scene of obsessive neatness. Nothing littered the desk, which contained a single open volume.

"Ah, Mr. FitzHenry, welcome home. I'm truly glad to see you." He extended a hand with sausage-like fingers.

"Hello, Professor Cowles. Fine it is to be back."

"And just in time, too."

"In time for what, sir?"

"We're fortunate to have Dr. Finbarr Sullivan as Visiting Professor of Greek. He has come to us for winter term after a stint at Tübingen, by way of Yale. Your letter indicated you wanted more work on your Greek. A pity you didn't meet him while you were in Germany. But now you have the opportunity, right here in Charleston."

"Finbarr Sullivan?" Drayton was interested, but dubious. He'd done his undergraduate studies at the College of New Jersey in Princeton and still had the emotional bruises to show for studying in the North. And now, to willingly sit under a Yale professor... "He's a doctor?"

"Yes. The German universities are granting a degree of *philosophiae doctor* in Latin, or Ph.D."

"Sullivan. Then he's Irish?"

"Oh, yes, he's Irish. But nevertheless, a scholar of some repute. You won't mind sitting under an Irishman, will you?" he asked in all seriousness.

Drayton managed a thin smile, refusing to acknowledge the professor's attitude toward the country of his ancestors. Indeed, he was embarrassed for the man.

Cowles was discomfited by Drayton's disapproving silence. "I beg your pardon. Are *you* Irish?"

"Well, the paternal side of family have been in Charleston since 1801. My grandfather came from Wexford, in Ireland. He was *Anglo*-Irish. And we are Protestant. Anglican." *Of a sort*, he added silently.

"Ah, the Ascendancy. That's different." Cowles continued. "Think what you may, Professor Sullivan's reputation as scholar and classroom teacher is unequalled. Our college is more humble than your Princeton, but venerable. And we engage in no bias against Catholics. With Finbarr Sullivan we have the opportunity to take a step closer to first rank in the Classics."

Cowles had made no secret of his ambitions for Drayton to join him in the groves of academe. But as much as he loved the Classics, Drayton wasn't entirely sure he wanted to teach. Until now his studies had been learning for its own sake. Yet he couldn't remain a dilettante forever; he'd have to do *something* with his life. Cabell Junior was going into the law. Ranse loved country life and with some maturity could probably take over planting rice at Cypress Stand as their father aged. There were other family farms Drayton might inherit, but he was unsure about planting for a living. He wasn't sure what career would satisfy the nameless longings that stirred him. Perhaps he'd been avoiding a career choice simply by pursuing additional study. Professor Cowles had just given him a good excuse to repeat the exercise and put off a decision even longer.

Still, he hesitated from a certain weariness of mind and spirit. And there was the fever for secession one breathed in the very sea air of Charleston. The tumult was sweeping across the lower South, and there was even talk of war. To Drayton, war was unthinkable. North and South were both Americans, after all. But how could one make plans in such unsettled conditions?

"I didn't quite expect this." Drayton was unable to keep the hesitancy at bay.

"Yes, but you must seize opportunity when it comes your way. And it's a rare opportunity to study under Finbarr Sullivan. Moreover, it's only the ninth of January. You've returned in time to enroll in his class. Knowing your mind, I took the liberty of notifying Dr. Sullivan that you will join the course. You may sign up in the Dean's office today."

Professor Cowles was clearly embarrassed to bring up the final matter, as any well-bred Southerner would. "I assume," he said, clearing his throat, "that tuition will be no difficulty?"

***

Drayton reported to class to find he hadn't missed enough to put him seriously behind. Even though the course was designed for advanced students of Greek, Sullivan had found it necessary to spend the first week reviewing the basics.

Dr. Sullivan was tall and thin and dressed in black, with the frost of New England austerity about him rather than Irish loquacity. He might have lacked Southern charm, but Drayton admired his deep knowledge and teaching style and his patience with the slower students. They were working from the *Iliad*, and clearly the man loved his subject. There were only nine enrolled, few of whom were truly proficient in classical Greek. Soon he began to call on Drayton to translate, blinking and nodding like an owl in a live oak when he recited correctly.

On Friday, at the conclusion of class the professor closed his book and said with the first note of cordiality Drayton had heard, "Gentlemen, as you learned last week when the course began, it's my practice, and I may add, my pleasure, to invite my students to tea. I find that we can often learn as much in an informal setting as in class. Think of it as an old-fashioned tutorial. Please drop by again Sunday at 4:00 PM. Mr. FitzHenry, the address is Number 12 Glebe Street, at Wentworth." Although Drayton had planned to travel to Cypress Stand for the weekend, this seemed more a command than an invitation. He resigned himself to attending and left the building.

Sunday afternoon rolled around. Shrugging off his reluctance, Drayton arrived on the stoop of 12 Glebe at the appointed hour. A white woman with a Spanish accent greeted him at the door. Taking his hat, cloak, and gloves, she ushered him into a small but cozy parlor. The evening was seasonally cold, and a cheerful fire crackled on the hearth. The class was huddled round sipping tea while Sullivan engaged in a vigorous conversation with Robert Pringle. Drayton knew Pringle as another aspiring classicist.

A few years older than Drayton, Pringle was a member of Charleston's leading family. Pringle's uncle, Judge J. J. Pringle, reportedly owned the best library of Greek and Roman texts in all Charleston. Like most of his contemporaries, Pringle was proud and touchy, and fancied himself as more of a scholar than justified by his attainments. But Drayton made allowances for the upbringing which most Charlestonians of his class had experienced. He made an effort to like him.

Drayton settled into the last vacant place, a rigid side chair close to the fire. Soon he was too warm as well as uncomfortable, and began mulling over various excuses for an early departure. At least the conversation between Pringle and Dr. Sullivan proved interesting. The Professor was making the case that Hector, not Achilles, was the true hero of the Trojan War, even though the epic's author was Greek. Pringle was clearly a partisan of Achilles and the Greeks.

By now the tea cakes were consumed, and Drayton was wondering how he might make a courteous exit when the door to the kitchen opened. Into the room swept a young woman, a vision in green silk crowned with golden hair. The Spanish-speaking woman followed bearing a tray with more cakes, a decanter, and an array of sherry glasses.

All the occupants of the room drew in a breath and stood as she entered, smiling. She helped the serving woman transfer the tray's contents to the table and dismissed her with a smile and word of thanks. Then she said to the guests with a more mischievous smile, "'Dost thou think because thou are virtuous, there shall be no more cakes and ale?' Well, not ale, exactly. I hope tawny port will suffice."

Drayton was transfixed. All time and motion and color seemed frozen as he contemplated the girl. He wondered who she was, until Sullivan smiled with obvious affection. "Thank you, Cecelia. You're just in time. We were all out of cakes."

With a delicacy of motion that caught at Drayton's throat, she began to pour the wine. Robert Pringle stepped up to the table as if first in line was an inherited right. As he took a glass from her slim fingers, Drayton felt an inexplicable rage surge up from deep within. He stepped forward boldly and took the next glass, looking full into her face. Her eyes locked on to his. Something subtle and indescribable passed between them. She look startled.

She seemed to want to speak. Finally she blurted, "That's Fonseca port. I hope you like it, Mr....Mr....?"

"FitzHenry. Drayton FitzHenry," he said hoarsely. He inclined with a slight bow.

"Ah, yes, the late arrival." She replied with a slight curtsey. Regaining her composure and turned to the other guests, giving him an unguarded moment to study her.

The girl's hair was coiffed high atop her head in the style of the time; but a strand of coppery gold had escaped, and she swept it back with a graceful gesture. Drayton tried not to stare, yet couldn't keep his eyes off the burnished gold of her hair, the elegant hands, her slim shape, the refined features and especially the eyes. All he could tell was that they were large, they were dark, and they were expressive. Precisely what color he couldn't say. But there was more to the girl than her physical attributes, something powerful but intangible. He could only think of the inadequate word 'charm.'

Robert Pringle and the young men crowded around her at the table, and Pringle scowled at Drayton. Another student tried to elbow Drayton aside, but he nimbly side-stepped and kept his place. Several tried to impress her with braggadocio, but he remained quiet, remembering from some long-ago English novel that women preferred the strength that resided in silence. Besides, he would rather just look at her, taking in her beauty. Talk would come later, he hoped.

After what seemed like an age, she turned back to him. He said, "You have my name. May I ask yours?"

"Cecelia Sullivan."

"Cecelia," he murmured. "The patron saint of music." How fitting, he thought, since she was the human embodiment of music, a symphony of grace and loveliness.

She laughed. "Well, I love music, but I am hardly a saint." She turned the task of making sure all were served.

This can't be happening, Drayton said in the silence of his mind. There was a sharp poignancy to the moment, as if Love were announcing, *Yes, here I am, unexpected and wonderful; but I can only stay a little while.*

A whispered query to Pringle informed him she was the only daughter of the Professor, a widower. She had lost her mother while a child, another experience he shared with her. But when he registered Drayton's interest, Pringle backed away with a frown.

When Drayton had her attention again, she said, "Father tells me you're something of a prodigy. You've earned your B.A., and your Greek is better than that of most of his students."

"Yes, I graduated the College of New Jersey in 1858."

"Ah, Princeton. And then you went abroad. The Grand Tour, I believe you Charlestonians call it. It conjures up all sorts of images, some frankly comical."

Drayton smiled. "Some of my experiences were frankly comical. I was truly an innocent abroad. When I returned to Charleston I found the opportunity to sit under your father. But having met you, I also find that being able to conjugate a Greek verb in the aorist tense is no longer so important."

Cecelia smiled and accepted the compliment with a total lack of affectation. No dipping of the head and glancing sidelong from lowered eyelids. Drayton drank in her scent and admired the copper highlights in her hair where the fire shone just right. But her eyes...

Instinctively he knew it was the female who chooses whether to permit a male to pay court, perhaps from his observing waterfowl in the family's rice fields, even though the preening male may think otherwise. He kept quiet and let the others posture and strut.

Robert Pringle hovered nearby, observing darkly. He was handsome with his sunburn, grandiose mustache, and brass-buttoned blue uniform of the state militia. Drayton was heartened that Cecelia seemed unimpressed by the uniform.

When Cecelia moved away with a tray of sherry glasses, Pringle advanced on Drayton and said, "What is your interest in that young woman?"

"What an odd question." Drayton smiled.

"Is it possible you have misunderstood me?"

"Not only possible but likely."

"Then I will rephrase the question. What are your intentions toward her?"

Drayton said, "I have only just met her. I'm not sure I have *any* intentions, other than to know her better."

"Exactly. You have only just met her. I met her first. You are an...an interloper."

"You met her when?"

Pringle paused and colored slightly. "Last Sunday. At tea."

"Ah," smiled Drayton. "You move quickly. When is the engagement to be announced?"

"There is no engagement, of course."

"Then you have declared yourselves to each other and have reached an understanding."

"Well, no," said Pringle, clearing his throat.

"Then Robert, it seems there is no relationship into which I may... interlope. You and I stand exactly in the same position toward her, gentlemen-suitors." Glancing at the crowd, he added, "I daresay there are others."

Pringle stiffened. "I repeat, I was here first."

"With respect, one's week's bare acquaintance is too weak a claim for me to relinquish the field." He realized at once the use of 'field' was an error.

Pringle's frown deepened. "Are you saying you wish to meet me on the field of honor?"

It was just such intransigence and misunderstanding among the city's high-born that made Charleston the dueling capital of the nation, second only to New Orleans. Drayton was a product of the code, as well. He couldn't retreat from a deliberate affront. Unless both men chose their next words carefully, the *code duello* was likely to produce a formal challenge. Pringle was already a lieutenant in the South Carolina artillery and notorious as a crack shot on the dueling field. But Drayton was a fine fencer. If challenged, he would then have the choice of weapons, and the *épée* might be his only salvation. Yet the last thing he wanted was to fight a man he basically respected, despite their rivalry for Cecelia Sullivan.

Mustering as much good will as possible in the circumstance, Drayton said, "You are already in uniform. Since arriving home, I find everyone talking about war. God forbid it should happen. But if it does, our country can hardly spare any of its young men to a private quarrel."

Memories of John Brown's raid on Harper's Ferry, Virginia were still fresh in Southern minds. Brown's purpose had been to incite an uprising of slaves throughout the South, though ironically the first fatality in the episode was a free black man. In April, the National Democratic Convention was scheduled to meet in Charleston. It was the topic of heated conversation, though off in the corners, since Sullivan forbade political talk that included secession. The Democrats were already at one another's throats over the intractable issues of slavery and State's rights. Many Southerners feared the Democratic Party would fragment, opening the door to the election in November of a hostile and purely sectional candidate, a Republican like William Seward or possibly Abraham

Lincoln. If that were to happen, secession was inevitable. War might follow if the seceding States were not allowed to depart peaceably. Their indignation stoked by Abolitionist slander of all things Southern, many Charlestonians were already at war in their minds.

This recent history underlay Pringle's next remark. "The word has spread all over the city that you oppose South Carolina's independence. It pains me to say it, but I doubt *you* would be missed."

The word 'coward' remained unsaid but implied, and there was a sudden tension in the air. Drayton drew himself up proudly, but kept himself under rein. The two were on the cusp of something momentous; for once a challenge was issued, however unintended by headstrong young men, neither could draw back. Drayton sensed that Pringle bore him no real malice, but had been carried along by his passionate nature and the conventions of time and place. It was up to Drayton to de-escalate the encounter.

"You are misinformed," he replied. "It is not our independence but war I oppose. The outcome is never certain when men resort to armed violence. Whether between countries or individuals," he added, staring hard at his rival, whose own expression softened.

Drayton continued, "But that's beside the point. You are probably right. In such a pass I would not be missed. However, the Palmetto Guards would doubtless miss you."

Pringle replied with a laugh, and the tension passed. "I am the most junior of all the junior officers. You give me too much credit."

"Only what is due. Which is why I urge that we not argue," said Drayton. He felt some sympathy for the man, for Pringle was stationed on Morris Island, a desolate tract of sand and marsh at the entrance to Charleston Harbor, where the so-called Iron Battery was beginning construction. Morris Island was sun-scorched, wind-scoured, and fly-bedeviled, even in January.

He continued, "You're interested in the young lady, as I am. But neither of us has an acknowledged claim. Let us settle it by wager."

Relief flickered across the taut lines of Pringle's features. He wasn't looking for a fight, either, which meant he wasn't serious about the girl.

"How do you mean?"

"Race Week is next month." Drayton warmed to his idea. "The Pringles have a fine possible entry. This year it's the Judge's famous Calliope, I'm told. And my horse Beltane has expressed his desire to run. I propose a match race under Jockey Club rules. If your horse wins, I relinquish the field – and the young lady – to you. If I win, then you concede to me exclusive courtship privileges. Any pecuniary side bets; well, that's up to the bettors."

Pringle studied Cecelia for a moment as she served her guests with a singular charm. "Those are high stakes."

"More for me than for you. She is not a Charleston lady. She is not even a South Carolinian, but from the North. She is Irish and Catholic, which matters not to me, but likely does to you. You know as well as I that a Pringle would never marry outside his own circle. You'd really not be giving up much if you lose, only a transitory attraction."

"Yet a FitzHenry would marry her?"

Drayton shrugged with self-deprecation. "I labor under no such restrictions, if it should come to that. I simply want to explore the possibility."

Pringle turned and looked at Celia again, then studied the resolution in Drayton's expression. Finally he sighed. "Very well, I accept."

Chapter Six

Charleston, South Carolina; February 1860.

A scant month had elapsed between the issuance of the challenge and Charleston's most famous match race. For the rest of his life Drayton looked back on it as one of his most joyous times, not so much for what the present days contained but for what future days promised.

Though he hadn't mentioned the match race to anyone, word somehow seeped out. It was impossible to keep such a secret in a town mad for horse-racing. He found himself a romantic figure, a status to which he was highly unaccustomed. It wasn't long before Cecelia heard about the bet. That Sunday afternoon a month past he had acted on impulse, spurred by the first sight of her. His only thought then was to possess her, and he hadn't stopped to consider how she might feel about it.

A few days before Race Week they walked along the High Battery. Anita, her *dueña*, followed ten paces behind, a picture of propriety. A fellow Catholic, the Spanish woman had come into the Sullivan's employ in Germany as a refugee from the Carlist Wars. Anita served both as chaperone and language instructor. Drayton was impressed, if not a little intimidated, to learn that Celia spoke French and German, and was mastering Spanish in addition to her knowledge of the Classical languages.

They paused to enjoy the aspect of the Harbor, the surrounding islands, the small brick fort near the anchorage called Castle Pinckney; and the farther, larger Fort Sumter at the Harbor's mouth.

As Drayton peered silently into the distance at Fort Sumter, Celia seized the moment to say, "I hear I am the object of a wager."

Surprised, Drayton looked at her abashed. He could muster only a sheepish smile in reply.

"I ought to be offended," she said. "At one level I am. It's as if my wishes in the matter are of no effect. I am a mere item of barter. But I'm also flattered."

"Sensible girl."

"Robert Pringle, I'm told, is the most desirable catch in all Charleston, perhaps the entire South. Surely the war will begin in earnest if a Yankee girl should snag him," she teased. The accompanying laughter in her voice and eyes enchanted him. She was not in the least frivolous, yet seemed to take deep joy in the simplest acts.

He said, "You forget, dear Celia, that *you* are the prize, not Robert Pringle. Nor even I, for that matter."

"I'm afraid your Charleston belles don't see it that way. I have become the object of universal execration for taking you two out of circulation."

"It doesn't matter. When I win the race, all that will change. You will be regarded as one who was well worth pursuing. Others will place the same value on winning you that I do."

"Then, sir, see that you win." She wrapped her arm in his, snuggling closely against the chill sea air that swept in from seaward. "Mr. Pringle is indeed a fine man. But I can scarcely look upon that enormous walrus mustache without laughing."

Later, walking home after leaving Celia and her Spanish shadow at 12 Glebe, he tried to sort out his feelings. He considered himself a rational man. He believed in Socrates' famous dictum, *gnothi seauton*, know yourself. In seeking to know himself and in trying to inhabit the realm of reason, he acknowledged reservoirs of feelings that often burst through the container of pure thought. Pascal, another wise man had said, 'The heart has its reasons that reason knows not of.' What he was experiencing was not against reason, it was beyond reason. It was simply a matter of the heart. How else explain what had hit him like the proverbial thunderclap? Yet... doubts persisted and nagged. Was love at first sight really possible, or was he confusing it with the unsatisfied physical desire of a vibrant young man? There was no untangling the question, except that he just *knew.* His attraction to Celia transcended the purely physical. Despite the differences in their background and religion, something life-changing had happened. She felt it, too, which accounted for the confusion that occasionally left this poised and confident woman tongue-tied.

Now Race Week was nearly upon them, and he began to fret with an attack of nerves. The wager was an inspired idea, provided he won. She had begged him to win. But there was no guarantee in a horse race, in which fact lay racing's appeal. And if he lost? He already knew in his heart and with a tremor of self-reproach that he would not honor the bet. If he lost there was no way he'd abandon his suit of Cecelia to Robert Pringle, and that would surely re-open the possibility of a duel.

Charleston, South Carolina; February 1860, Race Week.

No other season filled Charleston with excitement like Race Week. Not Christmas or New Year, not the cock fights or bare-knuckle boxing. The event was hosted by the South Carolina Jockey Club at the renowned Washington Race Track, built on land given by Colonel William Washington in the early 1800's. William, a cousin of President George Washington, had been a hero of the Revolution, commanding the Patriot cavalry at the decisive victory of Cowpens in 1780.

The race course lay north of the city on the west side of the peninsula not far from the Ashley River. It boasted high wrought iron gates, graceful stands with fluted columns, and an elegant dining hall for the gentry.

By mid-February the city was filled with planters, traders in livestock, socialites, journalists, and visitors of every kind from everywhere who loved fast horses. Pickpockets, confidence men, and assorted scoundrels also trooped in, drawn by the large sums of money exchanging hands, since virtually every inhabitant, male or female, young or old, black or white, considered himself a racing expert and was willing to lay odds on his favorite.

Most businesses closed for the races and accompanying festivities. Free concerts were offered on Church Street. German brass bands played at White Point Gardens, and the latest plays opened at Dock Street Theater. Every hotel and inn in Charleston was full, and some citizens found windfalls in offering their homes to the overflow of visitors.

Even the so-called "Fire-Eaters" fell silent. The militantly pro-secession Charleston *Mercury* ceased inveighing against the Morrill Tariff and ran the daily odds on Race favorites. The Morrill law would raise import taxes by 250 percent on manufactured items needed in the South, what the editors called "undisguised economic warfare, a Yankee raid to plunder the South." Drayton agreed, as did most Southerners, even Southern Unionists. But like most, he expected reason to prevail and defeat this punitive tariff. In the meanwhile, he thought, let us have some respite from politics. Let us enjoy Race Week. And they did. Sectional politics gave way to horse-racing, especially the match-up between the Pringles' Calliope and Drayton FitzHenry's Beltane.

Race Week culminated in the Silver Plate Handicap. With three three-mile heats it pushed horses to the limit and sometimes burst their hearts. Individual matches, or grudge races, were less demanding, though tough enough, and were held on the fifth and final day. Each day of the week featured its own ball or banquet — the Hibernians, the German Friendly Society, with the penultimate Jockey Club Ball on the fourth night, and crowned on night five by the Saint Cecilia Society Ball. This was the height of Charleston's social season, and only the city's elite were invited. Drayton enjoyed the prospect of taking his own

Saint Cecelia to the Society's ball, for his race was scheduled the same day and she would be celebrated as the laurel crown of victory. Unless his horse lost. Yes, he might lose. But he had a plan for winning, a plan that would shock all Charleston. Since he could not afford to lose, shocking all Charleston was a risk he was perfectly willing to take.

***

Junius, the best horse manager at Cypress Stand, arrived in Charleston to help Drayton prepare for the race, now only two weeks away. Shadpole, the FitzHenrys' jockey, had come with Junius.

The margins were thin for a race of this magnitude – three heats of one mile each, with only an hour's rest between heats. Early on Drayton had preferred a private match to the horse-killing Silver Plate Handicap. He believed in his animal with good reason, but the demands of the private match, even if less than the Silver Plate and other handicap races, would be a grueling test of man and beast. He planned to take Beltane to the summer cottage on Sullivan's Island and run him on the beach. This was the best training he could devise away from curious eyes at the track.

Junius and Shadpole couldn't be spared from the Edisto River property for more than a few days. Since Drayton was not the master, only the son of the master, these arrangements had required the prior consent of his father.

Drayton and Cabell Senior rode uptown to Meeting Street Station in the barouche, and Drayton noticed his father was more taciturn than usual. Shortbread, twin brother of Shadpole, drove the two bays. Soon the engine with its chain of cars came wheezing into the station and sat heavily, emitting puffs of steam as if exhausted by the effort. A few dozen passengers alighted. Negro employees waited for the platform to clear, then extended a wooden ramp to the horse carriage. Junius and Shadpole hopped down from the car reserved for blacks.

"Mornin', Mas' FitzHenry. Mornin', Mistah Drayton." Junius waved cheerily, then turned to supervise the unloading.

"I'm very happy to see you, Junius." He gave the man a bear hug, while his father stood back with a frown of slight disapproval. Cabell Senior did not approve of familiarity with his servants. "I'm glad to see you, too, Shadpole," said Drayton, giving the younger Negro a squeeze on the shoulder.

Junius unloaded Sadie, a mare provided for Shadpole, then Palmetto, his own mount, a Shire cross. Beltane was still at East Battery. Drayton intended to pick him up the way to the Mount Pleasant ferry on the Cooper River, and travel from there to the beach cottage.

Observing the proceedings Cabell Senior said with some asperity, "I hope you didn't forget your horse sense while you were abroad. I understand you're going to need all of it."

"You mean the match race?"

"Of course I mean the match race. When I first learned of it, I thought it was merely the high spirits of a young man with an even more spirited horse. Horseracing is an appropriate undertaking for a young man of your station. But now I hear the object of this race is not to prove who has the better racehorse, but is… is — how can I state it delicately – is a race for a woman." His voice rose a whole octave.

"Well, Father, I regret to say that is not delicate enough. It is a race for the privilege of courting a particular *lady*. A very fine lady, I might add."

His father said nothing, only shook his head.

"Who told you?" Drayton asked. "Cabell Junior? Ranse." He assumed the irrepressible Ranse was the informant. With his romantic sentiments, a race for a lady's hand would be impossible to ignore.

"Neither. They have been commendably close-mouthed and loyal. And I do not spy on my sons. But word of this race is all over Charleston. I learned of it from Quinby, our factor."

"Well, Father, in any event, it's nothing to be ashamed of. Robert Pringle wanted the exclusive right to pay court. I merely suggested we allow the horse race to decide. The other choice was a duel. Surely you would prefer a horse race."

His father said wide-eyed, "Why, as to that… I had no idea." He cleared his throat awkwardly and continued, more in weariness than anger. "Certainly I would not want you risking your fool life in a duel, unless you or the Family were insulted, or an unavoidable point of honor was at stake."

He paused as Junius and Shadpole mounted from the baggage platform and prepared to follow the carriage. "I have always been an indulgent parent, especially since the passing of your mother. Too indulgent, it seems. You are a grown man. You will soon be 21 and free to go your own way. But this… I expected far better of you."

"Father, is it the race that troubles you, or the lady? Since you've raised no objection to my entering Beltane – after all, here are Junius and Shadpole with their mounts – I'm forced to conclude it must be the lady."

"I only learned a short while ago there is a female involved. Otherwise, I might have raised objections earlier."

"But why, Father? I assure you Cecelia Sullivan is entirely suitable. Her family, character, and accomplishments are beyond reproach. Did you truly think I would pursue someone disreputable?"

Shortbread hitched up the two bays and the carriage began to roll. "I don't know, Son. Since you came back from Princeton and then back from Europe… I feel I don't know you as I once did. You've … you've changed."

"I should hope so, Father. Surely that's the purpose of education and travel – to broaden a person, raise one's horizons, deepen one's understanding. If those aren't changes, then your money has been sadly wasted."

"Yes, but I mean changed in some way foreign to us. You are still one of us, despite your Northern education and Grand Tour. We stand on the cusp of something momentous to South Carolina, perhaps to the South as a whole. The FitzHenrys have always played our part, and I need to know that you will, too, if and when the time comes."

"Of course, Father, why should you doubt it?" Drayton hoped 'playing his part' didn't mean going to war. The war talk had rattled everyone – well, almost everyone. His father believed separation between North and South would occur without violence, so Drayton felt there was no deception in answering as he did.

Father said, "This… this affair of yours has given me doubts. Reluctant doubts about your wisdom. Our family have never had occasion to be ashamed. We have been leaders in South Carolina since 1801. I am a former Member of Congress and a delegate to the Democratic Convention in April. I am a vestryman of St. Phillips and Saint Bartholomew's Parish. It is embarrassment enough to have a son notorious for his lack of Southern patriotism. But now you have made a public spectacle of yourself running after a Yankee girl. And a Roman Catholic to boot. How can I hold my head up in the city?"

Drayton laughed, trying not to sound derisive. He raised his voice over the clatter of the steel-clad wheels on the cobblestones. "Now be honest, Father. None of us are terribly religious. There's little in our church life that moves any of us spiritually. Your vestry duties are more social than spiritual."

His father bit his lip in annoyance. "I can't dispute what you say, although I must point out that as a young man of limited experience of life you have no way to judge what lies in the depths of a man's heart."

Drayton bowed his head, acknowledging the rebuke. "You're right, Father. If I appear skeptical, be assured I remain equally skeptical of the rituals and dogmas of Catholicism, indeed, of all organized religion. But I am a skeptic only, not an unbeliever. That applies to matters of faith *and* politics."

"Very well," his father sighed. "I've said my piece, and you know my mind. We will let the matter drop, since you tell me you're only courting the girl and have no plans to marry. I wish you success in the race. Shadpole is a fine jockey and will ride a good race for you." He paused. "I must add, for all your faults you are a good judge of horses. I have bred and ridden them all my life and even raced a bit, and I must say this Irish fellow you brought home is the finest animal I've ever seen."

"Thank you, Father. I only wish you had equal confidence in my judgment of womanhood."

Chapter Seven

Charleston, South Carolina; February 1860; Final Day of Race Week

When Race Week rolled around, slaves usually got the first day off. But this final day of the event offered something different and exciting. The clamor grew insurmountable to witness the epic contest for a woman's hand between two of Charleston's finest. All but the most insensitive masters allowed their blacks the extra day to attend. The actual details had gotten buried in the welter of rumor and hearsay – that it was only a race for the right to pay court to a woman. Few stopped to reflect that the elusive and barely known Miss Sullivan was free to reject both suitors, regardless of who won.

Drayton arrived at the course in the one-horse trap with Junius and Palmetto in harness. Shadpole rode Sadie and ponied Beltane behind him on a long lead. The streets leading to the race grounds were thronged with people afoot, on horseback, or in elegant carriages. Many he knew, and they called out greetings or words of encouragement. As the riders passed through the filigreed wrought-iron gates and headed for the stables, scores of Negro children festooned the spreading branches of the live oaks to watch the pageant. They cheered Beltane and shouted bets to each other as enthusiastically as the white buckra inside the course.

After stabling their mounts, Drayton helped Junius give Beltane a good rubdown. Junius checked his legs and hooves, eyes and mouth, then saddled him with the lightweight hunt saddle. When all was ready, Drayton drew the two black men aside for his final strategy conference.

Shadpole's principal virtues as a rider were his small size and his ability to hang on. According to Cabell Senior he could cling to a palmetto frond in a hurricane. But Drayton didn't regard him as especially horse-smart, despite his father's opinion. Junius was extremely horse-smart, but too large and heavy to ride jockey. They huddled in conversation. Then post time drew nigh, and they strode to the mounting paddock with Junius leading Beltane. Shadpole, dressed in the family's jockey colors of red and black, switched his whip back and forth dejectedly. Junius wore a wry grin in contrast to Shadpole's hangdog frown.

Robert Pringle came into the paddock resplendent in his militia uniform.

His trainer, a white man, and Old James, his black jockey, followed him. Old James led Calliope, who snorted, pawed the earth, and tossed her head when Beltane entered the ring.

Drayton extended his hand and said, "An historic day. We seemed to have excited the crowd beyond all imagining."

"Yes, so it seems," said Pringle. After an awkward pause, he added, "May the best horse win."

"May the best *man* win," grinned Drayton. This met with a quizzical look. But Drayton only smiled. All would be revealed soon enough.

The bugle rang at the judge's stand for 'riders up!' As Old James swung aboard Calliope, hundreds of chattering spectators lined the paddock to catch a glimpse of the rivals, hoping perhaps for insights in placing last-minute bets. Junius' grin grew wider, and Shadpole's frown grew deeper. Suddenly Drayton stripped off his bottle green tailcoat and top hat and thrust them at the diminutive Negro.

"Will you keep my coat for me, Shadpole? And guard it carefully. It contains my wallet. You understand — in case I have to pay off any side bets. But I think we're going to win."

Shadpole's frown brightened into a semblance of a smile. "Yassuh. You kin trust me to hold 'em safe till de ridin' ober. You goan win, for sho." He passed the whip to Drayton.

"Now give me a leg up."

A titter of astonishment echoed through the crowd as Shadpole made a step with his interlocked hands and vaulted Drayton into the saddle. Old James wheeled his mount and stared in alarm at Drayton's taking up the reins and riding Beltane in a tight circle. The horse pranced, nervous at the unfamiliar sights and sounds of the near-frenzied spectators. Beltane had raced before, but never at the Washington Course during Race Week. Drayton soothed him with whispers into his pinned-back ears. Soon he softened. His ears went forward, and he arched his head in a workmanlike manner as if concentrating on what he soon had to do.

Old James was a picture of dismay. It was comical, but it also convinced Drayton he'd gained the mental and moral advantage. The Great Families owned the horses, trained them, raced them, and placed enormous bets on them. Sometimes entire fortunes rode on the backs of these Arabians and Thoroughbreds. But the sons of wealth and privilege didn't ride them. Black jockeys did the riding, although occasionally a white man in need of money would contract to ride.

Drayton's deed was revolutionary. In fact, as the word ran like a grassfire through the vast throng, half of Charleston was scandalized; the other half delighted, as they always were with anything new. Drayton knew his horse would run and win because of their mutual love. Why stick with an old tradition that risked losing Celia Sullivan, and only because that was the way it had always been done? Time to do it differently. For a slave jockey it was just another assigned task in a life of servitude, even if the master awarded a cash incentive. But no incentive could equal the sheer will to win that motivated Drayton.

Pringle strode forward shouting, "Here! Here! What does this mean?"

Drayton laughed from his height at the sight of Pringle's mustache quivering with indignation. With an elation he'd never felt before he replied, "It means that I trust no other rider with my happiness."

"You can't ride. It … It isn't … *done!*" Pringle tried to catch hold of Beltane's bridle. With a deft pressure of his leg, Drayton kept his mount dancing just out of reach.

"It's done now," Drayton replied. "There's nothing in the Jockey Club Rules that says I can't ride my own horse. The jockey is chosen 'at the discretion of the owner.'"

"Now just hold on," fumed Pringle. "We'll see what the Club stewards have to say about this."

The bugle rang from the judges' stand calling the riders to the start line.

"It's too late, my friend, unless you want to forfeit. The Stewards can't change their own rules on the spot. Or … you can ride Calliope yourself. Then it really will be a match."

The time for talk was over; it was time to ride. Without another word Drayton trotted out of the mounting paddock onto the groomed sand of the racecourse itself, and posted toward the start line. A roar went up from the stands. There were some catcalls, but mostly whoops of delighted surprise. He did not glance back, certain that Pringle couldn't at this stage refuse the challenge. Sure enough, a moment after he reached the start line Old James pulled up alongside him. Calliope had calmed down and looked formidable.

As they waited for the starting gun, Drayton felt he was riding on too long a leg, as for a hunt. Instinctively he shortened stirrup by two holes and immediately felt more leverage in the saddle. He settled his mind with recollections of his first meeting Cecelia, when the whole plan had come together like the goddess Athena springing fully armed from the head of Zeus. The chain of logic was irrefutable. *A wager is better than a duel, and what better wager than a horse race?* And then, *Beltane will do far more for me than for Shadpole on his back.* I *must ride him. I must ride him for the symbolism of the act as well as to be sure of winning.* And finally, he would ride as a South Carolina gentleman, not in jockey silks, which bespoke the hired man or servant. His only concession to freedom of movement was to remove his hat and coat. He had come dressed in his best riding boots of Spanish leather with russet tops, fawn breeches, a vest of pearl satin, an immaculate linen shirt, and green cravat of watered silk. He dazzled, and he knew it.

The stands were full to capacity, a surging sea of color, noise, and motion. The impact on the senses was so intense that for a moment his composure slipped. Drayton was a reticent man, one attribute he shared with his father, who had drilled into him from youth, 'Do not make a spectacle of yourself.' And here he had become the Low Country's grandest spectacle of the year.

Old James and Calliope were alongside him behind the start wire. The Negro jockey refused to look at him. Wearing an angry scowl, he appeared as offended by Drayton's flaunting of tradition as his white master. Veteran jockeys sometimes engaged in rough tactics, ramming an opponent, especially in the far turns, or slashing the other riders with the whip. Such tactics were now effectively neutralized, and Old James knew it. This race was going to be a matter of horse quality and horsemanship alone.

Everything seemed more intense as Drayton took the starting position — light, shadow, sounds, the myriad details of the scene. He smiled down at the line judge, an old Charlestonian in black swallow-tail coat and top hat. The man wagged his head from side to side as he raised the starting pistol, a single-shot percussion model of antique vintage.

"Riders ready?" he shouted.

When both riders nodded, he pulled the trigger. A throaty boom and spurt of black powder smoke. Drayton put heel to horse. Calliope, a veteran of many races, streaked ahead. Beltane leaped forward, a bit slow from the start. Drayton lengthened his stride and with a slight touch on the reins, stayed a neck behind, just where he wanted. Old James shot him a brief malevolent glance, then gave himself over to the race, stretched out over Calliope's withers, urging her on with hand and leg and an occasional flick of the whip. It was time to get down to business.

Pounding, pounding, pounding they came into the first turn, where the virtue of hanging on revealed itself. This was where riders usually came off, thanks to the centrifugal force generated by a thousand-pound animal galloping at full speed into an arc. Drayton gripped tighter with his legs, and the signal urged his champion to increase the pace. Gobbling up ground, they stayed close behind Calliope and Old James. But he felt his face stinging from sand thrown back at him by the mare's hammering hooves. Squinting through half-closed eyes to avoid the sand, he saw he'd fallen a full length behind. Suddenly it was two.

He'd been willing to give up the first heat, since Calliope was the faster horse, and only go for the win if it fell within his grasp. Beltane had 'bottom.' He would run Calliope hard enough to wear down the mare and bring Beltane's stamina into play in the second and third heats, even if it meant conceding the first. But his plan was to stay within a length, enough to maintain Beltane's confidence in himself; and – he hoped – to make Old James over-confident.

Out of the final turn and a quarter mile to go, the distance between the two horses remained at three lengths, as if they were joined by an invisible tie. Beltane was running well. Drayton had been holding him back, but he didn't want to lose by three or four lengths. He knew the time had come. Though he'd seldom put whip to the horse, he touched him lightly on the flank and barked, "Now, old boy, now!"

Beltane surged ahead. The gap closed. It looked for an instant as if they might even pass Calliope by a neck at the finish. But the wily old Negro wasn't a leading Charleston jockey for nothing. Age and experience trumped youthful passion, for Old James had obviously been holding Calliope, too. A brief glance over his shoulder at his opponent closing, then Old James began to whip and spur the mare hard. She had plenty left. She leaped forward, opening the distance and streaking across the finish line a full four lengths ahead.

Drayton couldn't hear the roaring of the crowd for the roaring in his head. Crushed and humiliated, he realized he'd underestimated Old James and had waited too late to make his move. Had he assumed an unconscious superiority because he was a planter's son and his opponent was a slave? Perhaps so. At any rate, it was not a mistake he'd make again.

Back at the barn, Junius tossed a loose-weave cotton blanket over Beltane, walked him for a time, then removed the cooler and rubbed him down vigorously. Next he massaged lineament into the joints of his legs from knee to pastern.

"Well, Junius?" said Drayton. "We have to win the next heat for sure, or it'll be two out of three for the Pringles and we're beaten."

"Mistah Drayton," said Junius. "That Calliope, she a fast hoss, but she a flash in the pan. Our hoss got lots more bottom than that Pringle mare. Don't you worry none. Just stay up with her close in de next heat. Den make yo move at de last turn, like you just done."

***

Drayton patted Beltane on the cheek and spoke a few encouraging words. Retrieving his hat and coat from Shadpole, without which no gentleman could freely walk the grounds, he went to the jockey's lounge to relax in privacy in the short hour between heats. He thought he could manage one Tennessee whiskey without impairing his riding, and was pouring a dram when his two brothers came in.

He glanced up, smiled an abashed smile. "Didn't exactly do us proud, did I?"

Ranse grinned conspiratorially. Cabell Junior looked uncomfortable. Then they stepped apart, turning halfway. Behind them stood Celia Sullivan, a vision in ivory silk and a fur pelisse. Her eyes were slightly downcast, and a ghost of a smile hovered about her lips. She looked directly at Drayton, who remained immobile and astonished and as always, transfixed by her deep grey eyes that seemed to hold some secret knowledge.

"Have I violated the terms of the wager by coming?" she asked. "After all, you have only raced the one heat."

"And what a miserable heat it was," he said, swallowing his surprise and striding forward to take her hands. "As to the terms of the wager, this eventuality never entered in."

"You mean, I am allowed to show partiality before the wager is concluded?" she smiled more broadly.

"I would say, not only allowed but encouraged. After the wager is concluded…. Well, depending on the outcome, there may be complications."

"Not if you win," she said.

"No, not if I win."

"Then you'll have to do better, dear Brother," said Ranse, his grin never fading.

"He will, I told you," Cabell interjected. Cabell regarded himself as an expert on horse racing, and Drayton knew he'd made some sizeable bets on Beltane. "You were only holding back to wear down Calliope. Am I not right, Drayton?" Both worry and hope were audible in the question.

"Yes, that was my plan. But it didn't include losing by four lengths." His misery was plain. Celia escorted him back to the settees and his tumbler of whiskey.

As the four of them sat, Drayton looked behind them to the entryway of the chamber, a place unaccustomed to the presence of women. In welcoming Cecelia instead of shooing her out, he had evidently broken another hallowed tradition. "Is Dr. Sullivan not with you?" he asked.

It was a question he realized only now he'd been dreading to face. He knew the Professor had high regard for him as a student. But this race-and-wager business might prove another matter. Celia dropped her head and colored slightly. The brothers looked away with troubled expressions.

"What's the matter? Please, someone, tell me," said Drayton.

"No, Drayton, he didn't come," Celia said at length.

"Tell him all of it," said Cabell, grim-faced.

"Oh, don't upset him," objected Ranse. "It might spoil his riding the next heat. Which he must win, I remind you." He seemed to be enjoying the unfolding family drama.

"I don't need to be reminded," said Drayton. "Now what's this all about?"

"Very well," Celia sighed. "Father was most disapproving when he heard about the wager. He doesn't really understand you Charlestonians. Wastrels and exhibitionists, he calls you. Rather than seeing any romance in the race, he seems to feel you and Mr. Pringle have made—"

"Made a public spectacle of you?"

"How did you know?"

"It's exactly what my own father said about me. Is there anything else?"

"Yes, besides being reduced to an object of commerce," she paused, frowning. "He forbade me to come to the race, as if I would have missed it on any account."

"Yet here you are."

"I have never before disobeyed my father. But this time... Well, I was frantic to come. But naturally I couldn't venture out alone, and I couldn't tell Anita. I didn't even know where the race was to be held. I sent a note to your brother Cabell. He and Ransome kindly offered to escort me. As you say, here I am, but without Father's knowledge or consent. I wanted to come to encourage you to win, and ... and to tell not to risk your safety, because even if you don't win... Well..."

"Will you stay for the decision?"

"I might as well be hanged for a sheep as a lamb. Of course I'll stay. Wild horses couldn't drag me away. Not even Beltane."

***

Drayton narrowly won the second heat. The crowd, already wild with anticipation, now went mad with joy or frustration, depending on their sympathies for the Pringles or the FitzHenrys – and on their bets.

As planned, he'd stayed close to Calliope with the intent to make his bid at the final quarter mile. But he'd taken the measure of Old James and was not going to under-estimate him again. He suspected the Negro had guessed his strategy. And since a key element of strategy is never to do what your opponent expects, Drayton abandoned it in mid-race.

After the first quarter mile he'd sensed a resurgence of heart and will in Beltane. This decided him. He put a light whip on the horse entering the backstretch, sooner than planned. Suddenly it was a reverse of the first heat. Stretching forth his neck, Bel settled into a rhythm and surged several lengths ahead, with Calliope struggling to catch up. Drayton spared a fraction of a second's glimpse behind him to see Old James whipping the mare brutally, trying to close the gap. The Negro's spurs drew blood from Calliope's flanks. But he never closed the distance, and Drayton won by a length.

Now it really came down to the question of which horse had the staying power. Drayton already knew the answer, and during the interval he reassured his newly beloved and his brothers, now more cherished than ever, that the result was a foregone conclusion.

Calliope ran with blazing speed the first half mile of the final heat, but seemed to lose heart when Beltane began to fly no longer on sand but on the wind. The valiant mare stayed a few lengths behind but then faded, until at the final quarter mile turn it was no longer a race but a rout. Beltane raced with joy in his own speed and power, and the joy coursed through his rider. In harmony with the surging motion and rhythmic thunder of hooves along the rail, Drayton experienced an exaltation he'd never known.

"I shall mount on wings like eagles, I shall run and not be weary!" he shouted at Old James, at the infield crowd, at the whole world. Drunk from the chalice of elation, he laughed to himself. *Man did not need God to give him wings, for God gave him horses.*

Beltane could hardly cross the finish line for the spectators who burst onto the track, laughing, shouting and waving. Drayton slowed to a trot to allow the cheering crowd to make a lane to the judges' stand. Junius, Shadpole, Ranse, Cabell Junior, and Celia met him there; she with moist eyes and tremulous lips. The black-coated judges swayed and jabbered on their platform like a flock of crows.

Drayton posted to a halt and dropped lightly from the saddle, grasping a hank of mane at the withers and struggling to keep his feet. He felt Beltane against his cheek, winded and sweating but proud. The horse seemed to revel in the triumph as much as his master. The grey Irishman possessed in abundance the virtues of the horse-kind, exulting in his strength and eager to please, but with a pride that also said, *I cooperate of my own free will, and then only with those I deem worthy.*

Mud-spattered and bone-weary, Drayton was sore in places that hadn't ached for a long time. But he felt something else that made him rejoice in the pain, something ineffably sweet. Not just the sweet taste of victory, not just the presence of Cecelia, but a taste of the sublime. Drayton put his arms around Beltane and laid his head on the horse's foam-flecked neck. Then, for a moment too brief for anyone to notice, he wept.

— END OF PART I —

PART II
Chapter Eight

Tusculum Cottage, West Bank of the Edisto; March 1913.

Cabell emerged from the cabin, sniffed the aroma of frying bacon and said to his grand-nephew, "Let's walk down to the River while your GramPa makes breakfast."

Tommy nodded. "All right, Grand-Uncle."

The boy offered a steadying hand as Cabell swung his leg awkwardly down the wooden steps to the lawn. They made their way down to the mysterious Edisto, flowing placidly, concealing inexorable power in its stillness. The water was tea-colored in the shallows and along the bank amid rippling grasses and rushes. Spring was on the cusp, bringing renewal. A flock of egrets, perennial neighbors, took white-shining wing as Tommy sprinted after them. They settled complacently a hundred yards away in a flooded rice field. Cabell's heart caught for an instant at the memory. This single rice field – and there were a dozen like it on the property – had produced thousands of pounds of 'Carolina Gold' before the War. Now its only crop was cattails and marsh grasses. Sparkles danced amid the herbage as the wind ruffled the surface and caught the sun. Recollections of those lost days sparkled and danced in a shut-away chamber of his mind. He sighed and stumped on.

"Look here, Tommy." Cabell pointed with his cane at the tadpoles swarming in the shallows. "See, they're growing their hind legs. In a few weeks those that survive will be mature. The bullfrogs will start booming out their love songs to the females every night."

Tommy watched fascinated at the tadpoles darting to and fro amid the submerged grass. He appeared to ponder the mystery of male and female with due consideration. Then he asked, "Grand-Uncle, did GramPa marry her?" He gestured with a nod toward the burial ground on the level space upslope behind them. "After the great match race, I mean?"

"Tommy, you always speak of 'her' as if you're afraid to say her name. Are you worried what GramMa Annalee might think?"

Tommy fell silent. He stared into the tannin-stained water, poking at the tadpoles with a palmetto frond. "I just wonder sometimes why nobody will tell me about her," he said after a pause. "GramPa started to yesterday, but he went all funny the way he does sometimes, and didn't finish."

Cabell placed a hand on the boy's shoulder. "Then I will. She was a wonderful woman. There's nothing wrong in being curious about her." Cabell spoke with more certitude than he felt. He knew, as perhaps his grand-nephew only sensed, that the story of Drayton and Cecelia had not ended with her death.

"Her name was Cecelia Sullivan. We called her Celia for short. When you speak of her – and there's no reason why you shouldn't – you can call her Celia, too."

"So GramPa did marry her?"

A wrought iron bench was emplaced on the bank for the purpose of enjoying the prospect of river, marsh, and forest. Man and boy sat for a while. Cabell stretched out his ever-aching leg.

"Yes, he did," Cabell said. "But first he had to overcome many obstacles. The horse race was only the first. Neither Celia's father nor our family approved the match. I'm ashamed to say I was opposed, too, at the start, until I came to know her better. But their love was too strong to be denied, even with the coming of the War. In fact, it was the War that joined them together. And sadly, the War put them asunder."

"What's a sunder, Grand-Uncle?"

"Asunder means apart. It's in the church order of marriage: 'what God hath joined together let no man put asunder.' The War ripped apart the lives of millions, North and South. Ripped them apart. Your GramPa and Celia were not immune."

"I wish it hadn't happened. Then I might have known her," said Tommy. "Couldn't anybody stop it?"

It was a discomfiting question. "Son, I have chewed that over and over in my mind for fifty years, and I confess I still can't come up with an answer. Some folks *did* try to stop it, your grandfather especially. But he was young, and few listened. There weren't enough people like him on either side, and so the War came. I would like to say it happened like a natural disaster, except that human decisions were involved."

"You mean people decided they wanted war, knowing what it might bring?" Tommy discarded the palmetto frond for a dry cattail stalk. He lunged forward, thrusting it like a sword.

"I suppose a few actually wanted war, though most did not," said Cabell.

"But no one could foresee what it would bring, for they had no experience of the kind of war we found ourselves in. It was a matter of people blindly making decisions that led to another, and that led to another, until we ended up fighting. Like a chain that couldn't be unlinked, and war lay at the end of it."

"It just doesn't make sense." Tommy walked forward to the water's edge and poked the stalk in the shallows, frowning as the tadpoles scurried for safety.

"Maybe it doesn't when you're looking back." Cabell smiled, too. "But we were in front of things that hadn't happened yet, and we couldn't know what the future held. You see, history can only be understood backwards, yet it can only be lived forwards."

"You said Grampa was against the war. *He* understood it forwards."

They stood and continued to walk along the low bank.

"Yes. He was a student of ancient history, and he used to say the past was the only sure guide to the future. Of course, some folks say we Southerners live too much in the past. But few of us had the long view that your GramPa had. We only saw the next link in the chain, not the whole chain itself and where it was leading. Bad feelings between North and South had been going on a long time. But when things really started to unravel, it took only one year until the guns of Fort Sumter; and then suddenly, somewhat to our surprise, we were in it." Cabell's prosthetic was sinking into the wet soil. He pulled free with some effort and walked a few yards to dryer ground. Tommy took his hand to balance him.

"What was the first link?" the boy asked.

"Well, people differ about that. Some people say the Kansas-Nebraska Act of 1854. Some say the Panic of 1857, when the North's economy suffered far worse than ours, and they cast their eyes south with a view to turning us into a colony. Many believe it was John Brown's failed slave uprising in 1859. Some people go all the way back to the founding of the country. But since we have to start somewhere, I'd say it was the Democratic National Convention in 1860."

"What was that, Grand-Uncle?"

"The Democratic Party, the largest of the country's political parties, came together to nominate a candidate for President of the United States. It was in April 1860, and it took place right in our own city of Charleston." Even now, more than fifty years later, Cabell could recall the tension and foreboding as great events were bearing down and about to change your life forever, yet you were helpless to avoid them or to hasten them.

"The firing on Fort Sumter came a scant year later, in April 1861, and the War was on. Your grandfather and I were there. For both events and the ones in between."

Charleston, South Carolina; April 23, 1860.

No one was quite sure why Charleston of all cities had been selected to host the Democratic National Convention. Some speculated it was a gesture to reassure the South and dampen secession fever. The city was tense with the expectation that something dramatic would happen. These were Democrats, after all. Would they nominate the presumed favorite, Senator Stephen A. Douglas? Or would the Party fragment into sectional feuding, which was Cabell Senior's main worry.

By the mid-April delegates had arrived from all over the United States. For most it was their first visit to the city of legend and romance, the cultural center of the Deep South. Charleston's streets rang with unfamiliar accents — New England twang, the flat speech of the Middle West, and the soft speech of the Southern Tidewater. Every inn and hotel was full, and the cost of board had shot up to levels never before seen. Nearby Hibernian Hall had converted its second floor to a dormitory equipped with cots. The Hibernians were raking in the windfall. Some delegates contracted to stay in private homes. Foreseeing the crush, Massachusetts and New York had come by steamer. Their accommodations were moored ten minutes away at Adgers Wharf, equipped with ample stocks of beer, liquor, and – it was rumored — women of easy virtue.

Cabell Senior, Drayton, and Ranse returned from the River where they'd repaired for the onset of the malaria season. Depending on the weather, mosquitoes vexed the coastal plain from early April until autumn's first frost. At Father's request, Drayton agreed to accompany his brothers to the opening speeches, 'to refurbish his political education after a long absence abroad.' Cabell Junior and his father were worried that Drayton was interested in only one thing. A young South Carolinian was expected to be hot-blooded, but for politics, horses, cards, and only then, women. Drayton confirmed their fears by bringing Celia to the Convention.

Cabell expected an airing of differences between Northern and Southern Democrats, but was still shocked at the vehemence of the scene. He shot a sidelong glance at Drayton and Celia. The girl sheltered under Drayton's arm, as if from a storm. Cabell sensed her disbelief at the unfolding spectacle, something like horror struggling with a polite desire not to insult her Southern hosts.

Except for Race Week, Cabell had never seen such a huge crowd in Charleston. Hundreds thronged the lofty Palladian entrance of South Carolina Institute Hall, the largest building of its type in the city. Others leaned out the high arched windows on the second storey and shouted down ribald jokes to those they recognized below. Knots of plump men in window-pane plaid, wool serge, and top hats gathered on the sidewalk laughing, gesticulating, and haranguing one another.

"It's like a bee hive's been kicked over," observed Ranse as the three FitzHenry brothers and Cecelia walked toward the entrance on Meeting Street. Cabell fished for their tickets in a vest pocket.

When she could be heard above the noise, Celia asked, "Who *was* that? Can he be serious?"

"William Lowndes Yancey," Cabell explained. "Head of the Alabama Delegation."

"One of Barney Rhett's partisans," added Ranse.

Celia asked, "Can he really want to extend slavery by law into the Territories? Does he expect Northern delegates to agree? It would mean their political suicide."

Cabell was surprised at her grasp of affairs. He replied, "You must keep in mind, there are now so many blacks in the South that we must open new territory where they may emigrate with their masters. Otherwise we are greatly outnumbered and face a racial holocaust, as in Haiti."

"But Cabell," she said. "In one breath you tell me how content the Negroes are in their servitude, and in the next you raise the specter of racial holocaust. Which proposition is true, since both cannot be?"

He gave her an appraising look. "My dear, you ought to be a lawyer, not I."

Drayton laughed. "Brother, you've taken the measure of her wit, as I have. But it's a moot point. In my opinion what Yancey and Rhett really want is to break up the Democratic Party."

"Won't that assure the election of a Republican?" Celia asked.

"Yes, William Seward or perhaps Abraham Lincoln," said Cabell. "But then, Yancey and Rhett will have created the conditions for the South to secede. If you look at it this way, slavery is the pretext for secession, not its cause."

"I don't think he can do it," said Celia. "Not all Southern delegates are with the radical Secessionists. Certainly not your father, from what your brother tells me."

"No, Father is not with them. In fact, most of the South Carolina Delegation would preserve the Union," Cabell conceded. His father was known as a 'Co-Operationist.' These were South Carolinians who believed secession was their right in principle, but they wanted to act only in concert with other Southern states, and only if all else failed.

Cabell Junior was proud of his father while struggling to find his own path. Cabell embraced secession while Father saw it as a last resort. But at a personal level, he shared his father's distrust of all-consuming zeal. Father said the radicals were becoming caricatures of themselves, bereft of reason, in both sections, for the North had its radicals, too. Their never-ceasing, ever-intensifying denunciations of the South were doing more to fuel secession fever than any other factor. Father never stopped urging all sides to remember that words had consequences as well as acts. He frequently quoted Proverbs: 'A soft answer turneth away wrath.' But soft words and sweet reason were being swept away by the rising tide of passion. Sooner or later the South's moderates would be forced to choose independence or loyalty to the Union. Cabell Junior had recognized this reality and had made his choice.

***

Now came his father•s turn to speak. The hall fell silent to hear this respected voice among South Carolina's "reasonable men." As he stepped to the podium, for the first time Cabell thought he looked old. When you're with someone often, you don't notice the small daily changes, he mused. But now he did. Father seemed to have faded slightly. He'd lost much of his old subtlety and resilience, and was pale pastel compared to the starkness of the Fire-Eaters, his suit of pearl-gray against their sepulchral black.

Father was a throwback to his Gallic, not his Anglo-Irish ancestors, with a hawk-like face and sharp blade of a nose under a widow's peak, his hair once dark and now silver, worn in an old-fashioned queue and tied with black ribbon. He bore a look of distress as if he alone were responsible for the world-shaking events unfolding before them, when all he really wanted to do was enjoy the life of a Low County rice planter. It was a laudable desire, but hardly strong enough to hold the ramparts against the feelings being aired in Institute Hall. Standing before the writhing mass of delegates, Cabell Senior recoiled as some cheered, some hissed. But it was minimal – many of the State's radical Secessionists were boycotting. In the vastness of the hall Cabell and his brothers strained to hear from the gallery. Finally the buzz and bustle subsided enough that they could distinguish Father's words.

He spoke in a level voice underlining the gravity of his appeal. "I do not suggest that any of us compromise our convictions, but let us at least moderate our tone. Angry words may lead to angry deeds. I beg the delegates, let us not quarrel past the point of no return. Democrats of North and South are not enemies, for we seek to preserve liberty in our respective states and communities. Our natural enemies are those who claim the Union is a consolidated national government under which the states are but subordinate dependencies. Our natural enemies are those who would harness the taxing power of a consolidated national government to benefit a favored few."

He was interrupted by a round of applause across sectional lines.

"Through high tariffs the South is forced to pay a disproportionate share of the expenses of the national government. Tariffs should be high enough to cover the legitimate expenses of government, those authorized by the Constitution, and no higher."

"Hear, hear!"

Father ignored the plaudits. "All of us here are attached to the Union both by sentiment and interest. But I urge this Convention to affirm that the Union exists for the general welfare, not for the welfare of the politically favored. The Union is a confederated republic of the several states, which retain their sovereignty. The states have conferred upon the central government limited and enumerated powers to act as their fiduciary agent. Only the sovereign states can check the abuses and usurpations of the central government. This is the Republic established by the Constitution. If we can agree on this proposition and remain loyal to the Constitution as it was written, then the issue of Negro servitude need not divide us."

At last he made a slight bow to acknowledge the sustained applause.

After hearing his father speak, Cabell lost interest in the rest of the proceedings, as did the others. He saw Celia whisper in Drayton's ear. His brother rose, drawing Celia to her feet.

Cabell said, "I know you've had enough. But let's wait on Father. He will expect to see you here afterwards." He pulled his brother's sleeve and whispered, "I confess Miss Sullivan is devilishly attractive. But she is not of our blood or place. Are you going to let her dictate your actions?"

"Only if she is in the right," said Drayton.

Cabell was taken aback at the unexpected reply. Then he accepted it. "All right. Then we'll leave together and collect Father."

"Splendid," said Drayton. "Let's go out and enjoy ourselves; leave this *Sturm und Drang* behind."

"Yes, let's," agreed Ranse, his eyes sparkling at Celia.

"Who can resist such an onslaught," said Cabell, standing. "All right, let's."

After waiting in the lobby for a quarter hour, the brothers spied Father emerging from the seething cavern of Institute Hall. As they praised his speech,

Celia stood in the background. The Father stepped forward and made a polite bow over her extended hand. It was the first time they had met face to face.

As they were congratulating Father, Convention Chairman Caleb Cushing of Massachusetts exited the Hall, indicating the session was in recess. The lobby chandelier above reflected off Cushing's bald head, and his plump belly strained against the fabric of his blue vest and coat. Cushing spied Cabell Senior with his family, smiled, and crossed the lobby to greet them. Father introduced his children and Cecelia. Cushing bowed as gracefully as any Charlestonian, lightly touching Cecelia's wrist with his lips. They settled to chat into red leather settees that lined the lobby.

The Chairman said to Cabell Senior, "Well spoken, sir. We must preserve a truly national party. The country cannot afford a sectional party ruled by special interests, as you pointed out. The Democratic Party is the party of all sections and all economic interests of the nation, while the party of Seward and Lincoln is the captive of Wall Street, the railroads, and the corporations."

Father nodded. Cabell noticed the worry lines that etched his father's brow, the web of wrinkles stretching from the corners of his eyes. Tired eyes.

Cushing said, "We Democrats are the only party that can hold North and South – hold the Union – together. *But*...you say we need only remain true to the principle of state sovereignty. However, the North cannot ignore slavery. The conviction exists in my section that you insist on state sovereignty only to protect slavery. It is your peculiar institution, yet you demand that the North and West assent to it."

"Demand? I demand nothing," said Father. "I only ask that settled laws and institutions be respected, and that the South shall not be plundered by an unjust tariff."

"Well, ah…" Cushing hesitated, obviously not sure how to frame his rebuttal, and not wanting to provoke any more enmity than was already palpable in the air. "If Congress acts, we must –"

"Truly?" Cabell Senior's voice rose. People in the lobby turned to stare, some frowning, some nodding in agreement. "Congress is bought by Wall Street, the railroads, and the corporations. And if they should pass a law that overnight plunders thousands of law-abiding Americans? Why should we Southerners give any further allegiance to a country that does this? Why should we feel any loyalty a government simply takes whatever it wants, irrespective of law? Then, if we refuse to comply you are going to send armed force against us and take our property, even our lives and our liberty? This is the very essence of war, Mr. Cushing. The words of Northern Abolitionists and tariff-mongers are a declaration of war against us, *de facto* now but *de jure* to follow. What redress is then left to us but to meet force with force?"

"Well, you have the reputation of a peacemaker," said Cushing, spreading both hands in supplication. "I beg you not to let your Southern compatriots divide this great party over purely hypothetical events. If you do, assuredly the Republicans will win the Presidency, and then—"

"And then the South will exercise its sovereign right to depart the Union," Father interjected. "In the same manner we entered it. *Voluntarily*."

Cushing shook his head and clasped his hands together. His eyes held a mute appeal to Cabell Senior. "Upon my soul, I fear this above all. It will surely lead to war. The Republicans will *not* let you depart in peace, which I understand is your dearest wish. You would face a war you cannot win. The North has more money, more ships, more men, more factories."

"I see no reason why separation must lead to war, Mr. Cushing," Cabell Junior interjected. "But if it comes to that, wars are not decided by material means alone. We are the sons of the men who beat the British at Kings Mountain and Cowpens. The British far outweighed us in men and *matériel*. In fact, the Revolution was decided in this very State, by men whose only means were courage and fortitude and love of liberty."

Father held up a stern hand. "Son, you forget yourself."

"Yes, perhaps your version of history is correct," Cushing said. "But remember. *We* are the sons of the men of Lexington and Concord, of Bunker Hill and Valley Forge. I beg you not to under-estimate the courage and fortitude of the North. If such men, North and South, ever clash at arms… Why, there will be a bloodletting as the world has never seen."

A cold wave of presentiment swept over Cabell at the ominous words. Father's face darkened, but he replied with a placating smile, "I say again, the South has no desire for war, unless the North attempt to coerce us."

Ranse chided them with a bright smile. "Must we talk about such gloomy topics here in gay Charleston?" He grabbed Celia's hand and spun her up from her seat and around in a circle, his hand on her narrow waist, grinning at her laughter. "We are supposed to be the best-mannered and most hospitable city in America. Let us live up to our billing and repair to Henri's for supper and dancing."

Drayton nodded. "A splendid idea. Except that *I* will escort the young lady. Won't you come, Father, and you, Mr. Cushing? Let us show you what Charleston is truly known for. And it is *not* strife and disunion."

"Yes, I will most gladly," said Cushing, heaving his bulk from the bench. "We Yankees seldom visit this fair city. I'm not likely to visit again soon, and I should like to make the most of the opportunity."

***

Cabell remembered that night of music and laughter with sweet regret, when New Englander and South Carolinian were still able to fellowship. They feasted on the last oysters of the season and cracked crab. The sommelier poured wine non-stop. But Nero was tuning up his fiddle while the incendiaries gathered to burn Rome. A few days after their convivial evening came the first harbinger of national calamity.

The conciliatory efforts of Father, Caleb Cushing, and other moderates failed to dispel the sectional venom. The Convention collapsed. Cabell saw more clearly than ever that North and South had grown apart into separate communities, and it couldn't be bandaged over by party politics. When the platform vote failed to satisfy the Fire-Eaters, they walked out of the Convention. South Carolina Democrats reluctantly followed. The remaining delegates tried to select a Party nominee, but after 59 ballots Stephen Douglas could not seal the nomination. In confusion and dismay, the delegates streamed home by horse, rail, and ship, resolving to meet again.

Senator Douglas' loyalists re-convened in Baltimore in May as the 'official' Party convention. He received the Democratic nomination, but all knew it was worthless.   Southern dissidents who had bolted the session in Charleston also met in Baltimore and nominated Vice President John C. Breckinridge of Kentucky. Other dissident Democrats formed the Constitutional Union Party and nominated Tennessean John Bell, favorite of the Upper South. With the Democrats split three ways, the Republicans could expect to win the White House no matter who they nominated.

The debacle of the country's largest political party transfixed the American people. In the meanwhile Abraham Lincoln was emerging as the likely nominee of the Republicans. Before entering the Congress Lincoln had been a lawyer for the railroads. Ample funds flowed into his war chest, and he began to eclipse rival William Seward. People joked that Abe Lincoln only split rails, while Steve Douglas split the Democratic Party. But it was hardly Douglas' fault. He had at least tried to bridge the unbridgeable gulf. The Republicans had never won a Presidential election, but now they appeared poised to change the course of history.

Chapter Nine

The Democratic National Convention ended on a Friday. On Monday morning Dr. Sullivan surprised his students at the College of Charleston. Drayton expected him to offer some innocuous comment on the day's news, as he often did. But on this morning he posed the question, "Who knows where the word 'idiot' comes from?" Instead of taking station at the lectern, he paced back and forth excitedly at the front of the classroom. He moved so rapidly his lugubrious gray morning coat ballooned out behind him.

An awkward silence followed. There was only a scraping of feet and clearing of throats until Selby Jenkins, not the brightest star in the firmament, raised a tentative hand.

"Yes, Mr. Jenkins?" He stopped pacing.

"Well, sir, it comes from the Greek," Jenkins answered feebly.

His fellow students snorted. A few laughed outright.

Dr. Sullivan was nonplussed. When the boy failed to elaborate, he said, "Thank you, Mr. Jenkins." The soul of courtesy, thought Drayton.

"Yes, the word does come from the Greek," explained the Doctor. "From *idiotēs*. In ancient Athens it meant someone ignorant of public affairs, or a private man who refused to enter into the civic life of the *polis*. Now, I hope none of us are *idiotoi*. If you observe what is taking place around us, then you must see something ominous happened here in Charleston last week."

Everyone seemed on edge. Something *had* happened, and grave consequences might well follow. There were many disproving scowls, but no one broke the icy silence.

The Professor took a few more strides, stroked his chin, then stopped and faced the class. "One reason we study the Classics, apart from the value of the knowledge itself, is for what they may teach us about our times. Therefore, I have decided to adjust the syllabus for this course in the few weeks that remain of term. We are going to lay aside Homer, and we are going to take up Thucydides and his account of the Peloponnesian War. As you should know, that was the conflict between the empire of Athens against Sparta and its allies, from 431 to 404 BC. It ended the dominance of Athens and the golden age of Greece.

"You will read of Athens at the height of her power and the flowering glory of Greek culture, yet an Athens full of hubris, believing herself unassailable, and willing to enslave others to gratify her pride and self-styled honor. You will learn of the dire consequences when war fever escaped the bounds of reason."

Robert Pringle interrupted without the normal courtesy of being called upon. "Sir, if I may ask – why this abrupt change?"

"I believe Thucydides is more relevant to our time and place," the Doctor replied.

"By that, Sir," said Pringle, "I take you to mean the South is like Athens in the time of Thucydides, and that we are to be blamed for enslaving those who were brought here from Africa. Brought here by Yankee ships, I might add. But I seem to recall that Sparta, the arch-enemy of Athens, was built on the servitude of its helots —slaves. Why then do you take the part of Sparta against Athens?"

"Young man, I take no part. *Je ne blâme pas, ni n'approve; je raconte.* The past is what it is. The Greeks believed the past was the one thing even the gods could not alter."

"Sir, with respect, I believe you are being disingenuous," said Pringle, standing upright by his chair. He'd exchanged his militia uniform for a well-tailored brown roundabout and yellow silk tie. His mustache quivered as he spoke. "In likening the South to Athens, you are assigning blame for a war that may come as a result of Northern perfidy. Moreover, I suspect you have just called us idiots, although I will allow room for your well-known subtlety and refrain from such an assertion outright. But I for one did not enroll in this course to be insulted."

"Mr. Pringle, if you feel insulted by a parallel with the past, I beg you, do not put the responsibility upon me. Rather try to learn the lessons and avoid the disastrous mistakes of our forebears."

"I'll not endure this a moment longer!" Pringle gathered his books and papers, turned and marched toward the exit. In the shocked silence, all but three of the other students stood and followed him, scowling and muttering *sotto voce.*

As Pringle passed Drayton he growled, "Are you going to stay then?"

"Yes," Drayton said. "Don't you think you're being unjust toward Dr. Sullivan?"

"I might have known," said Pringle. "Now we see where your sympathies lie. You'll sacrifice your own people for … for that girl."

Drayton's blood rose, but he kept a grip on himself. A good Hellenist should aim for balance and good measure. Quietly he said, "My sympathies lie with the truth, however imperfectly I may seek it." He hoped so, at any rate. It was also true he would do anything to win Celia, and that meant he had to win her father as well. But truth was truth. And truth was a duty that transcended any private interests.

"Truth? That's all well and good." Pringle lowered his voice from its usual growl. He spoke almost intimately. "But remember, my friend. Truth is grounded in your people, place, customs, and traditions, not in some Jacobin abstraction." He turned and led the parade out of the classroom.

The unexpected shock of the encounter left the remaining students staring at the floor in embarrassment. Finally Dr. Sullivan broke the awkward silence, tugging at his shirt cuffs.

"Well, thank you for that, Mr. FitzHenry. There's an old saying in my profession, 'Genuine education enables one to listen to anything without losing one's temper.' His gaze took in the remnant of his class and he assayed a frosty smile. "There may be hope for some of you yet."

Yes, perhaps there was hope. Perhaps reason might yet prevail. Yet Pringle's exiting words had struck deep. They continued to echo in Drayton's mind. Who could say who was right, who was wrong? How could you *know*?

Thomas Moore

Chapter Ten

Charleston, South Carolina; June 1860.

Arm-in-arm, Drayton and Celia enjoyed their daily promenade along Charleston's High Battery, commanding the tip of the Peninsula and offering a dramatic view of Fort Sumter, four miles away at the entrance to the harbor. The fort's brick mass reared straight up from the water with no surrounding land. At a distance it seemed to be floating on the surface. Drayton stared at it for a long moment, as if to puzzle out some secret it concealed. But he couldn't be preoccupied for long with Celia at his side. It hadn't taken long to know he wanted her as his wife. He won the horse race, but that only made him realize he also had to win over her father. He began to question her more about him. The more he knew about Dr. Sullivan, the more likely he could overcome the barriers between them.

"I suppose you heard what happened in Greek class," he began. "The Great Walkout."

"Oh, yes." Celia's eyes were bright as her smile. "I think he was more gratified than he let on that you stood by him."

Drayton took her arms and paced along the sea wall. "No doubt he attributed my loyalty to…" He peered at her and smiled. "…self interest."

He never tired of studying Celia. Her upper lip was slightly pursed over a full lower lip, revealing a tiny glint of her teeth. He couldn't look at her mouth without an urge to kiss it. She had a slim, straight nose and face that was perfectly shaped and proportioned oval. But the eyes were the thing that riveted him.

"Those eyes," Drayton said. "Those deep gray eyes of yours. They see everything, don't they?"

Celia laughed brightly. "Did I never tell you that's what Sullivan means: the one-eyed or the dark-eyed one? In the Irish it was *Suilleabháin.*"

"Do you speak the Irish as well as your other languages?"

"Oh, no, just a few words I've picked up from Father over the years."

"I heard only a little Irish spoken when I was there. It seems utterly incomprehensible, yet it persists. I suppose if one can master Irish, then ancient Greek is a simple matter."

She laughed gaily. "Well, Father has a gift for languages. It seems to be in our blood."

They watched delightedly for a few moments as some boys on the sea wall tossed up chunks up of bread for the sea-gulls to catch in mid-air. But her face turned somber when Drayton asked, "When did Finbarr emigrate? And why?"

She stared at the jetties lining the harbor, the veritable forest of ships' masts and rigging. "Because of the Great Famine. They left Queenstown near Cork in 1847. The true Irish refuse to call it that but use its old Gaelic name, *Cobh*, pronounced 'cove.'"

"Interesting," he mused. "That's where I sailed from last December. Dreadful weather. I visited my ancestors' old family seat near Wexford. It was in Ireland I acquired a certain horse of your acquaintance."

She smiled and nodded. "During the famine, Father's family were better off than most," Celia explained. "They had a farmstead which the lord coveted. Like so many, he wanted the land for grazing, since there was more money in sheep than the pittance the lord received in rents. And when the blight killed off the potato, tenants could scarcely eat, much less pay rent. Countless Irish were evicted, turned out on the roads to die of hunger and exposure. It was especially hard in the West, the Beare Peninsula, for example, where Father's family lived for centuries. He is a direct descendant of Donal Cam O'Sullivan Beare, a hero of the Nine Years' War against England in the 1600's."

Drayton took her hand and pressed it to his lips. "I thank God Finbarr's family was able to escape. Even if my gratitude has a selfish motive."

She smiled, but bleakly, and continued as they walked. "The lord paid them enough for the passage to America on what came to be called 'coffin ships.' The food was execrable, there was little sanitation, and emigrants were crammed into steerage with scarce room to turn. Finbarr's mother died in his arms *en voyage* while his father lay ill in the filthy hold. Finbarr was young and strong and remained healthy. When they arrived in Boston, the authorities refused them entry because of the fever, and his father would have died on board within sight of his destination had Finbarr not smuggled him ashore. His father had a cousin in New York who took them in and helped Finbarr receive a fine education. The rest you know. But of those who remained in Ireland, tens of thousands starved to death or died of disease after being weakened by hunger. The lucky few, if you can call them that, found shelter in the workhouses. But it was a kind of living death. Ireland lost half its population from death or emigration. His father never forgot nor forgave, and neither, sadly, did Finbarr."

"When I was in Ireland last year, no one talked about this. I'm sure the memories were still fresh. That was only thirteen years ago."

"Naturally not," she said, gripping his hand to descend the sea wall and pulling him toward the gardens nearby. "Those who suffered and survived don't wish to be reminded. Neither do those who allowed such a shameful thing to occur."

"By 'those,' do you mean the English? Or the Anglo-Irish landed class?"

"Well, I must be frank. That's what the historical record tells us. It's one reason Father has such a low regard for the Ascendancy Irish. And your ancestors were obviously of the landlord class – Anglo-Irish."

"How do you know that?"

She gave him an arch look, then stopped to sniff the gardenias blooming in profusion. Bees swarmed around the shrubs, filling their air with industrious buzzing.

"First, you are Protestant."

"Yes, I am. It's part of my heritage. But I think for my ancestors it was a matter of expedience more than conviction. When the English became Protestant under Henry VIII, my people in Ireland went along."

"All the more shame to them, then."

Drayton shrugged. "Perhaps. I wish there existed a better appellation than 'Protestant.' I myself am not protesting anything, except perhaps the artificial barriers that are thrown up to keep men and women apart who ought to be together."

She smiled with pleasure and agreement. "And your surname provides another clue. I say this not to offend – it's not true of you personally in any case. But your Father and Cabell Junior wear the 'Fitz' in the name as proudly as any French marquis with his 'de' or Prussian count with his 'von.'"

Drayton laughed. It was true. "You not only see, you hear. Yet 'Fitz' is only the Old French version of *fils*, 'son.' Like your Irish 'Mac' or 'O.' Any 'nobility' my family has attained came from hard work and wise management. In this country opportunity lies open to anyone who does the same. Even the Irish." He laughed again.

"Yes. But I beg you – it's no laughing matter. Because of what the Irish suffered Father has retained a hostility toward the Ascendancy as a class. They are not only Protestants; heretics in his mind, but also rack-renters, evictors; pitiless, greedy men who despoiled and oppressed the native Irish for hundreds of years. You say your ancestors achieved their status in Ireland by hard work and wise management. Father would say they achieved it by force of arms and ruthless conquest. I know it seems irrational, but the Gaels have long memories. The ancient grievances are passed down from one generation to the next. It's in his blood. In his mind the crimes against the Irish over the centuries demand recompense."

They strolled among high banks of azaleas, which had bloomed earlier in the spring and were now depositing a carpet of browning petals. "I certainly hope he won't take out his ancient grievances on me," said Drayton.

"He likes you, despite his hostility toward the Ascendancy. But remember, he also feels this way about Southern slave-owners, whom he assigns to the same class. In all honesty I share his opinion of slavery. And he detests it, as he does all forms of tyranny."

"Well, I detest it, too; but not enough to repudiate my own blood. And since you're being frank, so will I. We have inherited an institution that we know must end, but we don't know how to end it. And so we remain trapped in a kind of stasis."

"Yes, I can see that. I suspect even Father can, now he's here. I'm surprised he could be induced to sojourn in the heart of the slave-kingdom; even though the College of Charleston is a prestigious position. He did say he wanted to satisfy his own curiosity about your Peculiar Institution."

"And what has he decided?"

"Well, the reality is not the equal of *Uncle Tom's Cabin*, if bad enough. Fortunately for us, you expressed your own opposition to slavery early on and unprompted. Otherwise, his disapproval would have proven unsurmountable."

"I see," he said, tight-lipped. He was glad of Finbarr's approval, yet offended at the same time. The FitzHenrys were paramount in their kingdom by the sea and justly so. Did he really need the approval of an impecunious Yankee interloper; a landless, itinerant schoolmaster only a slight cut above the fugitive hedge-scholars of Ireland's yesteryear?

He sighed. "Well, I haven't read *Uncle Tom's Cabin*. I refuse. It's a caricature and a calumny on my people. I have read *Castle Rackrent*, by Maria Edgeworth. I believe it shows the day of the landlords in Ireland is ending, just as Negro slavery will end here, of its own inherent weaknesses and contradictions."

Celia frowned at the severity of his tone. "Yes, Maria Edgeworth was of the landlord class. She was wise enough to realize human oppression of any sort is not sustainable – not in Ireland, or America, or ultimately, anywhere. Her realization gives me reason to hope. In any event, I tell you these unhappy things so you may understand and not let his feelings get in the way of … of our friendship I have begged Father not to import old quarrels into a time and place where they don't belong. "

Drayton released her hand and gestured emphatically. "My grandfather Thomas FitzHenry stood for Ireland and against the English in 1798. That ought to earn a mark in my favor. Don't misunderstand — I'm not ashamed of my ancestors. They were not Englishmen. My early forbear was Meiler FitzHenry, a Norman knight who came to Ireland from Wales with Maurice and Raymond FitzGerald in 1169. He had no particular loyalty to England. The FitzHenrys became Gaelicized. They married the daughters of Gaelic chieftains. Within three generations the FitzHenrys were Irish patriots, speaking Gaelic, following Irish customs, and sponsoring bards and poets and sheannachies."

"*Hiberniores ipsis Hibernicis.* More Irish than the Irish?" She teased.

"Exactly."

"Except that their Norman lord, Strongbow, was a vassal of England's King Henry II. And the FitzGeralds were invaders who had no right to Ireland in the first place. They were no better than land pirates."

Even in disagreement Drayton reveled in the sharpness of her mind. But she was wrong about his Irish kin. He thought back on the tales he'd heard at his grandmother's knee. Her Tourville kin were among the first French Hugenots to settle South Carolina, yet she was equally proud of her FitzHenry connections. Drayton had never known his grandfather Thomas, but from his grandmother Tourville he'd learned how Thomas FitzHenry first came to Charleston in 1801. Thomas was a close friend of Lord Edward FitzGerald, who died in the rebellion of 1798 against the Crown. Earlier, in 1780 and 1781, Edward FitzGerald had fought with the British Army in the American Revolution. He was wounded at the Battle of Eutaw Springs in South Carolina, and convalesced in Charleston. The experience engendered a sympathy for the cause of American liberty, which he took back to Ireland. Recalling how FitzGerald had extolled Charleston and the virtues of South Carolina, Thomas FitzHenry emigrated there when he fled Ireland. Drayton didn't want to boast of his ancestry, but they were hardly pirates. It was good to be well-born, yet he refused to live on inherited glory. He would earn a reputation through his own accomplishments.

Finally he told Celia, "My forebears and yours, for all their differences, were on the same side, the side of Irish liberty, though maybe at different times. It was my grandfather Thomas FitzHenry who spirited Lord Edward Fitzgerald's wife Pamela and his papers out of the country to France. The FitzHenrys were proud, to be sure, but not predatory. They were generous-hearted. They endowed schools. They were patrons of the arts. One was a writer of note, a contemporary and friend of Swift. My people weren't just soldiers or landlords; they valued attainments of mind and spirit and helped build modern Ireland. Anyway, in those days everyone was vassal to someone else, unless he was a king. Sadly, those were the days when might meant right."

"Is today any different," she said, "with this mad rush to war? Father, I'm afraid, draws an altogether different set of conclusions from his Irish ancestry than you do."

Drayton was surprised and filled with a kind of leaden anxiety to find himself the object of Finbarr's prejudice, an experience he was not at all accustomed to. It was disconcerting to bear the animosity of an intelligent, thoughtful man because of what his ancestors might or might not have done.

"Well, Finbarr is wise," Drayton said after a long pause. "He's entitled to his conclusions, as long as he doesn't hold me responsible for the deeds my ancestors may have committed 500 years ago. *You* don't, do you?"

"No. But I must honor and obey him." Her eyes twinkled. "Within reason."

Chapter Eleven

Sometimes in a moment of self-awareness Drayton pondered the words of Robert Pringle. Was he becoming a dissident, aligning with men like James Petigru, out of true conviction? Or was it trimming his sails to a wind that would bring him to Celia? In any case, she was almost his, and he still couldn't believe his good fortune.

He'd heard of such things, of course, in legend, literature, and history. Helen and Paris, Pericles and Aspasia, Tristan and Isolde. But he'd never expected it to happen to him, a Great Love. He was too diffident, too introspective. He didn't carry off the dashing pose of so many Charleston bluebloods like Robert Pringle. He enjoyed a reputation as an intrepid horseman, but wasn't made of the stuff of heroes, or so he believed. Yet somehow, some*why*, she'd chosen him.

Perhaps it was his erect posture and carriage, the graceful way he sat a horse. Drayton was a good rider because he paid attention to his horse and made it a matter of study, unlike the rakehells who rode with abandon because they wanted to win a reputation. His reputation, which many sniffed at, was as a 'scientific' rider. But no one could sniff at his results. Or perhaps it was the self-assurance that came with generations of breeding, tradition, and the mystique of the landed classes. But then, Robert Pringle had the same attributes, and was wealthier and handsomer in the bargain.

He would study himself in the mirror from time to time for reassurance, and to tease out an answer to the mystery. He was not bad looking, he supposed, but nothing exceptional. Of medium height, he was trim and hard from hours in the saddle and rowing the Edisto, and more recently, hiking the Wicklow Mountains. He had a high forehead appropriate to a scholar, crowned by luxuriant brown hair, which he wore shorter than the fashion. Thanks to his maternal Hugenot ancestors, he boasted a fine Roman nose like his father's and a complexion darkened by his heavy beard. He shaved daily, contrary to the style which favored facial hair. His deep-set brown eyes wore a quizzical look, as if surprised by some chance encounter. Now he *was* surprised – surprised by Joy, as the poet said.

There was more at work here than mere sexual attraction. This was not going to be another dalliance, a lightly passing *amour*. He'd known enough of those to tell the difference. It was one reason he'd gone to Europe, to cool the hot blood. Yet, how could one truly *know*? Celia's physical attractiveness stirred him every time he looked at her. But there was far more to her than beauty. Everything about Celia suggested character, goodness, and integrity. Yet appearances could be deceiving. As the Scripture taught, even Satan – Lucifer — appeared as an angel of light. The Old Book warned in Jeremiah, 'The heart is deceitful above all things and desperately wicked; who can know it?' Yet the same Book said in Proverbs, 'The heart of her husband doth safely trust in her.' It was all so confusing. Certitude was elusive. The ancient Greeks had wrestled with this basic problem of man – epistemology. How do we know what we know? Or more precisely, how do we know what we *believe* we know? All he could do was to trust his heart. He knew he could trust her, not just in a juridical sense, but at the level of his very self, as she would learn to trust him.

Charleston, South Carolina; September 1860.

Finbarr Sullivan honored his contract with the College of Charleston, returning to teach the fall term, despite anxieties about the widening gulf between North and South. Drayton spent as much time as he could with Celia, uncomfortably mindful of a need to placate his mentor by advocating peace and reconciliation. And though it was a cause he believed in himself, he did little on its behalf except hold heated discussions with his brother Cabell whenever they came together in town or at the River. He approached his father several times on the subject. Father never took him seriously, admonishing him 'not to let that Northern woman' do his thinking for him. Drayton tried to demonstrate he was thinking for himself. Any sane man knew that peace was better than war if it could be avoided. Father would agree in principle that war must be avoided, and then allow himself to be drawn toward the camp of the militants.

After a few fruitless conversations with his family, Drayton let the matter lie. Celia was back in town, which was all that really mattered to him. He made his reports to Professor Sullivan to show he was making an effort, but even in his own ears they sounded perfunctory. Then he would sweep Celia away for a carriage ride up the Peninsula, or long walks on the Battery, or tea in St. Michael's churchyard. In his eyes her grave beauty, tinged with wit and good cheer, only grew deeper. At the same time he delved deeper into her mind, and was in awe of her knowledge and understanding. He had no doubts that one day soon she would become his wife.

By the middle of autumn Drayton felt the entire State had come down with a case of secession fever. It was especially virulent in Abbeville and Edgefield.

On the occasions when his brother came home to Cypress Stand or the East Bay mansion, all Cabell could talk about was Martin Gary, the formidable Butler clan, and when, not if, South Carolina might go its own way. Amicably, of course.

Charleston followed close behind in enthusiasm for independence. Waving palmetto fronds, citizens held torchlight parades and illuminations down Broad Street to the 'Four Corners of Law'. Bands played military airs and marches while hundreds gathered at White Point Garden for pro-secession speeches. Moderate secessionists like Cabell Senior began to realize they were being rendered irrelevant. Cabell Junior suggested Father swap his pale pastels for the unambiguous colors of the Fire-Eaters. The political impulse was strong to co-opt the militants by adopting as much of their program as he could abide. But who was really co-opting whom?

The inexorable motion toward separation intensified with the Presidential campaigns. Any sentient person could see that Douglas, Breckinridge, and Bell were slicing the Democratic vote three ways, while Lincoln and Hamlin conducted a shrewd, well-funded, well-organized campaign – except in the South. The more Lincoln tried to reassure Southerners, the more they regarded him as a minority sectional President under the sway of self-serving interests.

The campaign marching song of the Abolitionists, 'John Brown's Body,' was first heard in the North, with words set to a popular camp meeting hymn. Soon the song made its way south, courtesy of secessionist newspapers who never missed an opportunity to highlight Northern perfidy. The song praised John Brown as a saint and martyr, whom the South considered a traitor and madman. Brown's papers seized at Harpers Ferry in 1859 had proved he intended to raise a servile insurrection. Freed Negroes would be incited to torture and massacre white Southerners, as in Haiti in 1804 under the rebel Dessalines. Abolitionist editorials smoked with hatred toward the South. Now moderates became convinced the Abolitionists' goal was not simply to abolish slavery but to abolish the South itself.

Even worse to theologically conservative Southerners was the blasphemy of men like Thoreau and Emerson who extolled John Brown as a Christ-figure. 'Without the shedding of blood there is no remission of sin,' Brown had said, equating his own execution with the sacrificial death of Jesus Christ. Ralph Waldo Emerson wrote that Brown's hanging made '...the gallows as glorious as the cross...' Christians in the South began to see there was no common ground, no possibility of co-existing in the same polity with such people. America was indeed a 'house divided,' in Lincoln's words. Divided in more ways than he knew. And not just by Southerners.

The triumph of inevitability — Abraham Lincoln was elected 16th President of the United States on November 6, 1860. Stephen Douglas had campaigned vigorously, in the South as well as the North. But the three Democratic candidates, Douglas, current Vice President John C. Breckinridge of Kentucky, and John Bell of Tennessee split the opposing vote, as everyone had known they would. Lincoln's majority was only in the Electoral College. His popular vote was a million fewer than the combined popular vote of his three opponents. His vote in the South was hardly worth counting. The outcome proved the Republicans were not a majority national party. In fact, Democrats remained strong in both houses of the Congress.

South Carolinians holding Federal office in the state and South Carolina's entire Congressional delegation began to leave office in protest. Members of Congress and officers in the U.S. Army and Navy from other states also began to resign, some eagerly, some with sorrow. Secession rallies sprang up in Mississippi, Alabama, and Texas. Even the more deliberate Virginians, most of whom were Unionists, began to speak of joining the Lower South rather than see their sister states coerced by Federal bayonets. On November 10, the South Carolina General Assembly passed an act to establish a convention to consider secession.

November 22, 1860; Abbeville, South Carolina.

Drayton tried to keep abreast of the news through newspapers from the North arriving every few days by mail packet and he corresponded with old friends from Princeton. Most of the voices emanating from the North echoed the refrain. The North hoped the South would remain in the Union, but if it left, the South would have to satisfy the North for the lost revenue and Federal property. But the 'Abos,' the Abolitionists, were a different matter. Many of them were eager for the South to leave, ending 'the covenant with Hell' and cutting away the 'diseased member.' The more radical among them called for invading the South to free the slaves. Vile Southern planters as well as their slave system were to be exterminated.

Reading these articles, Drayton felt his gorge rising. He understood his brother's fury, and could hear the war horns, far-off but calling clearly. When he questioned his father, Cabell Senior dismissed the rhetoric of the radicals. The North wasn't listening to the Abos, he said. They didn't want their own section flooded with newly freed Negroes competing with free white labor. As long as Reasonable Men kept their heads, all would be well. Drayton nursed doubts. The vortex spinning around them all seemed to be accelerating. But his father's reassurances allowed him to concentrate on the matter at hand, courting Celia.

He and Celia spent part of each day together, and she pleased him and interested him as no other woman had – except in one respect. She was not a horsewoman. He purchased a gentle 15-year-old cob for her, a gelding and 'made' horse, which he stabled with Beltane for company at the Washington race course. There he could teach her the fundamentals of riding, which she took to readily enough. And there, several times a week, they would return to the place of his triumph, reminding her of his love.

But history would not stand aside for anyone's self-indulgence, not even a storybook romance. Tucked away in an obscure western corner of South Carolina close to the Savannah River lay the town of Abbeville, founded by Hugenots before the American Revolution and named for their home in France. In addition to its fiercely independent Hugenot settlers were a large number of Scots-Irish, who were even more fierce and independent. Abbeville District had been the scene of bitter resistance to the British and Tories during the Revolution. It produced one of the state's foremost Patriot leaders, Andrew Pickens, a master of partisan warfare. The Long Canes area of Abbeville District was the birthplace of South Carolina's great apostle of states' rights, John C. Calhoun, former U.S. Senator and Vice President. Shortly before he died in 1850, he'd made a major speech in the U.S. Senate advocating secession as the ultimate remedy against the abuse of one section of the country by another. Now dead ten years, Calhoun's words still echoed. His *South Carolina Exposition and Protest* was holy writ to those who believed the sovereign states were the only effective Constitutional check on usurpation of power by the central government.

In 1860 Abbeville vied with its neighbor Edgefield to lead the cause of South Carolina's independence. On a brisk evening in November several hundred citizens gathered under flaring torches on what came to be known as Secession Hill to call for the state's departure from the Union. Since the legislature had proposed a statewide convention to consider secession, Abbeville wanted to be first in the queue. Overwhelmingly, they adopted their own ordinance of secession and elected delegates to the convention to begin in mid-December, earning for their town the title 'birthplace of the Confederacy.'

Compared to towns like Edgefield, Abbeville, and Charleston, the city of Columbia was lukewarm toward secession. Wade Hampton, Columbia's foremost citizen and one of the South's richest men, was known to support remaining in the Union. Hampton urged his fellow Southerners to resolve the South's grievances through negotiation; and above all, peaceably. Though lukewarm, Columbia was South Carolina's capital, thus the proper venue for a statewide convention. Here the delegates began to assemble in mid-December to draft an ordinance of secession.

December 11, 1860; Columbia, South Carolina.

Drayton arrived at East Bay from a morning ride with Celia to find his father supervising Shortbread's packing a valise. He wore a worried frown.

"Father, you look as if you're about to undertake an unpleasant journey. What's afoot? Has something happened at Cypress Stand?"

"Not too unpleasant a journey, I hope. I'm off to Columbia."

"For the Secession Convention? But you're not a delegate." Drayton was incredulous.

"Yes, I am. A recent development. Mr. Montagu has fallen ill, and there's no time for an election to fill his place. General Jamison has prevailed upon me."

"But Father, I thought you were ambivalent at the very least. Now you're signing on to the cause of secession?"

"My boy, I say this with reluctance. Secession is unavoidable. Lincoln's election has made it so. Since it must needs come, General Jamison and others have persuaded me that the voice of moderation must have a seat at the table. Otherwise Reasonable Men will lose all sway over events."

Drayton bit his lip. "Father, that has already happened. Is there no way to prevent this? Does no one see it will lead to conflict?"

His father stared at him with eyes full of perplexity. Finally he said, "Son, it's gone too far and too fast to stop. But my hope is for a brief ordinance that simply rescinds South Carolina's ratification of the U.S. Constitution in 1788 and nothing more. No long list of grievances, no returning of Yankee insults. I believe we can dissolve the tie with the United States without whipping up war fever. On either side."

Drayton read of the opening sessions in Columbia's stately brick First Baptist Church, the largest meeting place in the city. David F. Jamison of Barnwell presided. Reports of an outbreak of smallpox couldn't dampen the excitement and the tension. By far the majority of delegates were committed to secession, or they wouldn't have come. The vast majority also believed South Carolina and her sister states could depart the Union without igniting a war.

By December 17 the threat of smallpox in Columbia was reportedly too great to ignore, although some suspected the rumors were fostered to justify moving the convention to a friendlier venue. The convention recessed, agreeing to resume in Charleston. Met by marching bands at the Meeting Street Station, the 169 delegates re-convened on December 18 in Charleston's Institute Hall, where the Democratic National Convention had met the previous April.

Charleston, South Carolina; December 20, 1860.

Drayton called for Celia at Glebe Street on the evening of December 20th.

A few blocks away the sounds of martial music and fireworks reverberated from Citadel Square. Maria watched disapprovingly from the doorway as Drayton handed Celia into the carriage. He nodded at Shortbread, who twitched up the horses, heading downtown to Henri's for supper.

"Have you heard the news?" he asked.

"One needn't have heard the news since one can hear the noise."

Cannon boomed from the Battery. A volley of musketry followed from Citadel Square, and voices cheered from ten thousand throats as people thronged the streets singing paeans to liberty and independence. Drayton feared the place had become an outdoor insane asylum, just as James Petrigru had once described it.

The Convention's delegates had voted unanimously to secede amid shouts of joy, artillery fire, and pealing of church bells. They had signed the Ordinance on the same table used in 1788 to ratify the U.S. Constitution. South Carolina was the first Southern state to take this fateful step – 'imminent suicide' in the words of disgruntled Unionists.

Drayton said, "I read that seven states of the lower South and Texas will soon follow South Carolina." He was neither triumphant nor downcast, only reporting the facts as he'd learned them.

Celia said with slow anger, "How easy it was after all. Simply meet in convention and pass an ordinance. Thus a hundred years of history are undone."

"Perhaps we are brought to this moment by a hundred years of history." He answered more sharply than intended. Somewhat to his own surprise he felt the tug of ancient loyalties more powerful than any political argument or personal desire.

Celia said, "My father may have has been right all along. I fear deep in my bones where this is leading us."

"Well, I have done my part. I've spoken to anyone who will listen about the dangers of this headlong course. The Convention delegates believe in all sincerity that we can leave the Union peaceably. I see no reason why that won't prove to be the case – unless we are forced to defend ourselves."

She stared at him with something like derision. "What we wish, we readily believe."

He didn't want to quarrel. It would be their first, and privately he knew she might be right. He'd begun to recognize the all too human tendency toward self-delusion. With mental discipline, one could limit its effects. But all people were susceptible to it.

Drayton murmured, "Even the moderates like Father are now put to a choice. He thinks he's swimming against the tide, but I think the tide is sweeping him out to sea. He doesn't want disunion, but also says that we Southerners have been provoked beyond all bearing. In truth, it's hard for me to dispute him."

"It grieves me beyond words to think the folly of civil war could come between us just as we have found each other." She paused and looked at him with a hard, level stare. "Unless we both go abroad."

Chapter Twelve

The United States Government controlled four installations in and around Charleston. First was Fort Moultrie, dating from the Revolution and located on Sullivan's Island covering the northeast side of the channel into Charleston Harbour. The original Fort Moultrie, made of sand and palmetto logs, had humbled the British sea-borne attack in June 1776, giving the symbol of the palmetto its place of honour on the state flag and encouraging delegates to the Continental Congress in Philadelphia to issue the Declaration of Independence. The more modern fort was built of masonry but in a state of disrepair – and more importantly, indefensible from the land side. A mile across the water from Fort Moultrie was Fort Sumter, a three-tiered brick edifice on a sandbar in the middle of the channel. Sumter's heavy guns could cover all of Charleston's maritime traffic. Closer inbound, near the tip of the Charleston peninsula, was a smaller and obsolete fort dating from 1808 called Castle Pinckney. Finally, there was the Federal Arsenal in the city proper, housing guns and munitions and staffed only by a storekeeper and a handful of civil servants.

In November 1860, the U.S. War Department had ordered Major Robert Anderson to Charleston to take command of the Federal garrison and the four U.S. properties, believing he was the right man to send into the volatile atmosphere. Even-tempered and diplomatic, he enjoyed a solid military reputation that appealed to South Carolinians. He was born in Kentucky, married to a Georgian, and known to have pro-Southern sympathies. But he was also devoted to the Union and determined to carry out his orders. But only he knew for certain what those orders were, though only the most ardent Secessionists believed he'd been sent to start a war. *But...*could he avoid one? This was the question that kept everyone in a pitch of increasing tension. Tightening the Federal grip on the forts while South Carolina and her sister states marched toward independence put the two sections on a collision course.

When South Carolina seceded, Governor Francis Pickens dispatched a commission to negotiate turning over the Federal property to the state. President James Buchanan, knowing he was on the way out, at first refused to meet them. Most Southerners, certain of the South's superior military virtues, professed not to care. Their self-assurance convinced even the more sanguine that the Yankees would not fight, but would depart after a period of temporizing and face-saving.

In the summer Cabell Junior had followed Martin Gary's lead and tried to join the Edgefield Hussars. But by then there were no longer any officer vacancies, and Gary insisted he must take a commission. Gary and his colleague Matthew Calbraith Butler, also practicing law in Edgefield, intervened on his behalf. Cal Butler was well-connected politically. His father had been a U.S. Congressman, one of his uncles had served in the U.S. Senate, and another was a former Governor and hero of the Mexican War. Within a few weeks Cabell had been invited to join the military staff of Governor Pickens helping organize the state's forces, although his military knowledge was limited to what he'd gleaned from a crash reading program, *Hardee's Tactics* and the like.

Governor Pickens' peace commission failed in its primary task, but was useful in gathering intelligence. In fact, the actions of the Federal authorities were largely transparent. South Carolina's military authorities knew that lame-duck President Buchanan was torn between several Northern factions. Though a Pennsylvanian, Buchanan felt some sympathy toward the South's view of state sovereignty. He did not want to ignite hostilities. Yet his oath of office and his own personal pride would not allow him to abandon the U.S. installations in the South. Troops in the U.S. forts had to be re-supplied, but not in such a way to provoke conflict. If Lincoln wanted war, which he assured everyone was not the case, he'd inherit the impossibly complex decision upon his inauguration in March 1861. In the meanwhile, Washington and South Carolina maintained a gentlemanly but uneasy stand-off.

On December 24 the still-sitting Secession Convention adopted Christopher Memminger's 'Declaration of Immediate Causes Which Induce and Justify the Secession of South Carolina.' Unlike the Ordinance of Secession, Memminger's declaration enumerated South Carolina's grievances against the Union. It made heady reading, and raised the public temperature considerably, already elevated over the state's newly declared independence.

But now it was Christmas Eve, and politics could wait. The state's celebratory mood was overlaid with holiday revelry. Like most Charleston families, the FitzHenrys celebrated Christmas with several days of parties and dinners, ending the merry-making on traditional Twelfth Night and the approach of Epiphany. Eggnog laced with 'stiffener' was abundant, along with mulled wine. Cabell Senior produced his finest brandy for the male guests and 20-year old port for the ladies.

On December 26 the FitzHenrys hosted a post-Christmas breakfast for their friends and relations at the East Bay mansion. By mid-morning gentlemen were deep in their convivial cups and cigars. The ladies had withdrawn to enjoy a more sedate observance of the season as befitting their sex and station. Drayton and Celia had found a quiet place to be alone in the adjacent library – with doors open to avoid impropriety. In the smoking room Father ordered rum punch served for a toast. He noticed that Ransome had gone missing.

He demanded loudly, in case Ranse was in earshot, "Where is that young imp? Can't he stay still long enough to take a cup of Christmas cheer with his kin?"

Drayton came into the hallway and said, "Father, he was just here a few moments ago. Then I saw him dart outside. Perhaps he heard a disturbance."

Father snorted with annoyance. "These days one is *always* hearing a disturbance." He returned to his drink and conversation with James Orr, former Speaker of the U.S. House, with whom he'd served in the Congress. A few minutes later the pocket doors rolled open with a rumble and in stepped Ranse, his face strained and white.

"Why, Ranse!" said Drayton, alarmed. "What can be the matter?"

His brother displayed none of his normal bravado. Ranse pushed past him and strode to the crackling fireplace where his father stood with James Orr. Cabell Junior was also in the small circle of revelers. Celia joined Drayton, taking his arm discreetly.

"Father! Mr. Speaker!" Ranse exclaimed. "I just heard from a patrol of the Washington Light Infantry on East Battery."

"Yes? What is it?" the older men chorused.

"Last night Major Anderson moved his men from Sullivan's Island and occupied Fort Sumter!"

A heavy silence hung in the air as the men exchanged troubled glances. Cabell Senior wore the look of a man whose handiwork has collapsed in ruins.

"Father, didn't you hear? The Yankees now hold Fort Sumter!"

***

When the United States Government sent Major Anderson to take possession of U.S. forts in Charleston, the War Department's directive was to defend himself to the last extremity if attacked. The orders were well known to the secession government in Charleston. But South Carolina also relied on President Buchanan's desire to avert war, even as the pace of events accelerated with the occupation of Fort Sumter. No one in Charleston had acted on the intelligence that filtered south from spies and newspaper reporters in Washington. It was an obvious military step and should have been foreseen. In the late hours of

Christmas night and early morning of December 26, Major Anderson spiked his guns at Fort Moultrie, sent the garrison's families into Charleston, and rowed his troops to Fort Sumter.

On December 28 South Carolina's peace commissioners finally were allowed to meet with President Buchanan, who told them, "Major Anderson's action was not only against my orders but against my policy." Yet Anderson remained in Fort Sumter. Official South Carolina wondered if President Buchanan was deliberately misleading them. Up 'til now he'd appeared sympathetic. But he'd refused to negotiate until, evidently, the U.S. Government had a firm grip on Fort Sumter. Was he being duplicitous? Had he turned his coat? If not President Buchanan, who was giving Major Anderson his orders? Army Chief General Winfield Scott certainly. But whose was the policy? President-Elect Lincoln's? Radical Republicans' and Abolitionists' in the Congress? The uncertainties raised Governor Pickens' anxiety. The result was a wait-and-see attitude, which in practical terms meant a kind of paralysis.

Well, thought Cabell, *we waited and now we see – the Union flag floating above Fort Sumter and blue-coated sentries pacing the barbette.* In a classic case of too-little, too-late, Governor Pickens ordered South Carolina troops to occupy Fort Moultrie on Sullivans Island and Castle Pinckney in the harbor. A mere squad was required to seize the city arsenal and courteously escort the Federal storekeeper and his civilian staff off the premises.

Cabell served as a liaison to the artillery battalion that moved into now vacant Fort Moultrie. They included experienced soldiers, West Pointers and Citadel men. He was impressed with how they sited their batteries and emplaced the big guns that followed by mule train. Negroes performed the heavy work, digging trenches, throwing up the sand into parapets, and reinforcing them with palmetto logs. They built brick ovens to heat projectiles for 'hot shot.' However skillfully conducted, the business left Cabell with a sinking sensation. Though no one spoke of it, they all knew Major Anderson had 'humbugged' them, as the Duke of Wellington had described Napoleon's surprise maneuver into Belgium before Waterloo. Fort Sumter was now the focus of contention between newly independent South Carolina and the United States. The tension could only get worse when the Lincoln Administration took office a few months from now. If only the Southerners had had the foresight to get there first, when it was unoccupied. If only! What futile, mocking words, thought Cabell. The history of war was a series of blunders and missed opportunities. Once missed they could never be retrieved.

South Carolina could not permit the Yankees to occupy the Fort indefinitely, where it commanded Charleston's vital trade. The Deep South states were expected to follow South Carolina in seceding from the Union and creating a new country. Perhaps the new Confederacy could intimidate Anderson into departing quietly, although it was unlikely. Cabell had no idea of the provisions available in Sumter. Perhaps the Yankees could be starved out. Otherwise they'd have to be blasted out. Or the Confederates would have to use force against a Yankee fleet sent to re-provision them. Either course meant firing on the Union flag. Either course risked igniting all-out war.

Chapter Thirteen

Charleston, South Carolina; January 1861

James Orr had invited the FitzHenry gentlemen to a discussion of the crisis at John Russell's Bookstore on King Street. In the rear of the store, the reading room drew a weekly meeting of Charleston's leading intellectuals, the nearest thing in Charleston to an old-fashioned literary salon. The sessions included such luminaries as the poets Henry Timrod and Paul Hayne. A frequent guest was William Gilmore Simms, the South's answer to James Fenimore Cooper and one of America's most celebrated authors. Drayton felt a near awe of Basil Gildersleeve, who was earning a national reputation as a Greek scholar and had inspired Drayton in his interest in the classics. These were the most influential men of letters, journalists, and leaders in all Charleston, some would even say the entire South. Cabell Senior was too disheartened by recent events to attend, and Cabell Junior had military duties. Drayton thought he would represent the family and offer a word of moderation. But such strong-minded men were not easy to influence. In fact, they were accustomed to influencing others. But he had to try. He slipped into the rear and settled into a comfortable club chair and listened intently.

Paul Hayne had the floor. "Why should the North get so exercised about the secession of the South? After all, in the War of 1812, New England wanted to secede because the war harmed their trade. Some New England states refused to send militia to defend the Union or pay their taxes to the government in Washington City. Massachusetts has been the South's most vocal critic. Yet in 1812 the Governor of Massachusetts entered into negotiations with the British to turn their coats. In time of war, that is a treasonable act. Yet they say we are traitors simply for wanting to go our own way, as we have every right to do under the Constitution."

Sagacious, bearded Gilmore Simms nodded. Though humble, his words a magisterial air. Everyone listened when he spoke. "All quite true, Mr. Hayne. But that was two generations ago. I fear the memory of Americans is short."

Hayne continued. "Everyone knows the South pays an unequal share of the national revenue. They tax our agricultural exports to pay for their industries, which in turn charge us higher prices for manufactured goods than we pay in Europe. Thus we pay twice. If we leave the Union, the Yankees lose the opportunity to plunder us. Will they go to war? Only if they believe they can prevail. We must convince them otherwise."

There was a moment's silence as the group pondered the implications.

James Orr had noticed Drayton entering. "Gentlemen, young Mr. Drayton FitzHenry has just joined us. You're acquainted with his father, Cabell FitzHenry Senior. You also know him perhaps as the hero of a recent horse race. But I know him as one who studied in the North and recently returned from traveling in Europe. Perhaps he has some insights to share. Mr. FitzHenry?"

Suddenly, Drayton was tongue-tied. These leading intellects in his community seemed almost indifferent to the prospects ahead. Why couldn't they *see*? He could see. How could they go on about politics and the tariff and secession and not speak of avoiding war? A war that would surely rip him away from Celia and fling him into the folly of violence and privation just as his life was beginning to find its meaning.

"Mr. FitzHenry?"

He cleared his throat nervously. "Thank you, Mr. Speaker. And forgive me, gentlemen. I'm new to the group, and don't want to presume to tell anyone what we ought to do."

Simms asked kindly, "How old are you? Twenty? Twenty-one?"

"Twenty, Mr. Simms. I'm wet behind the years."

They laughed, and Drayton continued. "You gentlemen are older and wiser. But as Mr. Orr said, I have studied in the North, and I have seen some of the wider world beyond the South. I love Charleston, as you all do. But it is not the cynosure of Western civilization; pardon my heresy."

Gilmore Simms chuckled. "Young man, you seem overly impressed by the North. For my part, Charleston *is* the high point of Western civilization."

They laughed again, Drayton with them. "I'm aware I lack the life experience of you gentlemen. But what I know, I know. And I tell you this. I believe in states' rights. But if we commence a war—"

The celebrated poet Henry Timrod interrupted. "But Mr. FitzHenry, it is *they* who are about to commence a war. Under cover of night the Yankees occupied Fort Sumter, a virtual act of war. Governor Pickens' peace commission got nowhere. Now the Yankees are organizing a fleet with men and arms to reinforce Sumter. Their stated desire for peace is not reflected in their actions. It's merely a cloak from behind which to prepare for war. Such perfidy is a deliberate affront when all we ask is to go in peace and to be let alone."

Drayton said, "Yes, we only want to be let alone. But let us not take up arms unless they invade us first. Then we will have the moral high ground. Not only will the rest of the Southern states rally to us, but also a great many in the North who sympathize. I assure you, we haven't the strength to prevail if we incite the whole of the North to war."

James Orr said, "Ah, FitzHenry, you give them far too much credit. Have we not the greater martial spirit and skill at arms? Are not our men born to command?"

Drayton said, "Yes, sir, I know. It takes ten Yankees to lick one Southerner, and twenty just to make him run."

His sarcasm stopped the discussion.

"At the very least," Drayton continued in a more humble tone, "let us swallow the provocation of Fort Sumter. It's meaningless in a purely military sense. We can afford to be patient. Let us see if they attempt to impede our trade in Charleston Harbor. If nothing else, it will force *them* to act the aggressor."

Black-browed Barnwell Rhett Junior was in the rear circle of seats. Drayton hadn't noticed him till now. As always, he was implacable. "Fort Sumter is decidedly *not* meaningless," he said almost casually, blowing smoke from a cigar. "No material calculation can outweigh this simple fact: to allow them to hold Sumter is an indignity and an injustice. As long as it is in their hands, the port of Charleston can be closed to trade whenever they wish. Its occupation symbolizes their continued sovereignty — in *our* country. We might as well let them make slaves of us." He said this without irony, considering the scores of black slaves he owned.

"Precisely," agreed Henry Timrod, thin, tubercular, with a feverish glitter in his eyes. "What would you have us do, Mr. FitzHenry? Submit to injustice?"

"No," Drayton argued, warming to the task. "But I would counsel that we act consistently with our purpose, which is to depart the Union in peace. If we fire on their flag, *we* will have commenced war. Then we will have given them the pretext they need to invade us. It will forfeit the good will that still exists in the North. I know the Yankees. They are not a fiery impulsive people like us Southerners. Most of our people are Scots or Scots-Irish. It will be another conflict between the Teuton and the Gael, and you know the outcome of those historic struggles."

Three-quarters of the Southern people, especially the yeoman farmers and small holders and craftsmen, were of Scottish, Scots-Irish, or British Celtic origin. Perhaps Drayton's blood gave him more coolness of reason, although his grandfather Thomas FitzHenry had joined the doomed revolt of the United Irishmen in 1798 and barely escaped with his life. And his maternal Hugenot forbears had been hot for the Revolution. One relative had signed the Declaration of Independence in 1776.

James Petigru, Unionist leader and editor, came to his defense. "Mr. FitzHenry is right. The Yankees are a cooler, more methodical people than we Southerners. What's more, we say all we want is to be let alone. *Ipso facto*, we are fragmented. We are a race of individuals. The North on the other hand wants all Americans to act in harness toward a common goal decreed from above; namely, Washington. That is what 'union' means to them. They are like a hive of bees working in concert, while we act singly, or in twos and threes. When aroused to act on behalf of their interests – their mercantile interests especially – they will move as one, while we are so independent-minded we can scarcely find harmony with our fellow Southerners. They will advance with the remorselessness of an avalanche, and with their vast resources they will overwhelm us in the end. I beg you, let us seek a resolution without resorting to arms."

Paul Hayne scoffed. "If only it were possible. But as Mr. Timrod has pointed out, they are preparing for war under cover of peace. Only our readiness to fight can convince them to let us depart in peace. Then, if they do not let us depart; if they persist in trying to coerce us, we shall have made ready for that unfortunate eventuality as well."

The men nodded. Congressman Orr said, "If that is what it comes down to, if that is *truly* what is going on below the surface, then we will have no choice but to fight."

The session broke up, and Drayton emerged from the bookstore onto King Street and turned left, toward Tradd Street and home, pondering. If it did come down to a fight, whether instigated by the South or forced on her by the North, the vast majority of Southerners would fight, whatever their opinions had been before hostilities. Then he'd be faced with terrible choices. He knew Celia wanted to go abroad while there was still time. But could he flee and live with himself? Wouldn't the reproach of 'coward' always whisper in his ear? And there were his brothers, whom he loved. Must he join his family in a war he held to be folly? There were no good choices, and yet he must choose.

Chapter Fourteen

Charleston Harbor and Morris Island; January 1861.

It seemed that Charleston was destined to set in motion the most fateful events of the time. First the Democrats' National Convention. Then the Ordinance of Secession. Each turn of the wheel brought the divided nation closer to war. By January 1861 the tip of the Charleston Peninsula and islands ringing the harbor sprouted batteries of artillery.

On January 7 a South Carolinian in New York telegraphed Barnie Rhett at the *Charleston Mercury* that the Federals were sending a vessel to re-provision Fort Sumter. Rhett immediately notified South Carolina authorities and headlined the story, further whipping up anti-Union sentiment.

A side-wheel steamer, *The Star of the West*, was under contract to make the supply delivery. The U.S. Government had promised Governor Pickens that only non-military subsistence would be sent while the two sides were seeking a settlement. But the informant in New York warned that 200 soldiers of the 9th U.S. Infantry were concealed below decks. Several more confirmations arrived, keeping the state's military command up to date. The mission was an open secret, and Drayton wondered why the Federals had made no effort to conceal *The Star's* destination or departure date. Only Major Anderson, cut off from communications in Fort Sumter, was unaware of the relief mission. Federal authorities later claimed to have sent him a coded dispatch on January 5. A man of honor, he claimed never to have received it.

In the early morning darkness of January 9, *The Star of the West* arrived off the mouth of Charleston Harbor. The captain had brought his own pilot from New York who was acquainted with the channels and shoals. But the Confederates had extinguished all lights in the vicinity. The pilot couldn't see the channel markers or get his bearings, and the captain lingered outside the harbor until a faint dawn began to show itself. As soon as the pilot could see, *The Star* steamed over the bar and up the channel.

Governor Pickens had stationed a guard boat, the *General Clinch*, to stand watch. The *General Clinch* caught sight of the intruder and steamed ahead of

The Star of the West, signaling with bells, lights, and rockets. The nearest battery was on Morris Island, manned by the battalion of Citadel cadets, teen-aged boys, but well-drilled. Their sentry gave the alarm, and the cadets sprang from their beds in the sand dunes and to their posts. The Southern defenses had long been ready – guns loaded and primed.

At the command of The Citadel's commandant Major Stevens, Cadet G. E. Haynsworth pulled the lanyard on his brass 12-pound Napoleon. These were field guns, not coast artillery. But they were what the boys had trained on, and close enough to the shipping lane to damage the soft-sided steamer. Haynsworth's gun was aimed to fire a warning shot across the ships' bow. The iron ball hit exactly where intended, throwing up a plume of spray across *The Star's* forward track. The only reply from the vessel was the sudden appearance of a large garrison flag at the foremast head in addition to the U.S. naval jack flying from her peak.

The cadets showed no hesitation in firing on the U.S. flag. Major Stevens ordered all guns to open up. Coolly, the cadets sighted their guns and fired as the ship bore. Heavy Southern artillery on Sullivans Island joined in, but fell short because of the range. The harsh barks of the Napoleons and flame-illuminated smoke spiraling from the cadet battery alerted Major Anderson in Fort Sumter. He ran out his guns. Later he explained that because he was unsure of his targets, he refrained from firing. He was determined to avoid blame to the U.S. Army for igniting the conflict.

Soon the cadets had the deflection and range. Several balls struck *The Star of the West* with audible 'thwacks,' hitting amidships and cutting a steam line. Another round hit the stern post, threatening her rudder and steering linkage. When Fort Sumter failed to provide covering fire, *The Star's* captain turned about, to the accompanying cheers of the cadets. She almost ran aground re-crossing the bar, but managed to escape without further damage.

The Star of the West was a civilian vessel. But she flew the American flag and was sailing for the U.S. Government. The rounds fired on the ship were arguably the first shots of the War Between the States. However, James Buchanan was still in office and did not want responsibility for opening hostilities. Major Anderson protested to Governor Pickens. But when Federal civil and military authorities learned *The Star* had ignored a lawful warning shot across her bow, they quietly dropped the matter.

South Carolina argued that the incident was a deliberate provocation, and that Major Anderson's threat to close the harbor to all shipping would be an act of war. The city was willing to supply Major Anderson with provisions until a negotiated settlement could be reached. There was no need for any more provocative relief missions. Amid their growing tension, South Carolinians actually felt a grudging admiration for the beleaguered Union garrison. Citizens sent gifts of delicacies to Major Anderson's men they had gotten to know before he transferred his garrison from Sullivans Island to the Fort.

The same night the Federal commander in Pensacola, Florida, moved from the mainland after destroying excess gunpowder and spiking his guns, and occupied Fort Pickens. This old brick fort had been built in the same period, on the same pattern, and for the same purpose as Fort Sumter.

February-March 1861; Charleston, South Carolina.

The pace of the unfolding drama accelerated. Drayton devoured reports in the Charleston *Courier* about events in Montgomery, Alabama, the new capital of a new nation. The recently seceded states sent delegates to Montgomery to form the Confederate States of America. The next day they elected Jefferson Davis, former U.S. Senator from Mississippi, as President. They also drafted a Confederate Constitution, which echoed the United States Constitution in many respects. But it provided greater checks against usurpation of power by the central authorities, and cemented the principle of individual state sovereignty. It also protected the 'right of property in Negro slaves,' while at the same time outlawing the importation of slaves from abroad.

Little war talk emanated from Montgomery. Most CSA delegates expressed the desire to depart in peace and maintain friendly relations with the United States. In the *Courier's* analysis, secession didn't automatically mean war, especially if the new Confederate government could keep its head and handle the departure with aplomb. Many in the North understood that the Union was a voluntary association of the states which had formed it. They accepted, if reluctantly, that the states were as free to depart as they had been to join. At this stage few Northerners outside of New England advocated killing their fellow Americans to coerce them back into the Union's embrace.

In March Abraham Lincoln was inaugurated at 16th President of the United States, and Southerners sifted for clues to the future in his first inaugural address. At one level the speech was conciliatory toward the departing Southern states. An effective piece of rhetoric, it was even moving in places, with undeniable appeal to Southern moderates.

Lincoln said, 'We are not enemies, but friends… bound by mystic chords of memory…' He invoked '… the better angels of our nature…' to heal the spirit of disunion. He promised not to interfere with slavery. But even Drayton, with less anti-Lincoln bias than his countrymen, could see the proverbial mailed fist inside the velvet glove. Lincoln held an olive branch in one hand, a sword in the other. He promised to use force against the South only if needed to '…hold, occupy, and possess the property...' belonging to the United States; the coastal forts, for example; and to '...collect the duties and imposts...'

By his own admission to Southern peace commissioners, Lincoln's primary concern was protecting the Government's revenues. It was no secret this was the concern of his principal backers, the railroads and Wall Street. In the circumstances, waving a rhetorical olive branch failed to impress the South, which paid most of the Federal revenue from import duties. Like most conflicts in history, this one was revealing itself to be about money – tribute from the seceded states enforced by Federal control of Southern forts like Sumter and the threat to shut down free ports in the South.

Lincoln also disputed the right of secession. For the first time Drayton encountered the theory that a mystical, theoretical union had somehow existed before the thirteen original states created it in 1789, and that once the states had voluntarily entered the compact, none could depart without the consent of all the others. In other words, for secession to be valid at all required the unanimous consent of North and South. It was ludicrous even to his non-legal mind, and he found his anger boiling over.

With Lincoln as President-elect, events began to outrun the ability of anyone to control them. His accession to office allowed people to personify the crisis. Individuals began to forfeit any feeling of responsibility because their views had so little effect. As Voltaire said, 'No single snowflake in an avalanche ever feels responsible.'

Confederate President Davis sent another peace commission to Washington. President Lincoln refused to meet. His only offer was to allow the errant states to return to the Union without prejudice. The way was clear for intransigent men on both sides. In early March 1861, the U.S. Congress, now freed of its ballast of Southerners, sailed headlong into the seas of avarice and passed the Morrill Tariff. It imposed exorbitant duties on manufactured goods imported from abroad, raising the stakes of Lincoln's inaugural threat to collect the duties and imposts. With the Morrill Act, Congress made it clear the purpose of tariffs was no longer revenue for the necessary functions of government, but to kill imports and protect Northern industry at the expense of the South's agricultural economy. Two weeks later in Montgomery, the new Confederate Congress established the policy of free trade. Southern ports would exact no import duties, which would jeopardize trade in Northern ports. Both acts together were a mutual declaration of economic warfare.

Almost at once, Drayton observed that newspapers in the North that had advocated letting the South depart in peace changed their policy. They began to clamor loudly for President Lincoln to keep his pledge to use force if necessary to enforce the tariff in the South, secession or no secession. Suddenly, to

Northern industrialists, coercion, invasion, and war was preferable to duty-free ports at Charleston, Wilmington, Pensacola, and New Orleans.

Drayton and Celia clung to the increasingly vain hope they might avoid getting caught up in a conflagration, and build a life together. One day they relaxed on a bench at White Point Gardens. Standing, one could see the ominous silhouette of Fort Sumter less than four miles away.

"We are still at peace," Drayton said. "Yet in my bones I feel it won't last. Couples are walking their children and dogs on the Battery, boats are sailing in the harbor without a care, the sun is shining benevolently. Yet one can feel the tempest gathering."

Celia agreed. "I feel the same, Love. It's unbearable knowing the storm will break yet being forced to wait for it. What will we do? Have you thought any more about leaving the country?"

"My Love, in the vortex of events I think about little else. My heart longs to go away with you to Europe, or anywhere peace prevails. But many things hold me back, things I can scarcely understand myself, much less express."

She smiled, and he was grateful as ever for her understanding. She said, "One thing I have learned about you South Carolinians – you are more firmly attached to your native soil than any other Americans, I think. I don't doubt you're equally attached to me, *to us*. But I think you are going through a process of cutting the bonds that hold you, one by one. I know it's a painful process. And a slow one. I only pray you complete it before we get swept up in your vortex, or before my father takes me away back North."

Charleston, South Carolina; late March 1861.

The last conversation with Celia penetrated more deeply than any previous. He thought perhaps he hadn't truly been listening up till now. Now it was time to resolve matters that hung suspended between each day's headlines. Arranging to have supper at the Sullivan's on Sunday evening, he arrived and whispered to Celia as she took his hat and coat, "Tonight we cross our own personal Rubicon, my Love."

Her eyes widened, but she said nothing. Drayton greeted Dr. Sullivan, who was cordial but guarded. They enjoyed a fine meal and an interesting conversation, ranging back and forth between the ancient and the contemporary. The Doctor was always a fascinating conversationalist, but Drayton felt he'd held his own.

Finally, when an opportune moment occurred. As the Professor sipped his wine appreciatively Drayton said, "Dr. Sullivan, with your permission I have something of great importance to discuss. And I will follow your admirable Northern practice of coming straight to the point."

The Doctor folded his dinner napkin on the table and sat more upright in his Queen Anne chair, as if bracing himself. "Very well. Go ahead."

"Cecelia and I have an understanding, one too deep for words. We are devoted to one another and wish to be married. As is right, I am asking for your consent, with respect and affection. I would be honored above all men to have her as my wife. But I add in the greatest sincerity, I would feel equally honored to be your son-in-law."

Dr. Sullivan sighed, and began to pull at his shirt cuffs. Celia smiled at the mannerism from behind her linen napkin.

"You do us both honor, Drayton." It was the first time the Doctor had ever addressed him by his first name. The lowered formality gave him an instant's hope. "I believe you would treat her justly and make her happy. She would have no bride's portion to speak of. We are not wealthy. Except in love," he added with a smile.

"Which I share," said Drayton."

The Doctor smiled kindly. "In normal circumstances I might find no grounds on which to object, except the difference in our faiths, which is no small matter, by the way. But these are not normal circumstances."

"Yes, sir. Sadly, I agree. But I have done my best to promote peace among anyone who would listen."

"Even your own family? 'People of influence,' you called them?"

"Especially my own family."

"Yet your father was a delegate to the Secession Convention, and voted to take South Carolina out of the Union."

"Yes, sir, that's true. But you must also be aware he represented the moderates at the Convention, and argued for a simple ordinance of separation, not a bellicose statement of grievances that would inflame North-South passions."

"Ah, yes," the Doctor said dryly. "That task was left to Christopher Memminger."

A surge of anger flared up inside, but Drayton suppressed it. Now of all times was not the moment to lose his temper.

"And now your brother Cabell has joined the staff of the new Confederate States commander in Charleston, this General Beauregard. If yours is a family of peace, could he not wait at least until you were invaded by the perfidious

Yankees?"

"Sir, he felt it was his duty to don a uniform. He believes the most effectual way to deter war is to show determination. Only the credible threat of force can give teeth to negotiating a settlement."

The Doctor shook his head. "I fear you have greatly misread your potential adversary. And what of the firing on *The Star of the West?* What about the attack on Fort Pickens? Were those not outright acts of war?"

"No, only limited acts of self-defense. Dr. Sullivan, they have not led to general hostilities. Perhaps there is reason to be encouraged, not despairing."

"You not only misread the North, you underestimate Abraham Lincoln. He is as wily and effective a politician as ever held the highest office. If there is another such episode, I assure you, it will not be the same as it was with President Buchanan."

Drayton bowed his head to the words he knew were coming next. "No, Drayton, I cannot consent to give you Cecelia's hand, not amid such dire uncertainties. But as you and your family no doubt pray for peace, so do we. I want to complete my class here at the College. I hope our heavenly Father grants our petitions. But if tensions proceed as they are now, Cecelia and I must leave here in May, at the end of term."

Cypress Stand Plantation, Colleton District, South Carolina; April 1, 1861.

The four FitzHenry men gathered at Cypress Stand to celebrate Drayton's 21st birthday. Its foundation was of tabby, a strong, durable material made by burning lime and sand mixed with crushed oyster shells, always in plentiful supply in the Low Country. Above the tabby arcade on ground level stretched a row of simple, square Doric-style columns enclosing the lofty gable. All was sheathed in white clapboard. On the veranda overlooking the River, Cabell Senior passed goblets of his special Bourbon punch to each son in birth order, and they offered Drayton a toast. He smiled with gratitude for the mutual love that warmed them in the March chill. Not all wealthy Low Country families enjoyed such cordial family feelings.

Cabell Senior drew in an audible sigh and said to his boys, "There is nowhere on the planet grander than this very spot. We are privileged to live in the best country, America, and in the best state, South Carolina. Charleston is America's finest city. Our Colleton District is the most charming place in South Carolina, and of all the plantations on the Edisto, our own Cypress Stand is the loveliest."

Many neighboring houses were more ornate, but Drayton admired the simplicity, symmetry, and proportion of the family mansion. It sat amid lush green on a slight bluff of the Edisto, harmoniously framed by spreading live oaks, now in their hundredth year of growth since his great-grandfather Tourville had planted them. A hundred yards from the veranda the sun glinted on the River as it set in the west amid cast shadows of the tall cypress along the bank. The vista of manicured lawns sloping down to the River, live oaks draped in Spanish moss, the rich earth of the drained rice fields beyond waiting to be seeded – the scene was bathed in a timeless radiance. To each of them it was a scene of ineffable peace and beauty, a place that bound them and all things in its spell.

"Father, we are truly blessed," Drayton said. "Yet our perfect world is hurtling toward the abyss, and we're doing nothing to stop it."

"Come, come, my boy," said his father. "The Yankees must let us depart in peace. But even if they don't, if war does come, how would they ever find Cypress Stand?"

"Because, Father, they are a seafaring people, among other things. They have ten ships to our one. If war comes they will first blockade and control our coast. The River is but a highway to that coast. If we can go downriver to ship our rice, they can come up."

"Well, they may be a seafaring people, but we Southerners are a *martial* people. I'm certain they don't want to tangle with us. If they invade… Why, the idea is folly. The whole Christian world would side with us."

"Yes, Father, but what if *we* fire the first shot? Then the whole picture is changed. And that's what the hotheads in Charleston have been demanding ever since Major Anderson occupied Fort Sumter. Even old Edmund Ruffin has come down from Virginia to agitate for an attack on the Fort. President Davis in Montgomery is under enormous pressure to do something to 'redeem Southern honor.'"

Always the exuberant one, Ranse bounced up and down on the joggling board without spilling a drop of his julep. "Brother," he laughed at Cabell Junior. "You once courted Lucy Pickens. Why she chose that old duffer over you is a mystery to all Charleston. Perhaps *you* should be the one to bear the message to the Governor."

Father said, "Son, I think perhaps your concerns are misplaced. What you hear is merely the prating of politicians before the mob. And barking dogs do not bite."

"I hope you're right," Drayton replied. "But Father, the Yankees *wanted* us to fire on the *Star of the West,* and we obliged. It was a kind of test. Otherwise they would have come in the dark of night with an armed Navy escort. It's an axiom of strategy — never do what your opponent wants you to do. But the *Star of the West* was not a sufficient provocation, and Lincoln was not yet in office.

Now he is. And he is reported to be mounting an entire fleet, not a single vessel. He wants the threat of relief to goad us into firing on Fort Sumter. *And* on the U.S. flag. That's why the Yankees seized the Fort."

"On Christmas night. While all Charleston dined and drank," his brother Cabell observed. "Drayton may be right, Father. It will go better for us if we are not the aggressors. You're a friend of Governor Pickens. Can't you speak with him, press upon him the vital importance of withholding our fire? The Yankees are running out of supplies anyway. They can't stay there much longer."

"They can if Mr. Lincoln re-supplies them by sea," said Father.

"Exactly," said Drayton. "Which is why the pressure builds to reduce Fort Sumter now, before the invasion fleet arrives. Father, can't you intervene before we come to blows? You've been a voice for reason. Speak to Governor Pickens. Write to President Davis and Secretary Walker. Go to see General Beauregard. Urge them to show restraint."

Cabell Senior stared thoughtfully into his silver goblet. Drayton was relieved to realize his father was considering the proposition.

"Yes," Father said at length. "I was distressed that no one on our side foresaw Major Anderson's move into Sumter. No one wants to avert war more than I. If it must come, we cannot afford any more such slackness. And I concede your point. If we fire on Fort Sumter and the Flag, we play into Lincoln's hands. But we must allow President Davis' peace commission to act first."

Cabell Junior grumbled. "None of our other peace commissions achieved anything. Why should we expect this one to succeed?"

At the College of New Jersey, Drayton had made close friends among his fellow students from the North. But he'd also experienced first-hand how some in the North detested landed Southerners, whom they saw as proud, boastful, and arrogant. In return, the South detested the Northern elites of the moneybag, whom they saw as cold, calculating, and uncouth. Each side believed it had achieved the best of all possible worlds – the North's, democratic and mercantile; the South's, aristocratic and agrarian. Yet each civilization was failing to restrain the angry passions, wounded pride, and threatened interests that made them circle each other like snarling dogs. Succumbing to their prejudices, people on both sides of the Mason-Dixon Line had given themselves over to the worst image they held of each other, and withdrawn into hostile camps where the light of reason hardly shone. Drayton thought if only they'd given themselves over to good will instead, the differences might be resolved. Good will. Human charity. How simple they seemed. How hard to practice. It reminded Drayton of his one major fall from Beltane. A year ago while hunting he'd tried to jump a high fence which too late proved to have been erected in a bog. The footing was soft and the horse sank up to his fetlocks, spoiling the take-off. The crash seemed to take place in slow motion, and Drayton was transfixed by the looming rails, as if the accident were unavoidable and he a mere spectator rather than participant.

He was not a fatalist, despite immersion in the lore of ancient Greece and Rome. He felt he could make a difference, and it was his duty to intervene and stop the accident, like a good neighbor rushing to warn the train engineer that the trestle had collapsed a few miles up the track. Or rather, trying to persuade others to help stop a runaway train. A titanic struggle was shaping up, so awful in its prospects of Americans fighting Americans that most observers, even wise men, lowered their eyes and refused to embrace the meaning of the unfolding events. He had just moved his father closer to taking action, yet Father still wanted to wait. Drayton felt the hopeful moment break, as if made of glass.

Observing Drayton's pained expression, Cabell Senior said gently, "Son, please do not think I'm oblivious to your views."

His father sipped his mint julep, deep in thought. Walking apart from the group, Father turned and surveyed the scene before him, river and forest in the background, horses grazing on manicured pastures in the foreground.

Finally he sighed, turned back to Drayton, and said, "My boy, surely you know that no one in his right mind truly wants war. But I fear we are in the grip of something … of some force that is stronger than any human will, and that is propelling us forward. I cannot explain it. It is only something I sense.

"But I will speak to Governor Pickens. I will even go to General Beauregard, hoping not to embarrass his staff officer Cabell Junior. I will wire President Davis. But I doubt it will alter the course of events. Keep in mind it is not we who are seeking this conflict, despite what you've said about the mobs in Charleston. We wish only to go our own way in peace. If the Yankees force us to remain in the Union by levying war…" He shook his head slowly. "North and South have become two different peoples. There are angry feelings on both sides, and they crowd out every other thought and impulse. Angry men, when goaded into action by what they perceive as injustice, lose all sense of anything save their own grievances."

Drayton replied, "Then we must be larger men than the passionate and the angry. We must rise above our grievances and demonstrate wisdom."

"Yes, in principle. But we are in a vise. The Yankees hold Fort Sumter, which threatens our shipping and represents an unendurable insult to the honor of a sovereign nation. As you noted, President Lincoln is preparing a fleet to relieve Fort Sumter. But it is not 'relief.' It is an invasion. Lincoln said at his inauguration he will collect the duties and imposts, by force if need be. He pledges to enforce the Constitution – which he himself has traduced – in the

South as well as in the North. Is that not a veiled threat of war? Why will he not acknowledge the popular will in the South and bid us farewell as friends? And are we to sit idly by while our dignity is trampled, our sovereignty abused, and our country invaded?"

"Yes, Father. But if it must come, let *them* fire first. Let the world see Lincoln invading, even if it means we sacrifice an early advantage. What we gain morally before all the world would more than compensate." Drayton fought against the feeling he was trying to argue the unarguable.

"We must play our hand as best we may," said Father. "But you must understand that powerful interests in the North are threatened by Southern secession. Railroads. Banks. Manufactories. And President Lincoln is their kept man. Our choice is to remain in an unholy embrace with the North and continue to be plundered. Or we can part company, despite their threats of force, while praying for peace."

Drayton said, "Dr. Sullivan tells me President Lincoln is the wiliest politician ever to occupy the White House. Hasn't it occurred to any of us: he knows that we hot-headed South Carolinians can be maneuvered into shooting first, giving him the moral high ground, an insult to the Flag, a legitimate *casus belli*?"

He looked his father in the eye, then at his brothers. He loved them all. He loved his home by the River. He loved Celia Sullivan. If war came he might lose the things he cherished most. And when all efforts to prevent the calamity were exhausted, he'd have to decide – flee abroad with his Beloved, which he began to regard as unlikely; or stand with his blood, his kin, his state. When the crisis broke he couldn't straddle the fence any longer. There were only these two unhappy choices and no other. But choose he must. In the theater of men's lives it was reserved only to God and the angels to be lookers-on.

Drinking deeply of the minty-sweet liquor, chilled and fiery at the same time, he raised his goblet. "If war is on the horizon, then all I can say is, we had better get serious. We had better plan realistically how we shall win. No childish romanticism, no Walter Scott, no Charge of the Light Brigade."

"What? No glory?" said Ranse.

"Ranse, I have no experience of war. But I'm sure of this – it is not like two well-bred men in a duel who fire their pistols harmlessly in the air, shake hands, and then retire to the club for a drink. Remember what Caleb Cushing said the first night of the Democratic Convention? It is not going to be like that at all. If there's any glory and romance, it won't last long."

Ranse scowled. "Well, glory is in the eye of the beholder. And I wouldn't know from personal experience, either, but I would imagine the romance is the one thing that makes war bearable."

"Thanks for making my point," said Drayton, angry at himself for belittling his beloved younger brother, especially on a day of celebration. "*Ne puero gladium.* Do not give a child a sword."

Chapter Fifteen

Charleston, South Carolina; April 11-14, 1861.

The night of April 11 was wet and raw. A cold wind swept in from the sea, flinging gusts of rain into the faces of the city's residents who scurried to find shelter. Their wild enthusiasm for secession had cooled; the seduction of military bands and militia parades had run its course. Reports true and false abounded, convulsing the city. Some Charlestonians had heard from relatives in the army that the fateful event was about to unfold. Confederate batteries ringing the harbor had been firing occasional ranging shots for days, rehearsals for the opening act. The periodic booms stretched nerves already taut. A handful of residents remained festive over the prospects of the grand new adventure, but most were sobered by what they knew would soon occur.

Unsettled by the rumors of war, Drayton decided to go straight to the source. After all, he had plans for his personal life. Cabell Junior was on the staff of the commander of Charleston's Confederate forces, and Drayton had to assume he could confirm or dispel the rumors. Walking home from another "weekly" at Russell's Bookstore, he decided to call on Cabell. Continuing to the foot of King Street to General Beauregard's headquarters, he passed a note to the corporal of the guard at the sentry post. Cabell emerged a few minutes later, looking harried and straightening his uniform.

"Have you come to join up?" Cabell said, not bothering to keep the sarcasm from his tone. "Or are you going to bolt?"

Drayton was surprised at his brother's insight. Or was it only a shot in the dark? "That depends. Am I needed? Are the reports true that you're going to fire on Sumter tomorrow?"

Cabell frowned. "Brother, you know I'm not at liberty to say. But Father has asked us to stay in Charleston. He's hosting a midnight supper for some friends. Aunt Meggs and Uncle Porcher will stop by."

Drayton nodded. "I get the picture. 'And 'mid the tumult heard we from afar, ancestral voices prophesying war.'"

"I prophesy nothing. But General Beauregard has hopes for a peaceful resolution." Cabell nodded, turned, and went back inside.

Drayton needed to be with Celia. He sent a note asking her to join him for the family supper, then called on her at Glebe Street at 8:00 PM. They returned to the East Bay mansion by hansom cab and found his father, Ranse, Aunt Meggs and Uncle Porcher, and the Misses Alston gathered for supper. There were also some visitors from the Edisto River country, neighbors of Aunt Meggs.

The guests ate sparingly of the buffet while huddled in quiet conversation. The dessert wine and coffee were subdued. Around midnight, and without anyone in particular proposing it, they all drifted upstairs to the topmost piazza and peered into the darkness of Charleston Harbor.

Drayton's old rival Robert Pringle arrived and adjusted a set of field glasses in the flickering light of the gas lamp. He was resplendent in the new uniform a lieutenant of the Palmetto Guards artillery, which manned the recently completed Iron Battery on Morris Island. Drayton wondered why he was absent from his unit on this night of all nights.

In reply to Drayton's raised eyebrows Pringle said, "I'm surprised to see you here."

He looked over Drayton's shoulder, and his eyes glittered as Celia stepped into view.

"How so?" Drayton replied. "This is my father's house." He tried to remain civil, since the owner's son shared the same obligations of hospitality as the owner. "I'm here quite often. Without needing an invitation. Who invited you?"

"Your brother Cabell. I'm awaiting transport to Morris Island. But my skiff was commandeered by General Beauregard's messengers sent to demand Major Anderson's evacuation of Fort Sumter. You know them. Captain Stephen D. Lee and Colonel James Chesnut. I was ordered to wait in the city, and your brother kindly directed me here."

"I see. And how long are we to enjoy the pleasure of your company?"

Pringle stiffened, gripping the pommel of his sabre. "I can't say. They just rowed to Sumter, and how long they may be no one knows. Colonel Chesnut has been delegated the authority by General Beauregard. If the Yankees don't agree to evacuate while the cartel is at the Fort, Colonel Chesnut may order our batteries to reduce it – before the invasion fleet arrives from the North. I think the Yankees will not agree to go. And then it begins." His words struck a chill in Drayton – his words and his unmistakable eagerness.

Drayton didn't try to keep the anger out of his voice. "And this you regard as a matter of celebration?"

Pringle drew himself up even more stiffly. The brass buttons on his uniform gleamed in the lantern light. "Ah, yes," he said. "I'd forgotten your rather peculiar views on fighting the Yankees. But by now I'd have thought you might feel differently."

Drayton said quietly, "War is sweet to those who have never experienced it." *Café patriots and carpet cavaliers*, he thought. *They are all the more warlike for having never seen a war.*

"I will not violate the obligations of a guest in your father's home to demand satisfaction here and now," said Pringle. "But you will hear from me later."

"Now, later, as you wish; it makes no difference to me." Drayton felt a sudden heat rise inside. "We should have settled matters between us last year."

Pringle's lips tightened into a grimace. His eyes narrowed. Drayton's mind spun round in a quick calculus. As the challenged party, he would choose the weapon, and it would be the *épée* rather than pistols. His years of fencing lessons might prove their worth, for sooner or later, this was going to end badly. Drayton resolved to increase his lessons at Monsieur Debordieu's Academy of the Sword to three times a week.

Cabell Senior overheard them. He stepped over from the railing. "Now, listen, you young fools. I will have no more of this, and not just because you are under my roof. There will be plenty of fighting ahead, and you will both be needed. You agreed to the outcome of the match race last year. Furthermore, you no longer have the luxury of indulging your personal feelings. You, Mr. Pringle, are already in uniform and under military discipline. Drayton, you soon will be. Your warlike impulses now belong to your country. Is that understood?"

Both men gave a reluctant nod. Drayton wondered, *Will I soon be in uniform, or on a steamer bound for Le Havre or Liverpool?*

"I want your word on it." When his father was stern, there was no disputing him. "And give each other your hand on it, too."

Drayton extended his hand, and Pringle shook it correctly, but without enthusiasm.

Ambrosia, the house servant who lived full time at East Bay, brought up a tray of coffee and cakes. The clocks downstairs tolled 3:00 AM. The sound was like drops of blood dripping from the corpse of the old Republic that had been won by so much sacrifice. Its life could be measured now in minutes.

Cabell Junior entered the house and clumped upstairs in his cavalry boots, his sabre clattering on the staircase. Entering the piazza he wind-milled his arms and said breathlessly, "It's come at last, a directive from President Davis and his cabinet. General Beauregard sent Colonel Chesnut with a final message requesting the Yankees evacuate the fort, and that our batteries would refrain from opening fire until he replied. Major Anderson replied that he and the garrison will depart by noon on April 15, unless he receives new orders or supplies."

"Humph," said Cabell Senior, "we all know the Yankee fleet is on the way. Even now it may be off the bar. This is simply more of their sordid temporizing."

"Yes, sir, exactly. General Beauregard thought so, too, as did the War Office and President Davis in Montgomery. The General delegated to Colonel Chesnut the authority to announce the commencement unless he received a satisfactory answer from Major Anderson. He did not. Consequently, he sat down in the Fort's guardroom and drafted a note in the name of General Beauregard informing the Yankees that we would open fire in an hour. Colonel Chestnut and his delegation have just returned. The ball can open at any moment."

"So, then. Let the die be cast," said Ranse.

Anerriphthos kybos, sighed Drayton. *Jacta alea est.* The ancient platitude returned to deceive modern men. "Let the die be cast. You don't know what you're saying," he growled at Ranse. Celia looked at Drayton with dark frightened eyes and clutched him tighter.

"Perhaps not," said his brother. "But I do know this. At least the suspense will soon be over."

Brother Cabell had brought up a bottle of champagne. The pop of the cork, clink of glasses, and a murmured toast punctuated the weighty silence. Drayton refused a glass, but took another cup of rich, steaming coffee. The wait was excruciating, and the minutes crept forward in the dark as though the cataclysm would never break. Drayton felt an angry incomprehension. Had God Himself blundered? Now that the moment was upon them, all seemed clothed in unreality. Their lives were about to alter course in ways no one could foresee, and here they were enjoying a rooftop *fête*.

As always, Celia was simultaneously thinking his thoughts. He marveled at how close two people could become when she said, "I cannot believe this is happening. Here we sit in peace and safety. Yet in a few moments we will step over the threshold into war. All will be changed, utterly and forever."

Drayton stared intently into the dark – at nothing. Why could so few see what disaster might lie at the end of the path they'd embarked upon so wantonly? Did Lincoln have no thought for the blood to be spilled as a result of his maneuvering? *But then, perhaps I misjudge*, Drayton thought. *Why should I cling to such certainty that I am right and all others were wrong?* Was it merely because he was a student of history? What men called history was an interpretation, and men could draw different conclusions from the same set of facts. That is, if they *were* facts. One couldn't be entirely certain even of that. His father and older brother had reminded him often enough that their forefathers had humbled the might of the British Empire, the greatest military and naval power of its day. Much of that humbling had taken place right in his home state in 1780 and 1781. Who was he to assert they couldn't do it again and humble the Yankee empire?

Despite the hour they weren't tired, caught up as they were in a pitch of suspense. Trembling slightly, Celia nestled in the lee of Drayton's arm when a damp penetrating wind blew in from the sea with low scudding clouds ahead of it. The mansion's upper story was exposed to the elements, and the family and guests pulled their wraps and mufflers tighter around them. He felt a surge of passion for her, along with a lurking sense of helplessness that he couldn't protect her from the mad flailing sweep of history. He clung to her all the more fiercely in anticipation of what was about to occur. Wordlessly, she hugged him back.

At 4: 31 AM – he recalled precisely because the men pulled out their watches in unison and checked the time – a bright orb trailing flame shot up from Fort Johnson across the harbor, followed a moment later by a dull boom.

"Thirteen-inch mortar," said Robert Pringle.

The shell arched high in the murky distance, lost itself briefly in the clouds, and descended with marvelous accuracy over Sumter. It exploded just above the fort in a shower of sparks and another boom, sharper and more ominous.

The hum of conversation, the clinking of glasses from their piazza and neighboring rooftops fell silent at the enormity of the moment. He shuddered at the recollection of Caleb Cushing's words during the Democratic National Convention a scant year ago. '...a bloodletting such as the world has never seen...'

The lone mortar round from Fort Johnson was the signal for a general bombardment. Forty-three heavy guns and mortars began to thunder forth. First echoed the deep-throated roars of Mortar Batteries One and Two on Sullivan's Island. Then the sharper reports of 8-inch Columbiads on Cummings Point. The din increased with the Ordnance Rifles of Fort Moultrie and the nearer Floating Battery. The guns belched flame and iron with echoing rumbles at regular intervals, like a mad gargantuan clock that roared instead of ticked.

Celia crossed herself and murmured, "Christ have mercy." For the first few minutes she winced and shuddered with each resounding boom, until finally she became used to the noise and sank deeper under Drayton's sheltering arm. Someone had brought chairs to the piazza, and they sat tensely to watch the drama.

For two hours the Confederate guns pounded the fort without an answering salvo from the Yankees. Robert Pringle said, "Either Major Anderson is a coward, or he is betraying his own side out of sympathy with the South. Why else does he not fire back?"

Cabell Junior scoffed. "Neither proposition is true. Major Anderson is a brave man and an honorable and loyal soldier. There are no lights in Sumter's casemates to aim its guns. Anderson is simply waiting for daylight. He'll do his duty when the time comes. Believe me, there will be ample fireworks anon."

His prediction was accurate. Shortly after 6:00 AM slanting rays of the sun began to illuminate the fort, its 60-foot walls now wreathed in smoke and dust from the projectiles pounding its brick surface. The FitzHenrys heard the hoarse bellow of the 32-pounders in Sumter's southeast gun ports. Through his pedestal-mounted telescope Father observed jets of flame and smoke from the lower tier, and described the action.

One massive Yankee ball struck the iron-plated *glacis* of the Iron Battery on Cummings Point. Thanks to the extreme slope and thickness of the armor, it failed to penetrate. The ball rebounded upward and curved back into the harbor in a plume of spray. In moments flame and smoke began to erupt from all faces of the fort as the Yankees fired back in earnest. Spectators and soldiers at White Point Garden and along the sea wall cheered the Federals. The Southerners had begun to feel a touch of shame at firing so fiercely upon an enemy who couldn't fire back.

Riveted to the scene, family and guests ate breakfast on the piazza, then lunch. By Friday evening the bombardment had become routine, even monotonous. Cabell Junior and Robert Pringle had reported back on duty. Celia no longer winced at each discharge, even the close ones that rattled the crockery. Drayton considered how odd it was — to have grown used to the sustained bombardment, but to find the chiming of wineglasses and tinkling of silver on china out of place. Townspeople began to go about their normal pursuits. Finally the FitzHenry party dispersed. Against the backdrop of echoing artillery Drayton prepared to escort Celia back to her home at the College.

While waiting for Shortbread to bring round the pony and trap, Celia said, "This morning when it began it seemed so unreal. Our own little city, known worldwide for its grace and charm and good manners, wracked by this incessant cannon fire." Drayton was pleased to note she had said 'our' city. "At first every detonation sent tremors through me. I was so comforted by your presence. And now... Now I hardly notice the gunfire at all."

"Yes, how easily we become accustomed to the unimaginable," said Drayton. *What else will we have to get used to before this war is over?*

Drayton handed her up into the trap, then sprang up beside her with the leads. The pony mare shook her mane and whickered, eager to stretch her legs. They remained silent during the short ride, overwhelmed by events and full of uncertainty what it meant for the country and for them personally. Dr. Sullivan, dressed in a black silk dressing gown, met them at the entrance, his face dark with anger and concern. Maria the dueña hovered wide-eyed in the background. Her father said nothing, and Drayton was impelled to break the awkward silence.

"You should know, Dr. Sullivan, that I did all I could to prevent this tragedy."

"Yes, Mr. FitzHenry. I'm sure you did. Nevertheless, war has come. And that means we can no longer remain here, Cecelia and I." He didn't invite Drayton into the house but kept them all standing in the entry foyer. He turned to his daughter. "I'm sorry, my dear, but you will begin to pack your things. We will take ship north as soon as this folly ends and the harbor re-opens."

"But, Father—"

"Let me hear no buts! Our sojourn here is over. It has had its sweet and pleasant moments, no doubt." He regarded Drayton with something more akin to envy than anger. "We might have preferred to remain, but the Fates have decreed otherwise. After Hubris comes Nemesis."

Nemesis *did* follow Hubris. The artillery battle for Sumter was only one day old, and already Lincoln had issued his call for the states, North and South, to muster 75,000 troops into Federal service to suppress the insurrection. It was obvious that the legislation and accompanying press statements had been prepared well in advance. The South had walked into Lincoln's trap. Lincoln had the moral high ground, his *casus belli*. Let Dr. Sullivan align himself with the other side if he must. But Drayton was not about to condemn his own people in the man's presence.

Drayton said in quiet sad voice, "With respect, sir, there is ample Hubris on both sides."

"That is as may be. But even if this dreadful war had not come upon us, remember that we are of different faiths. Had we remained, I understand at last I could not have consented for my daughter to marry a Protestant."

Cecelia laughed bitterly. "Why, Father, you haven't been to Mass in weeks. And you're not on speaking terms with Father Capers. Does the Catholic Church really stand in our way?"

The parish priest abhorred Irish Fenians, with whom Dr. Sullivan sympathized. Drayton had often argued that the cause of Irish independence was the same as the cause for Southern independence. Though there were parallels, the argument had not overcome the Doctor's prejudice.

Dr. Sullivan said to his daughter, "As far as I am concerned, it does. My relationship with Father Capers is irrelevant. My relationship with the Heavenly Father is the one that counts. And that is my final word on the matter."

Drayton nodded with a slight bow of respect. An idea, breathtaking in its boldness, was flowering in his mind. He gave Celia's hand a squeeze and turned to depart. But halfway through the door the inspiration had matured into a plan.

He stopped and said, "Dr. Sullivan, it will grieve me to see you go. And Cecelia, of course. Charleston will be the poorer for losing you both. But as the Ancients believed, even the gods do not contend against necessity. Since you must leave, may I please have the privilege of a farewell breakfast with Cecelia tomorrow morning?"

Dr. Sullivan appeared surprised, then suspicious, at the ease of his conquest over young love. But under the pressure of his daughter's pleading eyes, he relented.

"Very well, young man. You may call for her at eight. But come prepared to say your goodbyes."

***

The thunder of the guns continued. On Saturday morning a cold front marched in from the northeast, dispersing the rain and low-hanging clouds and bathing sea and land in brightness. The smoke clouds from the Southern batteries and Fort Sumter were fringed with gold. The clearing weather caused the reverberations of the guns on Mount Pleasant and Sullivans Island to shake the tall French doors and windows along East Bay Street. The relentless battering of the Confederate artillery had knocked huge chunks of masonry from Sumter's upper parapet. The mortars lobbed hotshot high into the air, plunging into the fort's interior and starting fires. The fort belched black smoke like a chimney. Some of the Yankee guns had been disabled, and Major Anderson's rate of fire had slackened noticeably. It was clear the contest could not go on much longer.

When Drayton returned with Celia from the College, the family group was down to Father and Ranse. Ambrosia had laid breakfast on the sideboard. By now it seemed the most natural thing in the world to dine on ham and grits and peaches and cream to the accompaniment of reverberating artillery that vibrated the glass panes in their sashes.

"Why is the fort not giving a better account of itself?" Celia asked.

"Because, my dear," said Cabell Senior, "Fort Sumter was designed to enforce the customs duty upon vessels entering the harbor, and perhaps repel an invading fleet. In other words, it was built to fight wooden ships to seaward, not fight against forts on land with heavier guns."

"The Southern guns are heavier?" she asked in all innocence, as if such a possibility had never crossed her mind.

"Yes, some are. And in the circumstances, the Yankees *are* giving a good account of themselves. Positively gallant, I would say."

In the privacy of his mind Drayton congratulated Southern officers for such a remarkable job in erecting their batteries and conducting the bombardment. It was military professionalism at its best. Many of them were West Point-trained or Citadel men and better at the technical aspects of war than he might have supposed. Still, like so many Southern enterprises – except perhaps for planting rice and cotton – there was an unstudied casualness about launching a major war. It reeked of improvisation. Organizing the new nation proceeded nonchalantly. Newly minted Confederate officials, civil and military, evidently considered this approach in keeping with Southern romance and imagination. Creating a new constitution and laws, a new army and navy were mere trifles. He sensed it dimly: little did they realize they were colliding with circumstances that cared not a whit for romance and imagination, which would soon be overruled by the implacable logic of numbers.

***

As Saturday ended, bright sputtering parabolas flamed against the night sky as the mortars continued their work. Cecelia gently chided Drayton that her father had consented only to breakfast, which had long since come and gone. They had eaten dinner, and now the supper hour was approaching.

Drayton offered to send one of the house servants to Dr. Sullivan with a message that Cecelia was fine and that they were awaiting the conclusion of the artillery duel in the harbor. She demurred. Sending a slave would only antagonize him, she believed. This was fine with Drayton. His bold plan had finally resolved into details of implementation. He had no intention of returning her home.

He took her hand and took her aside into the drawing room, or *with*drawing room, whence its name. A spacious and handsome chamber with 12-foot ceilings, it boasted high bay windows overlooking the harbor that rattled with every discharge of the great guns. But now Fort Sumter spouted fire and smoke, and its flag was down. The Confederate fire had abated in response. The battle was at a lull, and Drayton knew the moment had come.

Touching knee to knee on a settee of blue watered silk, while portraits of his ancestors regarded them sternly, he said, "Dear Celia, as you know, in the Greek there are four ways of expressing the word love. Our poor English has only the one word. It does not allow me to express the breadth and depth of my feelings for you. But I think you know my heart. And I think you love me, too."

"As if you didn't know how I feel," she laughed. "I've loved you from that first night at the College."

"You mean, from our first meeting? But you didn't even know me."

"My dear, women know such things in their hearts. And that's where love resides, far deeper than the level of conscious thought."

"Yes, but—"

"'Where love deliberates the love is slight. Whoever loved who loved not at first sight?'"

"Shakespeare?"

"Christopher Marlowe."

"Ah, yes. Marlowe." Drayton paused, taking both her hands and probing deep into her eyes with his own. What he saw there, or believed he saw there, the depths of character and intelligence and passion, left him momentarily speechless. She was both Aphrodite and Athena. She would be more than a wife — lover, friend, confidante, and adventurous companion. Not a mere extension of her husband, but a woman of accomplishment in her own right.

She smiled, easing his awkwardness. "Then what are we going to do about it?" she teased.

Now it was his turn to smile. A torrent of emotion welled up. "There's only one possible solution to the dilemma. We must get married."

She said nothing, only smiled, waiting.

He said, "Will you be my wife, and allow me to devote myself to you for the rest of your life?"

She laughed, amused at the sudden foray into Southern manners. But these things had to be done in the right way. "Yes, Sir Knight. Most gladly."

They grinned at each other, reveling in their mutual discovery and in their shared sense of humor. Then he kissed her, and felt her tremble.

"My love, I'm not sure you understand. I mean, get married at once. Without your going back to Glebe Street. Your father said he would never consent to our marrying, but now that war is upon us, I believe my father will. He will allow you to remain here until we can make arrangements. *Immediate* arrangements."

Her eyes widened. As she hesitated, Drayton pressed her hand. "I will not take you back and allow Finbarr to rush you out of Charleston, perhaps never to see you again. These are extraordinary times and they call for extraordinary measures. If we don't seize the moment, we may lose it altogether. We may be separated across the battle lines and lose our chance for happiness."

"An elopement," she murmured, as if to herself. "Not exactly how I envisioned my wedding day."

"Nor was the beginning of a war how I envisioned mine. Father is always saying we must play the cards that fate has dealt us. And I say, love is trumps."

She sighed, and he looked at her with slight reproach. World-changing events were sweeping them up in a tempest. In the circumstances they shouldn't be preoccupied with their personal lives. Expressions of love seemed trite in comparison to the magnitude of the moment. But since they were in love and committed to one another, he was unwilling to let anything impede their happiness.

He was relieved that she didn't press him for a decision about quitting the state and going to Europe. She seemed to accept him without conditions or reservations. Good! That gave him a little more time to decide, even as her unconditional love tipped the scales in favor of leaving.

Ranse had gone outside to investigate, and he burst into the house, eyes blazing with excitement. "Fort Sumter has surrendered! The Yankees have hauled down their flag!"

A crowd collected on the Battery a short distance away. A storm of cheers rolled over the lower Peninsula. A new patriotic song, 'The Bonnie Blue Flag,' swelled from a thousand voices. Church bells began to peal from St. Michaels and St. Phillips. The unprecedented emotion and excitement were contagious, and Drayton experienced an involuntary thrill. It was a once-in-a-lifetime event as the Confederate States of America took its place among the nations of the earth.

Drayton looked at Celia, who stared back with frightened eyes. "Today we are ringing the bells," she said. "Let us hope tomorrow we are not wringing our hands."

Chapter Sixteen

Drayton found Father in the small first-floor study between the library and smoking room, twirling a tumbler of bourbon in his fingers and staring at the jarring headline "War!" in huge type on the front page of the *Mercury*.

Cabell Senior's frown deepened when Drayton entered. "Do not say it. In fact, I prefer you to say nothing at all."

"I wasn't going to say anything, Father, except to ask your blessing and permission."

"Blessing and permission for what? No, don't tell me. I know." His stiff back softened. He turned in the swivel chair and faced his son directly. "You are twenty-one. You have no need of my permission."

"Then I covet your blessing, Father. And your permission to keep her here while I make arrangements. You may not be aware, but her father opposes the match."

"Then he is wiser than I," he said, draining his glass. "But I've always been an indulgent father to my sons. Too much so. You're stealing her away, then? An elopement?"

Drayton stood in silence for what seemed like an eternity. He wanted Celia, but he also wanted his father's respect. And as practical matter, he needed the consent of the *paterfamilias* to shelter his new bride at East Bay. He would resort to a hotel if he had to, but he very much wanted to keep her at home. There was no answer but the plain truth. He drew in his breath.

"Yes, Father, though I wouldn't call it 'stealing.' She is of age, as I am. We are determined to marry. If I take her back to Glebe Street I will lose her. It's that simple. *Ergo*, I will not take her back."

His father sighed deeply. "You may not know this, but your mother and I..." His voice trailed off. "Well, suffice it to say there were some who opposed our marriage. I was much like you in 1839. And war talk swirled around us then, the possibility of war with Mexico."

Cabell Senior stared into his empty glass. "Very well, you have my blessing. But let us not add insult to injury. I *must* send Dr. Sullivan a note. You and she are both old enough to make your own decisions, but I will not be a party to an elopement without informing him. One father owes that much to another. In which case, he may show up here with the sheriff and demand her return. Have you a plan in case he does?"

Drayton said with relief, "We will both write him, too, begging his blessing. It may be only wishful thinking, but I'm certain he will, ah, let his erring daughter go in peace."

Father smiled faintly. Then his face took on a stern expression. "You will not have long for a honeymoon before you enlist."

Drayton could think of nothing to say. He stared down at the Persian carpet, counting the leaves on the lotus plants.

After a long awkward silence Father said, "Were you perhaps thinking of leaving the country with her?"

"Father, I have to speak truthfully. You have not raised a liar. I grieve to cause you pain, but we have considered it. No decision, but we couldn't help but discuss it."

"Well, I'm glad to know I didn't raise a liar. But it would grieve me worse to learn I had raised a coward and traitor. Your country is now at war. Any moment from now on we may hear of 75,000 Lincolnites invading our country. You will *not* disgrace your family or your name. I dread to think of losing any of my sons in the coming days. But death is preferable to dishonor. If you choose this Northern woman, as is your right, then she must cast her lot with you and your people. Does she love you so much?"

"Yes, and we have wrestled with the coming of war more than I can say. I never committed to her that I would run away to Europe or anywhere. I suppose we were waiting in hopes this possibility might never come to pass. But since it has, she knows I must stand with my State, with my brothers. I must be true to myself, despite my doubts about the wisdom of this war. How can I be true to her if I can't be faithful to other things with a prior claim?" His moment of choice had arrived, just as Cabell had described his. "When the time comes, I will enlist. I hear Wade Hampton will raise a cavalry regiment. Perhaps he'll have me and Beltane."

"Then you have my blessing, and my permission to live here or at Cypress Stand until you are called to duty. I know Colonel Hampton will be pleased to have Beltane at least." He smiled a wry smile, and the tension of the moment evaporated.

"But Father, I must tell you, my heart is not in it."

His father regarded him with a speculative stare. "I daresay your heart will be in it when the rest of you is in it."

***

The Very Reverend Ainsley Rutledge, Dean of St Phillips Church, performed the ceremony in the drawing room at East Battery. Since Fort Sumter the Dean had presided over numerous hasty weddings. He conducted the ceremony with tact and understanding. A High Church Anglican, he made it less obvious Celia was marrying a Protestant. Dr. Sullivan had refused to attend, nor did Maria the dueña. Cabell Junior, Ranse, Father, Ambrosia, and Shortbread stood as witnesses. Miss Julia Alston stood as bridesmaid.

Celia had worn a charming dress when she'd first arrived at East Bay, but had brought nothing else. The dress was suitable enough for an impromptu wedding, but they both regretted there'd been no time to shop for a trousseau or white silk wedding gown. Still, none of these details seemed to matter as they both intoned, "I do," and the Reverend Rutledge declared them man and wife. *Whom God hath joined together, let no man put asunder. No man, no army, no navy, no war.*

***

"It's not Saratoga Springs, but I suppose there are far worse places for a honeymoon." Drayton gestured with a wide sweep of his hand at his spacious bedroom. The huge rice bed draped with tulle netting to ward off mosquitoes. The silk counterpane. Plush Nain carpets. A brass-mounted Chippendale highboy. Bookshelves groaning under gold-embossed leather volumes. Hunting prints in elegant frames. A Purdy shotgun on the wall. Every detail bespoke quality and comfort.

Celia said, "My Love, it is extraordinary. Beautiful, yet masculine. It's so... so *you*. There is nowhere else I'd rather be."

He turned the gaslights low and lit a candle on the bedside table. A few moments of awkwardness followed as she came forward and gave herself for the first time. "I regret I have no alluring lingerie," she whispered, breathlessly, smiling.

"I can't imagine any lingerie more alluring than your natural state," he said, his heart racing. He was soon in his own natural state. He was pleased to find she suffered no false modesty. She was free, open, at ease with him. He wondered if perhaps it had something to do with being Catholic.

Beneath all the layers – silk over-gown, second and third skirt, shift, and stays — she was far more exquisite than he had imagined, gold and ivory, except for a roseate glow on her upper chest, throat, and cheeks. All he had ever known of women, and they were European women, was a thrusting and grasping that had been, well, adversarial. But this. No birds of prey tearing hungrily at flesh. It was a harmonious yielding of flesh and a deep fusing of souls. It was...*connubial*, just as it ought to have been.

He was dazzled by the treasures she opened and spread before him, for a moment paralyzed with rapture. Then they began to explore together, embarking together from trembling tenderness to fierce passion. She arrived before him, uttering soft cries to guide the way. He followed like a wave of the sea, lifted up and out of himself and crashing in ecstasy upon her shore.

***

Two mornings later a note arrived at East Bay addressed to Señora Cecelia *FitzHenry*. Celia read the note propped up in bed while Drayton, in his dressing gown, poured coffee at the sideboy.

"It's from Maria," she said. "She tells me she risks Father's displeasure to inform me they are departing Charleston today at noon on the steamer *Theodosia,* bound for New York. She begs me to present myself and say farewell, to ask his blessing — at the risk of his withholding it. Also, she wants to wish me farewell and Godspeed. May we go, please?"

"Yes, of course."

"You'll go with me?"

"Certainly. Do you think I'd cower here and let you face his wrath alone? We've done nothing to be ashamed of, even if we have gone against his wishes. We are both of age. I am proud to have married you, and prouder still that you consented to marry me."

They dressed leisurely, for by this time Drayton had acquired a splendid wardrobe for her, delighting in her girlish pleasure at each new garment purchased. She wore a green silk dress that brought out the gold in her hair and highlighted her complexion of berries and cream.

Shortbread drove them the few blocks to Adgers Wharf, where the ship's cargo boom swayed baggage onto the forward deck. Crewmen sorted it on deck while a blue-uniformed purser began to check passengers aboard at the gangway. Maria stood with Dr. Sullivan on the platform, straining to look back toward East Bay Street. Drayton noticed the Doctor seemed in no hurry to go aboard, but then stiffened and frowned when they drove into view.

Celia alighted from the carriage, with a smile of pure joy as she strode confidently toward her father. Drayton loved the way her hips swiveled ever so slightly as she walked. He closed up at her elbow. Maria curtseyed. Celia embraced her and spoke a few inaudible words in her ear. It sounded like Spanish, though Drayton didn't know the language. Celia curtseyed in perfect Charleston fashion to her father, remaining in a humble pose. She looked up and probed his eyes, which to Drayton seemed close to swimming with tears.

"Father," she said softly, "I ask your forgiveness for marrying without your consent. But this is the man I love above all earthly things, above life itself. I ask your forgiveness and your blessing on our union."

For what seemed like an age the Doctor stood rigidly. He stared at her at his feet, then at Drayton, than back at Celia. His body shook, but he remained rigid. Finally he extended a hand and lifted her up. She bent forward to kiss him, but he held her at arm's length.

He said in a voice that cracked, "You are my only child. Apart from my teaching and my faith, you have been my life. It breaks my heart to leave you here on the eve of war, in this place which has started it all and which will surely be the target of a terrible retribution."

"Father, you know how much I love and revere you. But this is my husband. You know that someday each one must leave father and mother and cleave to one's mate. I have sworn a vow to him: whither he lodges, I will lodge. His people shall be my people. And his God, my God."

"Even if he is your country's enemy!" Finbarr thundered.

She became severe in turn. "Father, in the end there is no country but the heart. *He* is my country."

Suddenly Drayton saw that this proud, austere, wise, and lonely man was broken indeed. The Doctor lowered his head, suppressing a sob. Tears welled up in Drayton's own eyes, but he turned and wiped them away.

The boat's steam whistle began its raw wail for passengers to board. It was a few minutes before noon. She knelt again and said in a low voice, "Your blessing, Father. And your forgiveness. I beg you not leave full of bitterness."

Dr. Sullivan lifted her up again. This time he drew her into his embrace. He said, "Our Saviour enjoined us to forgive not seven times, but seventy times seven. Can I not forgive my own beloved daughter?" As he pulled her close, his tears finally spilled out, leaving darker spots on the shoulder of her green dress.

Drayton stepped forward, extending his right hand, his hat in his left. He inclined his head toward his dear old professor, whom he'd likely never see again. He said, "Can you also find room in your great heart to forgive me as well? Is to adore Cecelia so great a sin?"

"In myself I cannot," her father replied. "Only by the grace of God can I find it in me to forgive you. You have taken the most precious thing from me. But I know she was not mine. People do not possess one another. Not parents their children, not husbands their wives. She was only given into my keeping for a little while. Now I reluctantly give her into yours."

"And I will keep her with all the love and devotion I can muster," said Drayton.

He and the Doctor shook hands. "I believe you will."

"And your blessing?" Celia asked.

"Ah, Daughter, that is another matter. You have married outside the Church. It is not up to me in the circumstances to bless your union. That is up to God. But I pray that He will. May we meet again after this foolish war is concluded. Perhaps the exigencies of war will bring your husband to the true Church."

With that he embraced his daughter wearing an expression that said, *This may be the last time we meet in this life.* He did not look back as he and Maria climbed the gangplank and went on board. Drayton and Celia remained while the crew warped the *Theodosia* away from the dock. The port sidewheel began to lash the water. The starboard wheel turned in reverse. She pivoted slowly into the harbor, toward the Atlantic Ocean and points north.

***

Well, 'twas a famous victory, thought Drayton. Major Anderson had surrendered Sumter. Now the South had to organize itself for war. This was as serious an undertaking as could be imagined, yet they were amateurs, beginners. As the lines were drawn, North and South had to recruit armies and amass the resources of war. At the same time they tried to claim the moral high ground, like two schoolyard bullies taunting each other, 'You started it!' 'No, *you* did!' Drayton marveled that the Union should gain such moral advantage from being fired on at Fort Sumter, a largely symbolic act in which no soldier was harmed. It paled compared to invading the South and levying mass war against fellow Americans. But one couldn't underrate the power of a piece of embroidered colored cotton hoisted on a pole, which if sold in any marketplace wouldn't net more than a handful of silver.

When Lincoln called for 75,000 volunteers, his summons went to all the states except the eight that had seceded, including the Upper South and pro-South Border States. They refused. Instead Virginia seceded, followed by North Carolina and Tennessee. Kentucky tried to secede, but the state split into pro-Union and pro-Confederate factions, each with its own government. Its proximity to the rest of the Union kept Kentucky from effectively joining the South. Drayton read that in Richmond, state officials offered command of Virginia's forces to a man named Robert E. Lee, a West Point graduate and former superintendent of the Military Academy. Rumor was that General Winfield Scott had offered Lee field command of all Federal forces. He had declined, resigning his U.S. Army commission and promising never again to draw his sword except in defense of his native state. Lee was well known and respected in Charleston from an earlier tour of duty, when he had inspected defenses along the South Carolina coast for the U.S. Army.

In 1861 the North had nearly twice the population of the South, 18 million to just under 10 million. The North had two-thirds of the railroad, rolling stock, and engines. It possessed most of America's developed mineral resources and eight times the industrial capacity—cannon foundries especially. The North inherited 700 of the 1000 Regular officers of the U.S. Army and more of its experienced Navy officers and sailors. The South's advantage, apart from an array of talented leaders like Robert E. Lee, Albert Sidney Johnston, *et al*? She was fighting against an invader for her homeland and way of life, not for an abstraction called the Union.

Drayton knew all this but was resolved not to let it overshadow their diminishing time together. He and Celia continued their hurried honeymoon at the family cottage on Mount Pleasant. They rode gaily along the surf where the sand was hard-packed. They took long walks hand-in-hand. He'd never imagined such joy and harmony were possible. But the outside world could not be ignored forever. A few days after Doctor Sullivan's wrenching farewell, they sat on the seaside porch of the cottage, lulled by the roar of the surf. She had been unusually quiet, and Drayton knew something weighed heavily on her mind. It was not hard to guess what.

"My Love, we can't make reality go away by pretending it doesn't exist," she said. "Events of historic significance are bearing down on us, like the incoming tide, whether we say yea or nay."

"I know, my Dear."

"And yet…" she began, then fell silent, drawing a knitted shawl about her shoulders and turning to stare at the sea.

"Yet?"

"Oh, Love, you have means, and you have an education in the classics that could find you a position almost anywhere. Let us leave here, put the onrushing madness behind us. We can go to Europe, South America, anywhere. You could write and teach—"

She was right; it would be so simple. Throw a few clothes and books into a valise. He had some money – British gold sovereigns he'd begun to stash away a year ago when war clouds began to gather. He knew of a steamer lying at Vendue Range waiting for cargo, the *Jeanne la Pucelle*, destination Le Havre. But though he'd made vows to his wife, he'd also given his word to Father. He hadn't shared that conversation with Celia. But duty bound him fast whether he'd given a promise to Father or not. He was caught. And though the trap was not of his own making, he was caught nonetheless. He could no longer hide the reality of the choice imposed on him by fate from himself or from her.

"Love, I would live anywhere for your sake. But this is where I was born and raised. I'm not an undifferentiated drop in the sea of mankind, I'm rooted here, in this place, part of this community. My brothers are going off to war—"

"Are you your brothers' keeper? Must you hazard your life in this folly because they are too foolish to see where it must all end? You *do* see. How can you go, knowing what you know?"

"How? How can I abandon my kin? They are my blood, and this is my state. My people are about to be invaded and I must stand with them. Folly or not, it's as simple as that. Can I repudiate my honor, my own self?"

"We women have our honor, too. It is what keeps the race alive, that suckles children and nurtures men. Ours creates, it doesn't destroy. Ours is the very beating heart of civilization. Don't speak to me of honor if it means you are lost to me, that there can never be a life for us."

There was no gainsaying this argument. In fact, it was beyond argument. Never had he felt so torn. But despite all, Drayton knew he must go, too.

She relented. "Very well. Say no more. For all your doubts and inner turmoil, you *want* to go. It's the grand adventure, for the doubter like you as well as the firebrand like Cabell. If you must go, you must, although I confess I don't understand this war at all. The Spartan women told their men as they marched off to fight, 'Come home with your shield, or on it.' I know you're enamored of all things Greek, but we are a Christian people, not pagan. So I will say to you only, come home in God's good time and by His good favor."

"Most men by far come back, Dear. Otherwise war would lose its appeal."

"I don't know much about war, my Love. As I have been told by many here in Charleston, I am only a woman and am not expected to know much about it. But this I *do* know: war changes men. It hardens them, coarsens them. Necessity is always their plea, and they do things they wouldn't think of doing without the excuse of war. I worry that this conflict will tarnish our love. I beg you to come back as you are to me now, insofar as it is possible — fine and good, not hard and coarse. Will you make me a pledge?"

"Yes, I will." He replied without hesitation, and his promise hung like an echo in the still air. She had made an enormous sacrifice to marry him, abandoning her father, her home, all that was familiar. He was going to repay her faith in him with faith in her. "What must I pledge?"

"Only this. In battle, do not forget God; show mercy, for your own sake if not that of an enemy. Engrave these lines on your heart: "Where Mercy, Love, and Pity dwell / There God is dwelling, too.""

— END OF PART II —

Thomas Moore

PART III
Chapter Seventeen

Charleston, South Carolina, March 1913.

Annalee heard the door in the rear squeak open. Late again! Her feelings were obviously of no account. Her husband was halfway through the kitchen when she sprang from the shadowed hallway.

"You lied to me!" She blazed away at him.

"I never lie, my Dear," he said. She saw him set his jaw. "But tell me — how do you think I've lied?" He leaned against the kitchen sink, arms folded, waiting.

"You promised me last week you'd given up this foolish notion of Gettysburg. Now I learn from the College you've spoken of going."

Though she had him dead to rights, she was surprised at her own severity. She hadn't intended to take such an aggressive tone, but this Gettysburg business infuriated her. She wanted to be kinder to him, but found to her dismay that she was powerless to behave differently. Something in him evoked memories of her father, whom she'd both loved and despised. Poppa had inherited the farm near Long Canes where she was born. Sadly, he was no farmer. To keep the family afloat he'd been forced to take a series of low-paid clerking jobs in Abbeville. His working 'in trade' humiliated her mother, who had visions of being a fine lady. She demonstrated superiority to her feckless husband by devotion to ceremony and lofty manner.

Momma ran the farm and increasingly the entire family – her father included – with an iron hand. Annalee would never forget the morning in her fifth year after a maternal rant when she wet the bed, as she had several times. Her mother made her stand in the corner with the reeking bedsheet draped over her head. Poppa came home for dinner and found his daughter in a deplorable state, the wet patch in her face. He ripped away the sheet. A terrible row followed, one of the few times her father stood up to her mother. In the privacy of her mind, Annalee cheered him on. After the violent argument an icy silence prevailed in the house for a week. And then one day, without warning or a word of farewell, he disappeared and never returned.

Nor would Annalee ever forget the night her husband sweated and stirred and moaned in his sleep in the grip of a bad dream. First she thought it was a nightmare of the War, common among Confederate veterans. But then Drayton had cried out, "Celia!" Even now, years after the episode, she recalled feeling the hard protective shell closing around her heart. She knew then he was going to betray her, just as her father had, just as Isaac Joyner had. All men betray; this was her one certainty in life. From that night she never let him forget that *she* was not the object of his dreams. His guilt was obvious to them both. As a result, she'd grown accustomed to his capitulating in shame when confronted. But to her chagrin, this time he didn't. Normally when she attacked he retreated. Or he failed to counter-attack. In her mind it was the same thing. Not this time.

His reply was slow in coming. "It wasn't a promise; it was only my inclination at the time. I've had an entire weekend to reconsider." He turned and went into his study, turning on the gas lights, and poking the banked embers of the fire.

Annalee followed. "Just so! An entire weekend alone with that malicious brother of yours. No wonder you broke your pledge." She wasn't going to let him wriggle out of this one.

"My Dear, there was no pledge. It's a principle of mine — I don't make pledges. And your field of view is too narrow. It was actually our grandson who inclined me to reconsider more than it was Cabell."

She pointed an accusing finger. "You will *not* take my grandson on such a foolish journey. I'm putting my foot down!"

In Annalee's case it was not just a figure of speech; she literally stamped her foot, an habitual act when lodging a complaint. He actually laughed at the gesture, which increased her fury.

"Tommy really wants to go, and I think it would be … be instructive for him. At any rate, it's not up to you or me. It's a decision his father must make."

"Then I'll see to it Preston refuses."

Normally at this stage his shoulders would slump in defeat. But of late she had perceived a change in his behavior. She feared she'd overplayed her hand. Instead of sagging he suddenly stood up straight before the fireplace, clasped his hands behind his back, and inclined his head, peering at her intently. She backed away slightly. He turned and laid a split log on the fire.

"I see you're determined to ignore my feelings in the matter," she said.

"Now, Annalee, you've made your feelings clear, and at every opportunity. Your opposition to this trip has been so disproportionate, it's forced me to wonder why." His voice was full of a resolve she rarely encountered, and filled the cup of her fury to overflowing. "The fact is, I haven't entirely made up my mind. If I followed my inclination, I wouldn't go. But Cabell thinks it would do me good. Tommy wants to go, and I think it would do *him* good." He stepped to his desk and sat in the leather chair. "Consequently, my Dear, I'm going to weigh all the factors, including your feelings in the matter, and come to a decision I think is best. And if I do decide to go to Gettysburg, then I'm going. And you can go to the devil."

***

After his wife stormed out, Drayton took advantage of Annalee's shocked silence to lock the door to the study and pour a snifter of brandy. Let her listen at the keyhole; it no longer mattered. His thoughts were his own – and silent. The drink was satisfying, celebratory as well as restorative. It felt good to have backed her down, a rare occurrence.

The episode was also a stimulus to self-examination and recall. Was it possible they'd been married thirty-odd years? His memory was good for details of contemporaneous events of the past. *Too* good, perhaps. They'd met in April 1876, eleven years from the end of the War, during General Wade Hampton's campaign for Governor and South Carolina's redemption from the rule of the Carpetbaggers. Three months before the Sioux and Cheyenne massacred George Custer. The same year that Heinrich Schliemann excavated the ancient Greek city of Mycenae, a discovery which Drayton had followed with great interest. They'd married four years after the first encounter, in May 1880, something of an anti-climax. It was now the spring of 1913. Their 33rd Anniversary was bearing down, and the elapsed years scarcely seemed real.

He found it hard to remember why he'd married her in the first place. It was easy to forget three decades of mutual disappointment. And it was mutual. She had as much reason to be disappointed in him as he in her. His brooding diffidence, his mournful air, his unhealed wounds of the spirit. He often woke her with nightmares of the War. In their early days together they'd taken walks along the High Battery. He would freeze into immobility staring at Fort Sumter and grip the iron rail on the sea wall so fiercely it left his forearms sore. These were hardly the ingredients of a satisfying marriage.

When the War began in 1861, most of his life lay ahead of him, with all its promise of love and fulfillment. Now, in 1913, most of his life lay behind him. Regardless of who was to blame, or if no one was to blame, in life's litany of failed expectations his marriage to Annalee Burr Joyner led the list. After Celia's passing he had no inclination to marry again. Then, inexplicably, he'd ended up in the kind of marriage he'd always feared in his youth — a business merger rather than a marriage. A relationship like his with Celia could only happen once in a lifetime, and only if one were preternaturally blessed.

Too few reminders of Celia remained to stir the memories. Her tomb at Cypress Stand. The battle-scarred, brass-framed miniature by Charles Fraser. A wedding gift in April 1861, it was also a gift of life, for it had saved him from enemy fire on the Second Day at Gettysburg. His old field glasses she gave him going off to the War, locked in the gun cabinet at the River. And one much-folded letter, near to falling apart at the creases, her dying testament. Let it fall apart. He'd committed the words to memory long ago. No other mementoes survived to mark their great love. That nothing more tangible remained was partly his fault. But more Annalee's.

Charleston, South Carolina, January, 1882.

He been married a few years and was living in Annalee's home on Church Street, which offered comfort and proximity to his teaching post at the College of Charleston. Perhaps that was one reason he'd married her. In exchange he offered her a fine old name and social standing in Charleston – a Faustian bargain, as it turned out.

The first harbinger came one evening at supper. A desultory conversation revealed something he wished he'd known before they'd wed. Flabbergasted at what followed, he'd forgotten what prompted her statement.

"All relationships are based on power," she said over her water goblet.

"*All* relationships?" He assumed she was speaking of politics.

"All relationships," she said.

"Even *marriage*?"

"Especially marriage."

Several months later he returned home earlier than usual to find Annalee searching through the personal items in his desk. Though startled by his unexpected appearance, she faced him down boldly.

"Why are you rummaging through my things?" he demanded.

She replied with a demand of her own. "Why are you keeping these letters?" She brandished a sheaf of pale green envelopes tied with bottle green ribbon. Her voice was a knife edge, and he recoiled as she read in her most sarcastic voice a note that trembled in enraged hands.

"'How you touched me, Darling, when you wrote, 'I am certain of nothing but the holiness of the heart's affections.' You have never written such a letter to me!" she hissed.

As she tossed the bundle on his desk, a flash of anger flared up inside him, then just as quickly died. He was weary of fighting. Now all he wanted was peace. Annalee had promised him refuge. Perhaps she was justified in taking offense. Let the dead bury the dead, and let the living occupy themselves with living. Besides, he had the one letter that counted most, kept separate from the others. It was Celia's deathbed letter, surviving like a flower pressed in a book; desiccated, but with the lingering fragrance of old times dead and gone.

When he remained silent, her eyes and nostrils flared wide in triumph.

"Burn them." Her voice was flat, insistent, minatory.

She gestured to the blazing oak logs in the fireplace. His protests died in his throat, and she gathered up the bundle of letters. Thrusting them into his hands, she motioned again toward the fire. "I said, *burn* them. This is … emotional adultery. Burn them at once or get out of my house!"

My house. When she asked for money for repairs and improvements, it was *their* house. Now it was *my* house. But dignity stopped him from saying it. He hated unseemly squabbles, and he was thrown off balance by her unexpected attack. He wanted to appeal to her better nature, until he remembered that all relationships, especially marriage, were based on power. Why didn't she just burn them herself? No, she wanted *him* to burn them, and while she presided. In that way his humiliation would be complete – and her power over him. He tried to glare back at her but couldn't meet her eyes. They glittered like a cobra's, rooting him to the spot. Never had he felt such revulsion for another human being. In the same moment he reminded himself of the danger of becoming the thing one hated. He'd lived through enough hostility to fill ten lifetimes. Hostility had killed his wife, his father, his brother, and countless thousands besides. When he returned alive from the War he'd resolved never to add another drop to the sea of antagonism that engulfed humanity. Almost involuntarily his legs moved, propelling him a few steps toward the fireplace.

Above the mantel was a gilt-framed portrait of Beltane, dead these five years. His neck and head were turned toward the viewer, capturing his liquid, expressive eyes. Annalee had always complained of a horse holding pride of place in her husband's study instead of his wife. Beltane looked down at him with pity and reproach. He seemed to say, *What has happened to you? You were a fighter, once.*

Bright yellow tongues lapped greedily at the hearth. "Burn them." Annalee's sibilant voice seduced him with its power. Slowly, tasting the ashes of defeat he'd known after the War, he shuffled with sad inches toward the beckoning fire. What must be, must be. He fed the envelopes one by one into the blaze, watching the edges curl up blackly before bursting into flame.

Chapter Eighteen

Cypress Stand Plantation, Colleton District, South Carolina; Late April 1861.

When they arrived at Cypress Stand, Celia presented Drayton the Charles Fraser miniature. A note on her marbled stationery of pale green accompanied the gift. Smiling with surprise, he read, 'How you touched me, Darling, when you wrote, I am certain of nothing but the holiness of the heart's affections. Now wear this image of me close to your heart.'

"My Love, you have made sure the setting was worthy of the gift," he said. "It's exquisite." Then he remembered. "Charles Fraser is not in the best of health, in addition to being in great demand. It must have taken weeks to schedule your sittings, and then the sittings themselves had to have been time-consuming. Just when did you begin this project?"

She blushed and lowered her head. "I beg you not to think me presumptuous."

"Why on earth should I think that?" Then he understood. "Is it possible you commenced the creation of this wedding gift before we were even engaged?

They'd honeymooned for a memorable few days in Charleston and Mount Pleasant. Now the time had come for her to visit his ancestral home by the River, especially while the weather blessed them with a cool dry spell that kept the mosquitoes in check.

Father had reservations about Celia and it was obvious to Drayton that he was about to put her to a test. Could she become the new *chatelaine*; a Northern-bred girl mistress of a Low Country plantation? To Drayton she was both Aphrodite and Athena. Could she add Ceres to the list and master the local rice culture? Father said he simply wanted to show her how things worked in case she were ever needed — where to find the storeroom keys, the medical chest, and how to address the servants. Drayton knew there was more going on in the background. He hoped she'd pass.

The family seat had started out before the Revolution as a simple farmhouse, two rooms on the ground floor bisected front to back by a central hallway. Over time as the family fortunes improved, it expanded upward and outward. But it was not magnificent, compared for example to the neighboring Boynton plantation with its high fluted columns topped by Corinthian capitals imported from Italy. Cypress Stand possessed only a modest portico supported by homemade square wooden columns, something approximating Doric with its molding at the top. Yet it was well-proportioned, a perfect and pleasing example of the Golden Ratio.

When Drayton walked Celia through the center hallway to the rear piazza, her delight came alive. She stood with rapture overlooking the terraced lawns sloping to the River, bordered by boxwood hedges, neatly trimmed. Some of the older shrubs had been sculpted into the shapes of deer grazing. Marsh grasses and cattails swayed one way then another as the breeze shifted, like a choir keeping time with celestial music only they could hear. Intersecting the expanse of marsh and woodland flowed the broad, placid, shining Edisto.

"Oh, my!" She exclaimed, clasping hands to her breast.

She laughed aloud when two wood ducks whistled overhead and dived into flooded timber across the water. She stood in silence, hands folded as if in prayer, while a great blue heron settled regally among the reeds at the edge of the lawn, then rested stock-still on one leg.

"It's breathtaking," she said, recovering her speech with a sigh. "Far more beautiful than you described. But for the house I'd think we were in the Garden of Eden. I can see why you love it so. I know you'll be sorry to leave it."

A frown passed over his father's brow and he cleared his throat awkwardly. Celia's innocent remark hadn't passed unnoticed.

"I hope you will be content with us while your husband…" Father stopped, as if perplexed. It was clear he assumed Drayton would soon be off to the War. "Well, I mean, for as long as you wish to stay. Warm weather will soon be upon us, bringing the malaria season, and then we'll return to Charleston. I recommend you remain with us there, on East Bay."

"Would you like to see some more of the countryside?" Drayton asked next morning after breakfast.

"Yes, indeed," Celia said.

"So far you've enjoyed the view of the River from the land. This time I'll show you how the land looks from the River."

They packed a picnic hamper and some bottles of wine into the currach, a long, shallow-draft boat made from a framework of ash, with a skin of canvas stretched tightly over the ribs and waterproofed with tar. It was an Irish design, brought to the Low Country by Thomas FitzHenry, Esq. of County Waterford and the United Irishman. Fitted with thwarts and brass oar-locks, it could be rowed or poled from the stern thwart in the shallow marshes and cypress flats.

As they were organizing the outing, Celia surprised Drayton with a request. He was eager for the time alone with her, but she said, "Let's invite Father along. He still has doubts about us. The more time we can spend with him, the better."

"Fine," grumped Drayton. "He can row."

Pleased at the unexpected invitation, Father joined them, sitting next to Celia on the stern thwart. Drayton sat amidships facing them plying the oars expertly. They glided downriver on a falling tide, while Father showed off his domains, the rice fields that stretched for several miles downriver, the pastures behind them with a few head of cattle grazing contentedly. He explained the intricacies of rice-growing, how the fields had to be flooded at just the right season, then drained before the grain ripened, how the trunks regulated the water level in the paddies in conjunction with the rise and fall of the tides.

After a twenty-minute cruise they arrived at the rice mill, a two-storey brick structure topped by an enormous four-sided brick chimney. Drayton rowed to the loading dock and tied off the currach's painter.

"How incongruous," said Celia. "To find such an artifact in the midst of the wilderness."

They picnicked on the grassy lawn alongside the mill. "We built it here," Father explained, "because up to this point the river is deep enough for seagoing vessels to dock when the milled rice is ready for market."

Drayton was proud of the plantation, too. He added, "Love, we ship rice all over the East Coast of the United States. I daresay the plantation feeds tens of thousands."

Celia sipped her wine from a silver goblet, silent and pensive, taking in the lush yet almost intimidating wildness of the landscape. It was a peaceful and perfect moment.

Drayton stood and walked to the river bank, studying the barnacle-encrusted pilings of the dock. "The tide is turning," he said. "We can ride it back upriver. It will make the rowing easier."

***

"Well, my Dear, now that you've seen most of it, what do you think of Cypress Stand?" Father asked as they skimmed along tea-colored waters. Drayton knew his bride, and noticed when she stiffened. He wished his father would leave well enough alone.

"It's ... quite lovely." There was a hollowness in her tone that Father could detect as well as Drayton.

Father stiffened in turn. "You damn it with faint praise. Please. Be frank and honest."

She remained silent for a while. The only sound was the swishing of the water along the bows of the boat and the rhythmic grinding of the oars in the locks.

Celia sighed. "Mr. FitzHenry, I am only a guest, and it ill becomes a guest to remonstrate with his host. I hope you'll forgive me, for I do want to learn and understand. You said to be frank and honest. I will. You have created something beautiful here, beautiful, majestic, and useful. I know that many people benefit from your efforts. And Cypress Stand is an image of Paradise. But it is a paradise with its dark side. Frankly, I feel uncomfortable."

"Uncomfortable? Have we not done everything possible to make you feel welcome?"

"You have indeed. You've shown me what Southern hospitality truly means. But I feel uncomfortable knowing I'm being waited on hand and foot by slaves."

She trailed her hand casually in the water, looking away as if embarrassed by her frankness. Drayton looked away, too, rather than witness his father's discomfiture – or show his own. He was sure that Celia was killing any prospects of Father's approval, even though their union was a *fait accompli*. He paid attention to his strokes – forward, pull, feather, recover. The boat fairly sped.

"We prefer the term servants," said Father. "And as valued servants, they are well treated and content with their station."

"Yes, sir, I can see they are well treated," she said with new resolve. "They have a kindly and compassionate master. Drayton could have no other kind of father and be the man he is." Drayton smiled inwardly at her diplomacy. She could charm a raccoon right out of its tree under a full moon.

"Thank you," said Father.

"And yet...," she continued.

"And yet?"

"And yet I question if they are truly content with their station."

"Their station is the one for which Nature his fitted them, as She has all her creatures. They must be content with that, as everyone must."

"But isn't it also true that Nature, by which I mean the Lord God, has instilled in all men a love of freedom? They yearn for it even in bondage; *especially* in bondage. It's a story as old as man himself."

Father frowned and shifted his weight on the thwart. Drayton could see his father cogitating on Celia's words. He kept his mind on the rhythmic stroke of his oars.

"There is something in what you say," Father replied at length. "But I have never seen evidence of discontent among my servants. They know they have a kindly master. They work hard, 'tis true, but all their needs are met."

"But, Sir, being sl— … Being in a condition of servitude, is it likely they would display their discontent? You're far wiser than I. Have you never asked yourself: do not all subject people display a deceptive contentment with their lot as a form of self-protection? Do they not feign affection for their masters, to whose will their existence is vulnerable, rather than show the resentment that festers in their hearts toward their servitude?"

Father's brow wrinkled in thought. "I must say, young lady, that I've never really considered the possibility. I suppose I ought."

She was not strident nor sanctimonious, but reasonable and discerning. She seemed to understand the complexities and moral ambiguities of their dilemma. But she made her feelings known in a way Father wasn't used to. Nor Drayton, for that matter.

"I know it must be galling" she continued, "for self-righteous Yankees to come south and lecture you on the matter of Negro …servitude. But you asked me what I thought and I answered honestly. Honesty also compels me to add this. The North has promoted, prolonged, and profited from slavery. We all know of the trade of molasses, rum, and slaves between the North, the West Indies, and Africa. Vast financial empires, especially in Connecticut and Rhode Island, have been built on the African trade. Some are even run by Abolitionists. Most are financed at high interest by Wall Street banks. Slavery is a national sin, not just a Southern one."

"If it is indeed a sin," Father said.

"Nor am I blind to other conditions in the North," Celia added. "Those same industrialists who look upon your slaveholding with smug condemnation…Well, they have *their* virtual slaves. Poor immigrants from Ireland living amid squalor and disease a dozen to a room in tenements reeking of filth. They are paid bare pennies a day for back-breaking manual labor on the roads or for garment piecework, while they are kept forever indebted to the company store."

Father nodded. He took the food hamper from Drayton, who was still in the currach.

"I appreciate your honesty," he said. "And your insights. And what do you think, my boy? I see the cogs turning in that fertile brain of yours."

Drayton stepped off the landing onto hard ground and took Celia's arm. "I think I married an extraordinary woman. What she says is certainly true about the North's involvement in the slave trade. She desires to mollify you, Father, and good for her. Nevertheless, it's only another form of the *tu quoque* defense. 'You, too.' A classic fallacy of logic. And, Sir, two wrongs don't make a right."

Back in their bedroom Drayton gather Celia in his arms and kissed her passionately. He felt her stir against him.

"I don't know how you do it," he said.

"Oh? Do what?"

"Somehow you made your case against slavery and at the same time won Father's admiration. Mine too, if it weren't already at its maximum. Why, I believe you almost persuaded him."

She broke away from him, stepped away, then turned and faced him, her face suddenly clouded. "I hope I can persuade you as well."

"Persuade me? Of what?"

"Oh, I can see the cogs turning as well as Father. The two of you are conspicuously silent on the matter of the War. But the struggle is written all over you. You're going to join up soon, aren't you?"

***

The next morning at breakfast Father sipped his coffee standing at the French windows looking out at the lawns and River. "Son, I want you to ride out with me this morning. I need to make my regular inspection. And let's see how that horse of yours is doing. I fear you've let him rest on his laurels since his famous race."

Celia had already gone out with Maum Biddy. It was a soft spring morning, a fine day for a ride. Junius had the horses – Beltane and Marvel, Cabell Senior's mare — waiting in the stable, saddled and tacked. Bel was restive in the presence of the mare, but quieted when Drayton entered and stroked his neck. The three men greeted one another warmly and Junius held the horses' heads while Drayton and his father mounted. Father and son rode away at an easy pace, keeping the eager horses on a tight rein. Drayton could feel the tension building, but waited patiently till his father was ready to unburden himself.

"Well, Lochinvar," his father began. "You have stolen away your Bride of Netherby and brought her here to us. I'm amazed I consented to such a scandal.

But I do like the young lady. I think she's adapting well to our life here. Old Joshua is ill again, and she's out with Maum Biddy to tend him. It's what your mother used to do, 'making the rounds.'"

Lochinvar was grateful for the welcome given Celia. Parental opposition to 'mere love matches' was all too frequent in his world.

"Yes, Father, I think she'll be happy here, for a time. Even in the presence of slaves."

They pulled their mounts aside on a high causeway so the field hands could pass. The Negroes sang as they marched to work and called out greetings to Drayton and his father. Unlike most planters, Cabell Senior didn't employ an overseer, but appointed leaders among five teams, and provided the overall supervision himself.

"Son," he said when they'd passed. "Let's take a page from Celia's Book of the North and come straight to the point. No use beating about the bush. What do you mean by 'for a time?' What did she mean yesterday about your leaving? I assumed she meant you're ready to depart for the defense of your country, since you are a FitzHenry, and both your brothers have joined. I also recognized you needed some time with your new bride, and I assented. But now the time has come to face your duty."

Father touched Marvel mare in the flank and they rode on, following the workers. Drayton remained silent, searching for the right words to placate his father, knowing there were none.

To fill up the awkward empty space, Father continued. "Cabell will take you in his troop; that is, as long as the vacancy remains, which will not be much longer. In the Beaufort District Troop you'll be among our friends and neighbors from Grahamville and Gillisonville and Coosawhatchee."

Miserable and not knowing what to say, but knowing he had to say something, Drayton replied, "This need not have come."

Father reined in, patting Marvel on the shoulder and withers. "Perhaps. But now it *has* come the question is, what are we going to do? I'm too old to fight, but I will support the cause in every other way I can, including giving my sons to the army. But how many? Will it be two or three? What are *you* going to do?"

"I think the war is a terrible mistake. I had hoped we could avoid such a pass."

"I had hoped it could be avoided, too. But now… Well, we will still try to go our own way and hope Lincoln and his extortionists will go theirs. But if we aren't free to leave, then we aren't free at all. We have re-claimed our sovereignty of passage in Charleston Harbor, and Lincoln used it as a pretext to call for 75,000 troops to invade us. Still, maybe it's a bluff. Perhaps our peace commission can settle matters before it comes to all-out war, especially if the Yankees know we are willing to fight. And so must you now be willing, too."

Drayton hiked up a leg on the saddle, pulled up its flap, and lengthened a stirrup. Bel stamped and pawed, wanting to do some real riding. The action bought a few moments. Cabell Senior was deceived by wishful thinking, clinging to the fanciful notion that the Yankees would let the South go in peace. If not, he believed the War would be limited to a few set-piece battles on the plain and then a treaty. Drayton believed they were rushing toward tragedy.

"Resorting to arms is a huge gamble," Drayton said finally, feet back in the stirrups. "In our Southern pride we're convinced we'll win. But what if we don't, Father? Is it a risk you're willing to take? To throw all you have, including your three sons and all this" – he gestured expansively – "into the wager? After Hubris comes Nemesis, and Nemesis will have her due."

"You over-state the risk. Our people are natural soldiers. We can shoot and ride better than any Yankee shopkeeper or factory drudge. You're a prime example. Our men were born on horseback."

Marvel walked on, until Father stopped to inspect the 'trunks,' large locks or valves of cypress beams set in the banks to regulate water flow into the rice fields.

"That may be, Father. But I tell you, in this war locomotives will prove more vital than horses."

"Locomotives! Whatever can you mean?"

Drayton remained silent, partly from filial respect, and partly from awareness of the futility of persuading him. His father was a product of his time and class. He could see things only in the way such men had for generations. Yet Drayton heard in the distant train whistle at Jacksonborough the tolling of the last hours of the Southern planter aristocracy.

***

Drayton was preparing for bed and watching Celia undress and don her nightgown with unconcealed interest.

"How was your ride with Father?" she asked, padding to him in bare feet.

"Fine, fine. Splendid. A fine day, really ...really splendid." He realized he was rattling on and clenched his jaw shut.

"As fine as all that, eh?"

"Yes, yes. Yes, indeed."

"Then why the hangdog expression?"

"I… ah. I…"

"My Love," she said with a short bitter laugh. "You are so transparent. But even if you weren't, I *know* you. Remember what you said on our wedding day? We are two hearts beating as one. I knew it yesterday when I saw it in your face – the inner struggle. Father is putting you under inexorable pressure to join the army. Your brothers have gone, and you feel you must, too. Yet you fear to tell me the moment has come. I don't envy your having to make such a choice. And though my love for you is boundless, I won't make it easier for you to choose the army. Come away with me to Europe. I know you love your family, your city, your state. And I applaud it. Yet, at the same time, you are different from them. Do you really want to risk your life to preserve the odious slave system? *Jeanne la Pucelle* sails in two days for Le Havre. Let's be on her."

He walked to the window and was diverted for a moment by the spectacle of countless tiny sparkles flashing on and off in the darkness.

"Fireflies," he said. "Come and look, Love. It's as if all the constellations of the heavens have gathered on earth."

"The country Irish believe night-time is when souls come out to play," Celia said, breaking into his musing. He circled her in his arms. "And there they are, sparkling. Seeing such a marvel, who can doubt the existence of the Creator? The earth is his palette." She fell silent.

Drayton filled the silence, slowly and deliberately unburdening his heart. "I planned to be a scholar, perhaps a writer, never a soldier. But sometimes the life of contemplation must yield to the life of action, including bearing arms to defend one's home. Socrates and Aeschylus served as hoplites in the Athenian army. They were proud to have fought in the front lines at Marathon."

Drayton hated war with a passion; yet he was being called to fight, and it was plain he'd have to go. He was not an atomized, deracinated individual. He was part of a family and a community, real and vibrant and nourishing for all their faults. Their spirit had been born in him from his conception; the life of his People was in his blood. On his father's side, it was the blood of Norman-Irish forebears who'd learned to love Ireland and fought for her liberty. On his mother's side were French Hugenots who'd defended La Rochelle. His ancestors had fought Indians and the British to carve out a home in the New World and build a civilization to rival the Old. The blood called insistently, even when the mind said, 'Folly!' He could not betray it for his honor, an old-fashioned concept to be sure. But could a man live without it, or live with himself dishonored? War was terrible, but shame and betrayal were worse.

"Yes," she took in his words, then said, "But later as you know, Athens and

Sparta went to war for their pride and greed. The golden age of Greece was destroyed, never to recover." She pulled away from his embrace and paced the floor with quick strides, arms folded across herself.

Drayton sighed deeply. The decision was not his; it had been made for him long before. "My Love, life often confronts us with a choice between the intolerable and the unbearable. I'm not wise enough to know how to choose between them. But I can no longer vacillate. In the end, despite my love for you, it's my duty to go. I have to stand with Cabell and Ranse in defense of my home. It was self-deception to think there was ever any other choice."

She said nothing, only shook her head slightly, and stared out the window.

"My Love, there's something I've come to perceive," he continued. "The best men of the South are in favor of emancipation – gradually, as the Negro is educated and made able to support himself. These same, these best men, are also the ones who will fight this war for independence. When it's over, these men will have earned the moral authority to govern and put a peaceful and orderly end to the slave system. The great paradox, my Love, is this: while many Yankees claim their war is to free the slaves; equally so, it seems, is ours. It will be my purpose, at any rate."

Cypress Stand, Colleton District, South Carolina, early May 1861.

Drayton felt awkward in his new uniform of the Beaufort District Troop. It was partly the uniform itself, and partly the feeling of being a fraud. The unaccustomed costume didn't make him a soldier, not yet anyway. He feared he might never be, despite how much he looked the part in the mirror. The black braid frogging down the breast of the woolen shell jacket, the brass buttons, and the cock feather in the black slouch hat were impressive. Still, it all seemed… well, too Napoleonic for his tastes.

He did like the cadet gray color. Many Southern regiments were choosing gray to distinguish their uniforms from Union blue. Even so, some of the proud old South Carolina militia units like Charleston's Washington Light Infantry refused to part with their traditional blue. "Let the *Yankees* pick another color," he'd heard some of them joking. "With yellow trim up the spine." Drayton had refused to join in the foolish levity. It was a case of whistling past the graveyard. Southerners might make better soldiers, but they would find out the hard way that Yankees weren't cowards.

Junius came into the bedroom for Drayton's kit.

"I'm glad you're coming with us, Junius. Although I don't know how Cypress Stand will operate without you."

Junius smiled, though dubiously, as he hoisted the leather valise on his shoulder.

"Well, Mistah Drayton, yo' Father he says I'm goan be freed after dis war ober. But I think I need to come along to Virginia with you young gente'mens, freed or not. Ya'lls goan be too busy fightin' to take proper care a dem hosses."

Drayton gripped his shoulder, and the big man swayed the dunnage downstairs to load onto the pack mule.

With no real knowledge of war, Drayton had packed the trunk with everything he thought he might need, starting with a few books. There was Suetonius' *The Twelve Caesars* to keep his Latin fresh, and Xenophon's *Peri Hippokes, On Horsemanship*, which he thought he might try to translate since there was no good English version. As an after-thought he threw in the Bible he'd received upon confirmation. He ought to read it more than he did, and it might provide some comfort in the coming trials.

He threw in several changes of linen and stockings, underwear, towels, and toiletries. He added flint-and-steel set, mess kit, sewing kit, a rubber-lined blanket, two wool blankets, and rain slicker. As a precaution he included woolen socks, long flannel underwear, and a knitted muffler. It was now May and the Regimental Letter had said to expect campaigning through the summer. But only a fool would fail to prepare for the coming winter as well. The Mexican-American War had begun in May 1846 and General Scott had captured Mexico City in September 1847 — a span of sixteen months. It was a poor benchmark, but it was all he had. This war could last sixteen months — or longer.

The moment for departure couldn't be put off any longer. Pulling on tan leather gauntlets, he walked down the front steps of the house to the mounting block, a chunk of tabby dating back to the Revolution. As he threw a leg over Beltane, he wondered how many FitzHenrys had vaulted into the saddle from this same spot over the generations and ridden away to fight Indians, British, or Mexicans. Now, sadly, his own countrymen were the enemy.

Junius was already astride Palmetto, and leading a mule with panniers lashed to an x-shaped frame of his own devising. The canvas cover bulged with their baggage, rations, extra tack, and farrier tools. No room of course for forge and anvil, but the Regiment would supply that essential equipment in its wagon train.

Father and Celia climbed into the barouche behind Shadpole, who sat tall and proud in the driver's box in FitzHenry red and black livery. Though the matched bays stood patiently, they glanced backward with worried looks at all the baggage being loaded. But the trip would not be long. The family would ride together the short distance to Jacksonborough, transfer the saddle horses, mule, and baggage to the train, and take the easy ride to Charleston. There the Low Country components of the new Hampton Legion were mustering for the rail trip north. They'd link up with Colonel Wade Hampton in Columbia, where he would complete organizing, equipping, and training his troops, mostly at his own personal expense. Cabell Junior was already in Charleston and would meet them for muster at The Citadel on Marion Square.

Drayton edged alongside the carriage, smiling down at Celia. Junius gave a hitch on the mule's lead. As the cavalcade moved out toward the oak-shaded lane and to the Jacksonborough Road, the FitzHenry family servants lined the pathway, nodding and calling farewell. A few barefoot boys whirled around with excitement, snapping their fingers. Some of the older women wept. Most stood impassively, clearly wondering what the war would mean for their future. They smiled and waved at Junius, but dubious over his good fortune. It was a fine thing to be free. But freed only after the war?

Junius reined in Palmetto. Leaning down, he stretched out a callused hand to Maum Biddy. She gripped it with spindly fingers. Drayton reined in, too, wondering what they were saying. Beltane pawed and snuffled, eager to be away; but Drayton had seen the grief and even something like anger in Maum Biddy's face, and he wanted to hear.

In a barely audible voice the old woman said to Junius, "Lawd knows I ain't never love a chile like I love you. An' it grieve my heart to know you ain't never coming back."

Junius bristled. "Now, Maum, don't say dat. I'se goan get through dis war and be comin' back soon enough."

"Yes, you goan git through de war. You goan live a long life, an' mos'ly a happy one. But, Son, you ain't never comin' back to Cypress Stan."

"Now how you know dat, Maum?"

"Don't ast me how I knows. I jus' knows, down deep in my heart. I pray de Lawd to keep you, wherever you goes."

Drayton was deeply moved. Until now, most of the Negroes on the place had remained in the background of his consciousness. They came when called, some surly, some cheerful. But now he saw them in the fullness of their humanity, experiencing the same emotions, the same loss, the same loves as the white buckra. This was a kinship of humanity that reached across a vast and seemingly unbridgeable gulf.

Junius retrieved his hand, smiled, and said, "De Lawd keep you, too, Maum. And *you* keep de folks, Mistah Cabell, Miz Celia, an' Cypress Stan." He turned his horse, tugged the mule's lead rope, and trotted off to catch up with Drayton and the carriage. "Come along, Mistah Mule," he sang out gaily. "We'se goan to Virginia!"

***

The order was to assemble with full kit and side arms at 8:00 AM on May 12 at the parade ground of The Citadel on the north side of the city. The officers carried a mixed array of sabers, mostly ceremonial. The enlisted soldiers would be issued their service sabers and Enfield carbines when they arrived in Columbia at the Cavalry Camp of Instruction. Some, like Drayton and Cabell, had already purchased revolvers, fine new Colts from Connecticut.

Father and Celia accompanied him to the muster, and he rode proudly but still self-consciously in his new uniform alongside the one-pony trap, which Father drove. No one had much to say during the short ride uptown to Marion Square. *This is how a man must feel on his way to his execution*, he mused. Though less than a mile, the journey seemed endless as they trotted up Meeting Street. Or rather, Drayton wanted it never to end, wanted to remain trotting endlessly alongside two people he loved, as if suspended in eternity.

He could hear a band playing before he saw Marion Square. In the past year he'd heard enough military marches to last a lifetime. All too soon the high crenellated walls of The Citadel loomed on the skyline, the perfect backdrop for a pageant of martial glory. A company of grey-clad Citadel cadets in black *kepis* was drawn up in ranks to see them off. The rest of the cadet battalion was in Columbia staffing the Camp of Instruction. The Legion's infantry was in the act of assembling to the long roll of the drums. Company first sergeants checked the muster lists and reported to company commanders, "All present!"

Drayton leaned from the saddle to extend his hand for one final gesture of farewell. Celia pressed his hand against her cheek, shyly almost, and handed him a package wrapped in brown paper. "I found these at Concord Street Maritime."

Untying the string, he found a leather case of rich cordovan cowhide. Binoculars! Quickly now; there wasn't much time. He popped open the clasp and withdrew the fine glasses. 'St. Aubin, Genève, Suisse,' was engraved on the brass frame between leather-covered barrels.

He tried to relieve the moment with a joke. "Concord Street Maritime? My love, I'm in the Army, not the Navy."

"The glasses would prove useful in either," she laughed. "But in the event you want to take a sea voyage with me…" She smiled ruefully, and he returned a wistful look.

He would be glad to be sailing on the *Jeanne la Pucelle* right now instead of here. But he was going to keep his good humor and make the best of it, whatever that could mean in the circumstances. War seemed like supreme folly. Yet people were fond of it. It was a perennial feature on history's landscape. Surrounded as he was by martial pomp and pageantry and the cheering crowd, he could understand why. Drayton had just enough time for a lingering grasp of hands. They'd exchanged all the kisses they could at East Battery before setting out. He feared too warm an embrace would make him desert, right in face of the muster.

He drew in a deep breath. "I love you and am loath to leave you with no more time than we've had together." He could barely speak.

"*Noli contendere adversum etiam deos nessicitas*," she said, suddenly tearful. Even the gods do not contend against necessity. "I love you. Go with God and my prayers."

He felt her fingertips slip though his, and the separation was accomplished. Laden with the conflicting emotions all soldiers feel at such times, Drayton's conflict was even greater. His compatriots believed in the war and were willing if not happy to go. He was there not because he wanted to be but because he had to be — unwilling to go, yet unable to stay behind. In a remote corner of his soul where such insight is lodged, he sensed the South was about to wager all, and perhaps lose it all.

With a touch of leg on Beltane, he rode to the cavalry assembly area, saluting smartly as he met his brother, who wore the shoulder straps of a second lieutenant. Cabell Junior was his platoon commander.

"I envy you," said Cabell. "You have someone to say goodbye to."

Drayton tried to smile, but was desolate inside. "It would be easier if I hadn't." But he had to put a good face on things and forced a smile. "I envy you your rank. At last you can give me orders and I have to obey."

"Ha! That'll be something to see."

With a creaking and rumbling, the artillerymen wheeled their guns to the limbers and hitched the trails. The drivers stood expectantly by the trace horses ready to mount. It was time.

Lieutenant Colonel Johnson, second-in-command of the Legion, would convey the Low Country contingents to join the rest of Hampton's men in Columbia. He swung into the saddle of his black Arabian, took out a pocket watch to verify the hour, then closed it with a pop. Riding to the head of the formation as the battalion staff fell in behind him, he sang out, "Company and troop commanders, form your companies!"

The commands "Fall in!" and "Mount" rippled down the line. The cavalry battalion heaved themselves into the saddle in relative unison, while the infantry dressed into line.

Johnson's next order reverberated down the line. "Praaaay-seeent, HARMS!"

Officers' sabers swept up and down, flashing together as blades caught the fire of the morning sun. Company guidons fluttered up sharply, then down, parallel to the parade ground. Four hundred pairs of hands slapped their muskets to the vertical, with 400 legs stepping back in unison. Citadel cadets had been drilling them, and while not quite up to the cadets' standard, it was still a creditable performance. To those untutored in military affairs, it was a stirring spectacle. Men cheered, women wept as the infantry ordered arms, went to the carry, and faced right into column.

"Battaaaaalions! In column of platoons, forwaaaard, march!"

In his oddly high-pitched voice, Calbraith Butler, commanding the cavalry, ordered, "By column of fours, forwaaaard, ho-oh!"

Knees pressed into horses' flanks. With a jingling of curb chains and creaking of leather, the cavalry swung from line into column, with four riders peeling away in sequence and heading at a walk toward Meeting Street. Some of the mounts caught the excitement of their riders and tossed their heads, eager to run. Beltane was forward, too, thinking this was another race. Drayton had to rein him and soothe him with a few words. Other riders did the same, making the movement ragged, but still impressive.

The drummers of the infantry began the rhythmic rattle of the *pas de marche,* while the Washington Light Infantry band struck up a rousing version of 'Bonnie Blue Flag.' Proceeding ahead of the infantry and artillery, the cavalry rode away in the manner of soldiers going off to war from time immemorial. To a man they wanted to look back at the crowd of well-wishers behind in the Square. Discipline and pride held them in check for a moment. They obeyed the stentorian, "Eyes front!" Finally it was too much to bear. Those with loved ones cast back a last lingering glance, a smile, and a wave.

Celia was holding herself tight with both arms across her midsection, as if in pain. At the last moment, before the column passed out of sight, she drew herself up tall and straight and raised her right hand in farewell.

Chapter Nineteen

Columbia, South Carolina; mid-May 1861.

Camps of Instruction had been established in various sites around the state's capital to train the South Carolina regiments that would soon join the Confederate army gathering in Richmond, Virginia, which had replaced Montgomery, Alabama as the new capital of the Confederate States of America. Individual recruits and organized units poured into Columbia from all over the state. Rawboned youths in homespun sauntered into camp clutching the family's precious fowling piece. Languid gentlemen in fine broadcloth arrived on horseback or in carriages, trailing a body servant and more baggage than a single man could handle.

Many of Drayton's comrades were away from home for the first time. Others, like him, had seen a bit of the world. Laughing and skylarking, Drayton's troop de-trained downtown amid a cacophony of sergeants shouting, steam hissing, and horses whinnying. They assembled in a muddy lot near the station after a half hour of mass confusion. The horses and pack mules descended a shaky boxcar ramp, some having to be angrily coaxed out of the dark, cool car and into the scorching chaos. The troopers were ordered to sort their personal kit and load it on the sole wagon. One wagon had broken down back in Charleston, and they jostled and elbowed and to get their possessions aboard, knowing all the gear wouldn't fit into one wagon, and highly reluctant to leave it. Their troop commander Captain Screven posted a guard on the *impedimenta* – his word. It sounded wonderfully military. They were acquiring a whole new vocabulary.

Drayton whispered to his brother, "We may be in uniform, but there's nothing military about this bunch."

Cabell was annoyed. "We'll get the rough edges smoothed off. In the meanwhile, just make sure you take care of yourself," he growled. No one else overheard, and Drayton was grateful not to get a dressing down in public from his own brother. It was the first time Cabell had pulled rank on him, and somehow that drove home the seriousness of the undertaking more than anything else.

The Troop tacked up horses, mounted, and followed their guides to the

Hampton Legion's bivouac east of town, not far from the Colonel's sumptuous estate, Millwood. Local lore said the mansion contained over 3,000 books. Drayton hoped he might get to browse among them in his off-duty time. If there was any.

It was a hot, listless day. Few clouds gave relief from the glaring sun. Hovering over all the camps was a miasma of wood smoke, cooking grease, horse tang, tobacco fumes, and human effluvia. Sweating and tired, the Troop off-saddled, herded the horses into makeshift paddocks, unpacked the mules, and began to erect their squad tents. They were called Sibley tents after their inventor, conical contraptions that reminded Drayton of Indian teepees. Nearby other tent cities mushroomed white and thick in the vacant spaces; their intersecting lanes churned to dust. The next rain would turn it into mud.

In 1860 Columbia's merchants had been lukewarm toward secession, but now found themselves warming to the cause and doing a brisk business, especially the purveyors of food and drink. Another industry, the world's oldest, enjoyed the windfall even more. But the city's clergymen, known statewide for their piety, prevailed upon the city fathers to move these establishments out of the city proper. Regimental chaplains worked overtime exhorting their flock, many away from home for the first time, to avoid the evil snares that were always attendant upon armies, even one as devout as the Confederate Army. But training was long and hard. Few of Drayton's comrades had the extra energy for off-duty pastimes.

If he had to go to war, Drayton counted himself lucky to be in the Hampton Legion.

Colonel Wade Hampton was an imposing man well over six feet tall. He rode a handsome bay stallion, Butler; and sat him easily and gracefully while his gaze took in everything. Though he never got bogged down with pettifoggery, he still mastered the vital details that could spell success or failure of his command. The Colonel was one of the wealthiest men in the South, with huge land- and slave-holdings in South Carolina and Mississippi. His resort property in Cashiers, North Carolina had made the region so popular with fellow South Carolinians that it became known as 'Charleston in the Mountains.' Millwood, his mansion outside of Columbia, boasted one of the finest private libraries anywhere. And his Greek revival home on Meeting Street in Charleston rivaled any in the city. Yet he was easy-going and unassuming, a humane and natural leader, who carried himself with regal dignity yet was approachable by all. When he spoke, his subordinates obeyed smartly, not from fear but from respect.

Hampton was dismissed by some as an amateur, a man with no formal military experience. Drayton heard considerable gossip about the Legion's being a 'family affair,' since his brother Frank commanded the cavalry battalion, and his sons Preston and Wade, Jr. were aides-de-camp. Unhappy as he was at being there, Drayton ignored the comments about 'Hampton's toy soldiers.' The Colonel had paid most of the cost of equipping two battalions of infantry, a battalion of cavalry, and an artillery battery. To be sure, the cavalry troopers owned their horses, and many had bought their own uniforms and equipment, defraying some of the expense to Hampton. But Drayton could only imagine the cost of four Napoleon brass cannon, limbers, horses, and harness for the artillery; 400 rifle-muskets for the infantry, and all the panoply of war that the Colonel paid for from his personal fortune. Quite extraordinary for a man who initially opposed secession and who called the slave traffic 'odious.' The causes of this war were not as simple as some tried to make it.

***

Colonel Hampton usually began the morning with an officers' call and informal briefing on the day's training. Cabell's chest swelled with pride to be in the company of such men, even if he was at the bottom of the commissioned chain-of-command. Cal Butler, Tom Screven, Martin Witherspoon Gary. And he fairly worshipped Wade Hampton, who conducted command lectures as if he'd been doing it all his life. His bushy chestnut beard and neatly trimmed hair reminded Cabell of Franz Hals' 'Laughing Cavalier,' especially the flashing eyes and mobile mouth that could be grim one moment and full of humor the next. He was strong and masterly, as one would expect of a man who hunted bear with nothing more than a sheath knife and rode like Bellerophon.

Hampton had the officers break ranks and crowd around. He would have towered above them in any case, but he stood on a wooden mounting platform to better be seen and heard. There was nothing self-consciously 'military' about the man. He addressed them as a father might address his sons, if he had 40 sons. He wore a waist-length shell jacket rather than the more formal officers' frock coat. Its unadorned grey was plain in comparison to the resplendent uniforms of the Beaufort and Edgefield companies. Cabell smiled to see manure caked on Hampton's boots from inspecting the horse lines. It seemed the Colonel was always inspecting the horse lines and putting the most searching questions to the troopers about equine care.

"We are a legion," Hampton said, pacing and turning in the confined space, "which means we are cavalry, artillery, and infantry. I'm speaking to you cavalry officers first, not because you take precedence, but because you need the most counsel." He grinned. "Being mounted gives you delusions of martial grandeur. Am I correct?"

There were a few nervous chuckles, showing his barb had hit home. "But, Sir, isn't it true that man for man, their cavalry can't match ours?" Tom Screven asked.

"Yes, it's true, for now. But they will field five times more riders than we. Their quantity may trump our quality, especially when they catch us up in horsemanship. And they will over time, under the exigencies of war."

"Sir, besides being better riders, wouldn't you agree we enjoy the advantage of greater skill in marksmanship? Moreover, we're hardier from life out of doors, and born to command," said Martin Gary.

"Born to command?" said Hampton. "Born to command slaves perhaps. But don't deceive yourselves. Leading Southern men in battle is another matter entirely."

Cabell nodded. Slaves had no choice but to obey, or be sold off to the harsh life of the cane fields in Louisiana or Mississippi. But the Southern yeomen of field and forest, poor but proud – they were a totally different proposition.

Hampton seemed to read his thoughts. "Southern soldiers must be led, not driven. Most of them are descendants of the Ulster Scots. They compose nearly three-quarters of our rank-and-file. Scots-Irish are the toughest and bravest, but most ornery and independent-minded people in the world. They are not brute beasts. They are not the off-scouring of debtors' prisons like the British Redcoats our fathers defeated in the Revolution. Indeed, the men we command are the grandsons of those Revolutionary fathers.

"If you haven't already observed, the Confederate soldier is not impressed with lordly airs, elegant uniforms, and lofty manners. You must earn his respect. Don't assume that command authority is issued with your rank. You must *win it* – win it by demonstrating courage and fortitude. Act professionally but not fanatically. Lead rather than drive your men to perform their duties. Use punishment but sparingly. I will have no martinets in the Legion. Fairness will strengthen discipline, for our men will then want to stand together and fight bravely for their officers and for each other. Insofar as possible, do all with good humor. Act in a cheerful manner, especially in adversity. Yet do not try to be the soldier's friend; you are his commander. You may – indeed, you certainly *will* – have to order him and his fellows into the valley of death. When that day comes you must act unhesitatingly and without a hint of favoritism. Those of you with friends, neighbors, and kinsmen in the ranks, pay special heed."

Cabell thought, or imagined, that Hampton's gaze lingered on him as the Legion commander's eyes swept the assembly. "Fortunately for our cause, I believe you're all equal to the task. You are Christian gentlemen. That is... Excuse me, Captain Moise. We do have one gentleman of the Hebrew persuasion among us, and welcome. At any rate, act according to your lights, and all will come out right."

***

"There ain't no animal in this mortal world more trouble than a horse," observed Sergeant Allen MacAllen, a lean, hatchet faced man, brown as shoe leather from a life in the sun and bow-legged from a life in the saddle. Drayton smiled to himself. His newly assigned platoon sergeant concealed a true cavalryman's affection for the animal.

The entire cavalry battalion was assembled on a broad meadow near camp for training in how to turn hunters and pleasure horses into cavalry horses. Colonel Hampton understood that the training of mounts was as essential as the training of soldiers. Perhaps *re*-training would be a better word. The novice cavalryman held the attitude, *My mount needs no instruction. Those others, maybe, but not mine.* Hampton clearly intended to dispel such notions. The battalion, composed of five troops of about 120 men each, had begun training early in the day, but in the South Carolina Midlands so had the sun. In the May heat and humidity, men and horses began to perspire. Soon the air was rank with the tangy smell of horse, human sweat, and wet wool. A fastidious man, Drayton found that the constant odors assailing his sensibilities were the worst thing about the army, aside from being separated from Celia. He could only imagine it would get worse in actual combat.

The Colonel's informal sessions sometimes included entire companies of the Legion, not just the officers. It allowed him to communicate directly with the men and avoided any uncertain 'filtering' through the officers, at least until the Colonel had learned how well his chain-of-command would interpret his guidance. Hampton ordered the horse soldiers to circle 'round. He had to stand up in the stirrups to make sure everyone heard. From time to time he'd turn Butler in a tight circle to make sure everyone was listening.

"Gentlemen," he said in his rich baritone. "I admonish you – do not to think when the shooting starts that you're going to 'rise to the occasion.' When shot and shell are screaming your way, you're going to sink to the level of your training. So then, let us train well. Now.

"You're all fine horsemen. But for a cavalry unit to be effective demands more than good riding. It requires the deepest understanding of the nature of the horse so that it may be employed properly in battle. It is a herd animal, and naturally fearful. Its instinct is to run with the herd. When a horse sees a mass of other horses coming at him, instinct says they're fleeing a threat. It wants to turn and run in the same direction. This makes it hard to stand a charge of the enemy. Superior horsemanship *and* proper training of the mount are the solution. Any questions?"

No one answered. There was only the jingle of tack, the occasional snorting and whinnying of the animals, and the munching of grass. Hampton didn't approve of grazing the animals in their tack, hard as it was to prevent; but this time he said nothing.

He continued. "Now, we are going to war soon, not to a fox hunt. This means your mounts are going to be exposed to something new and frightening — the sound of gunfire, especially artillery. Some may never get used to it and will have to be sent down for draft animals. I'm sure none of you wish to see that. Therefore, training is essential to accustom them to gunfire. I'm not worried about you lot," he grinned. "I'm sure you've all fought scores of duels over a lady, or have faced hostile gunfire from irate husbands as you decamped out the window."

Laughing, they moved off to one end of the field as directed, where a platoon of infantrymen waited to provide the required sound effects, after close inspection to ensure the cartridges contained powder only and no ball. The Beaufort District Troop was ordered to charge them at the trot. Fifty yards out the foot soldiers fired a volley into the air. At the same time the mounted men fired their pistols from the saddle.

The small arms exercise worked well enough. Most of the horses stood it, even those with the bad habit of shying and fleeing threats real or imagined. When they learned the unusual noise inflicted no harm, and feeling confidence flow into them from their riders, the horses soon overcame the instinct to bolt.

Hampton re-assembled the Troop for some added counsel. "When we train, we are sometimes learning more than one thing at a time. Your mounts stood the gunfire well enough, but your charge… Listen well, now. When you charge as a unit – and you will – stay together *as a unit*. By that I mean remain in line abreast to deliver the shock of your charge *en masse*. Some of your mounts are more forward than others. You must restrain the active ones and encourage the laggard ones sufficiently to stay in line. Whether you charge at the trot, at the canter, or full gallop is less important than that you remain together instead of falling upon the enemy in penny packets. Platoon and troop commanders, you must see that your men and mounts keep the pace of the charge. Remember, it is the impact of moral force, not just physical force, that wins the fight."

In the afternoon, they graduated from small arms to artillery fire. Hart's Battery had assembled at the end of the drill field. Drayton was not worried; Bel had always been willing to face anything. But in the event, as the guns bellowed and belched plumes of smoke, he learned that Beltane hated artillery fire. The horse sweated and shook, laid his ears back, and rolled his eyes. At the cannon's second discharge, Bel shied violently, whirling out from under Drayton, who took a tumble. He'd felt it coming the instant before it happened and managed a soft landing. Beltane stood trembling and regarded him wide-eyed. It was a rare event for Drayton to come off, and the horse was embarrassed - whether for himself or for his rider Drayton couldn't say.

Colonels Hampton, Johnson, and Butler watched as he scrambled to his feet and retrieved the bridle, soothing the nervous animal with circular caresses on his neck.

Hampton nodded, smiled a tight smile, and called out the first words he'd spoken directly to Drayton, "Nice landing, son. A horseman's most important skill."

Drayton didn't know whether the Colonel was serious or indulging his legendary wry humor. "Yes, Sir," he said. "It's what I've always believed. I've had a lot of practice."

Hampton rode closer, followed by his curious staff. The Colonel raised his voice high enough for the nearby troopers to hear. "Gentlemen, Private FitzHenry has just demonstrated how to fall properly. And he's a notable rider. If he can come off, the rest of us will, too. Mr. FitzHenry, please tell your compatriots the requisites of a safe fall."

"To be going slow," Drayton replied, without missing a beat.

Hampton laughed in his booming Franz Halsian style. "Yes, of course. But aside from that, how does one fall safely?"

Now serious, Drayton said, "Don't tense up, try to relax, and use your whole body to absorb the shock, instead of a protruding part, like a wrist or elbow."

"Very good," Hampton smiled. "We may not be able to avoid injury from the Yankees when we get there, but we can try to avoid injuring ourselves."

Drayton gathered up the reins, pulled the stirrup close, and prepared to re-mount.

In a lower, personal voice Hampton said, "It's a good thing you didn't come off during that famous match race of yours last year at the Washington course. I understand the stakes were high," he grinned.

"Yes, Sir, the highest imaginable."

"Well, I'm granting you twenty-four hours leave for the fine tutorial on how to take a fall. Sergeant Moore?"

James Moore, the Orderly Sergeant, spurred forward and handed Drayton a slip of paper, a printed leave form filled out with his name. Obviously planned before this unexpected incident.

Hampton explained, "Your prize is in Columbia, at Mrs. McCord's house."

Drayton was overjoyed, but instead of blurting thanks he could barely manage a surprised croak. "She's here in Columbia! And I have only twenty-four hours?" He felt the core of resentment flare up inside.

Hampton's eyes twinkled. With obvious sympathy, he said, 'I'm sorry, son. That's all the time there is. The Legion is moving to Virginia day after tomorrow."

***

Drayton trotted into Columbia westward along the Sumter road. As Beltane climbed the hill leading to the town center, Drayton tried to recall everything he could about the remarkable Louisa Cheves McCord. She was a contemporary and friend of Cabell Senior, who'd arranged Celia's visit. How like Father, thought Drayton – kind and thinking of others behind his pose of severity.

Louisa McCord was the daughter of Langdon Cheves, in his day one of America's most prominent public men. A leading lawyer in Charleston, Cheves had risen from humble beginnings and had befriended Drayton's grandfather Thomas when he arrived from Ireland in 1801. Cheves served as Speaker in the U.S. House of Representatives with John C. Calhoun and the 'War Hawks' who insisted on fighting Great Britain in 1812. He made Thomas FitzHenry his protégé, largely on the strength of Thomas' credentials as an Irish revolutionary. A self-made man himself, Cheves showed sympathy for the talented young refugee who was determined to rise in his new country. President Monroe appointed Cheves to head the 2nd National Bank of the United States, but he soon came to disapprove of a central national bank and returned to Charleston in 1829 to practice law. He was an early leader for secession and a mentor to Thomas FitzHenry's son Cabell Senior, helping him win his seat in Congress.

Louisa was the widow of the late Dr. James McCord of Columbia, and was known for her intellect and literary achievements – and for her passionate commitment to Southern independence. Clever of Father, Drayton thought, to lodge Celia with her. She lived on Pendleton Street across from South Carolina College in a simple but dignified two-storey Greek Revival 'cottage' enclosed by a wrought iron fence. The front of the house had a double portico with the top portion enclosed by a wooden railing to make a balcony overlooking the street.

As Drayton dismounted in front of the gate, Celia leaned over the upstairs railing and sang out, "I'm up here, my Love, with Mrs. McCord."

Louisa joined her guest and called down, "Welcome, Drayton. I'll send Cadmus down to stable your mount. Come right on up."

Drayton loped up the center stair, his sabre rattling against the wainscoting, and embraced Celia as she stepped into the hallway from the balcony. She laughed with delight and finally had to disengage from his bear hug. Taking his hand, she led him onto the balcony, where Mrs. McCord stood and held out her hand. Drayton bowed and kissed it in the old formal manner. She ushered him to a seat and poured lemonade.

"Iced lemonade!" he crowed. "You can't imagine how welcome this is after all the dust and powder smoke I've been ingesting."

Mrs. McCord was a handsome woman – he wouldn't call her beautiful – whose austerity was offset by a pair of twinkling eyes and merry disposition. It seemed that she and Celia had formed a bond already. The three chatted about old times and mutual relations. Drayton learned that Louisa's son was a Confederate officer already in Virginia. She was engaged in turning South Carolina College across the street into a military hospital, since all but a few students and many of the faculty had enlisted, and classes were suspended for the duration.

"Your brother Cabell Junior paid me a call recently," she said. "But I haven't seen you since you were a baby. How good it is to have you. I need only to meet that scamp Ransome to complete the set. And I'm especially happy to have this wonderful new bride of yours."

They spent the afternoon in animated conversation until the supper hour, when they repaired to the first-floor dining room. Louisa's charming daughters joined them for supper, and by the tone and tenor of the questions put to him, it was clear that younger brother Ransome was an object of romantic interest. But as the evening wore on, fatigue caught up with Drayton. He tried but failed to stifle a yawn. Ever the attentive hostess, Mrs. McCord declared the banquet at an end after coffee and strawberries with cream. Cadmus lit the lamps. Louisa took one and escorted Drayton and Celia to the guest bedroom, also on the first floor, in the rear of the house. She kissed them both on the cheek and bid them goodnight, wishing them a good rest. He felt like one of her family.

Drayton said, "First Father, and now Mrs. McCord. You seem to win the hearts of all you meet. Beginning with mine, of course," he added with a lascivious grin.

Closing the door softly and turning the latch, Celia studied him from lowered eyes. "Rest, the lady said. But just how tired are you?"

Drayton blushed as red as a cooked crab, but he said it anyway, and she smiled broadly in agreement. "I have only twelve more hours and it will go by in a flash. I suggest we not waste another moment."

***

Sated, warm, and languid, they lay in each other's arms. Drayton murmured, "We are too happy. We are not of this world. The gods envy such happiness in humans and seek to destroy it."

"Husband, you *are* a pagan!" She twisted toward him, laughing. But Drayton could hear a serious undertone. He realized he hadn't fully come to grips with her religion. It was authentic, not a mere social habit. He thought again of his promise, her way of sealing him into her own faith. "The one true God wants us to be happy," she said.

Drayton matched her light tone, but with a sub-stratum of his own. "Perhaps. But He demands self-sacrifice and self-abnegation. I want none of such a God. I'm greedy for you. I want to surfeit myself upon you. Yet I know that to do so courts disaster from the envy... well, if not envy from the gods, from some baleful principle by which the Cosmos operates to deny us our wishes and plunge us into misery."

"Nonsense. God is the principle by which the Cosmos operates. He loves us and only seeks our good, moral and material."

"That's the Book answer. But doesn't the Book say He is a jealous God and that none else must come before Him?"

"Yes, but—"

"Well, write me off as a contumacious sinner, for I put you before Him. I put *us* before Him. And anyway, this is hardly the time and place for a theological discussion. I have more important business in mind." He reached for her again, kissing her deeply. He felt her breath quicken under his roving hands. She stirred and rose to meet him, matching his passion with her own. Then they slept.

Military routine had given him the ability to rouse himself more or less at the appointed time. She was still sleeping soundly when he awoke, eased from the bed and dressed. A filament of dawn crept in at the window, and he watched her breast rise and fall softly. He pulled on his uniform quietly. He feared if she awoke and held him, he might not summon the will to go back. That would bring the Provost Marshal and disgrace down on him, his hostess, and his family. But he'd imbibed enough of a flicker of her faith to be grateful for the brief time they'd stolen from the exigencies of war. He offered up an unaccustomed prayer of thanks for such an extraordinary woman.

Thinking the Lord must be something like a powerful earthly politician who could be bargained with, he added, "I've not forgotten my pledge to her, Lord. I'll do my best to keep it, and I ask you to bring me home safe to her."

He stretched his hand out to caress her cheek, but withdrew it suddenly, fearing to disturb her sleep. Holding his pistol belt and scabbard close to keep them from clanking, and with one more longing look, he slipped silently out of the room.

Chapter Twenty

Northern Virginia; June 1861.

Do men make history, or does history make men? It was the topic Cabell had argued with Drayton the evening before they entrained for Virginia. "We're about to find out," Cabell had promised.

Just getting to the war was an ordeal in itself, a long, hot, uncomfortable train ride with many stops to change engines or water the boilers, take on fuel, and to water and feed the precious horses. At every opportunity Cabell led the way back to the horse car to soothe his Jolly and Beltane. The animals managed to arrive in Manchester, just across the James River from Richmond, Virginia, in good condition. They de-trained to the accompaniment of a military band playing 'The Bonnie Blue Flag.'

Not every horse arrived in good condition, and it was disaster for a cavalryman to lose his mount. Anyone cast afoot permanently was sent down to the infantry. It seemed odd to Cabell that horses were not assigned to the cavalry by the Confederate government, but were privately owned and had to be privately replaced when lost, another example of the idiosyncratic nature of the Southern army. Later the cavalrymen would joke about their debt of gratitude to their main commissary, the Union Army. As the War wore on, the Southerners discovered Yankees weren't the best riders, but they had the best tack and equipment and could usually be counted on to supply fine remounts as spoils of war.

The Legion went into bivouac at the old Ashland race track, which had first been built to tend a large number of horses. Thrown together with men he'd never have known in his pre-War life, Cabell was intrigued by the collection of new associates. The most engaging was his platoon sergeant Allen MacAllen, who had served in the old U.S. Army. One of the few in the troop with prior military experience, he knew as much as anyone about handling horses and far more about weapons and cavalry tactics.

At evening mess the troop could finally relax, enjoy a cheroot and a cup of coffee, which was already growing scarce. Cabell stretched out on his saddle blanket and sipped the scalding, invigorating brew. Sergeant MacAllen lounged nearby and lit up a cigar. The rest of his platoon sat in a loose circle, chatting and smoking.

As their officer, Cabell normally maintained some distance, but the Sergeant was a fascinating study. Cabell needed to get to know him better in any case. MacAllen was one of those Southerners — a common type, in fact — who affected the self-effacing, down-home simplicity of the rural yeoman. But the pose concealed a quickness and sharpness otherwise unsuspected.

"Sergeant, how did you end up in Beaufort District?"

"Well, Lieutenant, I wanted to try some of that famous seafood y'all are always bragging about."

"What I meant was, why are you fighting? Why did you volunteer?"

With a sly look, as if to avoid the sentimentality of a patriotic motive, MacAllen said, "My wife, she was a real hellion. Always throwing the crockery at me. I figgered I'd be safer here in the war."

Drayton was reclining nearby, cleaning tack. He looked up and said, "Then you're not fighting to preserve slavery?"

"Preserve slavery! Like hell! I don't own no slaves. Never have, never will. I'd like to free 'em all."

"I see," said Cabell, bemused. "Then what?"

"Give 'em a free one-way train ticket north. Let the Yankees take care of 'em."

"Well, in that case, what *are* you fighting for?" Drayton asked.

"I remind you, we ain't done no fighting yet. But mainly I'm going to fight because we been invaded. I don't rightly care for threats. I don't like folks coming down here with their superior airs and telling me how I ought to live. And if I refuse, why then, in their minds I deserve to be shot, and all my livestock taken, my farm burned, and my family turned out to starve. Who wouldn't fight in such a pass?"

"I suppose most of our men feel the same," said Cabell.

"Yes. But it ain't that simple. There's ... there's something else."

"There's what?"

"Well, it's the excitement and all. Down deep, I suppose I just like to fight."

"Good," said Cabell. "I'll be counting on it."

July 1861, Northern Virginia.

Cabell was sorry the troop missed the first major battle, Manassas. They'd been detached for picket duty on the flanks of the army assembled under their old friend from Charleston, General P.G.T. Beauregard. If Cabell was disappointed, Drayton appeared relieved, and that annoyed him.

The day after the battle Cabell called him out during horse inspection. When the troop had stood down he put on his gruff voice, half big bother and half platoon commander.

"You seem unusually cheerful this morning. I suppose it's because you missed the fighting." He didn't want to call Drayton a coward outright, just shame him into greater enthusiasm for the cause.

"Sir," said Drayton, with sarcastic emphasis on 'sir,' "I just go where they tell me. Anyway, I suspect we'll get our turn soon enough."

Cabell glared at him, then turned away

The same day came the shocking news that their own Lt. Col. Johnson, Wade Hampton's second-in-command, had been killed by a Yankee shell from the far side of Bull Run. He'd joined the cavalry's counter-attack by a Virginian named Jeb Stuart that added to the rout of the Yankees from the battlefield. The next day they were further shocked to learn that General Barnard Bee of Charleston had died of wounds, but not before conferring an immortal sobriquet upon an officer who would be heard from again and again, General 'Stonewall' Jackson.

The Legion's cavalry battalion went into camp along the Occoquan River, a rough demarcation between Union and Confederate territory. There they patrolled and scouted and suffered the usual tedium of camp and fatigue duty. Combat was episodic and small in scope – squad or platoon level encounters, which they always won. These skirmishes offered just enough danger and excitement to break the tedium. They even lost men occasionally. But the main benefit was the captured supplies and mounts, which the Yankees had in abundance.

For every hour spent in the saddle, the cavalry soldier spent about four hours in horse care. Equine diseases were common and had to be treated with means that were usually inadequate. Injuries to the mounts, including combat wounds, were equally common. Horses were complex living organisms, not mechanisms like a steam engine or threshing machine that could be satisfied with a shovel-load of coal and a squirt of oil. Fresh oats, hay and fodder, and especially clean water were never-ending requirements. Since water was heavy to haul, units camped whenever possible near a stream or pond. Hoof care was especially critical for a thousand–pound animal suspended on such delicate structures as the equine leg and foot. Horseshoes would come loose in sucking mud or when the hoof outgrew them, and new shoes weren't always available. The troopers rode their mounts barefoot as long as they were operating on soft ground. But on stony soil bare hooves could crack or cause the animal to founder. Bare or shod, hooves had to be kept trimmed.

Cabell was a quick study and reveled in his post. Though he had no background in military matters, he'd devoured *Hardee's Tactics* and St. Leger's *Cavalryman's Manual*, and his lawyer's memory served him well. He had to learn the art and the science of war, how to act in concert without confusion; how to hit the enemy at the right place and at the right time with all his force. He was not as good a horseman as Drayton, but good enough to lead them. Much of what he learned to fulfill his office he learned on the job. That was true of them all. But he continued to worry about Drayton. His brother kept Bel fit and healthy. He was never insolent and never shirked his duties, but he continued to mope about in camp.

What is the true nature of my worry? Cabell asked himself as if he were on the witness stand. *Am I concerned that he will let down the side in some major way when it counts? No, not likely. Then is it simply that he doesn't defer to me sufficiently, that he embarrasses me?*

Cabell wouldn't care to say the War had been a disappointment so far, but neither was it what he'd expected. Missing First Manassas meant he'd seen no massed charges with guidons snapping in the wind. Their assignment was reconnaissance and patrolling the flanks and front of the army. By the end of 1861 the war had become the pursuit of the mundane. His primary task as a leader had little to do with fighting but taking care of men and mounts. Their daily mission was scavenging enough to eat between irregular issue of rations, and scrounging another blanket or flannel underwear against the unaccustomed Virginia winter. He'd begun to enjoy his dram, eagerly awaiting the CSA whiskey ration or box from home with Maum Biddy's 'bounce,' a cordial made from corn liquor infused with sweet blackberries.

Their operational sector was in southern Fairfax and Prince William Counties, not far from where the Occoquon River flowed into Chesapeake Bay. The Bay brought cold winds with the smell of salt marsh, something these men from the Beaufort District were used to, if not the chill. One day Drayton came with a suggestion. Most of them had been raised on the South Carolina coast. And coast was coast. Why not send fatigues down to the Bay to fish, clam, and harvest oysters, something they'd grown up doing? An old-fashioned Low Country fish fry and oyster roast would be excellent for morale.

Cabell tried not to condescend from his position of rank. He wished he'd thought of it. "A splendid idea. I'm glad you're finally taking an interest in things."

"I always take an interest in eating when I'm hungry."

Cabell stiffened. "Brother, I'd hoped you would come around. But I see you're still wearing your arse on your shoulders. So tell me, Mr. Military Historian, if you're so dissatisfied with our mission, and I suppose that includes the leaders appointed over you; what would you do differently?"

"What difference does it make what I think?"

"I know you're here only from family loyalty. But I was hoping by now you had become more reconciled to serving," said Cabell, trying but failing to show more understanding.

"You mean, reconciled to leaving behind a wife whom I adore? Reconciled to the folly and madness of the War?"

"Yes, that's precisely what I mean."

"In your mind then it's better to be mad with everyone else than sane alone?" said Drayton.

Cabell laughed, breaking the tension. It was hard to stay angry with him. "Yes, I suppose that's what I mean. But look. Do you think you're the only one with a wife you adore? That you're the only one inconvenienced by this conflict?"

Abashed, Drayton hung his head. "I suppose I have been feeling sorry for myself. But see here, Brother, I'm no Thersites."

"Who?"

"Thersites from the *Iliad*. He was legendary for being the Greeks' worst soldier, always grumbling, questioning and even abusing his officers. Odysseus finally had to thrash him publicly."

"No, I suppose you're not that bad. So I ask you, what do you think of the War? How do you think we're doing?"

"It's my first war. I have no other experience with which to compare it."

"But you must have some idea. We've won every fight."

"Yes, but I don't have a strategic perspective. Like most private soldiers, all I see is what's in front of me, plus a few yards on either side. Anyway, one can win battles and still lose a war."

"You're more dyspeptic than ever," Cabell fumed. "And here I thought we were enjoying a grand new adventure."

"All right, then," said Drayton, collecting himself. "It has its good moments — the comradeship, mainly. It's long stretches of boredom relieved by intervals of terror. But mostly it reminds me of a menial job in a stable. Once in a while they throw in a horse race and pistol duel to break the tedium. I don't know if I'm doing it right, or if *we're* doing it right, nor can I say with confidence that our battle operations are wise or foolish. Fortunately, as a private, all I have to do is show up and obey orders, and hope my superiors know what they're doing."

"Well, don't take too much refuge in your lowly position. In the cavalry we often operate independently, alone or in two's and three's. Every man is expected to be his own officer, to use his initiative."

When his brother remained stubbornly silent, a burning annoyance welled up from Cabell's mid-section. He had never pulled rank on his brother, but now he'd reached his limit of frustration. "Trooper FitzHenry, this war is not a private matter, and you're not entitled to your private feelings. So get yourself sorted out. The sooner we all do what we must, the sooner we win and can all go home." Still scowling, he stalked away, feeling a dumbstruck Drayton staring a hole in his back.

***

In charge of the day's scout, Cabell ordered Drayton and Calhoun Sparks to patrol the area near Pohick Church, where George Washington had worshipped. The Troop maintained a nocturnal watch on Yankee activity in the area. The next morning Drayton rode into camp leading Sparks' mount, his comrade draped lifeless over the saddle.

Sparks was the first fatality in Cabell's platoon. He took the reins from Drayton's hands while several troopers lifted the body tenderly and laid it on the ground. His brother's face was a mask of anguish. Cabell had known sooner or later he was going to lose a man. He tried to remain calm and business-like.

"Well, Brother. I'm glad to see you safe. Tell me what happened."

Drayton dismounted stiffly, and Junius led both mounts away to be fed and watered.

"We were in a line of trees, dismounted to rest the horses, when an entire platoon of Yankees galloped up from behind. They'd been hiding nearby, keeping watch on us keeping watch on them. We sprang into the saddle and skedaddled, but they'd had the chance to get close. They opened fire, but didn't hit us – or so I thought. We turned a corner on one of your favorite trails at a gallop. Out of sight for an instant, we reined hard left into the woods, just like you rehearsed us, and jumped off behind a laurel thicket. We took the horses down and lay across their backs, ready to pop up mounted if we had to. I could hear the Yankees beating the brush a ways off and hallooing to each other. Finally they gave up and went home, or to Hell, or wherever they came from. We waited a long while to make sure they were really gone, and then I said to Calhoun it was time to show a clean pair of heels. He never answered. When I felt for him in the dark, I came across the bloody wound in his lower back. He was dead."

Cabell laid a consoling hand on Drayton's shoulder. "You did well. You did exactly the right thing. I'm truly sorry about Calhoun. It's the fortunes of war."

Drayton stared at Sparks remains as if he hadn't heard. Cabell knew his brother. He asked, "Is there more?"

"Look at his left hand," said Drayton.

Cabell knelt and took the hand in his own. The body was already stiff. The first two fingers of Calhoun's hand were bloody; white bone showed beneath the gashes. Cabell turned and looked at Drayton, puzzled.

"He was wounded, not killed outright," said Drayton. "He must have been in agony when we hid. He was single, but knew I was married. We couldn't be sure the Yankees would take us alive if they stumbled on us. You can see he bit down on his hand to keep from crying out in pain and giving us away. His teeth were clenched tight on his fingers when he died."

From that day on, Cabell had no more trouble with his brother.

White Oak Swamp on the Chickahominy River, Virginia; May 1862.

Union General McClellan had landed with his grand Army of the Potomac on the peninsula between the James and York Rivers. He had 110,000 men, an invulnerable supply base behind him at Hampton Roads, secure flanks resting on the two rivers, and naval gunfire support on both sides from the rivers. He would approach Richmond from the southeast, sweep aside the outnumbered and outgunned Confederates, occupy the Southern capital, and impose a peace. With such resources how could he fail?

Confederate General Joseph Johnston assembled his scattered army to meet the Federals. Despite all his advantages, McClellan moved slowly, bogged down in the swampy terrain. He paused frequently for his engineers, which the Yankees also had in abundance, to bridge streams and 'corduroy' the muddy roads, laying sections of timber across the boggy sections to create a trafficable surface. Occasionally his ponderous advance was interrupted by slashing Confederate attacks, but seemingly with no more effect than the attacks of the Chickahominy mosquitoes that swarmed the area. Annoying in the extreme, but not decisive. By May the Yankees were within six miles of Richmond. Johnston threw every man and gun into an attack at Fair Oaks. The only significant outcome was the wounding of General Johnston by a Union shell. He had to be relieved of command.

After Sunday services, Drayton was grooming Beltane, preparing for vedette duty while chatting with Sergeant MacAllen. Instead of attending Church Call the Sergeant had remained in camp. Soon after worship the black-bearded, black-eyed Manning Brown, the Regimental chaplain, came stalking through the bivouac to hunt down truants who neglected the state of their souls. He spied the Sergeant lounging on his saddle contentedly smoking a cheroot.

"Sergeant MacAllen, I'm afraid I won't be seeing you in Heaven."

Standing respectfully but retaining his cigar, MacAllen replied, "I'm sorry to hear it, Reverend. Just what have you been up to?"

Drayton chuckled as he brushed down Beltane. The Chaplain stumped off. The Reverend Brown was no drawing room pastor, but as tough as any Confederate trooper and just as determined to bring them the Word of God.

"Sergeant, I see you skipped Church Call," said Drayton. "You're not a pagan, are you?

"Not exactly. I'm a Baptist." He finished the cheroot and cast the stub into the fire pit.

Drayton paused, searching for an appropriate reply.

"You know what a Baptist is, don't you?" said MacAllen.

Drayton wasn't certain if he was serious or in jest. He suspected the latter. When he hesitated, MacAllen answered his own question. "A Baptist is someone who you know is doing it but you can't never catch him."

Drayton laughed heartily. "Sounds a lot like an Episcopalian."

"How's that?"

"Well, it's like this. You Baptists go in for good feelings; the Methodists good works, the Presbyterians good doctrine. And we Episcopalians... well, we're for good taste."

"Like the good taste to never get caught?"

"Exactly," said Drayton, laughing again.

"Then I'm right glad we discovered this spiritual bond between us. Speaking of spirits, have a pull. But only one. You're for the duty." MacAllen produced a flat bottle from his saddlebags.

Drayton took a swig and said, "I'm glad I could bring you over to the 'Whiskey-palians,' since I understand the Baptists disapprove of strong drink."

"We disapprove only on Sundays."

"Sergeant," said Drayton. "You must have been in a music hall or on the stage. Just how'd you end up in the South Carolina cavalry?"

"Oddly enough, by way of the United States cavalry." The Sergeant got up and inspected Bel's hooves while Drayton continued to curry him. "I served a stint out in west Texas, fighting Comanches and Mexican bandits with the 2nd U.S. Cavalry. That was real cavalry work, not like this play actin'. Guess they figured I had enough gen-u-wine service to be a sergeant in this mob."

"The old 2nd U.S. Cavalry. Say, wasn't General Lee in command of that regiment for a time? Of course, he wasn't a general then, only a colonel."

"Yes, he was. I served under him two years."

"Old Granny Lee." Drayton thoughtlessly repeated words from a hometown newspaper, the *Charleston Mercury*. The paper had printed a stinging rebuke of Robert. E. Lee after the failure of his first command, the campaign in Western Virginia, which left the pro-Union section of Virginia firmly in Federal hands. "The King of Spades," he added. The term referred to Lee's penchant for digging entrenchments, a task that white Southerners felt was beneath them.

"Now, Fitz," said the Sergeant. His jocular manner evaporated instantly. "I guess you don't know better, so I'll let that pass. But let me tell you, there ain't no finer man nor finer officer in either army, Yankee or Confederate. We're lucky he was given command. If the South has any chance to win this war, it'll be because of Robert Lee."

"I have heard he's a fine judge of horses and a graceful rider," said Drayton, backtracking to pacify the sergeant.

"Yep. And he's got a grey horse. Looks a lot like yours, matter of fact," said MacAllen, walking around the animal in close inspection. "You might get to see him one a these days."

"I don't reckon a mere private of cavalry is ever likely to have any dealings with the General Commanding," said Drayton. "Still, it's nice to know we have a horseman in charge."

Chapter Twenty One

Replacing the wounded Joseph Johnston, Robert E. Lee assumed command of the renamed Confederate army on the Peninsula between the York and the James Rivers, now the Army of Northern Virginia. In a series of fights known as the Seven Days Battles, the aggressive Lee drove away McClellan's vastly larger force by maneuver when possible and determined attacks when necessary. But the Confederates, now with the initiative, still had to learn in the hard school of trial and error. Coordination and communications remained spotty. Even the celebrated Stonewall Jackson, fresh from his stunning victories in the Shenandoah Valley, failed to arrive in time and turn the Yankee's exposed flank at White Oak Swamp. It was partly the Peninsula itself. In summer it was a God-awful place to do battle, with bogs and impassable roads, if you could call them roads, with glutinous mud that clung to human feet, equine feet, and wheels of the guns and wagons. Both armies battled incessant rain and swarms of mosquitoes as well as each other, often losing their way in the tangled and flooded thickets. War seldom chose congenial terrain in which to enact itself.

At a slight rise in the low-lying terrain called Malvern Hill, bad luck and poor coordination sent Confederates, including a South Carolina brigade, into deadly frontal assaults against massed Union batteries. From afar Drayton sat his horse with the Legion cavalry, hearing for the first time the eerie Rebel yell, like pagan war keening from an ancient time, a ululating wave as one regiment raised the high shrill cry and passed it on to the next. It was chilling, but it had no effect on the enemy's artillery. He watched horrified and helpless as the wheel-to-wheel batteries cut down attacking Confederates by the score. Cal Butler was chafing to attack in support of his fellow South Carolinians, but was ordered to await a breakthrough for the cavalry to exploit, in classic Napoleonic style. No breakthrough came, only broken Confederate dead at the muzzles of the skillfully-served Yankee cannon. Drayton sighed in relief that the order to charge was never issued.

Lee's re-organization divided the Army into two corps for more operational flexibility, the First under Lt. General James Longstreet, and the Second, under Lt. General Thomas J. 'Stonewall' Jackson. The Hampton Legion was broken up, its infantry and artillery battalions assigned to various brigades of Longstreet's First Corps. The mounted units were organized into an all-cavalry division under the command of Maj. General 'Jeb' Stuart of Virginia. Their beloved Wade Hampton would now be just another brigade commander, along with two other brigadiers from Virginia. Cabell and most of his fellow Carolinians were unhappy about the new arrangement. They had been serving with relatives and neighbors. Indeed, the Legion was more like an extended family than a military organization, operating as much by persuasion as discipline. Moreover, they enjoyed the Legion's identity as an elite South Carolina unit. Pride of place would now be submerged in regiments and brigades drawn from all over the South.

It also subordinated them to the Virginians who were ascendant in the new army organization. A rivalry sprang up, friendly for the most part, between the cavalrymen from Virginia and South Carolina. To the Carolinians, the Virginians acted as if they were the Army's sole horsemen. Cabell and his people chafed at what they regarded as a condescending attitude. But Stuart was a gifted leader of cavalry, and military necessity must take precedence over parochial concerns. Theirs not to reason why, thought Cabell, as he read the orders creating the 2nd Regiment, South Carolina Cavalry, from the old mounted battalions of the Hampton Legion. The former Beaufort District Troop was now 'C' Troop.

As a 'graduation gift' they were issued picket pins, which vastly simplified the problem of tethering horses when they were on a scout or raid and there was nothing to tie to. They often hobbled the animal in those circumstances. But hobbling could cause a horse to pull a tendon and was time-consuming to undo – a possibly fatal liability in the event of a surprise attack. Picket pins were three-foot iron rods sharpened on one end to be driven into the ground, with an eyelet at the other end for clipping or tying the lead shank. They could be deployed and recovered in a hurry. The troops thought they were a brilliant cavalry innovation, well worth the extra weight.

Cabell had become adept at hit-and-run tactics, the sudden slashing ambush, the pre-dawn raid behind enemy lines. And he'd been lucky – no wounds or debilitating illness. There was the moment when he'd thought he was a goner at Bristow Station, lying stunned on the ground with a broken saddle girth, the Yankees in pursuit and Drayton running away. For an instant he'd thought it was because of the argument they'd been having about the war. But his surge of fury had turned to gratitude when he realized Drayton was galloping to catch Jolly and bring him back for Cabell's escape, and under a hot fire from the enemy. It rankled, though, that Drayton later got all the praise for the feat instead of Cabell for leading a successful raid.

In any event, through operations like the one at Bristow, they'd become well-seasoned and confident. Once re-organized, they were to embark on more aggressive missions under the most offensive-minded commanders in military history, Lee and Stuart. But they had to do more with less. The Regiment was down to sixty per cent of its original strength. Death in battle, wounds, and above all – disease – had carried off the rest. And remounts remained in short supply. The leadership burden of keeping his men and horses healthy was as great as Cabell's combat role.

There was little he could do to reduce the odds of dying in combat. But illness was something he could control, to a degree. Cabell was determined to reduce the number crying off sick through the guidance of the Regimental surgeons, Doctors Taylor and Moore. Dr. Henry Moore he had known as a neighbor in Gillisonville. Though a graduate of Dartmouth Medical College, Moore had enlisted with his brother James as an ordinary soldier. 'Gentleman rankers,' such well-born privates were called. James Moore, or 'Jimsie,' was now a lieutenant and Regimental adjutant. But Henry's medical training was going to waste until he applied for transfer to the medical corps, and was appointed assistant surgeon of the Regiment with the rank of captain.

Quietly Dr. Moore went about imposing a new health regime. He began by making the troops wash hands after answering nature's call, after handling the horses, and especially before eating. Mess tins were to be washed in hot water whenever possible. Moore confessed he couldn't explain why, but he'd observed that clean hands and clean mess gear kept soldiers healthier. Dr. Moore maintained a cauldron of steaming water and lye soap in camp, and he constantly badgered officers and men to use them. As a result, the 2nd South Carolina Cavalry had a lower rate of dysentery than any other regiment; not a trivial accomplishment in an army which lost more men to sickness than to battle.

Thanks to better health practices, thanks to their battle-hardening, and thanks to a steady stream of captured supplies, the Regiment was in the best condition since its arrival in Virginia in July 1861. And with Stuart in command, it was time to show the world what Southern cavalry could do.

First was Stuart's astonishing ride around the entire Union army, taking the strategic concept of the deep raid to an extent heretofore unimagined. He employed half the Division, leaving only enough cavalry behind with Lee for essential screening and scouting duties. The operation was bold and risky and grueling for men and mounts, since no one rested for more than a few hours during the entire 48-hour mission. The troopers joked that they were commanded by 'General Consternation' because of the effect the raid created among the Yankees. The war booty, boost to morale, and intelligence on the enemy was immeasurable, and they returned feeling more proud of themselves than ever.

Then came Lee's equally bold strike at Manassas, where the war's first major battle had occurred in July 1861. With McClellan driven away from Richmond and back on his base, the Union threat shifted to a second Union army in northern Virginia under General John Pope. He was known for his pomposity and braggadocio, issuing orders from his 'Headquarters in the Saddle.' Southerners remarked afterwards that stunning defeat was foreordained for a Yankee general that didn't know his headquarters from his hindquarters.

Chapter Twenty Two

In camp along the Rappahannock, Virginia, June 9, 1863.

Chancellorsville was the most dramatic Southern victory in the War, but it exacted a high price which the Confederacy could ill afford. And Lee had lost his most trusted and able lieutenant, Stonewall Jackson. Despite the losses, the South was at a peak of confidence in Lee and his Invincibles; the North dispirited and reeling. Once again Lee had seized the initiative, and every man in the army knew Marse Robert was one to strike while he held the advantage. The troops went into camp near Culpeper, along the natural defense line of the Rapidan and Rappahannock Rivers, to refit, re-organize, and prepare for the anticipated move north. But the enemy still had a formidable force on the 'Yankee side' of the rivers. This could not go on much longer.

In June the 2nd Cavalry was encamped a few miles northwest of the Rappahannock River, which marked the informal boundary between the Union Army of the Potomac and Lee's Army of Northern Virginia. The Regiment had bivouacked in an arc below Brandy Station, a major junction on the Orange and Alexandria Railroad. Drayton's platoon of 'C' Troop had been designated the Regiment's ready platoon for the morning of June 9. Their orders were to stand-to at first light with horses bridled and saddled, with bits slipped and girths loosened but ready to tighten and mount in a moment if needed.

They might have to deal with a few probing Federal patrols, but expected no major action. The entire mounted division of Lee's army was camped in the same vicinity – the finest horse soldiers and horse artillery the world had ever seen, under an equally fine commander, General Jeb Stuart. In every cavalry fight to date the Southerners had prevailed, though usually outnumbered. The Yankees wouldn't dare attempt anything without a three-to-one advantage. Stuart's scouts were certain the enemy didn't have a mounted force of that size in the vicinity.

Reclining around the campfire, Drayton and his messmates drank 'Confederate coffee,' a vile concoction brewed from roasted corn and hickory nuts. Its only virtue was that it was served hot. Junius fried side meat and johnny cakes for breakfast, and the men chatted gaily. Other than the lack of real coffee, the main topic of conversation was the Army's impending move north into Maryland and possibly even into Pennsylvania, after Lee's stunning victory at Chancellorsville.

They also relived the grand review of the Division General Stuart had held the day before for General Lee. Ordered to turn out in their best and finest, 12,000 Confederate horse troopers and mobile batteries had assembled on the broad plain east of Brandy Station, forming into line abreast that stretched over a mile from end to end. Officers and men cheered wildly as Stuart and Lee cantered along their ranks in review, hats raised in salute. To behold the finest cavalry in the world assembled in one place was the most stirring spectacle he'd ever seen. For the first time in the War, Drayton had actually enjoyed himself. For the first time in the War he felt a sense of impending victory. Though the individual soldier revealed a touch of the worn and shabby from hard service, as a mass they were resplendent. And these were no grim, tight-lipped men. They were bright-eyed, smiling at Stuart and cheering General Lee, who waved his hat, smiling in return, dignified yet affectionate, like a father. No enemy could stand against such men and leaders as these.

But today reality poked its soiled fingers through the curtain of pageantry. The odor of war bothered Drayton in particular, though veiled for a moment by the aroma of sizzling pork. He took great pains to stay clean and had brushed his uniform thoroughly for the review. Still, he was sweaty and rank beneath the grey wool in the June heat. The thing he hated most about army life was always feeling dirty. Water in camp was too precious for the luxury of bathing, although in summer one might find a pond or stream to bathe in. He smelled and he knew it. His comrades smelled and they knew it. Though they dismissed it with good humor, the air of camp was always sharp with the pungency of human sweat and soggy wool.

With virtually every Southern cavalryman in the area, there was little chance of an emergency requiring the ready troop, and Drayton toyed with the idea of riding down to the river to have a wash. Cabell was attending a conference with Colonel Butler and the other captains. He had left Sergeant MacAllen in charge of the ready troop, though it was more of a platoon than a full troop.

"Sergeant, it's been too long since I bathed," said Drayton. "I smell so bad Beltane won't let me come near him. With your permission I thought I'd pop down to the river and get clean."

"Now, Drayton, you know I cain't let you do that. We're the designated ready troop this morning. Do you know what that means?"

"That we have to be … ah, ready?"

"I can see yore military education is coming right along."

"But ready for what?"

"Ready for whatever we need to be ready for," said MacAllen.

Drayton laughed. "I can't argue with logic like that. But we've got the whole cavalry division here in bivouac. Surely nothing's likely to happen."

"Most likely not," said the Sergeant. "But it's just when you start thinking that way that—"

A sputtering of small arms fire broke out to the northeast, in the direction of Beverly Ford. MacAllen's head shot up like a bird dog on point. Men and mounts pricked up their ears, straining to make sense of the unexpected early-morning volley. Soon the individual pops of pistol and carbine blended into a steady crackling roar, followed by the ominous rumble of artillery.

"That ain't no picket line skirmish. Ready troop, tighten girths and mount up," ordered the Sergeant. A bugle somewhere to the north began to call 'Boots and Saddles' with urgency. Still no orders came. MacAllen was about to ride north to the sound of the guns. This was every leader's standing order when the situation was uncertain and he had no commands to the contrary.

In that moment, as full day brightened, Private Boykin from A Troop came galloping pell-mell from Kelly's Ford to the east, where he'd been posted on vedette. He reined in sharply at the bivouac. His mount's hooves skidded in wet grass as Boykin leaned back in the saddle. Breathing heavily, he yelled "Yankee cavalry! Coming over the river at Kelly's Ford!" MacAllen frowned. Kelly's Ford was southeast, not north.

MacAllen took hold of the man's bridle and said calmly, "Pull yourself together. You've seen Yankee cavalry before."

"Never this many! And with artillery support. They killed or captured all our pickets in the dark. I'm the only one that got away"

Yankees at both fords of the Rappahannock and with artillery! It was more than a reconnaissance; it had to be a full-fledged attack. A flicker of uncertainty passed over MacAllen's face. The noise of battle was intensifying toward Beverly Ford. Should they ride northeast? But if the Bluecoats were simultaneously crossing in force due southeast at Kelly's Ford, they could outflank the entire Confederate position. They could roll up the Southern cavalry piecemeal and strike the bulk of Stuart's men from behind while the Southerners fought the attackers at Beverly Ford. From there the Yankees could also seize Brandy Station and cut the railroad that was so vital to supplying Lee's army.

The blood pounded in Drayton's head as MacAllen made his decision in a moment and a look of resolution settled in his eyes. It was all too sudden, from leisure in camp to action against an unknown number of the enemy. He'd fired his revolver many times, but always at distant or fleeting targets. He wasn't certain he'd ever killed a man. And that was all right. He'd do his duty the best he could, and he'd fight to protect his comrades, which meant killing if he had to. But he had no urge to kill.

"All right, boys," MacAllen said calmly. "We'll just pop down to Kelly's Ford and see what this ruckus is about. Boykin, you ride on back to the Regiment quick-like and tell 'em what you saw, that we're heading down there to take a look. Troop! At the trot, move out in line abreast."

'Boots and Saddles' was sounding over the scattered camps of the entire Division behind them. Drayton hoped the ready troop would soon be reinforced by the rest of the 2nd or by other regiments in the Brigade. But for the moment, his platoon was the point of the spear.

As they trotted forward, to his great relief, he heard the thudding of horses coming up behind. Twisting in the saddle, he saw Lt. Colonel Frank Hampton, Wade Hampton's popular brother and second-in-command of the cavalry brigade under Cal Butler. He was galloping toward them, waving and yelling inaudibly. *Thank God, the rest of the Brigade,* thought Drayton. But as Hampton drew closer, Drayton was incredulous. The Colonel was leading only six riders! Where were the rest of them? MacAllen had thirty. With 'Colonel Frank's' handful, they had thirty-seven men with which to oppose the Yankee incursion at the Ford, which could easily number in the hundreds.

Frank Hampton pulled alongside Sergeant MacAllen and reined in his big paint to speak. "Close up on the Colonel," MacAllen hollered. The line of trotting horses converged into a more compact mass. The horses were up, with tails high and ears pricked.

Colonel Hampton pitched his voice high. "They've caught us flat-footed, fellows. We're all that's ready to fight between Kelly's Ford and Brandy Station, until the rest of the Brigade gets in position. So ride like hell and fight like the devil!"

Amid of chorus of assent, Hampton drew his saber and yelled "At the canter, forward!" The Confederates spread out slightly but retained their wedge formation. They drew sabers, put heel to horse, and went thundering over the lip of the plain and down through grassy meadows toward the river. Drayton felt the motive power of Bel's mighty hindquarters flow into him. Together they were invincible. But he had a fleeting thought: *why sabers?* Southern horse soldiers almost always fought with pistols. The naked steel of sabers was for Wade Hampton's 'moral effect,' no doubt. Caught up in the drama and excitement, he gave himself to the moment. Beltane ran easily, and his confidence flowed into his rider.

In a few moments he saw dark blue figures emerging from a layer of mist along the riverbank. A handful had deployed into line, and two howitzers barked at the Confederates from a rise across the river. But most of the Federals – an entire regiment, it seemed – remained mired in mud and confusion, bunched up as they forded the Rappahannock and tried to sort themselves out on the Confederate side. The sudden appearance of Confederate cavalry bearing down on them and screaming like Cossacks threw them into further confusion.

The Confederates spurred their mounts harder and yelled even louder. In past encounters, it was in this moment of mental dominance though sheer aggressiveness that the Yankees usually broke and scattered. But not this time. The Bluecoats already deployed spurred forward, making room for the rest of their men to ford the river and fall into a line of attack.

Drayton's mind went blank, or rather narrowed into a tight focus on what lay ahead. At a controlled gallop the two sides closed within a few seconds. Flashing into his sight was a Union lieutenant, a fine-looking specimen of manhood as any Confederate cavalier. Now instead of running away, the Yankee officer pressed home the attack. Drayton was his target.

In the confused ebb and flow Drayton found himself in a saber duel with a weapon most Southern horsemen had found next to useless, except as a spit for roasting meat. The Federals however had been drilled in its use as the proper arm of a cavalryman for close combat. The cavalry saber was a primarily chopping weapon, and the Yankee was using it well, slashing at Drayton with strokes that could take off an arm or head. His heavy blows wore Drayton down by sheer strength and persistence. Drayton parried with his own saber, using the length of blade horizontally to protect his upper body from the fierce downward slashes. In the relentless power of the man Drayton saw his own death with mathematical inevitability, until an image appeared from youthful memory – the fencing lessons his father had insisted were necessary for a young Charleston gentleman. Part of his mind focused on the glittering point of his own weapon, part of it on the aggressive Yankee. He heard his old fencing master DeBordieu croaking, *Portez la botte! Make the thrust!* And something awoke in his heart for the first time in the war, the sleeping tiger in him, the sheer lust of battle.

Beating away the enemy's blow *en sixte*, he feinted, raising the blade upward as if to follow with a downward cut. But instead of slashing, with a deft twist of his wrist he leveled the saber, using it as a rapier.

His blade was one of those custom-made for the Legion cavalry purchased by Wade Hampton, a distinctive, double-edged, Prussian dragoon sword, well-balanced, and straight, not curved like the standard cavalry saber. It was a superior weapon for close-quarter combat, and especially for thrusting. In the right hands it was formidable.

The Yankee had greater strength and endurance, but Drayton had better swordsmanship and horsemanship. Beltane seemed to think his thoughts. Drayton lunged with the tip of his sword. The horse surged forward in the same instant, carrying the sword point deep into the blue coat just below the breastbone. The Yankee's eyes opened wide, as much with surprise as pain. To Drayton's astonishment he smiled as if to say, 'You win.' Then the eyes went blank, and he began to sway out of the saddle. Drayton tried to keep a grip on his saber, but the blade was stuck fast. The momentum of the fall ripped the weapon from his hand. In the haste of the charge he'd neglected to run the saber-knot over his wrist. The brave Yankee, now a corpse, toppled to the ground with the sword protruding from his midsection.

The young officer's sergeant, enraged at the loss of his comrade, spurred forward, screaming and chopping at Drayton in fury. The man had a good seat and used the saber with effect. Drayton dodged the first slash. But with no sword to parry the blow, he could measure the rest of his life in seconds. From somewhere the impulse spoke. He raised his left hand, while reaching with his right. The cut was excruciating, but the sacrifice of two fingers saved his life.

While the Bluecoat raised the blade for the stroke that would him finish off, Drayton drew his Colt smoothly and got off a hasty shot under his still upraised left arm. The man's forage cap flew off as the top of his skull erupted in a spray of blood, brain, and bone. Catapulting backwards over the cantle, the Yankee fell in a heap on the crimson-sprinkled grass a few feet from his dead officer.

Now Drayton began to reel in his saddle. The intense pain made him both dizzy and nauseated. His breakfast went spewing. Beltane, normally a model of steadiness, spooked at the unfamiliar noise and odor. As he was about to fall, Sergeant MacAllen rode up, catching the horse's reins while supporting Drayton in the saddle, and led him off the field. His last blurred, swirling memory was of his troop screaming like banshees, now with pistols popping, galloping forward into the retreating blue cavalry.

Holding Drayton precariously over Bel's withers, MacAllen removed him to a copse of trees off the road to Stevensburg. Drayton regained consciousness staring up in bewilderment at a spray of leaves against the June sky. The Sergeant was pouring a trickle of water over the mangled hand that stung and throbbed. As MacAllen wrapped it tightly with his neckerchief, Drayton noted with something like Olympian detachment that it was none too clean. But it did staunch the bleeding.

"Are we behind our lines?" Drayton asked.

"There ain't any lines, as such," said MacAllen. Mounted combat seldom resembled the clash of ordered ranks of an infantry assault. It eddied all around the field. "But we're safe enough here."

"We drove them off, didn't we?"

"Hell, yes. Them Yankee cavalry, they couldn't stop a pig in a ditch."

Drayton laughed through his pain, hoisting himself up on an elbow. He said to MacAllen and to himself with a leaden feeling of realization, "No, my friend. That might have been true once, but not anymore."

"Well, you made sure there's at least two of 'em we want have to worry about any more. That was the prettiest piece of fighting I ever saw. You took the starch right out of the whole mob."

***

As evening fell in camp near Brandy Station, Drayton sat musing and staring into the flickering coals of the fire. Junius sat with him in companionable silence. Doctor Moore had brought by a vial of precious laudanum, rare medicine in the blockaded Confederacy where such essentials had to be imported by sea. Drayton had handed it back, urging him to keep it for the more seriously wounded. Now he regretted his generosity. But at least he had a demijohn of corn whiskey to ease the pain pulsating in his hand.

Sergeant MacAllen held out his tin cup for a share. "I got to make sure my men are getting good medicine," he said.

"And your professional opinion?" Drayton asked.

"It'll do, it'll do. But I've known better."

"What's your favorite?"

"Well, I'll tell you a tale," grinned MacAllen. "I was with a fine woman oncet and was always trying to get her to have a drink of corn likker. You know, to make her more friendly-like. She kept saying, 'I'm a lady. I never touch the stuff. I've never had a drop in my life.' But I kept on persuading and I finally got her to take a tumbler. She raised it real delicate-like to her lips, sipped a little, and said, 'Why, you've given me Tennessee sour mash!' Ever since then I've had a strong preference for Tennessee sour mash."

Drayton laughed. "I prefer Napoleon brandy. But we were lucky to get this moonshine from the Virginia mountains. And after today we're lucky to have any at all."

"Yes," agreed the Sergeant. "I overheard Captain Screven talking with Colonel Butler. They was congratulating one another on 'retaining possession of the field,' allowing us to 'claim another victory for the valor of Southern arms.' What they really meant is that we didn't git run off by the Yankees and were lucky to retain possession of our wagon train and supplies, including the medicinal whiskey."

"I suppose it was a victory," said Drayton. "But you know and I know and I guess most everybody here knows – we were surprised. And we nearly took a drubbing. As Frederick the Great once said, 'It is forgivable to be defeated. But surprised? Never!'"

"Well, I don't know this Frederick fellah you're speakin' of. Must be in another regiment. But he's got it right. What worries me now is what grand scheme Jeb Stuart is going to cook up to restore his reputation. Anyways, Private FitzHenry, you're out of it for a while, with them lost fingers."

Drayton held up the bandaged, throbbing hand in the firelight. It was a hard fact to accept: his fingers, a small but intimate part of him, were gone. The leather gauntlet had absorbed enough of the cut to save the other three. He shouldn't feel bitter over the loss, since the alternative was to have lost his life or his entire hand, not just his fingers. And he had killed two men. It was a case of *nike é thanatos*. Victory or death.

He couldn't help but recall the boy lieutenant, strapping and strong and well-fed in the manner of the enemy. The blonde Viking surely ought to have killed him. Recalling the details seemed incongruous at such a time, but there they were in his mind's eye – the brightness of his brass buttons, the cleanliness and fine fit of his dark blue coat, the bit of golden furze at his chin.

He didn't dwell too much on the Yankee sergeant, except for an irrational indignation that the man had almost killed him. But the boy lieutenant. He would never forget his almost-smile at the moment of his final defeat. The word 'gallant' was thrown about a lot in the Confederate army, as in 'the gallant Pelham.' This Yankee had been gallant, too, even at the moment of his death.

Drayton wondered about the man's past, his upbringing, his education. He tried to imagine the strange pathways of chance that had brought them together. And why had both sides used sabers? When he saw the Yankees armed with sabers Frank Hampton had drawn his instead of his pistol. Was it some romantic impulse of knight errantry? Some residual sense of sportsmanship? Only Lt. Colonel Hampton could say. He'd been gallant, too, and now he was also dead. Sad for the poor Yankee lad that fate had brought him face to face with a Charleston-trained fencer, when pistols would have evened the equation.

Listening to the murmurs of his comrades, Drayton suspected they were discussing his exploit. He picked apart a skein of emotions, remorse mingled with exhilaration. He separated each feeling out of the tangle, holding it up one by one for examination, as was his wont, explaining himself to himself. In the sudden encounter his pledge to Celia to show mercy and humanity had never entered his head. There had been no time. The entire episode, from the first sound of gunfire at Beverly Ford to his hand-to-hand combat, had been one of constant movement, a matter of ten minutes or less. He'd had to concentrate on surviving. Perhaps her request was foolish in the circumstances. Still, he hoped he'd never have to take another life, especially on such personal terms.

Despite the insistent pain, despite the fatigue and privations of the bivouac, he had never felt more intensely alive. It was a strange sensation, to be sitting here drinking whiskey when by rights he should be dead, knowing he would never be the same man, having killed not at a distance but face to face in single combat. He had truly experienced the vagaries of war — the martial splendor of the great cavalry review, the fight with the Yankees at Kelly's Ford, being wounded and surviving. And all this in less than twenty-four hours. He finally saw the paradox of war, why men loved it even when hating it.

Into the shadows above the campfire bright sparks danced upward, demarcating the burning moment of life between darkness and the deeper darkness beyond.

"Junius," he said. "D'you know what those sparks make me think of?"

"Yes, Suh, I think so. Dey's like de souls of dead men ascendin' into Heaven."

"How'd you know, Junius? How'd you know?"

***

Drayton didn't realize he'd dozed off until a clatter and clink by the campfire brought him awake with a start. Cabell Junior and James Moore, now a lieutenant and the Regimental adjutant, had stopped by to check on him. Moore was the brother of Doc Henry. MacAllen was gone to check the horses. Junius had remained. Lt. Moore motioned him not to get up but stay reclining on his saddle, next to which he'd dropped a burlap bundle. Moore and Cabell settled on empty ration boxes beside him.

The adjutant was responsible, among other things, for posting duty assignments in the regiment, although the 2nd Cavalry's commander, Colonel Butler, made the final decisions. Drayton knew that re-assignment from the Regiment was imminent because of his wound.

He was wrestling with that possibility when Cabell said, "From two dead Yankees, Brother. Two of them. *Mordu la poussiére.*" He gestured at the bundle.

Cabell and Moore nodded thanks to Junius, who passed each of them a steaming cup of his ersatz coffee, far better than anyone else's brew. Drayton took one, too. Heaven only knew what Junius made it from, but whatever it was, it was vaguely satisfying.

"We recovered your saber," Moore said, blowing across the scalding liquid.

"And here are the Yankee officer's personal effects." The dead on both sides were often looted before the corpses were cold. "Prioleau Henderson obtained them somehow. Said they rightly belong to you."

When Drayton made no move to inspect the contents, Cabell opened the bundle. He produced a gold watch, gold ring and locket, a pocket New Testament, and a sheaf of letters bound in twine.

"I've looked at the letters to see if there's any useful military information," said Moore. "They're yours now."

Drayton received his saber wordlessly, glad someone had thoughtfully cleaned it of encrusted gore. But his eyes lit up at the sight of a Spencer repeating carbine in the burlap. The Spencer was the latest thing in the Union arsenal, a compact, magazine-fed rifle firing seven rounds in succession with great accuracy.

"So the Yankee cavalry are now carrying these damn things as government issue," he said, looking it over. "Not good. Not good at all."

"Yes," nodded Lt. Moore. "Taken from the Yankee sergeant you killed. It goes into the Regimental armory."

"I got some fine new Yankee boots," Cabell said after a while. "A bit large, but mine were coming apart. I took the other pair over to Ranse, who was footsore from ill-fitting shoes. He said, 'With boots like these I ought to be given command of a regiment.'"

"Yes, that sounds just like Ranse. I'm glad I could be of service to you both." He didn't bother to keep the acid out of his voice.

Cabell could abide the solemn atmosphere no longer. Exultant, he said, "You're the toast of the Regiment, Brother. Killed two men in single combat. By God, it was like Achilles against Hector. Or rather, Achilles against the Fifth New York. You broke the back of their charge. Your platoon was the point of the spear, and you were the tip of the point. What possessed you to attack the whole Yankee regiment in such a manner?"

Ignoring the question, Drayton held up his bandaged hand and smiled ruefully. "Well, Achilles didn't lose any fingers. Or his breakfast." How could he admit to them he felt no pride in the deed? He'd been forced to kill to save his skin. He recalled Odysseus' words to Eurycleia after massacring the suitors in his hall: 'It is impious to glory over slain men.' The image surfaced again of the gallant boy's expression as he died, contrasted with the Yankee sergeant's mask of murderous rage. "As for the charge, I just followed the others. But Beltane is fast, as you know. He ran ahead without my remembering our training to charge in line. I got carried away, so to speak."

Lt. Moore broke in. "I was at General Stuart's headquarters when the Yankees attacked," he said. "I wasn't here for that part of the fight. Tell me about it; what you saw and did. I'll have to write the Regimental report, and I'll include your observations."

Drayton pondered for a moment, sunk in the lassitude that followed the excitement of combat. He tried to envision the whole panorama of the battle as it must have been – the grand sweep of the War's first all-cavalry battle. There must have been long waves of horsemen galloping in dressed ranks; flags flying gallantly, the sun flashing off swords, foes clashing in grand style. But it was only a battle imagined, not what he'd witnessed. He could recall only a confused and desperate struggle for survival. A few men cutting across his front and the shock of recognition when he saw they were in blue. Frank Hampton slumping in the saddle and led off the field by his bugler. Only fleeting impressions, fragments of images, ending with a handful of grey moss troopers bringing up the rear as he reeled from the battle in shock and pain. Allen MacAllen's wry smile as he regained consciousness in the copse of beech trees.

"Well? What about it? What did you observe?" asked Jimsie.

"I observed how green the beeches were," Drayton said finally.

"How's that?" said Jimsie, pencil paused in the air.

"The beeches. I was flat on my back observing the beeches. They were deep green against the deep blue above."

"Ah." Moore cleared his throat, obviously thinking Drayton was still in shock, or in his liquor.

"I hate to disappoint you, Jimsie," Drayton said at last. "But I didn't see much and I recall even less. All I remember is following Sergeant MacAllen down the road from Stevensburg. There were only thirty of us in the ready troop, and then Frank Hampton came up with half a dozen more. Suddenly a line of Yankee cavalry materialized in our front. There must have been a whole regiment crossing Kelly's Ford. They had artillery on the other side of the river covering their crossing. The Yankees had presented sabers – I think. I mean, they must have, because Colonel Frank drew his and hollered, 'Charge and take 'em, boys!' We pitched right into them. Without thinking I drew my saber and galloped into the melee. Time seemed suspended, but I suppose it was only a few seconds later I came upon those two Yankees, an officer and his sergeant, who were intent on killing me. It's only thanks to a good horse and good luck that I killed them instead. We just sort of rode through them, like a hot knife through butter. I remember the noise of blades clashing and both sides yelling. Suddenly I was fighting the two in front of me. I got this." He held up the mangled hand. "I almost fainted from the pain, but I managed to draw my Colt and take the second one. And then Sergeant MacAllen was leading me back the way we came."

"Did you observe Frank Hampton being hit?"

"No. But as MacAllen turned with me back toward our lines, I saw the Colonel leaning over in the saddle and his reins slack."

"He made it back to the Barbour home," said Moore, "where he died of a pistol ball in the abdomen and a saber slash across the forehead. He must have been first hit by the ball. Otherwise no Yankee swordsman could have touched him."

"I grieve to hear it."

"Yes, we have lost a fine officer. But his charge – *your* charge – saved the day. Your thirty-seven men broke up the flank attack of an entire Federal regiment at Kelly's Ford. And that in turn threw Gregg's whole brigade of Yankees into confusion. That's why I need more details."

"I'm sorry, Jimsie. It was all just a chaotic jumble."

"Yes, well…" said Moore, disappointed. "I was hoping for something more like the Scots Greys at Waterloo." Drayton thought, *Anything to take the sting out of a surprise attack. They surprised the whole Division while we held full dress reviews and enjoyed the music of the bones and Sweeney's banjo.*

Moore stood up, handing the guest cup to Junius. "Anyway, Doc Henry says you're for home. Might as well start packing your kit. Cabell will take your mount. That'll keep him in the family, at least."

Drayton bristled. It seemed a foolish insistence in the middle of war, but he was not about to give up Beltane. *His* property, not the Confederate States government's.

He growled, "Nonsense, Jimsie. We're right on the cusp of a great campaign, perhaps the greatest yet. General Lee will soon be taking us north, and the coming campaign may end this terrible war. Do you think I'd cry off wounded at a time like this? I can still ride as well as any man in the regiment. I ride with my legs more than my hands, anyway."

Moore peered hard at him, glancing at the bloody bandage on his hand, then back into his face. Moore seemed to be saying with his eyes, *You have an honorable wound. Seize the opportunity it offers. Go home.* Drayton stared back at him resolutely. He was puzzled at his own reaction. Jimsie was right: go home. Had he developed a sudden taste for battle after the fight at Kelly's Ford? Did he want to prove himself to the whisperers and doubters? Surely he'd just done so. But before he could re-consider, Cabell joined in on his behalf, and the moment passed.

"Jimsie, that horse of Drayton's has too high an opinion of himself. I probably couldn't ride him anyway."

Moore shrugged. "Very well. I'll make a recommendation to Major Lipscomb, Colonel Butler's successor. The Colonel lost a leg today. General Stuart's aide Captain Farley was killed by the same cannon shot. The Regiment lost forty men in this fight. Tiny Hazelton has just died from wounds. I don't suppose we can spare anyone who's not too bad hurt and is willing to stay."

"I'm sorry about Tiny. Jimsie, find me a post as a scout or courier." He didn't want to serve under Lipscomb if he could help it.

"All right. Perhaps General Longstreet can use another courier on his staff. He was born in Edgefield, though he seems to think we South Carolinians are too volatile. Still, if he accepts you, he'll have someone well mounted, even if you are slightly mad."

"In that case I'll keep this," said Drayton. "Call it a battle trophy." He reached and grasped the Spencer repeater with his good hand.

He stroked the carbine with a kind of awe, and studied the stock of ammunition. The Spencer repeater fired the revolutionary new 'fixed' cartridge. The projectile and powder charge were contained in a brass casing that loaded into the rifle's magazine. No Southern factory had the capability to manufacture such cartridges. The weapon was useful only as long as the ammunition lasted, and it could only be obtained from the enemy.

Moore's face wrinkled, but he didn't pull rank on Private FitzHenry. "Very well," he said at length. He looked enviously at the weapon. "It's really not my prerogative to let you keep it, but who'll dispute me? You certainly earned it. At least it'll go to someone who'll use it on the enemy." He smiled grimly. "I recommend it in lieu of sword-fighting."

Chapter Twenty Three

Frederick, Maryland; June 27, 1863.

True to his word, Lieutenant Moore arranged to have Drayton assigned to General Longstreet's First Corps staff. Before taking medical leave, Colonel Butler, commander of the 2nd Cavalry, endorsed the transfer with a personal note commending Drayton as an excellent scout and courier. He was not a natural-born killer, even though Brandy Station proved he could fight. But now his bravery was the talk of an army of brave men. In 1862 he'd distinguished himself as a scout along the Occoquan. Despite the wound he could still be useful as one of the most skilled horseman in the Army. He'd developed a good eye for terrain and a kind of sixth sense about the enemy's location and movements.

Orders came re-assigning and promoting him to second lieutenant for his exploit at Brandy Station, as was appropriate to serve with the lofty ones. He had to say goodbye to Cabell and Sergeant MacAllen. And Junius, who was after all, not his personal servant but a member of the 2nd Cavalry. Cabell enjoyed the privilege just before he departed of pinning a second lieutenant's shoulder straps on Drayton's jacket. 'Pumpkin rinds,' the soldiers called them irreverently.

Moore rode with him to Longstreet's First Corps headquarters, an array of tents and laagered wagons in a meadow west of Gordonsville, Virginia. With a crisp salute Jimsie presented Drayton's new orders to Major Moxley Sorrell, Longstreet's chief aide. He returned Drayton's salute and said, "You stand relieved from the 2nd South Carolina Cavalry. Good luck and Godspeed." The two men shook hands and Moore rode away.

Since the death of the legendary Stonewell Jackson, James Longstreet had emerged as Lee's leading subordinate. There was no formal second-in-command or executive officer in the Army of Northern Virginia. Lee had his personal staff, and dealt directly with his corps commanders, who differed in date-of-rank but who were in principle co-equals. Lee re-organized the army again, this time into three corps, with Longstreet retaining command of the First.

Longstreet, nicknamed 'Old Pete,' was a tall and robust man, phlegmatic like his Dutch forbears, with a dark bushy beard and probing eyes. His gray uniform coat was ill-fitting and the general's braid on the sleeve tarnished. But he took his calling seriously. Like many Southern officers, he concealed a dry sense of humor behind the no-nonsense manner of an experienced professional soldier. He'd insisted on interviewing Drayton before finally appointing him to his staff.

"Well, Mr. FitzHenry, I understand you're a real swashbuckler."

"An exaggeration, General."

"So then, you *didn't* cut down two Yankees at Brandy Station?"

"I was just very lucky."

Drily the General observed, "Never trade luck for skill. Welcome to the First Corps. We don't stand on ceremony here. Getting the job done is more important than military courtesy, although there's a time and place for that, too."

As everyone in the Army expected, the victory at Chancellorsville was the precursor to another campaign aimed at the North. Lee urgently wanted to shift the fighting away from Virginia's blasted countryside, as he'd tried to do at Antietam. The lush farmlands of Pennsylvania would provide a source of supply and fodder, and allow Lee to threaten Washington from the northwest. Drayton had no desire to go north. He'd hoped the crushing blow at Chancellorsville would have induced the Yankees to sue for peace. But it was not to be. As he'd always feared and warned, the Yankees had staying power.

Lee's Invincibles now began calling themselves Lee's Miserables after the popular novel *Les Misérables* by Victor Hugo. It was a name they took on with irony and affection, because to a man they'd come to love 'Marse Robert.' He'd not only given them a string of near-unbroken victories but also something else, a pride in themselves and a belief that under his command no one could stand against them. It was a potent weapon to take into Federal territory.

In mid-June they began to march up the Shenandoah Valley, a natural invasion route, pointed like a dagger at Western Maryland and Pennsylvania, using the mountains to the east to screen the movement. Lee held back a few squadrons of cavalry to guard the eastward passes, South Mountain and Thoroughfare Gap. The bulk of Stuart's Division he ordered to deploy on the far side of the mountains, that is, off to his right flank as he moved north. Stuart was to shadow the enemy movements while screening Lee's. The aggressive Stuart took his too-broad directive like a bit in his teeth. He made a bold sweeping move north toward Rockville, Maryland – and promptly disappeared. The Federals, now under George Meade, had gotten between Lee and Stuart, although Lee didn't learn this until it was too late. Drayton remembered MacAllen's prediction back at Brandy Station. For the moment, Lee was ignorant of Stuart's whereabouts and of Meade's. No news was good news. If Meade was moving to intercept him, surely the dependable Stuart would bring word.

After capturing war-torn Winchester, a key town in the Valley that had changed hands dozens of times, Lee's Miserables crossed the Potomac at Williamsport, Maryland, and proceeded north toward Pennsylvania. Longstreet's corps brought up the rear of the twelve-mile-long column. As the brigades began to ford the Potomac and cross into Maryland, massed regimental bands played 'Maryland, My Maryland,' and the troops raised the song. The male voices in their ragged chorus was stirring and poignant. It wasn't the song itself, although its lyrics were belligerent enough toward the Yankees. Nor the melody, which was the same as 'O Tannenbaum.' Bewildered Confederates from the hinterlands who'd never heard the alternate lyrics wondered why they were singing a Christmas song in June.

The infantry forded the river, waist-deep and sluggish, while the artillery and some of the cavalry used the pontoon bridges thrown up by Lee's engineers. The infantry took off their trousers, shoes, and socks — those who had shoes, holding them aloft in one hand and their muskets and cartridge boxes in the other. Drayton found it the strangest sight he'd seen yet in this strange war, like a vast Chinese laundry on the move. Laughing and joking, they seemed glad to be taking the contest to the enemy on his own ground for a change.

In bivouac in Maryland, just below the Pennsylvania line, Moxley Sorrel sent for Drayton. He reported to the Major and General Longstreet under a tent fly, where the two men surveyed a map spread on a camp table.

The General returned his salute with a wintry smile. "Mr. FitzHenry, we've heard nothing from General Stuart for several days. I needn't tell you, he's a reliable officer, and our cavalry are the best in the world. I don't like it, this prolonged lack of information."

Drayton didn't think he was expected to comment on Jeb Stuart's value as an officer. He remained silent.

"You have some reputation as a scout, in addition to your prowess as a sword-fighter."

Drayton assayed a smile. "Sir, I am actually better at the former than the latter."

"Good. Listen now. I want you to strike out to the east. Go over the Catoctin Mountains if you have to. Locate Hooker—"

"Sir," interrupted Sorrel, "Just a reminder. Hooker has been sacked. The Yankees are now under George Meade."

"Yes, of course. Thank you. Try to locate Meade. Spend a few days in the bush if you have to. But don't stay out too long. We'll be moving north, of course, so find us in southern Pennsylvania. Bring me word… about here, day after tomorrow. I want my own intelligence, at least in the area occupied by this Corps." He beckoned Drayton to the map and waited while he made notes and his own rough sketch.

"Commit that to memory, then destroy it," the General ordered.

Drayton packed his saddlebags with three days rations and a few quarts of oats for Bel to supplement his grazing. He said farewell and trotted east, checking his own map – minus any identifying marks. Mid-afternoon of the second day, evading the screen of Union cavalry and dodging from copse to copse and vale to vale, he spied a long column of dust-covered Union infantry. They were trudging north, more or less parallel to Lee. The column snaked in both directions as far as he could see. He counted regimental flags for a rough estimate of their numbers and concluded it was a corps, at least. He tethered Bel to his picket pin well back on the reverse crest, then wriggled forward on his belly. He wanted to identify actual units if possible, at least corps and divisions, by their badges. He had a fine pair of field glasses, far better than the normal scout's.

The dust and movement made it difficult, but when the marching columns took their prescribed five-minute break in the hour, some soldiers fell out on an embankment and took off their kepis. Above them on a slope concealed in broom sedge, tense and silent, Drayton focused on the badges sewn on top of their caps. They were 11th Corps. Theirs was the one badge he could neither forget nor mistake, a crescent in red, white, or blue, one color for each division of the Corps. The 2nd Division emblem was a white crescent on a blue field, identical to the South Carolina state flag. These were the unlucky chaps, mostly German immigrants, who'd occupied Hooker's right at Chancellorsville, the flank Jackson had crushed at Chancellorsville. The 11th Corps was commanded by Oliver Howard, reputed to be a man of deep Christian piety. When Drayton saw the river of men and guns flowing north, his heart ran cold. Voltaire had said that God was on the side with the biggest battalions. And here they had Christian piety in their side, too.

His dead reckoning was spot-on, and he found Longstreet's headquarters where he expected south of Greencastle, Pennsylvania. Saddle-sore, tired, thirsty, and dirty, he trotted into the lines, argued with the sentry for a few moments about the parole and counter-sign, then made his way to the bustling command bivouac.

His first act was making sure Bel was cared for properly. Then, taking only enough time to splash some water in his face and brush the dust off his grey jacket, he reported to Moxley Sorrel. The Major took him at once to Longstreet's tent. The General, dressed in a loose cotton shirt, sat around a rough plank table in conference with his Division commanders Lafayette McLaws, John Bell Hood, and George Pickett. He stood up immediately, saw Drayton and motioned him over to report.

Saluting and nodding to the other generals – he was never especially impressed or intimidated by generals — Drayton summarized his long trek to the east.

"General, I could only get so close, as you understand. But I saw a large body of Union troops, with all three arms, on the march north and northwest. They were really pushing along. I shadowed them for nearly a whole day, and by their badges I identified at least two corps, the 1st and the 11th. They are moving more or less parallel to our line of march east of the mountains."

"See!" Longstreet said, turning abruptly to his subordinates. "It's exactly what Harrison told us."

"General Longstreet, are you sure you want to trust the word of … of an *actor*?" said Pickett.

Longstreet smiled. "Being an actor is what makes him such a good spy. In any event, we now have confirmation from Mr. FitzHenry here. He's a hero of Brandy Station. Do you doubt his word?'

No one demurred. Then Hood asked in his rich Texas drawl, "Mr. FitzHenry, did you see any sign or get any word of our cavalry, of General Stuart?"

"Sir, I'm sorry to say, none."

"Where *is* Stuart?" Pickett said, snapping his gauntlets on the plank.

"I'll tell you where, George," said Longstreet. "Somehow the Yankees have gotten between us and General Stuart. No doubt he's searching for a way around. No doubt he'll find it. But with as any men as Meade has, and them all strung out in line of march, it may prove a longer way than even Stuart can manage in time."

"Well," said Hood, "with your scouts, we've at least got some idea of Meade's movements. Seems to me we're on a collision course and will have a fight on our hands in the next few days. A week at the most. I would so advise General Lee."

Drayton stood patiently while the council of war unfolded, waiting for orders. He understood the dilemma. No one wanted to discount the spotty intelligence, and no one wanted to jump to premature conclusions. They were used to the Yankees' dilatory responses to Lee's audacious moves. This rapid advance by Meade was unusual. Better to let matters develop a while for clarity's sake. But they couldn't afford to lose the initiative either. They all knew that much information obtained on the field was contradictory or out of date, much was false, and almost all was ambiguous. The art of generalship was to sift through it all and make an appreciation sound enough on which to act. It was as much a matter of intuition as much as analysis, a kind of sixth sense. Lee had it, as did Longstreet, though not infallibly. Their intuitions came to pass more often than not, one reason they made such a good team.

"I've already sent Harrison up to General Lee," said Longstreet. "I'll add Mr. FitzHenry's report confirming what he saw. And now, Lieutenant." He turned to Drayton. "Well done, well done indeed. Get a decent meal, rest yourself and your mount. I want you to go out again as soon as possible."

June 28, 1863; Waynesboro, Pennsylvania.

Going out again after a short rest and re-supply was taxing. It meant more of the same — little sleep and long, vigilant hours in the saddle. And it was nerve-wracking. No matter how alert he was, he could easily stumble across a patrol of Yankees. Nevertheless, he relished it. The role of independent scout was the perfect assignment to complete a personal scheme he couldn't have indulged if he were still in a troop unit.

Drayton went out far to Longstreet's right. Checking the map, he found a town that would serve his purpose. It was convenient, on the main road north, a neatly-kept village of clapboard buildings and packed clay streets. And not a soul in sight. He smiled to himself at the simple German farmers, terrified of the on-rushing Confederate hordes, like the panicked Romans crying *Hannibal ante portas*. Hannibal is at the gates!

General Lee had issued a Special Order warning his men to treat Pennsylvania civilians and their property with respect. For the most part, it was honored, although some passing units paid for commandeered food and drink with Confederate scrip, knowing it was worthless to the locals. But Drayton had a few captured Yankee greenbacks. He intended to observe the decencies and pay for the service he was about to engage.

After scanning the seemingly deserted town for a time with his glasses and locating his objective, he decided all was safe. He rode in from a wooded ridge behind the town, dismounted, and led Bel to the back door of the wooden frame building, where fortunately a hitching rail was located. He drew his Colt and entered, emerging from a shadowed hallway into the interior, lighted with oil lamps as the day's sun began to fade. Behind the postal service counter a balding man sorted mail into boxes. He was short and plump, almost cherubic, with a fringe of white curls at the temples accentuating his baldness. He looked up wide-eyed in alarm.

"Lord help me," moaned the Yankee postmaster. "You've got me dead to rights, Johnny Reb. But there's no money here, nothing of value."

"You have the wrong idea," said Drayton, holstering his pistol. He handed a packet wrapped in waxed canvas to the bald man. "Please note the address on the package."

"Yes, Sir. To the family of Lieutenant Noah Marston, Fifth New York Cavalry, 21 Old Liverpool Road, Syracuse, New York."

He paused and looked quizzically at Drayton with pale blue eyes. Drayton said, "I am the sender, as you see in the 'from' line."

The man read aloud, "From Second Lieutenant Drayton FitzHenry, CSA."

"May I ask what this is all about? I heard you Rebs were moving into Pennsylvania. You've been burning the post offices as government property. Are you here to burn me out?"

"I'm here for the same purpose as any other patron."

"You want to use the U.S. postal services?"

"Yes," said Drayton, amused at the incredulity in the man's voice. "I want to mail these personal effects of a … of a Federal officer. Also a note telling how he fought and died most bravely, a credit to himself and his people."

The postmaster studied him for a time. Then he cleared his throat. "How did you come by these effects?" Drayton said nothing. The postmaster asked, "Did you kill him?"

After another heavy silence Drayton answered. "Yes, I'm sorry to say. Well, I'm not *too* sorry, for he would surely have killed me otherwise. But I believe his family would want to know how he died and to receive these mementos, don't you?"

The postmaster stared long and hard at Drayton. He seemed to be looking for the trick, for the ambush that lay in wait. Finally he appeared satisfied that Drayton was sincere. The man's lower lip quivered. "Yes, I think they would, most certainly."

"I could think of no more reliable way to ensure they reach his family," said Drayton. "I didn't want to entrust the package to a random Federal picket or try to send it through the lines."

"Well, Sir." The cherub drew himself up to his full height, which wasn't much to start with. "You may depend on the United States Post Office."

"How much is the postage?"

The man's eyes misted. "There is no charge in the United States for mail posted by serving soldiers. In the circumstances I see no reason why that policy should not extend to … to you as well."

Drayton took the man's hand and squeezed it. "Thank you very much, Postmaster… Postmaster?"

"Rudolf Amman, at your service."

The man had a German accent, like many in this part of the state. "*Sind Sie Deutscher?*" Drayton asked.

"*Nein, ich bin aus dem Schweiz gekommen,*" said the Swiss Rudolf Amman proudly.

They chatted in German for a moment like old friends, though Drayton found the *Schwitzertüsch* dialect hard to follow. It was time to go. He extended his hand. The two men shook hands warmly. Drayton turned and retraced his steps to the rear exit, pausing warily and scanning the back street in case he'd been observed. Beltane nickered in the shadows.

Just before he stepped out of the building into the lowering dark, the postmaster called after him. "Lieutenant FitzHenry, I am loyal to the United States. I believe your cause is wrong, and I cannot wish you good luck. But I will wish you this much at least."

"Yes?" Drayton replied, turning back.

"My eldest son is serving in the Pennsylvania artillery. He would be moved by this act of yours. May you never encounter him or his battery in the course of this campaign."

Cashtown, Pennsylvania; June 30, 1863.

By now Lee knew he and Meade were on converging paths and that they'd come to grips in the coming days somewhere in southwestern Pennsylvania. But Lee still lacked precise information on the location, disposition, and numbers of the enemy. Drayton went out periodically to take a look, but all he could manage, he and the other individual scouts, was glimpses of pieces. As lone scouts they had to rely on stealth; they lacked the fighting power to get though the thickening screen of Union cavalry protecting Meade's movements from observation. Sometimes stealth was not enough. In the absence of thorough intelligence, Lee could only keep moving and try to dominate the key road junctions that would allow him to concentrate his army in a hurry if attacked.

Longstreet's preference was to find a town with a good potential defensive position, use its road net to assemble the army, then maneuver in such a way as to place the Army of Northern Virginia between Meade and Washington and across the Union line of supply. Then Meade would have no choice but to fling his army on entrenched Confederates —Fredericksburg all over again. Longstreet frequently consulted the map, his staff, and his scouts. It appeared there was just such a place eight miles north by east, a trim college town with roads radiating like spokes of a wheel, and with high ground that could make an impregnable position for the Confederates to defend. It sounded pleasant enough. Its name was Gettysburg.

Chapter Twenty Four

Gettysburg, Pennsylvania; the First Day, July 1, 1863.

The first of July dawned hot and airless, as if Nature was holding her breath at the unfolding epic. Two blind boxers, Lee and Meade, had been lashing out with unseeing blows, until one blow finally landed. Standing by with Longstreet's command group, Drayton heard a smattering of musketry to the east, toward Gettysburg. It increased in volume from a crackle to a steady roar, followed by booms of artillery. What had evidently started as a skirmish was now a full-blooded battle. Tensions rose, pulses beat faster, the pace of the marching brigades quickened forward.

Drayton pondered the baffling, random nature of war. Generals made decisions and issued orders, yet the outcomes hardly seemed subject to human agency. War's caprices defied efforts to impose their will, he thought, as here and now at Gettysburg, a place they had noted on the map but for certain hadn't intended to start a major battle in.

He observed intently as Lee and Longstreet conferred, and could see by Lee's animated stride and facial expression that the General's well-known fighting blood was up. As the two officers weighed the ever-shifting physics of space and time, mass and energy, Drayton thought he could almost duplicate the conversation in his own mind.

The mathematics of the problem is ineluctable: only so many men, guns, horses, and wagons can occupy a given stretch of road. The mass-volume equation means they can only travel so fast. How many men can we bring to bear at the critical point? Where *is* the critical point? How soon can we concentrate the army? How many of the enemy are we facing? Meade is facing the same math and must balance the same equation. But Lee hates to attack piecemeal, throwing in one brigade at a time. Ewell is here with his corps, Hill's corps is north toward Carlisle but turning around. Heth's division has been the first to engage, but he has been fighting only dismounted Union cavalry – Buford's men apparently. It should have been a small matter to sweep them aside. Yet, as additional Confederate units have gone into the fight, they have run into stiffening Yankee resistance. Infantry, including the famed 'Black Hats.' What exactly are we facing? Now Hill's leading brigades wheeling back south have hit the Yankees west of Gettysburg on McPherson Ridge. Only part of Longstreet's corps is up, the divisions of Hood and McLaws. Pickett's fine Virginians are bringing up the rear, still half a day's march to the south. The serpent has to coil itself fully before it can strike.

Lee hasn't wanted to fight here and now. Nevertheless, a significant portion of the army, but only a portion, is engaged. Should we disengage, wait till the entire army is assembled, then attack overwhelmingly at a time and place of our choosing? Or is it too late for that? The battle is joined. Drayton can tell Lee wants to commit with what's at hand, contrary to his usual methods. By hitting hard now we can gain a victory, though not the annihilation of Those People we seek. Longstreet's is waving his arm in a wide circle. He's arguing for a maneuver around, finding a strong defensive position, and forcing the Yankees to come to us and shatter themselves on our works. No, that forfeits the initiative. We must maintain the offensive. Lee's right fist smacks his open left palm. Only the offensive wins decisively. Intuition says that Meade has only a portion of his strength on the field, too. Pressing the enemy before us, driving the Yankees back upon the rest of Meade's army in disorder and dismay might present another opportunity to catch them unprotected. Destroying them in detail or in one massive blow matters less than that we destroy them. We are gambling, yes. But we need a decisive victory, an Austerlitz, not a half-victory. It's why we came here.

Gettysburg, Pennsylvania; the Second Day, July 2, 1863.

Longstreet, Hood, and Harry Heth, whose brigade had opened the fight the day before, sat on a fallen pine log while Lee paced. Southern regiments waited in the background, smoking, lolling on the ground, some grabbing a moment's sleep in the lull before the storm. Hood whittled nonchalantly on a stick. The mercurial Heth was crestfallen and ailing. A spent ball had hit him in the head. He'd been wearing a new hat which was too big, and he had filled out the hatband with newspaper. The extra padding had saved him from serious injury. Heth, Longstreet, and Lee avoided speaking or even looking at one another. Longstreet was frustrated, as was Lee,that the engagement had gotten away from them. Drayton could tell they blamed Heth. But they didn't want to rebuke him for his aggressive-mindedness. At least he had fought, and he'd led from the front, thus his wound. Confederate leaders were supposed to be aggressive. Lee would rather his commanders fight than forfeit the initiative by cautiously awaiting orders. That was one reason why the Yankees had been beaten on so many fields. Now Lee, the master improviser, was pondering how to exploit the situation. After all, they had driven the Yankees before them and seized the town. One of Meade's best subordinates, General John Reynolds, had been killed trying to stem the flood, a flood composed mostly of the hapless 11th Corps, the same fellows routed at Chancellorsville. From general to private, Confederates scoffed. The first day wasn't a major victory, but on the whole, a satisfactory encounter. Drayton worried that perhaps 11th Corps' greatest contribution was to fill the Southerners with over-confidence, Lee included.

The Yankees had withdrawn south and west of Gettysburg and had dug in along high ground ideal for defense, a spine-like feature called Cemetery Ridge. Their right flank was well-anchored on rocky, wooded Culp's Hill in the north. To the south their line rested on a rocky but bare eminence the locals called Little Round Top. On the map the Union line looked like an inverted capital J or a fish hook. Drayton grasped the significance at once. Once again, simple mathematics ruled. The Yankees' position gave them the advantage of interior lines. Meade could shift units quickly from one end of his line to the other wherever it was threatened, inside the J. And Cemetery Ridge would screen their movements from Confederate observation. Lee had to extend his lines over a greater distance to encompass the Union position, from the outside, so to speak; and would have to maneuver his troops around the outside of the J if he wanted to attack. That would consume more time because of the longer distance. It would also expose his movements to observation from the Union high ground, Little Round Top especially.

Drayton wasn't close enough to hear the generals clearly, but he could see Longstreet making wide circular motions again as he joined Lee's pacing. He was persistent in his desire for a sweep around the Union army to get between Meade and his base, forcing the Yankees to attack at a disadvantage. The ghosts of Fredericksburg haunted his thinking. The normally imperturbable Lee nodded politely as always, but the tight lines of his mouth and flashing eyes showed he was upset.

As they strode within earshot of the staff, Drayton heard Lee say, "We don't yet know what we are facing. If we adopt your proposal, we must be certain of getting around Meade's entire army, lest his remnant get behind *us*. You want to envelop Meade. But we must not risk letting him envelop us." The unstated but ever-present factor – the Federals always had more men. "Meade is cautious, but he will make no errors on our front. Where *is* Stuart?" The question was not only on Lee's lips but also of every man in Lee's army.

Longstreet's reply was muffled. Then Lee raised his voice. "No, we have found the enemy here, and we will strike him here." Unsaid but well understood by both: *We must crush the Yankees on their own soil. From here we can march on Washington and dictate a peace. Time and resources are not on our side. A decisive battle here will win the war. And it* must *end.*

Drayton could see the flicker of resolution crossing Lee's face, the sudden set of his jaw and shoulders, while Longstreet seemed to sag. He'd lost the tactical argument, but he would follow orders. The two men turned and paced the other way, Lee gesturing, Longstreet nodding. Lee called Colonel Marshall forward with his order book. He dictated while Marshall scribbled. Soon riders were galloping north, he supposed to convey orders to Dick Ewell and A. P. Hill. Longstreet walked back to his staff, his face a brown study.

"Mr. FitzHenry," Longstreet beckoned. When he put his hand on the pommel and looked up, Drayton could see the anxiety he was unable to conceal. "Ride south as quick as you can. The road is clogged with troops, but that hunter of yours can take you cross-country. Find General Pickett and tell him the rest of the Corps is going to attack. We will strike the Yankee left as soon as McLaws and Hood can deploy, while Ewell attacks that big hill on the Yankee's right, Culp's Hill. Tell Pickett to force-march if he has to. His division is our main reserve, and we need every man on the field in case of a breakthrough. Then get back here right away."

The waiting and the uncertainty were at an end. Suddenly the troops standing by were all business, a business at which they were unsurpassed. With a minimum of fuss and wasted motion, with the easy confidence of veterans, the brigades fell in and began to march away in obedience to their orders.

July 2, 1863. Afternoon.

Union General Dan Sickles had inexplicably moved his entire Third Corps forward of Meade's main battle line, causing a bulge or salient with vulnerable flanks. McLaws' Division attacked the salient with unprecedented ferocity across a field of standing wheat, while the Yankees defended themselves with equal fury. The battle was in full cry a scant quarter mile away when Drayton returned from messaging General Picket, yet here he was riding behind the lines more or less safely, part of the process yet not entirely of it. He felt like a property man working backstage while the cast bellowed their lines and the audience cheered and clapped or booed raucously.

As he rode to report to Longstreet near the Rose Farm, he saw familiar faces from South Carolina. It was Kershaw's Brigade, standing tensely at rest, awaiting orders to join the assault *en echelon*. On an impulse Drayton decided to seek out Ranse. Finding his regiment, he asked permission of the company commander, who called his first sergeant, who called Ranse. A very surprised younger brother stepped out from the ranks. Drayton slid down from Beltane and they embraced on the verge of the dirt track, ignoring the thunder of guns on the hills beyond.

"It appears we'll be going into action any moment now," said Ranse with forced casualness. "Good of you to stop by for a call."

"Yes, I was in the neighborhood."

Ranse reached out to stroke the horse's velvety nose. "Good old Bel," he crooned. "He's carried you far and kept you safe, Brother."

"Relatively safe." Drayton held up the maimed left hand.

"Yes, I heard about Brandy Station. Thank God it was only two fingers and not the entire hand. Or head. And thanks for the boots!" He extended a foot. The leather was dusty and scuffed, but intact.

There was an awkward pause. Both men glanced involuntarily toward the center of the Union lines where musketry and cannon fire intensified. What could one say at such a time?

Then Drayton noticed Ranse's new headgear. "Lawd-a-mercy, Ranse. Where'd you get that straw hat?"

"Ha! Bought it from a choleric German farmer on the march up here. In Shippensburg, I think it was."

"Bought, or stole?" laughed Drayton.

"Oh, I bought it. With Confederate money, of course. If we win the war and *mein gute Herr* wants to travel South, he can redeem it. I know it's most unmilitary, but it keeps the sun off. It's hotter up here in Pennsylvania than I expected. And you know how easily I get sun-burned."

In addition to his new hat of yellow straw bright with varnish, Ranse carried a toothbrush thrust in the top buttonhole of his grey shell jacket. Ever after, Drayton retained the image of the jaunty headgear and the incongruous toothbrush.

Bugles blared frantically in the middle distance. A galloper arrived at the Brigade staff and spoke breathlessly to General Kershaw. The orders filtered down the line of regiments to fall in, and soldiers who lay or sat on the ground stood up, shouldered their muskets, and took their place in ranks. A tense silence settled over the ranks. All joking and casual conversation ended at the prospects of going into battle.

There was time only for a hasty, "Good luck." The brothers shook hands. Ranse took his place in the front rank of his company. Drayton put heel to Beltane and cantered rearward to General Longstreet's command group. Musket and cannon fire swelled to a crescendo, but it couldn't drown out the high fierce howls issuing from a thousand Southern throats.

Sickles' salient had left his flanks exposed and beyond support of the main Federal line on Cemetery Ridge. Yet paradoxically, it also created a kind of breakwater. Longstreet's troops aiming at the Yankee left first had to eliminate this salient before they could come to grips with Meade's main line. They were determined to break through. Sickles' men were equally determined to hold. The *en echelon* maneuver ordered by Lee was difficult, requiring precise timing; and nothing was going quite as it should, all too common in battle. The Confederates continued to fall short by a few minutes or a few yards. It was not a fight Longstreet wanted in the first place, and he grew angry at the mounting losses. It was a carnival of destruction. Captain Hugh Gardner's Palmetto Light Artillery deployed forward to support the attack. One section of four guns lost every man and horse within minutes. Drayton's heart wept for the huge number of dead horses everywhere, mostly artillery teams. The poor horses. Men at least had a choice to be there at the risk of their lives. Horses did not.

The fighting had subsided, like the outgoing tide. Men can fight in a frenzy for only so long, then flesh and blood must have a respite. The Pennsylvanians, defending their home soil for a change, had driven Hood's brigade back across Plum Run, or Bloody Run as it was now called, on the far right. Hood was badly wounded. Command devolved to Evander Law, a Citadel man and South Carolinian, whom Drayton knew slightly. Brigadier General Law's exhausted Confederates tried to find a few moments of rest and shade amid the boulders of Devil's Den and under the trees on the adjacent hill, Big Round Top. On the far side of the creek and throughout the swale lay dead men and horses and detritus of battle. There was a handful of dead cattle from the nearby farmstead. All lay swelling blackly in the late afternoon July sun. The lull on this part of the field continued. There were not even any Union pickets on the far side of the run and at the base of the rocky hill. The fighting had shifted to the center of Sickle's salient.

During the breathing spell, Longstreet called Drayton to his command post at the Rose Farm. Moxley Sorrel brought the ever-present map and held it up against a rail fence.

His face grim and drawn, the General said, "Mr. FitzHenry, we have to find a way around their flank. This battering of strength upon strength is draining us and getting us nowhere. While you were with Pickett, General Lee's staff engineer Captain Johnson reported that hill yonder was crawling with Yankees." He gestured toward Little Round Top. "But when Sickles moved his corps forward, I believe he left it uncovered. Colonel Alexander has spotted a Yankee signal team, but no infantry or artillery. If they had guns up there, we'd surely know it. They'd have fired on us in enfilade as we attacked the salient. It's the key position on Meade's left flank, our right. If it remains unoccupied and if we can take it, their blunder will give us this battle. I want you to get up there and scout it."

"If it can be done, General, Beltane and I will do it."

"Good. I expected no less of you. And listen now. I need a live report, not a dead hero. Take no unnecessary risks, but scout it thoroughly. If my hunch is correct, I want that hill. We all want this battle. We *must triumph* here. Ride now, and may God ride with you."

Chapter Twenty Five

Drayton is excited to the point of trembling; his breath comes thick and fast. Maybe God has ridden with him, if God hasn't turned his face from this field of blood. He has made it to the summit safely and now views the battle from the most strategic height on the field – inexplicably and inexcusably empty of troops. None of their deadly Parrott guns. No Yankee infantry, only some rudimentary stone breastworks they'd begun to erect before moving off the hill and into the wheat field and peach orchard. He touches the blackened embers of their cooking fires. Still warm. All is unnaturally still. Even their signals team has disappeared to the rear slope – decamped when Porter Alexander lobbed a few shells up here. Sickles' reputation will never survive this shocking blunder.

The view from Little Round Top is the first time he's beheld a battle between entire armies and not just a confused brawl of a few men in his immediate vicinity. The panorama is stirring and breath-taking; a tableau of entire brigades on the move, miniature artillery and limbers jolting forward, the crews atop the caissons bent forward nearly double, tiny drivers whipping the horses into a gallop, wheels turning so rapidly they appear to be spinning backwards. He can see why Longstreet is fixated on Little Round Top. It dominates the entire Yankee position; it's the key to winning the battle. Empty and ours for the taking. If our people can get up here first…

Has God truly ridden with me to this place? How is it that I of all people am the one Fate or God or Chance has dropped here at the most critical place and moment of the war's most critical battle, the battle that will decide the outcome? Drayton FitzHenry, the unwilling warrior, the notorious skeptic, the dubious patriot will be the one to bring back word of this crucial opportunity. But why me? What blind motion brought me here? Is it because I had the best horse? Is my horse my destiny?

One final look and Drayton slips away, flitting downhill among the boulders. He is only a few yards downslope when he hears voices above, from where he was just standing. He stoops behind an outcropping, turns, and edges back a short distance uphill. There he finds a two vast stone plinths with a massive lintel laid across the top forming a natural aperture. He steps into the protected position where he can scan the hilltop.

A Yankee officer — no, two men – are standing on a shelf of rock that projects outward from the summit, speaking animatedly, though he can't make out the words. One of the men is dark, short, and slight; the other, tall and fair. Through his glasses he can see that they're both officers, but can't make out their rank. The fine saber and binoculars mark the smaller and older man as senior. He is gesturing and expostulating to the younger man. He sees what I saw, Drayton realizes with a leaden feeling – this vital hilltop, key to the battle, vacated by his own side. But where are *his* troops? He and the younger man are alone. There are no regiments falling in behind them. Is he simply a scout, like me, a staff officer sent to check, but with no troops under his command? But for these two, the summit is as empty as Drayton has found it.

These men must not be allowed to report back to Meade. Drayton stows his field glasses, pulls the Spencer carbine round from his back on its cavalry sling, raises the rifle and steadies it on the rock cleft where he's lurking unseen. An easy shot at this distance. And with a repeater he can take them both. He sets the sights at forty yards. He will shoot the senior man first. Then, while his companion is bending over to render aid, he will kill him.

He breathes in, lets some of the air out slowly, then holds it and tightens his finger on the trigger. The sights are aligned. Squeeze, don't jerk. He can see them falling in his mind's eye. Shot down cravenly from ambush, without warning, without a thought of mercy. Murder. Murder, pure and simple.

He hears Celia's voice speak from the best place within him, soothing and low but still insistent: "In battle, do not forget God; and show mercy whenever you can. 'Where Mercy, Love, and Pity dwell / There God is dwelling, too.'" A pledge of love to her, inseparable from extending mercy to others. The promise he made in all sincerity, but also in all ignorance of war.

It isn't possible to take them prisoner. Better they not know he's been there observing; they might feel less urgency in making their report. Time to lay aside doubts and get on with his duty. His finger releases its tension, then comes off the trigger. Now the deed was done – or not done. He slings the Spencer around to his back and makes his way down to Bel, who whickers joyfully at his approach.

I have the fastest horse on the battlefield, and Bel is only a short distance. I'm closer to Longstreet than they are to Meade. They will have to make their way down the long back side of the hill and all the way back to Meade to report. I can – I will —win the race.

***

Drayton stole a quick look at his watch as he mounted. It would be an important bit of data – how long it took him to report back. In the event, it was twelve minutes. There was no way the Yankees on the summit could have made it back to higher headquarters faster than that, even if they had departed at the same moment. He was glad for Celia that he'd granted the Union officer his life. He would not return to her with wanton blood on his hands. The officer on Little Round Top would never know he'd come within a heartbeat of death, or that a distant woman had saved him, or that a fast horse had made it possible for his would-be assassin to keep a pledge. Drayton was as reconciled to soldiering as he'd ever be. The sacrificial death of Calhoun Sparks had changed him. But that didn't mean he felt a moral obligation to shoot every Bluecoat he saw. He'd observed many Yankees from 'hides' during his scouting along the Occoquan and could have killed them unsuspecting. He could have ambushed any number of Yankees while keeping watch on Meade for General Longstreet. But he'd held back, as circumstances dictated. And now, here, he couldn't bring himself to shoot them from the shadows.

He took a moment to stop at Brigadier Law's command post by the huge jumble of rocks across Bloody Run from Little Round Top. Young, slim, and eager, Law was giving orders to his regimental commanders when Drayton galloped up breathlessly and laid out General Longstreet's intent and the opportunity awaiting them up the hill. Then he galloped to Longstreet and saluted proudly, dramatizing his arrival by reining Bel back sharply. The horse reared, pawing the air. Drayton stayed in the saddle. His report began to tumble out.

"Take a deep breath, Lieutenant," said the General, grasping the bridle near the bit.

Drayton took a deep breath. "General, the hilltop is bare of the enemy. It's ours for the taking. But I can't say how long that will last. There was a Yankee officer up there scouting, too. He saw the same thing I did, no doubt. It's the key to the whole Union line on Cemetery Ridge. I took it on myself to report this to General Law on the way back to you. His Alabamians and Texians are the closest and can get there the quickest."

"Very well. I thought so," said Longstreet. "Now, I want you to ride to General Lee's headquarters and tell him what you've just told me. My orders are to roll up the enemy's left, but he's given me the latitude to decide how. You're reporting my decision, not asking for the order. Taking that hilltop will surely roll 'em up and more, and it's within the scope of my instructions. Well done, Lieutenant. Now, ride again. I'll send another courier with orders to General Law to move forward at once."

Lee was not at his headquarters, a modest one-story dwelling on the edge of Gettysburg. The battle was not going well on the Confederate left or on the right, and Lee had gone forward to Culp's Hill where the fight had bogged down. Drayton reported to Colonel Venable, who promised to pass on the message. As he rode back to Longstreet he heard volleys of musketry and Rebel-yelling to the southwest, in the direction of Little Round Top. Clearly the attack was going in to seize the high ground. He'd done his part. The rest was up to the grim-eyed stalwarts from Alabama and Texas.

Chapter Twenty Six

Gettysburg, Pennsylvania; late afternoon of July 2, 1863.

Drayton trotted over to the 1ˢᵗ Corps artillery park and called on Porter Alexander, commander of the Corps artillery. It was late in the evening, and men who'd been fighting all day lay sprawled in all the postures of exhaustion.

"Colonel, General Longstreet's compliments." He saluted and handed over Longstreet's orders for the morrow, which would be the third day of this ghastly, interminable battle. He waited in the saddle, easing his back muscles, while Alexander read in the glare of a campfire. He nodded, scratched out a hasty reply from his own orders book, and handed it to Drayton.

Drayton observed the artillerist's questioning look. Alexander glanced around him as if aware he was sharing sensitive information with a mere subaltern. "Lieutenant, General Lee seems determined to break them one way or another while we have them fixed in place. I suppose we must, or else leave here and return as best we can to Virginia with our tail between our legs." He waved his new orders in the air. "Marse Robert and Old Pete have something big in store for tomorrow. Pickett's Division is finally on the field. They are fresh and eager."

Drayton had seen the slaughter in the Peach Orchard and Wheat Field. "Tomorrow! Could anything be worse than today?"

"We'll know soon enough." Alexander turned away to see to his duties. "Until then, sufficient unto the day is the evil thereof."

What Marse Robert had in store was not to Old Pete's liking. The attack on Little Round Top had failed decisively. Still, Longstreet wanted to disengage and try to maneuver around Meade, even though at this stage the possibility was questionable at best. Lee had decided, perhaps on dubious evidence, that the Second Day's attacks on the Federals' left and right had induced Meade to weaken his center. Now Lee proposed to fling Pickett's fresh division into a frontal attack on the Yankee's supposedly weakened center, which rested on Cemetery Ridge behind a conspicuous copse of trees and a low stone wall. Drayton remembered Malvern Hill, last of the Seven Days Battles on the Peninsula, almost exactly one year earlier, when Union artillery blasted massed Confederate columns as they attacked frontally. A massacre. The same had happened to the Yankees at Fredericksburg, though no one cited it by name. Still, Drayton wondered, had Lee learned nothing from those debacles?

Longstreet persisted in arguing with Lee. Drayton watched the discussion, but couldn't hear. It seemed to him that Lee was tired and drawn, not his vigorous self. But he appeared determined to prevail on this field, crushing the Yankees once and for all and bringing an end to this sanguinary struggle of American against American. As Drayton watched, he saw some current pass between the two men. He read it as a mutual recognition of the same feeling in the other. Drayton realized with a shock that it was …love. They loved the men they had to send to their deaths, and a deep reluctance inhibited them. *Our generals simply aren't bloody-minded enough*, he thought. *I am not bloody-minded enough. And that's why we'll lose.*

Pickett's division assembled in the woods along the Confederate center of Seminary Ridge. Though not as elevated as the Yankee's high ground, it gave them some protection from enemy observation and counter-battery fire. To support Longstreet's grand assault, Lee assigned remnants from Pettigrew's and Trimble's divisions, badly fought out from the previous day, but adding some punch to the assault and bringing Longstreet's battering ram up to almost 14, 000 men.

Porter Alexander had 180 guns from 1st Corps. He borrowed from other units to support the charge. At 1:30 PM his massed batteries opened a stupendous cannonade on Cemetery Ridge to soften the Yankees for the attack. When Alexander signaled his ammunition was running low, Longstreet reluctantly sent Pickett and the supports forward. The brigades swept out of the tree line and formed as if on parade. They passed their own batteries and the sweating, cheering, powder-blackened gunners. Reforming beyond the guns, they paced off the deadly beckoning mile toward the Yankee lines. They marched into a storm of destruction. They marched into immortality.

General Kemper's brigade on the extreme right approached the objective. As they approached, a regiment of Yankees further to the right began to exfiltrate forward of their lines clearly aiming to bring the Confederates under flanking fire as they pressed forward. Longstreet ordered Drayton to ride forward to warn Kemper. Just as he delivered his message, a projectile hit him in the chest, knocking him out of the saddle. Stunned and senseless, he came to some uncertain time later in great pain and struggling to breathe. Feeling at his chest for the wound, he realized the ball or piece of shell had struck the Charles Fraser miniature of Celia and saved his life. Still, he was hurt badly enough, and could only make it back to the Confederate lines with the aid of a retreating soldier and by clinging to Beltane. There was no need to ask the fate of the attack. He could hear the Yankees cheering behind him. He could see the lines of Confederate dead, sprawling flat and empty. The bodies were dun-gray, blending almost with soil and hay stubble, but marked with splashes of red, the blood almost black where it soaked into the earth. The sight was like that of the sea-wrack cast up at high tide on the beaches near Charleston.

General Longstreet walked over and looked down at Drayton on the litter. He said nothing, but his face held an expression that wasn't quite pity or grief, or even apology, but somehow a mixture of all three. Seeing his courier was all right, the General nodded and walked away, raising his glasses to survey the stricken field.

Major Sorrel nodded 'yes' to Drayton's agonized appeal to convey Beltane to Captain Cabell Fitzhenry in the 2nd S.C. Cavalry. Then he motioned for the medical orderlies, who hoisted Drayton's litter into a captured Yankee ambulance wagon. The vehicle lurched off, swaying and jolting over the uneven ground. The other wounded inside began to groan with each jolt. Drayton knew he was in for a long, miserable ride.

***

He managed to hold on to his personal kit and one of his .36 Navy Colts. The other he'd given to Major Sorrel. In the chaos of the retreat, he never expected to see his main baggage again. Farewell to the fine Spencer repeater. Goodbye to spare uniforms and clothing, books, and a bottle of Napoleon brandy. His baggage might catch up with him, but it was unlikely. He was utterly bereft – a wounded and defeated soldier, lying helplessly in the bay of a wagon that pitched violently through every rut and pothole. And then the rains came.

On the afternoon of July 4, as his ambulance passed through Cashtown, a storm broke over the two armies with all the fury of the three-day battle itself. Booming thunder and lightning dwarfed human artillery. Slashing torrents of rain, driven horizontally by the wind, made it almost impossible to see. In minutes the dirt roads were rivers of mud as the Confederates began their long trek back toward Virginia and the safety of the Potomac. Mud clung to the hooves of horse and mules, wagon wheels, and the tired feet of men, slowing the pace of the retreat to a tortuous crawl. Drayton was grateful for the canopy covering the ambulance, though it could hardly be called shelter. Rain blew in from the open back. It dripped on the wounded where the saturated canvas rested on the wooden hoops. They suffered in silence, though their torment was beyond words. Drayton discovered the old formula in suffering – the degree of misery is in direct proportion to the elongation of time. He struggled upright, took off his rain slicker, and draped it over a feverish soldier on the top tier of litters most exposed to the leaks in the canopy. The man had lost a leg above the knee, was fevered and delirious from the inflammation of the wound. Drayton feared he didn't have long to live, and tried to make him comfortable. Then he collapsed in pain and exhaustion onto his own swaying stretcher.

Drayton had received a dose of laudanum on the Hagerstown Road before the wagon train began the retreat south. Was the scarce drug a privilege of serving on Longstreet's staff? Back when he was in a troop unit, like most line soldiers, he'd resented the staff wallahs who got the best of everything. But now he was too grateful for the relief to care. He allowed himself a few sips from his pocket flask of whiskey, severely self-rationed, and fell into a fitful sleep despite the jolting of the ambulance and the clamor of the storm. Hours later he awoke in darkness when the wagon halted. A tumult, an indistinct noise of shouting and gunshots, erupted somewhere down the line of retreat. Dull with drink and chest throbbing in pain, he struggled to the rear of the ambulance. His fellow passengers stirred, all but the man on top under Drayton's raincoat. He couldn't say how he knew, but the man had died.

He poked his head out and peered into the gloom and rain. It seemed the wagon train was under attack. Union cavalry, no doubt.

A few riders came sloshing up the muddy track from the rear of the column. Drayton called out, "What's happening?"

The horsemen reined in and a voice called out from the gloom. "We need every man who can stand on his feet — teamsters, the wounded, medical orderlies. Do you men have any arms?" In a flash of lightening on the horizon, Drayton recognized the officer; Captain James Hart, the Citadel man who'd commanded the Washington Artillery in the old Hampton Legion.

"Captain, it's Lieutenant FitzHenry. Late of Butler's 2nd Cavalry. I have my Colt." Painfully he descended from the ambulance. Every breath was an effort. He stood only by bracing himself against the rear wagon wheel. The rain had subsided, but he was still wet through and through.

"Mr. FitzHenry, well met. I heard you'd gone up to Longstreet. I'm sorry to find you among the wounded. But now we need every man. Local bucks from Greencastle and the Pennsylvania militia are attacking the trains all along the line. General Imboden is covering the rear with his cavalry, and I've got my Blakely guns posted back a-ways. But strung out like this, we're still vulnerable to being hit from the flanks."

Most of the casualties in the wagon were too hurt to move. But two lean and lanky wounded clambered down from their cots and joined Drayton. One had been shot in the jaw, and his head was swathed in bloody linen. "We ain't got no guns," his comrade growled. "But we still got our Bowie knives."

"They'll have to do. Mr. FitzHenry, you take charge of this wagon. Teamster," he called to the driver in the dark, "Are you armed?"

"Yes, sir. Shotgun."

"Stand by to use it, then. But stay up there in case you need to move off in a hurry. The attackers are trying to cut the traces and disable the wagons. Shoot anyone who tries. But for God's sake, be careful with that scatter gun. Don't hit your own mules. Good luck." Hart and his small troop splashed off into the dark.

Drayton and his comrades waited tensely, unable to see much, but straining to hear. *My first combat command*, Drayton laughed grimly to himself. *Two walking wounded and a muleskinner.*

Before long they heard loud pops and saw the muzzle flashes down the track toward Cashtown. Amid the sporadic gunshots they heard howling like wild Indians, cries of pain and rage, and triumphant rebel yells.

"They're comin' this way," said the wounded man who could speak. He and his companion twirled their huge blades that glinted wickedly with each streak of distant lightening.

The rolling skirmish kept their attention fixed behind them, up the track. It was the teamster who saw ghostly figures flitting from a stand of pines directly alongside the wagon.

"Look to yore left!" he yelled.

Before Drayton could react, the muleskinner discharged both barrels of his shotgun. The crew of the wagon in front of them fired at almost the same instant. Muzzle flashes revealed what appeared to be men in civilian dress running toward them. One carried a double-bitted axe, as if to chop the spokes of the wagon wheels. Drayton's heart rose in a sudden fury at this mad interruption of his ride home. Though it was impossible to pick his targets in the dark, especially moving targets, he squeezed off two shots blindly into the shadows where he heard the strange war whoops. He heard an even sharper yelp. *I hit one, by God.* Seized with battle rage, he stepped forward, firing off the rest of his cylinder. He had a glimpse of figures scuttling back into the darkness like cockroaches exposed to sudden light. His breath shortened. A vast iron fist gripped him. His head spun. His last thought as he collapsed into the mud was that he'd been shot again.

***

It was daylight when he woke in the ambulance, now blessedly at rest. As his vision slowly focused, he found himself staring quizzically into the rough bearded face of his wounded comrade leaning over him.

"No, Lieutenant, you ain't dead," said the grinning man. "And I ain't the Angel Gabriel.

"If I'm not dead, then where am I?"

"We jes' pulled into our lines at Williamsport."

"What about the pontoon bridge?"

The man snorted. "We jes' come through Noah's Flood. Ain't nary a bridge. Guess we'll have to stand and fight, and with our backs to the river." He examined the edge of his Bowie knife with something like ferocious glee.

The litters, the wounded, the entire inside of the wagon bay, were soaked and dripping. Drayton struggled to sit up, feeling the weight of his sodden clothes. The sharp pain had subsided to a sharp ache. He noticed someone had draped him in his rain slicker. A glance upward revealed the top cot was empty.

"Didn't you get a bellyful of it at Gettysburg?" he asked his companion.

"Wahl, that was a right sharp fight, shore enough." The man exposed a left leg wrapped in bandages. "Damn knee cap shot off. The doc like to've taken off the whole laig, but the ball come at it sideways and didn' leave no…uh, *particles,* he said. I was dumb lucky, I guess."

"Who were you with?"

"Gen'l Barksdale." He extended his hand. "Combs, Ezra Combs. Sergeant, Company H, 21st Mississippi."

Drayton shook hands. "Drayton FitzHenry. General Longstreet's staff. I assume you know General Barksdale is dead."

"I know. An' most a mah regiment. too. But we tore into 'em somethin' fierce. I don't rightly know why we had to come all the way up north to give them Yankees such a whuppin'. But if'n they follow us…Wahl, we'll jes' have to finish 'em off raht here."

"Well," said Drayton, fighting to catch his breath amid waves of pain. "I don't mind telling you, for the time being they've knocked all the fight out of me."

"That's all raht, young fellah. We'll fight 'em till Hell freezes over. Then we'll fight 'em on the ice."

***

Lee's engineers performed a prodigy of combat engineering to bridge the Potomac River, now in full spate after the torrential rain. The army assumed Meade was hot on their heels, but Lee was never dispirited, never fearful. Boldly he dug in at Williamsport until the makeshift bridge was thrown across the river. The wounded, the wagon train and stores crossed first, while the bulk of Lee's men remained behind their fortifications, almost daring Meade to attack. Once across, the leaden steps of the exhausted draft animals barely quickened. Some were no longer able to put one plodding foot after another and had to be abandoned. The wounded pleaded not to be left. Many drivers, in less fear now of pursuit by Gregg's or Buford's cavalry, stopped to take on as many of the marooned as possible. But General Imboden's officers hurried them along with harsh words. Drayton could follow the trail of the army by the detritus of war — broken wagons, discarded weapons and equipment, dead draft animals. Lee's Miserables were miserable indeed. He thought, *This is the path of glory.*

His driver told him that Butler's Cavalry had been part of the rear-guard covering the retreat. Before that, the man told him, Stuart's entire cavalry had fought a brutal all-cavalry action on the Third Day, east of Gettysburg and behind the main Union positions on Cemetery Ridge.

Once Stuart and his Division had finally found their way back to the Army on July 2, Lee had ordered Stuart to fall on Meade's rear the next day, in coordination with the assault by Pickett and Pettigrew on the Union front. It was an audacious plan, typical of Lee. It might well have worked but for the presence of Gregg's Federal horse troopers, more numerous and fresher than Stuart's men and horses, exhausted from their long pointless ride of the previous week. And the Yankees had been armed with those cursed Spencer repeaters, giving them a firepower advantage of five to one.

The driver added that General Wade Hampton had been badly wounded in the fight. He was somewhere in the same ambulance train headed for the Confederate military hospital in Charlottesville. He prayed Cabell had survived the cavalry battle, and that Beltane was safe in his care.

Thomas Moore

Chapter Twenty Seven

The General Military Hospital, Charlottesville, Virginia; July 1863.

In Drayton's view army hospitals were where people went to die, not to heal. But this one was far better than he expected – clean, well-managed, and providing a level of medical attention as good as could be found, given the South's shortages of drugs and medical supplies. Food was adequate. The patients lay on decent cots in the long wards. High ceilings and tall French windows kept the summer heat at a bearable level and dissipated some of the odor of suppurating wounds and lye soap.

He was pleasantly surprised to find himself under the care of a cousin, Dr. James Cabell of the University of Virginia medical faculty. The doctor packed lint around the fractured sternum to pad and immobilize it, then wrapped his thorax in a long cotton cingulum.

"Unless you subject it to stresses of motion, the fracture will heal of itself," the doctor advised. "The bruised heart is more troubling. You should refrain, insofar as possible in times like these, from undue excitement."

It was a hospital that a writer of children's fables might have designed, for it had an eccentric air about it. At times it seemed slightly absurd, peopled by odd characters straight out of Aristophanes or Aesop. Among the civilian volunteers who came to supplement the staff were the Moon sisters. One of them read devoutly from the Bible while the other, an atheist and feminist, campaigned for female suffrage, urging bemused Southern soldiers to do the same when they returned home. One old Charlottesville gentleman stopped in daily, volunteering to write letters for the wounded, but interrupted the patient constantly asking how to spell even the most commonplace words. Dr. Barton Smith, called from retirement and the enjoyment of his senility, often forgot what ward he was assigned to. A medical orderly had to lead him where he was supposed to be. But Dr. Smith could suture a wound or amputation with enormous skill. Since medical silk and catgut were scarce, he began using horsetail hairs, boiling them to make them soft and pliable. Dr. Cabell couldn't explain why, but he observed that using boiled horsetail hairs resulted in radically fewer inflammations of the wound, fewer even than with the standard material. Soon all sutures were of boiled horsetail hairs, and mortification of wounds dropped noticeably.

Many patients had heard of Drayton's survival at the height of the Great Charge. Those who could walk stopped by in a constant stream to marvel at the shattered miniature. Drayton indulged them as much as he could, enjoying their pet theories – theological or purely scientific – how the brass oval had saved his life. He noticed their examinations lingered over the dark eyes in the image that had survived the impact. In fact, the image was now mostly just a set of eyes, more alluring and mysterious than if the entire face had remained intact.

The owner of the doe-eyes, her face, form, and dewy translucent skin, visited him often in his dreams. Not infrequently he awoke in a state of tumescence, glancing around the ward with embarrassment and hoping no one had noticed the telltale bulge under the sheets. Not that it was unusual in this company of sex-starved men. *What strange creatures we humans are*, he mused, sexual desire existing in the midst of pain; life asserting itself amid constant death.

The best thing of all was letters from home for the first time in weeks. He was reading one from Celia when he heard a scuffling of feet and a nervous clearing of the throat. His eyes dropped from the page to the floor. He recognized the new boots at once. Yankee cavalry boots.

Looking up, he smiled. "Hello, Cabell. I hope you're not here as a patient."

***

Cabell found his brother looking comfortable and well fed. But there were dark circles under Drayton's eyes. Deep lines had etched themselves from the corners of his nose down to either side of his lips and chin. Permanent furrows creased his brow. Unbuckling his belt with sword and pistols and laying them aside, Cabell mustered all his moral courage. *He's in pain from his wound,* he thought. *In a moment he'll be wounded even worse.* Cabell settled on a three-legged stool close to his brother's cot. Up close, Cabell saw he'd been shaved recently; there were bloodspots on his chin. He wore a pallor despite the past weeks under the summer sun.

"I called on our cousin Dr. Cabell before stopping in the ward," said Cabell. "He tells me that with rest, you'll recover."

He cleared his throat nervously, searching for the right words. "The Regiment has been directed toward Culpeper again. We may even end up at your old battlefield at Brandy Station, guarding the fords of the Rappahannock. We lost a lot of people and especially mounts in the Pennsylvania Campaign. We have thirty men on leave to procure new horses."

"Brother, I know you, 'said Drayton unexpectedly. "What's wrong? Is it Beltane?"

For an instant Cabell felt a flood of relief. Drayton's question gave him another moment's respite. "No, the old boy is perfectly fine. He was nicked in the right shoulder, probably the same action when you were hit. But he's fine, truly. Taking his ease and grazing on lush Virginia grass with the remount company."

"Then it's Ranse." Drayton's voice cracked.

Cabell's words caught in his throat. But he had to tell him. He clutched Drayton's forearm and said, "Yes." He drew in his breath. "He'd dead."

"O, Cabell. Dear God." Drayton strangled on his words. "It was on the Second Day, wasn't it? I… I saw him. I was taking a message from Longstreet and we spoke for a moment before… before they went in." His brother's tears flowed unashamedly, and Cabell thought, *Drayton was always the emotional one. But I have lost too many friends to have many tears left, even for Ranse.*

"Then you saw him just before he died," Cabell said, his voice businesslike and even. "He was killed in Kershaw's charge on Sickle's Third Corps soon after. It was a slaughter, on both sides. Almost half his brigade was lost. I understand they call the place the Peach Orchard. What innocuous name for such a place of death."

Drayton's face twisted in pain. "Do you recall how he loved fresh peaches?"

Cabell's memory swam back to a place and time that now seemed unreal. "Yes," he said. "As a boy he used to climb up into the trees when the fruit ripened down on the River. He claimed the best peaches were at the top. Father was always sick with worry he'd fall and break his fool neck."

Drayton smiled through his tears. "Father would assign Old Joshua to walk around under the branches to break his fall just in case. But Old Joshua would lie down under the tree and go to sleep. We'd come out to the orchard later and find them both asleep, with Ranse nestled in Old Joshua's arm."

"And Ranse would explain it was because he didn't want Joshua to get into trouble."

They sat in a lengthy silence with their memories. Then Cabell came to his feet. He had to get back to the Regiment to help organize the move east. "I must go," he said. "Do you need anything?"

"Just take good care of my horse."

Cabell nodded. He didn't voice the envious thought, *Your war is over, Brother. You won't be needing him again because you won't be coming back to the Army.* He said after a moment's hesitation, "I have something to ask of you."

"Yes?"

"The Regiment will be in movement for the next few days and perhaps go into action. I want you to write Father. You have the greater skill with words, although there are no words to make the news any more bearable."

Drayton didn't answer, and Cabell began to wonder if he'd refuse. As the elder brother, it was more properly Cabell's responsibility.

"All right," Drayton said at last. "I don't want to, but I will. You will need to follow with your own letter, of course, when you're able."

"Of course." Cabell took is brother's hand and squeezed it. He turned on his heel and strode away, his boots resounding with hollow echoes on the wood-plank floor.

**

Drayton asked the hospital orderly to locate someone in Kershaw's Brigade who might also be a patient. If possible, he wanted to include some last comforting detail in his letter home, or a recollection from someone who knew Ranse. That evening a young man from Ninety-Six District, Lieutenant Francis Bedenbaugh, dropped by his ward. He had lost his right arm at the elbow in the same charge where Ranse had lost his life. In the circumstances, Mr. Bedenbaugh considered himself fortunate. They spoke quietly for an hour and the man left.

With a heavy sigh, Drayton took up pen, ink, and paper. *It takes twenty years of peace to make a good man, and twenty seconds of war to destroy him,* he thought. The grief of losing Ranse was so great that his hand shook as the pen scratched along the page. He wrote as though not with ink but his heart's blood:

The General Military Hospital
Charlottesville, Virginia
July the 14th, 1863

My Dear Father,

On behalf of Cabell Junior and myself, and because he is assigned to such active duties as to make letter-writing impossible, I write to you now with an insupportable grief.

Your dear son and our beloved brother Ransome is no more. In His inscrutable design it pleased God to take Ranse from us on July the 2nd inst, on the second day of the great battle fought in Pennsylvania at the Town of Gettysburg.

So many other fine young men fell there, Father – oh, so many! – in three days of the most desperate fighting, that one hesitates to express the heartbreak we cannot help but feel; for our loss is but one drop, though a cherished one, in a vast sea of the slain on both sides. The collective voice of anguish from the loved ones of the maimed and lost, plus the battle being lost, must resound at the gates of Heaven with a clamor seldom heard. I can offer no other comfort but that Ranse has passed on to that better World for which he was created.

I am greatly consoled to have had the opportunity to speak with him moments before the fatal charge that took his life and nearly half of Kershaw's Brigade. Father, if only I could tell you how he went smiling into the fight after our brief meeting. He was wearing an odd (and most unmilitary) straw hat against the broiling sun that he had procured from a Pennsylvania farmer. The image is indelibly printed on my memory how he turned and waved the hat gaily to me, smiled, then turned back and charged with his Regiment into a veil of smoke and dust. I did not witness his end, but learned later that he picked up the fallen flag, and with a laugh and a cheer as was his wont, guided the Regiment in its attack on the Yankee Third Corps. The pall of powder smoke made it impossible even for his comrades to observe all that befell that stricken field. Yet there is no doubt he is gone. The straw hat was found in tatters. He is carried among the killed on the rolls of the Regiment. It also grieves me to tell you his body was not recovered before the Army was forced to retreat back into Virginia.

Tho' I have endeavour'd to give you an accurate account, you can understand that a perfect reconstruction of events is not possible, as the action was obscured by the smoke and confusion of battle. I can only pray that our Lord, who holds in His hands the Destinies of all men and who has promised to comfort all who mourn, will assuage the pain of his loss. And may you also be comforted by the knowledge that no father ever raised a nobler or more gallant son. He was indeed the best of us.

I am, dear Father, your obedient and loving

Drayton

P.S. Father, on July the 3rd I was wounded in the breast by a Minnie ball or a round of canister at Gettysburg during General Longstreet's final grand assault, which lamentably failed with a great slaughter of our men. The projectile struck the brass-mounted miniature given me by Cecelia, which I wore at my heart. Thus armored by God's grace and her forethought I was not terribly much hurt, although the surgeon says my heart is bruised. With rest and good care I am expected to make a full recovery, for which object I am to be released when well enough and sent home to Charleston on medical furlough, and for such duration as may prove necessary. I can't say when this will be, but I hope to see you soon.

He felt slightly sickened by the conventional phrases of comfort. They were so inadequate as to seem indecent. But custom and habit were strong, and he could only hope they provided solace for his father. Yet, he asked himself, could he say in good conscience that there was any 'inscrutable design' which had taken Ranse – and nearly 8,000 others, North and South? And that was only the preliminary toll. Hundreds more would succumb to wounds. Could he truly believe it 'pleased God' to take the life of Ranse or any other soldier? Surely if the Christian religion meant anything, God could not be pleased. He must Himself be weeping over the crimes and follies of His creatures.

Drayton laid down the page and picked up a fresh sheet to write his wife and set her mind at ease. Telegraphed versions of the great battle had probably arrived by now in Charleston. She would be worried.

***

Sophia Hill, a Dublin-born woman had accompanied her brother's regiment of Louisiana Zouaves, the "Tigers," and mothered all the Charlottesville patients while her brother recovered in hospital. She'd become the unofficial matron of the entire establishment, and the men loved her. At the end of his second week, Mrs. Hill stopped by Drayton's cot and settled on the three-legged stool with a swish of taffeta, bringing forth a bottle from the folds of her dress.

"Will I pour you a measure?" she asked.

"Certainly," said Drayton, surprised, but glad of the unexpected largesse. He sipped, and was delighted to taste smooth and mellow Kentucky bourbon, not the Virginia mountain potstill stuff he'd been drinking.

"Now then," said Mrs. Hill. "Show me the miracle."

"The miracle?"

"The miracle brooch that saved you from the Yankees. I was told ye'd only show it for the price of a drop."

It was the first time he'd laughed since Gettysburg. Physically it hurt. Yet how therapeutic it was. He held out the miniature.

"By the Saints!" Mrs. Hill chortled. "A marvelous thing altogether. The Lord God was holding you in the palm of his hand surely. And such eyes the girl has. Irish eyes."

"Yes, she is my dark-eyed one. Do you know how to say that in the Irish?"

"Do I not? *Suilliabhean*. I'm told she holds to the true religion."

"Aren't they all true, in their way?"

"Indeed not. 'Tis her faith that covered and saved you, no doubt." She poured another finger of bourbon. "Aside from the good cheer," she brandished the bottle, "and the good company, I bring you good news."

"I can always stand a spot of good news."

"Dr. Cabell says you will survive and with the Dear's blessing, live to a ripe old age." She broke into a wide smile, but her teeth were cracked and jagged, like fangs. Drayton had to look away. "Lieutenant FitzHenry, you're for home."

Chapter Twenty Eight

Charleston, South Carolina, August 1863.

The train ride home from Charlottesville was uncomfortable and interminable. Decrepit engines had to be replaced in Danville, Charlotte, and Columbia, with stops for wood and water at many lesser towns along the way, whose names he forgot as quickly as the train departed. His bunk was primitive, one of a tier of planks hastily nailed into the interior of the carriage. The mattress was rough canvas stuffed with straw, but a luxury compared to sleeping on hard ground, as he grown used to in active service. He often went hungry. But the medical orderlies were kind. They made sure their patients at least received plenty of water, the only commodity in plentiful supply and much needed in the August heat.

The bumping and swaying along the rickety tracks tested his endurance. But eventually the tired locomotive puffed into Charleston's Meeting Street Station, where Celia, his father, and Shortbread and Shadpole waited with the barouche. Tenderly they transferred him to a litter, then to East Bay Street, and up to the comforts of his own room. After everyone had offered their few joyous words of welcome, Celia shooed them out, Father and servants alike. She stripped off his filthy hospital cottons, and began to sponge him down with warm water and castile soap.

She stroked his week's growth of beard. "That will have to come off. It makes you look older."

"I *am* older. And not just by the calendar."

Someone set down a tray of refreshments outside the door with a clatter but didn't disturb them.

"My Love," he sighed, stretching cat-like in the welcome embrace of his feather-bed. "I don't bemoan the wound I received at Gettysburg, for it's given us this time together, a time that the outbreak of war denied us. There were moments when I thought I might never see you or this place again."

"I never doubted." She smiled contentedly. Her warm wet sponge reached his nether regions. "Hmmmm," she said, arching her eyes.

"Love, my heart is bruised. I'm under strict doctor's orders to avoid undue excitement."

"Let me manage, Dearest. I'm sure we can stop just short of 'undue.'"

***

The family were at dinner one afternoon on the upper piazza, where Ambrosia had set up the meal service to catch the cooling sea breezes that wafted even in August. Uncle Porcher and Aunt Meggs, Drayton's mother's sister, had dropped in to pay homage. Uncle Porcher was sharing the latest news from the Charleston *Courier* about the enormous draft riots that had broken out in New York City. In mid-July tens of thousands of New Yorkers had risen in violent protest against conscription. They were mostly poor immigrants from Ireland and Germany and working class men who couldn't afford the $300 to pay a substitute for the Union army. They burned the draft office and Republican newspapers, assaulted and murdered local police and Federal officials. They had also turned in violence toward the city's Negroes. Dozens had been lynched. They were blamed for the conflict, and for taking the laboring jobs the urban whites must give up to fight in a war the Democratic city opposed.

Uncle Porcher, his face red with drink and anger, flourished his newspaper. "James Gordon Bennett writes that what has been going on in New York is the largest land battle in the country after Gettysburg!" He fairly screeched. "The Union government are sending troops to put down the insurrection. The Lincolnites will have to seek a negotiated peace with the South. They can't fight a war against the South *and* fight against their own people at the same time." He looked hopefully toward Drayton for confirmation.

Bundled in a settee despite the warmth, Drayton stared morosely at his uncle, then the rest of the group one-by-one, then off in the distance, toward the Harbor, where the Union fleet patrolled implacably.

"No, Uncle," he said. "We are caught in a trap, North and South. The more lives that are lost, the more blood must be shed to justify the loss. The Yankees will crush the New York insurrection no matter what, just as they will crush us in time."

Father was pouring some chilled white wine. He frowned at Drayton, holding the bottle suspended.

"I don't think such defeatist talk is called for," he said, "although if anyone has earned the right to his opinion, it is you, Son."

In that instant a loud crash reverberated from somewhere southwest of them on the Peninsula. Startled, Father dropped the bottle, scattering the serving dishes. "What in God's name!" A half-second later there followed an even more resonating boom that shook the ground and rattled windows. A column of smoke spiraled upwards from the area above the Battery. All eyes turned to the south, searchingly, fearfully. Then they turned to Drayton, now the resident expert on warfare.

"I think it's a round of heavy artillery, Yankee artillery. Fused round, which explains the second boom," he said. "If it's followed by another… well, then we'll know."

It was.

***

Early in the War the Federals had seized Hilton Head Island, routing the Southern defenders of Fort Walker and establishing a base for their naval blockade and other operations along the coast. In 1862 they laid siege to Charleston itself. The fighting had been confined to the approaches to the city — the Sea Islands and outer harbor. It had been mostly a naval campaign, with the new Yankee ironclads attacking the ring of heavily armed forts protecting the anchorage, including Fort Sumter, now in Confederate hands. In June 1862 the Federals had also struck at the city by land with an assault on Secessionville, on nearby James Island. Confederate defenders had thrown them back with heavy loss. Until now, the city itself had been spared the direct consequences of the siege. But suddenly it appeared Charleston was within range of long-range guns on Morris Island. This was as close as the Yankees had been able to come to the city.

Cabell Senior went at once to General Beauregard's headquarters. He was a long time returning; four more rounds exploded in his absence. He came back in a fury and gave orders to the servants to begin packing. They would leave for Cypress Stand as soon as possible.

A loyal Negro on James Island had brought in a report that the Yankees had erected a heavy siege gun on a platform of palmetto logs, virtually floating in the marsh on Morris Island, and elevated at a high angle for maximum range. They called it the 'Swamp Angel,' presumably for the Angel of Death. The gunners used the silhouette of St. Philip's Church steeple, in the heart of the city, as their aiming point. Beauregard's engineers and artillerymen believed its shells could reach no farther than the lower Peninsula, but everything and everyone within its range was at risk. The Yankees had also imprisoned a hundred Confederate officers in front of the battery to discourage Southern gunners from firing back. The prisoners languished in Medieval conditions, unprotected from harsh weather and voracious insects. There was nothing Charleston's defenders could do to stop the destruction. General Beauregard had sent an angry remonstrance to the Federals condemning the wanton shelling of civilians. It was a breach of the laws of war and the usages of Christian civilization. The best the Yankees would do was to give Beauregard twelve hours' respite to evacuate non-combatants.

As he struggled downstairs on Celia's arm, Drayton sighed. "It has come to this, the indiscriminate bombardment of a civilian population. It's clearly against the laws of war. But then, so much else that has happened in this war violates the laws of man and God."

"What did you expect?" Celia said quietly. "*Inter arma, silent leges.*" In time of war the laws are silent.

Later they learned that the gun had burst. The Yankees erected another Marsh Battery with four eight-inch Parrott rifles. Their shells turned lower Charleston into a ghost town of gutted houses. Yet somehow the mansion on the Battery escaped damage.

Doctor Moore had told him the deepest wound was inside and not visible, more worrisome than the fractured sternum, and that was the shock to the heart. If he didn't let the bruised heart heal, it could fail at any time under a strain. There was no better place to recuperate than Cypress Stand, even though mosquito season was at its height. Maum Biddy had concocted a surprisingly effective herbal potion for the white folks to discourage the wretched creatures, the bane of the Low Country. Purple martins were beginning to arrive on their southward migration. Each bird could consume its weight daily in mosquitoes, and colonies of bird tenements made from dried gourds erected on poles were readied for their welcome arrival.

They brought him upstairs to his room, and Celia helped him into the high rice bed. He reclined gratefully and took her hand. "Ah, Love," he said. "Words can't begin to convey the horrors I've seen. And if they could, you would not believe them. But I have tried to remain true to your charge."

"My charge?"

"Yes, my pledge. When I first went away, you charged me not to sink into brutishness, not to descend into the horror, not to become a man of blood. And out of my deep love for you, I promised to show mercy whenever I could. I've done my best."

"Yes, I remember. I feared you might not."

"But it has exacted a price. There was this one Yankee officer atop a hill called Little Round Top at Gettysburg. I came close to shooting him down – from ambush, as it were. He never knew I was there, hiding in the rocks. And I never learned who he was. I'm glad I spared him, yet he haunts me still. I dream of him, and some nights he laughs and scoffs at me as a coward. On others he nods and appears grateful. Either way he disturbs my sleep. He was alone, except for an aide. I had them both in my rifle sights, and in easy range. Yet for your sake I couldn't shoot. It would have seemed an act of murder. I didn't want to come back to you with blood…" He held up his hands. Unlike others, who looked away when presented with his raw, maimed fingers, Celia took his left hand, held it tenderly, and stroked her face with it.

"God will bless you for it," she said. "I know He will preserve you for this act of mercy."

"Why should He spare me when He has taken the lives of countless better men?" Her words made him angry instead of comforting.

"*He* hasn't taken their lives. Besides, don't you know your Scriptures? 'I will make all my goodness pass before thee. I will be gracious to whom I will be gracious, and I will show mercy on whom I will show mercy.'"

Drayton was speechless for a while at his wife's unplumbed depths. Finally he nodded. "Yes, from Exodus." But it provided no reassurance. *Why should He show mercy to me, of all men, and not to Ranse or to so many others, on both sides?* It made no sense. "At any rate I've been safe enough. Thanks largely to Beltane I was assigned as a scout and courier. I was not in direct contact with the enemy."

"Well, the enemy certainly was in direct contact with you." She touched his wounded hand. "And here." She touched him lightly where his chest was bruised.

"It was simply a stray piece of shell. They weren't aiming at me specifically."

"What a relief to know that," she said with a sarcasm she seldom showed. "At any rate you're home, and you're done with the War. Come what may, from now on we'll be together. And together we can face anything."

***

A few days later Father knocked on Drayton's door. "I must speak to you. I have sad news." Celia gave a slight curtsey and made to leave the room, but Father restrained her lightly by the forearm with a sorrowful smile. "No, Dear. Don't go. This matter touches you, too."

Drayton was sitting up in bed. His father pulled a cane-back chair close and extracted a letter from his coat pocket. Arms crossed over her chest, Celia paced the room. Father adjusted his glasses and prepared to read. "It's from Colonel Chesnut in Charleston."

My Dear Cabell, I regret to inform you that the son of our friend Judge Pringle, Captain Robert Pringle of the 1ˢᵗ South Carolina Artillery, was mortally wounded commanding his heavy battery at Fort Wagner on Morris Island. As you know, Wagner has been under constant bombardment. On August 19 Robert was inspecting a gun dismounted by enemy fire when a shell from a Yankee monitor exploded in front of him. A fragment passed completely though his midsection, leaving him only a few moments to say his goodbyes before he expired. He was a splendid young man. He gallantly exposed himself to the relentless fire of the enemy in order to keep his guns in action. Judge Pringle has informed me the funeral will take place at St. Michael's, which so far remains beyond the range of the Yankee Swamp Battery, on August 23, with interment to follow at Magnolia Cemetery.

"In the present circumstances I do not see how we can attend," Father said, "but I thought you would want to know." He left the letter on the edge of the high bed and softly quit the room.

"My old rival." Drayton picked up the letter, read it again, and let it fall to the floor. He said with more bitterness than intended to his wife, "There's that word again – gallant. They said it of John Pelham, who died needlessly last March at Kelly's Ford. Ranse died gallantly at Gettysburg. They even said it of me after Brandy Station. Little did they know. And now Robert Pringle."

Celia walked to the letter, picked it up, folded it reverently, and laid it on the side table. She placed a cool hand on Drayton's cheek. "I must see about dinner." She left the room.

At dinner Father was unusually quiet, and Drayton had little to say. His joy at returning to Celia hadn't overcome his moroseness. With no one to talk to, Celia ate silently. Shadpole brought tea and sponge cakes, which they decided to take on the verandah, as the evening was fine with a breeze that swept the mosquitoes away. They settled pensively with their teacups to enjoy the view of the River, which never failed to give pleasure, no matter how many times they saw it. A clutch of black children were running and playing in the lawn along the verge, chasing butterflies. Their carefree laughter annoyed him – in fact, *any* laughter annoyed him, Drayton noted. But he was powerless to change. The youngsters should have been working. Even slave children had chores, like minding the geese, bringing hay to the draft animals. Father seemed not to care. Drayton wondered if he'd begun to neglect his otherwise careful management of the plantation.

Without preamble or warning, Father turned to Drayton and said, "I want to know about Ranse. Judge Pringle at least has his son to bury. I don't. How do I even know that he's... he's dead?"

"Father, I wish I could tell you more. It's certain that he died. I regret deeply we couldn't bring him home for burial." Until they did, Father might never find the acceptance of the loss that he needed to go forward.

Despite the totality of the war, Northern newspapers still managed to find their way through Southern lines and were devoured by Confederate soldiers famished for news. While in hospital in Charlottesville Drayton had read the Hartford, Connecticut *Courant* making its rounds in the wards. The lead article said that the U.S. Government had contracted with a Gettysburg man named Basil Biggs to bury the Union dead at Gettysburg for $1.69 per body. With thousands dead Mr. Biggs stood to earn a princely sum. Of course, he wasn't expected to do the job single-handedly but to hire local labor. The reporter explained it was too much to ask the gravediggers to treat all the dead with the same dignity. When they came across 'traitor rebs,' they shoveled them into unmarked mass graves. Only those who had 'died for freedom' merited an effort to identify them through their personal effects. In due time they'd be given a dignified burial in the new Gettysburg National Cemetery when it was ready. Like many Confederates, Ranse was left in enemy country, with nothing to commemorate his sacrifice or mark his final resting place.

Drayton's musings led him to an idea. "Let us erect a cenotaph for Ranse."

"What's a cenotaph?"

"Well, Father, it's a tomb or monument for someone whose remains lie elsewhere. It comes from the Greek words *kenos*, meaning 'empty,' and *taphos*, meaning 'tomb.'"

Father's eyes wandered absently over the Negro children, still laughing and skylarking. Then his eyes wandered to the slight rise above the River where Drayton's mother and maternal grand-parents lay buried behind a low brick enclosure.

"Yes. A cenotaph," said Father. "That's what we'll do."

***

Inflation of Confederate paper money was running apace, and prices for everything were high, both the marble from Caesar's Head and the stonecutter's services. As always it was a matter of supply and demand. The stonecutter had more trade than he could handle as the war's toll mounted. But Cabell Senior managed a simple monument, a four-foot tapered plinth with a pyramidal cap, resting on a plain square base. The cenotaph was inscribed with Ranse's date of birth and the legend:

Died on the Field of Valour at Gettysburg, Penna, July 2, 1863

As they waited at the monument for the Right Reverend Pierpont to arrive for the memorial service, Father said, "Our Reverend seems to be delayed. While we have some time, tell me again about Ranse, how it happened, what his comrades said."

"Father, I've told you twice." Drayton knew he sounded cranky and almost disrespectful, against his own inclination. *What's the matter with me?*

"Yes, I know. But perhaps you left out a detail. And I'm getting old, you know. Sometimes I have to hear something more than once to retain it."

"Very well." Despite his occasional severity, Father had unusually tender feelings for his family, unlike some patriarchs of the plantocracy who were distant and remote. Cabell Senior's love for his wife had been legendary in an era when many marriages were mere dynastic arrangements. Before the War Aunt Meggs had told Drayton how his father became more humane and compassionate upon the death of his wife. Now he observed Father's softening at the death of Ranse. Drayton had feared the loss would be more than he could bear. What do you do when given more than you can bear, yet still must bear it? Die of anger or a broken heart? Unravel by slow degrees? Simply fade away from lack of will to live any longer? Then he'd worried Father might become embittered against all things Northern, including Celia. But it hadn't happened. If anything, their shared suffering had brought Father and Celia closer together.

Drayton took a deep breath. "Well, as you recall from my letter, most of what I learned came from an officer who was there, a Mr. Bedenbaugh from Ninety-Six, whom I met in hospital. The task of Longstreet's Corps, which included Kershaw's Brigade, was to seize a portion of the line held by Sickles' Union Third Corps. Sickles had inexplicably moved his Corps forward so that it protruded from the main Yankee position on Cemetery heights. This salient was vulnerable, and General Lee ordered Longstreet to attack *en echelon*, that is, with each brigade following on the flank of its predecessor after an interval to draw away the defenders, like a wave of the sea striking the shore."

"Yes, I recall."

"The 69th New York was across the field — the "Fighting Irish" — and I knew Ranse and his fellows faced a terrible time. The combat was intense and brutal. As Ranse's regiment went in, they were rocked back by Yankee volleys. They paused for a moment as if gathering their resolve. Many fell, including the flag-bearer. Since each regiment guides on its colors, they are always a prime target. Ranse seized the fallen flag in his right, raised it high, and with his musket still in his left, called out, 'Now are you fellows coming or not?' He turned and plunged forward into a curtain of powder smoke. The regiment cheered and followed. In less time than it takes to tell, Mr. Bedenbaugh came upon him, sprawled on his back. When the Lieutenant stooped down to take up the flag again, he noticed the toothbrush Ranse always carried thrust in the buttonhole of his uniform. It was his signature, so to speak. You know, Father, how fastidious he was. On an impulse Lt. Bedenbaugh plucked the toothbrush, intending to send it to the family as a memento of our loss. Then he too was hit, in the arm and right thigh. As he went down, the attack swept past him. The contested ground changed hands many times in bloody combat, often hand-to-hand. His people were never able to recover Ranse's body as the tide of battle moved back and forth."

"Call me an old fool, but I cherish the hope he may still be alive, languishing in some Yankee hospital or prison."

"Would to God it were so. But no, Father. Here."

Drayton pulled an object from his inside breast pocket, swaddled in brown paper. He had intended to keep it for himself, his own personal keepsake of a beloved brother. But now he realized it was more needed elsewhere. He handed it to his father, who unwrapped it slowly. It was the toothbrush, the handle made of polished cow horn and embedded with stiff pig bristles.

"Did he suffer much?"

"No, Father. He died instantly, so quickly in fact there was not even time for the smile to fade from his lips." Drayton didn't reproach himself for the lie. It was half true, anyway. But he couldn't repeat what Lt. Bedenbaugh had told him in the hospital: *His head was taken off by a cannon ball. The body fell on its back, the blood pulsing horribly from the stump of the neck. I could only tell who it was for the toothbrush in the buttonhole of his uniform blouse.*

At last Reverend Pierpont, pink and plump in his dusty black soutane, arrived in a one-horse shay driven by an ancient Negro. Drayton watched the grizzled old man loose the traces, soothing the animal with whispers while his master officiated. The Reverend's clerical collar was yellow and frayed. His hands trembled slightly as he opened his book.

A slight breeze riffled the surface of the River, and the sun glinted on the tops of the wavelets. Drayton listened to the lugubrious ooo-ooo-oohing of the doves roosting in the pines west of the farm. *Mourning doves. They are well-named.*

The familiar ritual provided little of the comfort it was supposed to. To Drayton words *meant* something. They were not mere noises to fill up the empty space in the heart scoured away by grief. Thinking back on his letter from the hospital, he resolved when his moment came in the service he wouldn't offer the usual platitudes. Instead a black rage welled up from his soul. To think what Ranse might have been, might have accomplished. What a terrible waste of a promising life. *Where are your gibes, your gambols, your flashes of merriment that were wont to set the table on a roar?*

Celia squeezed his hand as the Right Reverend Pierpont concluded his homily with a verse from The Revelation. "And I heard a voice from heaven saying unto me, Write, Blessed are the dead who die in the Lord." Almost instantly a subsequent verse in the same chapter spoke in Drayton's memory: *And the winepress was trodden without the city, and blood came out of the winepress, even unto the horse bridles.*

Now it was Drayton's turn to read. In his mind's eye he saw Gettysburg's Cemetery Ridge across the lethal distance, its heights bristling with artillery. He saw waves of the South's best men flinging themselves upward on the North's best men. He saw maelstroms of fire, leaving behind on the crest only the wreckage of human beings and the wreckage of Southern hopes.

Turning the pages to his marker, he read. "Thy glory is slain upon thy high places. How are the mighty fallen!" Involuntarily his voice rose to a high pitch. "Ye Mountain of Gilboa, let there be no dew, neither let there be rain upon you, nor fields of offerings, for upon you the shield of the mighty is vilely cast away." Suddenly the words were blurred by a film of tears. Celia put her arm around him as he closed the Bible. He could speak no more.

All prayers, all readings, all possible words were at an end. Reverend Pierpont folded up his prayer book, inclined his head with a slight bow to the family, and walked away. The old Negro gave the horse an affectionate pat, and handed the Reverend up into the carriage that swayed and sagged. Father, his face a mask of anguish, stepped forward and laid an object on the cenotaph. He turned and followed the vicar without looking back. Drayton stared hard, at first not able to see what the object was. Then, blinking his eyes clear, he saw the toothbrush.

Chapter Twenty Nine

The funeral left Drayton mentally and physically drained. Back in his bedroom, his refuge, he threw off his coat, loosened his tie, and kicked off his shoes. He poured a large tumbler of brandy and settled into the wing chair at the window overlooking the Edisto. His old friend, the great blue heron, picked its way along the shallows on awkward stilt-like legs. Celia followed him in and settled wordlessly on a stool at his side. She took his hand and pressed it against her cheek. Finally she spoke, softly.

"I know there was much you didn't tell Father about Ranse. For that matter, there's much you haven't told me about your own ordeal."

Drayton remained silent.

She tried again. "I don't want to cause you pain by making you re-live it. But you must share the burden. You must let out the anguish. You had nightmares again last night."

"I'm sorry I disturbed your sleep."

"No, dear. It's *your* sleep I'm concerned about." She put a soothing hand on his knee. "And your health in general. You will not heal of your wound unless you can rest. And you've hardly rested well since you returned home."

"I don't dispute it. But I have no control over what happens in my dreams." He answered in a sharp tone, almost a bark, wondering at the same time why he flared into rages at the one he loved above all.

"Please understand, my Love," she replied. "I'm not criticizing or complaining. I only want to help you."

"You can help best by leaving me alone."

She looked at him with a calm, level stare. She didn't smile, but there was healing in the stare. "No, Love, leaving you alone will *not* help, not help at all. In addition to your nightmares and insomnia, you are cross all the time, even with me, and especially with the servants and Father. You were never that way before. And you have this vacant look in your eyes. You sit for hours at a time on the veranda, staring blankly at the River, yet you don't really see it. When I converse, or try to, you answer in monosyllables. If I try to engage you further, you say, 'What does it matter?' or you become angry. No, Drayton, I love you too well to leave you alone. I believe you're suffering deeper wounds in your spirit than in your body. And I believe you can only relieve the suffering by talking the demons out." She took his hand in her right, and stroked his cheek with her left. Then she smiled faintly.

Her serene strength was what he needed. "Perhaps you're right. No, you *are* right. I must talk about it, yet I cannot."

"Won't you at least try? Make a start? I know about the lost fingers, but tell me how you were wounded in the breast. You've never spoken of it."

He suppressed a shudder, but it escaped as a groan. "I was only wounded, when so many others died. I came home to the bosom of my family, when so many others – braver and better men – will never come home. They lie in unmarked graves in the enemy's country. My own brother..."

"There *is* no braver or better man than you. I know how you rescued Cabell from the enemy charge at Bristow when his saddle came off. I know how bravely you fought at Brandy Station." Her tone hardened. "This is only your guilt speaking, a self-imposed guilt you do not deserve."

"That men could do such things to one another. Who's to say whether it's deserved or not?"

"I say! And I will not let you destroy yourself when God has brought you back to me. Now tell me about Gettysburg," she prompted. "Purge this poison from your soul. On the final day the battle climaxed in a grand charge. According to the papers it was the greatest of the War. An assault by Longstreet's men, of whom you were one. Isn't that so?"

"I was only a courier on General Longstreet's staff. But yes, there was a charge on the Federal center on the Third Day. It was... It was a stirring spectacle, until it became a brutal slaughter."

"And you rode into this slaughter on a horse, when all the others were on foot, knowing you would be a more conspicuous target? For myself, I devoutly wish you had not. But don't then tell me you were not courageous."

No, he was not the only mounted man. He remembered Dick Garnett, almost too sweet-natured to be a brigadier general. Garnett disappeared into the smoke leading his brigade of Pickett's Division, and like Ranse, was never seen again. Only his wounded horse, galloping back in panic.

"Perhaps you're right," he said. "But courage fails me now. I...I don't know if I can tell what I witnessed. I had seen savage combat the day before, and especially on the Second Day at Gettysburg, when Ranse was killed, though I didn't know he was dead until later, when I was in the Charlottesville hospital. But soon afterwards on the Second Day I rode all the way to Little Round Top and proceeded to its summit on foot without being fired upon, so I was not prepared for what happened on the Third Day."

"Perhaps there is nothing that could prepare anyone for such an event," she said.

How much could she have learned from the newspapers? He would not give her a full picture of the carnage, the chaos. Even if he could tell the tale, he'd spare her the appalling details. There was no explaining in terms she could comprehend anyway. How could one convey the madness of marching shoulder to shoulder straight into the muzzles of massed Yankee batteries without flinching, knowing the guns were double-shotted with canister; and to accept the inevitable — being blown to pieces and piled three deep?

At his long pause, she prodded him gently. "Tell it as you would a tale from antiquity, of a battle before the walls of Troy. And as with any story, begin at the beginning."

"I'm not sure where the beginning lies. I do know that sooner or later war robs you of your humanity, by putting you in a situation where you must either kill perfect strangers or be killed by them. I often think of the young man I killed at Brandy Station. He and I might have even been friends had we met in different circumstances." He said nothing to her about mailing the dead man's effects home to his family in New York. He wasn't sure why. It seemed like something he ought to keep private, even from his wife, with whom he normally shared everything.

"And then, a few short weeks later, I was at Gettysburg. It's impossible to convey the horror and confusion of those three days, the smoke, the incessant noise, the stench of blood and death."

"How could Lee have let this happen?" asked Celia. Even she, a Northerner, had embraced the mythos of Robert E. Lee.

"I admire General Lee. I would even say I love him, as we all do. But he is not infallible. We desperately needed a victory at Gettysburg, a decisive victory on Union soil that would end the war, as it surely would have. He thought his men were invincible. Yet the battle was lost on the Second Day. Longstreet knew this. But where he saw only calamity, General Lee saw opportunity. It was one of the few times I can say this of him, but he was wrong."

How could he explain to one who wasn't there that the fierce valor, because it was housed in flesh and blood, eventually must give way to the storm of lead and iron. The critical moment, once lost, could not be retrieved by gallantry and self-sacrifice.

He concluded, "Lee took all the blame and asked to be relieved. I can't think of another general in this war, North or South, who has accepted responsibility in such a manner. The usual conduct is to blame others, rightly or wrongly. Lee said himself that 'things got out of hand.' Events began to out-strip coordination, planning, and orders. Improvisation became the order of the day, but improvised decisions made in the dark, because our cavalry wasn't there to keep Lee informed of Meade's movements. General Stuart is much to blame. Yet Lee never reproached him, at least not publicly. He just said, 'It is all my fault,' then skillfully extricated us."

"If Stuart had kept Lee informed, would the outcome have been different?"

"Ah, Love, who can say? If Lee had possessed better intelligence, there likely wouldn't have been a Battle of Gettysburg. Even so, we came so close. It was a battle of the narrowest margins. A few more men here, a few more minutes there, and victory would have been ours. You always think you will have more time – time to reorganize, to plan, to prepare, to recover. And yet that one glimmering moment of opportunity, when gone, can never be recovered."

"All right then," she said, taking his hand gently. "I think I understand the broader picture. Now tell me *your* story, not that of the generals."

Gettysburg, Pennsylvania. July 3, 1865. Afternoon of the Third Day

Pickett's Division of Longstreet's First Corps finally arrived. Men of Virginia, they were fresh, for they'd been providing the Army rear guard and protection for the supply trains, and had missed the fierce fighting of the first two days. Moxley Sorrel directed them into position in the woods along Seminary Ridge, the spine of the Confederate position. Early in the morning of July 3, the Virginians, along with regiments from Pettigrew's and Trimble's brigades, began to assemble. Their orders were to lie down and avoid enemy observation from the heights to their right front, a hill called Little Round Top. They were warned to shelter from Union counter-battery fire that would lash their position once the Confederate artillery opened up to prepare the way for the infantry assault.

Southern armies were used to cheering their leaders when they rode by, especially Robert E. Lee. And while they were indomitable fighters, Confederates were not the most disciplined individual soldiers. But the seriousness of the impending attack had sobered them. When Lee, Longstreet, and Pickett and their staffs trotted down the lines inspecting the recumbent brigades, the men uncharacteristically obeyed orders. They didn't cheer. Instead they stood and removed their hats, holding them aloft in silent tribute. To Drayton the silence was more moving than cheers.

As a new member of Longstreet's staff, Drayton had gotten to know Edward Porter Alexander, commander of the First Corps artillery, 'Ned' to his contemporaries. Though their acquaintance was brief, Drayton had come to regard him as the most talented soldier in the Army. A young man of 28, a West Pointer and engineer, he was adept at almost all technical aspects of soldiering, from artillery to field fortifications to signaling. He displayed none of the self-importance and literal-mindedness of many engineers. In fact, though serious about his duties, he possessed a puckish sense of the absurd – especially the absurdities of war. An unspoken sympathy grew up between them. Now was Ned's hour to excel, and Drayton waved to him with doffed hat as Longstreet and staff rode up to his battery.

With his own First Corps artillery, Alexander had coordinated the fires of the batteries of other Corps along Seminary Ridge to support the attack. At 1:30 PM two 12-pound howitzers of the famed Washington Artillery sounded the commencement. Then 180 cannons in a line a mile long unleashed their barrage on the Federal lines. The bellowing was like nothing Drayton had ever experienced. The massed guns vomited coils of powder smoke stabbed with flashes of flame. The guns rocked back from the recoil, and the sweating gunners, faces smudged with powder smoke, wrestled them back into place. Shock waves buffeted the senses, rising to a crescendo of roaring the likes of which he'd never heard in two years of combat. The Parrott and Ordnance rifles spoke with sharp cracks in contrast to the softer booms of the brass Napoleons. Beltane laid his ears back. With wide eyes and flared nostrils, he sweated and paced nervously.

Alexander's bombardment invited retaliation. Union batteries a mile away on Cemetery Ridge opened fire. Soon they had the range. Their round shot plunged into the trees and shells burst over the troops tensely awaiting the order to go forward. Scores of Confederates hugging the ground were killed or wounded before the assault began.

Wreathed in smoke and dust, the Union lines on Cemetery Ridge were barely visible. An occasional breath of wind lifted the veil; otherwise it was difficult to ascertain the effect of the Southern artillery on the Yankees. But their artillery began to fall silent. A few Yankee guns were seen limbering up and withdrawing over the crest of Cemetery Ridge. Had they been knocked out of action by the Southern cannonade? Or were they simply conserving their ammunition for the assault everyone now knew was to follow?

Alexander sent word that his ammunition was almost exhausted. Unless the attack began soon, he would not be able to support it. In effect, Lieutenant General Longstreet had delegated the decision to attack to a lieutenant colonel.

Eyes flashing and pomaded ringlets bouncing under his kepi, General Pickett rode up to Longstreet, who sat on a rail fence. Drayton had never seen the Corps Commander so obviously depressed. He was not as good as Lee at presenting an air of confidence he didn't feel.

"General, the Yankee artillery fire has slackened, and Colonel Alexander reports he is running low on ammunition. Shall I advance?" Pickett's shrill voice carried above the thunder of the barrage.

Longstreet's distress was etched in his face, his mouth pursed, eyes narrowed. Drayton sensed he foresaw disaster and couldn't bring himself to speak. With only a slight nod at Pickett, he bowed his head.

"Then I shall lead my Division forward, sir." Pickett paused, seeking a clear confirmation. Head lowered, Longstreet only nodded again, almost imperceptibly. Picket put heel to horse and wheeled dramatically. Followed by his staff and flag-bearer, he cantered to where his men lay sheltering in the trees.

Amid the din Drayton couldn't hear Pickett's commands, much less Pettigrew and Trimble farther down the long battle line. Pickett's saber flashed in the sun. He stood in his stirrups waving it dramatically, which made his ringlets spin about his shoulders. His prim lips opened in a wide rictus under the waxed mustache, but to Drayton it was a wordless pantomime.

Because the roaring cannonade filled up all audible space, the troops fell into ranks seemingly without a sound. They simply materialized from the verge of the trees; first the skirmishers, then two lines of battle, one ahead of the other, with officers and flag details taking post in front. Their butternut gray blended into the shadows from which they emerged like ghosts. But they were not ghosts. They were not impersonal anonymous beings, even though he'd never met a one except George Pickett, Dick Garnett, and Lewis Armistead. Still, he felt he knew them all. Every man was his brother, uniquely valuable in his humanity, his courage, his patience and good humor in the face of hardship. No doubt the men across the valley, waiting in awe of the spectacle unfolding before them, were equally decent and brave. But these were his people. Drayton felt an overwhelming solidarity with them, admiration for their valor, and grief for what he suspected was about to happen. But perhaps the worst might not happen.

The cannon fire began to slacken, and now he could hear patches of drums rattling between the detonations. Tight-lipped and grim-visaged, with apprehension in their faces rather than fear, the brigades stepped off in perfect alignment, business-like, as men whose trade this was. They had done it on many a battlefield and knew no Yankee army could stand against them. He hoped fervently with every other Southerner on the field that they were invincible as

Lee believed, that this would be the last great assault of the last battle, and that victory would soon be in their hands. There had been other doomed, valiant charges into the face of destruction, but this grand assault stood out in his recall as he told the story to Celia. Around it glowed a halo of tragic glory. All their hopes were marching with the men of this Great Charge. Onlookers and participants alike sensed this was the climactic moment of two years of bloody conflict. If Longstreet's assault could pierce the enemy center and roll up each severed wing, then press on to the vulnerable lines of communications in the Union rear, the war might – *might* – end in the next hour or less.

Seeing them move away, each brigade taking its assigned place in an irresistible wave, he could only imagine the fearful wonder with which the Yankees watched the wave of 14,000 men coming toward them, muskets at the carry, flags fluttering, as if on parade. An eerie silence suddenly prevailed as the bombardment ceased altogether, allowing the infantry to pass in front of the guns. Drayton was surprised to realize the bands had been playing during the whole assembly. The drummers drummed them a few hundred yards; then stopped as ordered, remaining in the rear to bear away the wounded. There was no cheering, no rebel-yelling, only the clink of equipment and rhythmic tread of feet.

The brigades flawlessly executed the passage of lines, changing formation to pass through the artillery positions, then reforming their parade ground ranks. The day had grown hot, with humidity to match. Longstreet remained seated on his rail fence, watching Pickett's men march forward. His face remained impassive but flowed with rivulets of sweat – as did all their faces. The Corps commander retrieved an incongruous red handkerchief from his rear pocket and mopped his face. In that unguarded moment Drayton noticed the near-despair in his eyes.

Pickett and his staff rode about twenty yards to the year of Armistead's brigade, which followed behind Garnett's on the left and Kemper's on the right. Kemper's brigade composed the extreme right of the assault lines, which stretched a mile north along the front of Seminary Ridge, with Pettigrew's division in the center and Trimble's division on the far left. Pickett barked the command, "Left Oblique, March!" His division executed a precise 45-degree left turn to close on Pettigrew's men on their left. Then the command came, "Guide Center! Forward March!" The regiments and brigades re-aligned on their colors. Brigadier General Armistead, a short man barely visible to the rear ranks of his brigade, placed his black slouch hat on the tip of his sword, lifting it high for his men to guide on as the tense ranks approached the Emmitsburg Pike.

Then the long-range Federal artillery opened fire.

A few Yankee guns had been disabled on Cemetery Ridge. But smoke had concealed the majority still in action. Now they began to let fly with solid shot and explosive shell, ripping bloody holes in the neat Confederate ranks. By far the worst damage was from the artillery on Little Round Top, rifled guns by their sharp reports. As Pickett's men moved doggedly forward, their right flank was caught in enfilade from the rocky hill. The shells from these guns sped down the length of the butternut lines, obliterating a dozen men with one shot. A vast mournful mutter arose from the battle lines, which were beginning to lose their alignment under the horrible pounding. But stolidly, bravely, the Confederates stepped around the bloody fragments, closed up the gaps, guided on their colors, and pressed forward.

As they reached the Emmitsburg Pike they had to break ranks and clamber over the rail fence in their front that paralleled the Pike. Drayton could see them surge up and over the barrier, which was too solid to simply brush aside. As they climbed they were more exposed than ever to enemy fire. Sheets of flame and smoke erupted with a roar from the Union lines, and scores of men were flung backward or dropped in their tracks. With incredible courage and determination, ignoring their shocking losses, the Southerners halted on the other side of the Pike, re-dressed their ranks, and resumed their march into the storm.

At this point Longstreet stood up on his perch on his own rail fence, glasses in hand. "Look there!" he called out to no one in particular. "Kemper's brigade is going to be flanked. Pickett can't see it from his fold in the ground." The staff followed the General's pointing finger and saw a regiment of Federals detaching themselves from the main line of resistance and filter forward on the far right of Kemper's troops. Kemper's decimated brigade had edged to the left to close up the gaps blasted in the lines and aim for the main objective, a low stone wall and copse of trees in the center of the Union position. They were exposed to the enfilade musketry of the Yankees moving forward on their right.

"Major Sorrel, get a message forward to warn General Kemper his right is about to be turned. Ride straight to him; there's no time to go through General Pickett."

Drayton's heart turned to a lump of ice as all eyes turned toward him and Beltane. His courage, or lack of it, was on display before the entire Army. There was no deciding. The choice had been made for him long before. Not another word needed to be said. Blood pounding in his ears, he dashed a salute to Longstreet, turned Beltane with a twitch of his leg, and bounded forward into certain death. As he sailed gracefully over the rails along the Emmitsburg Pike he vaguely heard the cheers of the wounded men who lay at the foot of the fence.

Unscathed, he reached General Kemper, a large man, face begrimed with powder smoke and a look of granite in his eyes. "General! Compliments of General Longstreet. Look to your right! You're about to come under flanking fire from those Yankees on the rise there. Can you refuse your flank and form a firing line?" He pointed, and Kemper nodded, valiantly but vainly. What could he do but continue to go forward?

Drayton's last memory before being struck down was a collage of permanent images, hazy around the edges and in sepia tones, like an old daguerreotype. He recalled a dark slouch hat on a sword raised above the throng. Guns, hats, haversacks, and body parts flung into the air by blasts of grapeshot or exploding shell. A flying, trunkless arm and hand still gripping its saber. A musket spinning skyward, turning end over end before plunging down to stick upright in the earth on its bayonet. It swayed back and forth for an instant like the pendulum of a clock tolling doom. Then came the blow, the burst of pain in his chest, and the darkness.

When he regained consciousness, he couldn't tell how long he'd been out. Not long, it appeared, since Confederates were still on the field. They streamed back in small clumps, many limping, some supporting others or using their muskets as crutches. Their lips and jaws were stained oddly black. He realized it was gunpowder spilled from biting off the ends of the paper cartridges to load their muskets. Beltane had checked and stood waiting for his master. A passing soldier helped him to his feet, and he clung to the stirrup leather and managed to hobble back to Southern lines, despite the struggle to breathe and the sharp pangs that accompanied each breath. The other man's tears made visible tracks through the layered dust and soot on his cheeks.

***

Now it was Drayton's turn to weep. He emptied himself with sobs so deep that at first they strangled soundlessly in his throat.

Celia encompassed him in lithe, strong arms. "Go ahead, weep, my Love. Weep for them. They are worth your tears."

He was ashamed to cry so abjectly before a woman, especially his wife. But he gave himself over to the sorrow that scoured the depths of his soul and left no remnant of an emotion as unavailing as shame.

"You're feeling guilty because you survived. I beg you not to. Accept it for my sake, if nothing else."

Her insight astonished him. He hadn't fully realized the guilt until now. But she was right. And she was right about the catharsis of recounting the experience. As she'd predicted, the spasm of grief passed. He pulled himself together and felt, if not better, at least able to live with the memory. In the end it was her strong, loving touch that healed him, in body and spirit. The germ of a thought intruded: how distressed she'd be to know her healing would only enable him to go back to face the same thing again.

Hours later he lay in bed, spent and weakened from the strain of his catharsis. Celia sat by him in her shift, hair pinned up, and unwrapped his dirty cingulum. She gave him a sponge bath, then dabbed raw honey on the chest wound.

"Let's allow it to air," she said. As she worked she hummed a tune he thought he recognized.

"What's that song? Isn't it Irish?" He asked.

"Yes. I hardly realized I was humming. It's an old folk song, 'She Moved Through the Fair.'" Then she sang in her rich clear voice,

I dreamed last night that my true love came in
So softly she came that her feet made no din
She stepped up to me and this she did say
It will not be long, love, till our wedding day.

"It's a sad song of lost love."

"Well, sing no sad songs to me of lost love. We have found our love."

"Yes," she agreed. "God has been good to us. Still, life is not the way it ought to be by our reckoning; it is the way it is. How we cope with it is what makes all the difference."

He pondered that for a moment while she rinsed and dried him and wondered what she meant. Celia was perhaps not a representative example – a Southerner now by marriage and not by birth. But she and countless others who were Southern-born put the lie to the old caricature of the lisping Southern belle, fainting flowers exuding only the scent of affectation and insincerity. Why, they had proven tougher than the men, and with the kind of courage he couldn't imagine, waiting in dread and uncertainty for tragic news, while keeping homes and farms and industries functioning.

She broke his train of thought. "Now I understand how grateful I am that you are a horseman and went into the cavalry. Any service is dangerous enough. But from what you have told me, service in the infantry line seems certain death."

"Not certain, but the odds of death or serious wounds are greater."

"How can men do such things? How can they willingly march into the maw of the enemy guns knowing the chances are so high that they will not survive? I had always imagined that each man thinks he will be spared. He believes some other must pay the inevitable price of war. But it's not how I had imagined after all. Any soldier observing the carnage about him must know – *know* — his turn may be next. How can they do it?"

"I'll tell you how," he said. "Many have their spiritual faith, of course. They believe their fate is up to their Maker. Live or die, it's in His hands, and if they are killed, they will go home to be with Him in eternity. That's a consoling belief. But there's something else. I asked the same question you've asked of a wounded infantry officer in hospital. He told me this. The best soldiers give themselves up from the beginning as lost, he said. They decide in advance that they are already dead; and then, paradoxically, they no longer worry or live in fear. The matter has been decided. This officer said such men are happier; they are better able to live while they have life. They are free of anxiety, except for their fellows; whom they love and desire to protect. They are braver and fight more fiercely. This doesn't make them foolhardy or suicidal, for they still seek victory, and that means exacting from the enemy the highest price for their own death."

"Did you ever give yourself up as lost?"

He hated to lie to her, one with whom he'd always had perfect understanding. But he didn't want to upset her. Truth was the first casualty of war, in more ways than one. There had been a moment at Brandy Station, a scant fraction of a second when face to face with the Yankee horsemen and almost certain death. An impulse had seized him to submit, to let it happen, to go to his fate without a struggle. But in the same millisecond another impulse had supplanted it, something primordial, atavistic, deeper than conscious thought — the impulse to fight and survive.

"No, my Beloved. I could never do that. I desire victory for the South, although I know in the marrow of my bones – after Gettysburg the war is lost. But I'm too selfish a creature and too poor a soldier. In you I had too much to live for to give myself up as dead. And I was coming back to Cypress Stand. I knew it."

"How could you be so certain?"

"You'll scoff, but Maum Biddy told me. A few days before I left in '61 she held my hands and looked into my eyes in her far-seeing way and told me I would come back. Junius said she made a similar prophecy for him – that he'd survive the war and live a long life, but that he'd never come back here. I know that's not much reassurance to cling to. But, Beloved, she has the Sight. I can only repeat what she said: 'Doan ast me how I knows. I jus' knows.'"

"And you believe this… this clairvoyance?"

"Yes, I do. And not just because I wanted so desperately to come back to you."

Life – and love, which made life worth living – would go on, war or no war. He would make no concession to the folly of men who preferred fighting to loving. He and Celia had found more joy than either thought possible, and had therefore waited for life to exact its inevitable payment. He made a partial payment. But sooner or later he knew the balance of the debt for their happiness would come due.

Chapter Thirty

Cypress Stand, Colleton District, South Carolina; late April 1864.

Drayton sat in a reclining wicker chair on the terrace overlooking the River. The view itself was healing, physically and mentally. Father emerged from the French doors of the drawing room that gave onto the terrace. He settled in the adjacent chair and offered his son a cheroot. Drayton declined, but enjoyed the rich aroma as his father lit up. Spring had come to the Low Country with a stirring of bird life in particular. New blossoms broke bright on the marsh, and redwing blackbirds clung to plants that swayed and bowed to earth under their weight as they ambushed mayflies. He breathed in the earthy smell carried on a southerly breeze of pluff mud and spartina grass, which smelled like nothing else or nowhere else under the sun.

"Where is your bride?" asked Father. "You spend too much time alone these days."

"I fear I've frustrated her best intentions. She was here a while ago encouraging me to talk. But I'm emptied of talk."

"Well, men are not talkers like women. We do not like to reveal our innermost selves in the best of circumstances. Women can afford to indulge their emotions, while we men must bear things as they are."

"Yes, I suppose that's so. But it's women who make things as they are worth bearing."

The implied rebuke made Drayton wish he wasn't so combative with his father, a man whom he loved and respected in spite of their differences.

"I feel another argument coming on," said Father, turning toward him with a reproachful look. "Are we fated always to be at odds?" Again he offered a cigar from his coat pocket.

"Not by choice, Father, only it seems from some unavoidable predisposition. Yet you have been most patient with me."

"Son, you think I'm oblivious to things. Youth always undervalues long life and hard experience — until Youth itself becomes Age. I suspect you blame me for your having to go to war, or in some vague way, for the War itself. But history has its tides and currents, like the sea. I believe it was fated and thus inevitable."

He pointed to a rare pileated woodpecker that settled in a tall cypress and began its comical characteristic dance around the bole, looking for the best place to begin drilling for grubs. Father smiled and nodded, and they watched for a few moments.

"Once again, Father, we disagree," Drayton said. "But no, I don't blame you for anything. Yet I must say this: I have studied the Greeks, who were great believers in Fate. For all my admiration of their achievements, I differ with them on this point, as I do with you. War is not a natural phenomenon like a hurricane or earthquake. It's a choice, a choice made in the minds of so many thousands or millions that it may seem like an inhuman, inexorable force. But it's a human choice nevertheless. We simply made the wrong choices, North and South. We can't shift responsibility for the tragedy onto the shoulders of Fate."

"Well, that's a question we poor mortals must leave to God. What *is* left to us is what we do in this life, in the time given us, and with the abilities God endowed us with."

"On that we do agree, Father. And I've tried to do my best in those circumstances, to do my duty as I've been able."

"Yes, you have. I remarked earlier that men don't like to reveal their feelings. It's even harder between fathers and sons. You contemplated leaving the country after eloping with Cecelia, back in the spring of '61. Only the outbreak of hostilities at Fort Sumter forestalled you."

"Yes. I told you that, I recall."

"And I insisted you stay and serve, on pain of being disowned. Yet I knew how deeply you love our Celia. And how deeply she loves you. I regret that this war came between you."

"Would you have stopped me from leaving?"

Father stood up, pacing and stroking his chin. He puffed thoughtfully on the cigar, staring out across the meadow, marsh, and river. "I truly can't say. Probably I would have tried. But for your sake, not mine. I'd have pointed out that you would have found no new lands over the sea, for the land of your birth would have followed you – accusingly. Once you had ruined your life here, in this little corner, you would have ruined it in the entire world."

"Yes, I can see that. Perhaps I'm wrong about Fate versus human choice. I – Celia and I and all of us – have been caught up in something vastly greater than ourselves. I really had no choice but to go with Ranse and Cabell, did I? No choice now but to do my duty and see it through to the end, come what may."

Father had been holding himself taut, but now he seemed to relax into himself a little. He tapped a bit of ash from his cigar into a brass ashtray. "Every man worthy of the name must come to that realization when the circumstances are thrust upon him," he said. "And now I must tell you: though you and I have had our differences, I have never lacked of love for you. Indeed, you are more like your mother than … than Ranse or Cabell. Perhaps that's why I've shown you a degree of partiality greater than I've shown to my Firstborn." He turned and sat again, looking levelly into Drayton's eyes. "It must be said, and ought to have been said before now, for you might have been… been lost, like your brother, without knowing my …my feelings." He paused and dabbed his eyes with a handkerchief. Drayton feared at this most critical moment Father's reserve and restraint might block up his heart, but after a moment he continued.

"Yes, Father?"

"I am enormously proud of you. You have demonstrated as much courage as anyone in the Confederate Army, yet somehow you have not let the warrior eat up your humanity. Wounds and sacrifice and the loss of our beloved Ranse have not embittered you. I find that marvelous."

"You have Celia to blame," he smiled.

"No, I think she only brought out what was already in the man. In any case, you have my blessing, from Father to son." He laid a firm hand on Drayton's shoulder. "My approval of you as a man. My blessing, as from Abraham to Isaac, and from Isaac to Jacob."

Drayton hung his head, moved and speechless. In all his years this is what he'd wanted from his father above all. How strange that it took a war to bring it about.

His looked back at his father, feeling the freshening afternoon breeze from the River. He reached out and took his father's hand. "Thank you, Father, I will always strive to be worthy of being your son. I will always cherish your blessing, and this moment."

His Father stood again, backing away from the emotion that lay naked now that he'd said what he came to say. "This was a fine cigar. Cuban. Brought through the blockade. One of the few pleasures left to us. You should have tried one." He paused and placed an envelope in Drayton's lap. "And now, Son, ask for God's blessing, too."

The envelope lying heavy in his palms was addressed to Second Lieutenant Drayton FitzHenry, Confederate States Army. In the upper corner it bore the name and seal of the Confederate War Department in Richmond.

***

Celia was in the upstairs sewing room rocker, smocking a corselette. She was singing another plaintive Irish air as he mounted the steps. His delight in hearing a woman's song in the house made what he had to do all the more bitter. She looked up from her work and smiled gently as he entered. "I saw you speaking with Cabell Senior on the terrace," she said. "And this time you seemed to avoid an argument."

"Yes. It's never my desire to argue with anybody." *Especially you,* his eyes told her. She dipped her head, wearing the same sad gentle smile. "It just seems to happen of its own accord."

"What were you talking about?" *Courage,* his father had said. It took all the courage he possessed to drop the envelope in her sewing basket. With agonizing slowness she laid down needle and thread, set the fabric aside carefully, and retrieved the documents inside.

"Uh, that page is an endorsement from Major Moxley Sorrel," he said, with something like guilt. "I've told you of him. General Longstreet's staff."

"I see," she said icily. "And the endorsement is to this set of orders from the War Department. It seems they want you back, wounds and all."

"Yes, it seems so."

He expected her to bow to the inevitable as she had in 1861. Instead she flung the papers to the floor and stood up abruptly. Clutching herself with both arms around her midriff, she stalked to the window overlooking the River. "This cannot be. I can't believe God will allow this if He desires the happiness of His creatures."

"If only His creatures would heed Him, they might find happiness instead of slaughtering one another."

"If you really believe that, and with two honorable wounds, how can you go back?" she shouted. He had never heard her raise her voice this way. "Can it be you've *enjoyed* the slaughter? Has the adventure of war spared you the tedium of living at home with a clinging, desperate wife, fearful every moment you'll be ripped away from her? Tell me!" Her voice reached a pitch he could hardly believe. "Tell me you enjoy it, that you *prefer* it, and at least then I'd try to understand."

It was the folly of men to oppose feminine emotion with male reason. "No," he replied. "I can't say I enjoy it. But I have discovered the paradox of war. We are asked – no, ordered — to commit the most unspeakable acts against our fellows, acts of cruelty and violence that we'd condemn in any other circumstances. Yet war brings out the best in men at the same time. Fortitude and self-sacrifice, loyalty and good humor."

"There! I knew it. The good humor of male comrades is preferable to the love of a good woman!" She strode back and forth across the rear of the room. When the rocker stood in her path, she kicked it aside violently. It careened into the sewing table, sending buttons, lace, and linen cascading.

He stepped toward her, reaching for her hand. She snatched it away from him and paced until he cornered her in the rear of the room. Enfolding her in his arms, he simply stood, holding her until the anger drained away in wracking sobs.

"I must go back," he said.

"Couldn't you find a doctor who'd find you unfit for duty?"

"That's just it, Love, I am fit."

"I've been waiting for this. I knew that wounds would not hold you. Nor love."

"Then you knew more than I. My intention – my hope – has always been to remain. You have my whole heart. But the wound is healed, and Dr. Memminger has declared me fit to return. Physicians are under great pressure from the government to eliminate malingering. *Ergo*, I'm faced again with the same question we faced in 1861, when I couldn't turn my back on my people or my duty."

"Except now you know the war is lost. After Gettysburg and Vicksburg, there is no way the South can win. The idea that the British or French will intervene is a foolish hope. You are no fool. You know I speak the truth."

"Yes, it's true."

"Then why go back, if the war is lost?"

"It is precisely *because* it's lost that I must go back."

She stared in bewilderment. "That's madness."

He guided her to the box window seat and settled her, this time holding both her hands in his. Her face glistened wetly in the afternoon light from the window. She no longer hung her head in dejection, but still seemed combative. If reason and logic were to be his weapons, why, she would enter the lists on his terms and beat him.

"It makes no sense," she insisted.

"No. And yet it does, my Love. Remember when I told you about the men falling ill from drinking unclean water, and how Doctor Moore reduced illness in the regiment by boiling water to wash our utensils and making us wash our hands? And how Doctor Smith in Charlottesville reduced the inflammation of wounds by boiling horsetail hairs for sutures? And we know that mosquitoes somehow cause malaria, which is why we keep them off with Maum Biddy's concoction, and why we build mass tenements for the purple martins."

"Yes, I remember."

"And you said to me, 'Clearly there is an unseen world which is responsible. The medical men say there exists some kind of organism too small for the human eye to detect, which nevertheless causes illness, unless its influence is avoided by boiling water and keeping clean.' And I said, 'Perhaps, but I'm not sure what you're getting at.' And you said, 'We are speaking of the physical world, but the same principle applies to the spiritual world. There are unseen – indeed, unseeable — factors at work which determine our spiritual health.' In spite of myself, my Love, you convinced me: there is something in the unseen spirit world of yours that calls, and I must answer."

Celia shook her head as if she'd been struck in the face. "I'm dumfounded. You've gotten two wounds. You have fought your fight and done your part. No one will fault you for not returning."

"No one but myself."

The next morning was fixed for his departure. To hear her weep did more violence to his spirit than anything else he had seen or done in the war. Soon he'd have to say goodbye to his aging, ailing father, and to the one he loved more than life itself. Her Gaelic blood was strong; her anger hadn't dissipated. He tried to be especially tender with her as they undressed for bed. He stroked her shoulder, but she pulled away and murmured, "You are too good for this world and all its works, of which war is chief among them. I had no such presentiment when you went away in 1861, but this time I know in my soul I shan't see you again."

"I have an equal presentiment that I *will* come back," he said. "After Gettysburg and the wound in the breast, I feel as if nothing else can touch me. And you know what else? In 1861 I didn't want to go, but now I'm glad I fought," he said with unusual vehemence. "It will be those who fought who set things right afterwards. For all its flaws and mine, I have come to understand I love the South enough to fight for it. You have to love a thing first before you can reform it."

Celia lapsed into silence as they prepared for sleep. The unaccustomed restraint hung awkwardly between them. Spring had come 'round again, bringing heat, humidity — and worst of all, battalions of mosquitoes. The purple martins reported for duty conscientiously, but a few of the enemy always got through. Netting hung from the high bed frame provided some protection. Drayton had ordered the servants to erect an outer defense line, lengths of tulle tacked over the open bedroom windows. In theory, this let the breeze in and kept the bugs out. Though it was better than keeping the windows closed tight, the bedroom had still turned uncomfortable as the hot day wore on.

Defying convention, Drayton decided to sleep nude. As he slipped off his nightshirt, he felt a stirring on the other side of the bed. He assumed she was slipping out of her chemise to sleep more comfortably as he'd done. She was, but not for sleep. He felt her breasts press against his back. Her fingers reached around for him, and felt himself stiffen. In spite of the dismay the new orders evoked, in spite of the tension and silence that had followed, he turned toward her with a torrent of wanting. How could they ever have argued?

"I want to have your child," she whispered.

— END OF PART III —

PART IV
Chapter Thirty One

Beaufort, South Carolina; April 1913.

Returning from the River, Cabell stopped at Craven Street to drop Tommy. It was late afternoon, well after lawyers' hours, but the boy's father was nowhere to be found, not that he had much of a practice even during business hours. If Cabell had wanted to initiate a search, he presumed he could find Thomas Preston in a sodden heap in a tavern down on the wharves. Cabell took the boy home. Asking no questions, Nellie met them in the barn behind the house. They lived on Bay Street, a handsome three-storey Georgian overlooking the Beaufort River and with a stirring view of Lady's Island to the south.

While Cabell put away the harness and traces, Nellie rubbed down the Cleveland Bay. Tommy brought fresh hay while Cabell filled the water bucket at the back yard pump. Tommy helped him wrestle the heavy pail into the stall.

After supper Tommy went upstairs to read with a glass of cold milk and cakes. Nellie settled her husband in the drawing room's overstuffed leather chair. He sighed with relief as she unstrapped the prosthetic and propped his one good foot on the ottoman.

Nellie served him a cup of tea and took the adjacent chair. "A fine young man," she sighed. "Such a pity about his father."

"Not a pity," said Cabell in a savage voice. "A shame." He blew across the surface of the tea and took a sip. "And a disgrace to the family name."

"Well, the boy is no disgrace," Nellie said, passing a plate of his favorite benne-seed wafers. "It's a marvel he's turning out so well."

"Drayton has proven a better grandfather to Tommy than a father to Preston. Ever the anomaly, my brother."

Nellie paused, and Cabell felt her eyes searching his face for clues. Finally asked, drawing a breath, "Did The Anomaly accede to your plan?"

"What plan?"

"Come now, Dear. Remember whom you're taking to."

Cabell dipped his head, abashed. "Yes, my Dear, he did. He'll go to Gettysburg, right enough. But then he intends to travel on for a long spell afterwards. To Europe, to Ireland. And he plans to take Tommy. Maybe a year or longer. Like our Grand Tour of the pre-War years."

"Well," she smiled her slow, knowing smile. "You know the old saying: be careful what you wish for."

"Wise words," said Cabell. "Nellie, I wanted to learn his secret, not drive him into exile. He's not a young man. He may never return." Suddenly it was a bleak thing to contemplate life without his brother.

Nellie took one of the wafers and nibbled. "Husband, you have an unhealthy obsession with Drayton's past. Let it go. If the Gettysburg Reunion will relieve him of whatever burden he bears, then leaving Charleston and … that woman will be an acceptable price to pay."

"He seems prepared to pay it. But I'm his lawyer as well as his kin. I wish he'd consulted me about Annalee. She can make a lot of trouble if he just absconds."

"Dear, you expect more deference from Drayton, since you're the eldest. But he was never biddable."

Cabell set the teacup aside and poured a measure of port from the decanter on the end table. "No, never. But at least he plans to go to the Reunion. I believe that whatever has been troubling all the years since the War… Well, maybe Gettysburg will give him some peace at last." *And me, too*, Cabell thought. *Only our going back there together will open a door closed for fifty years. It will do us both good, for whatever burden he's had to bear in a way has also been mine.*

"And as for Annalee," said Nellie, refilling her teacup. "I'm not qualified to discuss the legal implications, but the marriage ended long ago, if indeed there ever was one in the true sense of the word."

Cabell pondered his wife's observations with mild wonder. To the women of his acquaintance, the inviolability of the marriage bond trumped all other considerations. They reflexively defended a woman wronged, perhaps from fear of finding themselves in the same predicament. But not his Nellie. She always saw into the heart of the matter.

"We talked about it yesterday and I must say Drayton seems oddly unconcerned. He promised to leave me power of attorney and instructions that will… take care of the problem."

Nellie nodded. "It's time. It's only decent now to bury the corpse."

"Well, something good came of it, at least. The boy. I'll go up and say goodnight."

"He'll ask for a war story."

"Yes, he will. I've about run out of my own tales. Lately he's been asking about Drayton's."

"And Drayton never talks."

"No, almost never."

To Cabell's surprise his grand-nephew did not request a war story. In his pajamas, nestled under the covers, Tommy asked, "Grand-Uncle, can you love someone even after they're dead?"

Cabell pondered the question for a moment, wondering what the boy's object was. "Yes, I suppose so. Why do you ask?"

"Well, GramPa has this book of poems in the River house, and I read 'em yesterday when nobody was looking. There was this one by a lady poet. I didn't quite understand it. The last line was underlined in ink, by GramPa, I think, so it must be important. I memorized it. It says, '...if God choose, I shall but love thee better after death.' So I was just wondering. He must have loved Celia a whole lot."

"Yes," said Cabell. "It was like something out of a legend. They got married just after the war began in 1861, and she died just before it ended in 1865. And during most of that time, your GramPa was off in the army. So they really had only one year together, when he came home after being wounded at Gettysburg. But I think they lived more fully in that one year than most people do in a lifetime."

"Then why did he marry GramMa Annalee if he still loved Celia?"

Cabell hesitated to answer, staring down at the carpet with a flash of recollection. Only a day ago he'd asked Drayton the same question when importuning him to attend the Reunion. His memories continued to unfold, back to the day when Drayton had met Annalee Burr Joyner, Charleston resident, woman of property, and widow of a Confederate soldier. Cabell had been there to witness their first encounter.

Walterboro, South Carolina; June 1876.

Cabell had traveled to the traditional stump meeting at Green Pond with their old commander Wade Hampton, with a stop planned in nearby Walterboro, seat of Colleton County. Arriving on the train with the General's entourage, he was surprised to see his brother present. Drayton had lived a recluse for nine years. He seldom ventured up from the River, and came to see Cabell and Nellie in Beaufort only once a year for Christmas dinner. Even then, though always polite, he was barely communicative. Today he was more animated than Cabell had seen him since the War, smiling and nodding at the locals like a lord as he rode into town. It seemed their old General's campaign for Governor had renewed his brother's interest in life. Hampton had held Drayton in special regard ever since the War, which Drayton reciprocated.

Beltane, though showing signs of age, was still splendid. He pricked his ears forward and picked up his feet proudly as the people cheered. A dignified Hampton in ruffled shirt and suit of light grey, descended from the carriage to the station platform, waving and giving a military salute to comrades from the War. Many of them wore shirts of red homespun, a symbol of Hampton's campaign. Drayton remained mounted at the rear of the crowd, keeping Bel under a tight rein. As Hampton was about to speak he spied Drayton, wearing an old corduroy coat and tie, not the emblematic red shirt.

"Why, there's my old scout Drayton FitzHenry," Hampton announced over the buzz. "With his famous horse. My friends, let me tell you about your neighbor and his big grey. He was the best rider and had the best mount of any man in Lee's army. He showed those Virginians they didn't invent horsemanship. We South Carolinians know something about it, too."

The voters cheered. A voice called out, "Whyn't you ride him, General! Show us if *you* know anything about it!" The throng roared with laughter.

Hampton's heavy beard parted in a grin. "Well, Drayton?"

Drayton laughed and urged Bel forward. The milling voters separated to make a lane. Smiling broadly, he reined in alongside the station platform. While Drayton dismounted a woman stepped forward confidently and held Bel's bridle and stroked his nose as if she knew something about horses. She was a fine-looking lady, tall and dark-haired, and wore the latest post-War fashion, a slimmer look than the old pre-War hoop skirts and pagoda sleeves. Over her dress of ivory silk was a charming bolero jacket, and as protection from the Low Country sun she wore a straw hat with a crest of cock feathers in the band.

Still a legendary horseman in his 58th year, the General swung easily into the saddle from the rail siding. Drayton lengthened the stirrups to accommodate the taller man.

"You always did ride on too short a stirrup," teased Hampton with affection. "Like a jockey. But then, you were. Once."

Patting Bel's withers and calming him with a few words, Hampton took up the reins and trotted down a length of track to get the feel, posting with the rise and fall of the gait. He stopped a hundred yards away, raised an arm in salute and motioned to the onlookers to stand aside. He rode back at a hand gallop, reining Bel in sharply till the horse reared on his hind legs. Hampton waved his broad-brimmed hat to the cheers of the onlookers. *What a fine statue that image would make,* thought Cabell. *But we've got to get him elected first.*

The General made Beltane stand still for a moment, relaxing the pressure on the bit. Giving Bel's withers another vigorous rub, Hampton dismounted to more cheers, handed the reins to Drayton and said a few inaudible words in his ear while patting his back. Cabell grudged him the moment. Drayton had been a favorite of Wade Hampton since the great cavalry clash at Brandy Station in June 1863. But it was the Great Beefsteak Raid at Petersburg that sealed Drayton forever in the General's esteem. Cabell had also fought bravely and had a missing leg to show for it. Now he was a leading Low Country lawyer, a contributor to Hampton's campaign, and a trusted confidant of Cal Butler and Martin Gary, two of the General's famous wartime subordinates. Yet Hampton looked on Drayton almost as a son, while Cabell was treated as another hanger-on. Fortunately for Cabell, his law practice was lucrative. He wanted no appointment from Hampton if he should win election. He only wanted to see the Yankees and Carpetbaggers driven from the state. But to be eclipsed by his younger brother wounded him more than he cared to acknowledge.

After the speeches and a rendition of 'The Bonnie Blue Flag' from a brass band slightly off key, the campaign party embarked on the train to continue on to Charleston. Cabell stumped aboard and saw his brother deep in conversation with the dark-haired lady. Both were smiling and nodding as if old acquaintances. Drayton had shown no interest in females since the War. He was sound and in his right mind — more or less. Still youthful at 36, he grew better-looking with age. Clean-shaven, he looked younger than most of the gnarled, bearded veterans. And he had an income, though modest, from his teaching and writing and occasionally guiding wealthy Northerners duck hunting in the Edisto marshes. Cabell knew ladies from Savannah to Georgetown who'd expressed interest in his brother. Some had actually made overtures. So many marriageable men had been lost in the War that even gentlewomen ignored the old conventions. Drayton had never shown any reciprocal interest. But now this woman seemed to have caught his attention. Cabell's moment of jealousy passed, and he was pleased for his brother.

Four months later Cabell was surprised to receive a note in the post that Drayton was getting married to Annalee Burr Joyner. It was to be a small event, with Uncle Porcher and Aunt Meggs, some of the Tourville cousins, and the elder Alston sister who'd married Major Hazelden, the brother of their dead 2nd Cavalry comrade 'Tiny.' Would he and Prioleau Henderson from the old 2nd Cavalry stand as Best Men?

Charleston, South Carolina; July 1876.

Cabell and Nellie traveled up from Beaufort for the ceremony, such as it was. Charleston was steamy. The Mills House, now fully restored from its wartime damage, had iced down the champagne, the wedding's one concession to the luxury of the old days. Cabell was surprised that none of 'the Widow Joyner's' family attended. Nor did Major Hazelden or his socially-conscious wife. An old-fashioned snub, apparently. It seemed a hurried, almost furtive affair, lacking the spontaneous joy of most other weddings he'd attended. Perhaps it was the War. Nothing had been the same since the War.

Cabell and Nellie had stopped at Jacksonborough to collect Aunt Meggs, now a frail widow. Meggs made some comment about the bride-elect's descent from Aaron Burr: she came from the best people. To Meggs it was supremely important to come from the best people, though Cabell knew that family lineages were often exaggerated.

Annalee wore a pale blue organdy gown trimmed with bands of navy, and Drayton looked like a British diplomat in his morning coat, striped trousers, and silk top hat, which he continually misplaced. The bride was civil but said little to family and friends.

When Cabell raised his eyebrows questioningly, Nellie giggled an explanation into his ear. "Dear, she appears wasp-waisted, but her corset is cinched down so tight she can scarcely breathe, much less converse."

Cabell noticed her hand trembling as she placed the ring on Drayton's middle finger, since the usual digit had been severed at Brandy Station. The disfigurement was still conspicuous, and the bride continually averted her eyes during the ceremony. But Drayton fawned over her as if she were a great find. Maybe she was special in the private way of married couples. Cabell decided there was nothing for it. He put the best face on the matter and wished them Godspeed as they departed on their wedding trip. Wade Hampton had invited them to honeymoon at High Hampton, his home in the North Carolina mountains.

On the train ride home to Beaufort Nellie and Cabell sat silent in the swaying, clacking carriage, both unwilling to relive the faint unpleasantness they'd just experienced. But finally Cabell couldn't contain his anxiety about his brother's happiness.

He took his wife's hand. "Nellie, I can't shake off the feeling that Annalee would rather have been at a funeral than her own wedding."

Nellie replied with a slight smile and a knowing look. "Dear, it was a marriage of …inconvenience."

"What do you mean?"

"Annalee, ah, suffers from a condition that only marriage can solve. Need I say more?"

Seven months later Cabell and Nellie received a note from Drayton announcing the birth of a boy, named Thomas Preston FitzHenry in honor of their grandfather Thomas FitzHenry and Wade Hampton's son Preston, killed at Burgess Mill in 1864. It was the same fight in which Cabell had lost his leg. The timing spoke for itself, although Drayton's note insisted that little Preston had been premature, after a most difficult birth in which both mother and child nearly died.

Nellie cluck-clucked her sympathies, passing over the putative seven months of gestation. Cabell merely smiled to himself, amazed at his wife's perspicacity. The new couple took refuge behind the comfortable veil of Charleston's good manners. Well-bred Southerners were adept at ignoring what mustn't be publicly acknowledged. During the War, when death hovered at everyone's elbow, it was understood that people would grasp a moment of illicit joy. It was too much to expect the South's rigid morality to restore itself all at once.

Chapter Thirty Two

Cabell considered himself a hard-headed man of affairs, unlike his brother, who was a romantic dreamer. Yet Cabell was romantic enough to recognize his good fortune in finding Nellie, in contrast to Drayton's bad luck in love.

In October 1864, Doctor Taylor had amputated Cabell's leg after the sharp fight at Burgess Mill. The amputation had not sent him into shock that killed so many who survived the initial trauma. But in Richmond's Chimborazo Hospital he developed pneumonia, which dogged him for weeks. Then the stump of the leg became infected, common in the days before medical knowledge could effectively battle sepsis. The fever and inflammation almost carried him away. He believed he would have died but for Nellie, one of several dozen volunteer nurses from local families.

She was born Penelope Pembroke, a daughter of the Ashland, Virginia Pembrokes. Somewhat plain, with dark hair pinned back severely in a bun, she had a sunny disposition. She smiled often, and Cabell had fallen in love with her, along with half the ward. At first she resisted his overtures. He thought for a time it was because she didn't want to get involved with a one-legged, broken-down Confederate. As their friendship deepened, he learned she was reluctant to marry someone out of state and leave her widowed, ailing mother. But he persisted, offering to make Hanover County his home, especially when he learned the fate of the FitzHenry properties in South Carolina – the farms on the Edisto River and in Gillisonville and Grahamville burned to cinders, the mansion on Charleston's East Bay looted and confiscated. He and Nellie married the day after Appomattox. The next day, when the Yankees began to occupy Richmond, Cabell took the Oath of Allegiance at the office of the provost marshal. 'Swallowing the dog,' Southerners called it.

They moved to the Pembroke home, a simple but spacious farmhouse on land once owned by Patrick Henry. In addition to a nurturing manner Nellie also had a ready wit. Refusing to be cast down by the catastrophe, she always found a way to make light of their condition and poke fun at the sanctimoniousness of their occupiers. Yet she wasn't frivolous. An educated and cultured woman, she could hold a conversation full of insight when the occasion demanded it. She continued nursing her mother and her husband. Her husband recovered and flourished. Her mother, now in her 80's and broken-hearted by the South's defeat, died in the spring of 1866.

Unlike most of their neighbors in war-blasted Richmond they had a bit of money, thanks to her late father's foresight. Distrusting Confederate bonds, he had buried a tobacco tin of U.S. $20 gold pieces in the back yard before he died in 1862. Nellie came up with the idea to use the money to capitalize a business. She employed former Confederates skilled in woodworking to manufacture artificial limbs for amputees like Cabell. Sadly, there were plenty of customers. Hickory wood, which worked best, was ample and cheap. But the crowning touch was Nellie's design for an 'articulated limb.' She learned of this invention reading about the Earl of Uxbridge, Wellington's second-in-command at Waterloo, who lost his leg to a French cannon ball. Her specially-designed prosthesis was a huge advance over the usual pegleg, shaped like a human leg, with hinges at the knee and ankle, allowing more natural movement. Cabell used the first one made, and though he still had to rely on a cane, he could get around reasonably well.

As the prosthetics business flourished, Cabell began to acquire some clients at law. By a stroke of good fortune, he'd passed his time in hospital with Leland Parkes, a lieutenant on the Confederate ram *C.S. S. Albemarle*, sunk by a daring Yankee raid on a deep October night in 1864. Convalescing in the adjacent bed, Cabell discovered that Parkes was expert in maritime and admiralty law. The naval officer spent months tutoring Cabell to pass the time and relieve the boredom. Cabell exulted that he'd fallen into a pot of gold. He learned all he could about navigation statutes, seamen's rights, salvage, cabotage, and prize law, knowing that there would be many such cases brought after the War. His foresight proved correct. In December 1866 Cabell was retained, along with several other admiralty lawyers, by Lloyd's of London to defend claims pressed by a Bermuda-based syndicate trying to cover their losses from blockade running. By the middle of 1867 Cabell and Nellie found themselves relatively well off.

At midday Cabell stumped upstairs of the carriage house he and Nellie had converted into a law-and-business office. Nellie was poring over the books in the light of the high window. She looked up and smiled her dazzling smile as if they'd just met. Cabell never tired of it.

"Dinner will be ready soon, Dear," she said. "In the meanwhile, there's post for you. From Charleston."

He sat in one of the office chairs and read the letter. Nellie looked at him with patient expectation. "It's what I've been expecting." He frowned. "The family home on East Bay Street is up for tax auction. $575.00."

Nellie's sunny smile didn't waver. "Then let's get it back in the family." She waved a slim hand over the accounts. "We can afford it."

Cabell stared at her with a mixture of gratitude and disbelief that he hadn't had to persuade her. "Are you sure, my Dear?"

"Yes, Dear. I want to care for my husband and raise a family, not run a manufactory. Your legal practice is growing and will keep us well. What better place for a maritime law practice than Charleston? Certainly landlocked Hanover County is not ideal."

Cabell nodded and reflected for a moment on the seriousness of such a decision. It wasn't just earning a living at stake. He wanted to redeem something of the old FitzHenry property from the Yankees. And truth be told, his law practice – and his effectiveness as an advocate – contained something of the avenging spirit of a conquered people. His battlefield with Yankee oligarchs was now the courtroom.

"Can we sell the prosthetics firm?" he asked.

Ever the astute businesswoman, she picked up a file folder. "It's already arranged, whenever we're ready," she said to his surprise. "We have an offer from Kyd Douglas representing a veterans' cooperative in Winchester, men from the Stonewall Brigade."

The wharf at Vendue Range, Charleston, South Carolina; September 1868.

The voyage from Norfolk to Charleston had been delightful, marked by warm, cloud-dappled days and moderate seas. Cabell and Nellie disembarked from the mail packet at Vendue Range, half-hoping to see Drayton in the crowd to greet them. Cabell had wired and written his brother, but with no reply. News only traveled fitfully in the still disordered times. The last they'd heard from Drayton was a brief note in late January 1867 informing them he was quitting his teaching post at the University of South Carolina. No explanation why, no word of his destination. They assumed he had returned to Cypress Stand and had addressed their communications to him there.

Now at the wharf were throngs of blue-clad Yankee soldiers, arriving or departing. There was also a horde of devouring locusts – carpetbaggers they were called in the most contemptuous tones; men in top hats, silk vests, and gabardine coats carrying fashionable luggage made of thick, flowered carpet cloth. Coarse, uncouth, but purse-proud, they swarmed over the South enjoying the patronage and perquisites of the Occupation – predatory tax collectors, property assessors, and parasites of every imaginable type.

"They're like bluebottle flies on a cadaver," Nellie whispered to her husband. Cabell fought to keep his composure and supervised the offloading of his own bags. Cheerful Nellie engaged a Negro porter. When she announced their destination, the courtly porter spoke to her with lowered voice, his eyes darting to each side.

"Ma'am, they ain't no rooms to be had at the Mills House. Nor any other hotel in Charleston. Doan matter if'n you got reservations. I just come from there and they's full up. Even them Yankee carpetbag men can't get no 'commodations."

Nellie looked at Cabell in despair. *It's your city*, her eyes seemed to say.

"The FtzHenrys still have friends here," he told her with as comforting tone as he could muster, for he wasn't sure himself. "We'll try the Alston sisters."

The porter loaded the bags in a mule-drawn hackney which drove them to the corner of Tradd Street and Rutledge Avenue. The Alston ladies were still there, though they'd been forced to quarter Union troops. They escorted Cabell and Nellie to the last available space, the former servants' quarters under the eaves of the fourth floor attic.

That afternoon the two hostesses served tea, a poor affair since they were destitute of all but the house itself. Their only income was the pittance of rent paid by the Military Governor. Cabell at once sent out for several basket loads of groceries, which the Alstons accepted with only a murmur of protest. Tea was delayed in favor of a full-dress supper.

"Now then," said Frances, the younger of the sisters, the one Cabell had always assumed his brother would marry. She proudly served the rice with a long-handled silver spoon. "We haven't seen Drayton in Charleston since 1864, when he returned to the Army after recovering from his Gettysburg wounds."

"We hear he's buried himself at the ruins of Cypress Stand," added Lily. "I've heard on good authority – it was an affair of the heart." She cast a sidelong glance at her sister

"Nonsense," scoffed Frances. "*I've* got it on good authority – he's secluded himself to write a book."

Cabell listened and fumed. Neither theory explained why he'd walked away from a prominent position at the University in mid-term, or why he'd failed to meet them when the mail packet docked.

***

Corruption among Occupation officials in South Carolina was so rampant that even many Northerners were scandalized and embarrassed. But it was too deeply entrenched, with too many beneficiaries, for anyone to do anything about it besides tut-tutting and hand-wringing. Homes like the FitzHenry's on Charleston's lower Peninsula were coveted spoils of victory; taxes were accordingly high. Only a jobbing Scalawag or thieving Carpetbagger could afford such properties. He had enough money, but Cabell knew an open bid in tax court would likely fail. Even though they'd 'swallowed the dog,' ex-Confederates rarely obtained justice from Federal Occupation courts. Most judges were political appointees, notorious swindlers and reprobates. Indeed, the courts were now the principal means of expropriating what little wealth Southerners had left after the War. And as a former Confederate officer and son of an Ordinance Signer, Cabell could expect short shrift.

If you can't beat 'em, join 'em, he decided. Paying the exorbitant tax, he bribed the tax assessor to put the property in the name of a blind holding company headquartered in Poolesville, Maryland, a state which had not seceded, though many Marylanders had fought for the Confederacy. He was able to incorporate before anyone noticed with the help of his friend from the War, fellow attorney Kyd Douglas. It took a few weeks to conclude the transactions, but in the end he regained effective ownership without revealing his name, unless someone grew curious enough to peel back the layers to the original documents in Maryland.

With Nellie's concurrence, he also decided not to occupy the mansion for a time to avoid scrutiny. His new 'company' hired a caretaker. An empty home near the Battery was a magnet for thieves, even though most of the furnishings and housewares had long since been plundered. Eventually the Yankees would have to leave the state. Then he and Nellie would move back in. Until they did, he set up a lucrative practice in Beaufort. Unlike battered Charleston, Beaufort was relatively unscathed, a maritime city equidistant between two other major maritime cities, Savannah and Charleston. Their estate agent rented the upper floors of the East Bay mansion and was allowed to keep half the proceeds, providing a financial incentive to take good care of the place. Cabell and Nellie said farewell to the Alstons, who would accept no remuneration for their generous three weeks of hospitality. Cabell made an anonymous deposit in their meager bank account anyway, enough to pay the year's tax on their home. Then he and Nellie departed for Beaufort on the Savannah line.

Chapter Thirty Three

Charleston, South Carolina, April 1913

D rayton resolved to explain himself more fully to Cabell in his own good
time, for Cabell was quite right. Annalee had made no secret of her feelings
about the Reunion — going to Gettysburg would push the tottering marriage
over the edge. And the bad ones notwithstanding, the War hadn't altered the
fact that marriage was the foundation of his society, a hallowed institution.
Divorce was considered a scandal. It offended the community's sensibilities
to just walk away. It was like repudiating his whole culture. But the choice,
however weighty, was his alone. Annalee's feelings were her own, and his were
his. She didn't get a veto, though she seemed to think otherwise. He'd taken
her trump card off the table years ago, in 1878. They'd been married only a few
years when he discovered her deepest secret. The knowledge threw her entire
persona, especially the public Annalee, into a different light.

By her account her first husband Isaac Joyner had gone off to the Western
theater of the War, a private in the Army of Tennessee. Isaac had never returned
and no word of him had filtered back. The Regimental returns from the 11th
South Carolina Infantry listed him killed in action at Shiloh in 1862. She came
to Charleston the following year seeking better opportunities than might be
found in the hardscrabble Upstate. She insisted to all Charleston that Isaac
had died bravely, and she'd basked in the halo of Southern patriotism that
accompanied her story. In those dreadful days thousands of men were swept
away in the vortex of destruction with no certainty of their fate. No one in
Charleston had reason to challenge her. Still, Drayton had always detected an
odd echo in Annalee's tale. Once it caused him to wonder if Mr. Isaac Joyner
had found the War an excuse to disappear conveniently. Even now he might be
living the good life in some distant hideaway. He recalled a certain satisfaction
the day he learned his intuition was correct.

Charleston, South Carolina; October 1878.

Drayton had lived in seclusion on the Edisto from 1867 to the summer of
1873, when he received a handsome offer to take over the Classics Department
at the College of Charleston. His books had brought him some income, some

local fame, and now brought him out of retirement. His secret burden still weighed him down, but he'd learned to live with it after a fashion. It was time to re-enter the land of the living. And Cypress Stand was always there as a weekend retreat.

The *Courier* had remarked on Charleston's good fortune '…in luring a scholar of such repute and a native of this city no less.' He'd given two well-received, after-dinner addresses to the Hibernians on the Young Ireland Rebellion and on Wolfe Tone. His presence in town was no secret.

It was Drayton's fifth year teaching at the College of Charleston and close to the end of term. He'd been married for two years. The Turks and the Russians were at each other's throats again, and Greece had joined the fray against the Turks. A madman had made an attempt on the life of the young Kaiser of Germany, Wilhelm I. And in the South, life was striving to return to normal after the end of Federal occupation and plundering Republican rule.

One afternoon as he left the College a tall man accosted him just beyond the quad. The stranger was lean and weathered like an old cypress post. But he was reasonably clean, smelling of castile soap, shaved and well-dressed in a faded Navy pea jacket, with a knotted kerchief instead of a proper necktie. In his hand he held a billed seaman's cap.

"Are you Mistah Drayton FitzHenry?" The man had a distinct Up Country accent, and for a moment Drayton thought the man might be related to his old Army friend Allen MacAllen.

"Yes, I am. What can I do for you?"

"It's more a question of what I kin do for you." The lanky fellow scanned the quadrangle furtively. Something in his words and actions put Drayton immediately on guard. He ran a hand into his pocket and gripped the derringer, his thumb on its hammer and index finger alongside the trigger. He took a step backward, remaining poised to strike if necessary.

"No need to get on yore high horse," said the stranger. "I mean you no harm and may be able to do you a good turn."

"Speak your piece, then. Who are you?"

"My name is Joyner. Isaac Joyner." He uttered a low mordant laugh while Drayton's blood froze. "You might say as we're kinfolks. Married to the same woman and all."

They withdrew under a spreading live oak in a quiet corner of the quad where the afternoon sun dappled the brick surface.

"The ghost of Shiloh," said Drayton, with a bitter I-knew-it amusement.

"The rolls of the 11th South Carolina carry you as killed in action." He lolled on a stone bench in the quad, crossing his arms. Joyner remained standing and paced to and fro.

"Well, as you kin see, I ain't kilt," the stranger said. "I was captured."

"Lit out, more likely."

"No, I was good and truly captured," Joyner replied. "They sent me to a god-awful hole of a prison camp in Illanoise. I like to died there a cold, starvation, and disease." His rawboned face creased deeper with a frown of recall. "Then they gave me a choice. Rot in that hellhole or join up. So I threw in with the Union. For the time bein'."

"A 'galvanized Yankee.' Mr. Joyner, I believe you're the first one I've ever met."

"No doubt. But I wouldn' agree to fight against our people. They sent me out West to fight Indians. Said it would free up real Amuricans to come fight the South. Anyways, I done that for a while. *Then* I lit out. I always wanted to travel."

"You kept going west?"

"Yes, sir. Went so far west I ended up in South Africa. Got there in 1871, just in time for the big diamond strike in Kimberly. Ever'body there – white men, that is – made fortunes."

"So that's where Annalee's money came from," Drayton scoffed. Feeling more relaxed with the man, he gestured for him to sit.

"Yes, sir. I had plenty at the time. And I felt bad. It was kind of a dirty trick to just disappear like I done. I sent her a handsome sum a money. Thought it might ease her grief some, not that she had any. It did ease *my* mind some." He sat on the end of the bench, circling one raised knee with both arms. He grinned conspiratorially, as if he expected Drayton to know exactly what he meant. Sadly, Drayton did.

"Did she sincerely believe you were dead?"

"Until 1872 I 'spose she did. You fought in the War, so you know how it was. We didn't have no reliable way of identifyin' the dead. And there was plenty a dead at Shiloh. You never saw so many folks blown to smithereens. It was easy to mix me up with a blasted corpse. I never wrote no letters, nor received any. I was sorta glad to be free – free of her, even as a prisoner of the Yankees, if you know what I mean." Joyner punctuated each statement with a flat, sweeping gesture, like a Cheyenne war chief.

"And after you sent the money, she never wrote you in South Africa, never asked you to come home and be a husband to her again?"

"She's a right shrewd woman," said Joyner. "She didn't want anything from me 'cept'n the money. And tell you the truth, I was makin' so much money there and enjoyin' the, ah, fleshpots, I never 'spected to leave. I promised I'd never darken her door again. I was half a world away. At the time it was an easy promise to make."

"Very well. Why have you come to me? Why have you reappeared after all these years? Or do I need ask? You must know turning up like this will cause us embarrassment."

The man shifted uncomfortably on his bench. "That's sorta my point, Mr. FitzHenry. You see, I ain't never been declared legally dead. The Regimental roll says 'missin and *presumed* dead.' I'm no lawyer, a course, but I checked the court records. Annalee submitted the Regimental muster rolls to have me declared dead. But that record alone don't make me legally dead. Point is, Mr. FitzHenry, since I *ain't* legally dead, or even approximately dead as you can see, then—"

"Then you're still legally married to her and I'm not her true husband. And she knew it when she married me."

"Yes, sir. But don't be too hard on her. She thought I was gone for good. I may be a pore man but I keep my word — till now's hard times, anyways. I don't aim to interfere with your, ah, connubial bliss. It's jes' that I find myself unexpectedly cast adrift here in Charleston, while on a world cruise so to speak. I need some funds to continue my journey, one which I'm sure the FitzHenry family would like to see extend well beyond these shores."

"What happened to all your South African money?" Drayton faced the visitor squarely.

"Well, I'm 'shamed to admit it, but I guess you could say I was … improvident. Anyway, I got nowheres else to turn at the moment, and I was certain you'd be willin'. Otherwise Annalee would have some major explainin' to do. And you, too, I'm sorry to say, for you seem like a fine feller. I'm sure the news of my miraculous resurrection would cause a major scandal in this city which is oh-so-proper. You will be scorned for cohabitin' unlawfully and immorally, and your good name as well as hers will be dragged into the gutter."

Drayton stood suddenly. "My name is secure enough from this kind of blackmail, for that's obviously your purpose."

Joyner shrugged with a kind of complacent leer, ignoring Drayton. "Folks will still ask, why'd you never verify my fate? They'll wonder — did her fine house and bank account look good to a pore schoolteacher, even one with an old Charleston name like yore's? And then there's yore son Preston to be considered." The man had obviously done his research. "He'll be regarded as—"

"A bastard."

"A harsh word, ain't it?" He twirled his billed seaman's cap casually around his index finger, trying to appear relaxed, as if hitting someone up for blackmail was a routine occurrence. "But I'm afraid it's the word the righteous folks here would use. Anyways, I'm sorry to hear you take that tone. Blackmail is another ugly word. I'm just a Southern sailor down on his luck. I could use some help from my... ah, new-found relative to find a room to wait in and a mess of pottage while one a them steamers makes up a crew. Then I'll sail away and you'll never be bothered by me again."

Well, well, Drayton mused. *So she has a shameful secret. Aside from our son, about all we have in common.*

The temptation to use the discovery was powerful. But there was his son to think about. And then, Drayton had no moral standing from which to reproach her. In the circumstances, honour demanded he say nothing – nothing to anyone, not even her. Perhaps it was a kind of perverse pride to know he could destroy her but wouldn't. She had never really had his heart – nor wanted it. He'd known passion and some of the depths of a woman. He knew she had never allowed herself any pleasure in his touch, for that would cede him power over her. In fairness, she was a casualty of the War as well as he, like the myriad Southern men and women who showed no outward wounds. They bore invisible lacerations of the spirit — the loss of dignity, the destruction of hope.

"I may have a good name, Mr. Joyner, but no money to speak of. We're still recovering from the War. But how much do you need?"

Chapter Thirty Four

Charleston, South Carolina; May 1913.

Drayton always returned from his River sojourns refreshed and restored for another week of classes at the College – and for his next bout with Annalee, which was sure to come sooner or later. In this case it was sooner. She was a discerning woman in her way, and she had to be aware that something was brewing in his mind, try as he might to conceal it. Had she divined his decision about Gettysburg? Not yet, he thought, but no doubt she suspected. His musings were interrupted by his wife at the far end of the dining table.

"Drayton! Your breakfast is growing cold. After the trouble I go to and fix you a good breakfast, the least you could do is eat it."

She was a fine cook and always put a good meal before him. She was solicitous about his health in general, and he was not unmindful of it. "Yes, dear. You feed me well. I suppose I was daydreaming again."

"You do that a lot." For an instant but an instant only, he detected a note of sympathy. Then she continued. "But you weren't thinking about me or your obligations to this household, I'll wager. You were thinking about the cusséd War again. As if you were the only one who suffered loss. At least you came home. Not like some…"

Did I hear the sub-text right? He mused. *Is she referring elliptically to Isaac Joyner? She has always wrapped herself in the mantle of his 'martyrdom.'*

His momentary good feelings evaporated. Gently but with repressed anger, he tossed his napkin on the table, got up without a word with his panama hat, and headed for the back door.

"Where are you going?" she demanded. "It's too early for school."

"I have errands."

He spoke truly; he *did* have errands. He needed new clothes for his trip and for Tommy, and had obtained his grandson's measurements, along with his grandson's promise to reveal nothing about the Gettysburg plans. Tommy wanted to go badly enough that Drayton felt he could rely on the child's discretion. Perhaps it was craven to conceal his decision from Annalee. But he would inform her when it was too late to intervene. Meanwhile, he was annoyed right down to his boots and just wanted to get out of the house. Her disparaging his Confederate service was a transparent effort to control him by belittling him. It wasn't effective any longer. Her insults might have been justified if she'd known his secret, but he was confident she didn't. No one did. He guarded it too carefully. Yet she still displayed an attitude, even though to many Charlestonians he was a minor celebrity, mainly from his role in the Great Wade Hampton Beefsteak Raid. And he'd suffered two wounds, one near-fatal, yet had returned to the Army in May 1864 when he might have cried off sick. In fact, it was almost forty-nine years ago to the day.

Charleston and points north; May 1864.

Drayton had only his loose cotton hospital clothes when he'd returned to Charleston in August 1863 to recuperate from Gettysburg. Now, a year later reporting back for duty, he had to acquire new uniforms and boots. Good wool serge in cadet grey was scarce, but he found some decent jeans cloth, a kind of wool-cotton blend aspiring to regulation grey. This late in the War many Confederates wore captured Yankee clothing, bleached and dyed with hickory bark and producing a brownish hue called 'butternut.' His new uniforms were closer to grey than butternut. The boots cost a king's ransom, but good footwear was a necessity, not a luxury. While the clothing and boots were being made he stopped in the empty East Bay Mansion. The place echoed ghost-like in its emptiness, and he wondered if he and Celia might ever return here. The gracious life the home and Charleston once offered was like something imagined from another place and time. Yet the widespread destruction of the city hadn't weakened the resolve of Charleston's defenders, only strengthened it, soldier and civilian alike.

A tedious three-day rain ride with many delays brought him to Richmond. From there he rode in a supply wagon to Culpeper, where the 2nd South Carolina Cavalry was in bivouac. He planned to retrieve his horse and then join General Longstreet and First Corps encamped to the south of the town. Knowing Cabell was riding Beltane, he'd brought Dial, a remount for his brother, a still-green fellow foaled in Camden. He trotted into a familiar scene, dismounted, and tethered Dial, whereupon Prioleau Henderson hailed him and shook his hand with exuberance.

"Where's our mob?" asked Drayton, embracing his old friend.

"Follow me," said Pree.

Allen MacAllen, now regimental sergeant-major, was with the veterinary surgeon and farriers, inspecting horses quarantined with glanders. When he spied Drayton, MacAllen strode forward, grinning. He and Drayton shook hands awkwardly. Then they embraced, pounding each other on the back.

"You smell like wood smoke," grinned MacAllen, washing his hands in a tub of lye soap. Drayton followed suit. They weren't sure of the causal mechanism, but were beginning to observe that dirty hands could spread disease to horse and man.

"Smoke and cinders from the locomotive. And you smell like horse. Speaking of which, where's Beltane?"

MacAllen jerked a thumb behind him. "Up at the horse lines. I can't speak for him personally, you understand, but I think he's been pining for you. Won't hardly let nobody ride him."

Tied to the picket line, Beltane began to bob his head, snorting and whinnying and stirring up all the other horses. Drayton arrived, addressing his equine comrade with the combination of kindness and authority that had served them well. As he stroked Bel's neck in large circles, there was no doubt in the mind of animal or man, as there had never been, who was the boss.

The horses were thin and gaunt, and some were sore-backed. Drayton looked at his comrades in dismay.

"It's them Jennifer saddles we went to war with," MacAllen explained. "They don't fit no more."

The standard-issue Confederate saddle had been fine until the animals lost flesh from too much work and too little forage. As they grew thinner, the saddle rubbed and chafed. Captured McClellan saddles were better in this regard, but still needed ticking or blankets underneath. Even that was lacking or worn out – or pilfered by soldiers outside the Regiment who had nothing and believed human needs preceded those of a horse.

Drayton saddled Beltane, thanked his former cavalry comrades, and reported to First Corps. And so it went on, the third year stretching tortuously into four. No one could imagine simply stacking arms and making peace. The blood already shed must be paid for with even more blood. It seemed the struggle would go on inexorably, until the last surviving Yankee and Confederate had fired their last remaining cartridges and then went at one another with the bayonet.

In the spring of 1864 President Lincoln appointed Ulysses S. Grant, victor in the Western Theater, to overall Union command, charging him to develop a coordinated strategy to crush the Confederacy. General George Meade remained in partial favor because he'd defeated Lee at Gettysburg. But, though grateful for Meade's victory, Lincoln had never forgiven him for failing to destroy Lee outright. Meade remained nominal commander of the Army of the Potomac, while the relentless Grant took charge of all the Union armies. He 'attached himself' to Meade, who became superannuated in effect, while Grant commanded the Army of the Potomac in reality.

In May the Yankees began a new drive on Richmond, traversing the fought-over lands south of the Rappahannock River. Lee marched eastward to meet Grant, who was crossing the Rappahannock into Virginia near the old battlefield of Chancellorsville. In early May 1864 the two armies collided in the broad expanse of scrub, thicket, and second-growth forest aptly named The Wilderness.

Tactical control in 19th Century warfare depended mostly on sight and voice. Keeping a unit together in a compact formation was considered necessary to mass its firepower. Fighting in 'open order' was frowned upon except in special circumstances. But in this awful terrain, commanders lost sight of their regiments as the men were swallowed in the underbrush. Voice and bugle command became impossible in the mayhem. Formations lost contact with their supports, and the battle degenerated into a chaos of small-unit firefights. Muzzle blasts ignited the dry brush, and disabled men burned to death amid the swirling battle.

Trying to bring order out of the chaos, Longstreet and his staff galloped across what remained of a coherent front line late in the afternoon. Drayton had just escorted Brigadier General Micah Jenkins forward to confer with Longstreet when a volley of musketry erupted from a nearby tree line. The Corps Commander grunted in pain, grabbed his arms, and slumped from the saddle. Drayton and several staff officers leaped from their mounts to attend the General while Major Sorrel rode forward shouting for the Confederates to cease firing on their own people. Longstreet was badly wounded but conscious. Micah Jenkins lay dead, shot in the skull, and by their own men, scant miles from where Stonewall Jackson had been mortally wounded a year ago by a Confederate regiment that mistook him and his staff for Union cavalry in the failing light.

The chaotic stand-off was inconclusive, although Grant appeared to be in retreat. But this time, instead of limping backwards as his predecessors had done, Grant side-stepped Lee to the east and kept on coming. In this remorseless new warfare, 'retaining possession of the field' meant nothing. Lee anticipated Grant as the two armies raced for the vital road junction at Spotsylvania Courthouse.

Lee named Dick Anderson, a West Pointer from South Carolina, to replace Longstreet as First Corps commander. Drayton found the quickest route for Anderson to Spotsylvania, enabling the First Corps to arrive a step ahead of the leading Federal brigades and fortify the vital cross-roads. Then followed one of the most appalling battles for its ferocity yet, a mad Saturnalia of blood and horror as innumerable waves of Yankees broke on the Southern breastworks. Fighting at the 'Bloody Angle' descended into a lust of killing as blue and grey battled across the thickness of a log wall. Soldiers discharged muskets in the faces of the enemy, passing empty guns rearward to be re-loaded and loaded guns forward to the front rank. Trampling their dead, they stabbed each other with bayonets and clubbed with musket butts in a frenzy. Over all was a constant roaring. Shouts of command, howls of agony, and gunfire blended into such harrowing clamor that it jarred the mind nearly senseless. How could men tear at one another with such savagery? Awful as it was, Gettysburg seemed sedate compared to this mutual annihilation.

In the rear, Drayton waited with the command group, struggling to keep Bel under control as shells exploded and solid shot ploughed lethal furrows. The Yankees, employing new assault tactics, broke the Southern salient. A flood of blue streamed through the breach, while a second wave turned to roll up the Confederate flanks. The life of the Army could be counted in minutes. On his bay battle horse, General Lee galloped forward from his post behind the lines to the head of his last reserves, a Texas brigade. He was going to lead the counter-attack in person. The Texians restrained him, calling out 'Lee to the rear! Lee to the rear!' His fighting blood up, Lee seemed determined, but consented when the soldiers refused to release his mount's bridle. With their beloved commander safe, the Westerners surged forward and sealed the gap, at great cost.

Balked but not defeated at Spotsylvania, Grant again refused to retreat. Marching around Lee's right he came on, and the two armies raced to the next vital spot. Once again, Lee got there first, digging in at an otherwise insignificant clearing near the old Seven Days battlefield known as Cold Harbor. The Union Army suffered one of the bloodiest repulses of the War. Even the sanguinary Grant was shocked at the losses his ill-planned operation produced, a series of senseless frontal attacks against Confederates behind log and earth breastworks. To the credit of the Union soldier, he accepted the appalling casualties and came doggedly on. At Cold Harbor the Yankees, knowing they were doomed, pinned their names and addresses on slips of paper on their backs before their suicidal charges. Surveying the field strewn with dead, their opaque eyes open and staring but the light gone out of them, Dick Anderson remarked, "Even the most savage must weep." An army fabled for their courage, the Confederates marveled at the unflinching bravery of their enemies. But they also wondered why Grant had learned nothing from the slaughter on other fields of massed frontal assaults against an entrenched enemy.

More soberly now, Grant tried to envelop Lee again, bringing the two armies into another collision at Petersburg in July 1864. The nine-month siege began, the penultimate act of the four-year drama. Grant had enormous resources with which to construct a vise and squeeze the South. While Lee's army hung on at Petersburg, far to the South Sherman marched on Atlanta. His 60,000 tough veterans were opposed by militia of old men and boys, leavened with a handful of Confederate regulars. They could do little to stop Sherman's burning and pillaging. Simultaneously, a Federal army advanced up the Shenandoah, destroying Virginia's granary. Benjamin 'Beast' Butler landed with 30,000 south of the James River to threaten Richmond from the rear. But somehow Lee held. As long as he did, the War would go on. He was truly equal to the myth, their Marse Robert in whom the South never lost faith. But the rumors grew of his heart pains and sciatica, as though a demi-god couldn't suffer from such mundane conditions. Not to mention dysentery, which they all experienced from the poor food and living filthy in the trenches.

Chapter Thirty Five

Petersburg, Virginia, 1864.

For three years of struggle Richmond had been the key to defeating the South. Now Petersburg was the key to Richmond. It was here the war of movement ended, the kind of war at which the Confederates had excelled, compensating for their weakness in numbers and resources. To protect Petersburg's vital hub of rail and roads networks, the Southerners entrenched behind log-thickened breastworks, log-lined "bombproofs," and obstacles of sharpened stakes called *chevaux-de-frise*. During Grant's brutal 'Overland Campaign,' from The Wilderness to Petersburg, Lee had inflicted losses of two to one. Union casualties equaled the number of troops in Lee's army when the campaign began. The North could afford its losses, the South could not.

As Lee and Grant settled into a siege, the War devolved into a matter of simple mathematics. The variables were time and distance, men and *matériel*. Grant was not going to squander lives as he had at Spotsylvania and Cold Harbor. With the Confederates pinned in their works at Petersburg, he could simply extend his lines, avoid major assaults, and force Lee to thin his own lines to avoid envelopment. Once the Confederates were stretched to the breaking point, he would punch through along the front or outflank Lee at a time and place of his choosing. Or both.

Until then, life such as it was dragged on. Hunger, disease, and death. There was little soap and water in the trenches. A bath was less an exercise in washing off the dirt than of rubbing it in. Amusements were rat-hunting and louse races. Country boys who'd grown up like deer in the woods had to learn latrine discipline, especially in a siege where they couldn't escape their own ordure. 'Fly stew' seemed to be the main item on the bill of fare. Snipers with new telescoped rifles on both sides proved deadly to anyone exposing himself above the parapets for more than a few seconds. And it was a wet death, in flooded trenches, dripping with blood. And the lice. *We don't have lice; they have us,* thought Drayton. The little devils preferred to nest in the seams and hems of their garments, and nightly the troops would run the seams over a candle to kill them.

Some of the cavalry units went into the trenches to spell the infantry, allowing the 'mud soldiers' a brief respite in the rear to get clean. It was a boost to morale to walk upright for a stretch without fear of a Yankee sniper blowing off the tops of their skulls. But Lee objected after a few days. The cavalry corps, now barely mustering a division, made up most of his reserves against a Union breakthrough, the likelihood of which grew daily as he had to stretch out his lines to meet Grant's ever-lengthening tentacles and avoid being out-flanked to the west.

General Longstreet returned, his arm permanently crippled, and perhaps sooner than he should have; but Lee needed competent leaders, and 'Old Pete' was one of his best. Too many capable commanders had been killed or disabled. Shortly afterwards came to plaintive cry through the lines that General Jeb Stuart was dead. The seemingly immortal Jeb Stuart, shot down by a Yankee cavalryman at Yellow Tavern northeast of Petersburg. The word crackled through the Army like flames leaping from tuft to tuft of dried grass. Stuart was irrepressible even in the darkest moments, with his red-lined cape and plumed hat, his pageantry, his retinue of bonesman, fiddler, and concertina player. Cal Butler disparaged them as 'Stuart's Traveling Minstrel Show' on the move and 'Stuart's Music Hall' in camp. But for all his theatrics, the Army had loved him. He'd been their Knight Errant, conferring a touch of romance to a war long since sunk into squalor. Drayton grieved with the rest of the Army, though he was a Wade Hampton partisan. From the beginning of the war relations had been sometime strained between the horse soldiers of Virginia and South Carolina. Yet despite the rivalry, despite Stuart's favoritism to his Virginia compatriots, the Carolinians respected him as a talented cavalry leader.

The static warfare of Petersburg flared up with occasional fights along the lines as Grant extended his line and sought to outflank Lee with superior numbers. But Lee always managed to get there first with just enough men, now armed with picks and shovels as well as rifles. In the circumstances there was not much for mounted soldiers to do except patrol the vulnerable flanks. Though well supplied from the Federal fleet commanding the James River, Grant's army was essentially isolated, a Yankee island in a Southern sea. Drayton found a certain irony in the Yankees' facing north — toward Petersburg — while the Confederates faced south. It reversed the strategic orientation of all previous campaigns.

Near Petersburg, Virginia; early September 1864.

Drayton resumed his role of independent scout, this time exultant, suddenly feeling what he'd never felt in the War, an eagerness to fight. He volunteered to probe behind the Union lines, a task at which he and Beltane excelled. It was dangerous work, for the Yankees sent out their own patrols to guard their unsecured rear. But it took him away from the tedium of the siege, away from the endless skirmishing by Hill's Corps and the shrinking Southern cavalry on Lee's right flank.

Drayton had gained a reputation for reading terrain and sniffing out the enemy. Longstreet was happy to send him on independent forays, knowing it suited his temperament. Solo scouting required a cold-blooded kind of courage, for any moment he might blunder into an enemy patrol. If that happened, and if he was lucky, they'd haul him in as a prisoner of war. Often as not, as the war descended in bitterness, patrols and pickets would gun a man down from ambush rather than capture him. It was tense, nerve-searing work, but better than the trenches. Preferable to the flies, lice, rats, mud, and stench. In time he'd come to accept the daily fear as a natural condition, even embrace it as a spur to keeping alert and centered, like a ship's ballast keeps the vessel righted. Now his worst fear was to be found deficient, useless, a pampered hanger-on at HQ, too obviously eager to save his own life. Off in the countryside he could scrounge an occasional meal from a sympathetic Virginia farmer who hadn't yet been plundered by the enemy. Of equal importance, there was more grazing for Bel beyond the siege lines. Camping alone and away from HQ, he had more time to give the horse a good rubbing down and grooming after a long ride. He was determined to keep Bel healthy, and had done remarkably well in three-plus years of conflict in which horses died at a higher rate than men.

Hunger and fatigue were insidious enemies, imposing a dullness almost impossible to avoid. Yet he had to keep his senses at their sharpest when roaming behind enemy lines. There was the incident back on the Occoquan in 1862, when Bel had saved him from death or capture by literally smelling the Yankees. Now, once again, deep in the Federal rear, Bel raised his head, laid back his ears, stiffened, and gave a low rumbling whinny. Drayton reined in and stood in the shadows, straining to hear. Keeping in the treeline, he eased forward with extra vigilance, till he heard the sound in the distance, the unmistakable sound of cattle lowing. Many cattle.

With light pressure, he edged Bel to the rim of pines bordering a large clearing, once a farm pasture from the sections of the board fencing still in place. In places makeshift repairs had been made with cut saplings. He popped Celia's glasses out of the case and scanned the site. Inside the enclosure he spied an enormous herd milling about hungrily and noisily as their keepers on the far side dumped hay in the corral. He scouted the area in detail, making note of the adjacent tracks and pathways and the disposition of the cattle guard, composed of thirty-odd Negro civilians and a company of cavalry or mounted infantry. Two soldiers rode the perimeter, but their attention was inward, checking for breaks in the fence. The rest of the Bluecoats took their ease in bivouac near the corral. Drayton caught a whiff of frying bacon as the Yankees prepared their evening meal.

While it was still light, Drayton drew a rough map of the layout in the shelter of the woods. As he sketched there swam into his mind a Greek myth, Hermes' theft of Apollo's sacred cattle. He salivated at the thought of a sizzling steak. Even when the South's decrepit railroads were working, the Confederacy could barely supply its armies. But now Sherman's horde was deep in the South attacking the sources of foodstuffs and the means to deliver them. The defenders of Petersburg had subsisted for weeks on hardtack, parched corn, pickled pork, and the flesh of horses and mules freshly killed in the shelling. *In extremis* they were content to eat rats that plagued them in the bombproof shelters. Most of the men accepted their lot cheerfully. But many did not. Hunger overcame patriotism and sense of duty, and men who were otherwise good soldiers slunk away from the lines, usually to be arrested and sent back by the provost marshal with a warning in lieu of punishment. The impact on morale of a few weeks of grilled beef would be incalculable. And here were thousands of cattle under a perfunctory guard. Though deep behind enemy lines, they were for the taking if the Confederates were bold enough.

The area west of the high ground that contained the cattle was mostly low terrain, bisected by numerous creeks and streams, with occasional hillocks of forested ground. It was not good cavalry country, yet good enough for this purpose, with plenty of cover in which to move concealed and assemble for the strike. All the disparate elements had come together in his imagination as if by their own accord into an orchestrated plan. Cook's Bridge on the Blackwater River was the key, if they could repair it in a hurry. Months ago, the Yankees had fired the structure to prevent its use. The river was too deep to ford there, its banks too steep and slippery. With the bridge destroyed, the Federals were no longer paying attention to this avenue of approach into their rear. But only the decking had burned, not the pilings, joists and braces. They remained standing starkly in the flood, singed but intact. If the bridge could be re-planked, the Southerners could use it to reach the objective and drive the cattle back to their own lines. He made some rough calculations. How long would it take the cattle and a few thousand cavalrymen to cross? And would the rudimentary repairs of which they were capable hold up under such a pounding?

Just after dark he reported to Moxley Sorrel at Corps headquarters and asked permission to take his proposal to Wade Hampton. General Longstreet, his wounded arm in a sling, emerged from his tent, and grinned fiercely when Drayton sketched out his concept of the operation.

"My compliments to General Hampton," the Corps Commander said. "Tell him I like my steak slightly rare." He waved him on toward Hampton.

Drayton cantered to the cavalry corps headquarters and dismounted.

Preston Hampton, the General's second son and aide-de-camp, greeted his friend warmly.

"I need to see General Hampton," said Drayton. "Urgently." The General's son motioned to follow as Drayton tied Bel to a picket line. He and Preston walked down to the horse lines where General Hampton was inspecting Butler, his big bay Thoroughbred, by lantern-light. The General was bent over with Butler's left forefoot cradled in his large strong hands. This was usually the work of a groom or enlisted soldier, not of a major general. But Hampton believed in personally inspecting his own mounts – within reason — and setting the example for his troopers. He looked up and grunted a barely audible greeting.

"Lieutenant FitzHenry. Glad to see you. It's been a while since Charlottesville. What brings you down our way?"

"Beef cattle, General Hampton, beef cattle. Near on three thousand head, I'd say."

Hampton set down the horse's foot, straightened up to his full six feet three inches, and peered hard at Drayton in the flickering light. "Then you must be speaking of Yankee cattle, for no such herd resides on our side of the lines. There may be no such herd in the entire Confederacy." He tugged at his thick brown beard; thought lines creased his brow. Despite the poor light, the angry scar across his forehead from Gettysburg was still visible.

"Yes, sir, exactly," said Drayton. "I think I know how we can rustle 'em." Motioning to the man holding the lantern, he pulled out his map, creased to the point of falling apart.

Thomas Moore

Chapter Thirty Six

Petersburg, Virginia, September 1864

General Longstreet issued a brief written order detailing Lieutenant Drayton FitzHenry to the Cavalry Corps under command of Major General Hampton 'for the duration of the proposed operation.' Hampton called a council of war with the brigadiers commanding his available brigades comprising 3,700 horsemen. It meant stripping the Petersburg defenses of virtually all its cavalry. The contingent included a company of mobile engineers, who would repair the bridge over the Blackwater River, and the skilled artillerists of Hart's Battery. After posting sentries outside the tent with orders to let no one within earshot, Hampton pinned his map on a frame of roughhewn boards and gestured to Drayton.

"Gentleman, this is Lieutenant FitzHenry of General Longstreet's staff. I know him personally and can vouch for his reliability as a scout. He has put an interesting project before me. You will no doubt agree it's a risky and daring venture. But if successful, it will bring great relief to our people. They are virtually starving in their works. Lieutenant, you have the floor."

Drayton stepped to the map. Tracing his recent scout with a willow twig, he said, "Gentlemen, as you know, the Yankee army is like an abscess driven into our side from City Point on the James River. They have our army invested around Petersburg, but their rear basically rests in the air. They are essentially open and unprotected in the south, except for occasional patrols of cavalry."

Hampton interjected, "And at present most of their cavalry are far off burning and pillaging with Sheridan in the Shenandoah Valley."

"Yes, sir. I have scouted the Union rear from our right flank on the Boydton Plank Road as far south as Ebenezer Church and as far east as the James River. That's where their right flank rests. I spent an entire day poking around as far as Coggins Point on the James. It was there I spied a huge herd of cattle."

"How huge?" asked Rooney Lee, son of *the* General Lee.

"Sir, they were milling about, of course, so this is only an estimate. Between twenty-five hundred and three thousand head." A long silence followed as the officers absorbed the implications of such a number.

"I know the place," Rooney Lee noted. "It's Edmund Ruffin's plantation. How well guarded is the herd?"

"Only a company of cavalry and about two dozen civilian drovers. The cattle are enclosed in an old farm pasture and the fencing is not in good repair. The troopers are more concerned about keeping the corral intact and the herd together than anything else. They are well behind the Union right and don't appear vigilant."

Hampton laughed grimly. "Gentlemen, most of us were with General Stuart's ride around McClellan in 1862 and on his Christmas Raid. I led a raid of my own around the Yankees all the way to Chambersburg, Pennsylvania in September of '62. And we went round the Yankee army in July of '63. One thing our cavalry are good at is striking deep into the enemy's territory and supplying ourselves from his goods. Now this operation certainly has its risks. But we cavalry are doing very little during this wretched siege. And think of the gain, of the benefit to our men. Three thousand fresh beeves. Moreover, they provide their own locomotion."

The officers grinned in assent. This was something they excelled at, not just because of their horsemanship and military skill, but because the romance and adventure appealed to their deepest natures. Drayton noted that Hampton didn't ask for agreement. He simply laid out the mission and then gave the necessary orders. "This then is how we will proceed," he said, using the map to sketch out the operation.

When he concluded, Hampton flashed his well-known smile that presaged battle. "Mr. FitzHenry, having Irish forbears, has referred me to a famous legend called *The Cattle Raid of Cooley*. It is evidently the great epic of Ireland, like the *Iliad* of ancient Greece. But gentlemen, the Irish raid involved only one animal, though it was a bull of legendary powers. We are about to capture thousands. Think what an epic that will be when one of our grand-children comes to write it."

***

When the brigade commanders departed to complete their preparations, Hampton clapped Drayton on the shoulder. "You'll have to give the briefing again," he smiled.

"Of course, General. To whom?"

"To General Lee. We're going there now."

Drayton felt his eyes bug out. To brief the commander-in-chief in person!

It was like a private audience with the Pope.

"I want you there," said Hampton. "You're the only one who's been over the ground. We're entrusting this entire operation with all its risks to your reconnaissance, to your judgment."

As Drayton and Hampton trotted into Headquarters camp, Robert E. Lee stepped out of his tent. An orderly helped him into his uniform coat. Lee remained hatless, returning a crisp salute to Hampton. General Lee was fastidious, with grey serge trousers tucked into high-topped cavalry boots, and a clean linen shirt and black stock tie under a brass-buttoned grey waistcoat. His grey beard and hair were neatly trimmed. The legendary commander seemed thin and worn under the grey frock coat with its swirls of gold braid on the sleeve. But somehow it only enhanced the dignity of the man. As they halted, Lee looked surprised, more at Beltane than at Drayton. He stepped forward and patted the horse's neck while Drayton and Hampton dismounted.

"Aha," Lee said, eyes twinkling. "I had heard there was another horse in the Army almost the double of my Traveller."

"Yes, sir. He might be Traveller's twin," said Drayton, handing the reins to an orderly.

Lee smiled again, and looked Beltane over with the knowing eyes of a horseman, stroking his chest and forelegs.

He nodded to Hampton. "Welcome, General Hampton. Is this young man another of your intrepid South Carolinians?"

"Yes, sir. Lieutenant FitzHenry, of General Longstreet's staff, seconded to me for an operation we have come to propose. Formerly of the 2nd South Carolina Cavalry, General Butler's people."

"Ah, you young men of the cavalry. You will be the bane of me, you Virginia and South Carolina horsemen, always contending for the pre-eminence." Lee looked archly at Hampton, his new Chief of Cavalry since the death of Stuart.

There was something playful in Lee's well-known reserve. Drayton felt encouraged by it to venture, "But General Lee, you are a Virginian."

"Yes, that's true. But until this war is over, I am privileged to command brave men from *all* the states. Still, it's natural to take pride in one's home." He fondled Bel's forelock.

Drayton found an unexpected boldness. "General Lee, I hope it's not a false pride. It seems to be the curse of our Southern race."

Lee smiled and nodded. His smile was like the man, both wistful and warm. "You may be right, Mr. FitzHenry. But I suspect it is pride – pride of the *proper* kind — that has brought us this far. The good Lord knows we have subsisted on little else."

"Another name for honor, then," said Drayton quietly.

Lee smiled like a schoolmaster commending a student who has just solved a difficult problem. "Adversity has made you wise, Mr. FitzHenry. Yes, let us call it honor rather than pride. Honor is what remains when everything else has been taken away." He looked off into the distance, as if divining the future. "And that they can *never* take away."

Hampton cleared his throat noisily, aware he was interrupting a special moment. "Let's not demand more of Southern honor than Southern stomachs can bear, General Lee. Thanks to Mr. FitzHenry, I have a plan to put beefsteak in the mess tin of every soldier in the Army, for several weeks if not months."

Lee's face brightened, and he laid a guiding hand on Drayton's shoulder. "Gentlemen, come have a bit of supper and tell me about it."

Since it was a fine afternoon in early fall, the General Officer Commanding dined outside. Lee insisted on living as austerely as his men to the frustration of his staff, who tried to make camp life easier. Lee ushered them to a plank table adjacent to his headquarters tent. Colonels Marshall and Venable of his staff joined them.

As the meal was laid, Lee gestured apologetically. "I'm afraid this is the last of the season's corn, and the ears are poorly." Each man had an ear of roasted corn, some hard crackers with 'US' stamped prominently on them, and a couple of rashers of fried bacon, mostly fat.

Drayton had heard that Marse Robert's camp fare was as lean as his soldiers'. He was known for passing a gift of ham or a turkey to the hospital or to one of his regiments that had performed an exemplary act. But the paucity of food at the General's table was still shocking. There were no culinary temptations to distract them as Wade Hampton proposed the operation. Drayton repeated the briefing he'd given earlier. Lee nodded approvingly as each element was discussed in turn and woven into an overall plan.

Lee's brow furrowed as he studied the map and the proposed route. He said to Hampton, "General, when you return, your corps will be strung out in line of march and embarrassed with many cattle. You will want to guard against Those People coming down Jerusalem Plank Road and striking you in the flank. Some fresh beef will be welcome. But it is a risky operation. Having you back safe is equally important."

Dinwiddie Court House, Virginia; September 1864.

With mounted skirmishers ahead and on the flanks, they moved out at dawn along the Boydton Plank Road, a muddy track, hardly a road, that marked the far right of the Southern defense. Silence and stealth were the order of the day. The first night they bivouacked in the cold and dark – no fires – on Rowanty Creek, with a cheerless supper of fried corn cakes. The horses enjoyed a rare ration of oats and a brisk rub-down. Troopers stood-to an hour before dawn, first sergeants changed the vedettes, and they rode eastward, with Drayton guiding. They crossed serpentine Rowanty Creek again at Wilkinson's Bridge, now well behind Union lines, timing their arrival at vital Cook's Bridge on the Blackwater just before dark.

The horsemen dismounted, pulling well off the track and slipping bridles and easing girths. Engineer wagons, piled high with broad oak planks, passed through the cavalry to the threshold of the ruined bridge. Drayton watched with admiration as the sappers unloaded the wide boards, and – God only knew where it came from in the impoverished South – coils of steel wire. Working as quickly as possible in the half-light, they replaced a few of the deck joists, laid fresh planks from end to end, and lashed the whole array together with the stout wire. The result was nearly as secure as nailing the planks, but without the hammering that might alert the enemy. By dawn the bridge was passable, a marvel of combat engineering. After strewing a thick layer of straw to dampen the sound of crossing, the sappers remained behind to guard their prodigy. Hampton's men trotted over with a muffled drumming of hooves. Hart's gunners had wrapped their wheels in crocus sacks to deaden the noise.

Alternating between a trot and a walk to spare the horses, the long column plodded through a dreary landscape of scrub pines and stunted oaks, intersected by numerous bogs and marked by the musty odor of rotting vegetation. To find the solid pathway through the fens was a feat in itself. Hampton nodded gratefully to Drayton as they emerged onto higher ground far in Grant's right rear. At the rally point, Drayton pointed out the routes where the division would divide. Hampton told off the three attack columns. Rooney Lee took the largest force and the horse artillery to the left to blocking positions at Prince George's Court House. Hampton and Tom Rosser went up the middle to seize the cattle. Dearing's regiment took its post on the right to guard against an attack from the east. Lovick Miller's squadron remained in reserve. Drayton accompanied Hampton and General Rosser with the middle detachment.

There was an old saying among veteran soldiers: no plan ever survives contact with the enemy. The uncertainties of war reveal themselves at the worst possible time — a cloudburst that turns roads into clinging mud, an impassable ravine not on any map, an encounter with the enemy who weren't supposed to be there. This is when real soldiers earn their pay, through innovation and improvisation. Yet so far Hampton's Great Beefsteak Raid was coming off without a hitch. It was too good to be true and therefore couldn't be expected to last. Soon they'd be within striking distance of the cattle corral. Had they really achieved total surprise, or would they ride into an ambush?

Drayton studied General Hampton, the easy way between him and his sons Wade Junior and Preston, elegant in their gray, somehow having avoided the splashing mire. Hampton gestured with a toss of his head at Rosser's Virginians, who deployed from column of fours into battle line. Now they waited, the hardest part. It wasn't long til they heard the booming of Confederate guns to the north, along the front at Petersburg. Marse Robert had launched a demonstration to divert the enemy's attention from Hampton's presence behind their lines.

Hampton nodded at General Rosser. His horsemen emerged from the pines in line abreast at a brisk walk, pistols at the high ready. The cattle noticed their approach before the Yankee guard and bellowed in alarm. Union cavalrymen began to shout and scurry about in confusion. Only a few were mounted, but the shock of seeing a thousand grim Confederate riders materialize in their rear was too much. They fired a few rounds and galloped away. The others in bivouac tried to mount, but Rosser's troopers surrounded them at a canter. The Confederates rounded up scores of prisoners, got them all mounted, hitched the mules to wagons full of fodder and other supplies, and began the withdrawal. Those detailed to herd the cattle had broken down the fences on the south side and were aiming the animals southwest along the track with cries of 'Hup! Hup!' and sharp cracks of their bullwhips.

There was a spate of small arms fire to the north, from the direction taken by Rooney Lee, and then from the east, where Dearing's men provided a block. They heard the sharp crack of Hart's three-inch Ordnance Rifles. Hampton ignored it, intent on getting the cattle and the rest of the booty headed back toward the Blackwater and Cook's Bridge. He needn't have worried. Soon Rooney Lee's brigade came trotting down the track from Dinwiddie Courthouse, joined shortly after by Dearing and his people. The re-assembled commands took their assigned posts as a rear guard for the drovers, the cattle, and captured wagons, a cavalcade now a mile long.

At the junction of Jerusalem Plan Road, as General Lee had warned, a regiment of Federal cavalry descended on the strung-out division. But Hampton had anticipated them. He met the Union attack with a violent counter-charge of his reserve, spurring forward at the head of Lovick Miller's troopers, his two sons at his side. The rest of the staff and some of Rosser's men followed closely, cheering. The Yankees turned and fled, but a few, braver than the rest, stood the attack. Drayton was galloping forward and view-hallooing like the rest when he spied a big, bushy-bearded Bluecoat siting on his horse calmly and taking aim with his Sharps carbine at Preston Hampton. The entire tableau seemed to unfold in slow motion. He hadn't fired his Colt for lack of a clear target. Even though it was a long pistol shot and made more difficult by the horse's motion, Drayton put heel to Bel's flank and dashed across the Yankee's line of fire. He leveled his revolver and fired three times, visualizing almost tranquilly the split second before the strike of the ball that dropped the big Yankee. The man recoiled as two rounds hit him square in the chest. His carbine discharged harmlessly in the air and fell from lifeless hands as the man toppled sideways from his horse, with his right foot caught in the stirrup. The panicked mount darted away, dragging the body a dozen yards before it came free in a muddy heap. An ashen-faced, wide-eyed Preston Hampton turned to Drayton and tried to speak a word of thanks, but was cut off by his father's roar,

"Preston, get that horse!" Captured remounts were invaluable. The General reined in and ordered his bugler to sound recall, shouting after Miller's and Rosser's aggressive troopers, "Let 'em go! We have other work here!"

The mounted herdsmen, mostly Westerners, had been chosen for their experience with cattle and knew their business. Before reaching Cook's Bridge, they slowed the lumbering animals to a walk and thinned the stream to two or three abreast. The herd thundered across without a single cow being shouldered into the stream. It also took longer for them to cross – twice as long as Drayton had originally estimated. By then the Confederates were cocky with success and indifferent to the Yankee's giving chase, a dangerous bit of bravado, in Drayton's view.

General Hampton remained on the 'Federal side' until every trooper and beast, wagon and cannon, were safely over the Blackwater. He waved his staff and scouts onward and was the last man to cross, grinning fiercely. Immediately the engineers who'd remained behind fell into a row about what to do with the precious bridging material. The bolder ones wanted to disassemble it and bring it along, though that would take hours. The more cautious, worried about pursuit, wanted to burn it in place. Both looked to Hampton. He laughed and said, "*They* burned the first bridge, not us. Leave it and come on. We may want to use it again — when the Yankees replace the herd!"

That evening Hampton hosted a celebratory dinner. Beef was on the menu, and the General invited Drayton as a special guest. The officers had managed to scrounge a score of potatoes, baked and smoking in their jackets, and a demijohn of 'Blackwater Rum.' Hampton laughed as the jug made its rounds. "Who says Southerners lack Yankee ingenuity?" They were past masters at distilling strong drink and had made a heady liquor from the local blackstrap molasses. While they were eating, Yankees in the opposing trenches began to call out asking to be invited over for supper since they were now reduced to eating salt pork from moldy casks. With equal wry humor the Confederates called back with a welcome, urging the Yankees to get a long leave of absence first.

Wade Hampton offered a toast. "Gentlemen, I drink to one of the most successful cavalry operations this Army has ever conducted. We rode for three days deep in enemy territory, covering 100 miles. We fought two sharp fights, brought in 2800 head of cattle, 300 prisoners, and hundreds of fresh remounts. We captured a thousand blankets and a week's precious hay and oats for the horses. I congratulate you. Every man in this Army thanks you. And a special tribute to Mr. FitzHenry here, without whom we'd be eating rancid salt pork like those fellows across the way."

"And glad to get it," observed Tom Rosser with a chuckle.

The stunning raid, on the lips of every Southern soldier for weeks, was not without cost. Hampton reported ten killed and forty-seven wounded. He did not need to add how grateful he was that his son Preston wasn't numbered among them. Drayton recalled the Catholic liturgy from Celia's missal: in the midst of life we are in death. But the reverse was also true. In the midst of death there was life, even in a terrible war. Life asserted itself in countless ways, from the louse races and rat hunts to the nightly banjo serenades. Now it was found in the laughter in Southern trenches as the delicious aroma of grilling beef wafted over the lines. What could be more life-affirming than a juicy steak in every mess tin, cooked to order *sanglant* or *au point*, with the crusty rim of fat perfectly charred? Drayton had never enjoyed a meal more.

Chapter Thirty Seven

In the lines before Petersburg, Virginia; October 1864.

Drayton had found a small strip of canvas and was sewing knee patches onto his breeches where they had worn through from rubbing the saddle. He looked up from his perch on a cannon trail to see Prioleau Henderson. He stood and shook hands, noting his friend's long face.

"Hello, Pree. Take a seat and have a sip of what passes for coffee around here. Roasted acorns flavored with gunpowder, I fear."

"I believe I will have something." But instead of taking up the coffee pot Henderson produced a flask from his pocket and poured a dram for both of them in the mess cups.

Drayton knew in his bones this wasn't a mere social call. Taking a deep sip and a deep breath, he voiced the question he feared to ask. "Is he dead?"

"No. Badly wounded, though."

"Thanks be to God. It would destroy Father to lose another son, especially his first-born and namesake. How bad?"

"He has lost his right leg. Roundshot, I suppose. Took his leg almost clean off above the knee and passed on through Dial. We had a pretty rough fight yesterday at Burgess's Mill."

Drayton remained silent, well aware that the wounded man could survive the initial shock of wounding only to die days later from infection or gangrene.

To fill the awkward silence, Henderson said, "Poor old Dial. A fine horse. Cabell had begun to hope the animal might make it through to the end." Drayton said nothing. He was glad of the liquor to combat the sick feeling in his gut.

Henderson continued. "Doctor Moore thinks he'll recover. He said if you have to lose a limb, it's better this way. The wounding and the amputation were simultaneous and clean. He only had to snip a few strands of tissue instead of the … the usual ordeal. He doesn't think the leg will mortify. Cabell treated the matter as if it were beneath notice, until he fainted from the pain."

"Where is he now?"

"On the way to Chimborazo Hospital in Richmond. And we've been ordered home, did you know?"

"Home then, is it?"

"Yes, General Butler's brigade is relieved from the Army of Northern Virginia. Governor Bonham has been pestering the War Office to detach South Carolina regiments for the defense of the state. There's nothing to stop Sherman in South Carolina but old men and boys. And *les mutilés de guerre.*" Pree rested a booted leg on the cannon trail.

Drayton grimaced. "Your so-called brigade is down to little more than a squadron. Does anyone think a single depleted brigade of cavalry on worn-out horses will stop him? Sherman has 60,000 battle-hardened veterans."

"Well, we might annoy him a bit. Anyway, there's no one else to spare. And now that we've rieved all the Yankee's cattle, there's not much for us to do here." Henderson stood up straight, pouring the rest of the whiskey into Drayton's tin cup. "Here. You keep this."

"No, you— There's more bad news, isn't there?"

Henderson drew in his breath and looked away. Finally, as if mustering the strength to speak he said, "Preston Hampton was killed in the fight at Burgess Mill. He was galloping forward, cheering our attack, and was shot in the groin. His brother Wade stopped to render aid, and he was hit in the back. Wade Junior will survive, but Preston died in his father's arms. He was a staff officer. He had no business rushing forward into the attack that way. I know he was a particular friend of yours. If only he'd..." The sentence died in his throat. Henderson laid a consoling hand on Drayton's shoulder and walked away.

If only, thought Drayton. If only this, if only that, these might not have died, those might not have been horribly maimed. 'If only' had become the *leit-motif* for the War. A few weeks ago he'd saved Preston's life, shooting down the Yankee horseman at Jerusalem Plank Road, only to lose him now. You might postpone your fate, but not escape it.

With three-to-one superiority in numbers, Grant massed two corps and sixty guns on Lee's far right at Five Forks. In late morning of April 1 after the fog lifted, the well-fed, well-equipped Federals attacked. Virginian George Pickett of Gettysburg fame commanded the right-most Confederate division, but he and his regimental commanders were in the rear enjoying a shad-bake. Anomalies in the terrain and vegetation cloaked the sound of the attack while it rolled forward against the uncertain Confederates. Lt. General A. P. Hill, Corps commander and hero of a hundred fights, rushed forward to restore order and was shot out of the saddle. Under their junior officers the Confederate conducted a skillful fighting retreat – but still a retreat. Lee's Petersburg line had finally been turned, although as happened so often, the Yankees failed to exploit their advantage. Relieving Pickett from duty, Lee evacuated Petersburg and began to withdraw along the line of the James River. From that moment the Army of Northern Virginia had one week to survive.

Appomattox, Virginia; April 9, 1865.

Drayton would never forget the long nightmarish retreat from Petersburg. Broken-down wagons, foundered horses, artillery without ammunition, and exhausted men littered the route. There was no food, little clean water, and above all, no respite from the exultant Yankees close on their heels. Yet the Army never disintegrated. They moved west, ever west, but to what end no one knew, except there were rumors of a trainload of rations at Amelia Courthouse. Drayton was scouting forward and escaped the debacle at Sayler's Creek, when a third of the Army and most of its wagon trains were captured. His baggage was taken along with the rest. Now he possessed only what he carried in his bedroll and saddlebags.

Though it had been only a week, the exodus from Petersburg seemed interminable. Finally the Army's exodus ground to a halt. A large force of Yankees out-marched them for once and blocked the road farther west. Lee had hoped to escape the closing net and join forces with General Joseph Johnston in North Carolina. But the net closed. The Confederates camped near a little village called Appomattox.

Drayton awoke in a cold, dew-soaked blanket to hooves pounding at dawn, then the long roll of the drums beating assembly. As the sun rose, he heard a rumbling of artillery. The Southerners were now outnumbered five to one and starved of food and ammunition. Reduced to little more than spirit, the grey ranks nevertheless summoned up the last reserves of courage. They deployed from column into a thin line of battle, and the maneuver was followed a few moments later by a scattered musket volley and rebel yells.

By 1862 the horrors of the war had convinced Drayton that honor and glory were mere words, cynically employed to impel men to senseless slaughter. Now he surprised himself with the thought: if such things as honor and glory existed, here they were, in the pure distilled spirit of man, something irreducibly transcendent in the human heart, not in the panoply of war, with brass bands and serried ranks. These gaunt scarecrows were ready to keep fighting, although there was no possibility of escape, much less victory. But if it was glory, it still carried the taste of ashes. After a few minutes the desultory firing sputtered to a halt. Duty had been satisfied and there were no more lives left to expend on the day's account books. Drayton knew it was the last Confederate volley he'd ever hear. For the final time he thrilled to the fierce, high rebel yell, rising then fading like the flames of a dying torch as it gutters out. A heavy silence hung over the field. *Actum est ilicet periit,* he said to himself. The deed is done; it is all over. Abject but relieved at the same time, he thought, *who will possibly understand all this a hundred years from now?*

Soon orders came for the remnant to stand down from line of battle. The Bluecoats retired beyond musket-shot, sat down in ranks, and kindled cooking fires, tempting the Southerners with the aroma of brewing coffee. Few Confederates had any illusions about the meaning of the cease-fire; and sure enough, within minutes the word 'surrender' rippled through the lines.

Hours later Drayton spied Lee and his aide Colonel Taylor trotting down the muddy lane from Appomattox Courthouse. In their wake followed the moment of heartbreak of an army that now had to accept defeat after fighting with such valiant self-sacrifice. Grown men lined the road, weeping unashamedly. They pressed in on Lee, reaching out to touch him or Traveller. Some called out they'd give it another go if only he'd say the word. Lee had never encouraged personal veneration, but he understood the need of his soldiers and so had never forbade it either. He was always a man of balance – perfect courtesy, perfect affection, and perfect dignity. Impassive, he doffed his hat to his men and extended his arm, the better for them to reach him. Drayton's heart filled with pride and pity. He felt the urge to go forward and tell him it was all right, that no other man could have waged the fight so well. Strange how Lee evoked that feeling of wanting to be comforted by him and to comfort him at the same time, as if he were their father.

Drayton guided Bel to the edge of the road. He took off his own hat as Lee passed by, holding it aloft. Drayton saw the flicker of recognition in Lee's face as he passed. The General smiled and inclined his head, perhaps remembering the few weeks of beefsteak he owed to his young subordinate with a great grey horse like his own.

To the Commanding General, to the disconsolate Confederates, to himself, Drayton intoned the lines:

Come, Lacedaemonians, let no one see us weeping
Or behaving in any way unworthy of Sparta.
At least this is still in our power.
What lies ahead is in the hands of the gods.

Chapter Thirty Eight

Wearing his best shell jacket, patched breeches, and newly cleaned boots – a matter of pride not to appear before the victors like a street beggar —- Drayton signed the Federal parole and collected rations for himself and a sack of oats from the Yankee commissary. The sympathetic Yankees handed out ample supplies from their stores, including a thick new wool blanket. Drayton said a muted farewell to Major Sorrel and the staff. General Longstreet, his barely-healed arm thrust into his uniform coat, motioned him over with his good arm. Drayton saluted, but Longstreet shook his head and extended his good hand. Imperturbable as ever, the General smiled his mordant smile.

"You might as well strike out for home," the General muttered. "There's no need to witness the final act. The surrender terms are generous; we are allowed to keep our mounts." There was no cavalry left to speak of. The infantry and artillery were ordered to parade in the morning into the village of Appomattox, stack arms, and deposit their colors. Then they could start the long trek to whatever remained in their blasted homeland.

"Yes, sir," said Drayton. "I don't think I could bear to see it, and there's no point in waiting. I never enjoyed... ceremony."

Suddenly there was no more war, and it took some getting used to. He was going home. And barring accident or disabling injury, he could count on Bel to take him all the way, though the way was long. He had a good supply of oats, and the grass was coming in green and lush. With the horse there existed a *relationship*, just as one would spend time cultivating a relationship with a human. Daily for years he'd stroked him and groomed him, talked and sung to him, tended to his needs. Now he was the best friend Drayton could have in the circumstances, not a mere conveyance.

With a last wistful look around the smoky bivouac, Drayton mounted, and trotted west. The skies had been lowering since dawn, and at mid-morning they let go with a heavy, relentless downpour. Progress was slow and miserable, and the horse tired from plodding through muddy tracks. Sick at heart and sweating in his slicker, Drayton followed the Appomattox River, always westerly.

In spite from the rains, the river rushed furiously over shoals, then broadened and turned placid and serene, like Homer's image of the two rivers in Hades, one of creation, the other of destruction, flowing in uneasy balance. Life gave forth gain and loss, but not always in equal measure.

He'd received neither tale nor tidings since early in the year and his thoughts strayed continuously to Celia and Cypress Stand. The surrender at Appomattox had been on April 9. He was near Bedford, Virginia when he recalled today was his wedding anniversary, April 15. Almost four years to the day since the firing on Fort Sumter.

Bedford, Virginia; April 17, 1865.

South of Bedford he pulled off the still-muddy lane to let Bel graze and enjoy a rubdown. He removed his boots to clean them. He spread his wet wool jacket over a rhododendron bush to dry in the sun that had finally shaken itself free of the clouds. As he sat on the bank soaking up the welcome warmth, a young woman in a wagon drew alongside. Whatever she was hauling was covered under canvas in the cargo bed. Attractive though ill-clad in homespun, she kept a double-barrelled shotgun close by her side as she stopped and eyed him curiously.

Drayton stood awkwardly in his stocking feet, holes at his heels, with a muddy boot in one hand and a cleaning twig in another.

"Good day, Ma'am. Thought I'd take this rare moment of sunshine and clean myself up. Hope it's all right to graze my horse here."

"The owner won't mind." She spoke in a cultivated accent, but with a note of sadness.

"You're sure?"

"Oh, yes, I'm sure. He died at Gettysburg. One of Pickett's men."

"I see." It was best to let the matter drop.

Something in his tone made her ask, "Where you there, too?"

"Yes." He gave her the veteran's level stare which said, *No more questions.*

"Were you at Appomattox?" She asked.

"Yes. Somehow I made it through to the end, and now I'm riding home."

"You're only the second one I've seen since the surrender. You've got a fine animal there. I suppose that puts you ahead of the parade."

"I hope to keep him that way. South Carolina is a far piece. I plan to let him graze his fill."

"When's the last time *you* ate?"

"Yesterday. Enjoyed an Easter feast of Yankee hardtack and tinned beef. Poor fare, to be sure. But I'm trying to make it last."

She reached under the wagon seat and extended a paper-wrapped bundle. "Guess I can share some of this. The Yankees passed through Bedford, but they didn't burn all the farms like they did up the Shenandoah." She watched him enjoy the ham sandwich, with thick slabs of buttered bread and succulent slices of meat. "And take this poke along with you. It's got some fresh-baked, buttered cornbread."

"You're very kind, Ma'm. I'm grateful. But I don't want to deprive you."

"I can get more. Assuming the Yankees don't come back."

"Why would they? The War's over. At least here in Virginia."

"They may come back, with blood in their eye. I expect you haven't heard, then."

"Heard?"

"Abraham Lincoln is dead. Shot Friday evening in a theater in Washington City. The assassin was the actor Booth. Was a Confederate spy all along, they say. They also tried to kill Secretary Seward. The Yankees are searching high and low for Booth and the others. They're detaining everyone and none too nice about it. A lone Confederate on a good horse... Well, you're bound to attract attention. That's why I stopped. To warn you."

"A Confederate spy?" He was shaken by incredulity. His spirits had lightened over the few days of travel since Appomattox. The awful news plunged him back into a state of gloom. "It makes no sense," he said. "Lee surrendered on April 9. The War was already lost."

Confusion and dread rose in his breast – and ambivalence. On the one hand, he felt a certain bitterness toward the man he believed mainly responsible for the War. Lincoln had refused to let the South depart in peace; had refused even to discuss peace. Then the wily Lincoln had manipulated the South into firing first so that *he* would have the moral high ground from which to launch a war of aggression. On the other hand, Drayton acknowledged Lincoln would have been kinder to the defeated South. 'Let 'em up easy' was reported to be his post-War policy.

The woman was intelligent and well-informed. "The new President is Andrew Johnson, from Tennessee, a Unionist Democrat," she said. "With Lincoln gone, Johnson will have no power to stop the Radical Republicans. He'll be lucky to hold on to his office. But it's bad luck for the rest of us."

Drayton nodded. Representative Thaddeus Stevens and Senator Charles Sumner, leaders of the Radicals, were known for their implacable hatred of the South. Sumner hated South Carolina in particular for the beating he'd received on the floor of the Senate at the hands of South Carolina Congressman Preston Brooks in 1856. The Radical Republicans would sup full on revenge. And Abraham Lincoln, ward-heeling politician, tool of the railroads and corporations, and yet with qualities of greatness he may have not suspected in himself, killed on Good Friday, would enter history as America's martyred Christ.

As the woman drove away, Drayton pulled on his boots, debating whether to hurry on, or to lie up during the day and travel at night. As he saddled Bel he reflected on the lugubrious side of Lincoln, a man known for his jokes and anecdotes. Yet, in photographs and newspaper accounts, Lincoln's sadness always came through as his defining characteristic. Faced with the necessity of winning the War, he must have suffered regrets at the loss of life. It was clear to any discerning person, North or South, that Lincoln had counted on a show of force, at most a brief punitive expedition, to end the sectional dispute quickly in 1861. Both sides had miscalculated, and a minor constabulary action had turned into a mutual slaughter of unprecedented ferocity. It was almost a mathematical equation: incompatible aims plus intransigence multiplied by miscalculation inevitably equaled war. And once war was unleashed, no one could foresee the outcome or the costs.

***

From Bedford Drayton turned south toward Martinsville, Virginia, relying on his fine compass but less-than-ideal maps, and on guidance from the locals who also shared a scanty meal from time to time. In Martinsville he caught a ride on one of the few trains of the Manchester Line still running. He huddled miserable and hungry with Bel in the jolting boxcar. The horse managed to snuffle a few strands of hay left in the carriage. They passed through Charlotte, North Carolina to Rock Hill just below the South Carolina state line, where they had to de-train. From there southward to Columbia Yankees had ripped up the rails and piled them onto burning ties. When the rails were molten hot, the raiders had twisted them around trees into 'Sherman's hairpins,' making the tracks impossible to repair without new rails.

Sherman's main force had marched on to North Carolina, where General Joe Johnston surrendered the remaining Confederates east of the Mississippi in late April. The second surrender included Wade Hampton, Cal Butler, and their cavalry. In Upstate South Carolina the Yankees had left behind only small units of roving provost marshals seeking Southerners on the 'wanted' lists. Drayton had slipped through Union patrols on myriad other occasions. It would be even easier now that hostilities had ended. The invaders were less vigilant, and lone returning Confederates weren't of particular interest. Yet his horse always excited admiration. Some chance encounter with a Yankee patrol and he might lose Beltane. But by now he was out of food and famished. Though rumors abounded about the fate of Columbia, he had to chance it. If he could reach Louisa McCord's, he could find shelter and sustenance, and recover for the last phase of his odyssey.

In early May he descended the Fairfield plateau, passed Killian's Mill, a charred ruin, and entered Columbia from the north. Though he'd timed his arrival for early evening, the spectacle of destruction was visible enough. The center of the once-lovely city was a desolation.

Columbia, South Carolina; May 1865.

To his inexpressible relief, the McCord home stood undamaged, along with most of the dwellings along Pendleton Street. The street formed part of the perimeter of South Carolina College, which had also been spared. Cadmus, looking more grizzled than ever, answered his knock with a stump of candle in hand. It shed little light, and Drayton had to identify himself.

"Cadmus, it's Drayton FitzHenry, your mistress' friend from Charleston."

Louisa McCord emerged from the shadowed hallway, lowering a fowling piece.

"Drayton FitzHenry. Thanks be to God." Handing the shotgun to the old retainer, now a free man, she embraced Drayton warmly. "Come in the house. I won't ask if you're hungry; you feel like a bag of bones. Cadmus, please take care of Mr. FitzHenry's horse. Then we'll have a late supper in the kitchen. There's some cold chicken in the larder and johnny cakes in the breadbox. And Cadmus, uncork a bottle of the claret."

"That's the last of the claret, Mizz Louisa," Cadmus complained.

"Yes, Cadmus, so it is. So it is."

In the flickering light of an oil lamp Mrs. McCord poured the wine without a sign of regret. Indeed, she seemed pleased to be able to offer such sumptuous hospitality, a meal which in earlier days would have been considered barely fit for the servants.

"We generally eat here in the kitchen now," she said. The dim light accentuated the lines and the pallor in her face, her lifeless gray hair. "We have so little lamp oil and firewood, it saves fuel."

"From what I saw entering Columbia, you're fortunate to have anything at all," Drayton said.

"Yes, thanks to General Oliver Howard, and thanks to the good Jehovah, whose special servant General Howard deems himself to be."

"Tell me about it. If you can bear to," said Drayton.

"Oh, I can bear to well enough," said Mrs. McCord with a deep sip of wine. "I shall tell any and all who will listen of the enormities visited upon poor Columbia."

"As on many other Southern towns."

"Yes, sadly," she nodded. "We were determined that Columbia should not meet the same fate. Like Atlanta. When Sherman's army arrived across the Congaree River in February and began to shell the town, the mayor saw any defense was hopeless, as did General Hampton. Resistance would only bring destruction, without any military gain. Our soldiers departed and the mayor went to Sherman to surrender the city, receiving his pledge it would be spared. The Yankees marched in, and the next evening they began to fire the place."

"Was it by Sherman's order?"

"In all honesty, I cannot say. Many of the incendiaries were drunken, throwing off all discipline. But their officers made no attempt to restrain them. I'm convinced the conflagration was by Sherman's connivance, if not by his direct order. One Yankee major told me that South Carolina, having sewn the wind, must reap the whirlwind. Wade Hampton's men did fire some of the cotton in a canal warehouse as they withdrew. It provided perfect cover for the Yankees to spread the flames. Within an hour private homes, business, and public buildings far from the waterfront were blazing."

"I recall Columbia had a modern fire brigade," Drayton said as he enjoyed his first decent meal in nearly a week. He drained his wineglass, noting how low they had sunk to drink claret with chicken.

Mrs. McCord nodded. "Yes, we did. But despite the brave efforts of our firefighters, the flames grew out of control. Yankees near the scene used their bayonets to poke holes in the fire hoses, laughing at the frustration of the firemen. When the mayor appealed to Sherman, the General was said to have ordered a whole regiment to construct a fire break – but with a wink and a nod. His men removed cotton bales from the warehouses and piled it at strategic points. Then they used kerosene to make sure it took fire, all the while protesting how indebted we should be for their help. It was this mocking cynicism infuriated me more than the crimes themselves. But they couldn't be everywhere. Some individuals were able to save their homes – with the help of loyal Negroes, I must add."

She smiled at Cadmus, who shared the meal with them but refused the invitation to sit, instead standing by the wood stove. "Still, if left to General Sherman and his men, I believe the whole city should have been destroyed. Then Sherman had the effrontery to blame Wade Hampton for the conflagration."

"General Howard intervened on your behalf?"

"Yes. This street would likely have gone up in smoke and flame, too, but for General Howard. He's a devout Christian and displayed a measure of what passes for kindness in the Yankee army. He made my home his headquarters, posted guards, and promised me it would not be harmed."

Drayton gathered his courage to ask what he'd been dreading to ask. "Tell me, is there any news of Father or of Cypress Stand?"

"No, my dear boy. I'm sorry. There has been no reliable word or mail from anywhere since Sherman crossed the Savannah River. But I have heard stories of widespread destruction along the coast."

Drayton remained at Louisa McCord's for three days. He would have left sooner, eager as he was to see Celia, but Mrs. McCord and Cadmus persuaded him that Beltane needed more rest and feed. It would make no sense to forge ahead prematurely, only to have his beloved horse founder before reaching his destination.

Before the War Louisa Cheves McCord had been one of America's foremost female authors, and Drayton found it refreshing to be able to discuss more than the War – history, literature, and horses. And they shared the loss of loved ones. Her husband David McCord had died in 1855 and her only son had been killed early in the War in Virginia. Before long they defaulted to the topic that loomed over the conversations of all Southerners. Why had they lost? What would happen now?

She sounded one optimistic note. "Sherman left the College standing. Most of the buildings were in use as a military hospital. There were too many patients for them to shift so they couldn't fire the place. Even the Yankees wouldn't burn down roofs over the heads of helpless men. I believe the College will resume operations in due time. When it does, you should consider coming back to teach. You could lodge with me. What could be more convenient?"

"Mrs. McCord," he said. "It's a kind offer and I thank you. But I don't think so. Ranse is dead and Cabell Junior has lost a leg. He has always intended to practice law, if any law remains to us in the coming days. And now we'll have to find some other way to farm. Though I'm no planter, it will be left to me and Celia to help Father run Cypress Stand."

Thomas Moore

Chapter Thirty Nine

Colleton District, South Carolina; June 1865.

R iding south from devastated Columbia, Drayton decided to bypass Charleston, now headquarters of the Union Army of Occupation. He had his parole, but hostile encounters still occurred between returning Southerners and Federal troops. This would mean slower progress, and he was churning with impatience to see Celia. He savored the anticipation of arriving home to his wife – home! what a satisfying word – to the point he began to push himself and his horse harder the closer he came.

North of St. George he left the main north-south road, aiming for Walterboro, seat of Colleton District, where could lay up for a day of rest. Sherman's rampaging Yankees had spared Walterboro, and Drayton's hopes soared that they might also have bypassed Cypress Stand. But 14 miles from Walterboro he reached Jacksonborough on the west bank of the Edisto, five miles from home. There he passed a scene of devastation as bad as Columbia though on a much smaller scale. His dread intensified.

He turned off the River Road toward Cypress Stand. There was no victorious homecoming, rather a kind of furtive slinking down the unkept driveway. No one ran up the lane with outstretched arms to fling herself into his embrace. There was only neglect, a weed-grown, broken-down fence – and silence.

At least he reached a slight rise from which he could spy the house, and his heart sank. No gleaming white walls and lofty portico, only blackened chimney tops above the terrain. He'd had no warning except his own imaginings. Yet he felt no great surprise after the ruins of Columbia and other towns, the shells of burnt homes that had marked his way. He wondered where Celia and Father had found refuge.

At the wrought-iron gate a small figure detached itself from the landscape and came forward. It was Maum Biddy. She wore a red kerchief on her head like a turban, and carried a basket on her arm. He hoped it contained something to eat. He pulled up in front of the sooty ruins, a piece of wall here and there, the chimneys, and now roofless columns of the portico scorched at the top.

As Maum Biddy set down the basket and prepared to speak he blurted with foreboding, "Where are they, Maum? Where's Miz Celia? Where's Mistah Cabell?"

Maum Biddy's face twisted into a frown. She clasped her hands together, looked down, and said, "Well, Mistah Drayton, she dead. Mistah Cabell, he dead, too. 'Ain't nobody left on Cypress Stand 'cept me. And now you."

He was stupefied; he couldn't absorb what she was telling him. He heard the words but they carried no sense. Dismounting in a daze, he dropped Bel's reins, forgetting to knot them over his withers. He staggered forward. The horse followed, placing his feet carefully to avoid stepping on the dangling reins.

"I sho is sorry, Mistah Drayton."

"Where are they?"

She gestured with a sweep of her wizened hand. "They buried up in the family plot, under those spreadin' oaks."

With heavy tread he climbed the little knoll. Maum Biddy thoughtfully remained behind. The mounded graves had been there long enough for grass to have covered the spaded earth. Two cypress headboards marked the spot. Carved into the wood was the still raw lettering: *Cabell Heyward FitzHenry , 1801-1865. Cecelia Sullivan FitzHenry, 1841-1865.*

Some tragedies are so cruel that the human spirit can't immediately absorb the impact. The blow carries its own power to numb. But sitting at their graves, the shock began to wear off, bringing inexpressible grief and a leaden sense of loss. How long he sat there bereft, with memories cascading through his mind, he couldn't say. But after a time he felt Maum Biddy touch his shoulder. Her claw-like hand was surprisingly gentle.

"How'd it happen, Maum? I never got word. There was no mail for weeks. I came straight here after the surrender, never knowing. I was so eager to get home."

Why would there be any mail? With the Yankees surging across the South, rail lines, bridges, and towns destroyed; when vital war materiel couldn't get through, why should he have expected mail to get through?

The black woman settled beside him with her basket. "Miz Celia, she took sick helpin' the Confederate soldiers in de hospital up at Jacksonborough. She caught the typhus fever, and your Aunt Meggs take her home to Pon Pon. Aunt Meggs tend her good, but the fever too strong. And Mistah Cabell, he... Well, the Yankees what come an' burn Cypress Stand, they whup him pretty bad. That's when he die, back in January. I think he die of a broken heart. Then Miz Celia, she die in April. Now you drink some a this here potion. You feel better by and by."

"No, Maum, I don't want to feel better. I want to die, too."

"Yassuh, dat's 'zactly what Miz Celia say you goan feel. And she ast me to beg you to keep on goin' fo' her memory sake. She say you gots to keep y'all's love livin' on beyon' the grave."

He stared at her in wild surmise. "You mean, she had time to leave me a message? She knew she was dying?"

"Yes, suh. And she lef' a letter. She make me promise to stay here till you come back and deliver it."

"Give it to me."

"No, suh. Not till you drink a little this potion and settles yo'self."

Like an obedient child he took the flagon from her hands, a fire-hardened gourd. He pulled deep, letting the warming liquor spread its healing presence throughout his body. Strangely, he began to feel better.

"Thanks, Maum. And now please let me have her letter."

"You eat a little this here pone lessen that lettah ruin yo appetite. They ain't no mo,' so you gots to eat it. An' drink a little mo' this potion."

He complied, and saw the wisdom in the old woman's ministrations.

"Now here Miz Celia's lettah. I goan leave you alone."

Celia's letter was wrapped in an oilskin covering sealed with wax. He got up and moved to the low brick wall enclosing the burial ground, resting his back against the bricks to read. Even seated he felt unsteady, vertiginous but for Maum's potion. Breaking the seal, he extracted the sheet of foolscap covered with Celia's elegant hand.

Pon Pon; April 2, 1865

My Beloved,

We are leaves on the wind and go not where we will, but where the wind blows. Yet in those moments when we are airborne, not earthbound, we see things from a great height, clearly and completely.

In 1860 I was blown south by Providence and a year later you were blown north by the winds of war. Too short a time we have had together. I was fearful and angry because I wanted so desperately to keep you here with me after Gettysburg. I would not be consoled at your departure a second time after the risks you had already survived. But now I see, as you once told me, that extraordinary times impose extraordinary demands. You had to go back. You could not be true to me unless you could first be true to yourself. Moreover, had you been here, you would have tried to prevent the Federal raiders at Cypress Stand even though wounded, and you would surely have been killed for your pains. That I could not have endured. I see now, clearly and completely as from a great height, and am grateful you did not succumb to my appeals to stay. All my fear and anger are faded, leaving only the deepest wanting of you.

I lament the passing of your dear father more than words can express. Time is said to be an anodyne for pain, yet the past two months have not begun to assuage my sense of loss. Despite his misgivings about our marriage he was as loving and kind to me as my own natural father.

The news from inland is as dreadful as from the coast, hardly to be credited, yet the evidence of eyewitnesses cannot be gainsaid. General Sherman's army is wreaking destruction across the State even worse than in Georgia, reducing the inhabitants to privations that language fails to convey. Barnwell is but ashes and cinders. Last week Columbia was burned to the ground, although it had surrendered without resistance. Everything edible and valuable is carried away or destroyed. Can it be possible a civilized army would perpetrate such outrages on their fellow Americans merely for seeking a political separation? If before I failed to understand why you took up arms, however reluctantly, I understand it now.

I am in the good care of your Aunt Meggs and Uncle Porcher and am trying so hard to get well, for I know you will come home. As Maum Biddy says, don't ast me how I knows, I just knows. But in the event our good Lord does not grant me recovery, I have extracted a pledge from Maum to wait at Cypress Stand until you return and to make sure you receive this letter. Shadpole is also here with me at Pon Pon, but he grows restless to leave by the day.

Please do not think I am suffering, except for missing you. I am in little pain, but am weak, too weak in fact to write more.

May God keep you safe until He blows you back to me. I enfold you from afar in all my dearest Love.

Celia

Idly, he tried to recall what it was he'd been doing in Virginia on April 2. It seemed important somehow. Where was he while his Beloved was releasing her grip on life? He hoped it was something meaningful and not trivial. Then he recalled. On April 2 had come word of the defeat at Five Forks. Immediately he'd marched with General Longstreet's whittled-down Corps to shore up the crumbling Petersburg defenses, only to have the Yankees break-through in overwhelming numbers at the Boydton Plank Road. General A. P. Hill died the same day trying to stem the flood. And on April 2 the retreat began that ended a week later at Appomattox.

In 1863, after returning wounded from Gettysburg, he and Celia had salvaged a short but radiant ten months together. Before shots were fired in April 1861, he'd feared the War's casualties would extend beyond the dead and wounded to encompass the death of the good things of the South – reason, civility, and grace. He hadn't foreseen that Celia would be his greatest loss. A brief tide of tears welled up in him, providing some relief at last. He gripped the futile earth, knowing the earth would not give up its dead. But the deepest grief recoils upon itself and contains itself. Tears are too cheap for such a grief. Consumed by a piercing emptiness, he stared dry-eyed at the grave with its rough wooden marker. He'd have to place a permanent stone for Celia and Father. Perhaps he could find the same stonecutter who'd chiseled Ranse's cenotaph. He observed dully and without emotion, for he was drained of feeling: the monument had been defaced. Someone – someone? — the Yankee raiders, of course, had used axes to hack wedges off the corners and mar the carved letters.

How long he sat there he couldn't say. He was called back to the moment by the lugubrious oo-oo-oohing of the mourning doves seeking their afternoon roosts. And the wind sighing in the pines. It was his own heart's cry he heard, dropping into sibilant depths and echoing faintly as it died in the blackness. The War had ended as he feared from the first day of Fort Sumter, in total calamity, the enthronement of ruin. And these deaths, an affront to nature. The pages of his heretofore happy history were seared by the loss of all he held dear, eluding his futile attempt to squeeze some sort of meaning out of the tragedy, to discern some abiding principle, impose some kind of order on the randomness of the destruction.

He felt Maum's hand on his shoulder again. "Mistah Drayton, you been sittin' here and grievin' long enough. Time to get on with the bidness of livin.' That what Miz Celia would want. That's what a FitzHenry gentleman does."

Yes, where was the gallant young paladin of Brandy Station, the Cuchulain of the Great Cattle Raid of Petersburg? He was a FitzHenry and as blood-proud as all his kin. It was strange to be rebuked by a slave – well, an ex-slave. But Maum was right. He sipped again from the flask, observing the rips and dirty patches on his uniform, and felt the week's growth of beard and his tangled mass of hair. He looked for Bel and saw that she'd unsaddled him and tethered him to the picket pin, where he grazed contentedly. A wooden bucket of water stood next to Bel's forefoot. Instead of storing up a reservoir of bitterness from a lifetime of slavery, somehow Maum had stored up kindness. Now she showered it on him and his horse which he'd momentarily forgotten in his grief. He wanted to show her kindness, too.

"Maum," Drayton said, "I want you to know Junius is all right. I saw him a few days before the War ended. He was captured, but unhurt. It happened at a place called Sayler's Creek. The whole Army was in retreat and strung out in a long line. The Yankees had far more troops. They caught us crossing this creek and swooped down on the rear guard. Junius was driving a mule team, part of the wagon train with our supplies. He was captured, along with several thousand men. But General Lee surrendered the rest of the Army three days later, so Junius won't have been long in a prison camp. He has survived, I'm sure of it. He may already be released and on his way home."

The old woman nodded but with a frown. "Oh, yes, suh, he survive, all right. That boy got gumption. He goan do all right. But he ain't never comin' back to Cypress Stan.'"

Chapter Forty

The ruins of Cypress Stand on the Edisto, late1865.

Beltane was worn and thin from the long ride home, and he'd outgrown his shoes. Drayton pulled them and trimmed his hooves. He turned him loose in a hastily re-fenced pasture, and made sure the cypress drinking trough was full. Thankfully the invaders had left the well alone; fresh water was plentiful for humans and animals. The grass had come in abundantly, and the horse would have a fine place to recover.

The cypress-ribbed currach had also survived, thoughtfully hidden by one of the slaves in the rice fields. After two days the most urgent chores were done and he'd restored himself with Maum Biddy's cornpone and home brew. Drayton dragged the boat over the paddy dike and down to the river's edge. He planned to row up the Edisto to visit Aunt Meggs, his mother's sister Margaret, and her husband Bayard Porcher. For reasons lost in time, the family called him by the surname Uncle Porcher – Por-CHAY — instead of his given name Bayard. Their farm at Pon Pon lay six miles upstream, near Parker's Ferry. Maum Biddy assured him the Yankees hadn't raided north of Jacksonborough and that Meggs' place had not been harmed.

It was strenuous work pulling the currach against the current, for in his impatience he'd launched before the tide had begun to turn. But the repetitive rowing was soothing in its way, taking his mind off darker matters. In due course he arrived at the dock at Pon Pon. Uncle Porcher met Drayton at the landing and tied off the boat's painter as Drayton stowed the oars. With a long arm draped over his nephew's aching shoulders, he escorted Drayton to the house, a two-story clapboard dwelling with little ornamentation.

Meggs and Porcher had always been devoted. Now, in poverty and despair, they clung to one another closer than ever. Porcher had grown vacant-eyed and reed-thin while Meggs had grown stout, as if she were taking up the space he was vacating. She sat wringing her hands and sighing deeply while her husband filled the gaps in Maum Biddy's account of the predations of the Federals, whom he called Lincolnites.

With command of the sea and secure bases on the coast, the Yankees' forays up South Carolina's Low Country rivers had met with little opposition. Drayton learned they carried lists of 'traitors;' those who'd signed the 1860 Ordinance of Secession or were leaders in the Confederate cause, singling out their property for special savagery.

"Your father died on the first of February," Uncle Porcher said. "We attended his burial and urged Celia to return and live with us here at Pon Pon. She thanked us warmly but refused. Said she had to remain at Cypress Stand and take care of your people who remained, bring what order she could from the disaster. Also, she was closer to Jacksonborough, where an army hospital had been set up at the train depot. She felt obliged to help nurse wounded soldiers."

"Two months later she got sick in Jacksonborough," Meggs added. "The typhus, they said."

"She sent Shadpole with a message to us at Pon Pon," said Uncle Porcher. "I went to fetch her in the buggy, and Shadpole helped me bring her here."

Thank God for extended family, Drayton thought.

"She was clearly sinking, and she wrote you a letter half-sitting up in bed and bade us leave it with Maum Biddy," said Meggs. "She was certain you'd make it back home. Then she asked for a priest. Well, I was beside myself." Meggs twisted her handkerchief into a knot. "That meant she believed she was dying. But I didn't know any priests or where to find one. Then Uncle Porcher thought of riding to Catholic Hill. It's about 30 miles, as you know, so he left at once. I despaired of his returning in time, or with a priest at all. But that evening he arrived with a Father Loomis. He had all his... well, his paraphernalia. And he went into her – she was so weak and barely conscious despite all I could do – and gave her the last rites. He put this cloth around his shoulders and shooed us out for her confession. Then we were allowed back in. He sprinkled water over her, then took oil from a little vial and put it on her forehead and lips and hands. Then he made that cross sign over her they always make."

"Then she died in the consolation of her faith," Drayton said.

"Yes. And I'd been reading the Good Book all the time I was tending her. She seemed greatly at peace after Father Loomis had done. There was a soft smile on her face, and no sign of pain or distress, except that..."

"Except that what?"

"She called out your name twice. And then she ... she passed on, even before the Father had finished putting away his things. Passed so softly that at first we didn't realize she'd gone. I'm so, so sorry, dear nephew. We did all that could be done." Meggs proceeded to collapse in wracking sobs.

Drayton held her in a close embrace. "I know you did, Aunt Meggs. It was especially kind of you to find a priest. I'll always be grateful."

Later, while Meggs prepared a meal, Uncle Porcher pulled Drayton aside privately. They stepped out of the house to catch the afternoon breeze. Porcher smiled awkwardly.

"Drayton, I know Meggs is a flibbertigibbet. But she took wonderful care of Celia; hardly ever left her bedside. It eased her suffering, though nothing could ease the regret of not seeing you again. I sat with her often, too; and she said to me shortly before the end…" He paused, and Drayton had to prod him with a look. Uncle seemed to feel like an intruder upon an intimate scene. "She was worried about her father and hoped you'd contact him. Then she told me the one year with you after Gettysburg was worth a lifetime with any other man. 'If love could hold me, I would stay.' Those were her last words to me before I left to fetch Father Loomis."

Drayton remained silent for a long time, staring at the River, which narrowed here and flowed through higher, forested terrain markedly different from Cypress Stand. Even the smell was different – fresher and cleaner, lacking the pungency of the brackish marshes.

Porcher filled the silence. "I hate to add to the woe of this loss, but there's more I think you need to know."

"About… the raid on the plantation?"

Yes." A note of stark anger replaced the tenderness with which he'd recounted Celia's final hours. "The bastards came upriver. Their target was the rail depot and military supplies at Jacksonborough. Cypress Stand was right on the way, and…"

"And?"

"They had your father's name."

Uncle Porcher was clearly reluctant to continue, but Drayton insisted.

"This is what Celia told me," said Uncle. "They put a noose about Cabell's neck, raised him up as if to hang him while demanding to know where his money was stored. When he refused to talk, they jerked him up, then let him fall before he choked. They repeated this half-hanging over and over. The officers laughed and called it 'enhanced interrogation.' Celia tried to intervene, but they physically restrained her. Finally, half-choked to death, your father appeared to relent; said he'd show them where his money was. They untied him and dragged him into the big house. He staggered into his study and opened a strongbox hidden under the floorboards. With a mocking laugh, he showed them his Confederate bonds. Enraged, they took him out and beat him insensible with a rope's end, saying this was fit punishment for a slave-driver.

"Then they fired the house. Celia told us she tried to save the Reynolds portrait of your mother and ... well, some of the library. She brought out the painting and went back into the burning house for an armful of your books. By the time she emerged the Yankees had shredded your mother's portrait with their bayonets. Your father could barely move after being half-hanged and beaten. But when they destroyed your mother's portrait, he boiled over with indignation. It was as if her living person had been assaulted. He somehow roused himself and attacked the vandals with his bare hands and teeth. They laughed and beat him to the ground with musket butts. This time he didn't get up. He died a few hours later holding Celia's hand. He was a prince, your father. I'm truly sorry."

"Did... did they harm Celia?" He scarcely dared utter the question.

"Not in the way you mean. When she came out of the burning house with the books, they ripped them out of her arms and threw them back in the fire. But she managed to hold on to these two. She told me later they would be the foundation of your livelihood after the War. Very wise, that young lady of yours." Porcher stepped inside and returned with the surviving volumes, Laud's *Lexicon of Classical Greek and English, With Marginal Notes*, and Julius Caesar's *Commentarii de Bello Gallico*.

"If she refused to flee, hide, or shrink from their presence, I must ask you again. Was she abused in any way? I've heard terrible stories of the outrages perpetrated upon women, especially the black women they ostensibly came to save." Porcher shook his head. "She was not abused." Drayton could tell he was speaking the truth. "When the Yankees first landed, your wife informed them she was a citizen of New York. The white officer said, 'All the more shame to you, then.' As the raiders were carrying off the edibles, even from the slave quarters, she rebuked them: 'The Gospel says, *It is not good to take the bread of the children and cast it to the dogs.*' The officer didn't care for that one bit. And when she tried to prevent their mistreatment of your father, they twisted her arms behind her, laughing evilly. She feared the worst. But the white officer and Negro sergeant kept the men in hand when it came to ... to the women. The white woman, at any rate. The black women were raped."

Drayton's grief was replaced by a savage rage. He was glad of the Yankees he'd killed at Brandy Station and the Cattle Raid. Seething with a hatred that came too late, he wished he'd killed more. He remained silent in impotent fury.

Porcher continued. "Thanks be to God the Yankees didn't come this far upriver. At least our home still stands, and we have some livestock left, and the kitchen garden. Come stay with us, Drayton."

"Thanks, Uncle. If I have to, I will. But for now, let me go back to Cypress

Stand and see what can be done with the place."

"Where will you live? You can't sleep in the outdoors, although I suppose that's what you've been doing all during the War."

Drayton laughed dolefully. "Yes, I'm well used to it. But the Yankees left the overseer's house. Maum Biddy and Celia fixed it up a bit for her use after the burning. And Maum is still there, in her old slave cabin."

"Maum Biddy is a wonder. Known all along the River as a root doctor. But what will the rest of them do now?"

"God only knows, Uncle."

They went back into the house to retrieve food parcels Meggs had prepared. Porcher and Meggs followed Drayton down to the dock as he stepped into the currach, with the precious books in a waxed canvas satchel provided by his uncle.

"The freed Negroes are... Well, it was cruel to raise their expectations so," said Porcher. "Hundreds of them, maybe thousands, followed Sherman as his army marched across the lower State from Savannah. The Yankees destroyed all the foodstuffs and livestock, what they didn't carry off. So there was nothing to eat for white or black. Most of the Negroes believed the Yankees had come to liberate 'em and couldn't understand why they were being abandoned to starve. I heard from my cousin Kinloch who lives at Sheldon. The Yankees threw a pontoon bridge across the Salkehatchie. The army went over and hundreds of Negroes tried to follow. Damn if the Yankees didn't break the bridge down with the black people on it. Needed to take along the pontoons, they claimed. The poor folks was on the bridge fell in the river and drownded, and the crowd rushing up from behind pushed those on the bank into the river and *they* drownded. Kinloch said that upwards of three hundred Negroes died. And the Salkehatchie wasn't the only river crossing where that happened."

Drayton paused before setting the oars in their locks. "What about your people?"

Porcher waved his arms. "Most of my sawyers and mill men stayed, 'cause we wasn't burned out, I guess. I've promised 'em wages when we can get back in business. Others have drifted back to the farms and plantations, even the burned out places. What else could they do? Where else could they go? But there's no work, almost no food or shelter. There's scarce even a church to sleep in. The Yankees burned most of them, too. All is destroyed, and the blacks are looking to us for ... for..." His voice rose in anguish. "What do they expect *us* to do for 'em? By God, I never thought I'd see such misery."

Drayton could find no answer. Here was a kinsman, hard-working and shrewd, but used to a comfortable and stable existence. Now it had all been shattered, not just the system of Negro slavery, but the Old Republic itself. With an aging wife and scant resources, how would he adapt to the collapse of his world and all its former certainties? For that matter, how would Drayton?

Drayton pressed Porcher's hands and embraced Meggs. "Don't be too hard on them, Uncle. They have known no other life except bondage. When the moment came to be free, naturally they seized it, as you or I would have done in like circumstances."

He settled himself on the thwart of the boat and took up the oars, realizing that Porcher, a man of limited imagination, couldn't grasp the idea of 'like circumstances.' As he untied the painter and cast off, Aunt Meggs said, "Bond or free, they still have to eat, don't they?"

It was pointless to continue the conversation, but from politeness Drayton answered. "Yes, they have to eat, as do we. Now the fighting's over, I hope the Yankees will provide some kind of relief. We have nothing left and will be lucky to survive ourselves." Drayton set the oars in the locks, musing. Black and white together, once as master and slave, now both as mendicants.

"When our two races became intertwined," he said as began to pull, "tragedy lay ahead for both. Now we have to help each other." *We're going to face worse problems under Yankee despotism*, he thought. He nodded goodbye, let the current carry him away from the dock, and turned the bow downstream.

The effects of the tide diminished this far upstream, and Drayton had an easier ride with the river's flow back to the farm. As always when on the River, his thoughts flowed freely with the current. *We were defeated*, he mused, *and we must accept it. I won't say fair and square exactly, but defeated nevertheless, not victims of some cosmic fate.* How could Southerners explain it? They had to explain it to themselves if no one else, for sake of their self-respect. What a fragile thing is human dignity, yet how we struggle to maintain it, or fight to affirm it. Anything to avoid humiliation. At the very beginning shrewd Lincoln had understood this Southern pride, inflaming it to induce the Confederacy into firing first. Now they'd lost, they'd have to find a way to subsist, even if it meant applying for Federal charity along with their former slaves, and not even at the head of the queue. At least he'd have a place to sleep out of the rain. The Yankee raiding party had burned the big house, the rice mill, barn, and dependencies. But they'd left a dozen slave cabins and the overseer's dwelling, because they'd shifted the sick Negroes there as a temporary hospital when the plantation infirmary caught fire from blowing sparks. And as for something to eat now Maum's cornpone was consumed... Well, maybe he could glean something from the ruins. The kitchen garden had been ravaged but not totally destroyed. Perhaps something more could be harvested.

He drifted into the dock and tied the currach securely. Maum Biddy emerged from the overseer's cottage and to his surprise, gestured with a large serving spoon. "Come on up and get sumpfin to eat," she called.

They sat on the steps of the cabin, watching the setting sun's rays turn the River to gold. "Maum, you're a magician," said Drayton, with a steaming, savory bowl in one hand and his mess kit spoon in the other. "I feared the Yankees had taken all the food."

"Mistah Drayton, they did took 'most everything. But this rice bog we eatin' come from the seed rice. It was in barrels in this here cabin. They didn't touch nuffin in here." Drayton recalled the two hogsheads of seed rice his father had put aside for next season's planting. Reluctant at first to eat it – it was a deeply ingrained family principle never to consume the seed for any reason – Drayton grasped that without Negro labor the days of the Low Country rice culture had, like so much else in their world, come to an abrupt end. Rice planting was a labor-intensive form of agriculture. Never again would the planters command the large crews needed to maintain the dikes and trunk valves, to flood the fields and drain them in season, plant the seedlings and harvest the grain. There would be no teams of bird minders to scare off the vast flocks of bobolinks that swarmed over the stalks at the critical 'milk stage.' And even if an adequate, trained work force could somehow be reconstituted, the rice mill downstream had been burned along with the plantation. A lofty brick chimney thrusting vainly into the sky marked all that was left. Now they were consuming the seed, despite its once venerated status. With a few surviving vegetables from the garden, they had a food source that would last for weeks at least

The rice bog was tasty and filling. "Thank you, Maum," he said. "I don't know what I'd do without you." For dessert he shared the wedge of blueberry pie Aunt Meggs had sent with him.

Maum Biddy took up the empty bowls for washing. "Mistah Drayton," she said. "I ast you doan call me Maum Biddy no more. Dat was my slave name. But I ain't a slave no more. Call me by my Christian name Dinah."

"All right, Dinah. I'll try to remember. But old ways are hard to break."

"Won't be hard fo' me. Now I'se a *free* woman." She went into the cabin and plunged the bowls into a pail of water.

Drayton felt grateful to her, but he wasn't going to pander. "Well, Mau—Dinah," he called after her. "Freedom is not as easy as you think. It carries responsibility."

"Cain't be no worse than bondage," she sniffed, putting the clean bowls in the overhead cupboard.

"Maum, it may come as a surprise to you, but a lot of us white folks hated slavery, too. We just didn't know what to do about it."

She joined him on the stoop with two wooden cups and a gourd of scuppernong wine.

"Is dat true of Mistah Cabell?"

"Father? It wasn't his desire to enslave anybody. When he married Mother he inherited this plantation and a hundred of your people. That's how you came into… into the family, with Mother. He felt a responsibility. Suppose he had just up and freed you and said, 'Go on; clear out. You're on your own.' What would you have done?"

She sat in thought, taking her time to answer. "Most of us would of stayed on and worked for Mistah Cabell for wages," she said. "And we'd of worked better, bein' free. Them who wouldn't work; well, they wouldn't eat, jus' like the Good Book says."

He was tempted to tell her that had been his advice to the family before the War. But to share it now would somehow seem disloyal to his dead Father. Still, he wanted to understand her mindset if he could. "If you hated us so badly," he asked, "why did you and Shadpole and the others remain at the farm after everyone else ran off?"

Her face wrinkled in surprise at the suggestion. "Well, Mistah Drayton, we didn't hate y'all; we just hate our bondage. An' anyway, them Yankee men, they didn't want us."

"Did Junius feel the same way?" Suddenly it was important to know. He sipped the delicious homemade wine.

Maum paused for a moment in thought. "Mistah Cabell was wrong to send him off to the fightin', Mistah Drayton. That was a white man's fight, not the colored's."

"But Dinah, he wanted to go with us."

"Oh, he *say* he want to go, all right. He believe fightin' for the white folks goan get us black folks freed. No one goan keep us slaves once de war was ober. You see, he believe fo' sho' y'all goan win. I 'spose all us black folks believe it. We want y'all to win and we didn' at de same time. Sho was a mixed up feelin'."

And still is, Drayton said silently.

Chapter Forty One

The ruins of Cypress Stand, 1865-1866.

D rayton remained in the overseer's cottage, slightly uphill and apart from the one-room slave cabins that stood in a neat row, their primness and fresh coat of whitewash mocking the blackened ruins up the hill. The cottage was more spacious, but as the weather warmed Drayton found it overrun with fleas and other vermin. The slave cabins were actually cleaner, thanks to ancient folk remedies and herbal repellents. But he would not live in a cabin once inhabited by slaves. He was still the son, grandson, and great-grandson of slave-owners. Maum Biddy graciously scoured his quarters with herbs and vinegar that brought the pests under control. But the episode only accentuated what he'd lost. And there had occurred a subtle but undeniable shift of roles between ex-master and former slave. Though Maum Biddy never said anything to remind him, they could both see that when it came to the practical challenges of survival, she was in charge. Yet she couldn't possibly know how it felt to be greeted every morning by the sight of the home where you were born burnt to the ground, to have to poke through its cinders for anything useful. All your possessions, including the finest classical library outside of Judge Pringle's incinerated; the Reynolds portraits and finest art, the English-made furniture, the Sevres porcelain and china, Nain and Isfahan carpets, all the artifacts of a high civilization — gone. Nothing left except what you carried home with you. Even your family's gravestones battered and broken.

Now he began to experience the dark side of his paradise. Summer heat and humidity came on hard, bringing swarms of insects and the dreaded malaria season. The Negroes were less susceptible to malaria than the whites by nature, but not immune. Maum made a paste from the juice of a wild plant she showed him in the pine forest undergrowth. "This is pennyroyal weed. You crush the leaves and till the juice come out and smear 'it all over yo'sef. That keep the skeeters away."

The juice worked reasonably well, but even with the mosquitoes at bay the plantation was not an idyllic place in summer. How had the blacks been able to stand it? Their intimacy with the natural world was surely a factor. Father had been right: growing up, Drayton had gladly enjoyed the benefits of the slave system without looking deeply beneath the surface.

As Maum trained him to survive off the land, Uncle Porcher lent him an old muzzle-loading fowling gun for which he had to improvise ammunition, using some of his precious remaining black powder. He was a good wingshot and bagged a few summer ducks. Maum helped improve his fishing. Deer were plentiful and he killed two, salting and smoking the extra meat to preserve it. Maum taught him how to forage edible wild plants like cattail roots, dandelion greens, and 'poke salad.' ("But doan never eat the poke berries!") He subsisted on arrowhead roots or 'duck potato,' wild scuppernongs and muscadines, blackberries and raspberries, burdock, yarrow, and amaranth greens, which they called 'pigweed.' Why, the whole outdoors was a fresh market if you knew what to look for.

Shortage of manufactured items was taken for granted: wicks and oil for lamps (go to bed early, rise early); tanned leather to make traces and harness for plowing. There was only one surviving water bucket. No rope, canvas, hand tools, spades, hoes, files or whetstones for tool-sharpening. Nothing except the few items obtained by barter. Still and all, he managed. In fact, he discovered a vast difference between what they had once considered necessities and mere luxuries.

One morning in late September Maum failed to appear. He called and called, using her name Dinah. He poked his head in every one of the empty slave cabins. He mounted Bel and rode to Jacksonborough, where the depot was being re-built to serve the partially repaired railroad. Men and women, black and white, sifted through the ruins, stacking re-usable brick and lumber aside. Everyone, black and white, knew Dinah Tourville, for her home remedies and scuppernong wine had benefitted many of them at one time or another. But no one had seen her. As she'd hinted months earlier, her moment had come and she'd moved on. She was a free woman, after all. What better way to assert her freedom than to simply move on when *she* willed?

Columbia, South Carolina; January 1866.

The Irish-inspired boat turned out to be one of Drayton's most valuable possessions. He daily whispered a prayer of thanks for the unknown slave who'd concealed it in a rice field. The currach gave him mobility on the great highway of the Edisto River and access to the best hunting and fishing in North America, which kept him fed. This January the waterfowl migration had been sparser than usual, but he'd reached some of their favorite habitat before dawn and had bagged a brace of pintails and a black duck. He returned to his cabin and was plucking them clean when Jeremiah Porcher, his uncle's former slave, now a salaried employee, arrived on a lethargic mule. "Mistah Drayton," he said, "this lettah come fo' you while we was at the post office in Jacksonborough. Mistah Bayard he tell me fo' to bring 'em right away."

"Thank you, Jeremiah." He offered the young man a dash of whiskey from a recent trade of a haunch of venison, scanning the letter while Jeremiah sipped and took his ease. The mule wearily cropped the dry winter grass.

At length Drayton said, "Jeremiah, you can head on back. There won't be an answer, at least not now."

Marked urgent, the letter was from Louisa Cheves McCord.

Columbia, South Carolina
December 1st, 1865

Dear Drayton,

You must return at once to Columbia, for the man and the hour are met. South Carolina College will re-open its doors in the New Year— in a much reduced state, to be sure, but nevertheless re-commencing instruction. No longer content to be a College, it now aspires to the august title of University. It presents a rare opportunity, the kind that seldom knocks more than once.

Maximilian LaBorde of Edgefield is Chairman of the Faculty and de facto President. Professor Rivers chairs the school of ancient languages and literature. He takes meals with me almost daily, and laments daily the poor preparedness of his prospective students. He fears being reduced to a mere instructor of the rudiments and wishes for an assistant who can lay the foundations upon which he may erect a towering edifice in keeping with his reputation. Moreover, since most of those now enrolling are former Confederate soldiers, he seeks a veteran who can impart Homer, Xenophon, and Thucydides with the authenticity impossible to a non-veteran. I mentioned you to him. He is aware of your reputation in the Classics and wishes me to write you at once, indicating he will follow with a letter offering an interview. As he is a man of indolent habits, I urge you not to await his invitation, but come straightaway on your own initiative.

You are welcome to board with me at Pendleton Street. Write soon of your willingness, and I will begin preparing your rooms. There is ample stabling for that splendid hunter of yours — if he will condescend to lodge with draft animals. There will be no concealing from him that my nag is not Gentry. My blood horses were stolen when Sherman's Mongol horde swept through burning and plundering. In the circumstances I was fortunate to acquire anything sound enough to draw my carriage.

Need I say how terribly sorry I was to learn of the loss of your dear father and wife, and of the sacking and burning of Cypress Stand? You know of my own

Thomas Moore

loved ones lost in the tragic War, and thus may be assured of the sincerity of my condolences.

Your devoted friend,

Louisa Cheves McCord

Chapter Forty Two

The University of South Carolina, Columbia; early February 1867.

Late one February afternoon Drayton walked across campus to Louisa McCord's, eager for the comforts of his new home. The day's classes had gone reasonably well, and he found he possessed the gift of teaching. Moreover, Mrs. McCord's prediction had proven true: all but one of his students were former Confederate soldiers. They respected him as a combat veteran and appreciated his ability to frame ancient events in terms of the Late Unpleasantness.

He crossed the University's Horseshoe, the central grounds of the college about which were grouped the principal buildings. A sharp wind coiled through the Horseshoe, funneled down its length by the six-foot brick wall enclosing the area. Drayton had thrust his hands deep into the pockets of his shabby Confederate greatcoat, wishing for some gloves and a muffler. With his head withdrawn turtle-like into the folds of the garment, and sunk equally deep in thought, he collided with a passerby. The man was tall and bearded, clad like Drayton in a soiled grey uniform topcoat and slouch hat, and carrying an armful of books.

"I beg your pardon," Drayton stammered. "I was trying to escape this blasted cold and wasn't being attentive."

"No, my fault entirely," said the other. "I was lost in the theorems of Pythagoras – or rather, how to explain them to young men who'd rather swap war stories. Say, I beg *your* pardon. You don't happen to be one of them, do you?"

"One of whom?"

"One of my mathematics students. You're in Confederate gray, like most of my class."

Drayton laughed. "No. Actually, I'm teaching here, too. And I consider myself fortunate to have any kind of overcoat, gray or otherwise. The Yankees got all my kit at Sayler's Creek."

"Sayler's Creek! A sad day, among many sad days. And you were there, too." The man was blessed with a muffler, and when he extended his head in animation, Drayton recognized him at once.

"Why, you're General Alexander. I heard you were teaching here."

"Yes! And you look familiar. But forgive me. I can't connect you with a name."

"I'm Drayton FitzHenry. I was a courier and scout on General Longstreet's staff. I was only a subaltern. You were a lieutenant colonel in command of the First Corps artillery. You would hardly remember me—"

"Oh, but I do, now. I recall we spoke at Gettysburg. On the Third Day. Briefly, though. I was ... ah, occupied." They shook hands warmly.

"Yes, you were," said Drayton. "I'd never seen the like of it, and God willing, never will again."

"No, I imagine not. It's been termed the greatest cannonade in history." Alexander smiled a self-deprecating smile. "At least with respect to the noise, even if it wasn't terribly effective. I recall now. I saw you that very afternoon. You were just riding off to reinforce General Pickett single-handedly. I heard you were killed in the Charge, then only wounded, and then, *mirabile dictu*, a year later you were back with General Longstreet. "

"Yes, I returned to duty in May of '64, shortly before General Longstreet was shot in The Wilderness. By then you'd been promoted to brigadier."

Alexander slapped Drayton's back with sudden recall. "And it was you," he grinned, "that we had to thank for the weeks of fresh beef at Petersburg."

Alexander was a tall robust man, handsome in the bluff manner of the Scots-Irish, with a neatly-trimmed beard. The large cranium bespoke his fabled intelligence. He took Drayton by the elbow as they continued to walk, battling against the biting wind.

"You say you're teaching here?" Alexander asked.

"Yes. The Classics, with Professor Rivers. And you?"

"I *impersonate* a professor of mathematics." Alexander raised his arms skyward, in mock entreaty to Heaven. "That is to say, I do teach and most assiduously. But do they learn? Learning, I fear, is purely notional."

Drayton laughed. "You ought to see them construing their Greek. Where are you residing?"

"At McCutcheon Faculty House. At least until I can bring Bettie and the children over from Augusta. And where are you living?"

"With Mrs. McCord on Pendleton Street."

Alexander smiled. "Not even a musket shot. Come by one evening and we'll pull a cork." He clapped Drayton again on the back. "I have some fine old Kentucky bourbon from a student who I suspect was seeking to compensate for his deficiencies in algebra. We can drink to old comrades. Or to better times ahead. For my part, I prefer the latter."

"Thank you, General—"

"Oh, call me Ned, as y'all did back then. I was only a jumped-up brigadier general, anyway. It's a promotion I never sought."

"I'll come. And I'll ask Mrs. McCord to invite you," Drayton said. "She'll be honored to host such an illustrious guest."

Alexander's laugh was infectious. He gestured at his soiled and patched topcoat, his scuffed boots. "Illustrious? No. Just another penniless Confederate vagabond."

***

In the pre-War days of the state's wealth and ascendancy, South Carolina College had been a highly regarded institution. This could hardly be said of it now; or, to be fair, of any Southern college, all of which had to cope with the Federal invasion, destruction, occupation, and poverty. Porter Alexander was an enormously gifted man who could have found employment anywhere, yet he'd come to Columbia to teach. Graduating near the top of his class at West Point in 1857, he'd been commissioned in the engineer corps. He specialized in battlefield innovation in the pre-War U.S. Army and later in the Confederate Army. He had perfected field signaling with semaphore flags, a key element of the South's first victory at Bull Run. During the Peninsula Campaign he was the first Confederate officer to ascend in an observation balloon. He commanded the artillery that supported Pickett's Charge at Gettysburg, and was one of only three Confederates to rise from the artillery to general officer rank.

It was an unlikely friendship. Drayton was a widower at 25. Ned, 33, was married with a five-year old daughter and toddler twins. Drayton was skeptical of all things military, Alexander a professional soldier – until Appomattox anyway. Drayton's realm was ideas; Ned's was technology. The principal bond between them was fighting for the South from the beginning to the end, and improbably, surviving. And Alexander's sense of fun made him good company, unusual in an engineer and a counter-point to Drayton's melancholy. Then there was his willingness to skewer sacred cows. He happily criticized the decisions of all the combatants, North and South, including himself. Even General Lee.

They met for lunch at the Faculty club, and Louisa McCord entertained him at supper on Pendleton Street. Two weeks into their renewed acquaintance

Drayton visited Alexander in his rooms for a drink and reminiscences. It was a martial environment, and Drayton wondered how Ned's life would change when his family arrived. A shotgun was propped in the corner. A sabre and pistol belt hung from a peg by the fireplace. Several bottles of whiskey decorated a side table, lending a sweet pungency to the air when decanted, in competition with the aroma of pipe tobacco. And on every available surface lay stacks of books and file folders, many bulging with clippings from newspapers and magazines.

"You seem to be going into competition with the College Library," Drayton observed lazily from the comfort of an overstuffed club chair.

"Not by design," smiled Alexander from the depths of a matching chair. "Only compiling the sources I need for my memoirs. The War was the defining event of our lives. Nothing before it, and likely nothing hereafter will hold the same significance. I intend to make a record."

"Good," Drayton nodded. "Perhaps now we'll discover if the pen really is mightier than the sword."

"Everyone says so, but no one acts as if they believe it." Alexander laughed, then turned serious. "Say, you were at Gettysburg. Surely you have some insight into General Longstreet's actions. Are you aware the Virginians are blaming him for the loss at Gettysburg and thus the entire War? Jubal Early opened the hue and cry, but General Lee refuses to join the chorus. Longstreet hasn't helped his own cause by his friendship with General Grant."

"A lot of our people feel kindly toward Grant," said Drayton. "Lee himself. Grant's terms at Appomattox were generous." He took a satisfying sip of bourbon, recalling the surrender and the long ride home afterwards. It was Alexander who'd suggested to Lee that the Confederates scatter into the bush 'like rabbits,' making their way to General Johnston in North Carolina, or wherever Confederates were still in arms. Lee had emphatically rejected his advice.

Drayton stood to replenish his glass, walking to the decanter which stood on a side table laden with files. "The smoke has scarcely settled on the conflict, yet already so much is being published," he said.

"Well, you're a student of history," Alexander replied. "You know that events must be recorded while memories are still fresh. That's why I'd like to hear your thoughts."

The flue in the old building drew poorly, and the smoke from the fire left Drayton's eyes stinging slightly. He was glad of the bourbon. It was like memory, harsh and bracing at the same time. He sipped and walked about the room idly, scanning the books, enjoying the camaraderie with this warm and fascinating man.

Finally Drayton said, "I'm perfectly happy to share my thoughts, for what little they're worth. The problem is my limited perspective. I was only a second lieutenant, after all. But I do recall that General Longstreet didn't want to make the assault on the Third Day. He was torn between his duty to obey Lee's orders and his certainty it would fail, and fail disastrously. He was right. I don't see how Jubal Early or the Virginia cabal can fault him for that."

"Good," said Alexander, grabbing up a notebook and stub of pencil. "This is the kind of personal observation I need."

"I was in the background," Drayton explained, "trying to steady my horse – he never learned to stand artillery well — and waiting for the General's orders. Longstreet sat on a split rail fence during your cannonade and mopped his face from time to time with a red handkerchief. The cannon fire was deafening, of course. One could scarcely think."

Alexander scribbled a few lines. "Yes. And?"

Drayton took a long draught of liquor. As always when recalling that Day, he began to tremble slightly. "Your note arrived. Longstreet read it and his face fell further than before. We gallopers came forward in anticipation of orders; we heard the exchange above the din. The General showed it to Pickett, who grinned and vaulted onto his horse. 'Well then,' Pickett said with his usual exuberance. 'Shall I go forward, General?' Longstreet bowed his head. He seemed in pain almost. Pickett asked again, 'Shall I lead my Division forward?' Longstreet looked up at him with a stricken expression. He couldn't bring himself to speak. He merely nodded. Pickett wheeled and spurred his horse, followed by his staff. You'll recall he was a showy rider. 'Come on then!' he shouted, and galloped to the woods where his Division waited, along with Pettigrew's and Trimble's people. Soon the drums began to beat the long roll. The troops emerged from the trees and fell into ranks, as if on parade. The rest you know."

As Alexander busied himself with note-taking, Drayton stopped at the baroque pedestal table laden with news clippings, magazines, and journals. He had a vague sense his host was asking him a question, but the words faded into the background as his gaze fastened onto a page of newsprint and the photograph of a Union officer. The likeness was eerily familiar. It seized him with a rush of confusion, followed by ... by something he couldn't put a name to. All he knew was that the image hung sharp and indelible in his memory. The profile in the picture was undoubtedly the same man he'd seen on the afternoon of July 2, 1863 on Little Round Top, down to the brimmed hat and walrus mustache, the officer's frock coat, the field glasses and saber. He was confronted again with that fateful moment of decision, re-living it in a flash:

Steady. Settle in behind the rifle. Breath in, out, in again, then hold it. Squeeze the trigger, don't jerk. He aligns himself with the inevitable wobble of the muzzle. The range is short and there's no need for much hold-over to account for the bullet drop. He can visualize the perfect shot, the wide-eyed surprise at the moment of impact, then the eyes growing filmy as the man crumples and life ebbs. Immediately he'll chamber another round and bring down the second man, an aide or courier, before he recovers from his astonishment. His finger tightens. Then... his finger softens, releasing tension on the trigger. Cecilia's face assumes its well-loved shape in his mind. And her words. 'Where Mercy, Love, and Pity dwell / There God is dwelling, too.' He lowers the weapon. The moment passes.

He hadn't given the incident much thought in the chaotic days that followed. The smoke-wreathed, blood-soaked tide of Pickett's Charge, shattered on the slopes of Cemetery Ridge. His wounding at its climax. The ghastly retreat in the ambulance as they creaked along in a driving rain, fearing Meade's pursuit. Later he'd wondered — had the man on Little Round Top survived? And now, here was his photograph. Drayton was about to digest the article when an inner voice warned: *Don't. What does it matter? It was just another random episode, like so many in the confusion of battle. Let sleeping dogs lie.* Good advice. He laid the page with the photo back on its stack.

"I'm sorry," Drayton muttered. "I was distracted. What did you say?"

"I said, you really ought to try your hand at journalism. It's a way to pick up some extra income." Alexander held out his empty glass. Drayton retrieved the decanter, walked toward his friend, and poured a generous measure.

"Is that what you're working on, Ned? I thought you were writing a memoir."

"Yes, but the memoir is a long-term project. In the interim I'm working on an article for the Southern Historical Society in Richmond. They have asked for a series on pivotal moments, when the South might have changed the outcome of the War. For example, Jackson's failure to attack in a timely fashion at White Oak Swamp in the Peninsula Campaign. Lee's plan was brilliant. Why, had Jackson acted promptly, we might have bagged MacLellan and his entire Army. The War might have ended with a Southern victory in June of 1862."

"Even the mighty Jackson failed," noted Drayton. "It softens the criticism of Lee at Gettysburg, does it not? I mean, the horrible waste of Pickett's and Pettigrew's men on the Third Day?"

"It does, perhaps. But Gettysburg was already lost by then." Alexander sat forward, clearly animated by the sudden turn in the conversation. "It was lost on the Second Day, when we failed to take Little Round Top."

Drayton felt his face growing hot, and the sweat prickled under his collar. His words came forth in a croak. "How so?"

Gesturing with his drink, Alexander sat back in his chair with a professorial expression, obviously in his element. "Since Lee was determined to attack Meade in place instead of the wide flanking movement many of us preferred, Little Round Top became vital. Surely you were aware of Longstreet's eagerness to seize the high ground on Meade's left flank – Little Round Top. Had we done so, and with my artillery on the heights, we could have enfiladed the entire Union line. Meade would have been forced to withdraw in disorder. It would have been a critical defeat on Union soil, if not an annihilation. The Lincoln Administration could not have survived the loss. Without a doubt it would have paved the way for a negotiated peace."

Drayton glanced back at the accusing article on the top of its stack. "Could you have trundled your guns up that steep rocky hill?"

"I don't see why not. We did at Harpers Ferry during the Sharpsburg Campaign, and on worse terrain. The Yankees did at Little Round Top. Hazlett's Federal battery got up there in the nick of time and helped drive off Hood's – or Law's —Texians and Alabamians. Here. Read this. Alexander got up from his chair, walked to the table and found the article Drayton hadn't dared to read, thrusting it into his hands. Drayton had no choice but to ignore the warning voice. He felt himself growing hot again, then cold as he read.

A Tribute to Brigadier General G. K. Warren
By William Swinton
Special to The New York Times
July 4, 1865

On this second anniversary of the great Battle of Gettysburg, when so many are enjoying their well-deserved laurels, let me add to the plaudits the Battle's greatest unsung hero.

The Battle was lost to Lee when the sun went down on the bloody field of Gettysburg the evening of the second day, the 2ⁿᵈ of July, 1863. While the issue was still in doubt on July 2nd, General Gouverneur Warren, chief engineer of the Army of the Potomac, had ascended the height now known as Little Roundtop upon a solitary reconnaissance, aware it had been uncovered by our troops when General Sickles moved his III Corps forward of the Army into the Wheatfield and Peach Orchard. His quick military judgment and an engineer's feel for good ground informed him at once the importance of the height. With the hill in our possession, the Army's left and thus our entire line, was safe. In the possession of the enemy our line was not tenable for a moment.

With an eagle's eye, and standing exposed to the enemy fire on the bare, rocky promontory, General Warren spied a body of Southern troops in the valley below. These afterwards proved to be men of Longstreet's Corps, rallying and re-organizing after the bitter struggle at the base of the heights, in the hellish, well-named rock feature called Devil's Den. In a matter of minutes these rebels could begin moving forward to where he stood on Little Roundtop, and into position to capture the unprotected hill.

General Warren was a member of General Meade's staff, and as such, commanded no troops. He had with him only his aide, Lt. Ranald MacKenzie. Nevertheless, he took it upon himself to hasten the nearest Federal units to the summit despite his lack of authority to give any such order. The stalwart men of Hazlett's Battery and the V Corps brigades of Strong Vincent and Steven Weed arrived scant minutes before the Rebels, and valiantly repulsed their many determined assaults.

'Just a staff officer!' has oft been the plaint of the line soldier. 'Those blasted engineers and their pettifogging obsession with detail!' Thank God for it, and for Gouverneur Warren. Only the soldier who grasps the sudden unexpected chance of battle ever wins one. Warren was such a soldier. By his quick forethought, his acuteness of perception, his initiative and boldness in assuming responsibility, General Warren secured the vital point and thwarted the enemy movement barely in time, which if successful would have brought disaster to our arms at Gettysburg. More than any single man besides George Meade himself, Gouverneur Warren saved the Army of the Potomac from defeat at Gettysburg on the afternoon of July 2nd, 1863. In so doing, Warren saved the Union.

Drayton stopped reading and felt his heart seize up with a painful leadenness. An attack of vertigo spun him around as the blood drained away to wherever it goes in times of profound shock. The news clipping fell from his fingers and fluttered to the floor. He sank into the armchair, fearing his damaged heart might fail. *Only the soldier who grasps the sudden unexpected chance of battle ever wins one. Why had I spared him, as if some outside force reached down and stayed my hand?* It was easy to blame an Outside Force. But in that instant he saw the blame rightly lay on him. With shocking clarity he grasped the meaning of the moment on Little Round Top. Think what he might have done, and what a difference it might have made. Might have! What useless, contemptible words. He wanted to rationalize it as an act of humanity to balance the other acts of violence he'd committed. Now he was forced to see it not as an act of decency but an act of betrayal, one that arguably condemned his whole people to defeat and degradation. One that made possible the deaths of his father and his beloved Celia. "We are betrayed by what is false within." *But was I false, or simply true to the wrong thing? Aren't they the same?*

Alexander regarded him with alarm. "Drayton, what's the matter? Are you taken ill?"

Drayton remained immobile in the chair's deep embrace. Taking the decanter from the sideboard, Alexander poured a glass, came forward and handed it to Drayton. "Why, you're white as a ghost. And sweating. What's come over you?"

"Thank you." It was an effort to speak. His breath came in spasmodic gasps, and he thought he might really be having a heart attack. Finally, he got himself under a semblance of control as Alexander peered at him deep in worry.

"I fear it's an old war wound. You may not know I was hit in the chest by a bit of shell or canister at Gettysburg. An object I wore at my breast is all that saved me. A common tale, but true. Sometimes shortness of breath overtakes me." He forced himself to take long, controlled gulps of air, letting it out slowly.

Alexander poured some water from a basin in the corner, wet a towel, and laid it across Drayton's brow as he sat back in the chair. "Why, you're burning up," the General said. "You're sweating like mad." He went to the washstand, splashed water into a glass, and returned. "Drink this. No more bourbon for a while."

"No, I'll be fine." Drayton waved it away. "Whiskey is just what I need at the moment."

He felt ashamed to concoct such a tale for a man he admired. Well, it was partly true. But there was no way he could explain, and certainly not to Porter Alexander, who wrestled with his own responsibility for the failure of his artillery bombardment to clear the way for Pickett's Charge. Drayton saw with awesome stunning clarity that if he'd killed Gouverneur Warren the day before, that fatal Charge need not have happened. Thousands of the South's best men would have been spared. The sudden weight of the realization was more than mind and heart could bear.

Struggling to keep his voice normal, he said, "Surely it is the decisions of the commanders in the aggregate that determine the course of a battle, not the acts of one man." Drayton had been a civilian in arms; Alexander the finest of professional soldiers. He desperately needed some exculpating word from his new friend. But it was not forthcoming.

Alexander said, "So we tend to believe, but it's a fancy. It's not so much the aggregate of command decisions that determines the outcome; it's more a matter of cumulative errors. The commander who makes the fewest mistakes is likely to be victorious."

Drayton persisted. "Nevertheless, it seems improbable that one man could make such a difference, as this article suggests. Battles on this scale are won by men acting *en masse* – brigades, regiments, perhaps even companies, but certainly not the sole individual." He hoped he'd kept the pleading tone out of his voice.

Alexander appeared not to notice his tone. As far as he was concerned, they were simply reminiscing about their combat experience, as hundreds of thousands of veterans did routinely. "In general I would agree," Alexander said. "But battles are as much a thing of chance as of design. In the exigencies of combat sometimes the sole individual, or a very few men, have determined the outcome, when chance sets them down at a decisive place and time."

"For instance?"

'Well, the Battle of Saratoga, for instance, in the Revolution. Timothy Murphy, a crack shot with his Pennsylvania long rifle, climbed a tree and killed British General Fraser at 300 yards at a critical moment, causing the collapse of the British. The American victory at Saratoga was the turning point in the Revolution, for it brought France into the war on our side. Murphy's exploit is called 'the most important rifle shot in history.' Then there's the battle of Waterloo that brought about the final fall of Napoleon. The Duke of Wellington said it was the nearest run thing he'd ever experienced. He also said the victory turned on the closing of the gates at Hougoumont by two men, Sergeant James Graham and Colonel MacDonnell. Two men of the Coldstream Guards changed the course of the greatest battle in the 19th Century – until Gettysburg, that is."

"I had no idea." Drayton continued the struggle to gain control of himself.

"You're an Irishman, I recall," said the General with a wide sweep of his glass.

"My grandfather emigrated from Ireland," Drayton said. "He was a member of the United Irishmen and came to Charleston after the rebellion of 1798."

"Well then, you might be interested to know Murphy and Graham were Irishmen. What do they call that mad island of yours – the Isle of Destiny?"

"Yes, *Inish Fail,* the Isle of Destiny. Do *you* believe in destiny?" Drayton asked, full of hope for an affirmative answer.

Alexander laughed. "Not I. But then, I'm an engineer. I believe in individual responsibility, armed with intelligence. Even then, chance still is trumps." He laughed again.

Was it the cruelty of Chance that placed me there on Little Round Top, or was it Design? Drayton remained silent, brooding but breathing heavily. He could see Alexander was troubled for him, but puzzled equally.

Finally his friend said as if to lay the matter to rest, "These battle exploits do get exaggerated. But the Yankee writers are saying it was Gouverneur Warren who won the battle. I think they have a case. And Colonel Oates of Alabama seems to agree." Alexander stood, rummaged through the same sheaf of papers, and produced another clipping. "Did you know Oates, who commanded the 15th Alabama?"

"Yes," said Drayton in a quavering voice. "I met him that afternoon, before he attacked Little Round Top."

Alexander summarized the article. "Colonel Oates was of the firm opinion that if his regiment had been able to take Little Round Top, we would have won the battle and possibly marched on to take Washington. Based on scouting reports, his Division commander, Brigadier General Law, reported the hill was unoccupied. You'll recall that Evander Law replaced General Hood when Hood was wounded. Thus Oates was surprised when he encountered the Yankees in strength and determined to defend the hill that the scout had reported empty of Yankees. But the Union brigades of Vincent and Weed got there just in time. The Alabamians went up against Colonel Joshua Chamberlain and the 20th Maine, at the extreme left flank of the Union line. Oates writes, and I quote: 'Colonel Chamberlain's skill and persistency and the great bravery of his men saved Little Round Top and the Army of the Potomac from defeat. Had we won Little Round Top, it would have forced Meade's whole left wing to retire.' He concluded, philosophically, that 'great events sometimes turn on comparatively small affairs.' So you see—"

"Then Oates agrees with this Swinton fellow. Thus you could say—"

"That General Warren's quick action won the War? Yes, I suppose you could." The silent accusation echoed and re-echoed in his mind. *Then I am the one who lost it.*

Chapter Forty Three

Drayton had no memory of walking home from McCutcheon House, or how he found himself in his room at Mrs. McCord's. Perhaps Cadmus had put him to bed, thinking he'd come home drunk. In a manner of speaking he had. Sure he'd not been in his right mind. Now he awoke still in his clothes, his greatcoat laid over him. The fire had died to embers, and a chill had settled over the room, clearing his head. He lay there reliving the conversation at Porter Alexander's.

How long had he scouted Little Round Top on July 2nd? A half hour, ample time to see the hill was devoid of enemy troops. He'd wasted no time reporting back, first to Brigadier Law, then to General Longstreet. But there was one huge difference between war and peace – the importance of time. Generally, in our peacetime lives we can afford to be late by a few minutes without penalty. We might miss a train or be docked a few minutes' pay by an employer. But the stakes are minimal. In war, however, a few minutes can spell the difference between victory and defeat. The Second Day was imprinted on his memory, and he went over it step by step, searching urgently for some circumstance which absolved him of responsibility for the choice he'd made. But there was none. Of his own volition he had let a man live, an officer whom Fate had placed – like him —at the most critical place and moment on the battlefield. Perhaps he'd acted from the most laudable of impulses, but he'd spared the man when it lay within his power to silence him. Then that enemy had on *his* own volition rushed troops to the vital hilltop even while Dayton was in the act of reporting back to Longstreet. The Union officer had done his duty, while Drayton had failed in his. The Yankees had won the battle and thus the war. Drayton's side had lost, and he had lost Celia, Father, his home, his country, his future. The motto on the FitzHenry coat of arms mocked him. His people had always taken such pride in it: *spectemur agendo. Let us be judged by our acts.*

At breakfast he toyed with his meal, eating a few bites for the sake of politeness. He somehow got through the school day, and retired early to his room in the evening, evading Louisa McCord's questions, for she had obviously detected his troubled state. He paced back and forth in his room until the lampwick burned down to a glow. Cadmus brought him a hot brick wrapped in flannel to warm the sheets. Tossing some split logs on the fire, he undressed and climbed into bed, drained in body, mind, and spirit. Yet he couldn't sleep. He envisioned the scene on Little Round Top over and over, as if repetition might provide some answer. It didn't. Two paths forked ahead of him, a choice of which to take, what to believe. One path would relieve him of blame for the consequences flowing from his act of mercy. The markers on this path asserted that all was random, echoing the words of Porter Alexander, a professional soldier prepared to leave all to the fortunes of war. In the soldier's world, decisions made in the fog of battle had no moral significance, only tactical impact. But, could he accept the broader implications of that choice? If what we *do* is meaningless, then what we *are* is equally meaningless. Life itself has no significance. Everything in him cried out against such a proposition; not so much in his mind but in the heart, where the deepest reason resides.

***

Three days later he called on Professor Rivers after his last class. The portly Rivers motioned him to a settee under the tall French windows that gave onto the Horseshoe. He offered Drayton a glass of sherry, which he accepted gladly, aware he'd been consuming too much of the harder stuff in the past few days.

"We're quite happy with your performance, Mr. FitzHenry," the Professor volunteered before Drayton could speak. "But I must say – lately you don't seem too happy with us. Is there anything I can do to make your passage here more congenial?"

"I regret very much I must tender my resignation. Most unwillingly, I should add. But I must".

Rivers' eyes widened in alarm. He reached out and gripped Drayton's forearm. "Ah, please don't say such a thing!" Drayton lowered his head, observing the older man's stomach straining against his waistcoat, which was stained with wine. Biscuit crumbs hid in its creases.

"I'm deeply sorry, sir. I never should have applied for the position. You see, I was struck in the breast at Gettysburg. It's a wonder I survived. But my heart was bruised, and I find it's giving me trouble. Physically I'm not up to the task."

The excuse wasn't entirely a lie; still it left him ashamed. But it was a credible excuse, and Rivers appeared to accept it. He wanted to bare his guilt before this slightly shabby but otherwise admirable man. He wanted to say, *How can I stand up in front of these men and pretend I'm fit to be in their company? To look at Davison every day with his stump of an ear and patch over an eye, lost at The Crater? Or Knollys raising his one good arm to ask a question, the other sleeve*

352

made empty by a Minié ball at Spotsylvania? Or continue to stare at the empty seats that might have been filled by those who died along the way, from Gettysburg to Appomattox, knowing I am responsible?

Chapter Forty Four

Cypress Stand; now Colleton County, May 1867.

By May the unusually cold winter and spring had given place to an unusually hot summer. But for Beltane, Drayton lived alone in the overseer's cottage at Cypress Stand, obtaining sustenance from the land as Maum Biddy had taught him. There was some solace in the beauty of the River for his self-condemnation. But he didn't seek solace, only the courage to bear the pain, trying to penetrate to the heart of this curse and discern what it meant. He had little traditional faith, more of a cultural habit. But he clung to the belief, groundless or not, that such torment over an act of mercy that changed the course of the War must mean something. It *must*.

The daily struggle to survive was a welcome diversion. Two years after Appomattox there was still little commerce, scarcely any money, and little to buy if one had it. Confederate paper notes were useful only to light one's cooking fires. U.S. 'greenbacks' circulated widely, but this *fiat* currency was steadily losing its value. The most desired money was coin, specie; the few U.S. $20 gold coins available, British sovereigns, and Mexican 20-pesos. U.S. silver dimes and quarters bought more than their nominal face value.

Barter was the principal means of exchange, and he was able to trade an occasional deer carcass or brace of ducks for the things he couldn't supply from the land. Before the War wealth had been measured in land, and secondarily, in whatever it took to make the land produce. Slaves, in the case of rice and cotton farmers. Livestock in the case of dairymen, and draft animals for tillage farmers. Now he had land, but mostly old rice fields. Still, there was enough tillable acreage to support one man and a horse. He'd bought a spade and hoe before departing Columbia. At least he could maintain the vegetable garden. Grass was plentiful for Beltane, though he'd have to figure out how to store hay for the winter, along with some supplemental grain. He began to dismantle the now useless slave cabins, sorting and stacking the cypress lumber, some for barter and some for later use in a new cottage he had in mind when he could afford it. In the things that mattered most he counted himself a wealthy man.

Plunging from wealth to poverty in a few short years revealed in most

Southerners something that couldn't be measured in money. To the conquerors this elusive something was manifested as a stubborn pride, a refusal to humble themselves in their spirits.

The South had once set a national standard of elegance and cultivation. In defeat a dispossessed gentry paid the continuing price of defeat — to be mocked by the arbiters of culture in the North, the same who had once regarded them from afar with envy. The ruling elites of the North tried to make the Southerner an object of national ridicule, his accent, his religion, his archaic codes, his nostalgia for a lost world. But they never quite succeeded. They never understood 'the unbought grace of life' that infused Southern culture; didn't understand it precisely because it couldn't be bought. And what they couldn't understand they hated. They also failed to reckon with the sense of fair-play among all Americans, North and South, that translated into a natural sympathy for men who'd fought so valiantly against long odds. Robert E. Lee became the most revered man in America, in the North as well as the South. But even the simple Southern farmer and backwoodsman stood forth in a kind of heroic luster. When the *bien-pensants* failed to make them objects of ridicule, it infuriated them all the more.

The looming question now was, could Drayton stay on his land? The Occupation government was seizing the most desirable properties one by one. For the time being, Cypress Stand attracted little attention, perhaps because the big house had been destroyed. Most of it was rice field, now deteriorating and weed-choked without regular maintenance. The farm's tax bill was a relatively modest $400, although it might as well have been $4 million, for all the money Drayton had. Sooner or later some enterprising crony of the corrupt Carpetbaggers or an officer of the Federal occupying forces would pay the tax and snap up the title at a tax auction. He figured he had a year, fifteen months at best, before he might have to quit the place. The idea filled him with despair, but there was nothing he could do about the future except apply himself in the present. Writing a book was the only way he could think of to keep hold of the land. He made great strides on *Man of the Hour*, an account of Rome's great champion of the failing Republic, Marcus Tullius Cicero. He found himself composing an historical narrative with the drama, pace, and emotional impact of a novel. His days were full – hunting or fishing or gardening, grooming and exercising Bel, and tending the family graves. But half the day he gave to writing, swept along by words and ideas flowing from his loss, and dimly aware his abyssal wound conferred on his text a passionate energy.

One Friday morning Drayton trotted Bel to Jacksonborough Station to do a little trading. The Methodist congregation had made an offer for some of his cypress siding to repair their burned church. The local postmaster had made a better offer, but the man was a Federal appointee, and Drayton refused to do business with him or any other Scalawags. He was musing on the un-wisdom of the decision during the leisurely ride home. After all, the man had to make a living the best way he could in straightened circumstances, as they all did. Lost in thought, he and Bel were already through the lofty wrought iron gate, Cypress Stand's one surviving structure, when he saw a horse and buggy tethered at the lawn jockey. He couldn't recognize the rig, and visitors were rare in any case since his self-imposed isolation. Above the brick wall of the burial plot he saw the upper half of a man in silhouette, tall and thin. He rode on to the site and his heart began to pound. It was Finbarr Sullivan, standing at Celia's grave.

In a mixture of trepidation and uncertainty, he dismounted, knotted the reins, and let Bel free-graze. The Doctor met him at the entrance to the enclosure, tall hat in his left hand, his right extended.

Drayton took his hand, hesitantly at first, then pressed it warmly. He was surprised he was able to look him directly in the eye. "Dr. Sullivan, of all the people I never expected to see…"

"Of all the places I never expected to come," said Finbarr, with his glacial Yankee smile.

Wordlessly they turned and paced back to Celia's grave. Drayton hadn't yet been able to replace the cypress headboard — lack of money, stonecutters defunct in the depressed post-war economy. And now here was her father. The lettering was carved skillfully but not deeply and had begun to fade. Looking at the weathered marker, he felt a twinge of shame, knowing the Irish attached great importance to honoring the dead.

"I… I haven't—"

"Drayton, you needn't say a word. I understand what you've been confronted with. You and the entire South. I saw much devastation on my journey here. I trust you'll provide a more permanent monument when you're able."

Finbarr looked sympathetically on the ruins of the big house. The scorched boxwoods and camellias next to the burnt mansion were coming back. The vital life of the place could not be entirely suppressed, although the Yankees had made a prodigious effort.

"Yes, that's my devout wish."

Finbarr nodded, continuing to contemplate his daughter's resting place.

"Cecelia begged me to leave the country in April 1861. Had I been gifted with foresight…" He gestured to the grave.

"This is part of the human plight," said Dr. Sullivan. "Wisdom often comes too late to do us any worldly good."

"I didn't really believe it would happen, until it did, and suddenly I found myself in it," said Drayton. "I was just a transient figure flitting across history, like an embarrassed scene-shifter who's caught onstage when the curtain rises unexpectedly."

That was only partly true. He was still reeling from what he'd learned at Porter Alexander's; that he had unwittingly played perhaps the most pivotal role in the entire war. But he couldn't share that with Finbarr. Not with anyone. Not ever. "I didn't really believe Americans could do such things to one another," he added.

"Then you didn't learn the lessons you studied so hard to master," said Dr. Sullivan. "Any people can commit any outrage against their fellows when money and power are at stake. Just ask the Irish."

"I did. I married one. You should know that as she lay… lay dying, she expressed the wish that I would contact you and let you know what happened. I did write you, but life has been so chaotic, and I wasn't sure of your address, so I couldn't be sure it reached you. May I say, Sir, in humility, how glad I am that you came, as hard as it must be for you."

Finbarr walked to the brick wall and settled his long frame, placing the tall hat carefully beside him. Drayton perched next to him, and they continued to regard Celia's grave. He related the story of Celia's last months as he'd learned it from Meggs and Porcher.

"Your letter pursued me for some months," Finbarr said after a time. "But it did arrive eventually. Naturally I was grief-stricken beyond words. She was my only child, and after her mother, the one I loved most in the world. For much of my life I've taken refuge in my faith. I pray the rosary daily, I go to Mass and confession, I study the catechism and guard against unsound thoughts. When Cecelia's mother died, it helped me through the worst. But then Cecelia married you and remained here, and I sailed away, partly forgiving yet still angry. I couldn't understand her marrying outside the Church. I was bitter toward you, though in truth you had done me no wrong unless it was wrong to love the most lovable creature God ever created. At length I saw that creeds are not enough. To be a Christian is a matter of right conduct as much as of right creed."

Drayton remained silent, feeling part of his burden lift at these encouraging words. "You should know," he said, "that she died in the consolation of her faith, with a priest at her side and all the proper rites of absolution."

Finbarr laid a hand on Drayton's forearm, the closest he'd ever come to an affectionate gesture. "You can't imagine how glad I am to hear that. Thank you. Perhaps you should turn to the true Church and find your own consolation."

"Perhaps. In God's good time. But not until I first understand a few things."

"You have the order of things backwards," said the Doctor. "Trust in God first, *then* comes understanding."

Drayton stood down from the wall with a jerk, pacing and gesticulating. "How can I believe that, when nothing turned out as promised? They said, love God and your neighbor, honor your parents, do good, observe the laws and customs, and all will be well. It was all… all an illusion. My world seemed so solid, so imperishable. Yet now I'm left alone in this scorched rubble, with only her tomb for company. And I won't have it for long. The plantation is on the block for the taxes."

"How much?" Finbarr asked, folding his arms.

"$400. It might as well be four millions."

This time Finbarr gave him a shrewd, sly look. "It could be worse, I must say. It seems your legendary Cypress Stand is low on the list of coveted properties. The Carpetbaggers know the mansion is a cinder, that the rice culture is ended forever, and that you have only a modest amount of land available for tillage."

Drayton was astonished. "How could you possibly know that?"

"I *am* an historical researcher, you know, among other things. I visited the County Tax Assessor. Finbarr reached inside his frock coat and drew out a heavy manila envelope. Drayton opened it with curious, trembling hands.

"Why, it's a deed for the property. In your name, but made over to me!" Drayton fairly shouted with incredulity. "And a receipt for the taxes. Paid for two years."

"Yes, and a few greenbacks left over," said Finbarr. "I'm sorry to have to do it this way. At first I intended only to pay the tax and secure the land from auction. But I realized the officious thieves were determined to seize the property, however impaired, from the heir of a traitor who signed the Ordinance of Secession, from a notorious Confederate cavalier who prolonged the war at Petersburg. Do you know one of those vile creatures had the effrontery to suggest your land would be fit recompense for their cattle you stole on the banks of the James? Oh, yes, I've heard the epic tale. Everyone has. But I played their game. Not for nothing have I studied the wily Greeks. My Northern credentials were impeccable, and I commiserated with them, suggesting what could be more condign punishment than to convey the land to a die-hard Yankee like me." He laughed one of his rare laughs. "Being strangers to the area, they knew nothing of our connection."

"Dr. Sullivan, I'm… I'm speechless. How did you possibly come up with $800?"

"On a poor professor's salary? A valid question. Will I tell you? I did contribute a small share. But most of it comes from your former classmates and professors at Princeton, of which faculty I am now privileged to be numbered. It is offered with the hope you will be able to continue your scholarship and writing and perhaps one day reflect credit upon your alma mater."

Drayton's heart was too full to speak. Finbarr looked on him kindly and took his arm, turning toward the carriage. "Did you think I wouldn't move heaven and earth to protect my daughter's tomb? A new owner from the North would likely have obliterated the graves and used the brick as a foundation for some alien structure. If Cecelia had to be taken from us, this is a meet resting place. She loved you, and she loved her home here by the River. Yes, it was her home. It's beautiful here, like the banks of the Shannon or the Erne. I know her grave will always be well-tended in your care. And with this financial matter settled, you will be able to emplace a proper monument."

Drayton walked with him toward the carriage. Bel looked up from his grass to make sure all was in order, then resumed his grazing. "I'd planned a stone simple and elegant like Celia herself. With your blessing, the epitaph will be, *If love could hold me, I would stay.*"

Finbarr frowned. "No verse of Scripture? No testimony to her faith?"

"Those were her last words," Drayton said.

Finbarr nodded his assent. "She will be well remembered."

"Yes, she will be. Her legacy will live on. In a way you can't imagine," he added involuntarily.

Finbarr searched him with a look, and Drayton could see the question forming on his lips. Then he appeared to think better of it. Finbarr's compassionate look seemed to say, *There is more you haven't told me, but I'll respect your privacy.* He tugged out his pocket watch and said, "I must get back to Jacksonborough or I'll miss my train."

They shook hands briskly. Drayton wanted to embrace him, but there was still too much history and too much sectional reserve in the way. Drayton walked him to the buggy and Finbarr laid a final consoling hand on Drayton's shoulder. "I was once where you are," he said. "I suffered the same doubts. Remember, I lost a beloved wife, too, though Cecelia was a great consolation for her mother's death. Perhaps we only find God in the brokenness that comes from loss and defeat. I will pray that you will. *Beannacht Dé agat.*"

"Sir?"

"May God bless you." He climbed into his hired buggy, and the old horse looked over his shoulder disconsolately. "Come and see me in Princeton," the Doctor called out over his shoulder as he gave the leads a twitch and trotted away.

Chapter Forty Five

Charleston, South Carolina; May 1913.

The Reunion was approaching. Facing it now with equanimity, Drayton began to tackle a list of items to prepare for a long absence — financial and legal arrangements, a power of attorney to Cabell, and a will. He had to give notice at the College. He had to get his son Thomas Preston's' agreement to take Tommy away for a year. He and Tommy needed a travel wardrobe. And there was mental preparation as well, a reckoning with the irrevocable step he was about to take. Southerners often hid unpleasant truths behind the veil of good manners. He could do that no longer. Time to face the truth about Annalee, his Medea. He thought back to July 1876, when, in her mind, she bestowed herself upon him. In fact, they'd had to get married. Well, 'had to' was not entirely true. You always had a choice in such cases, if you could dispense with your sense of honor. Yet that was one reason honor existed, for the difficult cases.

After meeting her at the Hampton gubernatorial rally in Walterboro, he'd begun to pay calls in Charleston, and things had just followed their natural course. No planning or forethought, just a surprising, spontaneous moment. He couldn't quite recall the exact circumstances, in fact; but he supposed they'd employed the normal biological process. At first he warmed to the idea of being married again and having a son. Annalee's strength appealed to him, and he nursed hopes she might come to care for him, too – for himself and not just the old Charleston name and social standing that came with it.

What little affection Annalee showed him changed with the Great Charleston Earthquake of 1886. She had invested heavily in Charleston real estate, including rental tenements for a steady source of income. No one in Charleston foresaw that an earthquake would undermine investments that were otherwise sound and lucrative. Most of her holdings were destroyed; and with so many simultaneous claims, the insurance companies went bust. She collected only a few cents on the dollar. The buildings that survived demanded large sums for repairs, including the Church Street home. It required costly 'earthquake bolts,' long threaded rods passing from one wall to another and tightened down to stabilize the structure.

Though she still owned her home free and clear, now she was forced to depend on Drayton's livelihood from teaching and writing. He was happy to share what he earned.

But she seemed to resent him for his generosity, assuming the role of a wronged and vengeful woman. To be sure, she *had* been wronged — in marriage by Isaac Joyner, by life's throwing Drayton FitzHenry into her path, and in 1886 by a wanton act of nature. Drayton believed everyone was wronged by something. All humans were wounded, blighted, disappointed in one way or another. All were doomed to die and knew it — the worst trick of all. Shouldn't we then live, truly live, while life remained in us? But Annalee refused to embrace life. He'd not done so well at living fully with his own secret burden. But neither had he forced her to bear his burden, while she seemed in some perverse way to blame him for her misfortunes.

Facing the truth meant accepting his own responsibility as well as apportioning hers. He had to acknowledge he hadn't truly loved her; at least nothing compared to his love for Celia. At the beginning there had been friendship and affection, and he'd hoped love might grow from that. Yet instead of growing and deepening, their relationship began to wither from the start. By slow degrees, and masked by convention, religion, and pride, it soured. She became colder and more censorious, an attitude made worse by her failing finances. If the earthquake were not enough, she suffered more loss in the great hurricane of 1893 and the panic and depression that same year. The looming Gettysburg trip was an effect, not a cause, of their discord.

Drayton always took great pleasure in his weekends at Cypress Stand. He'd fixed up the cottage comfortably and urged his wife to join him. But after an initial visit, part of their honeymoon, she consistently refused. He understood why – Celia's presence, though he wasn't about to disturb his first wife's grave just to placate his second. He'd burned Celia's letter, to his eternal shame. That was as far as he'd go. His journeys to the River were less frequent, and that seemed to please her. But there was always a simmering of resentment when he departed – on her part because he was going and on his because she held it against him. And then there was the day she refused, when he really would have been comforted by her presence…

Tusculum Cottage, Colleton County, South Carolina, September 1879.

During the school week, Drayton paid Jeremiah Porcher to tend the horses. Jeremiah was no Junius, but he was responsible and thorough, and he truly cared for the animals. He received a modest wage and the right to exercise them, except that Bel was never to leave the farm. Otherwise, Jeremiah was free to ride Ajax or Lord Fairfax to Jacksonborough and impress the ladies. Drayton even gave him a pair of English riding breeches and boots, which he kept buffed to a blinding gleam and wore more proudly than any of the white 'buckra.' But when home by the River Drayton took over the horse care and stable maintenance. It was no small task – hauling and stacking hay, filling water buckets, mucking stalls, grooming, cleaning tack. But he enjoyed it, and it gave Jeremiah needed time off.

One morning at the end of summer he found Bel lying in his stall, his chest heaving. Immediately Drayton slipped on a halter and lead shank, urging him to get up and moving. Bel strained loyally to rise for a few tries, made it as far as the adjacent paddock, then sank back to earth. His eyes were glassy, his nostrils flaring. Finally Drayton understood. It wasn't colic or a temporary ailment. His friend's great heart had finally given out. Drayton cradled his head in his lap and crooned the old Irish songs that had comforted Bel across the stormy Atlantic in the winter of 1860. Bel whickered and muttered low. With a twist of his head, as if to look up at his companion in arms one last time, he spasmed and fell still and silent.

He had learned much about life from Beltane. Now he was learning further how to deal with unbearable loss. Where does the longing go that can't be requited, yet won't subside? One by one he was being stripped of the things he loved most. First Ranse, then Father and Cecelia. His son Thomas Preston was likely to drink himself into the grave. If that happened, where would his grandson Tommy go? And now he'd lost Beltane. What would be left of him when nothing was left that he loved?

Drayton rode Lord Fairfax to Walterboro to pay a call on the Reverend Proffit, the Episcopalian vicar, a Low Church man. Drayton could never figure out where he stood with his Anglican co-religionists. Some considered themselves reformed Catholics; the High Church fellows, mostly. Other Episcopalians considered themselves Protestants, leaning heavily toward Calvinism and Low Church ecclesiology. Unless one was prepared to make a deep study – and he wasn't – it was too complicated for the layman.

The Reverend Proffit demurred. He squirmed uncomfortably, but was adamant.

"We don't perform …funerals for horses."

The air in his small office was stuffy. He was sweating and fanned himself with a pew-fan.

"Why not?" Drayton said. "At hunt meets Episcopalians bless the hounds, the horses, and the quarry. Why not a funeral?"

"A funeral is for God's creatures that have souls."

Drayton snorted. "From what I've seen of men, I'd say the horse has the nobler soul."

"So you're saying that horses will go to Heaven?" The vicar wore a pained expression.

"Where else would they go?"

"Be facetious if you wish, but I tell you, there will be no horses in Heaven."

"I tell *you*, they will be there before any of us." Drayton practically barked at the man, and was annoyed with himself. It was no way to attain his purpose.

Stiff and offended, the vicar stood and said, "I'm sorry for your loss. But you are being quixotic, and I must stand on the Word of God and the teachings of the church. I'm afraid I can't attend you. It's all I can do to meet the needs of my human parishioners."

The minister extended a moist, insincere hand. Drayton shook it tepidly. He supposed the good reverend was right, at least in a theological sense. Perhaps animals didn't have immortal souls. But perversely, as he rode home from the town, he resolved to go ahead with his plans. However inscrutable, there was a moral order to the Cosmos. And to observe Beltane's passing was to pay tribute to this moral order.

Drayton conducted the funeral, certain that God not only wouldn't mind, but that He'd bless the proceedings. His faith was merely an ember, struggling to stay alight amid his doubts, but this he believed. Annalee had declined to attend, on the same theological grounds taken by Reverend Proffit. But Cabell was there with Tommy. And Prioleau Henderson, who'd returned from an involuntary sojourn in Savannah. In the lawless year of 1868, black Union League Club militia had murdered Pree's father and stolen his prize Arabians. Pree had exacted revenge on one of the killers, then was forced to flee until Wade Hampton was sworn in as Governor. Now Pree lived close by in Walterboro.

Drayton considered it a matter of honor to dig the grave himself, not hire it done. Of course, it took him twice as long as it would have Jeremiah or anyone with a stronger heart and stronger back. He did ask Jeremiah to find help and move the carcass into the grave. Four local black men and Jeremiah prised Beltane gently into the pit and covered him with bricks from the ruins of the old manor house to keep out the carnivorous forest creatures. Bel rested on the slope under the spreading live oaks near the family plot. One tree had been struck down years ago by lightning, but the other two stood sentinel by the graves of his dear ones – Celia, Father and Mother, and Ranse's cenotaph, finally patched. The oaks had grown old and gnarled much like himself, and their limbs had spread outward. Now heavy with years, some of the boughs rested on the ground with their leafy ends turned upward, like the hands of supplicants.

Beltane lay not in the brick enclosure, hallowed ground where only those whom the preacher said had souls could be interred. He lay just east of it, where – perhaps; who could say nay? — he would be the first to rise on Judgment Day, waiting to give Drayton a ride up to Heaven, for by that time Drayton expected to be resting there, too.

Cabell and Prioleau Henderson and the Negro grave-tenders all took off their hats. Drayton took a deep breath. Until the actual moment he hadn't known what he would say. But then the words came readily.

"We have laid to rest one of God's noblest creatures. No living being ever had more courage, more loyalty, more open-hearted generosity. He came from The Curragh near Kildare, where the finest horses in the world are bred. His breeder said he had never seen the like; that he must have descended from the ancient stock of Ireland, from Enbarr of the Flowing Mane. Enbarr was the horse of Manannan mac Lir, god of the sea. He could gallop over land and sea and never be wounded by mortal man.

"He won me the woman I loved in his first and only horse race. He was my boon companion through the dark days of the War, he saved my life on more than one occasion, he brought me home safe, and he was my friend until he died. Horses are not merely transportation, they build character. All I know of courage, fidelity, fortitude, joy, and wonder, I learned from this great horse."

His voice broke slightly as he opened the Bible. Clearing his throat, he read from the Book of Job. *"Hast thou given the horse his strength? Hast thou clothed his neck with thunder? He paweth in the valley and rejoiceth in his strength. He goeth out to meet the armed men. He mocketh at fear and is not affrighted, neither turneth he back from the sword. He saith among the trumpets, Ha, ha! He smelleth the battle afar off, the thunder of the captains, and the shouting."*

He repeated the last lines with sudden surge of feeling, recalling the trumpet calls at Brandy Station, galloping headlong into the fight, his fear and excitement, and Beltane's eagerness. The horse had seemed to know exactly what to do, and Drayton had survived.

"He saith among the trumpets, Ha, ha! He smelleth the battle afar off, the thunder of the captains, and the shouting."

While he felt immense loss, he also felt peace. He was glad he hadn't left Bel's ending to formal religion. His friend had lived a long and useful life. Who could ask more? Neither man nor beast lives forever in this world, and when they reach the end, we must be content.

Cabell and Pree Henderson smiled, and he nodded at each of the old cavalrymen who grasped a handful of the sandy soil and dropped it in the grave. Drayton tossed in a handful, and they retired to the cottage, where he served drinks all around. Jeremiah and the black neighbors, facing more warm work to fill the grave, asked for beer. Drayton had thoughtfully left a dozen bottles cooling in the springhouse.

Chapter Forty Six

Charleston, South Carolina; June 1913.

Annalee was in the kitchen frying pork chops when Drayton sneaked in the back door. Her feet hurt, her back ached, and she had been lamenting they could no longer afford a cook and housekeeper, just when age imposed need of them. Drayton's teaching load had long ago been reduced, and she understood why his College income had diminished. But his income from book royalties was actually increasing. She knew because she'd taken a look at his correspondence one day while he was out – it was certainly her right as his wife to do so – and had found the accounts from his publisher in a folder in his desk. And he'd leased the hunting rights to Cypress Stand for an ample sum. That was as far as he would accede to her demands that he sell the place. Rich Northern industrialists were buying up old rice plantations by the dozen for the waterfowling. He could have made a fortune. Yet he never seemed to have any money. Was he supporting a mistress on the side? Gambling? Unlikely. He prided himself on his Southern honor. She was willing to indulge his little conceits, but it wasn't her fault she was in a querulous mood when he entered, arms full of parcels wrapped in brown paper. Now they were sleeping in separate rooms, he obviously thought he could stash the items without her noticing. She waylaid him at the door.

"I see you've been shopping behind my back," she said. Over the years she'd found it useful to put him on the defensive at the outset.

"Well, you weren't with me, sure, but that doesn't mean it was behind your back."

"Didn't we agree that we'd consult one another before spending money?" She took up her combative stance, legs spread slightly, one hand clasping the spatula to gesture with.

"We agreed to confer on matters related to the house, not personal matters," he said. "Must I obtain your permission every time I purchase a bar of soap?"

"So all those packages are 'personal'?"

"Yes, strictly personal."

"What are they?" she demanded with narrowed eyes. She felt her lips draw into a tight involuntary line. At similar moments in the past Drayton would look away, unable to meet her accusing stare. Now she was disconcerted to find him staring back, without a hint of contrition. She sighed. The days had gone when she could intimidate him with a look.

"These are things for my trip."

"Your trip! You're going to the Reunion after all. You'll use any pretext to avoid your responsibilities; to me, to our home!"

He stiffened under the onslaught. Foolish man. Words were but weapons, meant for attack and defense.

"I believe you're being unreasonable," he said.

"Unreasonable!" she shouted. "You told me earlier you would not go." It was an accusation, not a question. As far as she was concerned, this *was* what he'd told her.

Slowly he answered. "You keep invoking a commitment I never made. At first I was not disposed to go. But the more I thought about it, the more—"

She whirled, showing her back and letting the spatula fall in the sink with a clatter. She jerked the skillet off the range, hoping he got the message — he could prepare his own supper. But he continued on through the kitchen to the hallway, forcing her to turn to him again, "The more you thought about it, the more you decided to disregard my feelings. You keep this from me, then you skulk around like a thief making his escape." He froze, clutching his parcels. He *did* look like a thief; she had him dead to rights.

"I didn't disregard your feelings," he said. "I considered them, along with all—"

"I have been nothing but good to you from the day we met. I've made a good home for you, cooked for you" – gesturing at the stove – "tended you when you were sick, put up with your glooms and moods and nightmares."

"Yes, so you have," he sighed, walking on. She'd meant to add, 'loved you' to her catalogue of virtues, but the words had rushed too quickly ahead of her thoughts.

"Is that why you married me?" She demanded. Her reproach stopped him again in mid-stride. "To have a glorified housekeeper? To enjoy my hospitality while giving nothing in return? And when were you going to tell me of this deception. When the hansom cab arrives to take you to the station?"

There was no possible answer to that; her barb had hit its target. But to her surprise, he laid down his purchases on the hall table, advanced on her a few steps, and said in a quiet voice, "I planned to tell you when it suited. Suited *me*. And this conversation suggests the door of the hansom cab might be the best time." He stared with cold but obvious anger, inviting her to continue. The conversation wasn't following the usual pattern, but no matter, she wasn't done yet. She had to keep him off balance, change tactics.

Adopting a solicitous tone she said, "You think me harsh for seeking to deprive you of this … this ill-considered adventure. But you should be aware that I have only your interests at heart. I know something dreadful happened to you at Gettysburg, something from which you have never recovered. I only sought to spare you pain. I believe going there will increase your nightmares and your brooding."

"Have you considered," he said, "that going to Gettysburg might have the opposite effect? It might relieve me of the troubling memories."

Ha! He'd fallen into the trap, confirming her suspicions.

"Then I was right," she said in triumph. "Something *did* happen there. Perhaps you're not the hero you've made yourself out to be, Wade Hampton's fair-haired boy, the darling of the Confederate cavalry. What did you do at Gettysburg that needs resolving? Run away at the first sound of the guns? I wonder if all the other tales of your so-called heroism are made up."

She thought maybe she'd over-reached. But he only replied in that same low, collected, infuriating tone. What did it take to get him to lash out, lose control?

"I have never made myself out to be anything," he said. "Do you really think gratuitous insults are the way to persuade me? Until now I never thought you a fool. What makes you think you have the right to speak to me in this way?"

Her anger deepened by a sudden consternation at his failure to crumple. "I have *every* right. As your wife. And as the wife of a soldier who gave his life for the Cause. While you're celebrated as a hero, *he* never got anything but an anonymous grave in Tennessee. It seems to me your attitude mocks his sacrifice."

Drayton laughed, and she looked at him in alarm; a tremor of panic seized her. But a laugh could be interpreted in any number of ways, even a bitter, mirthless laugh. Maybe she hadn't lost yet. She busied herself with the chops while thinking desperately for something to add. But he spoke first.

"My dear," he said, with 'dear' uttered like a malediction. "You suggest I've made this decision just to hurt you. I regret any pain it causes, but it really has nothing to do with you." He retrieved his parcels and headed again for the staircase. She followed him, waving an accusing finger.

"That's all you've ever done – whatever suited you, and my wishes be damned!"

He turned and studied her as if seeing her for the first time. She put a hand to her face, knowing she'd grown old in her constant service to this man, enduring his moods, indulging his pining for a dead woman. He stepped toward her, leaning forward like a pugilist. But for the arms full of parcels she feared he might strike her. She wished he would. Then she'd retrieve at least moral victory.

"It's time you understood," he said, his jaw clenching. His stare bored into hers, and involuntarily she lowered her eyes. "We've been down all the possible highways of recrimination, and your invective has long since worn itself out. Resentment is a poison one feeds only to oneself. You have fed on it all your life."

"I have good cause to be resentful," she said through gritted teeth. "Now more than ever, with this foolish, wasteful, extravagant trip. No possible good can come of it. If you defy me in this…"

Well, it was finally out in the open; she'd arrived at the ultimatum, unstated but understood. *Submit to my will or leave my house. Endure scandal. Embarrass your kin. Tarnish the old family name.* She'd employed the same threat before, and he'd always capitulated.

"My dear, I am going to Gettysburg because I must. I must for myself," her husband said without rancor. His quiet tone made the reply all the more powerful. "You can accept it with good grace and wish me Godspeed, or you can engage in your usual unpleasantness. Either way, I am going."

He turned and went up the hallway to his second-floor bedroom. Seething, she watched his indifferent back retreating up the passage. *Please don't go,* she said plaintively, but only to herself.

— END OF PART IV —

PART V
Chapter Forty Seven

Gettysburg 50th Anniversary Reunion Encampment; Monday, June 30, 1913.

Cabell noticed that his brother became more taciturn the closer they drew to Gettysburg. By the time they alighted from the train he had spoken hardly a word in the last hour. Amid a tempest of old veterans laughing and chattering, the two men and the boy caught the tram from town to the encampment. As they descended from the tram, Cabell gasped in surprise at the vast sea of tents, pyramid-shaped and laid out with geometric precision in a grid. Each section of the grid was intersected by streets of packed dirt for access and to demarcate the cantonments of the various states, which were also marked by state flags flying from lofty flagpoles. He was equally surprised to see the Confederate battle flag with its St Andrews cross waving alongside the United States flag. Cabell was proud of the record of his people. The South had fought valiantly, lost without shame, and lived through the aftermath with dignity. Now Southerners were among the most patriotic of Americans. Even so, he hadn't expected to see the Confederate flag in a place of honor.

The detailed planning, expense, and labor involved in creating the encampment were clearly enormous. "I had no idea," Cabell stammered to Drayton as the three men each collected the one valise allowed Reunioneers.

"It's astounding," Drayton agreed. The expanse of bleached canvas, perhaps a mile long, was blinding white in the midday summer sun. At regular intervals stood elongated A-frame tents at the end of each state's section, far larger than the pyramidal squad tents. Queues of veterans were already forming for the midday meal.

"Those must be the mess tents," Cabell said, pointing them out to Tommy, who brightened at the thought.

"And look," said Tommy. "There's the hospital." The boy pointed to an even larger canopy with the traditional red cross on a white square.

They trudged toward the middle of camp along a long, wide macadam road that bisected the compound, appropriately named Long Lane. It passed through the largest state cantonment, Pennsylvania. State flags and the flags of

Pennsylvania regiments sprouted among the tent city on either side.

"What's that really big one?" asked Tommy. At the far end of the encampment a circus big-top poked its mass far above the constellation of smaller tents.

"I expect it's the venue for major events," said Cabell. "Lots of speeches. President Wilson is supposed to address us on the Fourth." He gave a sympathetic laugh when Tommy's face fell. "Don't worry. You won't have to go to any of them if you don't want to."

Red-cross-marked Army ambulances – motor trucks – plied their way along the lane. It was approaching the heat of the day, and Cabell wondered how many customers the Army Hospital and Ambulance troops would have to treat among this group of aged men. In fact, scores of Reunioneers had already clustered around large canvas bags that hung suspended from tall tripods at the head of each state or regimental cantonment. The odd structures held drinking ladles chained to the frame. When the Carolinians stopped to inspect, they learned it was called a 'Lister bag' after its inventor. It kept its drinking water cool even in the summer heat by means of evaporation.

A Boy Scout handed out complimentary copies of the *Gettysburg Ledger's* special Reunion edition. It provided a scheme of the encampment with key sites like the hospital and tram stops, and a schedule of the Reunion's principal events. The front page banner read, '*As America Celebrates Her 137th Birthday, Union and Confederate Veterans Celebrate Peace Between North and South.*' According to the report, 50, 000 were expected, a staggering number, 10,000 more than the original plans anticipated. But the reporter assured his readers the US Army and the state of Pennsylvania could handle the excess, the largest-ever combined reunion of Civil War veterans. The US Army's Chief Surgeon said of the event, 'Never before in the world's history had so great a number of men advanced in years been assembled under field conditions.'

The Army Quartermaster Corps, the Medical Corps, and the 5th Infantry Regiment were assigned by the War department to support the event. Pennsylvania contributed a brigade of its National Guard. The Army had field kitchens and bakeries and a commissary for the sale of common items like soap and stationery, all marked on the map. The newspaper informed veterans that the Army was prepared to serve three quarters of a million meals over the course of the next five days, including fried steak and onions, fried chicken, pot roast, roast pork sandwiches, baked potatoes, ice cream and Georgia watermelon, with the option of fried fish on Friday. High temperatures of 100 degrees were forecast, and veterans who needed treatment should report to the centrally-located 200-bed field hospital built and staffed by the US Army Medical Corps and Red Cross volunteers.

Drayton scratched his chin. "I can't help but wonder why all the trouble and expense. *Cui bono?*"

"The Federal Government needs us," said Cabell. "Needs Southern skill and courage in battle, needs our numbers and resources. Did you know that 'Fighting Joe' Wheeler and Fitz Lee served as major generals in Cuba in the late Spanish War?

"Which army? American or Spanish?"

Cabell explained, laughing, "Wheeler was in his 60's. When our fellows were attacking the Spanish in the Santiago campaign, he got excited and ordered his division to press forward. He shouted, 'We've got those damn Yankees on the run!'"

Hundreds of old men, some in UCV gray and GAR blue and some in civilian suits, sauntered up and down the wide central lane of the camp with the *Ledger* or with maps provided by the state veterans' associations, eagerly looking for their assigned areas. Scores of Army men in khaki rushed to and fro, laying in the final items of equipment, cots, blankets, and wash pails in the squad tents, which could comfortably house eight men. The impression of the entire camp was one of extraordinary energy, barely contained within bounds of meticulous planning and preparation.

The FitzHenrys found the South Carolina encampment next to West Confederate Avenue, a paved road that ran back into Gettysburg and provided access to the National Battlefield Park. The state's cantonment was sandwiched between Louisiana and Tennessee. Of the Southern states Virginia had the largest area, then North Carolina.

At first a certain hesitancy hovered between former enemies. But there was also an equal curiosity about the men they'd fought in the epic moment of their youth. This was an era when few people traveled beyond their home place. Most of them, Cabell wagered, hadn't been outside their respective states since the War. But soon Rebels and Yankees, excited as youngsters at summer camp, scurried laughing and skylarking from one state's area to another shaking hands and trading anecdotes. Cabell glimpsed they weren't content with simply showing good will toward former enemies *en masse*. They sought each other for individual ceremonies of reconciliation.

Cabell laughed to himself – and at himself – at the way Reunioneers were constantly asking, 'How's that again?' or 'What did you say?' It had taken them fifty years and the collective experience of the Reunion to realize they were all half deaf. During the War no one had paid attention to protecting their hearing, and the cumulative effect of gunfire had finally taken its toll.

Drayton began to come out of his isolation, looking excited and buoyant in spite of himself. Cabell believed his melancholy brother was actually having fun. His carefree chuckles at the unfolding spectacle were something Cabell had hungered for in the fraternal relationship. There was a lot of comparing of whiskers, followed by scoffing and beard-pulling to see if they were real. An oldster in UCV uniform pulled his own octogenarian beard and announced, "Back then it was blue and gray. Now it's *all* gray."

A number of uniformed UCV and GAR men had exchanged blue and gray headgear, and a contingent of incongruously clad Southerners was now pretending to show the *faux* Southerners how to march while one Confederate, younger than the rest and perhaps a drummer boy in his day, beat cadence on an upended water pail. Two former enemies, barely ambulatory, engaged in a mock but lively duel – with their walking canes. Cabell grinned at Drayton. There was no humor like the humor of old soldiers, who were grateful to be alive. He was one of them. They waited in a knot of veterans to process in, and Cabell listened intently to their conversation. They all seemed to be experiencing the same thoughts and emotions.

"Never thought I'd come back here."

"Never thought I'd *leave* here. Not in one piece, anyway."

"Well, I didn't. There's a piece a me over yonder, on Culp's Hill."

They exulted in the simple fact of being alive. It was not so much that they'd cheated Death, an expression often heard, but that Death had been so distracted with taking others that they'd been conveniently overlooked and were not about to quarrel with the outcome.

By the end of the day 8900 Southerners had registered, and 40,000 Northerners. The youngest veteran checked in at 61 and the oldest at 112, arriving on two canes strapped to his forearms and proudly refusing help from the Boy Scouts. The soldiers of Blue and Gray, black and white, even a handful of ex-Confederate Cherokee Indians, came with heads held high and full of war stories. The Pennsylvania hosts anticipated the presence of black Union veterans and had planned segregated quarters. But they hadn't counted on black Confederates attending and had no separate place to house them. To the surprise of the management, white Confederates made room for their black Southern brothers in their assigned tents.

***

Within the confines of the encampment Drayton could feel the loom of the old battle sites on the not-too distant horizon. It was like falling through a cleft in time. As his gaze explored the site, his eyes were drawn southeast, where Little Round Top presided over the southern flank of the battlefield. Cemetery Ridge, the objective of Pickett's Charge, limned the southern skyline and boundary of the camp. He felt the old tremors of peak experience, an instant of transcendence, that he'd felt in battle fifty years ago.

The turn of Drayton, Cabell, and Tommy came to sign in at the registration table operated by two Army sergeants in khaki and campaign hats. With some reluctance, the Army NCOs allowed Tommy to bunk with the veterans. Boy Scouts were supposed to stay together at Gettysburg College where they could be properly supervised and more easily dispatched on their duties in the encampment from a central assignment desk. But Cabell rapped on his wooden leg and pleaded the need for special assistance. The chief registration clerk, a staff sergeant, had looked askance at Cabell, then at Drayton's solemn expression, and reluctantly agreed to make Tommy a full-time *aide-de-camp* to his great uncle. Four South Carolinians from the Upstate filled the other four bunks in their squad tent. Each Reunioneer was issued a cot, blanket, pillow, wash basin with pitcher, and tin mess kit.

The long queues at the mess tent never seemed to end. The veterans had to eat in shifts since there were not enough places for all the attendees at one sitting. As they waited with their mess tins in hand, Cabell said, "Tommy, I smell the aroma of fresh beef. It reminds me of when we got some fresh beef at Petersburg and could forego trench rabbits for a time."

Tommy chimed in. "What are trench rabbits, Grand Uncle? Are they like the white ones GramMa Annalee raises?"

"No, not exactly."

"Like wild cottontails?"

The brothers began to laugh, and Tommy's face crumpled. Drayton gathered him in an embrace. "We're not laughing at you, son. We're just remembering. You see, trench rabbits really aren't rabbits at all."

"They're not? Then what are they, GramPa?"

Smiling, Drayton looked at Cabell, who said, "Young man, they were rats."

"Rats!"

"Yes, rats. And let me tell you, we were mighty glad to get 'em. When we could, that is."

"And don't forget the wonderful rock soup," said Drayton.

"Let me guess," said Tommy, his face contorted with suspicion. "First you boil water. Then add rocks."

"Right!"

"Any particular kind of rock?"

"No, any old rocks would do."

Cabell said, "But then, thanks to your GramPa, we got all the steaks we could eat. Steak and roast beef for the whole month of October. It might've lasted longer but we had no way to keep it from spoiling. So we just enjoyed it till it was all gone."

"Do you mean the Great Beefsteak Raid?" Tommy asked.

"That's right. Your GramPa was the brains behind it."

"Then maybe you'll tell me the story, Grand Uncle," Tommy replied with a note of command. "He won't talk about the War."

Chapter Forty Eight

Gettysburg Reunion, Monday afternoon and evening, June 30, 1913.

A bulletin board at the head of the regimental streets provided a schedule of each day's events – the Reunion-sponsored ceremonies and the informal side events. On Monday afternoon the state of Virginia hosted a dedication of the Virginia Monument. The Southern veterans assembled at the foot on Seminary Ridge near Lee's final command post during the Great Charge. Only the twenty-five foot granite pedestal had been emplaced. Artists' renderings were handed around to show what the finished work would look like. When the bronze figures were cast, the monument would include a statue of General Lee at the top, mounted on Traveller and looking east toward the Union lines on Cemetery Ridge. At the base were six infantrymen and a bugler flanking a mounted trooper carrying the Virginia state flag. With muskets at the ready they faced in the direction of Pickett's charge. It was an impressive concept, dignified, yet full of the battle's energy and drama — and pathos, considering that one out of four Virginians engaged in the battle was killed or wounded.

After the Virginia dedication, Cabell stayed to visit with South Carolina members of the UCV. Drayton and Tommy went to the cyclorama by French artist Paul Philippoteaux, a circular painting in which the beholder enjoyed, if that was the word, a 360 degree field-of-view from the center of the immense canvas. More than twenty feet high and nearly three hundred feet in circumference, it was housed in the newly constructed Cyclorama Building on Baltimore Street. The vantage point of the visitor was from the Union lines as Pickett's Charge crashed against the stone wall and Union defenders on Cemetery Ridge. The painting's verisimilitude was enhanced by the three-dimensional effect of life-size plaster figures, brick walls, artillery tubes, and foliage incorporated into the painting itself. It was so realistic that some viewers broke down in sobs. It was decidedly odd to view the Charge from the enemy's perspective, and for a moment Drayton found himself scanning the oncoming Confederates for a glimpse of himself and Beltane, carrying his dispatch to General Kemper.

They returned late in the afternoon for a rest and social time in camp, and were enjoying a slice of cold watermelon when a hubbub of cheers and applause erupted from the Pennsylvania cantonment across the way. Cabell and Drayton and some of their tentmates decided to pop over and see what it was about. Tommy followed. They found that General Dan Sickles had arrived, propelled in a wheelchair, and was holding an impromptu reception. Hundreds of Yankees and even a few dozen Confederates had gathered to greet him.

Drayton had no intention of fawning over Dan Sickles. It was his Corps that had killed Ranse and Kershaw's men in the salient on the Second Day. In fact, Drayton felt little of the conciliatory spirit he was supposed to feel. But he put the best face on the situation when the Pennsylvania Department of the G.A.R. invited him and his compatriots to stay for supper. This was a lavish meal furnished by Gettysburg ladies as a special welcome, and sure to be better than the camp fare, good as it was. Without a word of protest that they were intruding, the Carolinians took a place with alacrity at the long trestle table in the mess tent. Southerners from other states, learning of the special meal, had wangled invitations.

The GAR chaplain mounted the dais at the end of the enclosure to say grace. The unctuous tones of his prayer matched perfectly his black suit, high stiff wing collar, and string tie. Unlike most of his comrades he was clean-shaven and bald as an egret's egg.

"Oh, Lord," he intoned. "We pray you bless this gathering at table on a great battlefield of the war that preserved the Union. Keep us mindful that your hand was at work in every step of that cruel conflict. "

Drayton shot a quizzical look at Cabell, who merely shrugged.

The preacher continued. "How wonderfully do you ride upon the storm and direct it to the grandest ends! When the South fired upon our flag, some in the North foolishly said, 'Let the erring sisters depart in peace.' And when our valiant armies had conquered, including the vast struggle on this very ground, we were nearly shipwrecked by the folly of public men with their talk of peace and amnesty. Nothing enabled us to escape these dangers but your grace, Oh God. We give thanks for your providence that brought this nation through its trials gloriously and triumphantly, in the eyes of all nations!"

Drayton observed an uncomfortable stirring and muttering among the Pennsylvanians. A few glanced at him and their guests from lowered heads. The prayer must have gratified their sense of triumph, but the more sensitive among them realized it was a breach of hospitality. Southerners were present. The purpose of the event was reconciliation, after all. But they remained silent. No one wanted to profane a moment of prayer, however tendentious.

The prayer dragged on. "Here on this field," the preacher chanted, "You gave us the victory, O Lord, that sealed the fate of treason and rebellion. Slavery perished, traitors were cast down and submitted as a conquered people must. The Southern States have returned to the Union with rejoicing, and now America is the envy of the world."

Good manners were important, but silence was complicity. Drayton could stand it no longer. "Horseshit!" he shouted despite himself, and to his own surprise. Cabell looked at him wide-eyed.

"I beg your pardon? What did you say?" said the minister.

"Horseshit." Drayton stood upright in the aisle. "Everything you've said is horseshit. And believe me, I know horses."

After an angry stare of chastisement, the man continued. "Oh, Lord, as there are the disaffected still among us, let the waters of Lethe flow over the memories of the war. Let treason and rebellion be washed away by the returning tide of patriotism and prosperity. Let the siren call of State sovereignty perish, too. Never more any talk of secession and nullification. You have said in your word, 'The nation that will not serve me shall perish.' Our triumph over the rebellious South proves how perfectly your law is fulfilled. But let us not exult —"

"Come down from there, you Pharisee!" Drayton shouted, his truculence out of control. The Pennsylvanians began to mutter menacingly and shoot angry looks at the visiting Southerners.

"What is your name, sir?" demanded the minister.

Drayton cast off Cabell's restraining hand and walked forward a few steps in the aisle. "My name is FitzHenry, late of the 2nd South Carolina Cavalry and the staff of General James Longstreet, than whom no finer men ever drew breath. You insult the living and the dead with this so-called prayer. Say grace for the meal and have done, you hypocrite!"

A white-bearded fellow, short and stocky, and, it soon appeared, missing his right leg like Cabell, stepped out in the aisle inches from Drayton's face. "It's you god-damn South Carolinians who started the war. Sit down and shut up." The old veteran's lip curled in a sneer.

"And who are you?" Cabell demanded, standing with equal belligerence beside his brother.

Replying in the same cocksure tone Drayton had used, the man barked, "Hiram Wolfson, late private, 17th Pennsylvania Infantry. I lost a leg in the Peach Orchard fighting you damn fellers from South Carolina. Like to of died, but for the grace of God!"

Cabell answered quietly, "The Good Book says, 'God giveth grace to the humble. You don't seem very humble to me.'"

"I lost a lot of good friends on this field. I'll show you humble!" Hiram shouted, and lunged at Cabell. Despite his awkward prosthesis, Cabell sidestepped. Wolfson sprawled forward on the dirt floor, tripped up by his own unwieldy wooden leg. Drayton watched aghast, immediately regretting the results of his outburst against the Yankee minister. But, like the ill-considered firing on Fort Sumter, it was too late – battle was joined.

Cabell tapped his prosthetic, producing its peculiar hollow echo, and extended his hand to the fallen Pennsylvanian struggling to get back to his feet. "Let's make this a fair fight," he said, whacking his leg again, then laying aside his cane. He shed his suit coat, passing it to Drayton. The rest of the men inside the mess tent formed a cordon around the combatants, cheering, whistling, and cat-calling. Cabell and Hiram, now on his feet, circled each other, wary but awkward. Then with a roar, the redoubtable Yankee charged, or rather lurched forward, surprising Cabell with a bear-hug. The move overbalanced both men. They fell headlong, toppling the folding chairs, rolling on the dirt floor, yelling insults. Each man tried to get on top and pin his adversary, but neither could gain purchase with his injured limb, and the blows each rained on the other were too feeble to do serious harm. For a moment these two became surrogates for the grievances that still divided the nation. The ex-Confederates added their high shrill rebel yell to the fray as the two men rolled and flailed, knocking over the trestle table and sending the crockery flying. Grandson Tommy grabbed a fallen soup ladle and began to brandish it wildly at any Yankee who made a move to intervene. Instead of breaking up the fight, the old veterans continued to stand about cheering them on. But Drayton observed a younger man, looking vaguely familiar somehow, pushing through the cordon.

The man shouted, "Stop this, you fools! Stop it right now! Haven't we done enough fighting here?"

It was all the two combatants needed. Even they had grasped the comic absurdity of the situation, though each was too proud to be the first to cease and desist. But they couldn't contain their laughter. They roared with mirth, and the rest of the tent roared with them while helping the two ancient gladiators to their feet and brushing off the dust of battle. The laughter subsided into an embarrassed silence for a space until someone guffawed, and the uproarious mirth broke out again in rolling waves. Cabell produced a pocket flask and gave it to Hiram Wolfson. The Yankee passed it to Drayton, who took the first guest-sip, raising the flask in a toast to his now-friendly enemy.

"I should have known better than to come up here again and pick a fight with you fellows on your own soil," said Cabell, grinning.

Wolfson grinned back. "I should of known there was still plenty of fight left in you Southern fellers."

With the release of pent-up suspense and tension, former enemies shook hands. Drayton and his compatriots departed the Pennsylvanians' quarters and were headed back to their own when Drayton heard a voice.

"Say, hold on there, Mr. FitzHenry." He stopped and turned as the speaker added, "Drayton FitzHenry, Lieutenant, CSA."

It was the man who'd stopped the fight. Drayton hadn't given his full name or his rank. How did the stranger know? He was short, with a cherubic face, clean shaven and pink-cheeked, and a bald crown with a fringe of white. Also a strong man evidently. The thick cords of his neck strained against collar and tie. He was barrel-chested under white shirt and civilian vest of light blue serge, with sinewy arms under the rolled sleeves. He's kindly, Drayton thought, but commanding of presence, not a man to be trifled with, as evidenced by the instant compliance of the Pennsylvanians when he stopped the fight.

Drayton smiled. "Blessed are the peacemakers," he said.

The pink fellow smiled in turn. "Isn't that why we're here, to make peace?"

"Yes, so they say. But it was too terrible to forgive and forget easily, even after fifty years." Drayton peered at the man closely. "I know it's not possible, yet it seems we've met before. How did you know my name?" He offered his hand, and the Pennsylvanian took it in a firm grip.

"Walter Amman," the man said. "Late of the 57th Pennsylvania. Supernumerary."

"Supernumerary?"

"Yes, I was a drummer boy and flautist. And a medical orderly when casualties were high. But they wouldn't formally enlist me until the end of 1864."

"I see," said Drayton. "That explains your youth. You can't be much over 60. You were just a boy in 1863."

"Yes. I joined in 1862, after Antietam. I was twelve."

"Amman, Amman." Drayton pulled his chin, thinking hard. "Why, you're—"

"Yes. My father was Rudolf Amman, postmaster in Waynesboro, Pennsylvania. You stopped there to, ah, post a package in late June 1863, on your way to Gettysburg. My father often spoke of you. Papa used to tell me, '*Ich bin ein gute Menschenkenner.* I am a good judge of people. That was one of the finest young men I ever met. What a shame we must fight against them.'"

Drayton studied the man, astonished at this meeting after fifty years. He'd never forgotten the incident, but marveled that the Postmaster hadn't either.

Taking Walter's arm, he proceeded on toward his tent. "There was an older brother in the Pennsylvania artillery. Did he, ah, make it to the end?" Drayton asked.

"Yes, he did. He was wounded slightly in the cannonade the preceded Pickett's Charge, and wounded again at Petersburg. But he lived out his years."

"I'm truly glad of it. Your father said he hoped your brother and I would never meet. Meaning of course that I'd never meet him over the business end of his cannon." *Yet he may have fired the round that wounded me on the Third Day,* thought Drayton.

When they reached the South Carolina cantonment, Walter said, "My father spoke of your visit so often that your name and the details were engraved on my memory. But he heard you were killed at Gettysburg. He often expressed the hope that it was not by the Pennsylvania artillery."

"I remember him well. He was Swiss, and we spoke a bit of German together. I think we felt a kind of bond. He wished me well as I went on my way. You favor him. That's why you looked familiar." Swept up in the instant current of sympathy between them, Drayton said, "Come join us here for dinner tomorrow. Or rather, for lunch. We call the midday meal dinner and the evening meal supper."

"*Gern. Nach Mittag,*" Walter agreed, and they shook hands again, smiling broadly. Walter turned to go, then turned back again. "By the way," he said, as they parted. "It *was* horseshit."

Chapter Forty Nine

Gettysburg Reunion; Tuesday, July 1, 1913; Veterans' Day.

On Tuesday morning Reunioneers clustered around the notice boards for schedules and updates. This morning there were to be welcoming remarks from Alfred Beers, National Commander of the Grand Army of the Republic, and General Bennett Young of Kentucky, Commander of the United Confederate Veterans. A welcome would follow from Governor Tener of Pennsylvania, the Reunion host, and an address by Secretary of War Garrison. In the afternoon, unofficial lectures and group discussions were offered by the various state UCV Divisions: 'The North Carolina Regiments: First to Fight at Big Bethel, Last to Surrender at Appomattox,' and 'Lee to the Rear! The Texas Counter-Attack at The Wilderness that Saved the Army.'

But Drayton had his own program in mind. After breakfast he and Tommy caught the tram running to the lower end of the encampment and walked to the scene of the bitter fighting on the Second Day when Ranse was killed with nearly half of Kershaw's Brigade. Only a symbolic fraction of the peach trees remained. Most had been shattered by gunfire during the battle. The rest had been damaged by souvenir hunters until the creation of the National Battlefield Park extended legal protection to the site.

It was a tranquil spot; too tranquil, in fact. Drayton suddenly realized there were no birds singing, no crickets chirping. It was if the trauma of the battle remained imprinted with unnatural stillness on the landscape. For an instant he was disoriented by the memory of the Second Day, the din of gunfire still lodged in his brain, the screams of rage and pain, the coiling smoke, the carnage.

Tommy broke the stillness. "GramPa. I read about the fighting here in 1863. But it seems so peaceful."

"It does indeed, Tommy. One of our bravest enemies, General Joshua Chamberlain of Maine, wrote that on such battlefields something remains behind. He said that forms change, bodies disappear, but spirits linger to consecrate ground as the vision-place of souls. I like that expression, a vision-place of souls. Perhaps that's what you're feeling."

Tommy nodded with a solemn expression. "Were you here back then, GramPa? Right here, I mean?"

"Yes, I was." Drayton took Tommy's arm and led him to a slight declivity. His shaded his eyes and swept over the ground with his right hand. "It was right about here that I said goodbye to Ranse for the last time. His brigade was waiting to attack the Peach Orchard. I was fortunate to have five minutes with him." He paused, remembering the infectious grin under the incongruous straw hat, the toothbrush thrust in the buttonhole, the boots from the dead Yankee sergeant at Brandy Station. He continued, striving to be matter-of-fact and keep the sadness out of his voice, "We never recovered his body. The Confederate dead were mostly buried where they fell, not like the National Cemetery for the Union dead. Some were removed years later, but many remain. Ranse may be right here where we're walking."

Tommy maintained a respectful silence, and surveyed the field with renewed interest. Drayton had taught him not to walk over someone's grave. He appeared to think he might be treading on the last resting place of hundreds of fellow Southerners, and it evidently unsettled him.

"Uncle Ranse is one reason I kinda wanted to come here," Tommy said after a while.

Drayton nodded, and gripped Tommy's shoulder. In his tradition-bound world, the cycles of conduct had repeated themselves from generation to generation. And that was not altogether bad. Indeed, it had been a source of stability and of much comfort. Tommy needed stability in his life. But Drayton also feared over time it would decline into stagnation, like inland pools never replenished with fresh water and growing foul and fetid. He knew of families where there had been spousal and child abuse, and it was re-cycled down the generations. He knew of slave-owners who were cruel, and their cruelty spread out in ripples, creating more cruel people – sons, or freed slaves made bitter and angry at the entire white world, and then their blighted children passed on the anger down the generations. Many Southerners kept on doing the same old thing because it was the same old thing. It was the way great-grandpa did it, so we must, too. The War interrupted all that. The continuity of custom and tradition was broken because the society in which they flourished was shattered. The War swept away many of the old ways without, of itself, ushering in the new. The latter was up to the survivors.

Drayton said, "Tommy, I know you may not understand, but we're standing not just on a great battlefield, but on the threshold of the transformation of the age. I am of a different age, and my story is nearly over. Your story is beginning where mine ends. But before my sun sets, I can help put you on a path of living your life, living it *fully*. Would you like that?"

"I 'spose so, GramPa."

He studied his grandson carefully as they hiked forward toward the peach trees. "Tommy, what are the two most important things I've said you must do?"

"Be brave and tell the truth."

"Right. And sometimes they go hand in hand, because it takes courage to face the truth. Understand?"

"Yes, sir."

"Telling the truth is hard; it *will* cost you. Do you have an idea what I'm talking about?"

Drayton studied the child, fearing he was not getting through, or that Tommy was merely humoring him. But the boy's face was intent, expressive, without a hint of guile. He drew himself up tall and stared Drayton down. "Well, GramPa. I sorta do."

"All right. Tell me then." They paused to sit on a hummock of grass, dry and crackling in the summer heat.

Tommy paused for a moment and said, "Something happened to you here at Gettysburg. And it has something to do with me, too. The part about me I don't understand. But I guess so many men died here, people you knew back in the War, and Grand-Uncle Ranse; and it reminds you of things that are sad. Sad, but important. You want to teach me what it means before... before..."

"Before I die? Is that what you meant to say?"

"Yes, sir."

Drayton gave the boy's shoulder another affectionate squeeze. Tommy didn't like the gesture, but he endured it patiently. "

"I didn't want to make you uncomfortable," the boy said. He picked up a broken limb and stabbed a tuft of grass absently.

Drayton laughed. "Never fear, son. Anyone who's reached my age knows he has only a little time left to live. All the more reason for me to spend that time helping you understand. Only with knowledge and understanding can you truly live." He reclined, face up to the sun, arms linked behind his neck. Next to him, Tommy assumed the same posture.

"But GramPa," Tommy said. "Don't people have to find out things on their own? That's what Papa always says when I ask him about things. Why he's sick all the time, and what happened to Momma."

"Yes. He's partly right. But your father is impaired. He'd like to help you, but he has his lost his own way and can't help you, much as he might want to.

And young people sometimes need us oldsters to guide you. Do you remember my reading you the story of Theseus and the Minotaur?" Drayton sat upright.

"Yes, sir. It was one of my favorites." Tommy smiled with the recollection, sitting up and hugging his knees.

"You remember how Theseus had to slay the Minotaur to protect his fellow captives from being devoured?"

"Yes. The Minotaur lived in a strange place where nobody could ever find their way out of. I forget what it was called."

"The Labyrinth."

"Right, the Lab...Labyrinth."

"And how did Theseus find his way out after killing the monster?"

"The king's daughter gave him a ball of string. He unrolled it as he went in and then followed the string back the way he came."

"Right."

The boy looked at him questioningly, as if to say, *What's your point?*

Drayton paused, searching for the right tone, not just the right words. A red-shouldered hawk sailed over the landscape. Drayton pointed it out and they followed its course for a moment. Tommy waited patiently and Drayton said, "It's only a story. But stories like this represent real things; they help us understand life and deal with real problems."

"Yes, sir?"

"Well, you see, this story tells us that the hardest journey we can make is into the Labyrinth of ourselves, to slay the monster within. It's the most perilous – and the most necessary, if we are to truly live."

Tommy smiled, and Drayton felt he might have gotten through. "Will you give me a ball of string?" the boy said.

"Well, son, I'm hardly a king's daughter," Drayton laughed. "But yes, I can give you a ball of string. The way forward is also the way back. You can't live fully in the present unless you know where you came from, how you got here. And I can teach you. I can tell you the factual history and the myths and legends and stories. You see, our lives are a story, but the story has to be told and passed on, or those who come after will lose their way. Someday you'll tell my story to your children and grandchildren. And you'll include your own story. All our family's stories, of Great-Uncle Ranse and Great-Uncle Cabell and Celia Sullivan and your great-great-grandfather Thomas who came from Ireland. All of them."

"And GramMa Annalee's, too?"

"Yes, even hers."

"And your story about Gettysburg? And about the War?"

Drayton started to stand, his legs suddenly cramping. Tommy helped him to his feet and they walked on a few yards. "Yes. But the War is only a part of our story, and not the most important part. Love and faith, birth and life, all the deeds of our forefathers; these are the most important parts. And let me be clear. I'm not saying we should live in the past or become prisoners of the past. No, not at all. But you *will* become a prisoner of the past if you're ignorant of it. The man who has no past also has no future. It's what we grown-ups call a paradox."

Tommy nodded, and Drayton thought he might actually have understood. "Is that why you came to Gettysburg?" the boy asked. "GramMa didn't want you to come. And Grand-Uncle Cabell says you didn't want to come. Not at first, anyway."

For a moment he found it hard to unburden himself to a child, the natural impulse of the adult to maintain his superiority. Then he thought, who better than Thomas Preston, Junior? He would be the repository of their history, the guarantor of their truth. How better to confess all than to enter into the heart of this boy? Except ye become as a little child, ye shall not enter into the Kingdom of Heaven. Heaven was not some far place beyond the stars, but a place of peace within himself.

"Yes, it's true. I didn't want to come at first," Drayton said.

"Why not, GramPa? So you wouldn't be sad again? I mean, about Grand-Uncle Ranse and the others; what happened in the past?"

"In part, son, in part. But now it's my turn to tell *you* the truth, although it makes *me* uncomfortable."

The boy waited patiently, poking at an anthill with the toe of his boot.

"The main reason, Tommy, is that I was afraid of making this journey – afraid even though I understood I had to come back in order to go forward. And no one likes to admit being afraid."

A grimace of skepticism flitted across Tommy's face. "I've heard Grand-Uncle Cabell talk about what you did in the War. With General Butler and Wade Hampton and all. I can't believe you were ever afraid, GramPa."

Drayton put his am across the boy's shoulders as they began to walk back to the tram stop. "There are different kinds of fear, Tommy. I was afraid of what I might discover, or more precisely, of what I might *not* discover. And I was afraid of having to leave certain things behind when I went into the Labyrinth and came out again. You see, every person has a Labyrinth inside of us, and it's a very scary thing to penetrate into the heart of it. Even if you can make it out, you never come out the same way you went in. I was afraid, until I realized I also have my own ball of string to guide me."

"What's your ball of string, GramPa?" Tommy looked up at Drayton forthrightly, trustingly.

"Love and memory, Mistah Thomas. Love and memory."

Gettysburg Reunion; Tuesday, July 1, 1913.

Numerous brigade and regimental reunions highlighted the day's program. The Maine Brigades Association were sponsoring an address, 'Joshua Chamberlain, the One Man Above All We Wish Was Here.' The hero of the 20th Maine was a man admired by North and South. He had held the extreme left flank for Meade on Little Round Top against the ferocious assaults of the 15th Alabama. It was Chamberlain, promoted to Brigadier General, whose brigade had lined the road at Appomattox and who ordered his men to salute the passing Confederates on the way to the surrender site. He died just months before the Reunion.

In view of the forecast for early afternoon thunderstorms, the scheduled event at 1300 hours, the 5th U.S. Infantry's demonstration (non-firing) of the Springfield Model 1903 issue rifle vs. the Springfield Model 1861 rifle-musket, would be postponed until tomorrow at 1300. Reunioneers were glad of the rain – it washed the torpor out of the air while they relaxed in their tents, lounging on the Army cots, smoking, writing letters, or simply reminiscing. The rain held off, and thanks to the clouds, the rest of the day was pleasantly cool, without the humidity that might have been expected. Walter Amman turned up for the 1:00 PM serving of dinner. Drayton greeted him warmly outside the mess tent.

"*Guten Tag*," he smiled, then frowned as he noticed Hiram Wolfson bringing up the rear. But Southern hospitality must be upheld. "Hello, Hiram," he said. Some veterans had moved the mess tables outside to take advantage of the light airs. Drayton motioned for his guests to sit, and hung their suit coats on one of the guy ropes. "We've got a special Southern treat," he said, hoping to placate the man and avoid a repeat of last evening's scuffle. "We call it 'bounce.'"

"What's that?" Hiram asked, immediately suspicious. His good will of the previous evening appeared only temporary.

Cabell joined them at the plank table. "Old-fashioned white lightning from the Oconee County mountains," Cabell explained.

Drayton cut in, hoping to defuse any lingering animosity. "We wanted to show you some traditional Southern hospitality after last night. It's pot-still whiskey infused with peaches. And we snagged some ice from the Army field kitchen. We've been cooling it down, in deference to your visit."

Drayton stepped inside the tent and re-emerged bearing one handle of an ice-laden washtub with half a dozen glass jars nested in chunks of rapidly melting ice. Proudly wearing his Boy Scout uniform, Tommy carried the other handle. He and Drayton set the tub down beside the mess table. Tommy went back in the tent, re-emerged with a pitcher and glasses, set them on the table, and filled some with ice and water. Drayton poured the whiskey in the others. The afternoon light caught the peaches in the bottom of the jars and filled them with a soft amber glow. They began to enjoy ham sandwiches and sweet pickles followed by apple pie. Drayton watched as Hiram slowly downed a tumbler of bounce. A sense of foreboding welled up – this was not going to end any better than last night. A few minutes of desultory conversation followed in which all parties gingerly side-stepped any controversy, Hiram lurched unsteadily to his feet, raised his glass toward the American and Pennsylvania flags flying across the lane.

"To the flag," he toasted. "To *our* flag."

The four men and boy stood. At a respectful attention, Drayton and Cabell raised their glasses. Tommy gave a hand salute. Cabell glanced over his shoulder at the flags waving at the entrance to the South Carolina cantonment, the Confederate First National flag, called the 'Stars and Bars,' and the blue palmetto banner. Drayton drew in a breath as Cabell tactfully refrained from offering a reciprocal toast.

But Wolfson had noticed the gesture and the exchange of looks between the brothers. "Now why couldn't you fellers have done that fifty years ago?" His tone was a blend of belligerence fueled by alcohol. "Might've saved us all a lot of trouble."

Cabell reared back on his offended dignity, and Drayton thought it better to respond than allow his brother to join in another fray. But the words came out not at all as he intended. He realized as he spoke that his dignity was offended, too. "Well, Hiram, you Northern folks might have stayed home and saved *us* all a lot of trouble. It was you who invaded us, not us invading you."

"Yes, but you fellers from South Carolina, especially you Charleston hotheads, you're the bastards who started it all when you fired on the flag." He raised his glass again to the Stars and Stripes, then turned a baleful stare on Cabell and Drayton.

Drayton assumed a placatory expression. Good manners meant nothing if not observed in difficult situations like this. After all, this Pennsylvanian was both his host of a sort and his guest.

"I can't deny history," said Drayton. "We did fire first." He remembered all he'd done in 1861 to head off the coming conflict.

Sensing an advantage, Hiram said, "Then you admit you were traitors to fire on the flag and try to destroy the Union."

With a frown at Drayton, Cabell tried to pour oil on the waters. It was clear the Pennsylvanian hadn't vented all his spleen the previous evening. "Well, no, Hiram," said Cabell. "*Not* traitors. It wasn't our flag any longer. We didn't want to destroy the Union. We simply wanted to exercise our Constitutional right to leave, a right that was understood by all the states who joined it – voluntarily — in 1789. You still had your Union, minus the Southern states. But that's all behind us. We Southerners are as loyal now as any Americans, maybe more."

"So *you* say. Why should we trust you?"

Now Cabell's diplomacy gave way to an icy scorn. "You Yankees say you hated our arrogance and our high-and-mighty manner. Then you ought to've been glad to get rid of us. The North was like a man who cheats on his wife, beats her black and blue; but won't give her a divorce because he's upholding the sanctity of marriage. Why'd you want to keep us in the Union if we were so repugnant to you?"

While a red-faced Hiram rummaged in his mind for an answer, Walter Amman jumped in, surprising them all. "I'll tell you why. It was the revenue. It's a matter of record. The South paid most of the tariffs and imposts, but the North got most of the benefits. Remember, Hiram? In 1861 Abe Lincoln complained, 'If the South secedes, where will I get my revenue?'"

Hiram looked at his friend in alarm. "Whose side are you on!"

Walter answered his question with a smile, but a chilly one. "My friend, there are no sides anymore. Isn't that what this Reunion is all about? We're all Americans now."

Drayton had a moment of insight. Hiram had suffered from War, just as he and Cabell had. Simply winning didn't assuage the wounds. Hiram's scowl darkened. He drained his glass, then turned it upside down with a thump as Drayton offered him a refill.

Cabell regained his aplomb. In his best courtroom manner, he spread his hands and said, "Let's not remain enemies. The South just wanted to depart, which we believed was our right. But President Lincoln wouldn't discuss it, so it had to be settled by force of arms. Your side won, and we Southerners accept it. Yet the fact stands – whether it's an abusive marriage or a political compact like the Union, if you're not free to leave, then you're really not free at all."

"Yes, our side won," Hiram growled. "The Union won. Freedom won. I was gonna say I hope you never forget it, but you fellers don't seem to have gotten it in the first place."

Drayton sighed. There was no profit in continuing the conversation – nothing could really get through when embittered old men were set in their thinking.

Hiram pointed a long finger at them. "You Rebels think that anybody who ain't satisfied with how things go in a democracy can just pitch a fit, smash up the crockery, and walk out. You can't do that, whether it's a marriage or a country." His face contorted, he said, "I lost of lot of good friends here, fellers I grew up with." Drayton realized Hiram's grief was as fresh as yesterday. His anger, though genuine, was really a mask for his sense of loss.

Hiram stood again, breathing heavily, eyes blazing. "Walter, we saved the Union from these here traitors who'd have destroyed it. They're here at the Reunion only by our generosity. But if we have to teach 'em the same lesson again, we will. Or our grandchildren will." He cast a thunderous look at Walter Ammann, as if to include him in the lesson to be administered. "And the next time, we won't clasp the traitors to our bosom. Whoever's left after the smoke settles will be hanging from the gallows, not being treated to U.S. Army ham and apple pie!" Grabbing his cane from the table, he stumped off furiously.

The remaining men sat in stunned silence. Tommy's face was white, and he laid a hand on Drayton's forearm seeking reassurance. Walter stood, clearly embarrassed, and said, "I apologize for my friend. It's been fifty years, and we've only been here for a day. There was too much suffering to forget in one day. But I hope by the end of the Reunion our wounds will be healed." He shook hands and prepared to depart. "Thanks for dinner. I'd love to stay for a *digestif...*" – he cast a longing eye on the jar of bounce – "but I'd better go check on Hiram in case he has a seizure." They laughed. "No, seriously. I'm his personal physician, and he suffers from high blood pressure. I ought not to have let him have a drink. But one shouldn't have hurt him, and it was too good to pass up."

Drayton stood and Walter proposed in what seemed off-hand, "Drayton, why don't you walk back with me a ways, if you don't mind."

Drayton fell into step as Walter marched back to the Pennsylvania camp. Out of Cabell's hearing Drayton said, "I knew it was a mistake to come here." He expected Walter to commiserate. Instead his new friend demurred.

"No, on the contrary," said Walter. "You did well to come."

"I don't know what I hoped to accomplish."

"Oh, I think you do." Walter gave him a knowing glance.

"What do you mean?"

"I hope you don't mind, but I've been observing you. I couldn't help it, actually. I'm an M.D. and I notice things. I have to notice in order to heal people. I treat quite a few War veterans who suffer nightmares and depression, anxiety, bouts of irrational anger. Sometimes it's their bodies that need healing; oftentimes it's something else."

"Their minds, you mean."

Walter smiled, almost apologetically. "This isn't a scientific term, but it's *souls* that concern me, not just minds."

"Ah, souls."

"Please forgive me if I'm presuming on a short acquaintance," Walter continued. "But you behave differently from other Southern veterans, including your brother. They're just happy to be alive. They regard the Reunion as a celebration. You seem to regard it as a penance. They appear reconciled to the outcome of the War. You don't. Watching you just now with Hiram, I feared you would burst out of your skin. At first I thought it was simply a normal reaction to Hiram's rudeness."

Drayton stopped in the street and studied his new friend. "Nothing much escapes you, does it?"

Walter smiled and they walked on. "I feel for my father's sake – and frankly, my own – that I owe you my counsel. I suspect coming to Gettysburg has dredged up certain emotions you've repressed over the years. But you're not alone in this, not at all. Perhaps it would help to talk about it."

"Maybe it would," Drayton said. "I'll have to think about it."

"Join me tonight for dinner – supper, that is — with the Pennsylvanians."

"All right," Drayton agreed. "But please, no Hiram Wolfson. Or there'll be another brawl."

***

Drayton arrived and Walter alone, no Hiram Wolfson, directed him to the 21st Pennsylvania's chow line. Laughing and chatting like magpies, hundreds of veterans proceeded down one side of a long trestle table spread with the meal, holding out their mess tins to be filled by Army cooks on the other side of the table. Drayton was suddenly hungry, and his eyes lit up at the heaping portions of roast chicken in gravy with stewed carrots and potatoes, bread, and cherry cobbler, a far cry from meals served here fifty years ago, when he was lucky to dine on hard crackers and fatback. They found a quiet spot away from the crowded mess tables and sat cross-legged on a small rise under a beech tree. A warm feeling surged through Drayton. He was still in a state of perplexed wonder to have met the son of the Pennsylvania postmaster. All the more satisfying to find he was wise and sympathetic, though not intrusive. Walter had made the overture; it was now up to Drayton to respond —- or not.

"You've given me a lot to ponder," Drayton said as they finished the meal. "I'm grateful for your friendship. It's something I never expected, and in this least likely of places. I've thought of your father from time to time over the years. Perhaps he told you – he feared I had come to destroy his Post Office as Federal property. But it was a minor episode amid the cataclysm of the Gettysburg Campaign. Now here you are, and I wonder. Was it all mere chance? Or was there some purpose behind the encounter of fifty years ago?"

Walter set down his empty mess tin, retrieved a meerschaum pipe from his vest pocket, tamped in a bit of tobacco, and lit up. The rum-infused tobacco gave forth a delicious aroma.

"How can we be confident in what we know?" Walter replied. "Or rather, what we *think* we know? Is it the not-knowing that unsettles you? Or maybe you feel what many of us feel, a kind of guilt that we survived. Do you ask yourself why you lived when so many others died? I tend to think it was simple luck. But who am I to gainsay those who believe they were spared by some divine plan?"

Drayton said nothing. Walter's question had hit close to home, but he still wasn't ready to unburden himself fully.

After a long silence Walter tried another tack. "Did Hiram Wolfson make you feel you fought in a bad cause?"

Drayton began hesitantly. But this is what he'd come for, and the reckoning could no longer be put off. "When the War started, I did have doubts about our cause. I supported secession but opposed slavery. I worried not whether secession was right or wrong in the abstract, but whether it was prudent."

"Nothing wrong with that. My church teaches prudence is one of the four cardinal virtues. St. Thomas Aquinas ranks it first among the four."

"Well, perhaps. But in Charleston, South Carolina in the spring of 1861 prudence was not a virtue. I found myself in a terribly awkward situation. I had studied in the North and I knew their numbers and resources compared to the South's. I believed the South had the right to secede. That was implicit – and in some cases explicit – in the states' ratification of the Constitution. But I feared it would ignite a war we couldn't win. And like many Southerners, I retained a certain attachment to the old Union. After all, the Union was a product of the Southern states as much as of the North. Then I fell in love with a Northern woman, the daughter of my Classics professor and a splendid man. Right after Fort Sumter we married, despite the objections of both our fathers. Hers was an Irish Catholic. He hated slavery, which he equated with England's exploitation of Ireland. My father was a Protestant and a slave-owner."

"Your family owned slaves. How did you feel about that?"

"Again, a matter of being torn. I hated the institution; I loved my father. My bride Celia opposed slavery, too, like her father. But she loved me enough to overlook our family's part in the 'peculiar institution.' And she acknowledged that the North was equally guilty of slavery as the South. It was a national, not a regional sin. Yet History or Providence or Fate – take your pick —selected the South to be the atoning sacrifice for the whole nation."

"*Also, mein liebe Freund,*" said Walter. "If it makes you feel any better, I have wondered about *our* cause, or whether any political issue is worth the bloodletting that North and South endured for four years. Yes, we saved the Union, but a union for what? Is the Union an end in itself, or is it a means to an end? The Founders designed it as means – a means to secure the blessings of liberty. That's what the Constitution says, anyway."

Drayton nodded and sat silent again. A Boy Scout came round the mess area with a pitcher of iced lemonade and filled their metal cups. Drayton took a deep sip and said, "In the end, I went to war with my two brothers, despite my doubts. It was simple really, a matter of honor. Yet I was never free of the insurmountable paradox. We Southerners fought for our liberty, yet our liberty meant slavery for blacks. It placed us on the wrong side of history, and for this we must remain on everlasting stools of repentance as an exemplar of the North's moral superiority."

Walter laughed sourly, then turned solemn. "Yes, you fought for Southern independence but wanted to keep your Negroes in servitude. *We* fought to maintain the Union, but our revolutionary new union extended a form of servitude over all Americans. *There's* your paradox. I see it clearly now only after fifty years: our cause dictated that one group of men can compel others to submit to a government they don't want, and that refusal on their part makes them criminals and traitors. I can think of no other principle more fatal to liberty. Yet it triumphed in the field and is now assumed to be established. Slavery, instead of being ended by the War, has actually been expanded; for a man subjected by force to a government he does not want is a slave. There is no difference in principle, only in degree, between chattel slavery and political slavery."

Drayton drained his lemonade, then gestured with his empty cup for a refill. "Walter, I have to confess I'm amazed. I never expected to hear such sentiments from a Y—…from a Union veteran."

Walter smiled gravely. "You never know how the seed you plant will bear fruit."

"I'm not sure I understand." Drayton felt an undeniable bond of sympathy between them, but his skeptical mind still asked, *is he being sincere or simply trying to draw me out for his own inscrutable purposes?*

"Papa spoke several times of your visit," said Walter. He paused for a few puffs on his pipe. "Shortly before he died, he told me, 'That young man performed an unusual act of kindness in the middle of war. A people who produce such a man can't be the monsters we've been told. Perhaps their cause is not so terrible as people say.' As a Swiss, he was more independent-minded than the Pennsylvania Dutch, who actually aren't Dutch, as you know, but Germans. *Deutsch.* I took his words to heart; tried to see both sides of the conflict. There was so much death and suffering that we naturally want to make sense of it. We want to believe the sacrifice was worth the cost. And yet… I can't help but entertain certain doubts, especially in this watershed year of 1913."

"What's special about 1913, aside from the Reunion?" Drayton asked, then answered his own question. He did read the newspapers. "You mean the 17th Amendment?"

The 17th Amendment to the U.S. Constitution had just been ratified by enough states to go into effect the end of May. It authorized election to the U.S. Senate by the people instead of the state legislatures, as provided by the original Constitution.

"Yes," Walter nodded. "The Amendment kills off the last vestige of true state sovereignty, making the centralizing process nearly complete. And now the Senate will be subject to the same log-rolling, wire-pulling, and demagoguery as the House. But that's not all. There's the 16th Amendment. It went into effect in February and establishes a Federal income tax. It overturns the Constitutional provision on direct taxation, so now our incomes can be taxed, individually and directly. The initial tax rate is kept modest to avoid a backlash. But be assured – it will grow and grow until the taxman plunders us blind. And when you combine the power to tax with the Federal Reserve—"

"Don't tell me the Federal Reserve Act is going to pass?" Drayton struggled to take it all in.

"Yes. Before the year is out. President Wilson came into office a skeptic of Wall Street and the Money Trust, but he's agreed to sign the act into law. Then Congress will have turned over its Constitutional responsibility for sound money to a private banking cartel. This cartel is *not* Federal and it has no reserves, only the *fiat* money it will lend into existence."

Drayton recalled the hours he'd spent with Louisa Cheves McCord. "My grandfather's friend Langdon Cheves of South Carolina was appointed by President Madison to head the Second Bank of the United States in 1819. But Cheves soon quit. He feared a central banking power that would benefit government and lenders at the expense of everyone else, and would essentially become the ward of the state."

Walter nodded, then refilled his pipe. The Boy Scouts brought round another serving of lemonade. "He had foresight," said Walter. "But he couldn't foresee that the new Federal Reserve will make the state the ward of the banks. Eventually the income tax and the central bank will concentrate wealth in the hands of a tiny oligarchy and impoverish the rest of Americans. You and I may not be alive to see it, but I believe this year of 1913 marks a fundamental change in how Americans will live in the future."

What were they really celebrating, Drayton wondered, at this event organized at such trouble and expense by … well, by the state. Drayton realized Walter was trying to help him, but the awareness his new friend was imparting only deepened his sense of remorse for his actions at Gettysburg. He sighed. "A fateful confluence of circumstances. I wonder if our fellow veterans have any idea what they're really commemorating. Power transmutes into empire. Empire begets hubris. Hubris brings ruin."

Walter agreed. "I fear a future generation of Americans, proud of their fathers' victory over the South and with little understanding what it was really all about, will sink slowly into a new form of servitude to an all-powerful central state. They'll surrender without a fight, without a protest, without a murmur, beating their chests and proclaiming how free they are. And the rest of the world will only snicker."

Chapter Fifty

Gettysburg Reunion; Wednesday, July 2, 1913. Military Day

The second day of the Reunion broke hot and heavy, with the promise of afternoon rain as deep gray clouds piled up in the west. On the morning's official schedule was the dedication of a statue of Vermont's Brigadier General William Wells, who won the Congressional Medal of Honor on the Third Day. A demonstration of the M1903 Springfield rifle was re-scheduled, comparing it to the Model 1860 Springfield used in the Battle. But it would be cancelled in event of a storm. After breakfast, the program included a reception for General Dan Sickles, 94, last surviving Union general who fought at Gettysburg, where he lost his right leg but gained a dubious immortality for his actions on the Second Day. Whether he'd been right tactically or not was still a matter of debate, like the Lee-Longstreet controversy that still raged among former Confederates. Blue and Gray were invited to call on him at the rebuilt Rogers House, which had been his headquarters in July 1863.

In the afternoon the Reunion Commission planned a ceremony at the Angle, the apex in the stone wall that protected Meade's center during Pickett's Charge. Word went around informally in the typical Southern manner — the survivors of the Great Charge decided to arrive at the Angle and copse of trees in the same way they had fifty years earlier, by a charge. No arduous mile-long march for men in their 70's and 80's as in the original Charge. They assembled a few hundred yards west of the stone wall on Cemetery Ridge by the fence along Emmitsburg Pike. The hardy ones would assist the amputees and the infirm. On the crest of Seminary Ridge behind them they could see the gleaming base of the new but unfinished Virginia Monument, where Lee had observed the assault on July 3, 1863.

The re-enactors totaled about 120 men of the Pickett's Division Association plus an assortment of individuals from various regiments, Pettigrew's mostly, that had taken part in the Great Charge on the Third Day. Anyone who had participated in the original charge was invited, which brought the total to 200 bearded patriarchs, many in the Confederate gray of the UCV, some in civilian suits. At first the spirit was light-hearted, but as the men assembled and the hour approached, the mood turned somber. Drayton was glad he'd decided to participate, but also gripped by trepidation.

Cabell accompanied him to the assembly point, and Drayton was self-conscious as he began to perspire more than the hot day demanded. A faraway look came into the eyes of his compatriots. Some trembled and some tried to hide their anxiety with jokes and bravado.

Cabell stepped back and said quietly, "I suddenly understand something. It takes as much courage to re-enact this charge as it did to make the original assault."

Drayton nodded wordlessly.

Cabell said, "This is as far as I go. I'll see you tonight at mess."

"You're not going with us?"

"No, brother, I have no right. This is for the men who charged on that day. I was with Wade Hampton in the cavalry fight east of here. Besides, my wooden leg will only slow you down."

Drayton nodded silently. Then, in an odd gesture, Cabell put out his hand, as though Drayton was going to some distant place and would be absent from supper. Drayton shook his brother's hand and joined the remnant of the 28th Virginia, who were nearest. A little after 3:00 PM, like a school of fish, without any detectable signal or word of command, the old Confederates fell into line and began to march forward, some on crutches or canes, which slowed the pace.

The sun beat down fiercely as it had during the Charge, and by the time they stepped off from the Pike they were sweating profusely. Two men fainted from heat exhaustion and remained at the fence line. One Virginian had had the foresight to bring a canteen, which he proffered to his fellows. The first drank gratefully and sloshed a bit in his face. The other, a thin and much older man with a wisp of beard and one ear shot off, took a deep draught. He spit it out with a grimace of surprised anger.

"This is water!" he roared.

Most of the Southerners took off their coats and left them hanging on the fence, and the heat casualties were appointed to guard them. In a ragged line, the veterans started upslope toward the copse of trees and low stone wall. With a mixture of exultation and terror Drayton looked back at the stout fence line, reliving the moment when he had soared across it on Beltane with Longstreet's orders to General Kemper, and how the wounded strewn along its length had cheered his horsemanship. He recalled the incessant noise, and how bravely Bel had faced the rolling volleys of artillery fire which he hated above all else. He tried not to think of the moment of his wounding, and surprised himself with a thought that had never occurred to him – once unhorsed, how had he gotten back on the 'Confederate' side of the fence?

The old fellows approached to within the range at which the Union volleys had shattered the charging mass fifty years ago. Drayton found himself growing breathless from the heat, the exertion, and something more that he couldn't name, a kind of collective excitement that had taken hold of the entire formation.

The Southerners were now close enough to observe the hundreds of blue-clad Reunioneers who had gathered behind the wall. Drayton glanced down the length of the line and saw his comrades' spines suddenly stiffen. Heads up and backs straight, they marched forward resolutely, dressing their ranks. They began to cheer, the eerie rising and falling wail that came from some deep place of history and of blood. Former Lieutenant Stowell of the 19th North Carolina held his walking cane forward like an officer's sabre as guide. Former Lieutenant Holland of the 28th Virginia extended his furled umbrella towards the 'enemy.' Ignoring age and infirmity, heat and humidity and fatigue, the Confederates picked up the pace. Drayton found himself weeping involuntarily. Ashamed lest anyone notice, he cast a glance to his left and right. The Virginians and North Carolinians were weeping, too, even as they cheered and charged.

The distance closed. Twenty yards, now ten. He could hear the Yankees cheering, too; but whether for themselves or their erstwhile opponents, he couldn't tell. Then he saw the GAR begin to wave their blue kepis and slouch hats wildly in the air, and it was clear whom they were cheering.

Drayton hadn't made it this far in 1863 and he felt an irrational pride that he'd done so now. And then a strange thing happened. The Yankees stopped cheering, replaced their headgear, and began to clamber over the stone fence toward the advancing Southerners. It was only a foot and a half high. He saw the Yankees were weeping, too. Rushing toward each other, the two lines of former enemies met on eternity's side of the wall and embraced, sobbing and cheering one another and calling out words of mutual admiration and reconciliation he couldn't understand because there was a roaring in his ears and his heart beat so loud that it obscured everything else.

Drayton walked back alone to the main camp from the dedication of flags at the official ceremony at the Angle following the charge. He was suddenly hungry and eager for evening mess, eager to see his brother. He knew Cabell was intensely curious about his Gettysburg experience. He could never tell Cabell the whole story, but he could tell him that today… Well, something had happened. Something sublime.

.   Fifty years ago the men he'd just marched with and embraced, Blue and Gray, had fought fiercely on that stretch of field to kill other men whom they would otherwise have admired. If they could be reconciled, with themselves and with what they'd done in the place of slaughter, then perhaps he could find reconciliation in himself. The Confederate dead of the Great Charge no longer reproached him. In defeat they had entered into the pages of history's immortals. The launching of the original assault of the world's finest infantry with all the pageantry of war had for a moment convinced everyone on the field of their invincibility, a conviction soon dispelled in blood and fire. But what courage it had demanded to make the Charge. What courage, too, the Yankees had possessed to stand and receive it. The spectacle, then and now, brought Aristotle's wonder and pity to mind. But 1863 had been no stage drama like this impromptu re-enactment. Instead of Aristotelean catharsis, it had then generated only anguish of spirit. Now he could recall it without grief lacerating his heart. He still had some distance to travel to shed fifty years of guilt and self-condemnation. But he had found the courage to make a start.

***

Walter Amman came for lunch at the South Carolina camp – this time alone. Drayton and Tommy had been playing checkers on a barrelhead while waiting for the meal to be spread on the trestle tables. Drayton stood and greeted the Pennsylvanian warmly. A hundred or so UCV Reunioneers had congregated in the shade of a copse of trees to demonstrate the rebel yell for visiting journalists. After the meal, as the ululating cries split the air, the two men walked toward the town of Gettysburg, passing the camp of an Army battalion of the 5th Infantry. A detachment of cavalry was assembling for drill. Tomorrow they would go on duty as a ceremonial escort for Congressman Champ Clark, Speaker of the House, who was scheduled to make an address. With practiced eye Drayton paused to admire the mounted soldiers' turnout and horses as they went through their evolutions. Then he and Walter proceeded along their way. Drayton noticed with concern that his cherubic friend's face and muscular forearms had begun to turn bright red under two days of July sun. Finally Drayton broke the silence, as he knew he must.

"Walter, you gave me a lot to think about yesterday."

"My desire was to help. I hope I didn't intrude."

Laughing ruefully, Drayton said, "I imagine the whole point of the... ah, therapy is to intrude. And then I'm supposed to respond. Right?" He was more severe than he intended to be. He supposed his stressful reaction was an indication that Walter's probing was succeeding.

They paused at the Wisconsin camp to watch a spirited game of horseshoes between a blue-clad GAR veteran and a gray-clad UCV man. Several dozen spectators lounged on cracker boxes, grinning fiercely as other compatriots crowded round, shouting encouragement. When the Confederate's shoe clanged against the post, a shrill Rebel yell erupted. When the Yankee scored, the GAR men whooped and hollered. They turned south and skirted the town along West Street, passing the Army hospital that served the entire encampment.

"You keep looking up at Little Round Top" Walter said. The eminence dominated the plain of the encampment a mile to the southeast.

"Yes, Walter, I suppose I do." He wanted not to look, but the silhouette of the hill drew him involuntarily. The memory swam into his mind — the reconnaissance fifty years ago, the flicker of motion in the corner of his eye. Had he departed a minute earlier… The Union officers had reached the summit moments after Drayton had started to descend. If only he hadn't detected the movement, if he hadn't turned to investigate (though that was his duty as a scout). Any number of trivial circumstances might have spared him the guilty knowledge of fifty years. Then, as always, tumbled into his mind the memories ineradicable of what ensued. The bellowing of the guns, the terror that rode on the wind, and the long rows of dead, who seemed like nothing more than untidy piles of red-splattered rags. And the poor uncomprehending horses, mounds of dead horses, killed in their traces, or struggling to run away, screaming, with their entrails dragging.

"The hill looms over this part of the battlefield," Drayton said. "It's hard not to look at it."

"Yes, but when you look at it, you don't just look. You *stare*, as if the hilltop is the key to some mystery; and a strange expression comes over you. Did something happen to you there?"

"Yes. It haunts my dreams."

"Did you kill a man up there? Does *he* haunt your dreams?"

"It's the man I didn't kill who haunts me."

Turning right on Long Lane that bisected the camp, they continued on, then stopped at the North Carolina camp for a cold drink to combat the growing sun. Walter sipped from the ladle attached to the Lister bag, then said, "I can tell this is terribly difficult for you. In which case, why don't you let me go first? I have a story, too. We all do. None of us, Yankee or Rebel, was ever the same after what we did and saw here."

Drayton nodded and smiled. "I'm afraid I've been selfish, so wrapped up in my own troubles that I forget everyone here is re-fighting a battle. I'd like to hear your story."

"Good. Listen then." They found some empty wooden ration boxes in the shade of a stand of red oaks. "I was much younger than you at the time of the battle. I was a regimental musician, and we youngsters doubled as medical orderlies when needed. The carnage of battle was bad enough, but the horrors were … well, concentrated in a field hospital, or what we were pleased to call such dreadful places in 1863. As you know, the standard treatment for wounds to the extremities was to lop off the limb. It had to be done quickly or the patient would die of shock of the operation. Many died anyway. But the speed of the amputation seemed to me to be extremely callous, not merciful; and the surgeons seldom made any effort to save the limb. At my impressionable age I began to think they just wanted to amputate as many arms and legs in a short a time as possible, as if they were paid by the piece."

"Yes, I know," Drayton said. "You've seen my brother's leg. At least your side had anesthetics. The only anesthetic to help Cabell was a slug of whiskey."

Walter continued. "Our medical corps was overwhelmed by the casualties flowing in on the Second Day, after the bitter fighting in Sickles' salient. My orders were to remove amputated limbs from the operating tables to a place behind the field hospital, in this case a local's farmhouse. Other orderlies were doing the same, and before long the pile of bleeding arms and legs and feet had grown up to my chest. In correct military fashion we deposited them all in exactly the same place. In those days medicine had little understanding of the phenomenon of psychological shock, but that is what was happening to me each time I carried a severed limb to that ghastly pile, which I still see sometimes in my nightmares fifty years later. This is the main reason I became an M.D., and why I developed a special interest in mental trauma. A case of 'physician, heal thyself.'"

"You appear to have succeeded."

"Wounds may heal, but the effects linger. At any rate, I have little recollection of the episode after a certain point, but I was arrested by the provost marshal some distance behind the lines, crying hysterically and gripping a man's severed arm. They wanted to charge me with deserting my post in combat – *did* charge me, in fact. But because of my youth and the macabre circumstances, there was no court martial. I was sent home for a few months, where my parents' love and care brought me back to normal, more or less. And now I am coming to my point. My father was a wise man, and he encouraged me – no, insisted – that I not keep this terrible memory bottled up, but to talk of it, openly and often. At first I was too ashamed to do so, but with his encouragement I was able to ease the pain of recall, lessen the nightmares."

"I have made an effort *not* to remember, but the memories come unbidden," said Drayton. "I hoped coming here might help me exorcise the demons. It hasn't entirely. And frankly, though I know you meant well, your views on the meaning of this year of 1913 have only made it worse. If I could be convinced it was better for the South to have lost, it would be easier. But yesterday you convinced me otherwise, which makes my burden harder to bear."

"Forget exorcism. There's an easier way, I'm telling you. Confession is good for the soul. In your case, it's absolutely necessary, I believe. You can never be completely free of this… this burden, but you can ask others to help you bear it. You have a brother who obviously loves and respects you. You must take the risk and reveal your long-guarded secret. You *must* talk about it. This is your doctor speaking," he added with a smile.

Gettysburg Reunion; Thursday, July 3, 1913. Civic Day.

Thursday morning broke clear and warm, with no threat in the skies of another monster rainstorm. Blue and Gray milled around the vast encampment, sorting themselves out after breakfast at the bulletin boards, some making notes on the day's offerings. Some trekked off for the planned events. Others retired for naps, reported for sick call, played cards and checkers, wrote letters, and visited with their former enemies. Cabell was scanning the notice board and felt rather than heard Drayton at his side. He turned and nodded at his brother, then waved at the posted notice.

"Do you want to take in Mr. Clark this morning?" he asked Drayton. Congressman Champ Clark of Missouri, Speaker of the House, was scheduled to address the veterans at 10:00.

"No, I'll pass," said Drayton. "Two years ago the Speaker advocated that the U.S. absorb Canada. I assume he meant peacefully. But who knows?"

"Then we'll skip it," said Cabell. "How about President Wilson tomorrow?"

The highlight of the schedule for July 4, National Day, was the visit by President Woodrow Wilson, who would give a brief address in the Great Tent at noon. But it only held 15,000 in the audience, and was sure to be mobbed, unless the heat kept people away. He was the last speaker on the official program. The Reunion would formally close on the afternoon of the 4th.

Cabell noted, "The bulletin says the children of Generals Meade and Longstreet will be there. In fact, Mrs. Longstreet and her son are visiting the camp now. I just spoke to them briefly a moment ago. They were greeting General Teague and the South Carolina UCV in the mess tent after breakfast. Would you like to say hello?"

Helen Dortch Longstreet was their old First Corps commander's second wife, whom Longstreet had married in 1897. Those who knew the family praised Helen Dortch for her wonderful care of the 'Old War Horse' as he declined in health and then passed away in 1904. A vivacious and intelligent woman from

Georgia, she was active politically – a Teddy Roosevelt Progressive – and author of a memoir, *Lee and Longstreet at High Tide*, that tried with limited success to quell the criticism of her late husband's role at Gettysburg. Later Cabell wondered at the fortuitous confluence of circumstances: as he and Drayton discussed meeting Mrs. Longstreet, they overheard veterans promoting an event hosted by the Virginia UCV and the Pickett's Division Association. After the President's talk tomorrow there would be a lecture in the Virginia mess tent by Colonel John Leathers of the storied Stonewall Brigade. His topic: 'Lee's Sunrise Order: Did Longstreet's Insubordination Forfeit Victory at Gettysburg?'

Drayton found the item on the unofficial schedule, and stood in thought for an unusually long spell contemplating the notice. Then he said with unusual force, "Yes, let's go call on Mrs. Longstreet."

Cabell was attuned to his brother's occasional moroseness, and this social call departed from the pattern. Drayton was never eager to discuss his War service, but he especially avoided speaking of Gettysburg. He never attended UCV meetings or reunions of the old 2nd Cavalry. If anyone questioned him, he found a way to evade the matter. But *something* had happened, and judging from his pained reaction to the notice of Colonel Leathers' lecture, Cabell deduced Drayton's trouble involved General Longstreet, whom his brother had admired. Or perhaps Drayton had killed a man at Gettysburg. But he'd killed two men at Brandy Station, face to face and hand to hand in a sword fight, something uncommon in America's first modern war. He'd killed a Yankee cavalryman during the Great Cattle Raid. Those deaths never seemed to trouble him unduly.

Cabell took his brother's arm. "Come on, then." Drayton followed.

The Longstreet party had departed the South Carolina area by the time the brothers arrived. After a half hour's search they found them at the 5th Infantry Regiment parade ground near the main camp hospital. A khaki-clad drum and bugle detachment marched up and down playing a series of Sousa's marches.

Cabell removed his straw hat and smiled diplomatically with a slight bow. "Mrs. Longstreet, Gentlemen, I'd like to present my brother Drayton FitzHenry. He served on the General's staff as scout and courier. Drayton, this is Mrs. Helen Dortch Longstreet, the General's widow, his son Major Robert Lee Longstreet, U.S. Army, and the General's grandsons, James and John Welchel."

Drayton gave a slight bow to the General's widow, a tall handsome woman in an ivory linen dress and wide-brimmed hat trimmed with ostrich feathers. She extended a gloved hand and said, "Mr. FitzHenry, were you with my husband here at Gettysburg?"

"Yes, Ma'am, I was."

"Then you know of the controversy." She wore a proud but pained expression. "It started with General Jubal Early. And then General Pendleton picked up the drumbeat of criticism. The Virginians are saying that my husband was to blame for the loss of the Battle. Can you shed any light on the matter?"

"Perhaps," Drayton replied. "It's no secret that General Longstreet believed that he and General Lee had agreed to an operational concept... ah, decidedly different from what actually transpired. General Longstreet wanted to maneuver the Army between the Yankees and Washington, perhaps get astride their line of communication in a strong defensive position, and force them to attack us. Of course, it happened the other way 'round. We ended up attacking them in a strong defensive position. But once the conflict was joined, Lee abandoned the original concept and began to improvise. He felt we held the initiative, and he persisted in trying to destroy Meade piecemeal. He wanted to end the war here, knowing the South could not fight on indefinitely. And he believed, as he said later, that his men were invincible. Your husband believed otherwise. Sadly, he was right."

This was in accord with what Cabell had heard from Drayton during one their rare conversations about the battle. He found himself listening with renewed interest.

"But did this disagreement cause the General to disobey orders?" Major Longstreet asked. He was the product of General Longstreet's first marriage, tall and handsome like his father. Put a thick beard on him, mused Cabell, and he could be the General's twin. "They are saying he was insubordinate and refused to carry out Lee's sunrise order that departed from the original plan. They are saying that if my father had acted promptly as Lee directed, we would have driven Meade from the field."

Drayton remained silent for a moment's thought. Then he said, "Major, Mrs. Longstreet, I can tell you that the General believed the original concept of the operation still held, even after the battle was on. He had designs on Meade's left on the Second Day and hoped to out-flank the enemy without a frontal attack. We had all seen the futility of such attacks on an entrenched enemy at Malvern Hill and later at Fredericksburg. He had doubts that Lee's staff engineer Captain Johnston had adequately reconnoitered Little Round Top, the key to the Yankees' whole position. He wanted his own scout to go take a look to see if the Yankees were there or not. He sent me."

Cabell was stunned. He'd been vaguely aware of Drayton's role on Longstreet's staff, but had never learned the details. Cabell blurted, "You went up Little Round Top?" In all his years of trying to ferret out some detail of his brother's secret, this was the first time he'd made any progress.

"Yes, I did," Drayton nodded. "Earlier in the campaign General Lee had said to all his commanders, 'Meade will make no blunders on my front.' It was not Meade's blunder to leave Little Round Top undefended, but Sickles'. As you know, General Sickles moved his Third Corps forward toward the Emmitsburg Pike without orders from Meade, which created a salient in the Peach Orchard and Wheat Field." He gestured toward the sites and continued. "General Longstreet's intuition was that Sickles' movement had left Little Round Top uncovered, and he wanted to know what lay on the hill. He believed the scope of General Lee's orders would allow him to occupy it as part of his attack. In other words, he could employ his own tactical judgment without violating Lee's guidance. As you know, General Lee typically gave great latitude to his subordinate commanders."

"And what did you find up there?" asked Mrs. Longstreet, her face taut with suspense.

"I found General Longstreet was right. There were no Yankees occupying this vital position. No infantry, no artillery. Only a two-man scouting detachment."

Cabell noticed that his brother was oddly stiff and formal. *He's uncomfortable about this part of the battle*, he realized.

Major Longsteet looked at his mother pointedly, then smiled at his nephews, the Welchel boys. "Mr. FitzHenry, if I can secure a place on the program following Colonel Leathers, would you be willing to share your insights on this matter?"

Drayton nodded. "Yes. I feel I owe it to General Longstreet's memory. And thus to you." He smiled a thin smile. *But he's not happy at all*, thought Cabell. *He acts like a man who's just heard the death sentence pronounced.* And he realized, *He's hiding something.*

Chapter Fifty One

Gettysburg Reunion; Friday, July 4, 1913. National Day.

President Woodrow Wilson's address took place in the Great Tent in sweltering 100-degree heat, with an audience of 15,000. Wilson was Southern-born, had lived for a time in South Carolina, Georgia, and Virginia. Reportedly he had met Robert E. Lee as a youngster. Cabell enjoyed his brief remarks extolling national reconciliation. "We have found one another again as brothers and comrades in arms, enemies no more, our battles long past and our quarrels forgotten, except that we shall not forget the splendid valor of men once arrayed against one another, now grasping hands and smiling into each other's eyes."

Drayton passed up the Wilson event, and Cabell had agreed to meet him at the Virginia mess tent after the President's departure. The controversial lecture was scheduled for 3:00 PM, after the meal and serving items had been cleared away. Cabell was chatting with the Longstreet family when Drayton showed up at half past two, wearing an off-white linen suit which accentuated his white and drawn complexion under his normally healthy tan.

They engaged in a desultory conversation, and Cabell's curiosity nearly burst its bounds as his brother suddenly said to Mrs. Longstreet, "There's not a man here, North or South, who doesn't admire General Lee. I revere him supremely. In fact, I think this is the root of the controversy. To exonerate General Lee, people must blame General Longstreet. But Lee was a man, after all, not a god. He did make mistakes at the Battle. All the commanders on both sides did. *I* did."

Cabell found that odd, but he was more focused on what was *not* said – Longstreet's post-War reputation, which he believed explained the animus against him. The General had been friends with Ulysses S. Grant since West Point. They had served in the old Army together. Longstreet had been a groomsman in Grant's wedding, and had accepted a position in Grant's Administration after the 1868 Presidential Election. Many Southerners, embittered by Reconstruction, regarded Longstreet as a traitor to the South.

As expected, a capacity crowd began to file into the tent. When the seats were full, veterans lined the rear and side walls standing. A heavily bearded

Colonel Leathers, as whippet-thin as during the War, arrived with a uniformed Boy Scout carrying a briefcase. He greeted the Longstreets and FitzHenrys with impeccable courtesy, then took his place on the dais, inviting his fellow speaker to join. With an impassive expression Drayton followed, marching stiffly and without enthusiasm. A whiff of whiskey – the peach bounce, no doubt – followed in his wake.

My God, thought Cabell as he took his seat. *He's been in the tent drinking all this time. Pray God he doesn't embarrass himself, or the whole state of South Carolina. Or worse, lose his train of thought and bore us to tears. It's hot in here.*

Cabell took a seat next to the aisle on the front row of the audience, where the Longstreet party had settled next to former Brigadier General Evander Law. Helen Longstreet and the Welchel children fanned themselves with pew fans from the local Methodist church. A South Carolinian and Citadel graduate, Evander Law had commanded a brigade under Longstreet until John Bell Hood was badly wounded during the First Corps' attacks on the Second Day. Law had assumed command of Hood's Division. His troops, including men from Texas and Alabama, seized Devil's Den, but failed to take Little Round Top a short while later.

The Virginia mess tent was now full to bursting, despite the heat. General Bennett Young of Kentucky, National Commander of the UCV, introduced the event, then sat as Colonel Leathers took the podium. At the Colonel's nod, the Boy Scout produced a sheaf of papers. *Obviously well prepared,* thought Cabell. *And Drayton has no notes at all.*

***

Drayton was used to public speaking; platform appearances never unsettled him. But this would be the supreme public address of his life. He'd taken a glass of the special brandy secreted in his valise against just such an eventuality, though when he set out from Charleston on June 28, he couldn't foresee what was about to unfold. Indeed, by the time his bombshell was delivered, it might prove to be the key event of the entire Reunion. But that was for others to decide. He only had to get though the next hour. His past fifty years had been overshadowed by guilt and shame and anger. And yes, fear – fear of discovery. By the time one reaches his 70's, he mused, life itself has become a burden. For the aging, the accumulated weight of defeats, disappointments, and losses is rarely dispelled by life's occasional triumphs. To carry the millstone of age *and* the weight of fifty years of guilt and shame was foolish when he had the choice to discharge it. Suddenly he was eager for his moment. The burden was about to be shed. And his mind wandered – he needn't pay too close attention to Colonel Leathers because he knew what the Virginian was going to say – wandered back to April 1870, when Robert E. Lee had visited Charleston on his Southern Tour and offered counsel that would have relieved his soul – that was the word Walter Amman had used – if only he'd been wise enough then to accept the General's advice. General Lee was the only person ever to learn his secret. But that was all about to change, and in the most public and dramatic way imaginable.

Charleston, South Carolina; April 1870.

Drayton recalled the day the invitation arrived to dine with Robert E. Lee in Charleston. He was deep in seclusion and hardly left the farm except to shop in nearby Jacksonboro or Walterboro. He seldom received mail because he never sent any. But on this day in early April, as he nailed up strips of batten-board to repair the siding on the overseer's cottage, the postal carrier hove into view in a one-horse shay. The postman was black and a Republican appointee; Drayton was an ex-Confederate and, if anything, a Democrat. Yet they always greeted one another cordially. On this occasion he asked the man to wait in case a reply was needed. He seated the postman with a plate of cornbread and bottle of scuppernong wine while he ripped open the envelope and read the message.

General Lee was making a 'progress' through the South. After a stop in Savannah he would arrive in Charleston and remain two days with the Jefferson Bennetts at 60 Montagu Street. Old friends of the FitzHenrys, the hosts desired Drayton for supper 'with other leading citizens of Charleston' on April 29th. Drayton hardly considered himself a leading citizen of anywhere. But he was a recently published author and an eligible bachelor. The Bennetts had two sons at Washington College in Lexington, Virginia where Lee was president, and four daughters in need of husbands. Drayton had no interest in the girls, but he did want to see General Lee again – as did all Charleston.

On the morning of the 29th, Drayton left water and a few flakes of hay in the paddock for Beltane. Grass was coming in fine, and he'd have enough grazing. Drayton walked to Jacksonboro, and caught the train from Savannah to Charleston's Meeting Street station. He stayed at the Mills House, snatched a spot of sleep, then bathed, shaved, and changed into his best suit. It had been several years since he'd dressed up and ventured into society, and for the first time in a long time he was eager for human company.

The Bennetts' fine three-story home in the Federal style had escaped the great fire, years of bombardment, and Reconstruction. Drayton arrived at Montagu Street in time to hear Lee briefly address the immense crowd that had gathered below, filling the entire block. The Post Band played lively Southern airs, ending with 'Carry My Heart to Old Virginia.' The people cheered, and Lee spoke briefly but warmly from the second-floor wrought-iron balcony, then waved and went back inside. Drayton pushed through the throng, presented his card at the entrance, and was ushered in by a Negro butler in a black tail suit and crisp white shirt.

The table was laid with the finest china, crystal, and table linens, as if the War had never devastated Old Charleston. The guests gathered around their aperitifs, sipping and chatting with delight at this reminder of past glories. Then a voice whispered, "Hush. It's General Lee." The diners fell silent as Lee descended the broad curving staircase with his daughter Agnes on his arm, nodding acknowledgement with a slight smile.

Drayton stiffened in surprise at how the General had aged. He had last seen the grand old man riding back from the surrender at the McLean house at Appomattox, his ragged veterans crowding around to touch him or Traveller and render one final salute from choked voices. Lee accepted the Charlestonians' tributes with his accustomed dignity, looking almost frail in his dark civilian suit. His comportment was reserved, with neither aloofness nor familiarity. During the War Drayton had seen a fair bit of Lee, more than most, and enough to know the wistfulness about him that now bordered on sadness. But Lee did not bear himself as a tragic figure wreathed in sorrow. A man whose chief ideal was duty and self-abnegation, he evidently refused to yield to sorrow any more than he would to any other self-indulgence. As the guests took their seats at dinner, Lee smiled and joked, especially with the young ladies.

As the beef course made its rounds, Lee teased the Bennett girls, his eyes merry. "I see young Mr. FitzHenry is here. You must not neglect me in vying for his attention." The girls dipped their heads and twittered. Lee continued. "I know your work, Mr. FitzHenry. We recently acquired *Man of the Hour* for the library at Washington College." Drayton was surprised. But then, the General was known for a prodigious memory.

"I'm sure he would be a good provider for one of you delightful young ladies," Lee laughed. "I recall a time in 1864 when he provided for our entire Army. Thanks to him, I enjoyed the best roast beef I ever ate – until tonight, that is, Mrs. Bennett."

The guests clamored for an explanation. Drayton waved them away, and nothing would do but for the General to tell the tale of the Great Beefsteak Raid. Drayton smiled self-deprecatingly at the appropriate moments, but the account left him sinking into a guilty despondency. He hated to be put on display as a hero, a reputation he did not deserve. Yet when he declined the praise, his admirers gushed all the more.

The talk reached an ebb, and Mrs. Bennett said cheerily, hoping to ease the conversation along, "General Lee, I hope you are writing your memoirs."

Lee laid down his napkin and looked plaintively at his hostess, who awaited his answer with a bright, hopeful expression.

Lee said gently to spare her feelings, "No, Mrs. Bennett, I will not write any memoir. It is all I can do to edit my father's papers, a duty I feel I owe his memory." The General was speaking of 'Light Horse' Harry Lee, a hero of the American Revolution, who later fell into financial ruin and disgrace. Lee had just visited his father's grave on Cumberland Island the previous week.

Failing to take the hint, his hostess objected. "But General Lee, no one could tell the story of the, ah, Late Unpleasantness as well as you."

"Oh, many could tell it better, I am sure. In any case, I feel it would be trading on the sacrifice of my men, and this I will not do."

To fill the awkward pause that followed Lee's implied rebuke, Dr. Gibbes, the Episcopal rector, spoke up. "General Lee, may I say how much we admire your decision to become President of Washington College. You might have taken many more …more remunerative positions. I believe you are the most highly regarded man in the North as well as in the South."

It was true. Lee had won the heart of the entire nation as much by his conduct after the War as by his military leadership. Refusing to cash in on his fame, he accepted defeat with grace and dignity while urging national reconciliation.

"Well, I know nothing of that," said Lee. "I do know it was my duty to remain in Virginia. And it is our duty to put the War behind us. We must lay aside angry sectional feelings, train and educate our young people to build up our shattered country, and strive to live as good Americans."

Christopher Memminger, former Confederate Treasury Secretary, said, "That may require even more courage than fighting. But General Lee, you have set us the example. All in our world has been lost save honor." He tipped his wineglass toward Lee in an informal toast.

"Yes, the sun has set on the world we knew," said Lee, returning the gesture with his own wine. "Certainly the portion of it that rested upon African servitude, and for that we should be happy. But that was only a portion; it did not represent the entire South. The other, greater portion of courage and duty, honor, and civility has survived, and will enable our people to flourish again someday."

Charlotte Russe with rum-flavored whipped cream was served for dessert. The guests devoured it in an instant, then withdrew into the sumptuous drawing room with tea and coffee as the staff cleared the table. They crowded around Lee in subdued, respectful conversation. Lee chatted amiably, bathing the guests with a fatherly smile that leavened his gravity. Drayton envied how much at ease the man was – first, with himself, which allowed him to be equally at ease on a battlefield thundering with artillery or in a drawing room tinkling with teacups. At first Drayton had been content to admire him from a distance, but finally the impulse overcame him, the impulse that had led him to accept the Bennett invitation in the first place.

He made his apologies as he threaded his way between the adoring women, stepped up to Lee and said boldly, "General Lee, I beg your forgiveness, but may I take you away from these charming girls for a minute or two of private conversation? There's something of the deepest importance I must discuss with you."

Lee nodded, almost as if relieved. "I'm sure our hostess won't mind. Nor these young ladies." He smiled at them in his most winning manner. "After all, ladies, there are other young men here besides Mr. FitzHenry, whom I must sequester for a moment. You would be better served to visit with them than with a superannuated old Confederate."

Without waiting for the inevitable protests, he bowed them away and took Drayton's elbow. The two men retired to a quiet alcove off the drawing room. The butler came and refilled their teacups, and Drayton could scarcely believe he was alone with the man he admired above all others.

"I watched you at dinner," said Lee to Drayton's wonderment. "I knew something was troubling you."

"Yes, sir. There is something I must tell you. Frankly, General, I would rather not, yet I must. About something that happened at Gettysburg. On the Second Day."

Lee stiffened, but smiled. "Mr. FitzHenry, I am a member of the Episcopal Church. The office of Father Confessor does not exist in our denomination." There was no criticism in his voice, only wry assurance.

"I am, too, General. Nevertheless, I cannot live with the knowledge I recently acquired without some answers. Forgive my importuning, but you are the only one who can...who can—"

"Who can grant you absolution?"

"In a manner of speaking, yes."

Lee smiled faintly. "Well then, insofar as I have such powers I grant it, lest you take too much upon yourself. You were a junior officer. You commanded no corps, division, brigade, or regiment. The conduct of the battle was my responsibility, not yours. I alone am responsible for the results."

"Yes, sir, in principle. But victory in battle also depends upon the acts of individual soldiers."

Lee shrugged, as if to indicate he neither agreed nor disagreed.

"In this instance I was under General Longstreet's orders as a scout," Drayton explained. "A scout is expected to act independently and use his own initiative as the circumstances may dictate."

Lee remained impassive, awaiting the details.

"Sir," said Drayton. "You remember Colonel – well, later Brigadier General — Porter Alexander?"

"Yes, I remember General Alexander quite well. One of our best men."

Drayton told him of the Swinton article and Colonel Oates' letter he had read at Alexander's lodgings. He explained his mission for Longstreet to Little Round Top, his sparing the Union officer who then won the race to fortify the most vital spot on the battlefield. "When I went off to war, General Lee, I pledged to one I loved above all others that I would not return – *if* I returned – hardened and brutalized. I promised to show mercy whenever possible. I wanted to preserve our love by preserving the humanity that made that love possible. The irony is I had feared when going to war that I might have to live with shame for the acts I might commit, not for an act I did not commit."

Lee uncrossed his legs and leaned forward, his forearms on his knees with an intent expression. "Let me be sure I understand. You are telling me that the battle turned upon your decision to spare Gouverneur Warren when you were in a position to shoot him down from where you hid. It was General Warren who rushed the Federals to Little Round on his own authority, just in time to prevent its seizure by our people. You believe a timely attack by General Law's division would have occupied the high ground on this vulnerable flank and turned Meade's entire line. It would have won the battle and most likely the war."

"Yes, sir." Drayton waited for the rebuke that was coming, the rebuke that he deserved. Lee's courtesy was legendary, but so was his anger when aroused, as Benjamin Huger had learned after Malvern Hill, as Jeb Stuart when he returned too late at Gettysburg.

For a space Lee's face held a faraway look. "If you are correct, then the outcome of the battle flowed from an act of love and mercy." Lee mused. "For us, a *fatal* mercy."

He paused, sat back in his chair, and ruminated with an expression of wonder. Drayton hung his head in shame, wishing now he'd kept his secret. The General frowned as he absorbed what he'd just been told. Drayton could see him sifting the factors of time and distance, re-living the tactical situation at Gettysburg, for a moment perhaps visualizing victory instead of defeat, in his imagination even marching on to Washington and dictating terms to the Yankees. There in the silence of a Charleston drawing room both men could thrill to what it would have meant in 1863. Independence for the Confederacy. Peace. An end to the slaughter instead of two more years of death and destruction.

Finally, as if with effort, Lee spoke. "Mr. FitzHenry, I take with due seriousness what you have told me. But you must keep in mind the confusion and the fog of war. It's the nature of battle that one must act on incomplete or imperfect information. In battle time is everything, and yet there is often so little time to weigh one's course and to decide. There were many, many failures at Gettysburg, starting with my own. It has been said that all my major subordinates fell short in one way or another, at one critical moment or another. But they answered to me. Perhaps I was too … too gentle with them. Frankly, if you had taken the life of General Warren on Little Round Top, I'm not convinced it would have made such a difference as you seem to think. In any case, you must accept the outcome as the act of Providence."

Desperately hoping for more than a cliché Drayton said, "I wish I could, General Lee. It would be so much easier to bear if I could lay it all in the lap of Providence." He paused, searching, then added, "At Brandy Station I killed two Yankees in single combat; an officer, with my saber, and his sergeant, with my revolver. The sergeant left me this." He held up his maimed hand. "I killed another during General Hampton's cattle raid at Petersburg. Nor was it courage on my part. If I hadn't killed them, they would have killed me. I was no more deserving to live than they; I was just quicker. Was it Providence that brought those dead men across my path but left me alive? If so, why? So that I could in my turn forfeit our victory at Gettysburg? Are we then mere puppets in the hands of Providence? Or are we moral actors, with duties and responsibilities? I can't make any sense of it, except to regard what happened as a matter of personal responsibility, even if within the framework of chance. But if I am responsible, I can't live with the burden of it. How can one know?"

Lee placed his teacup on the side table with a clatter. Drayton noticed the slight tremor in Lee's hand as the General pondered and then spoke.

"Mr. FitzHenry, you ask the most difficult questions a man can pose of another man, of his Maker, of life itself." Lee sat back in his chair and sighed deeply. "But I'll give you my thoughts, for whatever value you may find in them. First, it may interest you to know that until Appomattox I was a soldier for 36 years. I served in the war with Mexico, on the frontier against the Comanche and the Apache, and in the War of Secession. And in all that time I never killed a man in single combat, for which I am grateful. My specialty has been ordering the killing of anonymous formations of men at a comfortable distance. I say this to assure you I'm entirely conscious of your distress.

"But I cannot think it was wrong to commit an act of mercy amid the dreadful things we were called upon to do. We had a duty to fight, to be sure, but with humanity. Christian charity must not give way totally to the exigencies of war."

"How does one reconcile Christian charity with a soldier's duty?"

Lee stroked his chin and said, "I believe we must do our duty above all. Yet sometimes our duty is not clear. We have a duty to God first, then to our families and our community. What if they conflict? We must do the best we can and leave the consequences to God. When I saw the men of Pickett and Pettigrew and Trimble streaming back from that terrible charge, I wanted to die with them. But duty came before my own desires, my own grief. I saw that ending the war at one stroke had failed at Gettysburg, and that it must go on for a while longer. There were so many occasions at Gettysburg where we fell short by just a few moments or a few yards and too few men. Victory was so near that all we had to do was close our grasp around it, yet it always eluded us. I think it had to be foreordained, not mere chance.

"In any case, it was my duty to command as long as ordered. The South's destiny as a people lies in the hands of God, not in mine, not in yours. It was He who created the best things in us, especially our valor. No soldiers ever showed more valor than our Southern men. I am glad to learn now that some showed mercy as well. What you have revealed gives me great comfort, in fact."

Drayton did not spare himself. "Perhaps it was mercy misplaced, General Lee. After all, in sparing a man I lost the battle."

The old chieftain paused long and thoughtfully, and Drayton saw that the lines etched in his face were not of sadness but of care, limned with acceptance. Mrs. Bennett came into the doorway of the drawing room, cleared her throat noisily, and stared at Drayton with reproach for monopolizing their famous guest.

"General Lee," she said. "Won't you please join us in the drawing room for some ten-year-old tawny port?"

"I would be pleased to," said Lee. "Presently." The General looked at her with a benign smile as if to ratify the justice of her unspoken complaint. But he remained in his chair, making it clear he was not ready to be dislodged. He turned back gravely to Drayton and continued the conversation.

"Mr. FitzHenry, if you expect me to answer such questions, you expect too much. I have struggled to answer these things for myself, and in the end I can only commit them to the God of history."

Drayton understood Lee's need to believe as he did, waiting as it were in the anteroom of Eternity. But Drayton could not be so sure, as much as he wanted to believe the same – and win the same acceptance, gain the same peace of mind his old commander evidently had found.

Lee passed a weary hand over his lined, bearded face, and sighed deeply. He leaned forward again, grasped Drayton firmly by the forearm, and looked into his eyes with surprising frankness. The banked embers of the older man glowed behind the legendary reserve. Drayton saw with a shock what he'd always suspected – Lee was not a man of marble but of fire.

"You are deeply troubled by your war experience, and you have my sympathy," said the General. "I have lain awake many nights reliving the war; my errors in particular. I think unceasingly of those brave men on both sides who died or were maimed, even though they were willing to risk all. I did risk all at Gettysburg and we lost. Do you think I'm not aware of what our defeat has meant and will mean, knowing that it is my doing? The triumph of Those People means there is no longer any check upon the central power, and in time the United States will become an empire, aggressive abroad and despotic at home. How do I reconcile this view with the proposition that God's will decided the outcome? Well, it is not for us mortals to know, much less to say."

"Then, Sir, are we just puppets in the hands of inscrutable Providence, in which case, why try to act morally or wisely or bravely? It is all decided." Drayton could not keep the asperity from his tone. But it was no way to speak to Robert E. Lee.

"It is commendable of you to face your responsibility," Lee sighed. Drayton observed with concern the tired lines in Lee's face, the shortness of breath, no doubt a result of his privations in the field. Like so many others, he was in effect a deferred casualty of the War. "But perhaps you take too much upon yourself. Of course we are obliged to act morally and wisely and bravely. But we must also accept that our perspective is limited. Can the finite explain the infinite? I think not. Consider yourself, and me, and all mankind, as droplets in a great river. The droplet sees only what is before and behind, but does not know the course of the river nor its destination. Shall the droplet then complain of its course and whither it goes? No. Those matters must be left in the hands of Him who formed the river. It is only for the droplet *to do its duty* and trust that it will arrive at the proper place in the fullness of time."

Drayton demurred. "'All the rivers run into the sea, yet the sea is not full.'"

"Yes," Lee nodded with his sad smile. "And the Scripture continues: 'To the place from which the rivers come, there they shall return again.' We the individual droplets cannot hasten this journey nor divert its path. In our sight the journey may seem full of inconsistencies and contradictions. Yet the march of history is in accord with God's will, not ours. Our desires are impatient. The life of humanity is long, but that of the individual is so brief that we see only the ebb of the wave and are thus discouraged. We must try to take the long view, Mr. FitzHenry, for it is history that teaches us to hope."

Drayton hung his head with stubborn impiety, his soul seared by the memories when he allowed his mind to go back there — the blonde-bearded face of the dead Union lieutenant at Brandy Station, the destruction at Gettysburg. How easy to off-load the shame and confusion onto God. But if it was all in His beneficent hands, then why the awful violence, the waste, the sacrifice of so many good men?

It was as if the General read his thoughts. "My young friend," said the General, reading his thoughts. "I have turned in my mind over the same questions you pose many times. We came so close to final victory so often, yet every time it seemed that Providence snatched victory from our grasp. Often in my heart I asked, 'Are we being punished for some great sin?' And yet in truth, I could not see the sins of the South as more scarlet than those of the North. If we were guilty of holding slaves, the North was equally guilty. Their ships and capital *were* the slave trade.

"Finally I came to see that had we won, we would have swollen up with pride. We might have claimed, 'We did this by our own martial prowess.' But God wanted to keep us humble, a people reserved unto Himself for His own future purposes, when our virtues will be needed by America, perhaps even the world, more than ever."

This time Agnes Lee came to fetch the General. She laid a slim white hand on her father's shoulder with a rustling of silk and a mild look of reproach. The interview was over. The background hum of conversation, the clink of glasses, intruded into their quiet corner. The old general and young subaltern laid aside the age-old questions that man had asked himself from the dawn of time. Lee stood, and Drayton with him.

"Please do not misunderstand me, Mr. FitzHenry," Lee added. "I am not speaking of dumb, brute resignation. I am trying, however imperfectly, to describe the deepest understanding. But your question cannot be answered to your satisfaction in this life," Lee said with sudden vehemence and a sweeping gesture. "I trust it will be answered in the life and world to come, when all things will be revealed."

There was nothing more he could say. Drayton stared mutely into his teacup, as if the sodden leaves could impart some hidden wisdom. But he had imposed on the old gentleman long enough. As he extended his hand, Lee said, "Mr. FitzHenry, you must find what comfort you can in believing your act of mercy was the seed of some good fruit yet to come. I believe it was, and I am grateful you chose to tell me. I will rest better now when contemplating my own role in the great battle."

Six months later, in October 1870, General Lee died at his home in Lexington. The Southern tour intended to restore his health had in fact left him exhausted, with adoring crowds seeking a word from him at every stop. Drayton mourned his passing, as did most Americans, including Lee's former enemies. Drayton gave thanks to God, if God was listening, for that final conversation. But for fifty years he had in essence rejected Lee's view. It had seemed too easy an escape, to blame it all on God. It had taken him fifty years and a trip to Pennsylvania to finally understand what General Lee had told him. But he wished he'd been able to follow Lee's advice at the time. It would have saved him a near-lifetime of anguish.

⁎

Cabell shifted and settled himself in his seat full of anticipation as stout and florid Brigadier General Teague, Commander of the South Carolina Division of the UCV, stood to introduce Drayton.

"Gentlemen," said Teague somewhat pompously, "you have heard from the estimable Colonel John Leathers of the Stonewall Brigade. Now I'm pleased to introduce for a different perspective a fellow South Carolinian. Lt. Drayton FitzHenry of Charleston, South Carolina enlisted in April 1861 in the Wade Hampton Legion. The Legion's cavalry battalion later became the famed 2nd South Carolina Cavalry Regiment. Mr. FitzHenry was at the point of the spear that broke up the Federal surprise attack over the Rappahannock at Brandy Station in June 1863, where he killed two opponents in single combat and was severely wounded himself. Forty per cent of his regiment became casualties that day. Refusing to take medical leave, he requested assignment as scout and courier on the staff of General Longstreet. He took part in the great battle here which we commemorate, including the Great Charge on the Third Day, where he was again badly wounded. He returned to duty in May 1864 and served to the end. Many of you owe him a debt gastronomical as the genius behind Wade Hampton's Great Beefsteak Raid at Petersburg."

Teague held up his hand and tried vainly to speak over the erupting cheers. "It was Lt. FitzHenry, scouting deep behind the Union lines, who discovered the vulnerable herd of cattle and conceived the plan to, ah, transfer them from the Federal Commissary to ours." Cheers and whistles and laughter continued for a minute or more.

Cabell watched Drayton intently, and for a moment he feared Drayton would balk. His brother remained rooted to his seat. But then he rose, swallowed vigorously, and took a deep draught of water from a glass next to the lectern. Cabell half expected to see him pull notes from his inside pocket, but he placed both hands on the lectern and began.

"Mrs. Longstreet, Generals Law and Teague, Colonel Leathers, Ladies and Gentlemen, and veterans North and South. I thank Colonel Leathers for his views. And I thank our Virginia compatriots for the opportunity to shed more light on the Gettysburg controversy. It still bedevils us former Confederates – need I add, bedevils us because we lost the battle. And once it was lost, the outcome of the war was no longer in doubt. Had we won, we would not be holding this conversation, for victory has a hundred fathers, but defeat is an orphan."

With surprise Cabell noticed his brother's set jaw and narrowed eyes. It was the same grim expression he seen many time in the past, as men about to go into battle gathered their courage and resolution. Drayton lowered his head for a moment, breathed deeply, then raised it and pressed forward.

"The Battle of Gettysburg was the epic moment of our youth. Nothing in our lives before or since came close to its terrible grandeur or produced in the combatants the sense that the issue between North and South was about to be decided. There is a magic in the otherwise ordinary place names that surround us, endowed with potency by such feats of valor that now, fifty years later, I still marvel at them. It was Hell with the lid off, and we who remain wonder how we survived. Too many beloved comrades did not. My own younger brother died leading Kershaw's charge against Sickles' men on the Second Day. The passage of time eases our grief but does not dispel it. Some of us may even feel guilt that we survived when better men did not. We have made peace with our former enemies and we have come here to celebrate that peace. But it is also a time to remember afresh our loved and lost. This is not only reunion of the living but also a muster of the dead."

Cabell lost himself in a moment of grief thinking of Ranse, until Drayton brought him back to the present.

"Our hosts have made the Reunion easier for us than it might have been. We who wore the gray have been welcomed here without rancor, credited with having fought honorably and valiantly for the principles we believed in – the principles *all* Americans once believed in. Our former enemies, fierce in battle, have proven magnanimous in victory. The mutual respect at the Reunion between Union and Confederate veteran, as we saw on Tuesday at the Angle, is a joy to behold."

Some veterans called out 'Amen!' A few cheered. Oddly enough, Cabell had never heard his brother speak in a public setting. Drayton displayed a simplicity and sincerity that connected. The audience was rapt.

"I have found our GAR hosts to be splendid fellows, and they evidently feel the same way about us. I didn't know quite what to expect, lingering animosity, perhaps. After a rough start, all I've encountered is good will and comradeship.

What a pity we couldn't have practiced it fifty years ago, before we came to blows. We have broken bread together, even broken a few heads, as you may have heard Monday evening." The tent erupted with laughter. Cabell grinned at the memory of old men with missing limbs, grappling in the dirt.

Drayton looked over the audience with a tentative smile. "Then we drank together and sealed the bargain of eternal friendship, wondering why, why, we ever tried to kill one another." Another chorus of cheers cascaded through the enclosure. Cabell was thoroughly enjoying itself, and as his brother warmed to his topic, so it seemed was Drayton.

"In fact, there seems to be more peace between Blue and Gray than between Gray and Gray. We former Confederates have argued over Gettysburg as we have over no other battle because the stakes were highest here. When Lee brought us to Pennsylvania he was looking not just to win a battle but to win the war.

"I took part in Longstreet's Assault or what is now known as Pickett's Charge on the Third Day, as a courier for General Longstreet. But as Colonel Leathers avers, the battle was already lost by then; it was lost on the Second Day, although we knew it too late. I can attest to this view, for I was there on the Second Day, too, when Fate ushered me onstage to play my pivotal role."

Cabell snapped to attention. *'Pivotal role?' He was only a junior officer, a scout and courier,* thought Cabell. *He commanded no troops. How could he have played a pivotal role?*

Drayton called him back to the moment. "*But ...* it is not my purpose to take sides in this dispute, neither to rebut Colonel Leathers and the 'Virginia School,' nor to defend General Longstreet." He looked over the expectant crowd with an expression Cabell had never seen before. "It is my purpose to reveal what really happened, to complete our understanding of why the battle ended as it did. The Apostle Luke records the words of our Saviour in chapter 12, verse 2: *For there is nothing covered that shall not be revealed; neither hid, that shall not be known.* I am subject to these words, as is every man. And my purpose is in keeping with the reason we have gathered at Gettysburg. We made a long journey to be here. But the longest, most arduous journey is the one we make into ourselves."

Cabell's heart leapt. He sat up straight in his hard folding chair and for a moment forgot the itching where his wounded leg sweated in its wooden socket. Now, at long last and totally unexpectedly, he was going to learn Drayton's secret, which had been the objective of his own secret campaign of fifty years. He could see in the expectant faces of the veterans that they, too, knew something momentous was coming.

Drayton continued. "This Reunion was organized for the purposes of peace and reconciliation. As soldiers we all did things we would never have done in peacetime, thus we must be reconciled with ourselves; we must find peace with our past. A fifty-year old controversy has come between us and the comfort we ought to enjoy in our final years. Despite the passage of time, many of us Southerners cannot accept that we lost. How could the Yankees have withstood us? We were the victors on so many other fields when we were out-numbered and out-gunned, hungry and barefoot. If there was no failure of courage and devotion on the part of the soldier in the ranks, then the failure must be laid at the feet of those higher up. Lee or Longstreet? Who was to blame? We torture ourselves with the question.

"Well, I knew them both. It is said that General Longstreet's refusal to carry out General Lee's orders cost us the victory on the Second Day, and that he failed to resolutely press home the Great Charge on the Third Day. I can assure you, it was not insubordination on his part. Rather, his training and soldierly instincts warned him of the limits of the possible, even with the finest infantry that ever marched. In attacking brave and resolute Yankees on their native ground, he foresaw the slaughter of the men he loved and the downfall of our cause. If he was dilatory, it was from seeking another way 'round. It was a case of humanity and compassion, not self-will or stubbornness. In this he was like General Lee himself. As generals, both men were brave and skillful in battle, resolute and audacious. But both men carried in their heart's center a fatal flaw for a military leader – love and pity."

Now Drayton's voice rose, and he seemed to grow in stature at the podium. "Why is the Virginia School so desperate to protect General Lee's reputation as a battlefield commander? No one can tarnish it; he was one of the Great Captains of history. But I think he was even greater as a man than as a general. The nobility of Lee's character has put an indelible stamp upon us Southerners, and he abides with us – *in* us – to this day. Those of us who were privileged to know him by service in his Army, and even those in the North, where he has become as revered a figure as any Union general, consider him the finest man America has ever produced – indeed, one of the most splendid men *any* country has ever produced. He has bequeathed us a portion of his dignity, and we do him no honor by pursuing this quarrel.

"I returned wounded from the Great Charge and glimpsed him at the base of Seminary Ridge when the shattered remnants came limping back. He rode among the survivors, comforting them, and saying, 'Too bad, ah, ah, too bad. It is all my fault.' Lee never tried to shift the blame onto his subordinates, although there was plenty of blame to go around. I am convinced Lee would have no part of what some of you have attempted — to make a scapegoat of General Longstreet when it is unjust, to safeguard the reputation of General Lee when it is unnecessary."

There was a rustling through the crowd as men shifted uncomfortably in their seats. The crowd, though stock still, seemed to be in motion as hundreds of hand-held fans oscillated furiously in the heat.

Drayton pressed on. "General Bennett Young told us on Tuesday that this Reunion marks the birth of a new nation, united and whole, echoing President Lincoln's Address here in 1863. You who wore the gray fought your best to give birth to the *Southern* nation. But if this is how it must be, then let us take comfort that the united and whole America was not re-born only in the hatred and violence of war as we suppose, but also in love and mercy. In many campaigns you witnessed prodigious acts of bravery and self-sacrifice. Did you perhaps also witness acts of love and mercy that moved your hearts even more than deeds of valor? I am now going to tell you of another act of love and mercy that clears up once and for all the controversy, and restores a posthumous fellowship between Jubal Early and James Longstreet. It is time for the shedding of burdens, time for all hidden mortal things to be revealed."

Cabell listened in incredulity as Drayton bared his fifty-year-old secret dispassionately. He told of his promise to Celia, not to return a man of blood… '…in battle, do not forget God, and show compassion and mercy whenever you can.' He quoted a line from William Blake that Celia had invoked in 1861: *Where Mercy, Love, and Pity dwell / There God is dwelling, too.* He continued in the matter-of-fact tone of an after-battle report, telling how General Longstreet ordered him to reconnoiter Little Round Top. There he spied a Union general and aide scouting the same vulnerable terrain. With the sights of his Spencer carbine on the two men, he was sure of his kill as he applied a steady pressure on the trigger. He paused, then lowered the rifle, gripped by the memory of a pledge he had made to his wife, and now, he realized, not just to her but to all that was true and good and beautiful in our existence, perhaps even to God himself. Unwilling to shoot down two unsuspecting men from ambush, he lowered the carbine and rushed back to report to Longstreet.

A kind of mutter followed by a collective sigh went up from the audience as they began to grasp the significance of Drayton's act. At the critical moment on the decisive piece of terrain when the battle might have been won, the moment was cast away.

Finally, Drayton said, "I am the man who lost the Battle of Gettysburg. I am the man who lost the War. If we had triumphed here, the War would have ended in the summer of 1863. My wife Celia might not have died, nor my father, nor all the countless thousands in the final two years of bloody conflict. My home in South Carolina would still be standing. So many of you here today lost your homes and lost friends…" His voice broke and he took a moment to compose himself. "…lost friends and loved ones who need not have died if we had prevailed on this field fifty years ago."

A shocked silence reigned over the assembly. Cabell's mind was awhirl. At last he understood. The most intolerable burden was to live in fear. It took a special kind of courage to accept the burden of what he had done and now give himself up to judgment, condemnation, or … to the unknown. Cabell was not sure how he felt himself. One corner of his mind burned with indignation against his brother, the other flowed with pity.

"Neither Lee nor Longstreet deserves your opprobrium," said Drayton. "Nor Heth nor Stuart nor Ewell. *I* am the one who deserves it. As General Lee said, it is all my fault. And I crave your forgiveness. If that's too much to ask, then know you cannot reproach me more severely than I have reproached myself. You Confederates traveled here to be reconciled with your former enemies, only to learn that your greatest enemy came – however inadvertently — from your own ranks. I hope you can be reconciled with me. If you can, then I am grateful. But whether yes or no, let us commit the matter to Him who shall judge among the nations; and they shall beat their swords into ploughshares and their spears into pruning hooks. Nation shall not lift up sword against nation, neither shall they learn war anymore."

Cabell clasped his hands in his lap till they hurt, watching his brother strip himself naked before the shocked veterans. Drayton trembled, and he was done. The remarks ended — quietly. Drayton remained standing at the lectern, mopping his streaming face and bracing himself for the collective fury of the veterans. At the same time he clearly hoped for their acceptance. The room was quiet as death. Not even the usual coughs or sneezes, not a foot shuffling or chair scraping. Even the pew fans were still. Cabell couldn't assess the reaction. Did they approve? Condemn? There was no applause. Even if they forgave, there would be no such acclaim, for what had just transpired was too profound for applause.

White-faced, holding himself erect as if with an effort, Drayton finally moved to descend from the dais. As he came abreast the front row, Cabell said to himself, *I can't let him bear this disgrace alone.*

"Hold up there," he called, grabbing his cane. He limped forward and locked arms with his brother. Drayton held his head high, and there was a sudden lightness to his step, but Cabell braced himself for the storm of invective that was sure to follow once the veterans got over their astonishment at Drayton's revelation. Arm in arm with The Man Who Lost the Civil War, Cabell held his brother tight as they began the long march of the condemned down the center aisle, which stretched interminably before them.

Cabell heard a motion behind him as he passed the front row. He turned to look behind him, and Drayton turned with him, frozen in place. General

Evander Law had come to his feet, erect as if on The Citadel parade ground. Law rendered an impeccable Corps of Cadets salute. Drayton nodded gratefully. The Longstreets stood, and he saw Helen Longstreet's ample cheeks glistening wet. One by one the old warriors began to stand. But for audible creaks of canes, crutches, and wooden limbs, complete silence reigned. Cabell and Drayton walked on slowly. Five, then twenty, then fifty rose, until the whole assembly was on its feet like waves lapping the shore, a thousand veterans, utterly still and at attention. And as they stood, they took off their hats or picked them up from the folding chairs and mess tables where they'd laid them, holding them across their hearts and turning to face Drayton as he passed, row by row, faces stern and solemn with vicarious suffering, in silent tribute.

***

Drayton rushed to a secluded corner outside the tent, bent over, and vomited violently. Cabell stumped forward and supported him while he retched three more times. Cabell held out his handkerchief, and his brother blotted his face bathed in sweat, then wiped his mouth. Drayton straightened up and smiled weakly. "Much better now. Thanks." Cabell extended the ubiquitous pocket flask. The pewter had absorbed some of the day and the whiskey was warm, but Drayton took a shallow sip.

"Just what the doctor ordered," he croaked.

"The universal remedy," Cabell agreed.

Cabell wanted to escape the vicinity at once, before being accosted by anyone offering blame or praise. He hobbled to keep up, but he needn't have hurried. Drayton hadn't gone far when he was stopped by a veteran in gray who offered him a drink from a hip flask, and by others who just wanted to shake his hand. Yet they said little, maintaining a respectful silence, as if they'd put themselves in Drayton's place and understood how much it had cost their compatriot to reveal what he had. And he marveled at Drayton's fortitude. He'd lived with his secret for 50 years! And told no one until now. How was that possible? In war, most men commit acts they wouldn't dream of otherwise, acts of wanton cruelty and violence. Then their conscience tortures them ever after, until they finally come to some kind of peace with the past. But not Drayton. He had always been at odds with everyone and everything. *He* had committed an act of mercy, and that had tortured him.

Yet in Cabell a residual anger simmered, competing with understanding and forgiveness. Drayton was right. We might have won otherwise, probably *would* have won at Gettysburg, Cabell thought, if we'd taken Little Round Top. And thus the War itself. There was nothing for it; what was done couldn't be undone. But his mind dwelt anyway for a moment on all the death and suffering that might have been prevented. Tens of thousands of fine young men, North and South. Father. Celia. He smiled and said to himself, reconciled at last. *Not to mention your leg.*

***

Drayton arrived at his tent to find Tommy and Walter Amman in deep conversation seated on camp stools. Walter stood and regarded him with an inscrutable expression.

"For years I carried a man's severed arm in my tortured imagination," said Walter "I can see it was nothing – nothing – compared to what you've been carrying for fifty years. When I urged you to share your burden… Well, I had no idea. I only hope it has given you the relief you need."

Drayton tried to smile, but feared his countenance remained rueful. Yet he wanted to reassure Walter. He said, "It may take some time to tell. If I can escape here alive, I'll write and let you know."

"Don't write," said Walter. "Come in person. Come visit me in Harrisburg. It's not far, and there's a train."

Drayton pondered the invitation. "Tommy and I will be leaving tomorrow. We'd planned to see the rest of Gettysburg and the place where his Grand-Uncle Cabell fought in the cavalry battle on the Third Day. Then we'll travel to New York, other points north, and then to Ireland. But thanks. I see no reason why we can't stop for a few days in Harrisburg. I haven't made a friend in longer than I care to remember. You've been a better friend to me than … Well, how can I possibly express what it means to lay this burden down? And we won't need the train. I've purchased a motorcar for the balance of our journey. I'm to pick it up in Gettysburg this afternoon."

President Woodrow Wilson had come and gone, but Reunioneers spoke more about the remarkable event in the Virginia mess tent than they did of the President's fine speech. Not all the Southerners were happy; there was some muttering and a few dark looks cast Drayton's way. But approving or disapproving, the veterans gave Drayton ample space to complete his catharsis. He sat quietly in camp in a checkers tournament with Tommy, Cabell, and their tentmates. After supper, the flags in the encampment were lowered to half-mast. Then a 48-gun salute by the Army's field artillery boomed over the site, followed by a solemn silence and the hush of peace. The Army band played 'Tenting Tonight on the Old Campground,' then 'Lorena.' A lone bagpiper's plaintive, skirling notes filled the camp with a pibroch called 'Lament for the Children.' Finally the Army buglers began to play 'Taps,' the bugle call that signaled the end of the day, and also honored the military dead. This time it was played echo-fashion by two buglers. One played a bar at one end of the camp, and the second echoed it at the other end, rendering it even more moving than normal.

Chapter Fifty Two

Charleston, South Carolina; July 6, 1913.

Annalee loved the banks of oleander she'd had planted along the Church Street façade. The clustered blooms of summer exuded a rich perfume. And she wanted air, oh, how she wanted the sea-and-flower scented air to waft through the closed house, ever since the salesman for woven wire screen had paid a call. It was a new invention that covered the doors and windows, allowing them to be opened to ventilation. Now that it was invented it seemed perfectly simple. But for hundreds of years Low Country residents had wrestled with how to allow cooling air in while keeping out the flies, sand gnats, and mosquitoes. It wouldn't be cheap to furnish all the doors and windows, and she needed Drayton's income. Her funds from... well, from the 1872 bequest – she would never speak *his* name nor even think it – were depleted. Moreover, there were still repairs from the Earthquake that had never been finished, cracks in the foundation that needed shoring up, more earthquake bolts to be run through the walls and then tightened down with flanges and huge nuts. They were a good investment against future earthquakes, but they weren't cheap.

For years she'd been skimming a portion of the monthly amount Drayton gave her for food and household expenses, building up a secret account against the day when she'd need to rely on her own funds. After all, women outlived men, and when he was gone, who knew how long she might have to subsist? It meant a certain plainness of fare, but Drayton never complained, one good thing about an academic for a husband, perhaps. It was the only good thing she could name, besides a certain social status. His head was always in the clouds. It was up to her to be practical.

Never had they experienced the thunderclap of First Love that he'd had with Cecelia. Supposedly that happened only once in a lifetime, and was something to be gotten over and out of the way. You couldn't depend on human beings. Love, if it existed at all, was fleeting, and was merely a biological trick Nature played on people to ensure the perpetuation of the species. But you could depend on money – hard cash. And if you didn't have it, why then, you could depend on being cold, hungry, miserable, and despised.

Drayton was due back in several days. Annalee experienced a sudden strange intuition as she balanced her accounts. Or perhaps it wasn't the intuition that was strange; it was Drayton's behavior. She planned to meet his train on July 9, hoping this small gesture of conciliation might ease the acrimony. She thought it would be wise to display her forgiveness. But then her indignation boiled over again. She could see him enjoying a raucous week of drinking and carousing with these foolish old men who lived in the past and had never outgrown their one moment of glory. And then there was that delayed echo in his words and behavior. The intuition led her to his study. It was locked, which only confirmed her suspicion that something was amiss.

The door was stout and solid, and the lock substantial. In frustration she called in a locksmith to open it. When he left, she scurried inside. To her shock, the bookshelves and side tables usually stacked with files were empty. Every volume had been removed. When had he been able to undertake such a move without her observing? She knew all that went on under her roof. She dashed to his desk. It was empty, too; but the shallow middle drawer was locked. She'd already dismissed the locksmith and was unwilling to face the embarrassment of calling him back. Her frustration turned to fury. She went to the kitchen, fetched a paring knife, and tried to pry open the lock; but it resisted valiantly. She went back to the kitchen and tried a larger knife. The defenses held, and the blade of the carving knife snapped in two.

Now her anger knew no bounds. She went out to the carriage house where Drayton maintained a workshop and set of tools. They were all in place, to her relief. She selected a claw hammer, returned to the study, and managed to insert the claws between the top of the drawer and frame of the desk. She was a strong woman, and she pried up with all her force. With a splintering of wood, the drawer popped open. It was empty but for a sheet of folded stationery lying alone. She sat in his swivel chair, unfolded the page, fumbled for her reading glasses at the end of their lanyard, and read with trembling hands Drayton's elegant copperplate :

I will not be coming back. It should be as clear to you as it is to me – we were fundamentally unsuited for each other. We made an honest mistake, yet still a mistake. How long must we pay for it? I've decided 37 years is long enough. If you choose to contest my decision, know that Cabell holds a sworn affidavit from Isaac Joyner, who approached me in 1878 for purposes of extortion. Thus we needn't go through the unpleasantness of a divorce. We were never legally married – you knew Isaac was alive at the time. But I was willing to overlook the matter for Preston's sake, indeed, for all of us, in hopes we might have had a marriage in spirit if not in law. Since that was not to be, the time has come to declare 'omnia persolutis,' paid in full. Thomas Preston Jr. will travel with me, and I have secured legal guardianship until his majority. Cabell has the details, along with documentation of the aforementioned. He is prepared to make it public in the event you use my departure to blacken the FitzHenry name. There is also a small allowance, which he will begin when he returns from Gettysburg. I wish you no ill, only happiness. Doubtless you can find it better alone than with me.

She read it again to see if there was an ambiguity or nuance in the text she might have missed to suggest anything other than an irrevocable decision. She read it a third time with the concentration of a Medieval scholar poring over a newly discovered Greek manuscript. There was nothing but the plain, brutal meaning of the words.

Chapter Fifty Three

Gettysburg, Pennsylvania, July 5, 1913.

The play was over, the last curtain call ended and bows taken, the spectators were streaming for the exits. Whatever lessons the drama held were tucked away in their kitbags to be savored later in the watches of the night. The three FitzHenrys dressed in the tent, said farewell to their tentmates, and assembled their meager baggage.

Drayton was grateful to his brother for dispensing with an interrogation, something he fully expected after yesterday's shock. Cabell acted as if nothing unusual had transpired. But when the silence itself became awkward, he asked, "How are you feeling this morning?"

"Not bad. I rested unusually well. And you?"

It was obvious Cabell wanted to talk, while trying to avoid The Subject. Cabell said, "I've been living with the prospects of this Reunion for almost a year. Now it's over… Well, I suddenly feel old."

Drayton nodded. This was a safe if uncomfortable topic. "I know. To feel your vital energy ebbing just a little every day. Marcus Aurelius wrote that every day is an assault on the inner citadel of the soul. It's an age-old question. Should you struggle against fate, knowing you must finally give in to the inevitable? Or do you heroically hold out as long as possible?"

Tommy sat outside on a camp chair. They both looked in his direction and Cabell said, "This is why Tommy is such a blessing. To teach and mold him… that would seem to be your purpose for the future. He will be our legacy. See you take good care of him on this trip you're about to make. I confess it worries me."

They grabbed their gear and walked the few hundred yards to West Confederate Avenue, where the new car was parked. Drayton had long known Annalee was skimming from the common household account. But the joke was on her, for he'd been turning over only a portion of his book royalties and putting the rest aside. He'd been skimming, too, if one could call it that with his own money. It had paid for the automobile and their travel fund.

At the station Cabell said, "You're planning a long journey. When I said it worries me, I selfishly meant, will I see you again? Neither of us is a young man anymore."

Drayton knew he might never return to the place he loved best, but his life-journey was not ended. The price of self-knowledge was exile, finding a place where he could wash off the dust of doubts, the encrustations of self-reproach, a place of peace and solitude – and above all, innocence. Home by the River had been such a place, where the beauty and order of the natural world converged with his inner world. More than any other place it had sustained him in his shame and guilt. But now it was time to move on.

"Thomas and I are going to Harrisburg to stay with Walter Amman for a while. He discerns the times and I want to learn from him. You're never too old to learn. Then to Philadelphia and New York. After that, Ireland, England, and the Continent. I want to show Tommy where his FitzHenry people came from. See if Beltane has any descendants. Maybe Ireland will explain why our family always ends up on the losing side."

"Well, Tommy needs to see a bit of the wider world beyond Charleston and the Low Country of South Carolina," Cabell agreed.

Before departing Charleston Drayton had shipped his excess baggage to the Gettysburg train station. As the Negro porter rolled the dunnage onto the platform, Cabell laughed. "Brother, you've got enough *impedimenta* there for a whole campaign."

They were early at Gettyburg station and decided to have a cup of coffee while awaiting the train. In the café Drayton said, "It's a lot of kit because I plan a long stay. If I'm still kicking after all that, I'll come back to the River. But not back to … to her. It's what I ought to have done years ago, had I possessed the strength and courage."

Cabell put down his coffee cup emphatically. "Brother, you have more courage than anyone I know. And courage of the finest type."

Drayton smiled. "I'm gratified. I was dreadfully afraid of forfeiting your respect."

"Never fear on that account. But what about Annalee?"

Drayton produced a large brown envelope from his portmanteau. "This is the file I promised you when we left Charleston. It contains my power of attorney, with instructions for the retrieval of all my assets I haven't already secured. I'll need you to forward some bank drafts while Tommy and I are traveling. Detailed instructions are here."

"And the Church Street house?"

"I've come to hate the house. And it was hers to begin with. Notwithstanding my renovations and improvements, she's welcome to it."

"But Brother, if she takes a desertion charge to a judge, she can trump all your plans for your assets; maybe even attach the River property."

"No, I have the trump card. It's in the packet."

"And that is?"

"A personal affidavit made in 1878 from one Isaac Joyner. Along with receipts of payments made to him the same year." Drayton glanced at Tommy and noticed he was listening bug-eyed. Drayton was hesitant about revealing the sordid tale to his grandson, but had resolved to be truthful with him insofar as possible. Hiding unpleasant facts from children was a too-prevalent characteristic of Southerners. And he'd concluded the boy was mature enough to handle the truth.

"Joyner? Wasn't that Annalee's married name?" Cabell was bug-eyed, too.

"Precisely."

"You mean—?"

"Yes. Her husband survived the War. He turned up in Charleston a few years after we were married – or rather, went through the sham of a marriage."

"She was still married to Joyner in 1876? Your marriage is invalid!" Both men regarded Tommy with concern. They could see the mental gears turning as he tried to figure out what this meant for his lineage.

"Exactly," said Drayton. "Moreover, the letters and copies in this file will strongly suggest, if not prove indisputably, that Annalee knew Isaac Joyner was still alive and mining diamonds in Kimberly, South Africa, when she and I went through our fraudulent ceremony in April 1876. When she learns of the contents of this package, I don't think she'll make any trouble for us at law."

Cabell shook his head in wonder. "You've guarded her secret for all these years, when you might have been free. *Why*, in God's name?"

"Why? Well, Brother, you know. A prisoner of tradition. And one of those traditions is to maintain the family name and dignity at all costs." He left unvoiced the thought — there was also his son Preston and grandson Thomas Preston to consider.

"Besides," Drayton added. "I don't think she realized herself the reason for her cruelty. She avenged herself on Isaac Joyner through her treatment of me. In any case, I had a secret of my own to guard; and in truth, I had no right to condemn her for wanting to keep hers. But now, here in this place, after so long… I am finally going to lay both burdens down."

"Honestly, I never understood why you married her in the first place."

"Beltane liked her."

"He was just being polite," Cabell laughed.

Chapter Fifty Four

Gettysburg, Pennsylvania, July 5, 1913.

After their goodbyes at the station, Drayton and Tommy had one more stop before embarking on their road trip. Drayton drove through the charming little town up Baltimore Street. He bore right on the Emmitsburg Pike for a few miles, which conveyed them to a parking area at the base of Little Round Top. He put the car in low gear and pulled the parking brake, breathing heavily. The blood pounded in his head. He sat still in the driver's seat for a moment while Tommy looked at him quizzically. Drayton smiled at Tommy and exited the car. Tommy climbed out of the Packard to accompany him, but Drayton said, "Son, do you mind terribly waiting here? This is something I must do alone." He inclined his head toward the summit.

"But GramPa, it's too hard for you to go up there alone. See how rocky and steep it is? Let me help you."

"Son, you've been splendid help this whole trip and I'm grateful. But now this is something I must do all by myself. Just help me across Plum Run. I'll go the rest of the way by myself."

"But *why*, GramPa?"

"My boy, I'm afraid I can't explain it to your satisfaction. It's just something I know, down deep inside. This is my personal Labyrinth." He placed a consoling hand on the boy's shoulder. "You must simply trust me in this, because I'm doing it in part for you. You are my future that I thought I'd lost, as I lost my past. But now I've found it and myself again."

Tommy helped Drayton down the slippery bank of Plum Run. As he grasped the hand with the missing fingers, Drayton saw him glance away, as if embarrassed. Once across, Drayton broke off a dry sapling to steady himself and began the strenuous climb.

They had trooped in their battalions, Blue and Gray, to Culps Hill, to Devil's Den and the Stone Wall and the Angle, to Little Round Top. He had waited till the last day, when the Reunion was ending so he could come here alone and undisturbed. The rainstorm of July 2nd had washed the oppression from the sky.

It remained a hot July afternoon, so quiet one could almost hear the sun's rays.

Of all the still-living men in gray he and only he came here, he thought. This particular, lonely spot, this natural stone window on the battle's turning point, this hinge of the fate of nations. It belonged to Drayton and to him alone. Now the moment had come which was as fraught as the speech before the assembled veterans on Friday — a private one, but equally laden with the fear of self-discovery.

Drayton had never been able to admit it to himself until coming back to Gettysburg, but in learning to forgive himself he saw also that he had to forgive Celia. He had harbored an unacknowledged anger for the position her pledge had put him in. As he said to the assembled veterans, *It is time for the shedding of burdens, time for all hidden mortal things to be revealed.* He'd hidden from himself the need to reconcile this residual anger with his love for her. The pledge contained an irony too deep for human comprehension: in exacting her promise she had ordained her own premature death. But now he could see all. Celia had played her role, too. It had fallen to her to insist on love and mercy as it had fallen to him to enact it. No, they were not puppets in the hands of some inscrutable, indifferent Fate. They'd been privileged to be assigned key roles in a cosmic drama by the Director himself. General Lee had tried to tell him so in 1870.

After much exertion and concern for his damaged heart, Drayton reached the rock bastion with its portal. The base stone seemed higher than he remembered. It was difficult to clamber up on it, but he managed. He peered through the window formed by the uprights. Forty yards above, on the pinnacle, stood the same man he'd spied in July 1863. Now he was a bronze figure, immortalized by the sculpture and by a lone Confederate's impulse of generosity in a world gone mad. The trilithon, though made by nature and not by the hands of man, reminded him of the cromlechs and standing stones in Ireland, the only monuments to a nameless people lost now even to memory. His stone at Little Round Top ought to display an inscription telling what had happened here. Drayton visualized the plaque, brass but with a green patina, raised letters rubbed shiny by the fingers of countless visitors down the years who would read it wonderingly:

At this place on July 2, 1863 the Battle of Gettysburg was won and lost, thus the Civil War was won and lost. The future was set in its course. This outcome flowed from an act of love in the midst of unspeakable violence and destruction. It is love that ultimately determines the course of history, not hate; for love is stronger than hate.

It would be a fitting epitaph for the South, a once-great people who would remain ever despised and denigrated by the ruling elites of the victor. Yet

Southerners had built a great civilization once, and they deserved at least a lament for their passing.

He rested his forearm on the granite and peered upward at General Warren, eternally standing sentinel. Yesterday the turmoil inside him had burst its bonds and flowed away like the ebbing of the tide. But as it departed, it didn't leave him empty. Instead he found himself full of something else, something he couldn't put a name to. But he was satisfied with the closing of a chapter in his life that had run on far too long. As endings usually are, it ought to be colored with sadness. Yet it was joyous, for in this ending was a new beginning, even though he knew his days were drawing short. For an instant had a bit of Maum Biddy's Sight. In climbing up this rocky slope he'd been climbing the stairsteps to the place from which all things emanate and to which all things return.

Here fifty years ago I let a man live by my choice. Did I act of my own free will, or was I an unwitting tool of inscrutable Providence? Yes and yes. Both are true. The immanence of the Godhead reconciles all contradictions, makes all things One. Now I lay my burden down. No more self-reproach and recrimination. Would that I had reached this understanding long ago, as General Lee encouraged me. But I refused to accept it in order to punish myself, when God himself was not punishing me, for my great error was that I wanted to be better than God.

It was not a rational moment, nor even properly speaking, theological. His private ceremony of self-forgiveness and acceptance he could only describe as a kind of … poetry. Some peace offering was needed to propitiate the spirits of the past. He drew in a deep breath, slowly fingering in his pocket the shattered Charles Fraser miniature that had saved his life fifty years ago, a talisman of his deepest wound. At first he was moved to lay it gently on the stone base of the trilithon. But it was too deep a part of him. He stared into the deep gray eyes above the cracked enamel, his memory supplying the rest of the beloved image. He spoke to her. "I kept my promise." He felt he ought to say something more, whisper a prayer, shed a tear. But there was nothing more to say that had not been said. And no tears came. Replacing the miniature in his pocket, he looked up, up, and farther up, beyond the crest of the rock-studded hilltop, beyond the stark silhouette of General Warren, and into the lowering sky.

How long he stood there he couldn't say. At length he clambered awkwardly from the standing stones and turned down-slope, half expecting to see faithful Beltane cropping the marsh grass and tethered to the distant fir tree which still stood. Time had collapsed in upon itself. In his soul he was young again, and Celia was home by the River, waiting for him on the grassy rise above the Edisto, wisps of golden hair fluttering in the salt-tinged air. Bel and the other horses were charging in line abreast to an imagined bugle, wheeling, flying uphill, then turning and charging again. Past, present, and future had condensed into this eternal, timeless moment. 'There is no past, there is no future, there is only Now,' Heraclitus had said. The fifty-year old question was answered, and now he could depart in peace. *Cursum perficio;* I have run the course. My journey ends here where it began. And Clio, the Muse of History, clucks her tongue in sympathy at the destruction of my people, which continues apace in spite of the reconciliation we have enjoyed at this Reunion. Like General Lee riding out to meet the broken remnants of the Great Charge, Clio murmurs, 'Too bad. Ah, too bad.' She can offer no other solace except to say, 'Your deeds are recorded in the Annals. *Non omnis moriar.* You shall not wholly die.'

***

Tommy circled the new car, admiring its lines, its gleaming fixtures, its power. He'd seen motorcars in Beaufort and Charleston, but had never ridden in one. And until now, after his inspection, he'd never realized the tires were made of rubber. He kicked them repeatedly, enjoying the recoil of his foot off the springy substance. It would be fun to ride with the top down all the way to Philadelphia, and beyond. GramPa would return soon, and he wanted to remember and try to understand all GramPa had told him. He wished GramPa had let him go up the hill.

He didn't think he'd ever understand adults or get used to living with their strange ways, his father especially, when he was drinking, and GramMa Annalee most of the time, and even GramPa, who was never unkind but had these gloomy moods.

GramPa was going to take him places he'd never seen, and Tommy admitted he was excited and scared at the same time. But there was no need to be scared as long as GramPa was there, who had fought so bravely, and who everybody at Camp was talking about because of something important he'd told them yesterday. But they always fell silent when he came into earshot. He wished somebody would explain. He'd ask him in due time. He knew his grandfather would be patient and make things clear, as he always did.

They were going to Philadelphia and New York, but the place that excited him most was Ireland. Everyone said Ireland was a fairy-land. They had lots of castles. They had the fastest horses, the most beautiful women, the bravest soldiers, and the greatest poets. He hoped he wouldn't feel out of place.

There he came at last. There was GramPa coming up the slope from Plum Run without any help like he'd needed going over. He'd thrown away the walking stick he picked up on the way to the top. Tommy saw him smiling in a way he'd never seen, kind of strange with a faraway look, and walking proud like a younger man.

GramPa came up and placed a loving hand on Tommy's head, as Tommy looked down in concern at the mud clinging to GramPa's shoes and good suit pants almost to his knees. GramPa looked down at the mud and pulled a face. They both laughed. It was good to hear him laugh.

"Did you make it back all right from the Labyrinth?" Tommy asked, glancing uphill and hoping he'd pronounced the unusual word correctly.

"Yes, I did." With an arm around his shoulder, GramPa ushered Tommy toward the car.

"Did anything happen up there?"

"Yes. Fifty years ago. And also just now."

Tommy knew there was no point in asking what. He would tell him when he chose.

"You seem happy, GramPa."

GramPa smiled again. It was a warm, affectionate smile, not bleak and sad like the ones Tommy was used to.

"Yes, I am, Thomas," GramPa said. "Very happy."

— The End —

Cork, Republic of Ireland

Aiken, South Carolina

Author's Note

This is a work of fiction, based on historical events and historical figures. Many of the people of the era are easily recognizable – Robert E. Lee, James Longstreet, Wade Hampton, Porter Alexander, and the Union Brigadier General Gouverneur Warren. But this is not merely a battle study of the decisions of the generals. I also wanted to portray something of the life of the soldier in the ranks. Ergo, there are several minor characters in the story not known to the general reader, who actually served and fought as depicted, including my own kin and their neighbors. (See below). Otherwise, no character in the story is intended to represent a real person. Any such appearance is a coincidence and the result of the author's imagination.

My principal goal was not just to write the best contemporary novel of the War, but also to place my protagonist in an excruciating moral and emotional dilemma and see how he would resolve his inner conflict. It could just have easily been another character in another war. But the Battle of Gettysburg, and especially the Second Day on Little Round Top, provided the perfect confluence for grafting my fictional scenario onto actual circumstances and drawing dramatic power from the underlying history. Here on July 2, 1863, a single man with less mercy in his heart might – might – have won the battle for the South and changed the course of history.

I consulted many of the standard sources on the War, including the battlefield itself in many treks over the terrain, and especially on the slopes and summit of Little Round Top, to make sure my fictional scenario could have occurred as depicted. My best written sources are the following works. I hope they have imparted authenticity to my story because they came from the pens of those who actually took part in America's great national epic – and greatest national tragedy.

Chained to Virginia While Carolina Bleeds: the Civil War Correspondence of Henry Woodbury Moore and James Washington Moore; letters of my great-grandfather and great great-uncle, who enlisted in 1861 in the Beaufort District Troop of the Hampton Legion Cavalry. Henry was a graduate of Dartmouth

Medical College and later became Assistant Surgeon of the 2nd South Carolina Cavalry. James Moore – "Jimsie" – served as Regimental Adjutant. Their correspondence was collected, annotated, and published by my late uncle, Henry Woodbury Moore, M.D., in 1996.

Autobiography of Arab, by E. Prioleau Henderson. The R. L. Bryan Company, Columbia, SC, 1901. Today little-known, but a splendid personal account of service in the Beaufort District Troop of the Hampton Legion, later Company C , 1st Battalion, 2nd South Carolina Cavalry. It's told from the point of view of Henderson's horse Arab, which in some ways is the prototype for Beltane in *A Fatal Mercy*. Both Henderson and his legendary Arab survived the War.

Butler and His Cavalry in the War of Secession 1861-1865: the South Carolina Regimental Series, by Ulysses R. Brooks. Gray Fox Books, Camden, SC, (reprint of the 1909 edition). Matthew Calbraith Butler rose to the rank of major general and commanded the South Carolina brigade of cavalry of "Jeb" Stuart's Cavalry Division of Lee's Army of Northern Virginia. This is also an authoritative source for a remarkable episode, the Great Wade Hampton Cattle Raid at the siege of Petersburg in September 1864. I must concede that I took considerable dramatic license by placing my protagonist Drayton at the center of the adventure. The real hero was Hampton's chief scout, a Texan named George Shadburne, who discovered the Yankee herd far behind their lines and conceived the plan. If Sergeant Shadburne has any living descendants, I hope they will forgive my appropriating the deed of their ancestor in order to dramatize this extraordinary episode, which I have never seen depicted elsewhere in Civil War fiction.

Fighting for the Confederacy: the Personal Recollections of General Edward Porter Alexander, by E. Porter Alexander and edited by Gary W. Gallagher. The University of North Carolina Press, 1989. Alexander was one of the most versatile and gifted soldiers in either army, and this is one of the best such memoirs. He did come to Columbia, SC in 1866-67 as a faculty member at the University of South Carolina, which survived Sherman's destruction of Columbia and re-opened soon after the War. Thus Alexander's friendship with Drayton FitzHenry, though of course fictional, is well within the bounds of historical plausibility.

Wade Hampton: Confederate Warrior, Conservative Statesman; by Walter Brian Cisco; Brassey's, Inc. Washington, DC, 2004. In my opinion the indispensable biography of a remarkable South Carolinian by a fine writer on other Southern themes.

Writing may be a lonely calling; but it is …well, a fiction to think that an author achieves anything worthwhile alone. I'm deeply grateful to my old friend and mentor Dr. Clyde Wilson, who inspired my first successful novel, *The Hunt for Confederate Gold*; and his colleagues at Shotwell Publishing, Paul Graham and Boo Jackson. Their goal, as is mine, is to produce first-rate books and restore to Southern letters the paramount place they once held in American literature.

I'm unable to express the fullness of my gratitude to my wife Rhonda for her encouragement and support, and who has literally made it possible for me to write; and to my sons Thomas Moore Jr. and Stuart R. Moore for their sound advice and counsel.

And finally, I owe an incalculable debt to Mary Morrissy, author and Professor of Creative Writing at University College Cork, Ireland. She not only gave me the validation every writer needs to keep slogging ahead, but also formal training in the craft of writing and self-editing. I hope *A Fatal Mercy* will reflect credit upon her tutelage, upon my colleagues in the Creative Writing M.A programme, and on University College Cork, arguably the best university in the most literary country in the world for its small size.

If you liked *A Fatal Mercy*, I hope you'll also enjoy *The Confession of John Dighton*, appearing in late 2020. It's not about the Civil War, however. Set in Tudor Ireland, England, and France, its sub-text is about the "Deep State" of the 15th Century, and thus of any century. The story itself is of an unlikely Irishman who stumbles on the answer to the greatest unsolved mystery of the time: who really murdered the two Plantagenet Princes in the Tower of London in 1485? Clue: it was not, as we are led to believe, their uncle, King Richard III.

About The Author

Thomas Moore brings 25 years' experience in Washington, DC in national defense, foreign policy, and international trade to his writing of fiction. He is the author of two previous historical novels, *The Hunt for Confederate Gold* and *No Villains, No Heroes*. A graduate of The Citadel, he earned an MA in National Security Affairs from Georgetown University in Washington, DC. He attended University College Cork, Ireland, where he earned an MA in History of the Irish Revolution and an MA in Creative Writing., both with First Class Honours. Thomas and his wife Rhonda live in Aiken, SC.

SOUTHERN LITERATURE is the glory of American culture. Faulkner, O'Connor, Warren, Lytle, Davidson, Gordon, Percy, Chappell, Berry will be known as long as Western civilization survives and long after today's politicians, "experts," and celebrity writers are forgotten. Another of the greats, George Garrett, wrote that "all signs indicate that Southern literature, far from being on its last legs and far from representing a falling off from earlier and better days, seems very much alive." Shotwell Publishing supports Garrett's witness by launching the imprint Green Altar Books—a collection of Southern fiction and poetry.

GREEN ALTAR BOOKS
SHOTWELL PUBLISHING

www.ingramcontent.com/pod-product-compliance
Lightning Source LLC
Chambersburg PA
CBHW031335070726
47496CB00017B/972